JEWISH BIBLICAL EXEGESIS
FROM ISLAMIC LANDS

BIBLE AND ITS RECEPTION

Rhonda Burnette-Bletsch, General Editor

Number 1

JEWISH BIBLICAL EXEGESIS FROM ISLAMIC LANDS

The Medieval Period

Edited by

Meira Polliack and Athalya Brenner-Idan

SBL PRESS

 PRESS

Atlanta

Library of Congress Cataloging-in-Publication Data

Names: Polliack, Meira, editor. | Brenner-Idan, Athalya, editor.
Title: Jewish biblical exegesis from Islamic lands : the medieval period / edited by Meira Polliack, Athalya Brenner-Idan.
Description: Atlanta : Atlanta : SBL Press, [2019] | Includes bibliographical references and index.
Identifiers: LCCN 2019032578 (print) | LCCN 2019032579 (ebook) | ISBN 9781628372540 (paperback) | ISBN 9780884144038 (hardcover) | ISBN 9780884144045 (ebook)
Subjects: LCSH: Bible. Old Testament—Hermeneutics. | Bible. Old Testament. Judeo-Arabic—Commentaries. | Jews—Islamic countries—Intellectual life
Classification: LCC BS1186 .J46 2019 (print) | LCC BS1186 (ebook) | DDC 221.6089/9240175927s—dc23
LC record available at https://lccn.loc.gov/2019032578
LC ebook record available at https://lccn.loc.gov/2019032579

The cover image shows a folio from Saʿadia Gaon's translation of and commentary on Job, held in the Cairo Genizah Collection of the University of Pennsylvania's Center for Advanced Judaic Studies Library.

Printed on acid-free paper.

In Memoriam
Ilana Sasson (1954–2017)
A Cherished Friend and Colleague
ת.נ.צ.ב.ה.

Contents

Abbreviations

AB	Anchor Bible
ABD	*Anchor Bible Dictionary*
Abr.	*De Abrahamo*
A.J.	Josephus, *Antiquitates judaicae*
AJSR	*Association for Jewish Studies Review*
Arab.	Arabic
Avod. Zar.	Avodah Zarah
b.	Babylonian Talmud
B. Bat.	Bava Batra
BDB	Brown, Francis, S. R. Driver, and Charles A. Briggs. *A Hebrew and English Lexicon of the Old Testament*. Oxford: Clarendon, 1907.
Ber.	Berakhot
BibInt	Biblical Interpretation Series
Bik.	Bikkurim
BJS	Brown Judaic Studies
BL	British Library
BNP	Bibliothèque Nationale, Paris
BSOAS	*Bulletin of the School of Oriental and African Studies*
Dial.	Justin Martyr, *Dialogue with Trypho*
EAJS	European Association of Jewish Studies
EBR	Klauck, H.-J., et al., eds. *Encyclopedia of the Bible and Its Reception*. Berlin: de Gruyter, 2009–.
EI2	Bosworth, Clifford E., et al., eds. *Encyclopedia of Islam*. 2nd ed. 12 vols. Leiden: Brill, 1954–2005.
EJJS	*European Journal of Jewish Studies*
EJIW	Stillman, Norman A., eds. *Encyclopedia of Jews in the Islamic World*. 5 vols. Leiden: Brill, 2010.
EncJud	Skolnik, Fred, and Michael Berenbaum, eds. *Encylopedia Judaica*. 2nd ed. 22 vols. Detroit: Macmillan Reference, 2007.

Eruv.	Eruvin
FC	Fathers of the Church
fol(s).	folio(s)
Git.	Gittin
Heb.	Hebrew
Hen	*Henoch*
HTR	*Harvard Theological Review*
IHIW	*Intellectual History of the Islamicate World*
IMHM	Institute of Microfilmed Hebrew Manuscripts
IOS	Institute of Oriental Studies, Saint Petersburg
IOS	*Israel Oriental Studies*
JA	*Journal Asiatique*
JAOS	*Journal of the American Oriental Society*
JBL	*Journal of Biblical Literature*
JCoptS	*Journal of Coptic Studies*
JIS	*Journal of Islamic Studies*
JJS	*Journal of Jewish Studies*
JJTP	*Journal of Jewish Thought and Philosophy*
JNL	Jewish National Library
JPS	Jewish Publication Society (Bible translation)
JQR	*Jewish Quarterly Review*
JSAI	*Jerusalem Studies in Arabic and Islam*
JSIJ	*Jewish Studies Internet Journal*
JSJSup	Supplements to the Journal for the Study of Judaism
JSOTSup	Journal for the Study of the Old Testament Supplement Series
JSQ	*Jewish Studies Quarterly*
JSS	*Journal of Semitic Studies*
JSSSup	Journal of Semitic Studies Supplement Series
JTS	*Journal of Theological Studies*
KJV	King James Version (Authorized Version)
LCL	Loeb Classical Library
LXX	Septuagint
m.	Mishnah
MasS	Masoretic Studies
Meg.	Megillah
MFOB	*Mélanges de la faculté orientale de l'Université St. Joseph de Beyrouth*
Mid.	Middot

MS(S)	manuscript(s)
MT	Masoretic Text
NLR	National Library of Russia, Saint Petersburg, Firkovitch Hebrew (Yevr. [= Еврейский]) and Judaeo-Arabic (Yevr.-Arab. [= Еврейско-арабский]) Collections
NLT	New Living Translation
NPNF	Schaff, Philip, and Henry Wace, eds. *A Select Library of Nicene and Post-Nicene Fathers of the Christian Church.* 28 vols. in 2 series. Buffalo, NY: Christian Literature Company, 1886–1889.
NRSV	New Revised Standard Version
NS	New Series
Or	*Orientalia (NS)*
p(p).	page(s)
PAAJR	*Proceedings of the American Academy for Jewish Research*
Pes. Rab.	Pesikta Rabbati
Q	Qur'an
QG	*Quaestiones et solutiones in Genesin*
r	recto
Rab.	Rabbah (preceded by biblical book name)
RevQ	*Revue de Qumran*
Rosh Hash.	Rosh Hashanah
RSL	Russian State Library, Moscow
RSV	Revised Standard Version
RU	Rijks Universiteitsbibliotheek, Leiden
Sanh.	Sanhedrin
Shabb.	Shabbat
SP IOS	Saint Petersburg, Institute of Oriental Studies
SP RNL	Saint Petersburg, National Library of Russia
Ta'an	Ta'anit
Tanḥ.	Tanḥuma
v	verso
VT	*Vetus Testamentum*
WMANT	Wissenschaftliche Monographien zum Alten und Neuen Testament
y.	Jerusalem Talmud
Yevr.-Arab.	Russian National Library, St. Petersburg, Firkovitch Judaeo-Arabic collection
ZAL	*Zeitschrift für arabische Linguistik*

Acknowledgments

We are immensely grateful to all our contributors, on whose interesting academic and personal backgrounds the reader can read more in the contributors section (pp. 343–51 below). More than half of the contributors spent a period as postdoctoral fellows or research associates in the international research project Biblia Arabica: The Bible in Arabic among Jews, Christians and Muslims, funded by the German research organization Deutsche Forschungsgemeinschaft. This internationally led project engaged about thirty researchers in Tel Aviv University and the Ludwig Maximilian University of Munich during 2012–2018. Its purpose was to uncover, chart, and describe the different Jewish and Christian schools and individuals that took part in the medieval scriptural translation enterprise of rendering the Hebrew Bible and New Testament into Arabic, including their aims and agendas and their styles and techniques. The project also studied the social and cultural implications of their innovative and ambitious endeavor, and, no less important, the Jewish and Christian dialogue with Islamic sources and reception in Islamic tradition. Scholars of the Bible in Arabic are still engaged in an attempt to organize and systemize the discussion of countless manuscripts and fragments that nowadays are found in monasteries throughout the Middle East and libraries across the globe; to analyze the different methods of translation from Hebrew, Aramaic, Syriac, Greek, and Coptic; and to examine the mutual influences, both religious and cultural, between the different religious communities. In doing so, they illuminate the wider historical and social repercussions of the unique interreligious discourse in the Arabic Bible versions and the ambitious endeavor of their translators.[1]

---

1. On the many activities and publications of the Biblia Arabica project, among them an annotated bibliography, please consult the website www.biblia-arabica.com. With the termination of the funding period, the ongoing work is now managed by a consortium of international scholars; see therein.

The preparation and publication of this volume would not have been possible without the concentrated research period allowed many of its contributors by the generosity of the Deutsche Forschungsgemeinschaft. We are hence grateful to it for granting the individual contributors the opportunity to specialize or develop their existing expertise and so to follow the direction pursued in this volume. We are proud, also, that alongside some seasoned veterans in Judeo-Arabic studies, several of the contributors are relative newcomers to the field. Around half of them finished their doctoral dissertations in recent years, while others come from established careers in biblical, Jewish, Arabic, or Islamic studies and have taken on the challenge of exploring a new terrain.

We are most grateful to the Society of Biblical Literature and to SBL Press for their continuous patience and support and their wholehearted embrace of this project and its publication. We extend special thanks to John Kutsko, Bob Buller, and Nicole Tilford.

We have striven for a text selection that would give expression to a pluralistic array of scholars. Not only do the contributors come from diverse academic trainings; they also come from diverse Jewish, Christian, and Muslim backgrounds. All of them honor and engage these materials as genuine and important expressions of Arabic literature and its wider humanistic heritage. We hope that the publication of this anthology by SBL Press will contribute to the dissemination of these texts and other such materials also among Arab and Muslim readers, who might see in it a fruitful bridge to the past and present and a common inheritance and legacy. Above all, we hope our text selection will arouse deep interest among readers from all over the world and provide a challenge to their understanding of the Hebrew Bible as well as the cultural and literary heritage of the Middle East. To repeat: the fact that medieval Jewish authors made a conscious choice to write in Arabic on their most sacred text, the Hebrew Bible, and to engage with concepts and terms deeply imbued in Islamic culture is, we think, inspiring, since it is not the obvious or most natural choice. This makes us think about the meaning of conviviality in all its intricate forms—not all of which were, or are, of course, of this creative or positive kind. The intellectual history and wider heritage of the Jews of Islamic lands is therefore interwoven with the texts chosen for this volume.

****

Last but not least, a luminous figure among the contributors was our dear friend and colleague Ilana Sasson (11 June 1954–15 October 2017), *Zichrona Livrakha* (may her memory be blessed). Both her parents emigrated from Baghdad to Israel, where she was born in Ḥolon. She cherished her background even after many years in the United States, where she specialized in the field and raised her family; hence she is a fitting embodiment of the long history and legacy of the Jews of Islamic lands. Perhaps it is through some inner eye that her Hebrew name designates "tree" (*ilan*) and "joy" (*sason*). A special privilege it was to have been able to discuss and receive her contribution to this volume in good time. Ilana left us too soon, as we say in Hebrew, "before her time," yet not before having fostered, during her unique and impressive career, strong connections and a lively dialogue with many of the contributors to this volume, in kindness of heart and generosity of mind and spirit, that all of us recall. It is therefore only befitting that we dedicate this book to her memory with much love.[2]

Meira Polliack and Athalya Brennar-Idan
Tel Aviv, autumn 2019

---

2. ת.נ.צ.ב.ה. = תהי נפשה צרורה בצרור החיים (lit., "may her soul be bound up in the bond of [everlasting] life"). Readers are welcome to consult all her available articles on her academia.edu website.

Major Judeo-Arabic Commentators
(Ninth–Twelfth Centuries)

In the following list the reader will find some basic information, for quick general orientation, on the major medieval commentators mentioned in this volume and some others whose work we were unable to sample in the excerpts. For expansive discussions on their lives and works, as well as other figures you may come across in the contributions to this volume, please consult the recommended surveys of Judeo-Arabic literature, as well as individual entries on commentators' names, in the following reference works (most of which can nowadays be accessed electronically).

Halkin, Abraham S. "Judaeo-Arabic Literature." *EncJud* 10:410–23.
Stillman, Norman A. "Judeo-Arabic History and Linguistic Description." *EJIW* 3:53–58.
Tobi, Yosef. "Literature, Judeo-Arabic." *EJIW* 3:271–78.
Vajda, George. "Judaeo-Arabic Literature." *EI²* 4:303–7.
Wechsler, Michael G. "Interpretation, History of: Medieval Judaism in Arabic-Speaking Lands." *EBR* 13:95–105.

Ninth–Tenth Centuries

Benjamin/Binyamin al-Nahāwandī. First half of the ninth century, Persia/Iraq. Karaite theologian and exegete. Few fragments of his biblical commentaries are extant.

Daniel al-Qūmisī/al-Kumisi. Last quarter of the ninth century and early half of the tenth century, Persia/Iraq and Jerusalem. Prominent Karaite communal leader and exegete. His major commentary on the Minor Prophets was written in Hebrew, with Judeo-Arabic glosses.

David ben Abraham/Avraham al-Fāsī. Late tenth century, Jerusalem. Major Karaite lexicographer and exegete.

Dāwūd ibn Marwān al-Muqammaṣ. Mid-ninth century, Iraq. Jewish philosopher (whether Rabbanite or Karaite is debated). Converted temporarily to Christianity.

Ḥiwi al-Balkhi. Ninth century, Balakh, Afghanistan. Sectarian Jewish philosopher, author of polemical questions on the Hebrew Bible.

Judah (ben David) Ḥayyūj (Abū Zakariyya Yahya ibn Dawūd Hayyūj). Last third of the tenth century, Fez, Morocco, and Cordoba, Spain. Influential Rabbanite linguist and biblical grammarian.

Judah ibn Quraysh. Second half of the tenth century, North Africa. Rabbanite grammarian.

Saʿadia (ben Joseph) Gaon (Saʿīd al-Fayyūmī; Heb. acronym: Rasag, Rav Saʿadia Gaon). Born in Fayum, Egypt (882), died in Baghdad (942). Spent some time in Tiberias (around 905). Appointed Head (Gaon) of the Sura Yeshiva (Jewish center of learning) in the area of Baghdad in 928. Prominent Rabbanite communal leader, philosopher, linguist, and exegete of the tenth century.

Sahl ben Matsliaḥ. Latter half of the tenth century, Jerusalem. Karaite exegete. Composed partially extant commentaries on the Pentateuch, Isaiah, and Hosea.

Salmon ben Yerūḥīm/Yerūḥam/Jeroham (Sulaym ibn Ruḥaym). Contemporary of Saʿadia, active around the middle of the tenth century, Jerusalem. Major Karaite exegete and polemicist.

Yaʿqūb/Yaakov al-Qirqisānī. First half of the tenth century, Iraq. Karaite theologian and exegete. Produced a massive compendia (summa) of Karaite history, religious praxis, and theology, known as *The Book of Lights and Watchtowers* (*Kitāb al-anwār wal-marāqib*), replete with biblical exegesis and discussions of exegetical methodology.

Yefet/Japheth ben ʿEli (Abū ʿAlī Ḥasan ibn ʿAlī al-Baṣrī). Died after 1004/5, Jerusalem. The most prominent Karaite translator and exegete of the tenth century. The first Jewish exegete of any persuasion to compose programmatic commentaries, as well as Judeo-Arabic translations, on every book of the Hebrew Bible, all of which are extant in manuscript.

Yūsuf ibn Nūḥ (Abū Yaʿqūb ibn Nūḥ/ibn Bakhtawayh/Bakhtawī). Latter half of the tenth century, Jerusalem. Karaite grammarian and exegete. Credited with founding a "house of study" (*dār li-l-ʿilm*) in Jerusalem, which served as the locus of Karaite scholastic activity in the city during the tenth–eleventh centuries.

Eleventh–Twelfth Centuries

Abū al-Faraj Hārūn. Middle of the eleventh century, Jerusalem. Major Karaite grammarian and commentator of this period.

ʿAlī ben Sulaymān al-Muqaddasī. Late eleventh century, Jerusalem. Karaite exegete. Much of his literary output consisted of abridgments, adaptations, and compendiums of the works by previous Karaite exegetes of the Jerusalem school, such as his digest of Abū al-Faraj Hārūn's and Yūsuf ibn Nūḥ's commentaries on the Pentateuch, and his abridgment of Levi ben Yefet's own abridgment of al-Fāsī's lexicon of Biblical Hebrew.

Aaron (ben Joseph) ibn Sarjado. Rabbanite exegete of the early eleventh century. Known as Saʿadia's pupil and may in fact have completed Saʿadia's commentary on the Pentateuch.

David ben Boʿaz/Boaz. Second half of the eleventh century, Jerusalem. Karaite exegete and communal leader.

Isaac ibn Barūn. Died ca. 1135, Spain. Hebrew Grammarian. Rabbanite.

Isaac ibn Ghiyyāth. Second half of the eleventh century, Spain. Rabbanite philosopher, talmudic scholar, and exegete. Only his extensive commentary on Ecclesiastes has survived.

Isaac ben Samuel ha-Sefaradi (ibn al-Kanzī). First half of the twelfth century, Spain. He composed commentaries on the Former Prophets, of which only his commentary on Samuel is extant (mostly on 2 Samuel), wherein he relied much on Yefet.

Jonah ibn Janāḥ (Abū al-Walīd Marwān; Latin: Marinus). First half of the eleventh century, Cordoba and Zaragoza, Spain. The most influential Rabbanite grammarian and lexicographer of this period. Author of the magnum opus *Kitāb al-tanqīḥ*, consisting of both a comprehensive grammar of Biblical Hebrew (*Kitāb al-lumaʿ*) and a comprehensive lexicon (*Kitāb al-ʾuṣūl*).

Judah ibn Balʿam. Second half of the eleventh century, Spain. Rabbanite exegete. Composed a commentary on the entire Hebrew Bible, focusing mainly on philological issues.

Levi ben Yefet (son of Yefet ben 'Eli). Middle of the eleventh century, Jerusalem. Karaite jurist and exegete.

Moshe ben Maymon (Mūsā ibn Maymūn; Latin: Moses Maimonides). Born in Cordoba, Spain (1135 or 1138), active in Morocco and Egypt, where he died in Cairo (1204); buried in Tiberias (lower Galilee). In Hebrew works to this day he is referred to by the acronym **Rambam** ("[Our] Rabbi Moses, son of Maymon"). The most prolific and influential Rabbanite communal leader, philosopher, legal scholar, and exegete.

Moses ibn Gikatilla. Second half of the eleventh century, Cordoba and Zaragoza, Spain. Rabbanite exegete and grammarian.

Sahl ibn Faḍl (Yashar ben Ḥesed). End of the eleventh century, Jerusalem. Karaite exegete.

Samuel ben Ḥofni Gaon. Rabbanite legal scholar and exegete of the early eleventh century, and Head (Gaon) of the Sura Yeshiva (Jewish center of learning) in the area of Baghdad (998–1013). He followed in the exegetical vein of Sa'adia and may in fact have completed his commentary on the Pentateuch (together with Sa'adia's other pupil Aaron [b. Joseph] ibn Sarjado).

Samuel (ibn Naghrella) ha-Nagid. First half of the eleventh century, Cordoba and Granada, Spain. Hebrew poet, talmudic commentator, and communal leader. Produced an extensive grammatical oeuvre, including a lexicon of Biblical Hebrew, of which only a few fragments are extant.

Tanchum/Tanḥum ben Joseph ha-Yerushalmi. Died 1291 in Fustat (Old Cairo). Prolific Rabbanite exegete. His work shows acquaintance with Yefet's writings.

Yeshu'ah ben Yehudah (Abū al-Faraj Furqān ibn Asad). Second half of the eleventh century, Jerusalem. The leading Karaite translator and exegete of the twelfth century. His extant works include both short and long commentaries on the Pentateuch, with Arabic translation. These reflect detailed acquaintance and thoughtful interaction with previous Karaite as well as Rabbanite exegesis, and significant influence by the Islamic Mu'tazilite school of theology.

Yūsuf al-Baṣīr (Joseph ben Abraham). Middle of the eleventh century, Jerusalem. Leading Karaite theologian and exegete.

Introduction

Meira Polliack

Since the 1990s we have been witnessing a renewed interest in medieval Bible exegesis written in the Arabic language by Jews from Islamic lands. This is especially evident in a large number of recent editions and detailed studies of their Bible translations and commentaries originally written in this language, also known as Judeo-Arabic. However, this interest is not a new phenomenon.

A Very Short History of Research

In Western Europe, the scholarly study of Jewish texts written in Arabic goes back to the early seventeenth century. At that time a growing number of Arabic manuscripts began to reach major library collections, often purchased through travels to the Middle East by scholars trained in Semitic languages, such as Oxford's first professor of Arabic, Edward Pococke (1604–1691).[1] The increasing access to Arabic texts led to a change of approach. While late-Renaissance scholars were largely concerned with ecclesiastical aspects of Arabic Bible versions, the growing physical access

---

1. Pockoke was an ordained priest in the Church of England and an alumnus of Corpus Christi College at Oxford. He spent several years in Constantinople and Aleppo, during which time he collected hundreds of oriental manuscripts (purchased by Oxford in 1693). The position of Laudian Professor of Arabic to which he was appointed was established in 1636 by William Laud, who at the time was Chancellor of the University of Oxford and Archbishop of Canterbury. See the delightful illustrated post by a contributor to our anthology, Michael G. Wechsler, "Edward Pococke and the Emergence of Arabic Studies in Late-Renaissance Europe," https://biblia-arabica. com/edward-pococke. On the Renaissance period and its shortage of manuscripts, see Karl Dannenfeld, "The Renaissance Humanists and the Knowledge of Arabic," *Studies in the Renaissance* 2 (1955): 96–117.

to manuscripts in the seventeenth century, compounded by the invention of moveable type, played a seminal role in the European flowering of Arabic studies. On the one hand, this was the era of the lavish polyglots, such as those printed in London (1653–1657) and Paris (1628–1645), which expanded general attention to the field and included Arabic Bible versions, too.[2] On the other, the valuable manuscript finds facilitated a detailed academic exposure to the precious literary heritage of Arabic and its scholarly appreciation. From the start, leading Semitists were not only concerned with Christian and Muslim Arabic sources, but also with Jewish Arabic literature that they cited profusely in their work, both in the original and in translation. Training in several Semitic languages—especially Arabic, Aramaic, and Hebrew (often in addition to a classical education in Greek and Latin)—was deep-seated in European scholarship. It enabled a wide comparative outlook on the spectrum of ancient and medieval sources of these three religions (nowadays often called "Abrahamic religions" in order to stress their common heritage). This training eventually led to a second peak in the study of Judeo-Arabic literature during the nineteenth century. The major scholarly figure of this era is Moriz Steinschneider (1816–1906), the Austro-Hungarian Jewish bibliographer and Semitist. His seminal and influential work, *Die arabische Literartur der Juden*, offered the first taxonomic attempt to describe the names, writers, and branches of Judeo-Arabic literature according to the manuscript sources available to him at the time (dating mainly from the thirteenth–fourteenth centuries).[3] Therein Steinschneider described his arduous search for manuscripts throughout

---

2. On the Arabic Pentateuch in early printed books, in some of which Saʿadia's Judeo-Arabic Tafsīr figures prominently, see the detailed survey by a contributor to this volume, Ronny Vollandt, *Arabic Versions of the Pentateuch: A Comparative Study of Jewish, Christian, and Muslim Sources* (Leiden: Brill, 2015), 108–38.

3. Moriz Steinschneider, *Die arabische Literartur der Juden* (Frankfurt: J. Kauffmann, 1902). See also the English adaptation of the same work, published in a series of articles as Steinschneider, "Introduction to the Arabic Literature of the Jews," *JQR* 9.2 (1897): 224–39; 9.4 (1897): 604–30; 10.1 (1897): 119–38; 10.3 (1898): 513–40; 11.1 (1898): 115–49; 11.2 (1899): 305–43; 11.3 (1899): 480–89; 11.4 (1899): 585–625; 12.1 (1899): 114–32; 12.2 (1900): 195–212; 12.3 (1900): 481–501; 12.4 (1900): 602–17; 13.1 (1900): 92–110; 13.2 (1901): 296–320; 13.3 (1901): 446–87. See also the recent appraisal of his work by Irene E. Zwiep, "Beyond Orientalism? Steinschneider on Islam, Religion and Plurality," in *Modern Jewish Scholarship on Islam in Context, Rationality, European Borders, and the Search for Belonging*, ed. Ottfried Fraisse (Berlin: de Gruyter, 2018), 202–17.

Europe since 1845, and he expressed his personal esteem for the unique Judeo-Arabic literary culture as follows:

> Arabic and German are the only languages and nationalities which have been of essential and continuing influence on Judaism. A statement of the extent and duration of the usage of the Arabic language by the Jews would, indeed, exceed the limits of what is here our principle subject, viz. the Arabic literature; but here I only give some hints of the life, customs, institutions, and their designations.[4]

The branches of Judeo-Arabic literature surveyed by Steinschneider included poetry, grammatical thought, philosophy, polemics, homiletics, translation, exegesis, medicine, astronomy, and even some specific sub-genres such as designated commentaries on the Ten Commandments. Considering the difficulties that faced him in obtaining manuscript sources and the fact that he had no occasion to avail himself to the Arabic and Judeo-Arabic material in the Cairo Genizah (which was uncovered in 1897), the fruits of Steinschneider's labor are impressive, both in scope and in detail. Much water has flowed under the bridge since then, and our readers interested in the wider picture are warmly encouraged to consult more recent and updated encyclopedic surveys of Judeo-Arabic literature. These include works by Abraham S. Halkin, George Vajda, Norman A. Stillman, Yosef Tobi, and Michael G. Wechsler.[5]

The eventual breakthrough in the sociohistorical and the sociolinguistic study of Judeo-Arabic literature and culture was inevitably linked to the hoard of new manuscript sources uncovered in the Cairo Genizah and in the Karaite *genizot* of the Firkovitch Collections, the bulk of which became fully available to scholars throughout the second half of the twentieth century.[6] The scholarly figure most connected with the reevaluation

---

4. Steinschneider, "Introduction," *JQR* 12.3 (1900): 481.

5. Abraham S. Halkin, "Judaeo-Arabic Literature," *EncJud* 10:410–23; George Vajda, "Judaeo-Arabic Literature," *EI*² 4:303–7; Norman A. Stillman, "Judeo-Arabic History and Linguistic Description," *EJIW* 3:53–58; Yosef Tobi, "Literature, Judeo-Arabic," *EJIW* 3:271–78; Michael G. Wechsler, "Interpretation, History of: Medieval Judaism in Arabic-Speaking Lands," *EBR* 13:95–105.

6. On the Cairo Genizah finds and research on them, see Stefan C. Reif, *A Jewish Archive from Old Cairo: The History of Cambridge University's Genizah Collection* (Richmond, Surry: Curzon Press, 2000); Adina Hoffman and Peter Cole, *Sacred Trash: The Lost and Found World of the Cairo Geniza* (New York: Schocken, 2011).

of this literature during this period is the German-born Jewish historian, Semitist, and ethnographer Shelomo Dov Goitein (1900–1985), known for his research on Jewish life in the Islamic Middle Ages. He was appointed professor of Islamic history and Islamic studies at the Hebrew University of Jerusalem in 1928, and in 1957 he took the chair of Arabic studies at the University of Pennsylvania, finally to become in 1971 a member of the prestigious Institute of Advanced Studies in Princeton. I focus on this meteoric career in order to illustrate the rise of the field and Goitein's immense contribution to its wider outreach and acknowledgment, including the training of a whole generation of leading scholars who worked on Judeo-Arabic materials in Israel and the United States (among them Mark R. Cohen, Mordechai A. Friedman, and Moshe Gil).[7] In bringing the field to the limelight of the sociohistorical school current at his time, Goitein recognized the insufficiency of classicist categories in describing the Judeo-Arabic oeuvre. He turned specifically to the documentary, everyday-type materials in the Cairo Genizah (personal letters, accounts, legal responses, bills, stock lists, etc.), as an alternative source for sociohistorical study, and less to Judeo-Arabic literature per se. Nevertheless, our readers are well-advised to consult his six-volume magnum opus, *A Mediterranean Society: The Jewish Communities of the Arab World as Portrayed in the Documents of the Cairo Geniza*.[8] While Goitein addressed literary Judeo-Arabic sources (including Bible exegesis) in his monumental work, especially in the fourth volume of *Mediterranean Society*, these became a primary focus of research onto themselves later in the 1990s.[9]

---

7. To gauge the spirit of the time, see Sabine Schmidtke's illuminating essay, "Near and Middle Eastern Studies at the Institute of Advanced Study: A Historical Sketch," in *Studying the Near and Middle East in the Institute of Advanced Study, Princeton, 1935–2018*, ed. Sabine Schmidtke (Piscataway, NJ: Gorgias, 2018), xxxi–xcviii.

8. Shelomo Dov Goitein, *A Mediterranean Society: The Jewish Communities of the Arab World as Portrayed in the Documents of the Cairo Geniza*, 6 vols. (Berkeley: University of California Press, 1967–1993).

9. On Arabic materials in the Cairo Genizah, see Geoffrey Khan, "The Arabic Fragments in the Cambridge Genizah Collections," *Manuscripts of the Middle East* 1 (1986): 54–61. On the Judeo-Arabic materials, see Colin F. Baker, "Judaeo-Arabic Material in the Cambridge Genizah Collections," *BSOAS* 58 (1995): 445–54; and Colin F. Baker and Meira Polliack, *Arabic and Judaeo-Arabic Manuscripts in the Cambridge Genizah Collections, Arabic Old Series (T–S Ar. 1a–54)* (Cambridge: Cambridge University Press, 2001); Meira Polliack, "Arabic Bible Translations in the Cairo Genizah Collection in *Jewish Studies in a New Europe: The Proceedings of the Fifth Congress of*

Looking back at these scholars, many of whom (such as Jacob Mann) I have omitted from this cursory opening survey, we generally miss the old European vantage point today. Now scholarly training for Semitists tends to be more narrow; combining Hebrew and Arabic to the same or close degree of expertise has become uncommon. Yet each age has its advantages too: in the past, Judeo-Arabic literature was not so much considered as a *sui generis* phenomenon which requires—indeed demands—independent tools of research. Its study suffered from the effects of its nineteenth-century portrayal as an "admixed" (then a dubious word) literature, addressing Jewish themes in an Arabic tongue or Arabic themes in a Jewish tongue, thus "impure" in its forms of expression and writing. As data, learning, and research trends change over time, we have become more careful of tendentiously and ideologically framing a culture, though perhaps not enough so. Generally, and in the present day, scholars make more of an attempt to understand the textual phenomena (such as the Judeo-Arabic literature represents) as literature produced by a multicultural, hybrid/mixed society, of the kind that no doubt existed in the premodern Islamic world, and without dismissing its historical development and complexities.

What might we mean by hybrid/mixed culture? Nowadays these terms tend to describe such a society as if it were a multicolored tapestry or mosaic of cultural and linguistic strands and identities. This is not to be confused with inauthenticity or lack of genuineness. Hence, the term *Judeo-Arabic literature* designates the rich oeuvre—literary, religious, popular, and scientific—created by the Jews of Islamic lands in the Arabic language during the medieval and modern periods (although the latter period does not concern us in this volume and, due to its special developments, merits a separate one).

The Judeo-Arabic Language

Essentially, this language is a form of medieval (also termed "Middle") Arabic that deviates from Classical Arabic in that it reflects some neo-Arabic dialectical features and pseudo-corrective elements. It is also distinguished by two other salient features that act as Jewish identity

Jewish Studies in Copenhagen 1994, ed. Ulf Haxen, Hanne Trautner-Kromann, and Karen Lisa Goldschmidt Salamon (Copenhagen: C. A. Reitzel, 1998), 35–61. On the Firkovitch Collections, see n. 28.

markers: the use of Hebrew rather than Arabic script in writing; and the occurrence of Hebrew and Aramaic words within the Arabic text, sometimes in Arabized form, such as *leshon qodesh* ("holy tongue"), *shabbat* ("Sabbath day"), and *al-torah* ("the Torah").

Accordingly, one cannot end this short stroll into the history of research without mentioning Joshua Blau's seminal studies on the linguistic features of Judeo-Arabic. These have contributed immensely to the flowering of research on Judeo-Arabic literary sources, above all his groundbreaking (and still the most definitive) *A Grammar of Mediaeval Judaeo-Arabic* and his foundational study *The Emergence and Linguistic Background of Judaeo-Arabic*.[10] Early in Blau's seminal works, the term *Middle Arabic* was used to describe Judeo-Arabic both chronologically (referring to its medieval stage, as a link between Old and New Arabic) and stylistically (in designating the admixture of Classical Arabic and vernacular elements akin to modern [spoken] Arabic). In the revised editions, Blau refined the definition of Middle Arabic texts as constituting "a continuum of a whole range of styles with infinitely varied mixtures of Classical and Neo-Arabic elements."[11] This is no small matter, as it goes to show the changing perspective on the linguistic features of Judeo-Arabic and its long history, both as a written and as a spoken language, that are reflected in its vast and important literature from medieval to modern times. The term *mixed* is thus increasingly used to give fair expression to the social functions (and agility) of its spoken and written forms. In his important sociolinguistic studies, Benjamin H. Hary convincingly and consistently argued over the last decades that Judeo-Arabic should be defined as an "ethnolect" or "religiolect" and that it reflects a state of "multiglossia" rather than "diglossia" since it is a mix of "elements of Classical Arabic, dialectal components, pseudo-corrected features and the standardization of such features."[12] Hary further stresses its distinctive nature:

---

10. Joshua Blau, *A Grammar of Mediaeval Judaeo-Arabic*, 2nd enlarged ed. (Jerusalem: Magnes, 1980); Blau, *The Emergence and Linguistic Background of Judaeo-Arabic: A Study of the Origins of Neo-Arabic and Middle Arabic*, 3rd rev. ed. (Jerusalem: Ben-Zvi Institute, 1999). For alternative sociolinguistic models in defining Judeo-Arabic, see especially Benjamin H. Hary's important works, including *Multiglossia in Judeo-Arabic: With an Edition, Translation and Grammatical Study of the Cairene Purim Scroll* (Leiden: Brill, 1992), 3–111; Per A. Bengtsson, *Two Arabic Versions of the Book of Ruth: Text Edition and Language Studies* (Lund: Lund University Press, 1995), 85–99.

11. Blau, *Emergence*, 217.

12. Hary, *Multiglossia*, xiii (quotation) and 55–69. Also consider, in this respect,

Judaeo-Arabic is not just a language, it is a Jewish language, typical of Jewish communities in the Diaspora which adopted a local language and wrote in Hebrew script with Hebrew and Aramaic elements penetrating the lexicon and the grammar. The language was used by Jews for Jewish readers and speakers and treated mainly Jewish themes in its literature. This, by itself, justifies granting Judeo-Arabic the status of a separate language or at least a separate ethnolect.[13]

In this respect, Judeo-Arabic belongs to the family of Jewish languages, including Judeo-Spanish (Ladino) and Judeo-German (Yiddish). These functioned—throughout lengthy periods and in defined geographical areas—as live oral and literary media for Jewish identity in the diaspora. In comparison to Ladino and Yiddish, it is possible to argue that Judeo-Arabic had the most formative and lasting effect on the spiritual and creative life of the Jewish people as a whole.

Why might we claim this? First, because, as Stillman states, "it was the medium of expression for one of the foremost periods of Jewish cultural and intellectual creativity."[14] Second, since it set an unprecedented and rarely surpassed range of branches, subject fields, and genres in nonfiction and fiction, which became the backbone of Jewish medieval literature, and without which we cannot envisage the development of modern Hebrew literature and Jewish thought as a whole.

Judeo-Arabic Literature

One may find a bird's eye view of the spectrum of Judeo-Arabic literature in the following short survey of its literary branches.

Theology, General Philosophy and Ethics. Includes, in this order, the major works of Saʿadia Gaon, *Book of Beliefs and Opinions* (*Kitāb al-ʾamānāt*

Blau's emphasis (*Emergence*, 49): "It was felt by the Jews themselves to be a distinct literary language. It was consequently used by writers who could equally well have written in more Classical language, had they so chosen, and its distinctive character finds expression in the possession of its own literary tradition."

13. Hary, *Multiglossia*, 105. See also Meira Polliack, "Single-Script Mixed-Code Literary Sources from the Cairo Genizah and Their Sociolinguistic Context," in *Jewish Languages in Historical Perspective*, ed. Lily Kahn (Leiden: Brill, 2018), 65–91.

14. Norman A. Stillman, *The Language and Culture of the Jews of Sefrou, Morocco: An Ethnolinguistic Study* (Manchester: University of Manchester Press, 1988), 3–4.

wal-'i'tiqādāt);[15] Maimonides, *Guide to the Perplexed* (*Dalālat al-ḥā'irīn*); and Maimonides, *Eight Chapters* (*Thamāniyyah fuṣūl*, originally his introduction to his commentary on Mishnah Avot, yet circulated separately).

Mystical Works. Reflecting Islamic Sufi influences alongside those of ancient Jewish mysticism, for example, Baḥya ibn Paqudah, *Duties of the Hearts* (*Kitāb al-hidāyah 'ilā farā'iḍ al-qulūb*).

Polemical Literature. Anti-Christian works such as "The Polemic of Nestor the Priest" (*Qiṣṣat mujadalat al-'usquf*).

Legal (halakhic) Works. Maimonides's Judeo-Arabic commentary on the Mishnah and many other monographs and compositions that discuss or enumerate religious laws in the Mishnah and Talmud, often by the *Geonim* (the heads of the *yeshivot*, the hallowed medieval Jewish learning centers of Iraq and Eretz Israel, such as Saʿadia, Hai Gaon, and Samuel ben Ḥofni Gaon).

Liturgy and Prayer. *Siddurim* (prayer books) by Saʿadia Gaon and Solomon ben Nathan of Sijilmasa (southwest Morocco). In these the liturgical instructions (rubrics) are in Judeo-Arabic, while the prayer text is in Hebrew. They also contain original Judeo-Arabic liturgy or translations of specific prayers, such as the Eighteen Benedictions.

Literature, Midrash, and Folklore. A common source of popular and ethical legends is Nissim Gaon's *Book of Comfort after Adversity* (known as *Ibn Shahin's Kitāb fī al-faraj baʿd al-shiddah*), which makes use of a known Arabic genre by this name and also derives from Hebrew midrashic literature. Similar in popularity, though more strictly adaptive of midrashic sources, is the Arabic compilation by David ben Abraham Maimonides known as *Midrash David ha-Nagid*. Proper Arabic translations of classical midrashim such as *Eikhah* (Lamentations) *Rabbah* are also available. A separate genre consists of tales (*qiṣaṣ*) on biblical or apocryphal characters such as Abraham, Joseph, and Hannah, sometimes in rhymed prose, which partly derives from late Muslim sources.[16] There are also popular historical chronicles, including the Alexander Romance and Arabic accounts of the Maccabee history, and literary works such as *The Thousand and One Nights* and *Kalila wa-dimna*, attested in Arabic and Hebrew script. To these may

---

15. Please note that, when transliterating from Arabic into English, except for Arabic book titles and some other cases, we have generally opted to leave out hyphens for long vowels, in order to facilitate the flow of the reading for those uninformed in Arabic. See further below on our editorial decisions.

16. Rachel Hasson's contribution on Solomon in our volume pertains to this genre.

be added transcribed sections of the Qur'an and the Arabic New Testament. The *maqamah*, gird poem (*muwashaḥ*), love poem (*ghazal*), and rhymed prose (*sajʿ*) are also attested, both in Arabic and in Judaeo-Arabic, as original compositions or as transcriptions from known Arabic works.

Poetics. This subfield is likewise represented, especially Moses ibn Ezra's *Book of Discussion and Conversation* (*Kitāb al-muḥāḍarah wal-mudhākarah*).

Science and Medicine. Including mathematics, engineering, astronomy, astrological almanacs, calendrical treatises relating to intercalation, and dream interpretation manuals. Magic and occultism fall under the wider conception of the sciences in the early medieval period. The medical literature is particularly rich and its subject matter varies considerably, consisting of medicine proper (such as the description of diseases, diagnosis and treatment, pharmacology) and paramedical material relating to the management of patients and the medical profession.[17]

Hebrew Grammar and Masora. This genre brings us closer to the subject matter of our volume. It includes grammatical and lexicographical works on biblical Hebrew, such as Jonah ibn Janaḥ's *Book of Roots* (*Kitāb al-ʾuṣūl*), Saʿadia's treatise on seventy Hebrew *hapax legomena* (*Kitāb al-sabʿīn lafẓah*), or David ben Abraham al-Fāsī's Hebrew-Arabic Dictionary (*Kitāb jāmiʿ al-ʾalfāẓ*);[18] and masoretic compilations, such as Mishael ben Uzziel's *Book of Differences* (*Kitāb al-khilaf*), which relates to the differences between Ben Asher and Ben Naphtali on the reading tradition of the Hebrew Bible. Grammatical commentaries that focus on syntactical issues, rare words, and etymologies, while commenting on a biblical passage, also belong to this category.

Yet most notable among all Judeo-Arabic branches is systematic *Biblical Interpretation*, to which our volume anthology is mostly devoted. About a quarter of the literary corpus that has survived in manuscripts belongs to this category. This proportion certainly reflects the importance of Hebrew Bible translations and commentaries in the reading and education system of Jews from Islamic lands. The commentaries are often divided into Rabbanite or Karaite works, or "schools" in various discussions of biblical reception history, yet early on we made the decision to

---

17. See the detailed introduction in Haskell D. Isaacs, ed., *Medical and Paramedical Manuscripts in the Cambridge Genizah Collection* (Cambridge: Cambridge University Press, 1994).

18. See Esther Gamliel-Barak's contribution about this dictionary (129–38).

present them here together, as part of the same cloth of Judeo-Arabic
Bible exegesis from Islamic lands. The Karaite movement, which emerged
mainly in Iraq in the late ninth century, was an integral part of medieval
Judaism. Its main ethos was scriptural and messianic: it espoused a full
spiritual and intellectual return to the Hebrew Bible and to the promised
land, and it indeed settled in Jerusalem where the Karaites established a
thriving learning center in the tenth–eleventh centuries. We shall return
to them later on, yet they are interlaced with Rabbanite authors in our
volume, quite intentionally. Readers will also note the interwoven aspect
of grammatical debate in many of the commentaries, and their overlapping with philosophy and theology. This is precisely the type of fusion
one will find in Judeo-Arabic Bible exegesis. It reflects the rich intellectual world of its authors: often they will discuss purely theological and
even philosophical themes, such as the nature of creation and humans or
a complex syntactical issue, as part of their insightful literary engagement
with various biblical passages.

The multifarious nature of Judeo-Arabic literature transpires even
from a short survey of this kind. It is the tendency of classification to
simplify complex, multilayered literary phenomena, and thus it can only
capture a glimpse of the intricacy and vastness of Judeo-Arabic literature,
whose creativity was fueled by the ability to transfer, transmit, and filter
various subject matter from Hebrew and Arabic into Judeo-Arabic. The
new literary forms created through this process—in fiction and nonfiction—were often born out of old forms (originally available to the Jews in
Hebrew, Aramaic, or Arabic literatures) by way of inversion, displacement,
and combination. The media of translation and adaptation functioned as a
sieve through which known classes of texts were passed and transformed
into something different and new. The norms of the recognizable old forms
retained visibility by being transgressed, and they were often revitalized by
becoming refashioned norms.

More on the Genre of Judeo-Arabic Bible Exegesis

Translation and adaptation were thus the activators of the various genres
of Judeo-Arabic literature. As the reader of this volume may note, the
classes of texts that were born of this process, among them Bible exegesis and translation, were often highly innovative and even subversive in
respect to the cultural horizons of their authors, a fact that allowed for
their development and growth.

No matter how complex the Judeo-Arabic text or commentary to which you are drawn in your reading, do keep in mind that in part it reflects a written or oral tradition, which in some intricate way came about through different registers of language, from Classical to Middle Arabic or vice versa, from Hebrew or Arabic into Judeo-Arabic. This is partly the reason for the difficulty in translating it into communicative English. The editors and various contributors have gone a long way towards this end, in order to enable a natural reading flow in English.

In Judeo-Arabic Bible commentary, earlier Jewish exegetical traditions inevitably went through a change of content, which mediated between them and the Arabic target culture as a whole, while new layers and insights were forged and sealed. The beginning and end of this process of transculturation are difficult to envisage, yet it was a process typical of Jewish existence in the diaspora as a whole.[19] From the earliest periods of encounter with host languages and cultures, long before the contacts with the Arabs, Jews applied the media of translation and adaptation (for example, into Greek, Aramaic, and Persian) as a means of bridging the gap between the old and the new, between the self and the other; thus they retained an independent, agile, and vibrant identity. It is likely that these long adaptive modes of cultural interaction were regenerated in the encounter with Arabic thought and literature, becoming a means of self-expression for any Jew who spoke or wrote in Arabic. If the boundaries of our world correspond to those of our language, then one who absorbs a bilingual or multilingual atmosphere from early childhood is likely to experience interchangeable mental boundaries. For such a person, reading a biblical commentary in Judeo-Arabic serves not only as a cultural outlet, but also as a psychological outlet of primary importance in that it enables some level of integration between different self-identities. It is apparent that Jewish existence in the world of Islam and the cultural flowering it inspired turned new modes into an essential medium of self-expression and creativity in various forms of Jewish language usage, whether spoken or written, sacred or mundane.

Yet setting this scholarly history aside, an informed reader may well ask several questions.

---

19. On the term *transculturation*, which designates transference on the combined levels of language and culture in all that they entail, see James Barr, *The Semantics of Biblical Language* (repr. London: SCM, 1981), 4. Consider also his general study on the contrasts between Greek and Hebrew thought (8–45).

(1) *Why did medieval Jews use the Arabic language for writing on
the Bible in the first place? Was not Hebrew their literary and consecrated
tongue?* The answer to this question has been partly supplied above, yet
it is complex. Yes, since ancient times and throughout their history and
in different places, Jews continued to write and read in Hebrew, though
often in conjunction with other host culture languages such as Greek and
Aramaic. In the medieval Islamic world, Jews also retained Hebrew for
prayer, liturgy, poetry, jurisprudence, and some personal correspondence,
as evidenced in the Cairo Genizah sources.[20] The Jews adopted Arabic for
nonfictional purposes, as did many Christians in the region, mainly in
their philosophical, scientific, and exegetical literature. This process was
closely and naturally linked to the advent and spread of Islam from the
seventh century CE, and to the diffusion and use of Arabic throughout the
Middle East and southern Mediterranean (not only as a spoken language
but also as a language of literary expression) from the eighth century. The
Jews took strongly to Arabic for many reasons, such as social mobility and
access to wider culture, but also due to its closeness to Hebrew. They began
writing and reading it, in Hebrew script, as early as the late ninth century.

(2) *Why did they not use Arabic script but preferred to transliterate
Arabic into Hebrew letters?* This is probably due to sociolinguistic as well
as cultural issues. Jews learned to read Hebrew as part of their religious
upbringing, whereas mastering Arabic script was not as compulsory or as
affordable for many. Intellectuals and professionals did, of course, learn
the more complicated calligraphy of Arabic writing.

(3) *Yet how was it that the Jews became so immersed in Arabic culture?* Here, too, sociology—namely, minority and majority relations,
social mobility, et cetera—is only part of the answer, as is Arabic's linguistic closeness to Hebrew and Aramaic. A lot can be said for the strong
influence and dialogue with Islamic literary and intellectual culture as a
challenging model for the Jews. Many of the conceptual, methodological,
and compositional elements of Jewish Bible exegesis are informed by this
model.[21] The readers will no doubt feel the imbued Arabic and Islamic ter-

---

20. On the Cairo Genizah, see nn. 6–9 above.

21. On this issue, see Rina Drory's seminal work, *The Emergence of Jewish-Arabic
Literary Contacts at the Beginning of the Tenth Century* [Hebrew] (Tel Aviv: Porter
Institute of Poetics and Semiotics, Tel Aviv University, 1988), 156–78; and Drory,
Models and Contacts: Arabic Literature and Its Impact on Medieval Jewish Culture
(Leiden: Brill, 2000), which contains a synopsis of certain sections of her work in

minology and notions in almost every text in our anthology. They should keep in mind that this was not a necessary choice yet was one which came naturally, whether consciously or unconsciously, to these medieval Jewish authors. It certainly tells us much as to how deeply they felt Arabic culture to be their intellectual home.

Lastly, one should also recall that in the broadest sense the history of Jewish Bible exegesis from Islamic lands, also called Judeo-Arabic Bible interpretation, extends well beyond the linguistic borders of works written in Arabic. It includes works written by Jews in Hebrew in which these distinctively Islamic elements are attested. Famous medieval commentators from the eleventh to thirteenth centuries such as Abraham Ibn Ezra or David Kimhi (RaDak), whose works eventually became canonized in the rabbinic Bibles printed from the sixteenth century, are also part of this story. They were addressing a Jewish audience in Christian Europe that was unfamiliar with Arabic, yet their personal and family roots lay deep in the heritage of Muslim Spain. They were well aware of the vast literature on the Bible originally written in Judeo-Arabic, and they transfused many of its concepts and notions into their Hebrew works. Above all, they retained many of the linguistic-contextual and rationalistic strands typical of "the school of Judeo-Arabic exegesis."[22] Nonetheless, for the purpose of

---

Hebrew plus additional materials; Miriam Goldstein, "'Arabic Composition 101' and the Early Development of Judaeo-Arabic Bible Exegesis," *JSS* 55 (2010): 451–78; Meira Polliack, "Deconstructing the Dual Torah: A Jewish Response to the Muslim Model of Scripture," in *Interpreting Scriptures in Judaism, Christianity and Islam: Overlapping Inquiries*, ed. Mordechai Z. Cohen and Adele Berlin (Cambridge: Cambridge University Press, 2016), 113–29.

22. For recent works that attempt an overview of this school's exegetical methodology, see Haggai Ben Shammai, "The Tension between Literal Interpretation and Exegetical Freedom: Comparative Observation on Saadia's Method," in *With Reverence for the Word: Medieval Scriptural Exegesis in Judaism, Christianity and Islam*, ed. Jane Dammen McAuliffe, Barry D. Walfish, and Joseph W. Goering (Oxford: Oxford University Press, 2003), 33–50; and also Ben Shammai's earlier "The Exegetical and Philosophical Writing of Saadia: A Leader's Endeavor" [Hebrew], *Peʿamim* 54 (1993): 63–81; Daniel Frank, *Search Scripture Well: Karaite Exegetes and the Origins of the Jewish Bible Commentary in the Islamic East* (Leiden: Brill, 2006); Miriam Goldstein, *Karaite Exegesis in Medieval Jerusalem: The Judeo-Arabic Pentateuch Commentary of Yusuf ibn Nuh and Abu al-Faraj Harun* (Tübingen: Mohr Siebeck, 2011); Meira Polliack, "Concepts of Scripture among the Jews of the Islamic World," in *Jewish Concepts of Scripture: A Comparative Introduction*, ed. Benjamin D. Sommer (New York: New York University Press, 2012), 80–101.

this volume we have restricted consideration to representing the reader with a tasting menu of exegetical texts written in Judeo-Arabic ranging from the tenth and eleventh centuries, also known as the "classical" and often "golden" formative period of Judeo-Arabic exegesis and creativity at large. Our purpose is to whet the palate of current Bible scholars and students by engaging them in discussions of texts and themes related to the three major divisions of the Hebrew Bible, structured accordingly under Pentateuch, Prophets, and Writings. We wish to open up this rich and perplexing world through first-hand and often first-time engagement with selected excerpts from this immense and thought-provoking litera-ture that is seldom engaged by the interpretive reading curriculum on the Hebrew Bible or in the study of its reception history. It is for you, our dear readers, to judge if we have done this successfully.

Not all of the major medieval figures are included in our selection, and hence it should not be read as a *definitive* anthology. Nevertheless, the major *Rabbanite* and *Karaite* exegetes of this era are well represented.

(4) *What do we mean by these designations Rabbanite and Karaite?* As already stated, the Karaites represent an intellectually powerful stream in medieval Judaism, which generally rejected the authority of the rabbinic traditions as canonized in the Mishnah and Talmud; they instead offered a return to the Hebrew Bible as part of their restructuring of a scriptural-based Jewish faith. The Rabbanites espoused rabbinic tradition, and the two groups engaged in intensive exegetical and polemical debates. Readers will sense the tension between Scripture and tradition as they delve into the pages of the different commentaries and excerpts. Many of the discus-sions offered by our contributors hinge on these issues as well.

(5) *Why did Judaism verge on a dogmatic split during this era?* Here again the answer lies in the surrounding culture. Something about the powerful encounter with Islam and its scriptural models led to intellectual unrest and a reexamination of the past.[23]

---

23. On Karaism and its history, see Meira Polliack, "Medieval Karaism," in *The Oxford Handbook of Jewish Studies*, ed. Martin Goodman (Oxford: Oxford University Press, 2002), 295–326, and further bibliography therein; Yoram Erder, "The Mourners of Zion: The Karaites in Jerusalem in the Tenth and Eleventh Centuries," in *Karaite Judaism: A Guide to its History and Literary Sources*, ed. Meira Polliack (Leiden: Brill, 2003), 213–35; Fred Astren, *Karaite Judaism and Historical Understanding* (Colum-bia: University of South Carolina Press, 2004), 1–123; Meira Polliack, "Re-thinking Karaism: Between Judaism and Islam," *AJSR* 30 (2006): 67–93; Marina Rustow, *Heresy*

Our Volume, and the Reasons It Has Come to
Fruition in the Here and Now

In early Jewish studies, as they developed in Europe and Israel, the medieval (secular) Hebrew poetry of the Jews of Muslim Spain (Andalucia) had always been regarded as one of the pinnacles of Jewish creativity, studied and taught as an expression of "the Sephardi Golden Era." In this conception were included some major philosophical and poetic works written originally in Judeo-Arabic that had entered the Hebrew canon already in the Middle Ages through medieval Hebrew translations such as *The Book of Beliefs and Opinions* by Sa'adia Gaon, *The Kuzari* by Judah Halevi, and *'Arugat Ha-bosem* by Moses ibn Ezra.[24] The medieval translation enterprise of such works (and also of the works by Sa'adia and Maimonides, surveyed above) from Arabic into Hebrew was mainly carried out by the Tibbon family of translators who worked in Provence during the twelfth–thirteenth centuries.[25] Nevertheless, the rich and varied Judeo-Arabic literature written in the Middle East and Spain—in the fields of science, poetics, philosophy and, most notably, Bible exegesis—which was not channeled into the Hebrew corpus by the medieval translators was generally left outside the sphere of scholarly interest, and in many cases it was only preserved in manuscripts or else lost altogether. Though the importance, even if not the extent, of this literature was certainly known in the nineteenth century and, as we have shown, even in the seventeenth century, its research was neglected, often as the result of the purist tendency to concentrate on classical Hebrew sources. Another reason for this relative academic neglect was the modern historical development of Judeo-Arabic literature amongst its native communities. Not only did much of it not reach print and only part of it survive in manuscript sources, but some of it became incomprehensible

---

and the Politics of Community: The Jews of the Fatimid Caliphate (Ithaca, NY: Cornell University Press, 2008), 3–288. On the threefold structure of the Judeo-Arabic commentary, see the final section of this introduction.

24. This medieval Hebrew adaptation represents only segments of Moses ibn Ezra's original magnum opus by the Judeo-Arabic title *Maqalat al-ḥadiqa fi ma'ani al-majaz wal-ḥaqiqa* ("Dissertation of the Garden on Figurative and Literal Language"). For a detailed analysis of this work, see P. Fenton, *Philosophie et exégèse dans le Jardin de la métaphore de Moïse Ibn 'Ezra* (Leiden: Brill, 1997).

25. On the Tibbon family translation enterprise, see the recent definitive work by Sarah J. Pearce, *The Andalusi Literary and Intellectual Tradition: The Role of Arabic in Judah Ibn Tibbon's Ethical Will* (Bloomington: Indiana University Press, 2017).

due to the adoption of spoken Arabic dialects or spoken Spanish (Ladino) in many of the Jewish oriental communities that had previously mastered classical Judeo-Arabic. This process began in the wake of the disintegration of the Muslim Empire and the great expulsions from Spain during the fourteenth and fifteenth centuries, when waves of Ladino-speaking Jews settled in Arab lands and changed the linguistic fabric of their Jewish communities. This process deepened once the colonial powers, who generally welcomed Jews and were favorable to their social mobility, had encouraged accomplishment in European tongues.[26] The most consistent exception to this rule was the Yemenite community, which up to modern times kept a live tradition of classical Arabic education, including the transmission and reading of Saʿadia's Bible translations and commentaries.[27]

As mentioned in our opening comments, during the last three decades Judeo-Arabic literature in general and Bible exegesis in particular have received wider recognition, although these subjects have certainly been on scholars' tables (so to speak) and continuously studied for over three hundred years. Beyond the complex history of research (which always has its highs and lows, its surges of energy and laidback periods), the current wave is also due to the growing academic and public legitimization of the cultural heritage of the Jews of Islamic lands, in Israel and outside it. There seem to be several factors behind this resurgence. Some are more scientific in nature, for instance, the renewed availability since the 1990s of Judeo-Arabic manuscripts housed in the former Soviet Union, especially those known as the Firkovitch Collections, has partly contributed to the intensification of research into this literature.[28] Other factors are more elusive

---

26. For further discussion of these historical-linguistic developments, see, for instance, Stillman, *Language and Culture*, 5.

27. On this unique tradition, see Doron Yaʿakov's contribution in this volume (89–100).

28. The newly available manuscripts (also dating from the tenth–thirteenth centuries) were collected in the nineteenth century from Karaite *genizot* in the Middle East by the Russian Karaite scholar and bibliophile Abraham Firkovitch. They are now housed in the Russian National Library; see Malachi Beit-Arié, "Hebrew Manuscript Collections in Leningrad" [Hebrew], *Jewish Studies* 31 (1991): 33–46; Menahem Ben-Sasson, "Firkovitch's Second Collection: Remarks on Historical and Halakhic Materials" [Hebrew], *Jewish Studies* 31 (1991): 47–67; David Sklare, *Judaeo-Arabic Manuscripts in the Firkovitch Collections: The Works of Yūsuf al-Baṣīr* [Hebrew] (Jerusalem: Ben-Zvi Institute, 1997), 7–16; Zeev Elkin and Menahem Ben-Sasson, "Abraham Firkovich and the Cairo Genizas in the Light of his Personal Archive" [Hebrew],

in nature, namely, the theoretical shifts that have occurred, mainly during the past decades, in the humanities in general and in biblical, Jewish, and Islamic studies in particular, including the proliferation and maturation of their subdisciplines and their entering into what may be called a "post-ideological" era.[29] Accordingly, the history of the Jews during the Middle Ages, particularly under Christendom, is not as bound as it was to the Zionist ethos, nor is it studied necessarily as an inevitable precursor to the horrific recent chapter of the age-old Jewish entity in Europe. Islam has always enjoyed a more positive image in this respect. Nevertheless, the study of the history of the Jews of Islamic lands and their literature was to a certain extent subdued under the effects of the modern Arab-Israeli conflict. As this conflict loses its earlier existential bite, it brings with it a palpable relaxation of the former reserve in recognizing the Arabic culture and literary output of the Jews of Islam as a phenomenon worthy of independent research and wider public recognition. The changing of historical consciousness and alternative discourses which have entered Israeli culture have in turn led to a review of the Ashkenazi-centric (European) orientation that characterized modern Zionism and the state of Israel in its first decades, giving way—particularly since the 1980s—to a pluralistic conception of its cultural heritage. This is partly the result of the successful struggle of Jews originating from Islamic lands (who make up a significant portion of Israel's Jewish population) to receive greater appreciation and access to positions of influence in politics, economics, and the academy. More than anything, the growing need for peaceful coexistence with the Palestinians and other Arab nations has also contributed to the maturing of Israeli society and to the loosening of its ideological constraints which identified Arab culture and language with the "enemy." Though isolationist voices still abide (however regrettably, in my view) especially in the political discourse, one can inevitably sense beneath and above the surface of Israeli society a new and welcome cultural openness, most notably towards Arabic music, cuisine, and wider culture. This most naturally converges with a revival of interest in Judeo-Arabic culture and in the long indi-

Pe'amim 90 (2002): 51–95; Olga Vasilyeva, "Documents in the Firkovich Collection: Valuable Sources on the History of the Jewish Communities in Europe and the Middle East from the Twelfth to the Nineteenth Century," *Karaite Archives* 2 (2014): 201–20.

29. See, in this respect, the remarks concerning the study of the Jews in medieval (Christian) Europe by the historian Israel J. Yuval, *Two Nations in Your Womb: Perceptions of Jews and Christians* [Hebrew] (Tel Aviv: Am Oved, 2000), 11–15.

vidual history of the major oriental (usually called 'Sephardi or 'Mizraḥi in Hebrew) communities in Israel (North African, Iraqi, Persian, Syrian, Yemenite), especially among second- and third-generation descendants.

Further Insights into the Choice of Commentaries and Our Editorial Policy

The term *Judeo-Arabic literature* is used to designate all fields of Arabic writing—whether fiction or nonfiction (literary or scientific)—in which the Jews of Arab and Muslim lands gave expression to their interests and creativity. However, our volume concentrates mainly on one of the branches in which this literature reached a peak of creativity: Bible exegesis and the interrelated fields of Bible translation, the study of Biblical Hebrew (its grammar and lexicon), masorah (its reading tradition), and biblical theology. Due to the vastness of this corpus, which stretches from medieval to modern times, most of the selected texts have been delimited to the medieval period, particularly to the golden or classical era of Judeo-Arabic literature (tenth–twelfth centuries), in which it flourished in all genres and subgenres. During this period, Judeo-Arabic spelling stabilized, emulating in the main Classical Arabic orthography with regard to the graphic representation of Arabic *matres lectionis* and other features. This stage is closely identified with the relatively stylized Judeo-Arabic of Saʿadia Gaon, whose works feature prominently in our anthology.[30] In fact, all of the texts in our anthology were written in this type of Judeo-Arabic, also known as Classical Judeo-Arabic.[31] We chose not to include the original texts but only their English translations, so as to minimize the usage of Hebrew and Arabic words for those who might be less familiar with them. We tried to open up these texts to different readers interested in biblical reception history and exegesis from all over the world, making the

---

30. See the five detailed contributions in this volume by Vollandt (75–87), Yaʿakov (89–100), Tobi (101–19), Mohammad (193–215), and Wechsler (321–41).

31. For a detailed survey of these historical stages, including the subdivision of the first stage into Pre-Islamic and early Judeo-Arabic and the third stage into Later and Modern (twentieth century) Judeo-Arabic, see Hary, *Multiglossia*, 75–82. On the orthographic distinctions between Preclassical and Classical Judeo-Arabic, see Joshua Blau and Simon Hopkins, "On Early Judaeo-Arabic Orthography," *ZAL* 12 (1984): 9–27; Blau and Hopkins, "Judaeo-Arabic Papyri–Collected, Edited, Translated and Analysed," *JSAI* 9 (1987): 87–160.

texts more user-friendly and accessible. For this reason, too, we chose a minimal transliteration policy of Arabic (and Hebrew) words into English when such words do occur; we distinguish consonants (though Arabic *alif* at the beginning of a word may be omitted at times) but not long vowels or the *shaddah* emphasis (with some exceptions allowed).

To a large degree, this user-friendliness was part and parcel of the primary intention of the Judeo-Arabic Bible commentaries. In the original setting in which they were composed, they were meant to be used as biblical study-aids for everyday readers, and they certainly functioned as such. For this reason, they were cast in a threefold structure, which is reflected in most of the manuscript sources. First, the biblical verse or a cluster of verses was quoted in Hebrew, usually in the form of an *incipit* (the first word or phrase of the given verse) but sometimes in full. Second, the verse was translated into Judeo-Arabic, so as to facilitate its comprehension.[32] In Karaite commentaries (such as those by Salmon ben Yerūḥīm or Yefet ben ʿEli) the translation was usually literal, imitating the grammar and the semantic range of the Hebrew. In Rabbanite translations (such as those by Saʿadia Gaon or Samuel ben Ḥofni), the rendering is more orientated towards the proper forms of Classical Arabic usage. In both traditions the translation is an instructive tool, meant to clarify the biblical Hebrew and its meanings as much as possible. Third, the verse was commented upon in Judeo-Arabic, including explication of matters of language, style, and content. The commentary followed the biblical passages systematically and rarely skipped any issue. This threefold literary structure appears to have entered and stabilized in Jewish writing on the Bible during the Muslim period and to have been influenced by parallel models of Islamic theological discourse and Qurʾanic exegesis.[33] We have deliberately retained this style in the excerpts from these works included in this volume. To facilitate reading we have supplied the Arabic verse translation, that is, the second layer described above, not in the original but in an adapted English version, often using the JPS 1985 translation as our base. We have also provided, in some cases, the Hebrew verse in a known English translation. When it comes to the commentaries (the third and widest layer), authors

---

32. For additional discussion of Karaite translation methods, see Meira Polliack, "Medieval Karaite Views on Translating the Hebrew Bible into Arabic," *JJS* 47 (1996): 64–84; and Polliack, "Medieval Karaite Methods on Translating of Biblical Narrative into Arabic," *VT* 48 (1998): 375–98.

33. See nn. 21–22 above.

did their utmost to invite readers to savor their range of topics and richness of expression. Do bear in mind, however, that these are often small tastes from gigantic works.

Due to various constraints, our volume clearly does not afford the full array of exegetes or styles active in this period. Many of these Rabbanite and Karaite exegetes, including Sa'adia, produced commentaries only on specific books of major interest to them or their public, such as Isaiah, Job, and texts of the Pentateuch. The one exception is the Karaite exegete Yefet ben 'Eli, who made it his proclaimed task to translate and comment in Arabic on the entire Hebrew Bible. He did so in Jerusalem, during the second half of the tenth century, and his commentaries were cherished by later generations as well, Karaite and Rabbanite, and hence survived in hundreds of manuscripts. It is therefore obvious that his portion within the anthology is significant. Not only did his commentaries give expression to linguistic-contextual as well as literary and theological methods developed by the Karaite school, they also collated the opinions of other commentators, and so they are very much a compendia of the variety of interpretive opinions known in this era. For the Karaites, translation remained a major medium in clarifying the literal meaning of the biblical text. The establishment of primary meaning was also the object of their grammatical commentaries on the Bible. Grammar and translation were linked in their system of interpretation: Karaite grammatical thinking had a clear hermeneutic function in elucidating the literal meaning of the biblical text. The scholar who has devoted several monumental works to this issue is no other than the leading European Semitist Geoffrey Khan.[34] He has especially highlighted how the Karaite concern with linguistic form

---

34. See Geoffrey Khan, *The Early Karaite Tradition of Hebrew Grammatical Thought: Including a Critical Edition, Translation and Analysis of the Diqduq of Abu Ya'qub Yusuf ibn Nuh on the Hagiographia* (Leiden: Brill, 2000); Khan, *Early Karaite Grammatical Texts*, MasS (Atlanta: Society of Biblical Literature, 2001); Geoffrey Khan, Maria Angeles Gallego, and Judith Olszowy-Schlanger, *The Karaite Tradition of Hebrew Grammatical Thought in Its Classical Form* (Leiden: Brill, 2003). Khan also devoted a volume to the Karaites' practices of transcribing the biblical text into Arabic characters and adding a translation and commentary in Arabic script. In his view, this reflects their wish to preserve the accurate reading tradition of the biblical text, especially in cases where contemporary medieval reading traditions were at variance with the Tiberian masorah. On this, see Khan, *Karaite Bible Manuscripts from the Cairo Genizah* (Cambridge: Cambridge University Press, 1990); and Khan, "The Medieval Karaite Transcriptions of Hebrew into Arabic Script," *IOS* 12 (1992): 157–76.

arose from the conviction that there was a direct link between form and meaning.[35] Grammar and translation served as the building blocks of the Karaite biblical commentaries, whose explicatory layer was usually devoted to what might be called forms of "higher criticism," namely, the discussion of structural, literary, and theological aspects of the biblical text together with additional references, at times, to their symbolic or messianic implications.

By far, the Karaite school produced many more biblical commentaries than did the Rabbanites during this period, for the Karaites were newcomers on the scene and espoused the return to the Bible as the focus of Jewish religion and life. This is why our volume contains slightly more Karaite than Rabbanite materials from these two centuries. Readers will amply sense that ideological tensions and a revamping of the Jewish understanding of biblical law and theology is also often at the heart of the debates—overtly and covertly—in the Karaite commentaries. In the Rabbanite sphere, Saʿadia Gaon's works became dominant early on. In as much as the reception tradition of Saʿadia's works reflects, they seem to have overshadowed the work of his contemporaries and students, although some of these (such as Samuel ben Ḥofni's works) have reached us in good form. We regret we were not able to give more exposure to these commentators in our text selections. Indeed, we focused on the formative era, and so more remains to be done in the future. Leading Judeo-Arabic exegetes active later on in the twelfth through fourteenth centuries, especially Isaac ben Samuel (al-Kanzī), Tanḥum ha-Yerushalmi, and even Maimonides (whose *Guide to the Perplexed* has many exegetical insights), fell beyond the historical horizon set for this volume, though they are sometimes mentioned or discussed. They shall await their turn of inclusion in other selections in due course. The reader is also invited, accordingly, to read more about them and their works in the recent multivolume and online *Encyclopedia of Jews in the Islamic World* and the *Encyclopedia of the Bible and Its Reception*. Basic details on the medieval authors included in our volume (and some others, too) will also be found in our separate list of "Major Judeo-Arabic Commentators" at the beginning of this volume and, of course, through the rich referencing provided in the various contributions.

---

35. See Khan, *Early Karaite Tradition*, 9–21, 13–33.

Most of the Judeo-Arabic excerpts provided in English translation have not been published elsewhere or, at the most, are available in distant editions, often without translation (to which references are supplied). The expert scholars who have contributed to this volume offer the very fine fruits of their expertise in the field. Along with select bibliography, they also supply a contextualizing preface and/or an embedded discussion on the interpretive nature of their chosen text. Indeed, we encouraged each contributor to choose where she or he would like to place their pick—bearing in mind, nonetheless, the criteria that the volume should provide an overall tour of the Hebrew Bible, a balanced selection from the Bible's three divisions and major genres, and a chronological focus ranging mainly from the tenth to the eleventh centuries.[36]

We hope this volume will arouse keen interest among a wide and diverse readership and that it bestow upon all of its readers, as well as upon the memory of past generations of scholars and readers, a sense of renewal, in the expression it gives to the continued intellectual and spiritual lives of Bible exegetes from almost a millennium ago. The fruits of their labors are in no uncertain terms still with us.

Bibliography

Astren, Fred. *Karaite Judaism and Historical Understanding*. Columbia: University of South Carolina Press, 2004.

Baker, Colin F. "Judaeo-Arabic Material in the Cambridge Genizah Collections." *BSOAS* 58 (1995): 445–54.

Baker, Colin F., and Meira Polliack. *Arabic and Judaeo-Arabic Manuscripts in the Cambridge Genizah Collections: Arabic Old Series (T–S Ar. 1a–54)*. Cambridge: Cambridge University Press, 2001.

Barr, James. *The Semantics of Biblical Language*. Repr., London: SCM, 1981.

Beit-Arié, Malachi. "Hebrew Manuscript Collections in Leningrad" [Hebrew]. *Jewish Studies* 31 (1991): 33–46.

Ben Shammai, Haggai. "The Exegetical and Philosophical Writing of Saadia: A Leader's Endeavor" [Hebrew]. *Peʿamim* 54 (1993): 63–81.

---

36. We are especially grateful to James T. Robinson for offering three contributions to this volume.

———. "The Tension between Literal Interpretation and Exegetical Freedom: Comparative Observation on Saadia's Method." Pages 33–50 in *With Reverence for the Word: Medieval Scriptural Exegesis in Judaism, Christianity and Islam*. Edited by Jane Dammen McAuliffe, Barry D. Walfish, and Joseph W. Goering. Oxford: Oxford University Press, 2003.

Ben-Sasson, Menahem. "Firkovitch's Second Collection: Remarks on Historical and Halakhic Materials" [Hebrew]. *Jewish Studies* 31 (1991): 47–67.

Bengtsson, Per A. *Two Arabic Versions of the Book of Ruth: Text Edition and Language Studies*. Lund: Lund University Press, 1995.

Blau, Joshua. *The Emergence and Linguistic Background of Judaeo-Arabic: A Study of the Origins of Neo-Arabic and Middle Arabic*. 3rd rev. ed., Jerusalem: Ben-Zvi Institute, 1999.

———. *A Grammar of Mediaeval Judaeo-Arabic*. 2nd enlarged ed. Jerusalem: Magnes, 1980.

Blau, Joshua, and Simon Hopkins. "On Early Judaeo-Arabic Orthography." *ZAL* 12 (1984): 9–27.

———. "Judaeo-Arabic Papyri—Collected, Edited, Translated and Analysed." *JSAI* 9 (1987): 87–160.

Dannenfeld, Karl. "The Renaissance Humanists and the Knowledge of Arabic." *Studies in the Renaissance* 2 (1955): 96–117.

Drory, Rina. *The Emergence of Jewish-Arabic Literary Contacts at the Beginning of the Tenth Century* [Hebrew]. Tel Aviv: Porter Institute of Poetics and Semiotics, Tel Aviv University Press, 1988.

———. *Models and Contacts: Arabic Literature and Its Impact on Medieval Jewish Culture*. Leiden: Brill, 2000.

Elkin, Zeev, and Menahem Ben-Sasson. "Abraham Firkovich and the Cairo Genizas in the Light of his Personal Archive" [Hebrew]. *Pe'amim* 90 (2002): 51–95.

Erder, Yoram. "The Mourners of Zion: The Karaites in Jerusalem in the Tenth and Eleventh Centuries." Pages 213–35 in *Karaite Judaism: A Guide to Its History and Literary Sources*. Edited by Meira Polliack. Leiden: Brill, 2003.

Fenton, P. *Philosophie et exégèse dans le Jardin de la métaphore de Moïse Ibn 'Ezra*. Leiden: Brill, 1997.

Frank, Daniel. *Search Scripture Well: Karaite Exegetes and the Origins of the Jewish Bible Commentary in the Islamic East*. Leiden: Brill, 2006.

Goitein, Shelomo Dov. *A Mediterranean Society: The Jewish Communities of the Arab World as Portrayed in the Documents of the Cairo Geniza*. 6 vols. Berkeley: University of California Press, 1967–1993.

Goldstein, Miriam. "'Arabic Composition 101' and the Early Development of Judaeo-Arabic Bible Exegesis." *JSS* 55 (2010): 451–78.

———. *Karaite Exegesis in Medieval Jerusalem: The Judeo-Arabic Pentateuch Commentary of Yusuf ibn Nuh and Abu al-Faraj Harun*. Tübingen: Mohr Siebeck, 2011.

Halkin, A. S. "Judaeo-Arabic Literature." *EncJud* 10:410–23.

Hary, Benjamin H. *Multiglossia in Judeo-Arabic: With an Edition, Translation and Grammatical Study of the Cairene Purim Scroll*. Leiden: Brill, 1992.

Hoffman, Adina, and Peter Cole. *Sacred Trash: The Lost and Found World of the Cairo Geniza*. New York: Schocken, 2011.

Isaacs, Haskell D., ed. *Medical and Para-medical Manuscripts in the Cambridge Genizah Collection*. Cambridge: Cambridge University Press, 1994.

Khan, Geoffrey. "The Arabic Fragments in the Cambridge Genizah Collections." *Manuscripts of the Middle East* 1 (1986): 54–61.

———. *Early Karaite Grammatical Texts*. MasS. Atlanta: Society of Biblical Literature, 2001.

———. *The Early Karaite Tradition of Hebrew Grammatical Thought: Including a Critical Edition, Translation and Analysis of the Diqduq of Abu Yaʿqub Yusuf ibn Nuh on the Hagiographia*. Leiden: Brill, 2000.

———. *Karaite Bible Manuscripts from the Cairo Genizah*. Cambridge: Cambridge University Press, 1990.

———. "The Medieval Karaite Transcriptions of Hebrew into Arabic Script." *IOS* 12 (1992): 157–76.

Khan, Geoffrey, Maria Angeles Gallego, and Judith Olszowy-Schlanger. *The Karaite Tradition of Hebrew Grammatical Thought in Its Classical Form*. Leiden: Brill, 2003.

Pearce, Sarah J. *The Andalusi Literary and Intellectual Tradition: The Role of Arabic in Judah Ibn Tibbon's Ethical Will*. Bloomington: Indiana University Press, 2017.

Polliack, Meira. "Arabic Bible Translations in the Cairo Genizah Collection." Pages 35–61 in *Jewish Studies in a New Europe: The Proceedings of the Fifth Congress of Jewish Studies in Copenhagen*. Edited by Ulf Haxen, Hanne Trautner-Kromann, and Karen Lisa Goldschmidt Salamon. Copenhagen: C. A. Reitzel, 1998.

———. "Concepts of Scripture among the Jews of the Islamic World." Pages 80–101 in *Jewish Concepts of Scripture: A Comparative Introduction*. Edited by Benjamin D. Sommer. New York: New York University Press.

———. "Deconstructing the Dual Torah: A Jewish Response to the Muslim Model of Scripture." Pages 113–29 in *Interpreting Scriptures in Judaism, Christianity and Islam: Overlapping Inquiries*. Edited by Mordechai Z. Cohen and Adele Berlin. Cambridge: Cambridge University Press, 2016.

———. "Medieval Karaism." Pages 295–326 in *The Oxford Handbook of Jewish Studies*. Edited by Martin Goodman. Oxford: Oxford University Press, 2002.

———. "Medieval Karaite Methods on Translating of Translating Biblical Narrative into Arabic." *VT* 48 (1998): 375–98.

———. "Medieval Karaite Views on Translating the Hebrew Bible into Arabic." *JJS* 47 (1996): 64–84.

———. "Re-thinking Karaism: Between Judaism and Islam." *AJSR* 30 (2006): 67–93.

———. "Single-Script Mixed-Code Literary Sources from the Cairo Genizah and Their Sociolinguistic Context." Pages 65–91 in *Jewish Languages in Historical Perspective*. Edited by Lily Kahn. Leiden: Brill, 2018.

Reif, Stefan C. *A Jewish Archive from Old Cairo: The History of Cambridge University's Genizah Collection*. Richmond, Surry: Curzon Press, 2000.

Rustow, Marina. *Heresy and the Politics of Community: The Jews of the Fatimid Caliphate*. Ithaca, NY: Cornell University Press, 2008.

Schmidtke, Sabine. "Near and Middle Eastern Studies at the Institute of Advanced Study: A Historical Sketch." Pages xxxi–xcviii in *Studying the Near and Middle East in the Institute of Advanced Study, Princeton, 1935–2018*. Edited by Sabine Schmidtke. Piscataway, NJ: Gorgias, 2018.

Sklare, David. *Judaeo-Arabic Manuscripts in the Firkovitch Collections: The Works of Yūsuf al-Basīr* [Hebrew]. Jerusalem: Ben Zvi Institute, 1997.

Steinschneider, Moriz. *Die arabische Literartur der Juden*. Frankfurt: J. Kauffmann, 1902. Translated as "Introduction to the Arabic Literature of the Jews." *JQR* 9.2 (1897): 224–39; 9.4 (1897): 604–30; 10.1 (1897): 119–38; 10.3 (1898): 513–40; 11.1 (1898): 115–49; 11.2 (1899): 305–43; 11.3 (1899): 480–89; 11.4 (1899): 585–625; 12.1 (1899): 114–32;

12.2 (1900): 195–212; 12.3 (1900): 481–501; 12.4 (1900): 602–17; 13.1
(1900): 92–110; 13.2 (1901): 296–320; 13.3 (1901): 446–87.
Stillman, Norman A. "Judeo-Arabic History and Linguistic Description."
EJIW 3:53–58.
———. *The Language and Culture of the Jews of Sefrou, Morocco: An Eth-
nolinguistic Study.* Manchester: University of Manchester Press, 1988.
Tobi, Y. "Literature, Judeo-Arabic." *EJIW* 3:271–78.
Vajda, G. "Judaeo-Arabic Literature." *EI*² 4:303–7.
Vasilyeva, Olga. "Documents in the Firkovich Collection: Valuable Sources
on the History of the Jewish Communities in Europe and the Middle
East from the Twelfth to the Nineteenth Century." *Karaite Archives* 2
(2014): 201–20.
Vollandt, Ronny. *Arabic Versions of the Pentateuch: A Comparative Study of
Jewish, Christian, and Muslim Sources.* Leiden: Brill, 2015.
Wechsler, Michael G. "Edward Pococke and the Emergence of Arabic:
Studies in Late-Renaissance Europe." https://biblia-arabica.com/
edward-pococke.
———. "Interpretation, History of: Medieval Judaism in Arabic-Speaking
Lands." *EBR* 13:95–105.
Yuval, Israel J. *Two Nations in Your Womb: Perceptions of Jews and Chris-
tians in Late Antiquity and the Middle Ages* [Hebrew]. Tel Aviv: Am
Oved, 2000.
Zwiep, Irene E. "Beyond Orientalism? Steinschneider on Islam, Religion
and Plurality." Pages 202–17 in *Modern Jewish Scholarship on Islam in
Context: Rationality, European Borders, and the Search for Belonging.*
Edited by Ottfried Fraisse. Berlin: de Gruyter, 2018.

On the Pentateuch

Yefet ben 'Eli on Genesis 11 and 22

Marzena Zawanowska

In this essay I present a taste of Yefet ben 'Eli's complex and sophisticated exegetical approach to the Bible, as reflected in his translation and commentary on the Pentateuch, by foregrounding two passages: Gen 11:1–9 and Gen 22:1–2. The choice of these particular biblical passages was dictated by the fact that they both represent important conundrums and, as such, received much exegetical attention. Therefore, they provide excellent material for illustrating Yefet's innovative approach to interpreting Scripture, which draws upon and creatively transforms a large array of different sources, both Jewish (Rabbanite as well as Karaite) and Muslim. In addition, Yefet's treatment of the story of the city/tower of Babel and the opening verses of the Akedah narrative reflects his sensibilities and unique methods by encapsulating many features characteristic of his entire exegetical oeuvre.

I will proceed as follows. First, I shall cite the relevant biblical Hebrew passage in English translation (based on the English translation of the Jewish Publication Society [JPS] of 1917 and 1985), with slight modifications.[1] The citations will be given verse-by-verse (in italics). The next

I wish to convey my profound appreciation to the Center for the Study of Judaeo-Arabic Culture and Literature of the Ben-Zvi Institute for the Study of Jewish Communities in the East, housed in the National Library of Israel in Jerusalem, and especially to Dr. David Sklare, for giving me an opportunity to study working editions of many Karaite Bible commentaries compiled and stored in the Center.

1. I would have preferred to use the older JPS translation of 1917 as the base for my translation of the Hebrew text, since it better reflects the underlying Hebrew source text and thus also underscores the instances where Yefet's Arabic translation of the biblical verses differs from the original. For the reasons behind such a decision, see also Michael G. Wechsler, *The Arabic Translation and Commentary of Yefet ben 'Eli the Karaite on the Book of Esther*, Karaite Texts and Studies 1, Études sur le judaïsme

step will be my English translation for each verse of Yefet's Arabic translation to the Hebrew (in bold), followed by my translation of Yefet's Arabic
exegesis for the verse(s) (in regular font). The reason behind such a tripar-
tite structure is that it exactly reflects the three-layered division of Yefet's
Bible commentaries. Finally, at the end of both sections I offer short con-
clusions—a sort of gain-and-loss account—in which I try to address the
question of whether Yefet's wrestling with exegetical cruxes posed by the
story of the tower/city of Babel and the Akedah narrative has been done
successfully and whether he provides valuable and compelling solutions
also from a modern reader's perspective. My comments, discussion, and
additional comparative materials are presented in the footnotes.

Genesis 11:1–9

(v. 1) *And all the earth was of one language and of one speech* [Heb.
dəbārîm 'aḥādîm]

**And all the inhabitants[2] of the earth were of one language and
of one speech [Arab. *khuṭab*].**

We have already said [earlier] that the statement *every one after his tongue*
(Gen 10:5) refers to [the situation] after the generation of dispersion.[3]

---

médiéval 36 (Leiden: Brill, 2008), 151. However, since the 1917 translation on its own
would look quaint and archaic—even grammatically wrong at places—to contemporary readers, as signaled by the JPS decision itself to produce a newer translation that
accounts for both English-language developments as well as scholarly developments, I
settle here largely for a combination and a mixture with the newer translation.

2. For a similar addition in translation, provided by Saʿadia, see Joseph Deren-
bourg, *Version arabe du Pentateuque de R. Saadia ben Iosef al-Fayyoûmî*, vol. 1 of
Œuvres complètes de R. Saadia ben Iosef al-Fayyoûmî (Hildesheim: Olms, 1979), 18.
For an English translation, see Michael Linetsky, *Rabbi Saadiah Gaon's Commentary
on the Book of Creation: Annotated and Translated by Michael Linetsky* (Northvale, NJ:
Jason Aronson, 2002), 235.

3. Hebrew *Dōr ha-pəlāgā* ("generation of dispersion," "generation of split," or
"generation of separation [of races]"). According to the Midrash this generation was
removed two years from the generation of flood, as it is written, *Shem begot Arpach-
shad two years after the flood* (Gen 11:10). At this time the generation of separation
begun, though the separation actually took place only 340 years after the flood. See
Gen. Rab. 26:3; 38:2, 9.

And this chapter comes to explain to us how [did it happen that] many languages were created in the world as well as to indicate the reason why many languages were created.[4] Thus [Scripture] says that before their languages were confounded, all the inhabitants of the earth had one language. It was *the holy tongue* [Heb. *ləshōn ha-qōdēsh*] in which the Lord of the universe spoke to Adam and in which Adam called the names of animals and other things.[5] Neither he nor his children ceased to speak this language until the generation of dispersion, and they knew no other.

As to the expression *and of one speech,* it means that as long as their language was one language, there was no disagreement between them with regard to noun [forms] and in speech, [especially in terms of] verb declination, as [is the case with] the Arabs [who] disagree with regard to many nouns and in speech. So [Scripture] indicates that at that time

---

4. A similar historical-etiological explanation of the reason why the story of the tower of Babel was told and included in Scripture is provided by another Karaite exegete from Jerusalem, Yeshuʿah ben Yehudah. In his view, its aim is to explain the existing divisions of lands. See MS RNL Yevr-Arab. 1:3204, fol. 57b. For the emergence of historical sensibilities among the medieval Karaites as reflected in their interpretations of this pericope, see Marzena Zawanowska, "The Discovery of History in Medieval Bible Exegesis. Islamic Influences on the Emergence of Historical Sensibilities Among the Karaites as Exemplified in Their Innovative Treatment of the Story of the Tower of Babel (Genesis 11:1–9)," forthcoming. For a study of historicizing tendencies in Yefet ben ʿEli reading of prophetic literature, see Meira Polliack, "Historicizing Prophetic Literature: Yefet ben ʿEli's Commentary on Hosea and Its Relationship to al-Qumisi's Pitron," in *Pesher Nahum: Texts and Studies in Jewish History and Literature from Antiquity through the Middle Ages*, ed. Joel L. Kraemer and Michael G. Wechsler (Chicago: University of Chicago Press, 2011), 149–86.

5. Some other medieval Karaite exegetes, such as Yaʿqūb al-Qirqisānī, also upheld a view that Hebrew was the primordial language of humanity. In his opinion, this language was subsequently preserved among the religious people who keep divine commandments. See MS SP RNL Yevr.-Arab. 1:4529, fol. 23a. Others were uncertain about it. For example, in the commentary on the Torah written by Yūsuf ibn Nūḥ (and abridged by his student Abū al-Faraj Hārūn), known as the *Talkhīṣ*, we read that "the expression *of one language* (v. 1) means that at that time all the people spoke one language, either Hebrew, or Persian, or another." See MS SP RNL Yevr.-Arab. 1:1754, fol. 53b. For studies of the Karaites' exegesis of the story of the city/tower of Babel, and especially their discussions of the origin and nature of human languages, see Miriam Goldstein, *Karaite Exegesis in Medieval Jerusalem: The Judeo-Arabic Pentateuch Commentary of Yusuf ibn Nuh and Abu al-Faraj Harun* (Tubingen: Mohr-Siebeck, 2011), 151–61; Arye Zoref, "Yaʿqūb al-Qirqisānī's Position in the Debate over the Formation of Language" [Hebrew], *Ginzei Qedem* 12 (2016): 127–54.

there was no disagreement between them as to the matters of this sort.[6] But some say that the expression *and of one speech* means [that they were all] of one view and of one will, and therefore they did not disagree when one of them proposed, *Come, let us make bricks, [and burn them thoroughly]* (v. 3).[7]

(v. 2) *And it came about, as they journeyed from the east, that they found a plain in the land of Shinar and settled there.*

And it came about, as they journeyed from the east, that they found a plain in the land of Iraq and settled there.

[Scripture] has already indicated that the ark [of Noah] rested upon the mount Judi [Arab. *Qardu*].[8] Here it informs [us] that they journeyed from there, and when they came to this plain, they settled in it. It is possible that they headed for the land of Israel [Arab. *bilad al-Shām*],[9] or that they wandered the world in search of a place that would suit them. But since they found this plain suitable for them, they settled in it.

---

6. A similar explanation of the expression *and of one speech* (v. 1) as meaning a common pronunciation was expressed by the authors of the *Talkhīṣ* (Yūsuf ibn Nūḥ and Abū al-Faraj Hārūn), who also contrast this with the situation in Arab lands, where there are different manners of speech (dialects). See MS SP RNL Yevr.-Arab. 1:1754, fol. 53b.

7. Most likely, Yefet alludes here to a view expressed by Yaʿqūb al-Qirqisānī who, following an old midrashic explanation, interpreted this expression as meaning that the builders of the tower were of one opinion and one faith. See MS SP RNL Yevr.-Arab. 1:4529, fol. 23a.

8. Arabic *Jibāl Qarda* (lit. "mounts Qardu"). According to an early Christian as well as Islamic tradition, after the flood, Noah's ark came to rest on Mount Judi (Arab. *al-Jūdiyy*; Aram. *Qardū*; Syr. Qardū), traditionally identified with a peak near the town of Jazirat ibn Umar (modern Cizre), at the headwaters of the Tigris, near the modern Syrian–Turkish border. The identification of this mountain as the landing site (*apobaterion*, or "place of descent") of the ark is found in Syriac and Armenian tradition throughout late antiquity, and later on also in Islamic tradition (see, e.g., in the Qurʾan, Q Hud 11:44). With time, however, it was abandoned for the tradition equating this location with the highest mountain of the region, viz., Mount Ararat. For the sake of comparison, Yaʿqūb al-Qirqisānī does not try to identify the place, while the authors of the *Talkhīṣ* (Yūsuf ibn Nūḥ and Abū al-Faraj Hārūn) limit themselves to stating that it was "in the East of the land of Shinar." See MS SP RNL Yevr.-Arab. 1:1754, fol. 39a.

9. Arabic *bilad al-Shām*, a term denoting the entire region of Syria, but often used in medieval Karaite commentaries specifically in reference to the land of Israel.

(v. 3) *And they said to one another: "Come, let us make bricks, and burn them thoroughly." And they had brick for stone, and bitumen*[10] *had they for mortar.*

And they said to one another: "Come, let us make brick,[11] **and burn them thoroughly." And they had brick instead of stone, and bitumen had they instead of mortar.**

[Scripture] indicates that one turned to another in exhortation to make brick and burn them, so that they be the lightest and most durable [possible]. [It also informs us] that they made brick instead of [using] stone, which [usually] serves to raise [high] constructions [Arab. *dawāmis*],[12] and that they used bitumen instead of mortar to cover up with it the walls, so that the building be firm.[13] Thus they made brick and burned them and prepared the bitumen.

(v. 4) *And they said: "Come, let us build us a city, and a tower, with its top in heaven, and let us make us a name; else we shall be scattered abroad upon the face of the whole earth."*

Then[14] **they said: "Come, let us build us a city, and a tower, with its top in heaven, and let us make us a name; lest we be scattered abroad upon the face of the whole earth."**

---

10. Hebrew *ḥemār*, "bitumen." The JPS has "slime."

11. Yefet uses the singular here as a collective noun, whereas the Hebrew text has the plural.

12. Arabic *dawāmis*. For various possible meanings of this term, see Dionisius A. Agius, *Arabic Literary Works as a Source of Documentation for Technical Terms of the Material Culture* (Berlin: Schwarz, 1984), 214–15.

13. A similar explanation is provided by Yeshu'ah ben Yehudah, who posits that the builders used bricks not only because they were more durable than stone, but also because stone was unavailable to them. See MS RNL Yevr-Arab 1:3204, fols. 58a–b.

14. On Yefet's (and Sa'adia's) tendency to specify in translation the meaning of the Hebrew conjunction *vāv*, which typically opens biblical verses, see Meira Polliack, *The Karaite Tradition of Arabic Bible Translation: A Linguistic and Exegetical Study of Karaite Translations of the Pentateuch from the Tenth and Eleventh Centuries C.E*, Études sur le judaïsme médiéval 17 (Leiden: Brill, 1997), 102–18; Marzena Zawanowska, *The Arabic Translation and Commentary of Yefet ben 'Eli the Karaite on the Abraham Narratives (Genesis 11:10–25:18)*, Karaite Texts and Studies 4,

[Scripture] indicates that when they prepared the brick and the bitumen, they said to one another: "Let us build one city, that we may all live in it, and let us also build a tower rising into the sky, to make us a name forever, thanks to the building of this tower. And let us gather in this city, lest we should be scattered in the world and separated from one another."[15]

It [also] informs [us] that their intention was against the will of God, blessed and exalted, who ordered them: *spread out in the earth and multiply within it* (Gen 9:7), and said: *and replenish the earth* (Gen 1:28).[16] It [= this divine order] was beneficial to them, because [thanks to it], they [could] expand the place of [their] residence, and [also] because in every area there are mineral resources and fruits which are not [available] in another, and [thereby] people [could] diversify their means of living.

It [was] also so that they may see the wonders of the Lord of the universe in terms of the diversity of climates, grounds, mineral resources, and plants of [different] lands, as well as that they may contemplate the stars which appear in one region and district, but are invisible in another. Thus they would praise the Lord of the universe who created the creatures in diversity, the reason for [the existence of] them all being his wisdom. Yet, all these notwithstanding, they sought to gather in one place. Therefore, God scattered their gathering, and their wish was not fulfilled, as it says:

(v. 5) *And the Lord came down to see the city and the tower, which the children of men* [Heb. *bəney ha-ʾadam*] *built.*[17]

And the Lord of the universe came down to see the city and the tower, which the children of men[18] began to build.

Études sur le Judaïsme médiéval 46 (Leiden: Brill, 2012), 173, and further bibliography there.

15. When commenting on this passage, Yeshuʿah ben Yehudah adds another practical reason for the building of a high tower, "to be seen from afar, so that if someone goes out of the city and gets lost on his way, he [could] perceive [the tower] and head for it." See MS RNL Yevr-Arab 1:3204, fol. 58b.

16. Also the authors of the *Talkhīṣ* (Yūsuf ibn Nūḥ, Abū al-Faraj Hārūn) emphasize that the builders of the tower acted against the will of God as expressed in Gen 9:7. See MS SP RNL Yevr.-Arab. 1:1754, fol. 40a.

17. The JPS has "builded."

18. Yefet uses here the Hebrew *bəney ʾadam*—without the definite article *ha*. The MT here has, literally, *sons* of man.

(v. 6) *And the Lord said, "If, as one people with one language for all, this is how they have begun to act, then nothing that they may propose to do will be prevented from them.*

And the Lord of the universe said: "If as one people with one language for all, this is how they have begun to act, then nothing that they desired to do will be prevented from them.

(v. 7) *[Come], let us go down, and confound there their language, so that they may not understand one another's speech."*

[Come,] let us go down, in order to confound there their language, so that they may not understand one another's speech."[19]

The statement *And the Lord came down* (v. 5) refers to the angel of the Lord.[20] For it is the custom of Scripture [Arab. *rasm al-kitāb*] to use a concise style [= ellipsis] [Arab. *'ala tarīq al-ikhtiṣār*],[21] just like it says: *And the Lord came down upon Mount Sinai* (Exod 19:20), meaning by this [that]

---

19. Sa'adia adds his amendments already on the level of translation by rendering this verse with, "Let us go and I shall bring down an instruction of intimidation and I will disperse their language by it." See Derenbourg, *Version arabe du Pentateuque de R. Saadia ben Iosef al-Fayyoûmî*, 18. For an English translation, see Linetsky, *Rabbi Saadiah Gaon's Commentary on the Book of Creation*, 235.

20. Ya'qūb al-Qirqisānī also ascertains that it was not God himself who descended to see the city, but he enlists different buffer words than Yefet to distance the Creator from his creatures, namely "his order" and "his power" (Arab. *amruhu wa-qudratuhu*). See MS SP RNL Yevr.-Arab. 1:4529, fol. 25a.

21. Arabic *ikhtiṣār* ("ellipsis"). On different uses of the Arabic concept of *ikhtiṣār* ("ellipsis") in medieval Karaite commentaries, see Geoffrey Khan, ed. and trans., *The Early Karaite Tradition of Hebrew Grammatical Thought, Including a Critical Edition, Translation and Analysis of the* Diqduq *of Abū Ya'qūb Yūsuf ibn Nūḥ on the Hagiographa*, Studies in Semitic Languages and Linguistics 32 (Leiden: Brill, 2000), 48–49, 128–31, 147 (syntactic ellipsis); Meira Polliack, "The Unseen Joints of the Text: On Medieval Judaeo-Arabic Concept of Ellision (*iḥtiṣār*) and Its Gap-filling Functions in Biblical Interpretation," in *Words, Ideas, Worlds in the Hebrew Bible—The Yairah Amit Festschrift*, ed. Athalya Brenner and Frank Polak (Sheffield: Sheffield Phoenix, 2012), 179–205 (narrative gaps); Marzena Zawanowska, "'Where the Plain Meaning is Obscure or Unacceptable …': The Treatment of Implicit Anthropomorphisms in the Medieval Karaite Tradition of Arabic Bible Translation," *EJJS* 10 (2016): 1–49 (stylistic ellipses).

the glory of the Lord [came down]. It condenses, since the descent of the angel was upon the order of God and according to his will.

And [God] sent the angel so that he observed their [= the inhabitants of Babel] actions, just like he sent the messengers to Sodom, so that they observed their [= the inhabitants of Sodom] actions, as it is said *I will go down now, and see* (Gen 18:21). Likewise it says here: *And the Lord came down to see* (v. 5).

Two opinions are said with regard to the statement *which* [*the children of men*] *built* (v. 5). The first of which is that [Scripture] refers [here] to what they intended to build, since afterwards it says: *and they stopped building the city* (v. 8), and they did not build anything. The second of which is that they have already begun to build. And [if so], the statement *and they stopped building the city* (v. 8) means that they ceased building. It is a more likely [interpretation], since it says [*And the Lord came down*] *to see the city* [*and the tower*], and it would not have said *to see*, had not there been a visible construction there.

And [Scripture] rightly [specifies and] says *the children of men* (v. 5) [to avoid confusion], because in the same verse it mentions the descent of the angel, just like [God] used to talk with Ezekiel and with Daniel, and say *the son of man* [Heb. *ben 'adam*], since there were angels standing [there too].

Next [Scripture] indicates that when the angel saw their [= the inhabitants'] actions, he said: "These people gathered into one gathering and speak one language, and therefore they could realize what they intended to [do]."

[As to the statement *this is how they have begun to act* (v. 6), it means] that it was the first action by which they began to disobey [God]. But some say that it refers to the first construction that they began [to build].

As to the statement *then nothing* [*that they may propose to do*] *will be prevented from them* (v. 6), it means that until that time nothing of what they intended to do had been disallowed.

They said: *Come, let us make bricks* [*and burn them thoroughly*] (v. 3): "I let them make a free choice, and they fulfilled their will."

Next they said: *Come, let us build us a city* (v. 4): "I let them start to build; and had I let them, they would have finished the building. But let us go down for the second time in order to punish [them]."

So, for the first time the angel descended [merely] *to see the city* [*and the tower*] (v. 5). Afterwards, he descended for the second time in order to confound their language and scatter them in the world. And the expression [*Come,*] *let us go down* (v. 7) is like the statement *Let us make man*

(Gen 1:26), namely, it is a majestic plural [Heb. *ləšōn gədūlā*],[22] employed by all users of languages [Arab. *ahl al-lugha*].[23]

As to [God's] words, *and confound there* (v. 7), they mean the confusion of their language so that they may not understand one the language of another. Some say that, [as a result], every group had a language only of its own, that no one else [could] understand.

Next [Scripture] indicates that having confounded their language, [God] scattered them from the plain, so that they spread in the world, as it is said:

(v. 8) *Thus the Lord scattered them from there over the face of the whole earth; and they stopped building the city.*

Thus the Lord of the universe scattered them from there over the face of all the earth; and they were prevented from building the city.

(v. 9) *That is why its name was called Babel, because there the Lord confounded the language of the whole earth; and from there the Lord scattered them over the face of the whole earth.*

That is why its name was called Babel, because there the Lord of the universe confounded the language of all the inhabitants of the earth; and from there he scattered them over the face of the whole earth.

[Scripture] says, *and they stopped building the city* (v. 8) and omits [Arab. *ikhtaṣara*] mentioning the *tower*, since the *tower* is [included] within the city. It is possible that the statement *That is why was the name of it called*

---

22. Hebrew *ləšōn gədūlā* (lit. "majestic language") is used in the manuscript. On the use of *pluralis majestatis* in medieval Karaite commentaries, see Yair Zoran, "The Majestic Plural [*Pluralis majestatis*]: The Plural of Respect" [Hebrew], *Beit Mikra* 143 (1995): 402–3.

23. Arabic *ahl al-lugha* (lit. "people of language"). On this term as designating rather "language community" or "linguistic community" in the sense of "native speakers" rather than "philologists," "linguists," or "grammarians," see Daniel Frank, *Search Scripture Well: Karaite Exegetes and the Origins of the Jewish Bible Commentary in the Islamic East*, Études sur le judaïsme médiéval 29 (Leiden: Brill, 2004), 52. Cf. Goldstein, *Karaite Exegesis in Medieval Jerusalem*, 33 and n. 37 there.

Babel (v. 9) was [pronounced by] Noah, since he was the leader of the generation, but it is [also] possible that it was [pronounced by] the Lord of the universe. And [Scripture] indicates that the name Babel was derived from the event, but an additional [letter] *beth* [= *b*] was added to the name, because the root of this word [is composed of] only two letters: *beth* and *lamed* [= *b* and *l*], as per the statement, *and confound* (ונבלה) *there* [*their language*] (v. 7). Thus, despite that it says בלל, one of the [two letters] *lamed* [= *l*] does not belong to the root, just like [is the case with roots] שדד, סבב, בזז, and others like those.[24]

I have translated לא יבצר מהם (v. 6) as "nothing [that they desired to do] will be prevented from them," according to the context [Arab. *fī al-maʿanā*]. For the meaning of the word is "to be inaccessible to," and a thing inaccessible is prevented from people. Likewise is the statement [*I know that you can do everything,*] *And that no purpose can be prevented* [לא יבצר] *from you* (Job 42:2).

People disagree with regard to the time when their language was confounded. Some of them maintain that it occurred towards the end of the days of Peleg's life.[25] Others maintain that it occurred at the beginning of his life, which is more likely, since Peleg was called on account of the event, as it is said [*And unto Eber were born two sons; the name of the one was Peleg;*] *for in his days was the earth divided; [and his brother's name was Joktan.*] (Gen 10:25). And Joktan was born after that they had been scattered in the world.

Genesis 22:1–2

(v. 1) *And*[26] *after these things,*[27] *God tested Abraham and said to him, "Abraham," and he answered, "Here I am."*

---

24. A similar grammatical explanation is provided by the authors of the the *Talkhīṣ* (Yūsuf ibn Nūḥ and Abū al-Faraj Hārūn). See MS SP RNL Yevr.-Arab. 1:1754, fol. 39b.

25. This a is midrashic explanation. See Gen. Rab. 26:3.

26. Hebrew *wa-yehî*. The JPS, as well as other older translations of the MT, follow the KJV with the formula, "And it came to pass." See also, similarly, Yefet.

27. Hebrew *dābār* (pl. *dəbārim*) can mean both "word(s)" and "thing(s)." It is unclear how Yefet understands this expression ("after these things"): after all the events that he lists as having happened to Abraham or "after these words," that is, after all the announcements listed by the exegete in what follows.

And after these things, the Lord of the universe tested Abraham by that he said to him, "Abraham," and he answered, "Here I am."

(v. 2) *And he said, "Take your son, your only one, whom you love, Isaac, and [you] go [Heb. ləkh ləkhā] to the land of Moriah, and offer him there as a burnt offering on one of the mountains that I shall tell you of."*

And he said, "Take your son, your only one, whom you love, namely, Isaac, and you go to the land of Moriah, and offer him there as a burnt offering on one of the mountains that I shall tell you of."

The statement *after these things* (v. 1) is meaningful, for it refers to what God promised twice before to Abraham, may peace be upon him, with regard to Isaac. The first time, before Isaac was born, when he said, *But my covenant will I establish with Isaac* (Gen 17:21). The second time, when he ordered him [= Abraham] to expel Hagar and Ishmael, and said: *In all that Sarah has said to you, hear her voice; for in Isaac shall your seed be called* (Gen 21:12). After a while, and after the announcements, Isaac was born, and Abraham came to conclusion that Isaac would remain after him and occupy his place, and that all the [above-mentioned] promises were related to him [= Isaac]. He [= Abraham] thus announced that to Abimelech and others.[28] The *mudawwin*[29] [Arab. "compiler-editor" or "author-redactor"] is therefore saying that [only] after all these announcements, God said to

---

28. Nowhere in the Bible does Abraham explicitly inform Abimelech about Isaac being his successor.

29. On the Karaites' concept of *mudawwin*, see Haggai Ben-Shammai, "On *mudawwin*—the Editor of the Books of the Bible in Judaeo-Arabic Exegesis" [Hebrew], in *Rishonim ve-Achronim: Studies in Jewish History Presented to Avraham Grossman*, ed. Joseph Hacker, Benjamin Z. Kedar, and Joseph Kaplan (Jerusalem: Zalman Shazar Center for Jewish History, 2009), 73–110; Meira Polliack, "Karaite Conception of the Biblical Narrator (*mudawwin*)," in *Encyclopaedia of Midrash*, ed. Jacob Neusner and Alan J. Avery-Peck, 2 vols. (Leiden: Brill, 2005), 1:350–74; Uriel Simon, *Four Approaches to the Book of Psalms: From Saadiah Gaon to Abraham ibn Ezra* [Hebrew] (Ramat Gan: Bar-Ilan University Press, 1982), 67–95; Marzena Zawanowska, "Was Moses the *mudawwin* of the Torah? The Question of Authorship of the Pentateuch According to Yefet ben ʿEli," in *Studies in Judaeo-Arabic Culture: Proceedings of the Fourteenth Conference of the Society for Judaeo-Arabic Studies*, ed. Haggai Ben-Sham-

Abraham:"Take Isaac and offer him [there] as a burnt offering."[30] That is why [the *mudawwin*] opened [Arab. *ṣaddara*][31] with the expression *After these things*.

And his [= the *mudawwin*'s] words *God tested Abraham* (v. 1) with an "and" [conjunctive *vāv*] may be related to what was [ingrained] in Abraham's heart, namely, in his heart [he was convinced that] God's promises would be fulfilled in Isaac. But the Lord of the universe said to him: *take your son* (v. 2), contrary to what [was ingrained] in his heart.

And the statement *God tested Abraham* (v. 1) is a preface [Arab. *ṣadr*][32] which the *mudawwin* introduced before mentioning God's command to Abraham, so as to inform [us] that God's wish concerning this command was for no other reason than to test Abraham, and that his wish was not that Abraham would execute the deed [denoted by the statement] *and offer him there as a burnt offering* (v. 2). Therefore he opened with the statement *God tested Abraham* (v. 1), so that when the reader read, *and offer him there as a burnt offering*, and afterwards he read, *Lay not your hand on the boy* (v. 12), he would know that this statement was neither an abrogation [Arab. *naskh*] [of previous promises], nor a change [of God's mind] [Arab. *bidʿa*], but rather it was [intended] after the manner of a test.[33] The reader

----

mai, Aron Dotan, Yoram Erder, and Mordechai A. Freidman (Tel Aviv: Tel Aviv University Press, 2014), 7*–35*.

30. Yaʿqūb al-Qirqisānī also juxtaposes God's order to offer Isaac as a burnt offering with his promise, *for in Isaac shall your seed be called* (Gen 21:12), and he concludes that these (seemingly contradictory) statements were meant to make Abraham's trial complete (Arab. *tamām al-miḥna*), in order to demonstrate "Abraham's superiority [over other people]" (Arab. *li-yaẓhara faḍīlatahu*). See MS SP RNL Yevr.-Arab. 1:4529, fol. 47a.

31. This is a methodological comment reflecting Yefet's perception of the Bible as a text consciously and intentionally composed by the author-redactor, or compiler-editor (*al-mudawwin*). The exegete employs the Arabic verb *ṣaddara* not only to denote "preceding," "prefacing," or "opening," but also in the sense of "ordering" and "arranging" literary materials. For more on the term *mudawwin*, see the references above, n. 29.

32. Arabic *ṣadr* ("preface," "opening," or "beginning"), a literary term often used in poetry to describe the first hemistich of a poem, while in prose it denotes a preface, or opening. See above, n. 31.

33. While commenting on this passage, Saʿadia also opposes the idea of abrogation, or God changing his mind, but his line of argument is different, as he states that God is capable of resuscitating Isaac after Abraham's offering of him, in order to keep all his promises to Abraham valid. See Moshe Zucker, *Rav Saadya Gaon's Com-*

of the Scripture of God [Arab. *kitāb Allāh*] knows about this. But as for Abraham, may peace be upon him, he did not possess this knowledge—to wit that the order was after the manner of a test—for had he possessed this knowledge, he would have been neither praiseworthy for what occurred to him, nor deserved a reward [for what he executed].[34]

And we must know that God, blessed and supreme, does not need to try people, nor to test them, for he *declares the end from the beginning* (Isa 46:10). Rather, he tested [Abraham] for the sake of the inhabitants of the world throughout the generations. For he, the Almighty and Exalted, knew [in advance] that Abraham would obey him in everything that he would order him, as it is said: *and you found his heart faithful [before you], etc.* (Neh 9:8).[35] So he tested him for the sake of the inhabitants of the world,

mentary on Genesis [Arabic and Hebrew] (New York: Jewish Theological Seminary of America, 1984), 141. Furthermore, in his *Books of Beliefs and Opinions*, the Gaon, just like Yefet, juxtaposes the two seemingly contradictory verses—*and offer him there as a burnt offering* (Gen 22:2) and *lay not your hand upon the lad* (v. 12)—and says that the latter does not abrogate the former, since the order of God was to hand his son, Isaac, over for an offering ("to reserve his son as a sacrifice"); and when Abraham did so by preparing the fire and the wood and by taking the knife, God told him that it was enough and that he did not want from him anything more than that. See Saʿadia Gaon, *Kitāb al-mukhtār fī ʾl-amānāt wa ʾl-iʿtiqādāt* (*Sefer ha-nivḥar ba-ʾemunot u-va-deʿot*), ed. and trans. Joseph Qāfiḥ (Jerusalem: Makhon Moshe, 1993), 140 (3:9). For an English translation, see Saadia Gaon, *The Book of Beliefs and Opinions*, trans. Samuel Rosenblatt, 2nd ed. (New Haven: Yale University Press, 1976), 169. Cf. Andrew Rippin, "Saʿadya Gaon and Genesis 22: Aspects of Jewish-Muslim Interaction and Polemic," in *Studies in Islamic and Judaic Traditions: Papers Presented at the Institute for Islamic-Judaic Studies, Center for Judaic Studies, University of Denver*, ed. William M. Brinner and Stephen D. Ricks (Atlanta: Scholars Press, 1986), 33–46.

34. For more on Yefet's conviction that the righteous are sometimes submitted to trials so that they could be more rewarded in the hereafter, see George Vajda, *Deux commentaires karaïtes sur l'Ecclésiaste*, Études sur le judaïsme médiéval 6 (Leiden: Brill, 1971), 210. For Saʿadia also acknowledging that the trial should increase Abraham's reward, see Zucker, *Rav Saadya Gaon's Commentary on Genesis*, 140 [Arabic], 399–400 [Hebrew].

35. A similar argument for God's foreknowledge or his perfect omniscience is found already in Midrash Tanḥuma, whose authors ascertain that God tested Abraham so as to make known to the people of the world that Abraham had been chosen by God not without a reason. See Tanḥ. Vayera 4:46. Similarly, Genesis Rabbah interprets: "*For now I know*—I have made known to all—that thou lovest me, *and thou hast not witheld, etc.*" See Gen. Rab. 56:7. The English translation here follows Harry Freedman and Maurice Simon, eds., *Midrash Rabbah*, 10 vols. (repr., London:

in order to inform people of [all] the generations about his obedience to God,[36] that they might emulate him and follow in his footsteps, just like Job, may peace be upon him, was tested with respect to his progeny and his property,[37] as well as his own body, that his obedience and the excellence of his perseverance might become evident, that the people [who read of him] might [then] follow in his footsteps and persevere in trials.[38] God also brought about similar things [= afflictions] for his chosen favorites [Arab. *khawāṣṣihi al-mufaḍḍalīn*], that the inhabitants of the world benefit from that [= their example]. In addition, when he tests his beloved friends [or "the holy men"; Arab. *al-awliyāʾ*],[39] it benefits them [too] in [both] this world and the hereafter.[40]

Soncino, 1961), 1:497. For an English translation of the above cited passage from the Tanḥuma, see John T. Townsend, ed., *Midrash Tanḥuma* (Hoboken, NJ: Ktav, 1989), 1:130. For further bibliography see Louis Ginzberg, *The Legends of the Jews*, 5 vols. (Philadelphia: Jewish Publication Society of America, 1909–1928), 1:284; 5:252 n. 247. Medieval Bible exegetes generally followed this line of argument. Thus Saʿadia emphasizes that the trial was meant to demonstrate to people Abraham's perfect obedience. See Zucker, *Rav Saadya Gaon's Commentary on Genesis*, 140, 399–400. For the Karaite authors of the *Talkhīṣ* (Yūsuf ibn Nūḥ, Abū al-Faraj Hārūn) making a similar claim that Abraham's test was meant to demonstrate to people his obedience to God, see MS SP RNL Yevr.-Arab. 1:1754, fols. 279b–280a.

36. Arabic *ṭāʿa* ("obedience"), a term generally designating (in Islam) active obedience, as opposed to passive submission denoted by the term *taslīm*, profusely used in the religious context to indicate unquestionable submission and obedience to God.

37. Arabic *bi-awlādihi wa-bi-mālihi* (lit. "in his progeny and his property"). The combination of "progeny and property" appears repeatedly in the Qurʾan as a synonym for the most precious possessions in this world. See, e.g., Q Al-Kahf 18:46, where it says that "property and progeny are the adornments of life."

38. The comparison between Abraham and Job was made already in the Midrash. See, e.g., Gen. Rab. 49:9; Tanḥ. Vayera 4:7.

39. Arabic *al-awliyāʾ* (lit. "the forefathers"). For the meaning of this term as "exalted saints" or "chosen friends," see Frank, *Search Scripture Well*, 118.

40. In his comment on Gen 35:22, Yefet expounds: "Scripture records [Jacob's] story (*khabar*), so that we learn that in this world, the righteous are subjected to trials, as it is said *many are the afflictions of the righteous, etc.* (Ps 34:19), and that we ascertain that there is a place of retribution for the righteous, where there will know no suffering. Similarly, God benefits the wicked in this world, and they pass away from the world in prosperity, knowing no adversity, as it is said *They spend their days in wealth, [and in peace they go down to Sheol]* (Job 21:13), but their deeds are undoubtedly kept by God, who will recompense them for them in the hereafter, as it is said about both

But the difference between Abraham and Job was that Job knew that these blows [were after the manner of] a test, as it is said *he will laugh at the trial of the innocent* (Job 9:23), whereas Abraham did not know that it [was merely] a *test*. Accordingly, Job was afflicted without [exercising any free] choice in that [matter]. Rather, the test [described] in his story [Arab. *qiṣṣa*] [consisted of examining] the excellence of his perseverance [in enduring] blows that fell upon him, as well as his [ability to withstand] arguments with people, their slanders, and invectives. And he [= Job] remained firm in his religion, and excelled in his faith.

However, the test of Abraham, may peace be upon him, concerned the matter of order, the fulfilment of which involved [exercising] free choice.[41] And it is the most difficult order for a man [to be demanded] to take his dearest child, especially one like Isaac, and offer it [as a sacrifice] and burn it.

When the *mudawwin* commenced [Arab. *ṣaddara*] explaining what [Abraham] had been ordered [to do by God], stating, *and said to him: "Abraham"* (v. 1), he indicated that [Abraham] was called by [God] and so answered, *Here I am* (v. 1). Next he informed [us] what the Lord of the universe said to [Abraham]: *Take your son, your only one, whom you love* (v. 2).

And it was possible [for God] to say: "Now take Isaac, your son, and offer him there as a burnt offering," but he purposefully added [Arab. *zāda*] the words *your only one, whom you love*, to kindle in Abraham's heart [love] for his child, so that if he had carried out the order, his reward would have been doubled.[42] And it is so that when people give orders to their slaves or their children, they tend to formulate them in the easiest

---

[kinds of men] [*God shall judge the righteous and the wicked*], *for there is a time there for every purpose and for every work* (Eccl 3:17)." See MS SP IOS B 217, fol. 50b.

41. According to Mu'tazilite doctrine, all humans are endowed by God with freedom of choice and, consequently, are responsible for their own actions, on account of which they deserve reward and/or punishment. See Haggai Ben-Shammai, "Kalām in Medieval Jewish Philosophy," in *History of Jewish Philosophy*, ed. Daniel Frank and Oliver Leaman (Leiden: Brill, 1995), 115–48, esp. 119.

42. A similar argument is made by the Karaite authors of the *Talkhīṣ* (Yūsuf ibn Nūḥ, Abū al-Faraj Hārūn), who ascertain that the expression *your only son, whom you love* (Gen 22:2) was meant to increase Abraham's trial (Arab. *ta'ẓīm al-miḥna*). See MS SP RNL Yevr.-Arab. 1:1754, fol. 280a. Ya'qūb al-Qirqisānī, in turn, maintains that had there been no doubts engendered by God's order to offer a human being as a sacrifice, both Abraham's obedience to God and his perseverance in the trial would not have been so great. See MS SP RNL Yevr.-Arab. 1:4529, fol. 46b.

way [possible]. But the Creator, the Almighty [and] Supreme, does with his beloved friends [Arab. *al-awliyā'*] as opposed to that, so that if they carried his order out, and persevered, and [despite everything] praised [God], they would deserve his praise, and he would grant them a full reward, above the reward that he would have granted them had he formulated [his command] to them in the easiest way [possible].[43]

And he [= God] called Isaac [Abraham's] *only [son]* on the basis of what he said to him: *for in Isaac shall your seed be called* (Gen 21:12).

And when [God] said: *and you go to the land of Moriah*, he ordered him [= Abraham] to go to a place that he would let him know about.[44] He added [Arab. *zāda*] the word *"you"* [Heb. *ləkhā*], meaning by it that Abraham [alone] would go, and nobody [else] would be together with him. Therefore when Abraham approached the land of Moriah, he said to his two young man: *stay here with the donkey; whereas I and the boy [will go over there and worship]* (Gen 22:5).

And his [= God's] words *and offer him there as a burnt offering* literally [Arab. *bi-ẓāhir al-qawl*] mean the offering of him [= Isaac] [as] a burnt offering. Abraham had already known the laws of burnt offerings from the ancestors [Arab. *al-qudamā*], as it is said about Noah, *and [he] offered burnt offerings on the altar* (Gen 8:20).[45]

And his words *on one of the mountains that I shall tell you of* points at two things. First, that he [= God] did not immediately inform him [=

---

43. A similar idea was expressed by Saʿadia in his comment on Gen 12:1, where he states that in contrast with people who try to formulate their requests in the easiest way possible, God formulates them in the hardest way possible in order to afterwards increase the believer's reward for having executed the required deed. See Zucker, *Rav Saadya Gaon's Commentary on Genesis*, 114 [Arabic], 357 [Hebrew].

44. The authors of the *Talkhīṣ* specify that the land of Moriah is the one known from Solomon's narrative (Arab. *qiṣṣa Shəlomo*), where it is said *on mount Moriah, where the Lord appeared to David* (2 Chr 3:1), whereas the mount of Moriah is a place well known within the land of Moriah. See MS SP RNL Yevr.-Arab. 1:1754, fol. 280a.

45. This comment alludes to the conception of the antiquity of the commandments (Arab. *qidam al-farḍ*), according to which already the patriarchs were aware of and performed certain commandments, despite living before the revelation of the Torah; knowledge of these commandments was believed to have been transmitted orally until the time of Moses. For more on this subject, see Yoram Erder, "Early Karaite Conceptions about the Commandments Given before the Revelation of the Torah," *PAAJR* 60 (1994): 101–40, and further bibliography there.

Abraham] which mountain from among the mountains it was. Second, that there were numerous mountains in the land of Moriah.

And [the fact that] he said: *that I shall tell you of*, and did not say: "that I will show you," indicates that [God] had already directed to him words [not mentioned here, in the past] [wherein] he informed him which mountain it was. But it is [also] possible that he showed him the glory upon the mountain, and said: "Direct yourself to this mountain, and offer him [= Isaac] there." And [God] ordered him four things: (1)—to take Isaac alone [and no one else], as he said: *take your son*; (2) to go alone, as it is said *and you go to the land of Moriah*; (3) *and offer him there as a burnt offering*; (4) *that I shall tell you of*.

These [first] three orders God wished [Abraham] to fulfill, namely, the taking of Isaac, going alone, and directing himself to the mountain that God had told him of, whereas [his order] *and offer him there as a burnt offering*, God did not wish him [= Abraham] to fulfill, but rather he ordered him [to do] so after the manner of a test.

Now I need to dwell here for a while and explain how God's orders and prohibitions [Arab. *awāmir wa-nawāhī*], as well as his promises and his threats [Arab. *wa'd wa-wa' īd*], are formulated.[46] Thus I will say that they are divided into two types [of expressions]. The first one is a precise (or "clear," "unambiguous") statement [Arab. *qawl muḥkam*]; and the second one is a statement that bears two possible [meanings] [= allows for two possible interpretations].[47]

---

46. Arabic *amr wa-nāhī* (pl. *awāmir wa-nawāhī*; "orders and prohibitions"). This is probably a translation of the Hebrew terms denoting positive and negative commandments (עשה ולא תעשה; lit. "you shall," "you shall not"), which connotes the principal religious duty in Islam of commanding what is right or good, and forbidding what is wrong or evil (Arab. *al-'amr bi-al-ma'rūf wa-al-nāhī 'an al-munkar*). It is mentioned several times in the Qur'an (e.g., Q Al-Imran 3:104) and consists of commanding right (Arab. *ma'arūf*; lit. "known," or "familiar," and hence approved), and forbidding wrong (Arab. *munkar*; lit. "unknown," or "unfamiliar," and thus disapproved). In addition, the principle of enjoining good and forbidding evil is one of the five principles of the Mu'tazilite doctrine, to which the Karaites generally subscribed. The other four are: God's unity (Arab. *tawḥīd*); God's justice (Arab. *'adl*); God's promise and threat (Arab. *al-wa'd wa-al-wa'īd*); and the intermediate state of Muslim sinners (Arab. *al-manzala bayn al-manzalateyn*). See Ben-Shammai, "Kalām in Medieval Jewish Philosophy," 118; Michael Cook, *Commanding Right and Forbidding Wrong in Islamic Thought* (New York, Cambridge University Press, 2000).

47. On Yefet's creative adaptation of Islamic hermeneutical terms in this context,

As for the precise [statement], it is [the one] which [God] puts in the context [Arab. *qarīna*][48] indicating that it is a precise [statement]. [For example,] if there is no condition to it, [God] informs [us] that it is unconditional, as he said in [the story about] the flood, *I will not again curse the ground any more for man's sake* (Gen 8:21), and [thereby] indicated that this statement had no condition whatsoever. Another example [can be adduced from] what he said to Solomon, *Wisdom and knowledge is granted to you; and I will give you riches, and wealth, [and honor]* (2 Chr 1:12), which is an unconditional statement. Had it had any condition, [God] would have explained it, just like he imposed stipulation upon the forefathers [Arab. *al-awliyā'*], *if you walk in my statutes, [and keep my commandments, and do them],* etc. (Lev 26:3) *then I will give you rain [in due season],* etc. (Lev 26:4) till the end of the passage. Likewise, he said, *But if you will not obey me* (Lev 26:14), and the rest of the verse. And similarly [God] said to Solomon, *then I will lengthen your days* (1 Kgs 3:14), under

---

see Marzena Zawanowska, "Islamic Exegetical Terms in Yefet ben 'Eli's Commentaries on the Holy Scriptures," *JJS* 64 (2013): 306–25.

48. Arabic *qarīna* ("context"; lit. "proximity"). Islamic tradition distinguishes between two kinds of *qarīna*: verbal or semantic, and circumstantial. Linguistically, the term *qarīna* refers to a verbal or nonverbal element elucidating a part of speech extraneous to itself. The other meaning of the term *qarīna* relates to the circumstances of transmitting a given tradition. These two types of *qarīna* may converge in the same context to define a precise meaning of a certain sentence or word. See Wael B. Hallaq, "Notes on the Term *qarīna* in Islamic Legal Discourse," *JAOS* 108 (1988): 475–80. This exegetical tool, often used by medieval Karaite exegetes, may have been shaped under the influence of the rabbinic principle: דבר הלמד מעניינו ("something learned/proved by the context"; see, e.g., b. Sanh. 86a). It is included as the last principle of the Hillel's seven *middōt* and corresponds to the tenth principle of Ishmael's twelve *middōt*. Thus it seems that the Karaites used the Islamic term to denote a traditional Jewish concept. Indeed, Yefet employs the term *qarīna* in a literary-stylistic sense: to denote an (immediate) narrative context in which given words or expressions appear, and which helps define their meaning within an analysed verse or passage. See Yoram Erder, "The Attitude of the Karaite Yefet ben 'Eli to Moral Issues in Light of his Interpretation of Exodus 3:21–22" [Hebrew], *Sefunot* 22 (1999): 313–33, esp. 323–24; Meira Polliack and Eliezer Schlossberg, "Historical-Literary, Rhetorical and Redactional Methods of Interpretation in Yefet ben 'Eli's Introduction to the Minor Prophets," in *Exegesis and Grammar in Medieval Karaite Texts*, ed. Geoffrey Khan, Journal of Semitic Studies Supplement 13 (Oxford: Oxford University Press, 2001), 1–39, esp. 24–25; Zawanowska, *The Arabic Translation and Commentary of Yefet ben 'Eli the Karaite on the Abraham Narratives*, 118 n. 22, and further bibliography there.

the stipulation of obedience, thus making it a conditional promise. And this [promise] that I have mentioned [above] and similar [others], God formulated in a precise statement [Arab. *qawl muḥkam*].

Likewise in the case of [positive] command and prohibition [Arab. *al-amr wa-al-nahy*]. Sometimes [God] explains that they are related to a specific time and not another, or to a specific place and not another, or to a specific person and not another, and informs [people about] its conditional aspect, namely a stipulation that has to be fulfilled. That is the first, precise kind [of statement] [Arab. *al-muḥkam*] of which the worshipers are informed.

The second kind [of statement] that God directs to him [= his worshiper] is an imprecise [or "unspecified," "ambiguous"] statement [Arab. *qawl mursal*], and it bears two possible meanings [= allows for two possible interpretations].

(1) Sometimes God means by this the realization of his words, with no stipulation by him, as he promised the kingdom to Jeroboam son of Nebat, and [subsequently] granted him that, though this promise was not [bound] by covenant and oath (1 Kgs 11:31).

(2) Sometimes there is an [undeclared] condition by God [to the realization of his words], but the worshiper is informed [about it] only afterwards. Of this [kind] is God's statement [directed] to Hezekiah, *for you shall die, and not live* (2 Kgs 20:1; Isa 38:1), [the realization of which] was under the stipulation that he prayed and called [God] [= prayed privately]. Similarly, *Yet forty days, and Nineveh shall be overthrown* (Jonah 3:4), and many similar [others].

Now we will [return to interpreting the chapter and] say that when [God], may he be praised, promised Abraham and said: *Sarah your wife shall bear you a son indeed; and you shall call his name Isaac, and I will establish my covenant with him for an everlasting covenant, and with his seed after him* (Gen 17:19); and said, *But my covenant will I establish with Isaac, etc.* (Gen 17:21); and said, *For in Isaac shall your seed be called* (Gen 21:12)—he did not put these statements in a context [Arab. *qarīna*] indicating that they were precise statements, with no condition whatsoever. Therefore, when [Abraham] heard God's saying *and offer him there as a burnt offering*, [he thought] it possible that these promises, which [God] had promised him [before], had a condition by God, about which he had not informed him [yet]. At the same time, however, [he thought] it possible that God's words [directed] to him—*and offer him there as a burnt offering*—had no condition, and should of necessity be executed, unless he permitted him [otherwise]. This conviction [Arab. *i'tiqād*]⁴⁹ [= the fact that he thought it possible] made him [= Abraham] begin [performing] the deed in a belief that if God's words [directed] to him had a condition, and he [= God] did not wish him [to accomplish] the deed, he would [soon] explain it to him; but if they had no condition by him, he would leave his worshiper [= Abraham] to himself to execute the deed.

Abraham, may peace be upon him, acted in accordance with this assumption [Arab. *fa'ala 'ala hadha al-aṣl*; lit. "followed this principle"]— [namely,] he went being convinced that he would have to offer Isaac, unless God would order him otherwise and inform him [about] the conditional aspect, or the stipulation [involved in this order], provided that it had [any] condition or stipulation. This is a view to which we are disposed [to subscribe], and it is [consistent with] the way [in which] Scripture [expresses itself] [Arab. *maslak al-kitāb*].

As for the obligations that are imposed by reason and the commandments that were revealed through unambiguous statements [Arab. *'ala tarīq al-ta'akīd*], the [biblical] text [Arab. *al-nass*] has already clarified that [both these kinds of commandments] were everlasting obligations.⁵⁰

And as for the commandment [Arab. *farḍ*] related to [a specific] person, it follows [one of] the two principles, which we have mentioned in what preceded.

---

49. Arabic *i'tiqād* ("conviction," "belief," "faith," "trust," "confidence"). This should probably be understood here in accordance with Sa'adia's understanding of this term, viz., as a belief or dogma that underwent a speculative process, and only after having become rationally established in believer's mind, it acquired the status of conviction. See Sa'adia Gaon, *Kitāb al-mukhtār fī 'l-amānāt wa-'l-i'tiqādāt*, introduction, par. 4 [Arabic and Hebrew]. For an English translation, see Sa'adia Gaon, *The Book of Beliefs and Opinions*, 14. Compare Haggai Ben-Shammai, "Kalām in Medieval Jewish Philosophy," 130.

50. Following the *mu'tazilite* distinction, adapted also by some Rabbanite Jews like Sa'adia, medieval Karaites distinguished between rational (Arab. *'aqliyya*) and revealed (Arab. *sam'iyya*) commandments. The former, imposed by reason, or "planted" in human consciousness, were generally believed to have existed from time immemorial and therefore there was no need for prophetic revelation about them, whereas there were divergent opinions with regard to the latter which, if not for the revelation, would not have been known to humans. In his comment on Gen 2:17, Yefet ascertains: "What the reason imposes as an obligation is such forever; therefore it needs not be revealed." See MS SP IOS B 051, fols. 125a–b. See also Yoram Erder, "Early Karaite Conceptions about the Commandments Given before the Revelation of the Torah," and further bibliography there.

But another commentator maintains that the statement *God tested* [נסה] *Abraham* (v. 1) [means] that God honored Abraham, may peace be upon him, and he derives [this interpretation] from the verse, *for God is come to honor* [נסות] *you* (Exod 20:16).[51] And about the statement, *and offer him there as a burnt offering* (v. 1), he says that Abraham understood it [= this order] as referring to Isaac, while God, the Almighty and Exalted, [actually] meant by it [= this expression] the lamb, which he [= Abraham] offered. Yet God did not make this clear in his phrase [Arab. *lam yaṣraḥhu* or *yuṣarriḥhu bi-al-'ibāra*], leaving this statement unspecified [Arab. *qawl mursal*], until Abraham took the knife to offer [Isaac], and [only] then he said to him: "My wish was the offering of the lamb, however I did not inform you [about] my wish, in order to demonstrate to the people your obedience."

Another [commentator] says that from his words, *and offer him there as a burnt offering*, Abraham did not learn whether [God] meant Isaac or something else, since he said, *that I shall tell you of.* According to this commentator, his words—*that I shall tell you of*—are not related to [the phrase] *on one of the mountains that I shall tell you of*, but rather they are related to [the phrase] *and offer him there as a burnt offering*. He maintains that Abraham went being convinced that the offering of a sacrifice was necessary. Yet, [he thought] it possible that Isaac would be the sacrifice, but [he thought] it [equally] possible that it would be something else. And when [God] ordered him [= Abraham] to take Isaac alone and go [with him] to the place where he ordered him to offer, and [when he went there and] built the altar, and arranged the wood, and prepared everything he needed [for the offering], and did not see God ordering him to offer something else, but Isaac, he thought that [God] meant Isaac, since neither at first [God] ordered him to take something else, nor when [Abraham] finished [preparing everything] that he needed for the offering, [did] he say to him to offer something else, other than Isaac. Therefore [Abraham] bound him [= Isaac] and took the knife to offer him; and [only then] God informed him that [when he said], *that I shall tell you of*, he meant the lamb [and] nothing else.

Another [commentator] maintains that when God said, *and offer him there* [*as a burnt offering*], he referred to Isaac, [and] nothing else. And so

---

51. Yefet's understanding of the Hebrew root נסה in the *piel* ("to test") as נישא ("to honor") derives from the midrashic interpretation, reproduced also in Rashi's commentary on Exod 20:17. See, e.g., Gen. Rab. 55:6.

Abraham thought, but God's wish was merely to have him [= Isaac] put on the altar, and he did not want him [= Abraham] to execute his offering and his burning [= of Isaac]. But Abraham, may peace be upon him, acted according to the common [meaning] of the word [Arab. *'ala mashhūr lafẓa*] "burnt offering" and [therefore] he put him [= Isaac] on the altar and begun to offer him. Thereupon God said to him: "Indeed my wish was merely to have him [= Isaac] put on the altar, but I did not explain this to you at the outset, for I wanted your love [for God] and obedience [to him] to become evident."

Another [commentator] maintains that when [God] said, *and offer him there as a burnt offering*, he wished him [= Abraham] [merely] to prepare for the offering. So Abraham prepared the wood and the fire, and he built the altar and arranged the wood, and he bound Isaac and put him on the wood. Next he took the knife in his hand to wait for God's order. Had [God] ordered him to offer [Isaac], he would have offered [him], but if not, he would have abandoned [this idea]. And he [= this commentator] claims that this order resembles [a situation when] a governor orders his scribe to prepare for writing; he [= the scribe] has to prepare the inkwell, and take the paper in his hand, then stretch [the hand] and halt, in order to wait for what [the governor] will command him to write [down].[52]

This is all that has been said about this narrative [Arab. *qiṣṣa*]. The first view we have explained [in detail], since it is the most likely interpretation. But we have cited the [divergent] opinions of sages, at the request of [someone who is] asking to be informed about [different] opinions of people with regard to this account [Arab. *qiṣṣa*]. So we have cited them, but will not occupy [ourselves] with their refutation.

Now, we will return to our subject and conclude that Abraham, may peace be upon him, was convinced that [God's order directed to him] *and offer him there* [*as a burnt offering*] referred to Isaac [and nothing else],

---

52. Most likely, Yefet cites here an interpretation provided by the authors of the *Talkhīṣ* (Yūsuf ibn Nūḥ, Abū al-Faraj Hārūn), who also compare God's order directed to Abraham to offer Isaac to an order to prepare for writing directed to a scribe, and who maintain that God wished Abraham merely to prepare for a burnt offering by putting Isaac on the altar, upon the wood, taking the knife in his hand—and waiting for further orders. According to the *Talkhīṣ*, the test consisted of checking whether Abraham would be able (Arab. *imtiḥān al-qadr*), or ready and determined (Arab. *ma' al-'azm 'aleyhi*), to offer his son. See MS SP RNL Yevr.-Arab. 1:1754, fol. 252a. Cf. Goldstein, *Karaite Exegesis in Medieval Jerusalem*, 72, 157.

and that thereby [God] asked him [= Abraham] to offer and burn him [= Isaac], according to the assumptions [Arab. *al-'uṣūl*; lit. "principles"] that we have mentioned [above, in the first explanation]; and that his words, *that I shall tell you of*, referred to the mountain, and not to Isaac.

Further Discussion

Both passages present serious theological and semantic problems with which commentators of all times have had to grapple.

The amazingly compact account of the story of the tower/city of Babel leaves many important details unexplained, among them the paramount question of what was the sin of the builders that made them deserve divine punishment, and it challenges an important religious tenet of the noncorporeal nature of God. Yefet's approach to the former exegetical conundrum is very modern in that he tries to reconstruct the true history behind the text, as well as the history of the text itself, instead of focusing on the story's homiletic aspect, as is the case with earlier commentators. As a result, he many times provides answers not only to questions of who did what, when, where, why, and how, but also ponders the reason why the story was told and included in the Bible in the first place. His innovative answers notwithstanding, the very fact that he asks such questions reveals his unusual historical sensibilities to which we, as modern readers, are highly attuned. As to the latter *crux interpretum* of this story, posed by the implication of divine anthropomorphism, Yefet skillfully enlists his knowledge of linguistics to solve it by referring to the concept of ellipsis, thus offering a palatable stylistic explanation that sounds convincing even today.

The Akedah narrative is undoubtedly one of the most theologically difficult as well as morally disturbing passages in the entire Hebrew Bible, invariably leaving its readers perplexed and distressed. It undermines the traditional conception of the all-benevolent, omniscient, and perfectly just Deity on the one hand, and, on the other hand, it puts the "fundamentalist"—uncompromising and blind—faith of Abraham under a question mark. Yefet's treatment of this narrative is marked by scholarly honesty in that he pinpoints and minutely discusses all its puzzling aspects one by one. While doing so, he investigates and assesses a sheer variety of different interpretations—a method, well-known in present day research too, that allows us to better comprehend the full scope of the problems engendered by this pericope.

The main innovativeness of his approach, however, consists of providing a consistent and comprehensive literary analysis of the story,
which brings Yefet's reading significantly closer to modern literary
approaches to Scripture. This is borne out, inter alia, by how he clearly
distinguishes between the figures of the text's author, protagonists, and
readers—all of whose diverging perspectives he explores individually,
while also closely scrutinizing the story's overall structure as well as its
narrative building blocks. He also delves deeply into the stylistic nuances
of the text, among other things discussing the idiosyncratic features of
divine discourse. With the aid of all these sophisticated literary and linguistic tools Yefet successfully contrives to improve the Creator's image.
Nevertheless, his evident admiration for Abraham's obedient response
to the divine order to offer his own beloved son—which, in the exegete's
view, should serve as an exemplum for future generations of believers—
can hardly be considered universally convincing.

Therefore, we may conclude that Yefet's chief contribution to the
reception history and exegesis of both sections consists of his systematic
engagement with scientific (historical, linguistic, and literary) methods
of interpretation. In so doing, he anticipates modern approaches to the
Bible; this makes his commentaries interesting not only as a reflection of
his own medieval *Sitz im Leben*, but also as a source of valuable—original,
insightful, and inspiring—solutions to old cruxes which remain valid for
us today.

Bibliography

Manuscript Sources

Ya'qūb al-Qirqisānī, *Commentary on Genesis*, MS SP RNL Yevr.-Arab.
    1:4529.
Yefet ben 'Eli, *Commentary on Genesis*, MS SP IOS B 051.
Yefet ben 'Eli, *Commentary on Genesis*, MS SP IOS B 217.
Yefet ben 'Eli, *Commentary on Genesis*, MS SP IOS B 222.
Yeshu'ah ben Yehudah, *Commentary on Genesis*, MS SP RNL Yevr-Arab
    1:3204.
Yūsuf ibn Nūḥ and Abū al-Faraj Hārūn, *Commentary on the Torah* (the
    Talkhīṣ), MS SP RNL Yevr.-Arab. 1:1754.

Printed Sources and Studies

Agius, Dionisius A. *Arabic Literary Works as a Source of Documentation for Technical Terms of the Material Culture.* Berlin: Schwarz, 1984.

Ben-Shammai, Haggai. "Kalām in Medieval Jewish Philosophy." Pages 115–48 in *History of Jewish Philosophy.* Edited by Daniel Frank and Oliver Leaman. Leiden: Brill, 1995.

———. "On *mudawwin*—the Editor of the Books of the Bible in Judaeo-Arabic Exegesis" [Hebrew]. Pages 73–110 in *Rishonim ve-Achronim: Studies in Jewish History Presented to Avraham Grossman.* Edited by Joseph Hacker, Benjamin Z. Kedar, and Joseph Kaplan. Jerusalem: Zalman Shazar Center for Jewish History, 2009.

Cook, Michael. *Commanding Right and Forbidding Wrong in Islamic Thought.* New York: Cambridge University Press, 2000.

Derenbourg, Joseph. *Version arabe du Pentateuque* de *R. Saadia ben Iosef al-Fayyoûmî.* Vol. 1 of *Œuvres complètes de R. Saadia ben Iosef al-Fayyoûmî.* Repr., Hildesheim: Olms, 1979.

Erder, Yoram. "The Attitude of the Karaite Yefet ben 'Eli to Moral Issues in Light of His Interpretation of Exodus 3:21–22" [Hebrew]. *Sefunot* 22 (1999): 313–33.

———. "Early Karaite Conceptions about the Commandments Given before the Revelation of the Torah." *PAAJR* 60 (1994): 101–40.

Frank, Daniel. *Search Scripture Well: Karaite Exegetes and the Origins of the Jewish Bible Commentary in the Islamic East.* Études sur le judaïsme médiéval 39. Leiden: Brill, 2004.

Freedman, Harry, and Maurice Simon, eds. *Midrash Rabbah.* 10 vols. Repr., London: Soncino, 1961.

Ginzberg, Louis. *The Legends of the Jews.* 5 vols. Philadelphia: Jewish Publication Society of America, 1909–1928.

Goldstein, Miriam. *Karaite Exegesis in Medieval Jerusalem: The Judeo-Arabic Pentateuch Commentary of Yusuf ibn Nuh and Abu al-Faraj Harun.* Tübingen: Mohr Siebeck, 2011.

Hallaq, Wael B. "Notes on the Term *qarīna* in Islamic Legal Discourse." *JAOS* 108 (1988): 475–80.

Khan, Geoffrey, ed. and trans. *The Early Karaite Tradition of Hebrew Grammatical Thought, Including a Critical Edition, Translation and Analysis of the Diqduq of Abū Yaʿqūb Yūsuf ibn Nūḥ on the Hagiographa.* Studies in Semitic Languages and Linguistics 32. Leiden: Brill, 2000.

Linetsky, Michael, trans. *Rabbi Saadiah Gaon's Commentary on the Book of Creation. Annotated and Translated by Michael Linetsky*. Northvale, NJ: Jason Aronson, 2002.

Polliack, Meira. "Historicizing Prophetic Literature: Yefet ben ʿEli's Commentary on Hosea and Its Relationship to al-Qumisi's Pitron." Pages 149–86 in *Pesher Nahum: Texts and Studies in Jewish History and Literature from Antiquity through the Middle Ages*. Edited by Joel L. Kraemer and Michael G. Wechsler. Chicago: University of Chicago Press, 2011.

———. "Karaite Conception of the Biblical Narrator (*mudawwin*)." Pages 350–74 in vol. 1 of *Encyclopaedia of Midrash*. Edited by Jacob Neusner and Alan J. Avery-Peck. 2 vols. Leiden: Brill, 2005.

———. *The Karaite Tradition of Arabic Bible Translation: A Linguistic and Exegetical Study of Karaite Translations of the Pentateuch from the Tenth and Eleventh Centuries C.E.* Études sur le judaïsme médiéval 17. Leiden: Brill, 1997.

———. "The Unseen Joints of the Text: On Medieval Judaeo-Arabic Concept of Ellision (*iḫtiṣār*) and Its Gap-filling Functions in Biblical Interpretation." Pages 179–205 in *Words, Ideas, Worlds in the Hebrew Bible—The Yairah Amit Festschrift*. Edited by Athalya Brenner and Frank Polak. Sheffield: Sheffield Phoenix, 2012.

Polliack, Meira, and Eliezer Schlossberg. "Historical-Literary, Rhetorical and Redactional Methods of Interpretation in Yefet ben ʿEli's Introduction to the Minor Prophets." Pages 1–39 in *Exegesis and Grammar in Medieval Karaite Texts*. Edited by Geoffrey Khan. Journal of Semitic Studies Supplement 13. Oxford: Oxford University Press, 2001.

Rippin, Andrew. "Saʿadya Gaon and Genesis 22: Aspects of Jewish-Muslim Interaction and Polemic." Pages 33–46 in *Studies in Islamic and Judaic Traditions: Papers Presented at the Institute for Islamic-Judaic Studies, Center for Judaic Studies, University of Denver*. Edited by William M. Brinner and Stephen D. Ricks. Atlanta: Scholars Press, 1986.

Saʿadia Gaon. *Kitāb al-mukhtār fī ʾl-amānāt wa-ʾl-iʿtiqādāt (Sefer ha-nivḥar ba-ʾemunot u-va-deʿot)*. Edited and translated by Joseph Qāfiḥ. Jerusalem: Makhon Moshe, 1993.

Saadia Gaon. *The Book of Beliefs and Opinions*. Translated by Samuel Rosenblatt. 2nd ed. New Haven: Yale University Press, 1976.

Simon, Uriel. *Four Approaches to the Book of Psalms: From Saadiah Gaon to Abraham ibn Ezra* [Hebrew]. Ramat Gan: Bar-Ilan University Press, 1982.

Townsend, John T., ed. *Midrash Tanḥuma*. Hoboken NJ: Ktav, 1989.

Vajda, George. *Deux commentaires karaïtes sur l'Ecclésiaste*. Études sur le judaïsme médiéval 4. Leiden: Brill, 1971.

Wechsler, Michael G. *The Arabic Translation and Commentary of Yefet ben 'Eli the Karaite on the Book of Esther*. Karaite Texts and Studies 1. Études sur le judaïsme médiéval 36. Leiden: Brill, 2008.

Zawanowska, Marzena. *The Arabic Translation and Commentary of Yefet ben 'Eli the Karaite on the Abraham Narratives (Genesis 11:10-25:18)*. Karaite Texts and Studies 4. Études sur le Judaïsme médiéval 46. Brill, Leiden 2012.

———. "The Discovery of History in Medieval Bible Exegesis: Islamic Influences on the Emergence of Historical Sensibilities among the Karaites as Exemplified in Their Innovative Treatment of the Story of the Tower of Babel (Genesis 11:1-9)." Forthcoming.

———. "Islamic Exegetical Terms in Yefet ben "Eli's Commentaries on the Holy Scriptures." *JJS* 64 (2013): 306-25.

———. "Was Moses the *mudawwin* of the Torah? The Question of Authorship of the Pentateuch According to Yefet ben 'Eli." Pages 7*-35* in *Studies in Judaeo-Arabic Culture: Proceedings of the Fourteenth Conference of the Society for Judaeo-Arabic Studies*. Edited by Haggai Ben-Shammai, Aron Dotan, Yoram Erder, and Mordechai A. Freidman. Tel Aviv: Tel Aviv University Press, 2014.

———. "'Where the Plain Meaning is Obscure or Unacceptable …': The Treatment of Implicit Anthropomorphisms in the Medieval Karaite Tradition of Arabic Bible Translation." *EJJS* 10 (2016): 1-49.

Zoran, Yair. "The Majestic Plural [*Pluralis majestatis*]: The Plural of Respect" [Hebrew]. *Beit Mikra* 143 (1995): 402-3.

Zoref, Arye. "Yaʻqūb al-Qirqisānīʾs Position in the Debate over the Formation of Language" [Hebrew]. *Ginzei Qedem* 12 (2016): 127-54.

Zucker, Moshe. *Rav Saadya Gaonʾs Commentary on Genesis* [Arabic and Hebrew]. New York: Jewish Theological Seminary of America, 1984.

Qirqisānī's Exegetical Method and Commentary on Genesis 18:1–22

Nabih Bashir

Introduction: Qirqisānī's Exegetical Method

Like contemporary Muslim and Christian *Kalām* philosophers who belonged to the Muʿtazila movement, the Karaite Yaʿqūb Qirqisānī (first half of the tenth century CE) established the foundations of his exegetical method on reason and logical argumentation. This is to say that the criterion of what is reasonable (Arab. *al-maʿqūl*) serves as the main and basic measure in the exegesis of scriptural verses, in his case the Hebrew Bible. In his words, "The Reasonable is the foundation on which every statement is based and from which knowledge [Arab. *ʿilm*] is derived" (Qirqisānī, *Kitāb al-Ānwār*, 1:4).[1] There is no contradiction between philosophy and the Hebrew Bible, in his view. On the contrary, one feeds the other and confirms it: religious faith is strengthened through rational thinking and study (1:75); rational thinking and study is a religious obligation (1:66–75, 150–51);[2] and the distinction between right and false is made valid only by thinking, study, and examination (1:73, 108–9). However, we should not conclude from this that reason precedes religious belief, as some of the *Kalām* philosophers contend. Rather, Qirqisānī sees reason as an instrument to establish, nourish, and strengthen belief. Whoever does not adopt this path in the gaining of knowledge will find himself or

---

1. Text follows the edition Yaʿqūb Qirqisānī, *Kitāb al-Anwār wal-Marāqib—Code of Karaite Law*, ed. Leon Nemoy, 5 vols. (New York: Alexander Kohut Memorial Foundation, 1939–1943); all translations are mine.

2. Haggai Ben-Shammai, "The Doctrines of Religious Thought of Abū Yūsuf Yaʿqūb al-Qirqisānī and Yefet Ben ʿEli," 2 vols. (PhD diss., Hebrew University of Jerusalem, 1977), 1:8–35.

herself relying on tradition and imitation, without any kind of individual or critical thinking.[3]

The main two instruments for study and examination are the innate faculty of discernment (Arab. *al-tamyīz*) and analogical reasoning (Arab. *al-qiyās*), and they can be acquired through rigorous learning. Furthermore, the theoretical-examinational effort of human intellect in Qirqisānī's method "is the only basis for knowing the truth, particularly the religious truth."[4] Qirqisānī rejects the Muʿtazili[5] differentiation between commandments based on reason and commandments based on revelation, which Saʿadia Gaon (a contemporary of Qirqisānī) introduced into Jewish thought. According to this division, the "revelational commandments" are not drawn from reason and cannot be derived or examined logically, whereas "rational commandments" are derived through analogical reasoning. In opposition to this, Qirqisānī argues that what Saʿadia classified as revelational commandments are actually necessities (Arab. *ḍarūrīyatun*), namely, axiomatic foundations (Arab. *'uṣūl*), which are at the basis of the so-called rational commandments (Qirqisānī, *Kitāb al-Anwār* 1:86–101). Further, Qirqisānī does not seem to hesitate at all, throughout his code of law (*Kitāb al-Ānwār*), to examine rationally the Karaite as well as the Rabbanite religious laws. And so he says: "We are obliged to apply the (logical and critical) study and examination of the commandments, and we are obliged to accept the outcome of this study and examination in this respect, no matter whether it reflects the Rabbinic or the Karaite opinion" (1:3). Accordingly, he rejects all forms of anthropomorphism (1:15, 31–38, 42), regardless of the fact that he and other major medieval Karaite exegetes generally followed the "literal sense of the text" (Arab. *ẓāhir al-naṣṣ*) as their main exegetical approach.[6]

The following excerpt, from Qirqisānī's exegesis on the beginning of the *parashat Vayera* (וירא, "The Lord Appeared," Gen 18:1–22:24), gives expression to four main exegetical traits that are common in Qirqisānī's work.

First, Qirqisānī makes ample use of the views, opinions, and commentaries found in rabbinic literature. Qirqisānī presents these as legitimate

---

3. Hatwig Hirschfeld, *Qirqisani Studies* (London: Jews' College, 1918), 14.

4. Ben-Shammai, "Doctrines," 1:109.

5. See further Marzena Zawanowska's essay in this volume, 49 n. 46 and 52 n. 50.

6. Meira Polliack, "Major Trends in Karaite Biblical Exegesis in the Tenth and Eleventh Centuries," in *Karaite Judaism: A Guide to Its History and Literary Sources*, ed. Meira Polliack (Leiden: Brill, 2003), 363–415.

opinions and ideas that are not obligatory, thereby omitting the aura of holiness from them.

Second, in accordance with the tendency of Karaite exegetes at large, Qirqisānī uses the method of literary analysis to elucidate the biblical verses as detached from extratextual authority.

Third, Qirqisānī's exegetical approach is philological-historical, sometimes mixed with ideas drawn from the dominant philosophy of his time, Neoplatonism.

Fourth, similarly to other medieval Karaite exegetes, he seeks to avoid and rule out any attempt to denunciate and defame angels, particularly with regard to their sanctity. This is probably because such denunciation may affect the degree of prophecy through which the biblical materials have been conveyed and have come down to us. It is worth noting that this is also the dominant position of the Muslim and Christian *kalām* philosophers who belonged to the Muʿtazila movement during this epoch, and so we see how Qirqisānī fully partakes in the wider intellectual milieu of his time, applying many of its notions to the study and elucidation of the Hebrew Bible.[7]

The Manuscripts

Qirqisānī's exegesis of *parashat Vayera* (Gen 18:1–33) appears in two different manuscripts, but only one (Yevr.-Arab. 1:4529, marked as A) contains the whole exegesis, whereas the other (Yevr.-Arab. 1:3198, marked as B) contains only part of it and suffers many omissions. There are no exegetical differences between the two manuscripts; therefore, I chose not to include an apparatus. Our main exegetical section appears in manuscript B (seventeen folios altogether) only in two folios (39v and 40v, where folio 40r is missing). Manuscript A, containing 104 folios, is part of Qirqisānī's commentary on Genesis (also known as *Kitāb al-Riyāḍ wal-Ḥadāʾiq, Book of Parks and Gardens*; henceforth *Riyāḍ*). The exegesis of *parashat Vayera* starts in 36v and continues to 38v.

Please note: in the following, texts that appear in round brackets are added by me in order to complete the translation, whereas what appears in square brackets, while also my additions, refers to the biblical source or

---

7. See my "A Reexamination of Saadya Gaon's Dictum 'Humankind Is More Sublime Than Angels'" [Hebrew], *Ginzei Qedem* 14 (2018): 9–54.

completes the biblical verse. The English translations of the MT biblical verses are based on the 2009 JPS translation.

English Translation of Qirqisānī's Commentary on *Parashat Vayera*

And the LORD appeared unto him by the terebinths of Mamre [Gen 18:1]

In this section you were informed that God has appeared to Abraham and manifested himself onto him[8] at this place (called) the terebinths of Mamre. And as it was argued, this place (is located) in southern Jerusalem, near the tombs of the fathers, peace and mercy be upon them (= Hebron). And Mamre is one of the three men, as Scripture tells, who was one of the allies of Abraham, peace be upon him. Hence, it was told, "Now he dwelt by the terebinths of Mamre the Amorite brother of Eshkol, and brother of Aner; and these were confederate with Abram" [Gen 14:13]. And regarding the verse "And the LORD appeared unto him" and the verse "and he lifted up his eyes" and so on, if one might ask whether the meaning of the word "appeared" is what has been expounded later in the follow-up story of the three men, or rather, there is another meaning for the word. After all, people differed on this subject. Some of them were of the opinion that every story of both stories is different from the other,[9] because God revealed to him (to Abraham) from what he had expounded (later) regarding this topic. So, when Abraham lifted up his eyes toward those three men and saw them, he said to God: "if it please you, do not go on past your servant" [Gen 18:3]. That is to say, he asked God for the appointed time to forbear him until he does his duties toward them, since he was fully aware of their excellency and uprightness and that they are angels of God. Therefore, he approached and asked them: "Let now a little water be fetched" [Gen 18:4]. Others were of the opinion that both of the stories are just one[10] and that whereas he said "and the LORD appeared unto him," he expounded and illustrated this in a way that this revelation and appear-

---

8. It seems that Qirqisānī follows R. Issi in this matter (Gen. Rab. 48:3, Soncino ed. 407). On the other hand, Sa'adia Gaon uses only the verb "revealed" (*tajallā*) as a translation-elucidation for the Biblical Hebrew verb "appeared" (*yera*).

9. Qirqisānī might be referring here to some of the sages, the Midrash, and Sa'adia Gaon, who adopted this exegesis. For example, see b. Shabb. 127a.

10. See b. Shabb. 127a; Gen. Rab. 48:4 (Soncino ed. 407).

ance was his dispatch of those three men to him, who stood over against him. So, he (Abraham) ran to meet them and bowed down. This is evident from the verse "he ran to meet them" [Gen 18:2] that precedes the verse "do not go on past your servant." This disproves the first exegesis. And if someone refers to the verse "do not go past"[11] and argues that it is in the singular form, although they were three, we reply to him that it is possible that he approached one of the three, because it said "wash [your feet, and recline under the tree]" [Gen 18:4–5]. And if someone asks and says about the verses calling them "men" [Gen 18:2], and later on calling them "the LORD" [Gen 18:13–14]: Therefore, it must be rather a creator or created being. If he was a created being, then how is it possible that the created got the same name of the worshiped? And if he was a creator, then how is it possible that a human being could see him? Beginning so, we say that the angels and the prophets could approach humans in some instances on behalf of the Creator, may his glory be exalted, while their sayings are being said in their names; but the intention is to speak on behalf of the Creator, may he be glorified and exalted. We have already expounded this in the response to Binyāmīn's[12] argument regarding the angel in the book focusing on religious obligations.[13] For example, the angel approaching Hagar stated: "I will greatly multiply your seed" [Gen 16:10],[14] not that the angel really will do this, but God will greatly multiply her seed.

Furthermore, Moses approaching the people of Israel declared: "that I will give the rain of your land" [Deut 11:14]. This speech is on behalf of God, and the meaning is not that Moses will really do this. There are various similar examples in this regard we have already mentioned there.[15] And, in a similar way, the angel approaching Moses from the fire of the bush: "I am the God of your father" [Exod 3:6]. He is not the God of his father, rather this verse was reported on behalf of the Creator, may his

---

11. Manuscript B begins here.

12. Binyāmīn is the eminent proto-Karaite scholar Benjamin al-Nahāwandī (originally from Nahāwand, Persia, first half of the ninth century). He became very famous for adopting the theory of an "angel creator." Elsewhere I argue that this theory was not his but was widespread among some Jewish, Christian, and Muslim cults and sects. See Nabih Bashir, "Angels in the Theology and Exegeses of Saadya Gaon: Human Being as the Purpose of Creation" [Hebrew] (PhD diss, Ben-Gurion University of the Negev, 2015).

13. Qirqisānī, *Kitāb al-Anwār* 1:55; 2:319.

14. Qirqisānī, *Kitāb al-Anwār* 2:319–21.

15. Qirqisānī, *Kitāb al-Anwār* 2:319.

glory be exalted. As has been said here: "and the LORD appeared unto him," and the seeing indicates someone has been seen and someone who saw, then the verse "and he lifted up his eyes" necessitates the verse "and looked." This is another indication that the two stories are one and that the second story came to expound and illustrate the first one. Regarding Abraham, it has been told that he saw twice: in the first [instance] it was written, "and he lifted up his eyes and looked"; and in the second, "and when he saw them he ran to meet them." It is possible also that the first verse, "and looked," indicates that he saw persons whom he could not know who they were; and the second look indicates that Abraham examined and knew that they were angels. Further, by naming them "men," he meant that they were in the image of humans, just like the saying: "And six men entered by way of the upper gate" [Ezek 9:2], regardless of the fact that they were not men, rather they were angels in the form of humans. Similarly, the saying: "the man Gabriel" [Dan 9:21]; and the telling of Manoah's wife: "the man has appeared to me" [Judg 13:10]. Therefore, the usage of "the LORD" [Gen 18:1] must be elucidated in the same way we just mentioned above. That is, if an angel was allowed to approach humans in such a way, then the prophet was also allowed to approach them in a way that his speech apparently seemed that he is talking for himself, but in fact the speech refers to God; and then they (= angels and prophets) were allowed to approach humans on behalf of God, even though it seems that they speak for themselves. In addition, we should not deny that an angel could have the name of the Lord. We already expounded this matter somewhere else.[16] And, if someone is asking: if in fact the three men were angels, then how is it possible that angels eat and drink? For it was said after all: "and set these before them; and he waited on them under the tree as they ate" [Gen 18:8]; and from the beginning of the story Abraham approaches them: "And let me fetch a morsel of bread that you may refresh yourselves" [Gen 18:5]? In addition, if Abraham knew that they were angels, is it (logically) permissible for him that angels eat? If it is (logically) permissible that spiritual angels eat food, then it necessitates that they defecate, hence they could be filthy and impure, and this assumes lots of things that are not possibly committed by the pure and holy spiritual beings.

---

16. See Ben-Shammai, "Doctrines," 1:238; 2:61, lines 31–32; Qirqisānī, *Kitāb al-Anwār* 1:178.

Hence, we say that people hold many different views in this respect. Some have the opinion that they were not angels but humans[17] and that Abraham recognized that they were trusted prophets. So, when he saw them, he dedicated himself to them and ran to meet them and bowed down to them as a sign of admiration and glorification. They [some commentators] further said: If someone denies this by saying that which human lived in that age that was more splendid than him (= Abraham)?

Then, we reply to him that Shem was a righteous prophet and Eber too was a prophet, and we have shown that he [Abraham] was a prophet. In addition, Melchizedek, who blessed Abraham and to whom Abraham gave a tithe, lived in that age. And nobody denies also that some other prophets lived in that age. They added that when Abraham saw them and recognized them, and they stood over against him—for the verse says, "stood over him"—then he knew that they were approaching him and he approached the most splendid of them in his speech: "My lord, if now I have found favor in your eyes" [Gen 18:3], which means "my sir," and later he approached them all at once in the saying: "and wash your feet" and the rest of the verses. He approached them by saying: "Let now a little water be fetched," because whoever goes a long way by foot and wants to relax used to wash his feet, hide in the shade, and lean back.

Then, Scripture follows that up by mentioning the food as an example of what must be offered to guests, and then they complied with his offer. On the other hand, those who argue that they were angels explain that the saying "and they ate" should not be understood in its original meaning, but that it refers to consumption, just as the verse "and you shall consume [Heb. lit. "eat"] all the peoples" [Deut 7:16], which means to extinguish. They further said that the angels pretended to Abraham that they were eating, but in fact they were not.[18] Whoever holds such a view seems as someone who escaped from a bad thing but was caught by another worse thing, yet was not saved from the thing that he fled from.[19] This is because

---

17. See, for example, Eliyahu Ki Tov, *Sefer ha-Parshiyot: Divre hakhamim Rishonim ve-Ahronim 'al Parashat ha-Shavu'a—Bereshit* [Hebrew] (Jerusalem: Yad Eliyahu Ki Tov, 1983), 293.

18. Some sages, the Midrash, Philo, Flavius Josephus, Sa'adia Gaon, and others hold such opinions. They are mentioned without attribution by way of indirect polemics.

19. It is likely that here Qirqisānī criticizes Sa'adia, who adopts such an opinion. See Moshe Zucker, ed. and trans., *Saadya's Commentary on Genesis* (New York: Jewish Theological Seminary of America, 1984), 124 for Judeo-Arabic, 375–77 for

that Abraham offered food to them indicates that he was of the opinion that they could eat; otherwise, it would be impossible for him to offer food and invite them to a thing that is impossible for them to comply with. Therefore, his approaching them: "that you may refresh yourselves," and their approaching him: "Do as you have said" [Gen 18:5], indicate that eating food is not impossible for them but, rather, it is possible for them. And it is even more amazing to discover that they were not really eating, but it was only an illusion and imagination. [Whoever holds such a view] attributed to the angels deception, that Abraham could not know that they deceived him, and this caused him to misapprehend the thing as different from what it really was. Others are of the opinion that the angels, who are animated, speech-enabled,[20] and rational beings, when almighty God is willing to send one of them towards the creatures, he dresses the angel in a terrestrial body that gravitates him down, and sends him to one of his prophets.

After fulfilling his mission, God takes off the terrestrial body from the angel, and after it was taken off, he [the angel] becomes an entity with a nature of the celestial body on his way towards heaven, and when he gets there he [God] takes off his heavenly body and gets the soul and the mind and ends up in the world of the intellect.[21] This way of examination is the way of the philosophers: examining the descending of the soul and the intellect together towards the physical world, their dressing the body,[22] their using nature until they get all the benefits; and then they ascend towards the world of the intellect. If it is so, then there is no need

---

Hebrew; for an English translation, see Michael Linetsky, ed. and trans., *Rabbi Saadiah Gaon's Commentary on the Book of Creation* (Northvale, NJ: Jason Aronson, 2002), 271. Sa'adia's commentary is based on R. Meir's opinion (Gen. Rab. 48:4, Soncino ed. 414–15).

20. The term *al-nuṭq* basically means "articulated speech," but conceptually it always has the meaning of "rational" or "endowed with reason." However, in our context it is more accurate that the author meant the basic meaning, because he added after it "rational."

21. In the manuscript: *min ʿālam al-ʿaql* (*from* the world of the intellect), the correction based on the entry "Khālūsā"; see Joshua Blau, *A Dictionary of Mediaeval Judaeo-Arabic Texts* [Hebrew] (Jerusalem: Israel Academy of Sciences and Humanities, 2006), 189.

22. The author of *Kitāb Maʿānī al-Nafs*, which is wrongly attributed to Ibn Paquda, mentions the idea of the angels dressing in terrestrial bodies, such as do the soul and the intellect, when they go down toward the earth, whereas they take off their terres-

to deny that, when an angel is sent to the terrestrial world, God composes in him a limb for using in eating and feeding. This is necessary in order to be able to eat and drink by what he was dressed of before his descending toward the terrestrial world. In other words, he wears two bodies: a celestial body, and a terrestrial body gravitating him down.

This terrestrial body could digest all the food that the angel eats and expel it without need of defecating and of filth. However, one of our sages said in this respect things without bringing solid proof, leading to that one of the three was an angel, the other two were humans, and Abraham approached in the first place the angel: "My lord, if now I have found favor in your eyes," and in this regard it was said: "and the LORD appeared unto him." He meant that God appeared to him [to Abraham] in the sense that God has sent to him this angel, after Abraham asked him: "do not pass," and he approached the two others who were humans, and said to them: "Let now a little water be fetched," and the rest of the things, until they approached him: "so do," and they were [those] who ate without the third. Afterwards, the two asked him: "Where is Sarah your wife?" and when he answered: "There, in the tent" [Gen 18:9], the third one, the angel, approached him: "I will certainly return to you when the season cometh round" [Gen 18:10]. This is the same one who approached Abraham: "And the LORD said unto Abraham: 'Why did Sarah laugh, saying...'" [Gen 18:13]. Do you not see how Scripture distinguishes between the speech in plural form and the speech in singular form? When it uses the singular form, it uses "LORD"; when it uses the plural form, it does not use [LORD]. Then, it delayed this use by notifying that the other two went to Sodom, and that the angel was left behind; about him was said, "And the LORD said: 'Shall I hide from Abraham'" [Gen 18:17]. Therefore, it was said: "but Abraham was still standing before the LORD" [Gen 18:22]. This exegete says: Scripture supervenes the angel together with them, and the angel got the same name of them (= men), as it said: "three men," just as said above: "six men" [Ezek 9:2]. This is also similar to what was said regarding Joshua: "[Joshua] ... looked up and saw a man standing before him" [Josh 5:13], with Scripture notifying that he is a "captain of the host of the Lord" [Josh 5:14]. We have already said that there are many more similar examples.

---

trial bodies when they ascend toward heaven. See Ignác Goldziher, ed., *Kitab Ma'ani al-Nafs* (Berlin: Weidmann, 1907), 59.

Discussion: Qirqisānī in His Context

The manifestation of God, as formulated in Gen 18, includes many textual, linguistic, and theological difficulties. In addition, such a manifestation appears unnecessary. It is not vital at all and adds no value or significance beyond the manifestation of the angels. In vain we search in the literature of the sages for any convincing interpretation for such a manifestation.

One of the rules of the biblical hermeneutics that the sages used to deal with such difficulties is *tiqqun soferim*, literally, "scribal corrections."[23] The *soferim* are the Jewish scholars/scribes of the postbiblical era. Occasionally, they emended biblical phrases to avoid expressions which could appear irreverent or inappropriate and to fix or overcome such difficulties.

For example, we read, "The men went on from there to Sodom, while Abraham remained standing before the LORD" (Gen 18:22), whereas earlier we read something different: "And the men set out from there and looked down toward Sodom, Abraham walking with them to see them off" (Gen 18:16). The former verse implies that Abraham was still at the same place, but according to the latter Abraham accompanies the angels some distance! Therefore, it appears that the Lord really was still standing "before" Abraham, since he is omnipresent; but, as it would be derogatory to his honor to say that he was standing before Abraham, as an inferior before his superior, it is reversed, as we are told by R. Simon: "This is an emendation of *Soferim*, for the *Shechinah* was actually waiting for Abraham" (Gen. Rab. 49:7 [Soncino ed. 425–26]).[24]

Saʿadia Gaon includes in his commentary the following unconvincing traditional interpretation: the purpose of the manifestation of God by himself in this chapter is to tell Abraham that "the cry of Sodom and Gomorrah is great." However, he adds the following as his own interpretation:

---

23. See W. Emery Barnes, "Ancient Corrections in the Text of the Old Testament (*Tikkun Sopherim*)," *JTS* 1 (1900): 387–414; Carmel McCarthy, *The Tiqqune Sopherim and Other Theological Corrections in the Masoretic Text of the Old Testament* (Freiburg: Universitätsverlag, 1981); Moshe Zipor, *Tradition and Transmission: Studies in Ancient Biblical Translation and Interpretation* [Hebrew] (Tel Aviv: Hakibbutz Hamecuhad Publishing House), 2001.

24. See also Gen. Rab. 49:7 in Theodor-Alback's edition, 2:505–7 (Hebrew) and n. 4 therein; and William G. Braude, trans. *The Midrash on Psalms*, 2 vols. (New Haven: Yale University Press, 1959), 1:251, on Ps 18:26.

Now it mentions the appearance of light before the passing of the individuals so that Abraham be certain that they are allies of God. Likewise, the purpose of the appearance of light (the manifestation of God in Saʿadia's terms) for the prophets is for them to be certain that what they hear is the words of God [...] Abraham says to them: "God, if I have found favor with you," with a concealment/ellipsis [iḍmār] of the word "allies" of God. This error, [i.e.,] that he thought that they are men, is all through [the story] because of how minimal the distinction is between prophets and angels.

As we can see, Saʿadia uses here a different hermeneutical rule, the rule of concealment/ellipsis (iḍmār). By this he implies that the biblical text lacks some vital words, so that it is less comprehensible. In addition, in the context of the revelation, he attributes an error to Abraham.

It seems that one of the main purposes of Qirqisānī's commentary on Gen 18 is to advance a polemic against the widespread conception in rabbinic tradition that "but Abraham remained standing before the LORD" (v. 22), as one of eighteen emendations of the scribes, "corrects" an original text that read, "but the LORD remained standing before Abraham" (Kitāb al-Ānwār 1:154).[25] In addition, Qirqisānī deals with some textual and theological difficulties by arguing that the verse "And the LORD said: 'Shall I hide from Abraham what I am about to do'" (Gen 18:17) belongs to an altogether different story (1:155). The same argument can be found in ancient Jewish Hellenistic commentaries, mainly in Philo and Josephus (see Philo, QG 4.1–20; Abr. 133–146; Josephus, A.J. 11.196–200), and in later commentaries such as Maimonides, who attributes to Rabbi Hiyya (the Great, d. 230 CE) the second interpretation that Qirqisānī adopts here (see above) and views it as the best interpretation.[26]

---

25. Qirqisānī explicitly presents and discusses the topic of the eighteen emendations of the scribes (Qirqisānī, Kitāb al-Ānwār 1:144–161). In addition, Qirqisānī accuses the Rabbanites of claiming that the Hebrew MT was written by Ezra "the scribe" (Qirqisānī, Kitāb al-Ānwār 1:15, 149–150).

26. "One of the sages, may their memory be blessed ... arrived at this great principle. It was Rabbi Hiyya the Great, when speaking of the text of the Torah: 'And the Lord appeared unto him by the terebinths of Mamre, and so on' (Gen 18:1). For after he had first propounded the proposition that God manifested Himself to him, he began to explain what the form of this manifestation was; and he said that at first he saw 'three men' and ran ... He who propounded this allegoric interpretation says of Abraham's dictum—'And he said: My lord, if I now have found favor in thy sight, pass not away, I pray thee, from thy servant'—that it too is a description of what he said in a vision of prophecy to one of them; he says in fact: 'He said it to the greatest

The church fathers used Gen 18 to strengthen the doctrine of the Trinity (e.g., Justin Martyr, *Dial.* 56.1–10).[27] It seems that Qirqisānī emphasizes that the three men actually ate and that the verse "And the LORD said: 'Shall I hide from Abraham what I shall do?'" belongs to a separate story, thereby weakening such Trinity-oriented interpretations. And yet, it can still be argued that if spiritual entities such as angels can be manifested and descend towards the physical world by being dressed in a terrestrial body, so to speak, including eating, therefore the same could be said about God's incarnation, as orthodox Christian doctrine tells us. In other words, Qirqisānī's interpretation of Gen 18 cannot in fact weaken Trinitarian interpretations. But, on the other hand, he guarantees three issues that are crucial for him as a Karaite exegete: safeguarding the accuracy of the biblical text; adhering to what he understands as the literal interpretation of the text; and removing the error that the Rabbanites attribute to Abraham, who at first thought the three angels were humans.

Bibliography

Albeck, Chanoch, and J. Theodor. *Midrash Bereshit Rabbah* [Hebrew]. 16 vols. Berlin: Z. Hirsch-Itzkowsky, 1903–1929.

Bashir, Nabih. "Angels in the Theology and Exegeses of Saadya Gaon: Human Being as the Purpose of Creation" [Hebrew]. PhD diss., Ben-Gurion University of the Negev, 2015.

———. "A Reexamination of Saadya Gaon's Dictum 'Humankind Is More Sublime Than Angels'" [Hebrew]. *Ginzei Qedem* 14 (2018): 9–54.

---

among them.' Understand this story too, for it is one of the secrets [...] This is quite similar to the story concerning Abraham, in which it at first informs us in a general way, 'And the Lord appeared unto him, and so on,' and then begins to explain in what way this happened" (Moses Maimonides, *The Guide of the Perplexed*, trans. Shlomo Pines [Chicago: University of Chicago Press, 1962], 2.42, p. 389). It should be noticed that this interpretation that Maimonides attributes to Rabbi Hiyya is not found in any printed editions of Genesis Rabbah, including the English Soncino translation (Gen. Rab. 48:10, p. 411), Theodor-Albeck's Hebrew edition, and the edition with the *Matnot Kehunah* (Jerusalem: Levin-Epstein, 1977), 1:55. In addition, the Islamic conception of God's manifestation is much closer to the conception presented here by Qirqisānī (see, for example, Q Hud 11:69; Ad-Dhariyat 51:24–30).

27. Saʿadia was fully aware of such use and tried to refute it. See Saʿadia Gaon, *The Book of Beliefs and Opinions*, 2:6.

Ben Naftali, Issachar Ber, ed. *Matanot Kehunah*. 2 vols. Jerusalem: Levin-Epstein, 1977.

Ben-Shammai, Haggai. "The Doctrines of Religious Thought of Abu Yusuf Ya'qub al-Qirqisani and Yefet Ben 'Eli." 2 vols. PhD diss., Hebrew University of Jerusalem, 1977.

Blau, Joshua. *A Dictionary of Mediaeval Judaeo-Arabic Texts* [Hebrew]. Jerusalem: Israel Academy of Sciences and Humanities, 2006.

Braude, William G., trans. *Midrash on Psalms*. 2 vols. New Haven: Yale University Press, 1959.

Emery Barnes, W. "Ancient Corrections in the Text of the Old Testament (*Tikkun Sopherim*)." *JTS* 1 (1900): 387–414.

Goldziher, Ignác, ed. *Kitab Ma'ani al-Nafs*. Berlin: Weidmann, 1907.

Hirschfeld, Hatwig. *Qirqisani Studies*. London: Jews' College, 1918.

Ki Tov, Eliyahu. *Sefer ha-Parshiyot: Divre hakhamim Rishonim ve-Ahronim 'al Parashat ha-Shavu'a—Bereshit*. Jerusalem: Yad Eliyahu Ki Tov, 1983.

Linetsky, Michael, ed. and trans. *Rabbi Saadiah Gaon's Commentary on the Book of Creation*. Northvale, NJ: Jason Aronson, 2002.

McCarthy, Carmel. *The Tiqqune Sopherim and Other Theological Corrections in the Masoretic Text of the Old Testament*. Freiburg: Universitäts-verlag, 1981.

Moses Maimonides. *The Guide of the Perplexed*. Translated by Shlomo Pines. Chicago: University of Chicago Press, 1962.

Polliack, Meira. "Major Trends in Karaite Biblical Exegesis in the Tenth and Eleventh Centuries." Pages 363–413 in *Karaite Judaism: A Guide to Its History and Literary Sources*. Edited by Meira Polliack. Leiden: Brill, 2003.

Qirqisani, Ya'qūb. *Kitāb al-Anwār wal-Marāqib—Code of Karaite Law*. Edited by Leon Nemoy. 5 vols. New York: Alexander Kohut Memorial Foundation, 1939–1943.

Zipor, Moshe. *Tradition and Transmission: Studies in Ancient Biblical Translation and Interpretation* [Hebrew]. Tel Aviv: Hakibbutz Hamecuhad Publishing House, 2001.

Zucker, Moshe, ed. and trans. *Saadya's Commentary on Genesis*. New York: Jewish Theological Seminary of America, 1984.

Sa'adia Gaon's Translation of the
Torah and Its Coptic Readers

Ronny Vollandt

Sa'adia's Judeo-Arabic translation of the Torah is not only one of the most influential texts in Judeo-Arabic culture but also among the best-known Arabic versions of the Bible. The frequent attestation of his translation in the Cairo Genizah shows that the Tafsīr, the name by which it became known, acquired an authoritative, even canonical, status among all Arabic-speaking Rabbanite communities. Soon after its creation, the Tafsīr could be found in communities throughout the Near East, North Africa, and Muslim Spain. But the Tafsīr did not only have Jewish readers; it was also read and transmitted by Samaritan, Muslim, and Christian scholars in the Middle Ages.[1] The source text that I present below appears to have been the written documentation of a series of regular meetings between a Jew, Abū al-Majd ibn Abī Manṣūr ibn Abī al-Faraj al-Isrā'īlī, who has been identified as the ḥazan and treasurer of the Babylonian congregation of Old Cairo at the time of the Nagid Abraham ben Maimon (1186–1237), and one of the leading Coptic scholars of that time, al-As'ad Abūl-Faraj Hibat Allāh ibn al-'Assāl.

The Text

The source presented here is from a preface found at the start of two Coptic manuscripts of the Tafsīr: Paris, Bibliothèque nationale de France, MS Ar. 1; and Cairo, Coptic Orthodox Patriarchate, MS Bibl. 32.[2] Both of these

---

1. Tamar Zewi, *The Samaritan Version of Saadya Gaon's Translation of the Pentateuch: Critical Edition and Study of MS London BL OR7562 and Related MSS*, Biblia Arabica 3 (Leiden: Brill, 2015). See also Ronny Vollandt, *Arabic Versions of the Pentateuch: A Comparative Study of Jewish, Christian, and Muslim Sources* (Leiden: Brill, 2015), 88–89, 105–8, 243.

2. The text has been published in Ronny Vollandt, "Flawed Biblical Translations into Arabic and How to Correct Them: A Copt and a Jew Study Saadiah's Tafsīr,"

are dated to the last decade of the sixteenth century, stem from the same workshop, and were copied from the same archetype that goes back to an original written more than three centuries earlier by al-Asʿad ibn al-ʿAssāl, more than three hundred years after Saʿadia. It recounts how al-Asʿad invited Abū al-Majd, a distinguished member of the Jewish community of Old Cairo and someone with whom he had obviously established a personal relationship, to help him copy a manuscript as accurately as possible and establish the correct transmitted text of the Tafsīr.

So, in the month of Shawwāl of 1242 CE, the two scholars sat facing each other and studied the text jointly. As the preface relates, each held his own copy of the Tafsīr. But while the Copt referred to a manuscript of Saʿadia's translation written in Arabic script, elaborating on its contents and characteristic features, the Jew read aloud from a manuscript that contained the same Arabic text in Hebrew letters. The Copt duly noted all textual variants between the two versions on his own copy, and incorporated his collaborator's explanations in the form of a sophisticated interlinear apparatus as well as marginal glosses.

The Context

Al-Asʿad ibn al-ʿAssāl had a vivid interest in Jewish texts. For example, he and his brother Muʾtaman are known to have read Maimonides's *Guide of the Perplexed* (*Dalālat al-ḥāʾirīn*).[3] They belonged to the ʿAssālids, one of those distinguished families (*buyūtāt*) who, often over several generations, attained high positions in the civil service and also ecclesiastical prominence, and exerted a profound influence on the internal affairs of the Coptic community.[4] The Arabic-language works by members of the

---

in *Studies on Arabic Christianity in Honor of Sidney H. Griffith*, ed. David Bertaina, Sandra T. Keating, Mark N. Swanson, and Alexander Treiger (Leiden: Brill, 2018), 56–90.

3. As shown by Gregor Schwarb, "The Reception of Maimonides in Christian-Arabic Literature" [Hebrew], in *Maimonides and His World*, vol. 7 of *Ben ʿEver le-ʿArav: Contacts between Arabic Literature and Jewish Literature in the Middle Ages and Modern Times*, ed. Yosef Tobi (Haifa: University of Haifa, 2014), 109–75; Schwarb, "Die Rezeption Maimonides' in der christlich-arabischen Literatur," *Judaica* 63 (2007): 1–45.

4. On these, see Adel Sidarus, "Families of Coptic Dignitaries (*buyūtāt*) under the Ayyūbids and the Golden Age of Coptic Arabic Literature (Thirteenth Century)," *JCoptS* 15 (2013): 189–208.

al-ʿAssāl family on jurisprudence, canon law, theology, philosophy, and linguistics were marked by a universalism of sources with a great intellectual openness, irrespective of their religious provenance. Al-Asʿad's father was a high-ranking government official; one of his brothers, al-Amjad Abū al-Majd ibn al-ʿAssāl (d. after 1270), was secretary to the *diwan* of the army. Al-Amjad's position required him to travel back and forth between Cairo and Damascus, which ensured a steady influx of books not previously available in Egypt, notably those by East and West Syriac and Melkite authors.[5] These books laid the foundations for the most famous book collection of the time, known as *al-khizāna al-amjadiyya*.

Al-Amjad and his three brothers, al-Asʿad Abūl-Faraj Hibat Allāh ibn al-ʿAssāl (d. before 1259), al-Ṣafī ibn al-ʿAssāl (d. ca. 1265), and Muʾtaman al-Dawla Abū Isḥāq Ibrāhīm ibn al-ʿAssāl (d. after 1270), all of whom he supported, appear to have been the nucleus of a close-knit scholarly network.[6] Georg Graf described them as "the center of the literary Golden Age of the Copts in the thirteenth century."[7] In their linguistic and exegetical endeavors, the members of this circle interacted with one another and shared a similar approach. Not much is known about Ibn Kātib Qayṣar ("the son of the secretary of Qayṣar," that is, of the Seljuk Amir ʿAlam al-Dīn Qayṣar, d. ca. 1260), a related figure in the circle, who excelled in theology and in biblical commentaries and translations.[8] Another member of the circle was Abū al-Shākir ibn al-Rāhib (fl. ca. 1250), whose father, al-Sanā Abū al-Majd Buṭrus b. al-Muhadhdhib Abū al-Faraj al-Thuʿbān al-Rāhib,

---

5. Awad Wadīʿ, *Dirāsa ʿan al-Muʾtaman b. al-ʿAssāl wa-kitābihi "Majmūʿ uṣūl al-dīn" wa-taḥqīqihi* (Cairo: Franciscan Printing Press, 1997), 66 n. 73.

6. To be precise, al-Asʿad and al-Ṣafī had the same mother. Muʾtaman was their half-brother, born after their father's second marriage. The most recent and comprehensive introduction on the ʿAssālids is Wadīʿ, *Dirāsa ʿan al-Muʾtaman*. See also Georg Graf, "Die koptische Gelehrtenfamilie der Aulād al-ʿAssāl und ihr Schrifttum," *Or* 1 (1932): 34–56, 129–48, 193–204; Alexis Mallon, "Une école de savants égyptiens au Moyen-Âge," *MFOB* 1 (1906): 109–31; 2 (1907): 213–64; Mallon, "Ibn al-ʿAssâl: Les trois écrivains de ce nom," *JA* 5 (1905): 509–29. On al-Asʿad's critical edition of the Arabic gospels in use among the Copts and its apparatus, see below.

7. Georg Graf, *Geschichte der christlichen arabischen Literatur*, 5 vols. (Vatican: Biblioteca Apostolica Vaticana, 1944), 2:387.

8. On Ibn Kātib Qayṣar, see Mark N. Swanson, "Ibn Kātib Qayṣar," in *Christian-Muslim Relations 600–1500*, ed. David Thomas, http://doi.org/10.1163/1877-8054_cmri_COM_25670; Stephen J. Davis, "Introducing an Arabic Commentary on the Apocalypse: Ibn Kātib Qayṣar on Revelation," *HTR* 101 (2008): 77–96.

had been the preceptor of the ʿAssālid brothers. An encyclopedist in his scholarly production, Abū al-Shākir distinguished himself as a theologian and the author of linguistic treatises, and composed a *Kitāb al-Tawārīkh* (*Book of History*).[9] This work was a major source for another Copto-Arabic historical treatise, the universal chronicle by Jirjis b. al-ʿAmīd b. al-Makīn (1205–1273), *al-Majmuʿ al-mubārak* (*The Blessed Collection*).

Participants in this scholarly circle, who showed great interest in Maimonides's *Guide of the Perplexed*, also read and frequently quoted another work of Jewish provenance—Sefer Joseph b. Gurion, a medieval historiographical compilation in Hebrew that later came to be known as Sefer Josippon.[10] Composed anonymously in southern Italy in the first half of the tenth century, it was soon translated into Arabic. The translation initially circulated in Hebrew letters, but it was later copied into Arabic script, which facilitated its dissemination beyond the Jewish community.

However, the most popular Jewish text among medieval Copts remained Saʿadia's Judeo-Arabic translation of the Torah, the Tafsīr. Coptic copies of the Tafsīr, transcribed into Arabic script, appeared at the very start of the Ayyubid period and soon supplanted Arabic versions of the Pentateuch translated directly from the Coptic-Bohairic.[11] It seems that the ʿAssālids actively promoted the inclusion of Saʿadia's Tafsīr in their studies. For example, the earliest extant Coptic manuscript of the Tafsīr (Florence, Biblioteca Medicea Laurenziana, MS Or. 112) was copied by

---

9. See Samuel Moawad, ed., *Chapters 1–47, Critical Edition with Introduction* [Arabic], vol. 1 of *Abū Shākir ibn al-Rāhib: Kitāb al-Tawārīkh* (Cairo: Alexandria School, 2016). The work has three parts: the first on calendar reckoning, astronomy, and chronography; the second on civil and ecclesiastic history, beginning with biblical history; and the third on the history of councils. A brief version of the work has become known by the title *Chronicon Orientale*. On the long debates about its authorship, see Adel Sidarus, *Ibn ar-Rāhibs Leben und Werk: Ein koptisch-arabischer Enzyklopädist des 7./13. Jahrhunderts* (Freiburg: Klaus Schwarz, 1975), 41–45; Adel Sidarus, "Copto-Arabic Universal Chronography: Between Antiquity, Judaism, Christianity and Islam," *Collectanea Christiana Orientalia* 2 (2014): 221–50.

10. See Ronny Vollandt, "Ancient Jewish Historiography in Arabic Garb: *Sefer Josippon* between South Italy and Coptic Cairo," *Zutot* 11 (2014): 70–80.

11. See the remarks of Ofer Livne-Kafri, "Appendix II: Some Notes concerning the Arabic Version," in *Topics in Coptic Syntax: Structural Studies in the Bohairic Dialect*, ed. Ariel Shisha-Halevy (Dudley, MA: Peeters, 2007), 685–94; Ofer Livne-Kafri, "A Note on the Energicus in a Coptic-Arabic Translation of the Pentateuch," *Acta Orientalia Academiae Scientiarum Hungaricae* 62 (2009): 405–11.

"the monk Gabriel"[12] who, before his elevation to patriarch of the Church of Alexandria as Gabriel III, had been the preceptor of al-Amjad and a secretary to the al-'Assāl family. He accompanied al-Amjad and his brothers during their travels to Damascus in search of manuscripts, transcribing many texts composed by them or important for their literary work. Another early Coptic manuscript of the Tafsīr (Vienna, Nationalbibliothek, MS Mxt. 664) was in al-Amjad's personal library, the abovementioned *al-khizāna al-amjadiyya.*

There are indications that the adoption of Sa'adia's Tafsīr into Christian canons happened progressively. The oldest attested Christian manuscript containing Sa'adia's translation is London, British Library, MS Add. 11855 (AM 740/1024 CE), in a group of early manuscripts of West Syriac provenance. However, these manuscripts only feature Sa'adia's translation of Genesis: the other manuscripts represent translations from the Peshitta (Exodus and Numbers) and the Syro-Hexapla (Leviticus and Deuteronomy).[13]

The only Christian manuscripts in Arabic script that contain a full set of pentateuchal books from Sa'adia's Tafsīr were produced by Coptic scribes. Indeed, it would appear that the text was already available to Coptic scholars some time before the Coptic-Bohairic Pentateuch was rendered into Arabic, since the Arabic translation of the latter exhibits a striking similarity to Sa'adia's text. Moreover, the Tafsīr can be found in a large number of copies from the first half of the thirteenth century onwards, and its transmission among Coptic communities is complex, with textual witnesses branching out in a number of different manuscript types, which can be referred to as (1) the basic type, (2) the revised type, and (3) the extended type.

(1) The first, most basic type of manuscript containing the Tafsīr takes the form of a running translation, without additions. We may assume that this type antedated the revised and extended types, not only because this is indicated by those manuscripts that have been dated, but also since it is implied by the textual basis itself. Codices of this type usually make explicit

---

12. As pointed out by Berend Jan Dikken, "Some Remarks about Middle Arabic and Sa'adya Gaon's Arabic Translation of the Pentateuch in Manuscripts of Jewish, Samaritan, Coptic Christian, and Muslim Provenance," in *Middle Arabic and Mixed Arabic: Diachrony and Synchrony*, ed. Liesbeth Zack and Arie Schippers (Leiden: Brill, 2012), 71–72.

13. On the relevant manuscripts, see Vollandt, *Arabic Versions*, 222–29.

that the text contained in it is "accurately copied from the translation of Saʿīd al-Fayyūmī [= Saʿadia Gaon], from Hebrew into Arabic" (Arab. *muḥarrara min naql Saʿīd al-Fayyūmī min al-ʿibrāni ilā al-ʿarabī*).[14] Despite this claim of accuracy, however, the text included in these manuscripts exhibits some fairly significant revisions that allow us to speak of a distinct Coptic adaptation. A particularly obvious example is that the chapter division follows the Coptic tradition, although in addition it retains an indication of the weekly Hebrew *parashōt*.[15] The earliest dated manuscript of this type is Florence, Biblioteca Medicea Laurenziana, MS Or. 112, copied in 1245/46 CE.[16]

(2) A revised version of the Tafsīr is based on the earlier basic type. It is represented in copies of the exemplar created through the Coptic-Jewish collaboration described at the beginning of this essay (and further below). Manuscripts of this type include a preface, which contains a long exploration of the features of Saʿadia's translation in comparison to those of other Christian, Jewish, and Samaritan translators of the Bible. Further, the preface's anonymous author introduces a system of rubricated marks. Variant readings, text-critical observations, etymological notes, and explanations of the Hebrew original are noted between the lines and in the margins. The whole enterprise was prompted by a wish to return to the original character of the Tafsīr.

(3) The group of revised manuscripts of the Tafsīr supplement the basic text with a set of additional texts. These manuscripts fall into two subgroups. In the first, the translation is preceded by an edificatory proem that elaborates on the abrogation of Mosaic law (Arab. *al-sharīʿa al-musawiyya*)—that is, the Torah—by the New Testament. Each book of the Pentateuch is preceded by a short summary of its contents, referred to as a "study guide" (Arab. *dallāl*). The manuscripts close with an account, called the "epilogue" (Arab. *al-khātima*), of how the Hebrew Scriptures were handed down through an authoritative, unbroken line of transmit-

---

14. E.g., Florence, Biblioteca Medicea Laurenziana, MS Or. 112, fol. 1r.

15. On the Coptic division, see Joseph Francis Rhode, *The Arabic Versions of the Pentateuch in the Church of Egypt: A Study from Eighteen Arabic and Copto-Arabic MSS (Ninth–Seventeenth Century) in the National Library at Paris, the Vatican and Bodleian Libraries and the British Museum* (Leipzig: W. Drugulin, 1921), 111–13.

16. Other manuscripts of this basic type include MSS Paris, Bibliothèque Nationale, Copt. 1; Oxford, Bodleian Library, Laud. Or. 272; London, British Library, Or. 422; Oxford, Bodleian Library, Hunt. 33; Vatican, Bibliotheca Apostolica Vaticana, Copt. 2–4; and Coptic Orthodox Patriarchate, Bibl. 2–5. For details on these, see Vollandt, *Arabic Versions*, 229–34.

ters, until they were eventually translated into a variety of languages and thus became corrupted. The epilogue elaborates further, and, fashioned after the rabbinic tractate of the Chapters of the Fathers (Hebr. Pirqe Avot), provides the chain of transmission, until the Scriptures were translated into Arabic. It recounts how, after being revealed (Arab. *anzala*) to Moses, the text of the Torah was passed on (Arab. *sallama*) through a long line of judges and prophets, from Joshua bin Nun through Ezekiel and finally to Malachi, the last of the biblical prophets. From there the Torah was passed on from Ezra to some of the tannaitic pairs, including Yehoshua b. Perakhiah and Nittai of Arbela, Yose b. Yoḥannan and Shimon b. Shetaḥ, and, finally, Avtalion and Shemaya. When Titus conquered Jerusalem (70 CE), the Torah was saved and transferred to Betar; and when Davidic descendants, identified as a family of exiles (Arab. *al-ashrāf min nasl Da'ūd*), escaped the destruction of Betar by Hadrian (135 CE), they took the Torah with them to Baghdad, where they reside to this very day in exile, as the text says. As the knowledge of the Hebrew language diminished, different Jewish factions rendered the Torah into Arabic and, by means of the translations, its text was disseminated among the nations. On the other hand, in those manuscripts belonging to the second subgroup of the revised type, Sa'adia's Tafsīr is interspersed with the commentary of Mark b. al-Qunbar.

It is, thus, not farfetched to conclude that the Tafsīr in Arabic script was in heavy use, indeed until quite recent times. That Sa'adia's version of the Torah was granted a canonical status of some sort becomes obvious not only from the sheer number of preserved manuscripts, but even more so in light of the textual creativity with which it was revised, augmented, and appended with thematically related introductory prefaces, short treatises, and commentaries by Coptic scholars. These manuscripts, of which only a very small number have undergone a thorough investigation, evidence that the Tafsīr was a popular object of study and that its transmission was carefully safeguarded. The function that the Tafsīr fulfilled in the Coptic church—and the reason it had to be studied and transmitted meticulously—finds its expression in the accompanying texts of the revised and extended manuscript types.

Al-As'ad ibn al-'Assāl's Preface to the Tafsīr: A Translation

From my readings and from the historical accounts it emerges that the seventy-two translators [of the LXX] rendered the Torah from Hebrew into Greek without any fault. Only thereafter, when it was translated from Greek into Arabic, did the insufficient knowledge of both languages became apparent. I, however, have never met a Greek [Melkite] who was of such education in literature that he could act as a reviewer with me by comparing the Greek source text with the Arabic translation.

Also the Jews who translated the Torah into Arabic fell short in these two aforementioned matters. However, as I perused the translation of the learned Rabbanite Sa'īd al-Fayyūmī [hereafter Sa'adia], I satisfied myself—owing to his style—that he is the most preferred of all translators and the most eloquent interpreter among the people of his confession. I found his concise Arabic diction, his overall eloquence, the consistent homophonic correspondence (*ittiḥād masmūʿ*) between the Arabic and the Hebrew, the rendering of proper names and countries, and the Hebrew terminology that was retained in the Arabic translation, as well as the absence of textual distortions (*taṣḥīf*) and his elegant transfer of obscure into clear words—to be very pleasing to the ear. Thus I copied his version in what follows this preface, and with the intention of editing (*taḥrīr*) it most accurately. For this purpose, I summoned to my aid one of the most notable Israelites, whose name is stated at the end of this copy. He had memorized the text and recalled its words skillfully. Further, he was well versed in the study of its expressions, its recitation (*tilāwa*), and everything related to the interpretation of its meaning and also grasped its underlying intention. In his hand, he held a copy in Hebrew letters, from which he read aloud in Arabic. In my hand, I held the present copy in Arabic letters, which is Sa'adia's translation that I intend to transcribe.

Furthermore, I had in front of me a number of additional Arabic versions of the Torah. Some of these were translated by notable Samaritan scholars from Hebrew into Arabic. Others are from the Greek, including the translations of al-Ḥārith ibn Sinān and ʿAbdallāh ibn al-Faḍl, and also an ancient one in which the name of the translators is not mentioned. Another is the copy of the priest al-Faḍl Abū al-Faraj b. al-Ṭayyib, including a translation and commentary from Syriac into Arabic. What is more, I had at my disposal a number of commentaries of Christian, Jewish, and Samaritan provenance. As for the Christian commentaries, there are those by John Chrysostom and Basil of Caesarea; both spoke with the help of the Holy Spirit. With regard to the Jewish commentaries, there are those by the learned scholar Abū al-Faraj b. Asad, the teacher Abū ʿAlī al-Baṣrī, and the prince Abū Saʿīd al-Dāwūdī. For the Samaritan commentaries, I had the commentary of the scholar Ṣadaqa al-Mutaṭabbib.

The comparison revealed to me that Sa'adia used a number of techniques in his translation. The first is the use of additional words in many instances to clarify the meaning, which I pointed out in this translation. In this copy, I have placed the letter *zāy* [= *ziyāda*, "addition"] as a rubricated sign over all additions in order to signal each such instance. Whenever you encounter this letter in red ink, know that something has been added by Sa'adia with the purpose of specifying, elucidating, and completing the sense in the Arabic language or to avoid anthropomorphism. This is illustrated in the narrative of Sodom and Gomorra (Gen 18:33): "And the LORD went his way, as soon as he had left off speaking to Abraham" [NRSV], which he translated: "And the messenger of the LORD [went his way, as soon as he had left off speaking to Abraham]," either to remove suspicion of anthropomorphism and undermine the arguments of the stubborn and skeptics; or for other reasons that will reveal themselves to one who observes closely, if he is knowledgeable.

Al-As'ad ibn al-'Assāl's Preface to the Tafsīr: A Short Commentary

In his preface, al-As'ad ibn al-'Assāl describes the great variety of Arabic translations that were in use among the Copts in his day. It did not escape his attention that each of them, being based on multiple source languages, had its own internal history, which had led to variations in the text. The motif of corruption in translation is prominent in many contemporaneous writings—mainly but not exclusively of Muslim provenance—where it was usually linked to the concept of *taḥrīf*, that is, the twisting and distortion of the divine revelation.[17] Transmission was flawed, he recounts, due either to an insufficient knowledge of the source and/or target language or to the translator's particular agenda.

He summarizes the account of Ptolemy, king of Egypt, who commissioned seventy-two Jewish scholars to translate the Torah into Greek,[18] which he could have known from the Arabic translation of Sefer Josippon. He mentions that he has failed to find a Melkite to help him study the Arabic translation in juxtaposition with the Septuagint. However, he praises Sa'adia's translation and finds it most excellent in terms of style,

---

17. Vollandt, *Arabic Versions*, 12 n. 30.

18. Abraham Wasserstein and David J. Wasserstein, *The Legend of the Septuagint: From Classical Antiquity to Today* (Cambridge: Cambridge University Press, 2006), 192–216.

eloquence, and accuracy. He arrived at this conclusion by comparing it with other translations and commentaries: Jewish, Samaritan, and Christian. The authors that are mentioned here in his preface fall in two categories: those who produced a translation (Arab. *naql* or *tafsīr*) of the Torah and those who produced a commentary (*sharḥ*) on it. Among the first group we find Saʿadia for the Jews; an unspecified Samaritan scholar (probably Abū Saʿīd [Egypt, thirteenth century]); and for the Christians al-Ḥārith ibn Sinān (Ḥarran, active before 956), ʿAbdallāh ibn al-Faḍl (Antioch, eleventh century), and finally Abū Faraj ibn al-Ṭayyib (Iraq, eleventh century). The first commentators he mentions are the church fathers Basil the Great (d. 379) and John Chrysostom (d. 407). In addition, he was familiar with Karaite scholars such as Yeshuʿah ben Yehudah (referred to by his Arabic name Abū al-Faraj b. Asad; Jerusalem, mid-eleventh century), Yefet ben ʿElī (Arabic: Abū ʿAlī al-Baṣrī; Jerusalem, tenth century), and David ben Boaz (Arabic: Abū Saʿīd al-Dāwūdī; Jerusalem, late tenth century).

Al-Asʿad's main interest was in the Hebrew original, which, were it not for Saʿadia's Tafsīr, would have remained a closed book to him. As is known, the Tafsīr is not a literal translation. In order to grasp the original meaning of the Hebrew, al-Asʿad had to first establish an accurate text of the Tafsīr and discern which parts of Saʿadia's translation reflect his translation technique and which the Hebrew source. For this purpose, he reports, he solicited the help of Abū al-Majd.

The second part of the preface describes four ways (*masālik*)—today we would call them *techniques*—that are prominent in Saʿadia's approach to translation. It is well known that the exegesis embedded in Saʿadia's Tafsīr is one of its major features. The Tafsīr attempts to reconcile the biblical text with halakhic practice and hermeneutic implications, on the one hand, and, on the other, by taking into consideration linguistic and stylistic requirements of the Arabic language by omitting repetitive elements, condensing the narrative, and providing referential links through the insertion of temporal conjunctions. Accordingly, the Tafsīr contains great liberties with the formal structure of the Hebrew source and is anything but a literal rendering of the text. An explanation must have been provided by Abū al-Majd.

The first technique consists of interpretive additions. As shown by the case of Gen 18:33, where Saʿadia's "and the messenger of the LORD" introduces a mediating agent, these insertions are often meant to eliminate anthropomorphisms. Other additions clarify or gloss part of the biblical verse in which they occur. Because they are extraneous to the Hebrew text, al-Asʿad as editor marked them with the siglum /zāy/. For example, he marks the text of Gen 2:17, which reads "for in the day that you eat of it you shall die" (NRSV) in the Hebrew. Saʿadia translates *tastaḥaqqu an tamūt*, adding "you shall be due [to die]" to reconcile with the fact that Adam does not die immediately as a consequence of the transgression. The end of Gen 4:7 deals with the duty to resist the impulse to sin ("but you must master it," NRSV); Saʿadia, using the terminology of contemporaneous rational theology (*kalām*) and in order to counter the notion of determinism, added *bi-l-ikhtiyār*, "out of free will," so that the end of the verse reads: "and you shall rule over it [sin] out of free will."

Bibliography

Davis, Stephen J. "Introducing an Arabic Commentary on the Apocalypse: Ibn Kātib Qayṣar on Revelation." *HTR* 101 (2008): 77–96.

Dikken, Berend Jan. "Some Remarks about Middle Arabic and Saʿadya Gaon's Arabic Translation of the Pentateuch in Manuscripts of Jewish, Samaritan, Coptic Christian, and Muslim Provenance." Pages 51–81 in *Middle Arabic and Mixed Arabic: Diachrony and Synchrony*. Edited by Liesbeth Zack and Arie Schippers. Leiden: Brill, 2012.

Graf, Georg. *Geschichte der christlichen arabischen Literatur*. 5 vols. Vatican: Biblioteca Apostolica Vaticana, 1944.

———. "Die koptische Gelehrtenfamilie der Aulād al-ʿAssāl und ihr Schrifttum." *Or* 1 (1932): 34–56, 129–48, 193–204.

Livne-Kafri, Ofer. "Appendix II: Some Notes concerning the Arabic Version." Pages 685–94 in *Topics in Coptic Syntax: Structural Studies in the Bohairic Dialect*. Edited by Ariel Shisha-Halevy. Dudley, MA: Peeters, 2007.

———. "A Note on the Energicus in a Coptic-Arabic Translation of the Pentateuch." *Acta Orientalia Academiae Scientiarum Hungaricae* 62 (2009): 405–11.

Mallon, Alexis. "Une école de savants égyptiens au Moyen-Âge." *MFOB* 1 (1906): 109–31; 2 (1907): 213–64.

———. "Ibn al-ʿAssâl: Les trois écrivains de ce nom." *JA* 5 (1905): 509–29.

Moawad, Samuel, ed. *Chapters 1–47, Critical Edition with Introduction* [Arabic]. Vol. 1 of *Abū Shākir ibn al-Rāhib: Kitāb al-Tawārīkh*. Cairo: Alexandria School, 2016.

Rhode, Joseph Francis. *The Arabic Versions of the Pentateuch in the Church of Egypt: A Study from Eighteen Arabic and Copto-Arabic MSS (Ninth–Seventeenth Century) in the National Library at Paris, the Vatican and Bodleian Libraries and the British Museum.* Leipzig: W. Drugulin, 1921.

Schwarb, Gregor. "The Reception of Maimonides in Christian-Arabic Literature" [Hebrew]. Pages 109–75 in *Maimonides and His World.* Vol. 7 of *Ben ʿEver la-ʿArav: Contacts between Arabic Literature and Jewish Literature in the Middle Ages and Modern Times.* Edited by Yosef Tobi. Haifa: University of Haifa, 2014.

———. "Die Rezeption Maimonides' in der christlich-arabischen Literatur." *Judaica* 63 (2007): 1–45.

Sidarus, Adel. "Copto-Arabic Universal Chronography: Between Antiquity, Judaism, Christianity and Islam." *Collectanea Christiana Orientalia* 2 (2014): 221–50.

———. "Families of Coptic Dignitaries (*buyūtāt*) under the Ayyūbids and the Golden Age of Coptic Arabic Literature (Thirteenth Century)." *JCoptS* 15 (2013): 189–208.

———. *Ibn ar-Rāhibs Leben und Werk: Ein koptisch-arabischer Enzyklopädist des 7./13. Jahrhunderts.* Freiburg: Klaus Schwarz, 1975.

Swanson, Mark N. "Ibn Kātib Qayṣar." In *Christian-Muslim Relations 600–1500.* Edited by David Thomas. http://doi.org/10.1163/1877-8054_cmri_COM_25670.

Vollandt, Ronny. "Ancient Jewish Historiography in Arabic Garb: *Sefer Josippon* between South Italy and Coptic Cairo." *Zutot* 11 (2014): 70–80.

———. *Arabic Versions of the Pentateuch: A Comparative Study of Jewish, Christian, and Muslim Sources.* Leiden: Brill, 2015.

———. "Flawed Biblical Translations into Arabic and How to Correct Them: A Copt and a Jew Study Saadiah's Tafsīr." Pages 56–90 in *Studies on Arabic Christianity in Honor of Sidney H. Griffith.* Edited by David Bertaina, Sandra T. Keating, Mark N. Swanson, and Alexander Treiger. Leiden: Brill, 2018.

Wadīʿ, Awad. *Dirāsa ʿan al-Muʾtaman b. al-ʿAssāl wa-kitābihi "Majmūʿ uṣūl al-dīn" wa-taḥqīqihi.* Cairo: Franciscan Printing Press, 1997.

Wasserstein, Abraham, and David J. Wasserstein. *The Legend of the Septuagint: From Classical Antiquity to Today.* Cambridge: Cambridge University Press, 2006.

Zewi, Tamar. *The Samaritan Version of Saadya Gaon's Translation of the Pentateuch: Critical Edition and Study of MS London BL OR7562 and Related MSS.* Biblia Arabica 3. Leiden: Brill, 2015.

The Yemenite Branch of Manuscripts
of Sa'adia Gaon's Tafsīr

Doron Ya'akov

Introduction

Sa'adia Gaon's translation of the Torah was widespread among Eastern Jewish communities for the first few centuries after it was written, but beginning in the thirteenth century it was gradually replaced by other translations.[1] Each community formulated a translation in a language that was similar to the vernacular of the community members. Only the Yemenite Jews continued using Sa'adia Gaon's translation until the last generation of Jews that lived there (mid-twentieth century). They studied the translation in their schools, generally as part of the weekly study of the Torah portion.[2]

Therefore, it is not surprising that nearly all the extant manuscripts of Sa'adia Gaon's translation are Yemenite. They number approximately ten thousand. Most of them are later manuscripts—from the seventeenth

---

Editor's Note: This essay examines the *language* of a specific Torah translation in a certain context in order to place it against a wider context. Therefore, it contains more examples in the original language (Judeo-Arabic in Hebrew script) than other essays in this collection.

1. Yosef Tobi, "Between Tafsir and Sharh: Saadia Gaon's Translation of the Bible among the Jews of Yemen" [Hebrew], *Studies in the History and Culture of Iraqi Jewry* 6 (1991): 128–31; Mordechai Cohen, "Bible Exegesis: Rabbanite," *EJIW* 1:442–57; Meira Polliack, "Bible Translations: Judeo-Arabic (Ninth to Thirteenth Century)," *EJIW* 1:464–69.

2. Tobi, "Between Tafsir and Sharh," 131–38; Eliezer Schlossberg, "Sa'adya Gaon's Commentaries in the *Ḥeleq Ha-Diqduq* of R. Yiḥya Ṣāleḥ" [Hebrew], *Tema* 5 (1995): 85–86.

century onward.[3] It stands to reason that earlier manuscripts were prevalent before the catastrophe that befell the Yemenite Jews in 1679, when, together with many other books owned by Jews, they were lost forever.[4] In more recent times, at least five editions of Sa'adia Gaon's translation were printed for Yemenite Jews. The first of those editions is very famous—printed in Jerusalem between the years 1894 and 1899 by Avraham an-Naddāf (1866–1940) and distributed in Yemen as well.[5] During the last generation of Jews in Yemen most of the study of the Tafsīr was from that printed edition.

In the research of the text of Sa'adia Gaon's translation, all the Yemenite manuscripts are referred to as stemming from one textual branch. According to researchers, the manuscripts vary only slightly, and therefore they can be grouped as one.[6] The Yemenite branch stands beside the Eastern branch, both of which transmit the translation in Hebrew script. Opposite them stand the Christian branch that transmits the translation predominantly in Arabic script and the Samaritan branch that incorporated additional components into the original Tafsīr.[7]

Researchers evaluated the Yemenite branch and expressed their views on its adherence to the original translation. Kahle thought that the fact the translation was transmitted in Hebrew script deemed it to be less than

---

3. Eliezer Schlossberg, "Towards a Critical Edition of Rav Saadia Gaon's Translation of the Torah" [Hebrew], *Talelei Orot* 13 (2007): 91.

4. Yosef Tobi, *The Jews of Yemen: Studies in Their History and Culture* (Leiden: Brill, 1999), 78–84.

5. Shalom 'Irāqi Kats and Avraham an-Naddāf, *Keter Tora, Named Tāj by Our Ancestors* [Hebrew, Aramaic, and Arabic] (Jerusalem: Zuckerman, 1899).

6. See, for example, Berend J. Dikken, "Some Remarks about Middle Arabic and Sa'adya Gaon's Arabic Translation of the Pentateuch in Manuscripts of Jewish, Samaritan, Coptic Christian, and Muslim Provenance," in *Middle Arabic and Mixed Arabic: Diachrony and Synchrony*, ed. L. Zack and A. Schippers (Leiden: Brill, 2012), 56–57.

7. Ronny Vollandt, "Christian-Arabic Translations of the Pentateuch from the Ninth to the Thirteenth Centuries: A Comparative Study of Manuscripts and Translation Techniques" (PhD diss., University of Cambridge, 2011), 182–204; Vollandt. *Arabic Versions of the Pentateuch: A Comparative Study of Jewish, Christian, and Muslim Sources* (Leiden: Brill, 2015), 221–44; Haseeb Shehadeh, *The Arabic Translation of the Samaritan Pentateuch*, 2 vols. (Jerusalem: Israel Academy of Sciences and Humanities, 1989–2002); Tamar Zewi, *The Samaritan Version of Saadya Gaon's Translation of the Pentateuch: Critical Edition and Study of MS London BL OR7562 and Related MSS*, Biblia Arabica 3 (Leiden: Brill, 2015).

authentic.[8] In his opinion the original translation was written in Arabic script. However, many other researchers challenged his premise.[9] Moshe Zucker, Yehuda Ratzabi, and Joshua Blau claimed that the Yemenite branch is extremely close to Saʿadia Gaon's original text.[10] Blau wrote that the most accurate manuscript of Saʿadia Gaon's translation is an Eastern manuscript (MS SP RNL Yebr.-Arab. 2 C) written shortly after Saʿadia Gaon's death.[11] The Arabic in that translation reflects a postclassical variety, close to literary Arabic. The Yemenite manuscripts reflect a text that is similar to that of the Eastern manuscript, which indicates their faithfulness to the original translation.[12]

However, there are many differences between the Eastern manuscript and the Yemenite ones, mainly relating to various linguistic features that typify the Arabic of the translation.[13] It stands to reason that over time there were changes that entered the text of the translation in Yemen. To a degree, those changes obscured the classical style and characteristics of its language. In many instances, the Yemenite texts were amended to reflect the spoken Yemenite Arabic dialect. In other cases, the text of the translation was adjusted to better agree with the Hebrew source.

Eliezer Schlossberg, in his introduction toward a critical edition of Saʿadia Gaon's translation, adopted Blau's view and considered the Eastern manuscript a primary source in the research of the text of the translation.[14] Schlossberg is aware of the fact that there are differences between the Yemenite manuscripts, and it appears that in his opinion the variations are primarily due to chronology, namely, that the earlier manuscripts are

---

8. Paul E. Kahle, *Die arabischen Bibelübersetzungen: Texte mit Glossar und Literaturübersicht* (Leipzig: Hinrichs, 1904), X.

9. Recently by Dikken, "Some Remarks."

10. Moshe Zucker, *Rav Saadya Gaon's Translation of the Torah: Exegesis, Halakha, and Polemics in R. Saadya's Translation of the Pentateuch* [Hebrew] (New York: Feldheim, 1959), 317; Yehudah Ratzaby, *A Dictionary of Judaeo-Arabic in R. Saadya's Tafsīr* [Hebrew] (Ramat-Gan: Bar Ilan University Press, 1985), 23; Joshua Blau, ed. *Judeo-Arabic Literature: Selected Texts* (Jerusalem: Magnes, 1980), 19; Blau, "The Linguistic Character of Saadia Gaon's Translation of the Pentateuch," *Oriens* 36 (2001): 2 n. 4.

11. Joshua Blau, "Saadya Gaon's Pentateuch Translation in Light of an Early Eleventh-Century Egyptian Manuscript" [Hebrew], *Lěšonénu* 61 (1998): 111–30.

12. Blau, "Saadya Gaon's Pentateuch Translation," 112–14.

13. Blau, "Saadya Gaon's Pentateuch Translation," 117–27.

14. Schlossberg, "Towards a Critical Edition," 95.

the better ones.[15] Even though, as stated earlier, research to date deems the Yemenite branch to be a single unit,[16] in my opinion more emphasis needs to be placed on the differences between the manuscripts. By doing so one might describe more accurately the Yemenite transmission of Saʿadia Gaon's translation and how that transmission developed throughout the history of its manuscripts.

In the following I set out to prove the claim that the earlier manuscripts are the better ones. To do so, I have examined a number of Yemenite manuscripts from different periods and compared the translations of a few select segments in the Torah (primarily from Genesis). I then compared my findings to the text of the Eastern manuscript. The results indeed show that the text of the earlier manuscripts is more faithful to the Eastern manuscript. The significance of that is that, on the one hand, the earlier manuscripts contain more elements from Classical Arabic and, on the other, they allow for a freer translation of the biblical Hebrew text.

Berend Dikken considered two manuscripts to be the earliest testimony of the Yemenite transmission of the Tafsīr.[17] Schlossberg referred to a different manuscript, and research has shown the latter to predate the other two.[18] For the purposes of this article I established three groups of manuscripts. The first group, manuscripts dated prior to the sixteenth century, will be group A. This group includes a manuscript from the British Library (A1) and the Oxford manuscript (A2).[19] In this group I also included photocopies of pages of a very early manuscript (held in private hands) that I obtained, that include some fragments from Saʿadia Gaon's translation. Based on the form and style of the script, the upper Babylonian diacritics and other considerations, it dates from approximately the thirteenth century (A3).[20] I examined two manuscripts from the seventeenth

---

15. Schlossberg, "Towards a Critical Edition," 98.

16. Many even considered An-Naddāf's printed edition an exemplification of the Yemenite transmission: Blau, *Judeo-Arabic Literature*; Blau, "Saadya Gaon's Pentateuch Translation"; Schlossberg, "Towards a Critical Edition," 92–93; Zewi, *The Samaritan Version*, 47–62 and 77–83.

17. Dikken, "Some Remarks," 56–57. In my opinion, the second manuscript that was referred to does not indicate the precedence that the first one does.

18. Schlossberg, "Towards a Critical Edition," 98.

19. A1: BL Or1041, from the fourteenth or fifteenth century. It includes only the text of the Tafsīr. A2: Bod. MS Opp. Add. Q4. 98, from the fourteenth century. It, too, includes only the text of the Tafsīr.

20. The segments I received include each verse of the MT with full Babylonian

century for the second group (B): a manuscript from the Jewish Theological Seminary (B1) and a manuscript from the British Library (B2).[21] The
third group contains a late manuscript from the nineteenth century from
the Jewish Theological Seminary (C1) and Avraham An-Naddāf's printed
edition (C2).[22]

I will present examples of variations between the groups. Most of the
examples are based on Blau's observations.[23] All of the English translations of the biblical (MT) examples are from the NRSV. I compared all
the Yemenite manuscripts to the Eastern manuscript (S), and its version
matches the first manuscript quoted in each case, unless otherwise noted.
There are three types of cases discussed: cases that relate to classical attributes in the Arabic of the translation; cases that relate to the parity, or
disparity, between the translation and the Hebrew text; and other types of
variations. The original Judeo-Arabic text (in Hebrew script) is printed in
bold; Hebrew Bible quotations are in regular Hebrew font.

Classical Elements versus Yemenite Spoken Dialects

In the earlier manuscripts, classical elements of Middle Arabic are retained
even where the spoken Yemenite Arabic dialects (and other Neo-Arabic
dialects) do otherwise.

(1) The sound masculine plural is usually ין–, in any syntactic position, in all Yemenite manuscripts, throughout all periods. So also in A, for
example: **ואלכנעניין ואלפרזיין** (A3, והכנעני והפרזי אז ישב בארץ), "the Canaanites and Perizzites were also living in the land at that time," Gen 13:7) as the
subject of the sentence. Gentilic nouns always receive this suffix, excluding

---

diacritics, followed by Onkelos's translation with full Babylonian diacritics, followed
by the Tafsīr with very partial Babylonian diacritics (mainly *shadda* and *ḍamma*).
These segments include Gen 6:5–19; 12:7–18; 18:5–19; Num 9:23–10:9; 11:10–16;
Deut 25:6–26:1.

21. B1: New York, USA, MS 9842, dated 1650. Manuscript B1 has a layout similar
to A3, but the MT is marked with Tiberian diacritics and cantillations. B2: BL Or2228,
dated 1655. This manuscript also includes the MT marked with Tiberian diacritics
and cantillations, Onkelos's translation with Babylonian diacritics, and the text of the
Tafsīr. The biblical verses are at the top right corner of each page, and the translations
surround them.

22. C1: New York, USA, MS 9065.1, dated 1807. It is named "Forosho" because it
includes Rashi's commentary as well. C2: Kats, *Keter Tora*.

23. Blau, "Saadya Gaon's Pentateuch Translation."

the name מצריון ("Egyptians") that consistently receives the suffix ‑ון.[24] But in A1 the verse continues: חי[ניד'] מקימן מקימן פי אלבלד; the predicate מקימן received the suffix ‑ן in accordance with classical grammar and with the text of S. This is a good indication that there was a strong tendency to end gentilic names with the suffix ‑ין even in earlier periods. The suffix ‑ון does appear at times in group C as well, particularly in nominal sentences after הם ("they").[25]

(2) In group A, the verb form before a plural subject corresponds to Classical Arabic: for example, והיה כי יראו אתך המצרים ,ראך אלמצריון (A1, "and when the Egyptians see you," Gen 12:12); רא[ו]ך אלמצריון (A2); ראי' אלמצריון (A, וייראו המצרים, "the Egyptians saw," Gen 12:14). In group B the first verb was amended: ראוך ... ראי. In group C the transition to the spoken dialect was completed: ראוך ... ראו.

(3) The accusative marker appears properly: אזואגא אזואגא ... ד'כורא ואנאת'א (A1, A2, שנים שנים ... זכר ונקבה, "two and two ... male and female," Gen 7:9); אזואגא אזואגא ... ד'כור ואנאת' (A3, B). In group C it was omitted in this verse, as in the vernacular: אזואג אזואג ... ד'כור ואנאת'.[26]

(4) At times the early Yemenite manuscripts reflect classical structures more than S,[27] such as the dual form here: ולם יטיקא אן יקימא (A, B, ולא יכלו לשבת, "they could not live," Gen 13:6, with regard to Abraham and Lot). In group C and S: יטיקו ... יקימו.

(5) Case markers in the possessive forms: in the earlier manuscripts the syntactic position affects the case. קאול קין הבל אב'אה (A, ויאמר קין, אל הבל אחיו, "Cain said to his brother Abel," Gen 4:8); קאול קין הבל אב'יה (B1); קאל קין הבל אב'יה (B2). But in C: קאל קין להבל אב'יה. In the later manuscripts the frozen form אב'יה appears in all syntactic positions, just as it is frozen in the spoken dialect (with the exception that the final vowel is ū, ʾaxūh).

(6) Classical conditioning of the verb suffix ‑ן in the future tense (dual and plural): ויציראן (A1, והיו, "and they become," Gen 2:24), ו/פיכונאן (A2, B1), but in later manuscripts ו/פיכונא (B2, C); also יכונן (A1, Gen 6:11), in all other manuscripts יכונו.

---

24. Probably because that form is used in the spoken dialect.

25. As in הם בשריון, "they are mortal" (Gen 6:3); or והם ואגעון (וגעון), "while all of them were still in pain" (Gen 34:25).

26. See Wolfdietrich Fischer and Otto Jastrow, eds., *Handbuch der arabischen Dialekte* (Wiesbaden: Harrassowitz, 1980), 87.

27. Blau, "Saadya Gaon's Pentateuch Translation," 127–28.

(7) Agreement between the relative pronoun and the antecedent: אלשגרה אלתי (A, B, העץ אשר, "the tree which," Gen 3:17). In C: אלד'י, as the pronoun is used in the spoken language.

(8) Retaining the rules of أَنَّ (إِنَّ) and her sisters: adding a pronominal suffix after אַן when not immediately followed by a noun: פאנה אלי' סבעה איאם (A, כי לימים עוד שבעה, "for in seven days," Gen 7:4); but in B and C: פאן אלי'.[28]

(9) An indefinite noun is not followed by a relative pronoun: כל בשרי פיה (A, B, C1, כל בשר אשר בו, "all flesh in which," Gen 6:17). In C2: כל בשרי אלד'י פיה.

(10) The classical form of the verb ראא (رَأَى) in the future tense: ליריה (B, לראות, "to see," Gen 2:19), ליוריה (A, C).[29]

Correspondence with the Hebrew Text

(1) ואדם אַיִן לעבד את האדמה. ואד יעלה מן הארץ והשקה את כל פני האדמה, "there was no one to work the ground, but streams came up from the earth and watered the whole surface of the ground" (Gen 2:5–6): ולא בכ'אר כאן יצעד מנהא, "and no steam came up from it" (A, B); C: ובכ'אר כאן יצעד מנהא. Sa'adia Gaon understood the negative אַיִן to refer to both verses, but later manuscripts amended the Tafsīr to reflect the meaning of the second verse as explained by other exegetes.[30]

(2) ותצחק שרה בקרבה לאמר ... למה זה צחקה שרה לאמר, "So Sarah laughed to herself, saying ... Why did Sarah laugh, and say" (Gen 18:12–13): פצ'חכת סרה פי נפסהא קאילה ... קאילה (A, B1, S with slight variation), namely, the participle קאילה is a circumstantial accusative (حَال). In B2 and C: קאילא,[31] as לאמר is translated elsewhere.

(3) ויתן להם יוסף עגלות על פי פרעה ויתן להם צדה לדרך, "Joseph gave them wagons according to the instruction of Pharaoh, and he gave them provisions for the journey" (Gen 45:21): ואעטאהם יוסף עגלא באמר פרעון

---

28. See William Wright, *A Grammar of the Arabic Language*, 2 vols. (Cambridge: Cambridge University Press, 1896–1898), 2:81.

29. Blau, "Saadya Gaon's Pentateuch Translation," 126. Here group B is seen to reflect an earlier version than group A.

30. See Schlossberg, "Towards a Critical Edition," 92–93.

31. There is a difference between the forms in the Yemenite rendering of the Tafsīr: *gāyilah* as opposed to *gāyilā*.

ו{ואעטאהם ... ואעטא} (A, B; C1: חזאדא ... ואזאדא :עגאלא). But in C2: ואעטא ... ואעטא
זאדא. The repetition of the verb agrees with the Hebrew verse.

(4) למען הציל אתו מידם להשיבו אל אביו, "that he might rescue him out
of their hand and restore him to his father" (Gen 37:22): לקבל אן יכ'לצה
מן אידיהם וירדה אלי אביה (A). B and C: לירדה אלי אביה. The form לירדה is
more similar to the Hebrew להשיבו.

(5) חטאו משקה מלך מצרים והאפה לאדניהם למלך מצרים, "the cupbearer
of the king of Egypt and his baker offended their lord the king of Egypt"
(Gen 40:1): אד'נבא לסיידהמא מלך מצר (B, C); אד'נבא לסיידהמא (A) ... אד'נבא מלך מצר.
Sa'adia Gaon, in accordance with his usual practice, does not repeat words
he considers duplicates.[32]

(6) חֹמֹתֶיךָ הַגְּבֹהֹת וְהַבְּצֻרוֹת, "your high and fortified walls" (Deut
28:52): אלשאמכ'ה אלחצינה (A, B). There are two asyndetic adjectives, as
is customary in Classical, and Sa'adia Gaon's, Arabic.[33] However, in C:
אלשאמכ'ה ואלחצינה as it appears in the Hebrew verse.

Other Types of Variations

(1) הן האדם היה כאחד ממנו לדעת טוב ורע, "See, the man has become like
one of us, knowing good and evil" (Gen 3:22): הוד'א אדם קד צאר כואחד
מנא מערפה אלכ'יר ואלשר (A1, B). In A2 and in C: מנא פי[ה] מערפה. The
variations stem from exegesis: the word ממנו, and therefore the entire
sentence, is ambiguous. One option is: "man has become like **one of us**,
knowing good and evil."[34] The other option is: "man has become as one,
and from him to know good and evil."[35]

---

32. Zucker, *Rav Saadya Gaon's Translation*, 267–69.

33. See Zucker, *Rav Saadya Gaon's Translation*, 265.

34. The cantillation signs support this exegesis; a *zaqef* is marked over the word
ממנו. Other commentaries support it as well.

35. Onkelos supports this option: הא אדם הוה יחידאי בעלמא, מניה למדע טב וביש,
as also Maimonides in his Commentary on the Mishnah, in the eighth chapter of the
introduction to Tractate Avot (J. Qafiḥ, ed, *Maimonides' Commentary on the Mishnah:
The Arabic Text with a Hebrew Translation*, vol. 4 [Jerusalem: Mosad HaRav Kook,
1965], 400). See also Yosef Ofer, "'Behold, the Man Is Become as One of Us, to Know
Good and Evil' (Gen. 3:22): Interpretation and Reading Traditions in Tiberias and
Babylonia" [Hebrew], in *Al Derekh Ha'Avot: Articles about Bible and Education*, ed. A.
Bazaq (Alon Shevut: Tevunot, 2001), 419–31.

(2) The spelling of proper nouns: the name שרה in A is always סרה. In B and C, שרה. In S the spelling is ³⁶ס[א]רה or סארה. But שָׂרִי remains the spelling in the Tafsīr as it appears in the Hebrew. אברהם is spelled אברהים in A, like the Muslim Arabic spelling of the name. But in B and C it is spelled אבראהם, reflecting the spelling of the Yemenite Jewish Arabic name.

(3) Rare nouns: ומחיתי את כל היקום אשר עשיתי, "and every living thing that I have made I will blot out" (Gen 7:4): ואמחו גמיע אלאנאם אלתי צנעתהם (A1). In B: גמיע אלאנאם אלד'י צנעתהם. In A2 and C: גמיע אלנאס אלד'י צנעתהם.³⁷ In S: גמיע אלאנאם אלדין צנעתהם. The rare word אלאנאם ("humankind") was replaced by a more common word that is graphically similar, אלנאס ("the people").³⁸

(4) Rare forms: והיו בך לאות ולמופת ובזרעך עד עולם, "They shall be among you and your descendants as a sign and a portent forever" (Deut 28:46): ופי נסלך אלמשאבהיך אלי אלדהר (A, B). In C: אלמשאבהין לך ("that are similar to you"). The later manuscripts amended the rare combination of a definite noun with an enclitic possessive.³⁹

(5) Matters of text: ואברהם הלך עמם לשלחם, "and Abraham went with them to set them on their way" (Gen 18:16): מאצ'י (A, B; in S: מאץ'⁴⁰). In C: סאיר.

ויעברו אנשים מדינים סחרים, "When some Midianite traders passed by" (Gen 37:28): פלמא מר בהם אלרגאל אלמדיאניין אלתגאר (A, B, C1; in S: אלמדיאניין). But in C2: פלמא מר בהם אלתגאר.⁴¹

(6) The vowel of the future tense prefix of form IV. The Yemenite manuscripts often mark the *ḍammah* (signifying a short *u* vowel) in the Tafsīr with a Babylonian *qibbuṣ* mark. In group A it is marked at times, in group B more so, and in C it is marked almost consistently. The form IV future tense prefix is not marked with a *qibbuṣ*, which indicates that the vowel

---

36. א marking a long vowel is sometimes elided in S in the spelling of common words (Blau, "The Linguistic Character," 123–24). It is possible that the set spelling סרה in the Yemenite manuscripts (in which the א is usually not elided) is in juxtaposition with the Hebrew spelling.

37. This part of the A2 manuscript is a later supplement.

38. See Blau, "Saadya Gaon's Pentateuch Translation," 122, regarding the modified noun in this verse.

39. Wright, *A Grammar of the Arabic Language*, 2:67.

40. Blau, "The Linguistic Character," 6.

41. Probably omitted accidentally.

shifted to correspond with the local Arabic dialects.[42] The current tradition of reading the Tafsīr has the prefix usually read with a vowel, probably influenced by form I. This pronunciation seems to be reflected in the later manuscripts that do not mark the diacritic, as stated earlier. Yet in A3, four verbs in form IV are marked with a *qibbuṣ*:[43] תֻכְּמִלְהָא, "finish it" (Gen 6:16); לֻאֶהלִךּ, "to destroy" (Gen 6:17); וֻאֻתְּ'בֻת, "I will establish" (Gen 6:18); אֻעטִיהָא, "I will give it" (Gen 13:17). This clearly indicates that the earlier reading of the Tafsīr maintained the classical vowel of the prefix.

Other Elements in the Yemenite Manuscripts

Despite all the examples above, even the earliest Yemenite manuscripts reflect a later Arabic in many regards, and frequently they do not agree to the testimony of manuscript S. Even the classical elements demonstrated above are not preserved consistently. For example, 'ט is always replaced by 'צ. I found no occurrence of 'ט in all of the Yemenite manuscripts. So too the numerals: they always appear in the frozen form, such as with the suffix ־ין.[44]

Summary

I have demonstrated some instances (and those are just examples) where the earlier the Yemenite manuscript is, it shows more compliance with Classical Arabic, while maintaining a freer translation that is not restricted by the literal text of the Bible. Based on manuscript S (and other testimonies), they are closer to the original language, style, and text of the Tafsīr. One has to bear in mind that the earliest extant manuscripts date from the thirteenth century; the translation had been written over two hundred years previously. As shown by the chronological gradation of the varia-

---

42. The use of form IV decreased significantly in the Neo-Arabic dialects (Fischer and Jastrow, *Handbuch der arabischen Dialekte*, 70).

43. For technical reasons, the Babylonian *qibbuṣ* sign was replaced with the regular *qibbuṣ* sign.

44. In group A numerals are often written in abbreviated form, for example in A3: ש' ד'ראע טולהא ונ' ערצ'הא ול' סמכהא, "the length of the ark three hundred cubits, its width fifty cubits, and its height thirty cubits" (Gen 6:15). Is it due to economy alone, or is it an attempt to displace classical forms?

tions between the manuscripts, it can be assumed that if we had had earlier manuscripts they would have been closer to the original Tafsīr.[45]

This claim strengthens the status attributed to the Yemenite manuscripts of Sa'adia Gaon's Tafsīr. They essentially agree with the text of the early Eastern branch and reflect an Arabic language similar to Classical Arabic. Both branches independently testify to Sa'adia Gaon's original language.

Another practical matter of significance is that any research of Sa'adia Gaon's Tafsīr that includes the Yemenite manuscripts should distinguish between the developmental stages of the Yemenite text. Work on a critical edition of Sa'adia Gaon's text should promote the earliest manuscripts. And it goes without saying that the printed edition C2 is not an adequate testimony of the Yemenite branch since it contains many flaws.

Bibliography

Blau, Joshua, ed. *Judeo-Arabic Literature: Selected Texts*. Jerusalem: Magnes, 1980.

———. "The Linguistic Character of Saadia Gaon's Translation of the Pentateuch." *Oriens* 36 (2001): 1–9.

———. "Saadya Gaon's Pentateuch Translation in Light of an Early Eleventh-Century Egyptian Manuscript" [Hebrew]. *Lěšonénu* 61 (1998): 111–30.

Cohen, Mordechai. "Bible Exegesis: Rabbanite." *EJIW* 1:442–57.

Dikken, Berend J. "Some Remarks about Middle Arabic and Sa'adya Gaon's Arabic Translation of the Pentateuch in Manuscripts of Jewish, Samaritan, Coptic Christian, and Muslim Provenance." Pages 51–81 in *Middle Arabic and Mixed Arabic: Diachrony and Synchrony*. Edited by L. Zack and A. Schippers. Leiden: Brill, 2012.

Fischer, Wolfdietrich, and Otto Jastrow, eds. *Handbuch der arabischen Dialekte*. Wiesbaden: Harrassowitz, 1980.

Halkin, Abraham, and David Hartman, eds. *Epistles of Maimonides: Crisis and Leadership*. Philadelphia: Jewish Publication Society of America, 1993.

Kahle, Paul E. *Die arabischen Bibelübersetzungen: Texte mit Glossar und Literaturübersicht*. Leipzig: J. C. Hinrichs, 1904.

---

45. The connection between Yemenite Jewry and Babylonia and Sa'adia Gaon is known from early periods. As an example, see Abraham Halkin and David Hartman, eds., *Epistles of Maimonides: Crisis and Leadership* (Philadelphia: Jewish Publication Society of America, 1993), 114.

Kats, Shalom 'Irāqi, and Avraham an-Naddāf. *Keter Tora, Named Tāj by Our Ancestors* [Hebrew, Aramaic, and Arabic]. Jerusalem: Zuckerman, 1899.

Ofer, Yosef. " 'Behold, the Man Is Become as One of Us, to Know Good and Evil' (Gen. 3:22): Interpretation and Reading Traditions in Tiberias and Babylonia" [Hebrew]. Pages 419–31 in *Al Derekh Ha'Avot: Articles about Bible and Education.* Edited by A. Bazaq. Alon Shevut: Tevunot, 2001.

Polliack, Meira. "Bible Translations: Judeo-Arabic (Ninth to Thirteenth Century)." *EJIW* 1:464–69.

Qafih, Josef, ed. *Maimonides' Commentary on the Mishnah: The Arabic Text with a Hebrew Translation.* Vol. 4. Jerusalem: Mosad HaRav Kook, 1965.

Ratzaby, Yehuda. *A Dictionary of Judaeo-Arabic in R. Saadya's Tafsīr* [Hebrew]. Ramat-Gan: Bar Ilan University Press, 1985.

Schlossberg, Eliezer. "Sa'adya Gaon's Commentaries in the *Heleq Ha-Diqduq* of R. Yiḥya Ṣāleḥ" [Hebrew]. *Tema* 5 (1995): 83–95.

———. "Towards a Critical Edition of Rav Saadia Gaon's Translation of the Torah" [Hebrew]. *Talelei Orot* 13 (2007): 87–104.

Shehadeh, Haseeb. *The Arabic Translation of the Samaritan Pentateuch.* 2 vols. Jerusalem: Israel Academy of Sciences and Humanities, 1989–2002.

Tobi, Yosef. "Between Tafsir and Sharh: Saadia Gaon's Translation of the Bible among the Jews of Yemen" [Hebrew]. *Studies in the History and Culture of Iraqi Jewry* 6 (1991): 127–38.

———. *The Jews of Yemen: Studies in Their History and Culture.* Leiden: Brill, 1999.

Vollandt, Ronny. *Arabic Versions of the Pentateuch: A Comparative Study of Jewish, Christian, and Muslim Sources.* Leiden: Brill, 2015.

———. "Christian-Arabic Translations of the Pentateuch from the Ninth to the Thirteenth Centuries: A Comparative Study of Manuscripts and Translation Techniques." PhD diss., University of Cambridge, 2011.

Wright, William. *A Grammar of the Arabic Language.* 2 vols. Cambridge: Cambridge University Press, 1896–1898.

Zewi, Tamar. *The Samaritan Version of Saadya Gaon's Translation of the Pentateuch: Critical Edition and Study of MS London BL OR7562 and Related MSS.* Biblia Arabica 3. Leiden: Brill, 2015.

Zucker, Moshe. *Rav Saadya Gaon's Translation of the Torah: Exegesis, Halakha, and Polemics in R. Saadya's Translation of the Pentateuch* [Hebrew]. New York: Feldheim, 1959.

The Bible as History:
Sa'adia Gaon, Yefet ben 'Eli, Samuel ben Ḥofni, and Maimonides on the Genealogy of Esau and the Kingdom of Edom (Genesis 36)

Yosef Yuval Tobi

Introduction

The sages of Israel in the Judeo-Arabic cultural context of the Middle Ages treated the Bible as a human literary work, without doubting in the slightest its essence as a divinely-inspired prophetic book. Thus, for example, Sa'adia Gaon does not hesitate to incorporate into his commentary on the book of Psalms linguistic, poetic, and structural comments that are accepted in literary analyses of human works of creativity, while at the same time viewing it as a prophetic book spoken to David by the mouth of God. One of the questions often pondered by the sages of Israel has to do with the status of the narrative-historical sections of the Bible, which in themselves contain neither practical nor supplementary instructions for performing one's religious duties. Just as Moshe Zucker has already noted, this question was also discussed by the Muslim scholars regarding the Qur'an.[1] As a matter of fact, the very question had already been raised by the talmudic sages, though not in the detailed formulation of an abstract idea, but rather in a specific reference to a particular matter.[2] In any case, like the approach taken by the Jewish sages in relation to the Bible, the accepted approach among the Muslim scholars was that the narrative parts of the Qur'an have also a moral function, that is, to learn thereby what is

---

1. See Moshe Zucker's preface in *Saadya's Commentary on Genesis* (New York: Jewish Theological Seminary, 1984), 62–63.

2. See further below.

considered a virtuous act for which a person will receive reward, and what is considered a nefarious act for which a person is liable to punishment.

Nevertheless, the sages' bewilderment over the Bible's integration of its historical parts was repeatedly raised as a fundamental question by medieval Jewish philosophers and commentators of the Bible, who, in their Judeo-Arabic cultural setting, rendered in layman's terms its plain meaning. In what follows, we shall discuss the attitude of four sages, all of whom rejected in one way or another the rabbinic midrashic literature, or else dismissed its literal interpretation:

1. Sa'adia Gaon (Egypt-Iraq, 882–942), whose attitude toward rabbinic midrashic literature was ambivalent: he adopted it in his liturgies but did not recoil from denouncing it in his commentary on the Bible,[3] much like other Geonim, such as Sherira Gaon and Hayé (Hai or Hay) Gaon, who were not afraid to answer those who turned to such literature that "we do not rely upon the words of Aggadah";[4]
2. The Karaite Yefet ben 'Eli the Levite (lived in the second half of the tenth century CE in Jerusalem), whose very association with the Karaite sect made him reject the words of the sages;
3. Samuel ben Ḥofni (officiated as the Gaon of the Sura Academy during the years 998–1013), who, in principle, adopted Sa'adia Gaon's approach; and
4. Maimonides (1138–1204), who argued that the rabbinic midrashic literature must be understood in the context of allegory, and even declared in several places in his works that his intention was to compile a book entitled *The Book of Homilies* for the said purpose of explication.

The position taken by Jewish philosophers was expressed in their philosophical works, for example, Sa'adia in his book *The Book of Beliefs and Opinions*, and Maimonides in his book *The Guide for the Perplexed*. How-

---

3. See Yosef Tobi, "Sa'adia's Biblical Exegesis and his Poetic Practice," *Hebrew Annual Review* 8 (1984): 241–57; Haggai Ben-Shammai, *A Leader's Project: Studies in the Philosophical and Exegetical Works on Saadia Gaon* [Hebrew] (Jerusalem: Mosad Bialik, 2015), 336–73.

4. See Yehoshua' Horowits, "The Attitude of the Ge'onim to the Aggadah" [Hebrew], *Mahanayim* 7 (1994): 122–29.

ever, exegetes of the Bible—and in this category we must once again number among their ranks Sa'adia, along with Yefet ben 'Eli, and Samuel ben Ḥofni—expressed their positions in their biblical commentaries. The philosophical writings of Sa'adia and Maimonides, as well as significant portions of Sa'adia's commentary on the Bible, have come down to us in manuscripts preserved by Jewish communities in the East and which have all seen print from the beginning in the nineteenth century. Sa'adia's commentary on the second part of Genesis, including this portion of *Vayishlaḥ*, have not reached us. Some say that he did not write a commentary on this particular portion at all. Nevertheless, Sa'adia refers to the issue discussed in his introduction to two books of the Bible, namely, Genesis and Psalms. In contrast, the commentaries of Yefet on the Bible, as well as that of Samuel ben Ḥofni on the Pentateuch, were only preserved in the Cairo Genizah. Fragments of Samuel ben Ḥofni's commentary were published from the Genizah manuscripts, while the extensive biblical commentary of Yefet is still largely preserved in the Genizah writings, although in recent years parts thereof have been widely published.[5] In any event, the commentary on Gen 36, which includes the genealogical lists of Esau and of the kingdom of Edom, has not yet been published.[6]

The Integration of the Genealogical Lists of Esau and of the Kingdom of Edom in the Biblical Narrative

The biblical portion of *Vayishlaḥ* (Gen 32–36) unfolds with the dramatic story of Jacob's encounter with his brother Esau in the vicinity of the Jabbok River valley in Transjordan, and which by its modern identification emp-

---

5. See *Rav Shemuel Ben Ḥofni's Commentary on the Pentateuch* [Hebrew], ed. Aharon Greenbaum (Jerusalem: Mossad Ha-Rav Kook, 1979); Eliezer Schlossberg and Meira Polliack, eds., *Yefet ben 'Eli's Commentary on Hosea* [Hebrew] (Ramat Gan: Bar-Ilan University, 2009); and Yair Zoran, ed., "Yefet ben 'Eli's Commentary on Obadiah" [Hebrew], *Ginzei Qedem* 8 (2012): 129–95.

6. It is discussed here according to a photocopy of a manuscript that was kindly given to me by Prof. Meira Polliack of Tel Aviv University, who also supplied the following details: "Yefet's commentary on Gen 36 has survived in two good manuscripts. One is in the second Firkovitch Collection, now housed in the Russian National Library at St Petersburg: MS SP RNL Yevr.-Arab. 1:23 [microfilm 53812 at the IMHM, National Library of Israel, Jerusalem]; and the other, in better and fuller shape, now housed in the National Library of France, Paris: MS BN 278 [microfilm 4326 at the IMHM, National Library of Israel, Jerusalem]. In this manuscript the original Judeo-Arabic text translated herein can be found on page 151 and following."

ties into the Jordan River near the Adam Bridge. The beginning of their encounter is fraught with great tension and with Jacob's unrelenting fear of Esau, although the episode has a happy ending. Jacob and Esau hug each other, kiss, and cry upon each other's shoulders. Esau also refuses to accept the gift offered to him by Jacob, and only after certain overtures does he eventually accept the gift. Furthermore, Esau offers to Jacob a military escort along the way, but Jacob gently turns down the offer with the argument that it would be an impediment to his progress as he slowly makes the journey together with his entire entourage. Each of the two brothers then turns to his separate way: Esau to the south toward Se'ir and Jacob northward to Sukkot and to Shechem, places that lie on the western bank of the Jordan River. Then, following the narrative of their encounter, there comes another dramatic episode whose beginning is marked by tranquility; but, as the story unfolds and ends, it becomes very disturbing: this is the story of Dinah in Shechem. Jacob is plagued with troubles. He flees for fear of "the Canaanite inhabitants of the land." Deborah, the wet nurse of Rebecca his mother, suddenly dies. Thereafter Rachel, his beloved wife, dies while giving birth. Rueben, his eldest son, lies carnally with Bilhah, his father's concubine. And finally, Isaac, Jacob's father, is gathered unto his people. Jacob's afflictions do not end there, seeing that in the biblical portion of *Vayeshev* (Gen 37–40) begins the tragic episode of Joseph and his brothers, which actually spans the remaining sections of Genesis.

Then, at the end of the portion *Vayishlah* (the whole of Gen 36), between the hardships that Jacob has had to deal with after the incident with Dinah in Shechem, and so on, as described above, and the story of Joseph and his brothers, beginning with the start of *Vayeshev*, the biblical narrative suddenly takes a turn and incorporates in a seemingly puzzling manner a completely unusual matter—the detailed history of Esau and the kings that descended from his posterity and who ruled over the land of Edom, while specifically emphasizing that their kingdom was "before there reigned any king over the Children of Israel" (Gen 36:31).[7] It is, of course, possible to explain this in a way that cannot easily be refuted, namely, that the narrative of the kings of Edom has come down in its proper place, seeing that it comes after the Bible says of Isaac: "And his sons Esau and Jacob buried him" (Gen 35:29). The *mudawwin* (the copyist or editor of

---

7. Biblical citations in this essay follow a combination of the KJV and, when the KJV presents a text too archaic for contemporary readers, the JPS 1985, even when KJV is quoted in the bibliographical sources.

the Torah, in the language used by the Karaite Bible exegetes and by the Rabbanites of the tenth century)[8]—who sought to foreground the history of the people of Israel as being the main subject of interest in the Bible, meaning, the history of Jacob after the death of his father Isaac—saw fit to recuse himself at this place from the necessity of having to render a detailed account of Esau's history, and by giving rather a brief genealogical account of Esau's progeny. So, too, in this manner, has the *mudawwin* conducted himself with regard to the sons of Keṭurah, Abraham's wife, and with regard to Ishmael his son, at the end of the biblical portion *Chayei Sarah* (Gen 25). Similarly, in the book of Chronicles the *mudawwin* presented an abridged account of Esau's genealogy (1 Chr 1:35–54), after the universal genealogy to Abraham, Ishmael, and the sons of Keturah (vv. 1–33) according to Gen 10 and 25, which comes before the genealogy of the Judah tribe of Judah (chapters 2–4).

The Genealogical Lists of Esau and the Kingdom of Edom in Midrashic Literature

As noted, the detailed genealogical lists of Esau and the kingdom of Edom have provoked a surprised response in rabbinic literature, as being something that is out of the ordinary and that is incompatible with the history of our forefathers. The main explanation given for this is the aggrandization of the name of Israel, God's chosen people, compared to the gentiles, while simultaneously pointing out the ethical differences in their conduct. The most detailed discussion of this matter is found in Tanḥ. Vayeshev 1:

> Alternatively: Why have the Scriptures endeavored to write down their genealogy? Was there nothing else that the Holy One, blessed be He, could have written, instead of the Duke of Timnaʿ, the Duke of Loṭan? Rather, it comes to teach you that from the beginning of the creation of the universe, the Holy One, blessed be He, has painstakingly traced the genealogy of idolaters and worshippers of the zodiac, so that they may have no recourse to a defense when mankind is informed about their origin and their vices.... To inform about their vices, in the sense that

---

8. Meira Polliack, "'Scribe', 'Redactor' and 'Author': The Multifaceted Concept of the Biblical Narrator (Mudawwin) in Medieval Karaite Exegesis" [Hebrew], in *Teʿudah 29, Yad Moshe: Studies in the History of the Jews in Islamic Lands Dedicated to the Memory of Moshe Gil*, ed. Yoram Erder, Elinoar Bareqet, and Meira Polliack (Tel Aviv: University of Tel Aviv, 2018), 147–76.

one sees that they are the children of promiscuity. Wherefore it says,
"the sons of Eliphaz were Teman, Omar, Ṣepho, and Gaʿtam, Qenaz, and
Timnaʿ and ʿAmaleq" (1 Chr 1:36), "And Timnaʿ was the concubine of
Eliphaz" (Gen 36:12), showing that he married his own daughter.... And
since all of them were the children of promiscuity, the Scriptures have
singled them out to make known their vices. However, as for Israel, the
Holy One, blessed be He, has drawn them near to him, and has called
them [his] "lot" and [his] "inheritance," and [his] "portion," as it says:
"For the Lord's portion is his people; Jacob is the lot of his inheritance"
(Deut 32:9).... Allegorically, it is compared to a king who had a gemstone cast out into the dirt and into the gravel. The king had to search in
the dirt and in the gravel to retrieve the gemstone from them. When the
king finally reached the gemstone, he put aside the dirt and the gravel
and occupied himself only with the gemstone. In this manner the Holy
One, blessed be He, has concerned himself with former generations,
including them all, but then laid them aside.... When he reached the
gemstones that are Abraham, Isaac, and Jacob, he began to be occupied
with them. For this reason, the section which treats on the dukes of the
sons of Esau has been juxtaposed against this section.[9]

Another exegesis that presents the same general thought is brought down
in Gen. Rab. 82:14 on Gen 36:

Rabbi Shimon bar Yoḥai said: Why is it that I must expound and say,
"And Timnaʿ was the concubine of Eliphaz?" It comes to make known
the praise of our father Abraham's house, to what extent the kingdoms
and rulers wanted to be joined to him. And what was Loṭan? He was one
of the rulers.

Certainly these homilies contain within them a related reference to the
kingdom of Rome, concerning which the sages of Israel have identified
with Esau, as in the legends about the destruction in b. Giṭ. 57b: "The
hands are the hands of Esau: this refers to the wicked kingdom that
destroyed our Temple, and that burnt our edifice, and that exiled us from
our country." The first midrash alludes to the mass-proselytization movement that swept across Rome after the destruction of the Second Temple,
whereas the second expresses an apologetic polemic with the Roman
kingdom.

---

9. The Tanḥuma translations are from *Midrash Tanḥuma* (New York: Horev, 1924);
all translations are mine.

The Purpose of the Genealogical Lists of Esau and the Kingdom of Rome in Sa'adia Gaon's Writings

In at least three places in his works, Sa'adia treats the different aspects of the biblical narrative in terms of their literary genre:[10] (1) in his introduction to the commentary on Genesis, related to a question that he raised, he wrote (translated from Judeo-Arabic): "And if a man should ever ask and say if the order that accompanies the composition is so important, why do we not find in this book, meaning to say in the Torah, the commandments and the legal rulings grouped together and arranged in chapters, and divided into individual parts and ranked according to their status? Instead, we see them scattered and haphazardly arranged";[11] (2) in the sixth essay of the *Book on Beliefs and Opinions* (3:6), in the matter dealing with scriptural references of "God commanded" and where "God warns" against doing a certain thing;[12] and (3) in his introduction to his commentary on the Psalms.[13]

Sa'adia's need to express this issue on three separate occasions, and especially his presentation of his position as an answer to a general question as to the purpose of the narrative parts that are included in the Bible—with the exception of those parts that contain the commandments—shows that he is actually responding to questions that were being asked in the contemporaneous Jewish world about the content, structure, and manner in which the Bible was written. There is no doubt that in his long and detailed response, Sa'adia answers those questions somewhat apologetically. Without referring to the specific *responsa* of the sages earlier alluded to, regarding the integration of the genealogical lists of Esau and the kingdom of Edom, Sa'adia actually adopts in principle the method of the sages in all his discussions on this question, to wit, that even the

---

10. Cf. Eliezer Schlossberg, "The Methods of Education According to Rav Sa'adia Gaon," in *Streams of Love (Yuvle Ahava), In Loving Memory of Yuval Hayman*, ed. Yosef Yuval Tobi, Shmuel Glick, and Renée Levine Melammed (Jerusalem: published by the family, 2016), 55–68.

11. Zucker, *Rav Saadya's Commentary on Genesis*, 167.

12. Yosef Qafiḥ, ed., *Beliefs and Opinions* [Hebrew] (New York: Yeshiva University, 1970), 129–31.

13. Yosef Qafiḥ, ed., *Rav Saadya's Commentary on Psalms* [Hebrew] (New York: American Academy for Jewish Studies, 1966), 19–21.

narrative parts of the Bible that do not contain commandments have a moral lesson to tell. Thus, we read in his commentary on the Psalms:

> And the third part [of the five biblical literary genres] is the narrative.... A narrative about people who had been aggrandized, as the accounts of Abraham, Isaac, and Jacob were narrated in the Pentateuch. And the intention of that was to oblige us to be like them.... However, the purpose of the narrative about the accounts of people who had been condemned was to prevent us from doing like their deeds. This is in reference to what is mentioned in the Pentateuch regarding the spies, and regarding those who complained and regarding the men who have joined in worshiping the Ba'al of Pe'or.... The aim of those two parts is the same, as it is known by God that people need to be guided by events; for this reason, he threatened them with these narratives.[14]

However, in the *Book of Beliefs and Opinions*, he presented a less pious and traditionalistic stance:

> And now I shall explain the matter of the Holy Scriptures and say that, for us, it is less understood than what it used to be in times past, [specifically] things that we should be educated by them to be obedient to him, and which he included in his book, and has added thereto his commandments, and after that the rewards that he would give them. All this has become lasting benefit to future generations, namely, that all the books of the prophets and books of the sages belonging to all peoples [an allusion to the Qur'ān?!]; in spite of their abundance, they contain three basic elements: the first in importance are the commands and admonitions, and they are one and the same; the second—the reward and punishment, which are likened unto their fruit; and the third, the episodic narrative, describing the person that acted uprightly on earth and succeeded, and the person who corrupted his ways therein and perished; for any instruction can only be had with these three things.
>
> And I have seen fit to mention specific instances relating to the veracity of the biblical narrative. Had it not been for the fact that the soul accepts that there exists in the world a genuine story, no man would hope for what he regularly hopes for after being informed about the success that he can have at a given mercantile venture, or the success that comes from the pursuit of a particular professional skill, seeing that man's strength and his needs are dependent upon his possessions. He

---

14. *Commentary on the Psalms*, 19–21. Here and in what follows the translation is mine from the original Judeo-Arabic.

would not even fear what he is being warned against, such as the danger of going out on a certain road, or at his being warned to avoid a certain action.[15]

Indeed, also in the third element there is moral lesson to be learned, albeit not in a religious, faith-based, or ethical context but rather in the context of one's economic well-being and of one's personal safety. This trend of being detached from the pure religious context is reinforced in Sa'adia's introduction to his commentary on Genesis, in which a simplistic approach to biblical interpretation emerges. Sa'adia counts eighteen matters in the Bible which are divided into three groups: (1) eight matters "that are connected to the [biblical] commandments and to the admonitions, which are the essence of the Torah"; (2) "seven [matters] that are one level below them," and whose relevance here is mainly to the narrative part of the Bible, whose usefulness is similar to the third element he spoke about in his introduction to Psalms; and (3) "the three last [matters] are at the lowest level, but these too have benefit, since it is impossible for the Torah to contain useless things."[16] By his words, in which he details these three elements, Sa'adia implies that in the Bible there exist details about which there is no readily understood ethical meaning, only the imparting of historical knowledge whose benefit is to improve the individual's personality and feelings:

> The first of the last three to complete the eighteen are events which merely give us a time reference. They have been made known unto us because he (God) was cognizant of the fact that people would be delighted and encouraged by knowing the number of years that have transpired since the creation of the universe until their own day. In addition, he has made known unto us their parts and their periods: such-and-such years from a particular generation, unto a particular generation, so that it might rest in our thoughts like a candle that illuminates and as a station that comprises one part of time before transitioning into a second part of time, just as everyone who has ever studied the Torah feels within his soul.
>
> The second of the last three deals with family genealogy, such as how the Scriptures have traced the patristic lineage of the seventy nations to the three sons of Noah, as also the lineage of Abraham and Ishmael,

---

15. *Beliefs and Opinions*, 129–31.
16. *Commentary on Genesis*, 175–80.

and of Jacob and Esau. The blessed Creator knew that men would find
solace at knowing these genealogies, since our soul demands of us to
know them, so that mankind will be cherished by us as a tree that has
been planted by God in the earth, whose branches have spread out and
dispersed eastward and westward, northward and southward, in the hab-
itable part of the earth. It also has the dual function of allowing us to see
the multitude as a single individual, and the single individual as a multitude. Along with this, man ought to contemplate also on the names of
the countries and of the cities.

The third of the last three deals with the number of people who are
mentioned therein, of which the children of Israel are enumerated in four
distinct places. The advantage by what we have been able to understand
(in this matter) is that one may know how the people had multiplied after
it had been a few in number, as it is written: "All the souls of the house
of Jacob, which came into Egypt, were seventy," and so on (Gen 46:27).
Moreover, that we may know just how great the multitude of people was
who had seen the miracles of the messenger, and who had actually heard
the words of God who spoke on the mountain, as it is written: "And all
the people saw the thunderings," and so on (Exod 20:18). So, too, that
we may know what great number of people were conducted (by God) in
mercy and who gave to them a leader, and who supplied for them food
and sustenance, as it is written: "The people are six hundred thousand
footmen," and so on (Num 11:21), as well as all similar things. To this
also belongs the number of spoils taken during war, as it is written: "Take
the sum of the prey that was taken," and so on (Num 31:26); and the
number of dedicated offerings given to the tabernacle, as it is written:
"This is the sum [donation] of the tabernacle," and so on (Exod 38:21).
For [a memorial of] these things, and things similar (in the Bible), there
are rational reasons that I shall explain in the book, God willing.[17]

The Purpose of the Genealogical Lists of Esau and the Kingdom of Edom in Yefet ben 'Eli's Commentary on Genesis

Yefet ben 'Eli the Levite, the renowned Karaite commentator and a young
contemporary of Sa'adia, explains in great detail and with a clear rational-
historical approach all the individual scenes described in Gen 36. However,
in doing so, he also presents a historiosophical approach that incorporates
national and faith-based ideas, aimed at repeatedly expressing contempt
for Esau and his descendants, as opposed to the lavish praises he heaps

---

17. *Commentary on Genesis*, 180.

upon Jacob and his household. Nevertheless, the fact that there is a synthesis between Esau's genealogical list and that of the kingdom of Edom is explained by reasons related purely to good editing.

> Before he [the *mudawwin*] begins the story of Joseph, which narrative continues unto Israel's descent into Egypt, he wrote down the genealogy of Esau, since it was not comely to stop in the middle of such narrative and to interject his genealogy. In this manner, he was able to convey Esau's genealogy near the same place where he conveyed Jacob's genealogy.[18]

Editing considerations also play a role for Yefet when explaining the difference between the integration of Esau's genealogical list and that of the kingdom of Edom in Genesis and in 1 Chronicles:

> Now this stands in contrast to the way in which he edited in the book of Chronicles (1 Chr 1:43–54), wherein he put Esau's genealogy before Jacob's genealogy. The reason for which is clear, being that he wanted to begin with Jacob, and therefore dealt with tribe after tribe, discussing his family's genealogy unto the end, which is the purpose of the book. He put first the genealogy of Esau since it was brief [as also with regard to the detailed account in the book of Genesis], and since it is not comely to write it in the genealogy that treats the family of Jacob. Notwithstanding, here [in the book of Genesis] he put the genealogy of Jacob first for the first of the two reasons that I have written.

As already noted, words of denigration to Esau are repeated often in Yefet's commentary on Gen 36. Thus in the place that reads "Esau is Edom" (v. 1), he states that it was said by way of mockery, seeing that this nickname derives from what he said to Jacob, "Please feed me with that red red pottage" (Gen 25:30). In this manner, in what was said concerning the wives of Esau, that they were "from the daughters of Canaan" (Gen 36:2), the intent here is to show the difference between him and Jacob: Jacob married women from his father's family, as opposed to Esau who took wives from the daughters of Canaan, for which the Scriptures hold him in contempt.

Yefet presents a rational explanation, coupled with words of praise for the land of Israel, along with a somewhat nationalistic proclamation, when commenting on 36:7, "And the land where they sojourned could not bear them because of their cattle":

---

18. For the Yefet MS used for the translation here, see n. 6.

His intent here is not to the entire land of Israel, but rather that place where they had their dwelling, seeing that the land of Israel is broad, capable of providing for all the tribes completely, and certainly was able to provide for Jacob and Esau. Even when Esau saw that he had no choice but to be separated from his brother, he left his place and went to Mount Se'ir, for two reasons: the first, because he knew that he had no portion in the land of Canaan, and that it belonged to Jacob; the second, he was well-pleased with his dwelling place in the region of Se'ir, insofar that he had already gone there and acquired for himself a place, having distanced himself completely from the Holy Land. For us, this matter was accentuated that we might know that God prevented him from dwelling in his land, and that he would have a portion in it, as it says: "And Esau I have hated" (Mal 1:3).

Yefet was also troubled by the fact that the land of Israel was given over to a foreign ruler, the Muslims, which made him take advantage of the narrative about Esau in this chapter to state that God strengthens one people over another people:

Dukes belonging to the indigenous inhabitants of Se'ir did not cease to exist in their places until Esau and his children took leave of their place and went unto them. After some time, the sons of Esau made war with them [the indigenous inhabitants of the land], and killed them and inherited their country and dwelt therein, as he says: "The Horites formerly dwelt in Se'ir; but the children of Esau succeeded them," and so on (Deut 2:12). [The *mudawwin*] has made it known that the Lord of the Universe had strengthened the sons of Esau over the inhabitants of Se'ir, until they uprooted them from their place, so as to fulfill the words of Isaac unto him, "See, your dwelling shall be the fatness of the earth, and of the dew of heaven from above" (Gen 27:39). In connection with this matter he has written for us the genealogy of the sons of Se'ir, that we might know that the Lord of the Universe strengthens one nation over another, until they have conquered their country and dwell therein, just as he strengthened the sons of Esau over the inhabitants of Se'ir, and in the same way strengthened Moab and Ammon over the Rephaim until they took from them their country and dwelt there.

In his commentary on Gen 36:31, "And these are the kings that reigned in the land of Edom, before there reigned any king over the children of Israel," Yefet presents the different views regarding how much earlier in time the kingdom of Edom had reigned than that recorded for the kingdom of Israel, based on different chronological tables that can be adduced from the Scriptures, and without any moral or ethical motivation for saying so, except for acquiring historical knowledge alone—similar to what we have found in the words of Sa'adia concerning the genealogical lists of Ishmael and Esau. In his later remarks, however, he points to the great difference between the grandeur and more spiritual kingdom of Israel and that belonging to the kingdom of Edom:

> He has mentioned concerning them eight kings, announcing that one reigned after the other, as it says: "And so-and-so died." He has also made it known that each one came from a different city, excepting Ba'al Ḥanan alone, where, regarding him, the name of his city has not been mentioned, and perhaps came from the land of Sha'ul. In addition, he has informed us that each reigning king was not the son of his predecessor, by which we learn that their kingdom was not a kingdom sanctioned by heaven, as it is with the kings of the house of David, and where each one of them reigned after his father, and all of them from one city, meaning, Jerusalem. As for the others, each one of them overcame the other and reigned in his stead. The son of the deceased king never reigned in his father's stead, but there came another potentate from a different city who became victorious through the sword and reigned in his stead, to fulfill the words of Isaac: "And by your sword you shall live" (Gen 27:40). It was on this account, therefore, that Moses (may peace be upon him) explained to us their ever-changing countries and their genealogies.

The national trend with respect to the land of Israel belonging to the people of Israel, broadly construed, emerges from the concluding section in Yefet's commentary on the chapter:

> Afterwards, he says: "These are the dukes of Edom, according to their habitations in the land of their possession" (Gen 36:43), which comes to inform us that that country was given to them as a possession, and that the sons of Esau would inherit it generation after generation, as it says: "For I have given Mount Se'ir to Esau for a possession" (Deut 2:5), and it shall not cease from being their inheritance in the future, when Israel shall invade them and not leave for them a living soul, as it says: "And the house of Jacob shall be a fire, and the house of Joseph a flame, and the house of Esau chaff, and they shall set them on fire and consume them, and there shall not be any remaining of the house of Esau" (Obad 18). After which, they shall destroy their country and not leave in it any trace unto them, while its portion will remain eternally destroyed,

as it says [in a prophecy concerning Mount Se'ir], "I will make of you
perpetual desolations, and your cities shall not return" (Ezek 35:9);
whereas, as for his portion, being its uttermost parts, Israel shall inherit
it, as it says: "And Edom shall be a possession, Se'ir also shall be a possession for his enemies; and Israel will be triumphant" (Num 24:18).
And he says elsewhere: "And they of the Negev shall possess the mount
of Esau" (Obad 19).

The Purpose of the Genealogical List of Esau and the Kingdom of Edom in the Commentary of Samuel ben Ḥofni on Genesis

Nothing has remained from the commentary by Samuel ben Ḥofni on
Gen 36 except a small fragment. At any rate, most of his words have been
copied from the commentary of Yefet ben 'Eli, including the explanation
which in principle is the editing considerations with regard to the integration of the genealogical lists of Esau and the kingdom of Esau in that
particular place in the biblical text. With that said, there is some novelty
in his comment: he contends that this happens to be the way of scribes, a
comment that stems from a new perception that infiltrated the literature of
Israel at the time, namely that a work is created and constructed upon the
basis of a logical structure:

> And since the purpose sought in these essays was to inform us about
> the status of good gentry, meaning to say, Jacob and his offspring, he
> began by mentioning the kings of Esau and shortened it, in order to
> distinguish him and that he might begin anew with a description of the
> genealogy of Jacob with an explanation and with a detail, and thus do
> they who are the ... by applying them to a part where it lends nothing
> to its purpose, and where they shorten it and abandon it. Afterwards,
> they expand in a chapter that has more to do with its purpose and their
> intended object. Now, in this manner, because its purpose was to clarify
> the genealogy of Shem, he forwarded the matter and says of him: "These
> are the generations of the sons of Noah; Shem, Ḥam, and Japheth" (Gen
> 10:1). Afterwards he says: "These are the generations of Shem" (Gen
> 11:10). In the same way he says: "And these are the generations of Ish-
> mael the son of Abraham" (Gen 25:12), and later he says by way of a
> protracted declaration: "And these are the generations of Isaac, the son
> of Abraham" (Gen 25:19).[19]

---

19. *Rav Shemuel Ben Ḥofni's Commentary on the Pentateuch*, 74.

The Purpose of the Genealogical Lists of Esau and the
Kingdom of Edom in Maimonides's *Guide for the Perplexed*

In the *Guide for the Perplexed* (3:50), Maimonides relates to the narrative parts of the Bible, in harsh critical reaction against those who do not interpret the Torah's words in the correct manner and perhaps even against those who cancel the value of those words altogether. In this context, it is incumbent upon us to mention his harsh statement concerning the verse "And the sister of Loṭan was Timnaʿ" (Gen 36:22), an individual case drawn from the genealogical list of Esau. For Maimonides there is to be found therein a sacred and virtuous status that is no less significant than that of the Ten Commandments:

> There are in the Law portions which include deep wisdom, but have been misunderstood by many persons; they require, therefore, an explanation. I mean the narratives contained in the Law which many consider as being of no use whatever; that is, the list of the various families descended from Noah, with their names and their territories (Gen 10); the sons of Seʿir the Horite (36:20–30); the kings that reigned in Edom (from v. 31); and the like. There is a saying of our Sages (b. Sanh. 99b) that the wicked king Manasseh frequently held disgraceful meetings for the sole purpose of criticizing such passages of the Law. "He held meetings and made blasphemous observations on Scripture, saying, 'Had Moses nothing else to write than, And the sister of Loṭan was Timnaʿ.'" (36:22).[20]

Generally speaking, Maimonides follows in the footsteps of Saʿadia regarding the importance of the narrative parts of the Bible, which, in essence, detail the religious and moral lessons that are to be learned:

> Every narrative in the Law serves a certain purpose in connection with religious teaching. It either helps to establish a principle of faith, or to regulate our actions, and to prevent wrong and injustice among men….
> The accounts of the flood (Gen 6–8) and of the destruction of Sodom and Gomorrah (Gen 19) serve as an illustration of the doctrine that "indeed, there is a reward for the righteous; indeed, He is a God that judges on earth" (Ps 58:12). The narration of the war among the nine kings (Gen 14) shows how, by means of a miracle, Abraham, with a few

---

20. Moses Mamonides, *Guide for the Perplexed*, trans. M. Friedländer (New York: Dover, 1904), 380–81.

undisciplined men, defeated four mighty kings. It illustrates at the same time how Abraham sympathized with his relative (Lot), who had been brought up in the same faith, and how he exposed himself to the dangers of warfare in order to save him. We further learn from this narrative how contented and satisfied Abraham was, thinking little of property, and very much of good deeds; he said, "I will not take from a thread even to a shoe-latchet" (Gen 14:23)....

Of this kind is the enumeration of the stations [of the Israelites in the wilderness] (Num 33). At first sight it appears to be entirely useless; but in order to obviate such a notion Scripture says, "And Moses wrote their goings out according to their journeys by the commandment of the Lord" (Num 33:2). It was indeed most necessary that these should be written. For miracles are only convincing to those who witnessed them; whilst coming generations, who know them only from the account given by others, may consider them as untrue. But miracles cannot continue and last for all generations; it is even inconceivable [that they should be permanent]. Now the greatest of the miracles described in the Law is the stay of the Israelites in the wilderness for forty years, with a daily supply of manna. This wilderness, as described in Scripture, consisted of places "wherein were fiery serpents and scorpions, and drought, where there was no water" (Deut 8:15); places very remote from cultivated land, and naturally not adapted for the habitation of man, "It is no place of seed, or of figs, or of vines, or of pomegranates, neither is there any water to drink" (Num 20:5); "A land that no man passed through, and where no man dwelt" (Jer 2:6). [In reference to the stay of the Israelites in the wilderness], Scripture relates, "Ye have not eaten bread, neither have ye drunk wine or strong drink" (Deut 19:5). All these miracles were wonderful, public, and witnessed by the people. But God knew that in future people might doubt the correctness of the account of these miracles. in the same manner as they doubt the accuracy of other narratives; they might think that the Israelites stayed in the wilderness in a place not far from inhabited land, where it was possible for man to live [in the ordinary way]; that it was like those deserts in which Arabs live at present; or that they dwelt in such places in which they could plow, sow, and reap, or live on some vegetable that was growing there; or that manna came always down in those places as an ordinary natural product; or that there were wells of water in those places. In order to remove all these doubts and to firmly establish the accuracy of the account of these miracles, Scripture enumerates all the stations, so that coming generations may see them, and learn the greatness of the miracle which enabled human beings to live in those places forty years.[21]

---

21. *Guide for the Perplexed*, 381–83.

Still, regarding the genealogical lists of Esau and the kingdom of Edom, Maimonides reveals an innovative approach. Unlike his predecessors, he does not make the matter contingent upon any ideologically-based, religious-moral lessons to be learned, nor on matters relating to good editing practices, but rather on a practical-halakhic approach—namely, the need to bolster the commandment calling out for the destruction of Amalek, without accidentally including all the descendants of Esau and Se'ir:

> The list of the families of Se'ir and their genealogy is given in the Law (Gen 36:20–36), because of one particular commandment. For God distinctly commanded the Israelites concerning Amalek to blot out his name (Deut 25:17–19). Amalek was the son of Eliphas and Timna', the sister of Loṭan (Gen 36:12). The other sons of Esau were not included in this commandment. But Esau was by marriage connected with the Se'rites, as is distinctly stated in Scripture: and Se'rites were therefore his children: he reigned over them; his seed was mixed with the seed of Se'ir, and ultimately all the countries and families of Se'ir were called after the sons of Esau who were the predominant family, and they assumed more particularly the name Amalekites, because these were the strongest in that family. If the genealogy of these families of Se'ir had not been described in full they would all have been killed, contrary to the plain words of the commandment. For this reason, the Se'rite families are fully described, as if to say, the people that live in Se'ir and in the kingdom of Amalek are not all Amalekites: they are the descendants of some other man, and are called Amalekites because the mother of Amalek was of their tribe. The justice of God thus prevented the destruction of an [innocent] people that lived in the midst of another people [doomed to extirpation]; for the decree was only pronounced against the seed of Amalek.[22]

Moreover, from the second part of the chapter, which details the names of the kings of Edom, Maimonides learns an important political lesson and connects it to the biblical command, "You may not set a stranger over you, who is not your brother" (Deut 17:15). According to him, mentioning each king's hometown comes to teach us that these were not the sons of Esau, but rather kings of another nation whom they had set over themselves, and that these kings "meddled with the sons of Esau and subdued them." There is no evidence from the Scriptures to support such claims; however, Maimonides concludes that one must learn a lesson from the

---

22. *Guide for the Perplexed*, 381–82.

deeds of Esau's progeny, and not set a king over the people who comes from another nation:

> The kings that have reigned in the land of Edom are enumerated (Gen 36:51, seq.) on account of the law, "you may not set a stranger over you, which is not your brother" (Deut 17:15). For of these kings none was an Edomite; wherefore each king is described by his native land; one king from this place, another king from that place. Now I think that it was then well known how these kings that reigned in Edom conducted themselves, what they did, and how they humiliated and oppressed the sons of Esau. Thus God reminded the Israelites of the fate of the Edomites, as if saying unto them, Look unto your brothers, the sons of Esau, whose kings were so and so.[23]

Conclusion

On the whole, five reasons are listed by medieval scholars in their discussions on the genealogical lists of Esau and the kingdom of Edom in the biblical section of *Vayishlaḥ*:

1. a moral-religious lesson;
2. a mark of distinction between the people of Israel and the gentiles;
3. good editing practices;
4. a way to impart historical knowledge; and
5. a way to bolster the commandment calling out for the destruction of Amalek.

Nearly all of the scholars whose work has been presented here concur with the first three reasons, which have already been conveyed in the writings of talmudic sages, although not in an abstract, or formulaic, principle. The reason of bolstering the biblical commandment to destroy the Amalekite nation is unique to Maimonides, and perhaps it should be viewed as some kind of humanistic approach. It seems, however, that the more interesting innovations that characterize the spirit of the tenth century in the Judeo-Arabic cultural context in the East are those which take into account editing considerations in what was relayed in the name of Samuel

---

23. *Guide for the Perplexed*, 382.

ben Ḥofni, and the idea of imparting historical knowledge which brings a sense of satisfaction to humans by means of expanding their general knowledge, as described by Saʿadia in his introduction to his commentary on Genesis.

Bibliography

Ben-Shammai, Haggai. *A Leader's Project: Studies in the Philosophical and Exegetical Works on Saadia Gaon* [Hebrew]. Jerusalem: Mosad Bialik, 2015.

Ben Ḥofni, Samuel. *Rav Shemuel Ben Ḥofni's Commentary on the Pentateuch* [Hebrew]. Edited by Aharon Greenbaum. Jerusalem: Mossad Ha-Rav Kook, 1979.

Horowits, Yehoshua. "The Attitude of the Geʾonim to the Aggadah" [Hebrew]. *Maḥanayim* 7 (1994): 122–29.

Mamonides, Moses. *Guide for the Perplexed*. Translated by M. Friedländer. New York: Dover, 1904.

Midrash Tanḥuma. New York: Horev, 1924.

Polliack, Meira. "'Scribe,' 'Redactor' and 'Author': The Multifaceted Concept of the Biblical Narrator (Mudawwin) in Medieval Karaite Exegesis" [Hebrew]. *Teʿudah* 29, *Yad Moshe: Studies in the History of the Jews in Islamic Lands Dedicated to the Memory of Moshe Gil* (2018): 147–76.

Qafiḥ, Yosef, ed. *Beliefs and Opinions* [Hebrew]. New York: Yeshiva University, 1970.

———, ed. *Rav Saadya's Commentary on Psalms* [Hebrew]. New York: American Academy for Jewish Studies, 1966.

Schlossberg, Eliezer. "The Methods of Education According to Rav Saʿadia Gaon." Pages 55–68 in *Streams of Love (Yuvle Ahava), In Loving Memory of Yuval Hayman*. Edited by Yosef Yuval Tobi, Shmuel Glick, and Renée Levine Melammed. Jerusalem: published by the family, 2016.

Schlossberg, Eliezer, and Meira Polliack, eds. *Yefet ben 'Eli's Commentary on Hosea* [Hebrew]. Ramat Gan: Bar-Ilan University, 2009.

Tobi, Yosef. "Saʿadia's Biblical Exegesis and His Poetic Practice." *Hebrew Annual Review* 8 (1984): 241–57.

Zoran, Yair, ed. "Yefet ben 'Eli's Commentary on Obadiah" [Hebrew]. *Ginzei Qedem* 8 (2012): 129–95.

Zucker, Moshe, ed. *Rav Saadya's Commentary on Genesis* [Hebrew]. New York: Jewish Theological Seminary, 1984.

Sa'adia Gaon's Commentary on Exodus 32:1–6: Why Did Aaron Agree to Build the Golden Calf?

Arye Zoref

Introduction

Sa'adia Gaon probably started writing his commentary on the Pentateuch at a later stage of his life and therefore never completed it. In many ways, his commentary on the Pentateuch reveals the insights and experience that Sa'adia had acquired during his life-long work as a biblical commentator. His commentary on the story of the golden calf demonstrates his creativity as a commentator and his spirit of innovation. Sa'adia's innovative commentaries on several biblical texts have stimulated the exegetical discussion over the centuries, but in many cases his suggestions were rejected by later commentators for being overly creative.

The translation of the text below is based on the Judeo-Arabic original according to Yehuda Ratzabi's edition.[1] Biblical quotations are translated according to the New Living Translation (NLT). The words in square brackets are completions and clarifications added by me.

The discussion includes quotations from several commentaries on Exodus in manuscripts:

- New York, Jewish Theological Seminary 8916. F49522 in the Jewish National Library. [David ben Bo'az]
- SP RNL Yevr.-Arab. 1:4531. F58215 in JNL. [Qirqisānī]
- SP IOS B 220. F69212 in JNL. [Yefet ben 'Eli]

---

1. Yehuda Ratzabi, ed. *Saadya: Rav Saadya's Commentary on Exodus* [Hebrew] (Jerusalem: Mosad harav Kook, 2013), 374–75.

+   London, British Library Additions 19657, F8408 in JNL.
    [Ghazal ben Abi Srur]

Translation of Sa'adia's Commentary to Exodus 32:1–6

Some people say, however, and hopefully God is leading me toward the truth, that the right way to understand this issue is this: Aaron complied with the people's demand in order to test the people so that he could distinguish between those of them who belong [to the group of sinners] and those who do not. The people crowded in front of him, as it is said: "They gathered around Aaron"[2] (Exod 32:1), and Aaron knew that some of them belong [to the group of sinners] and stubbornly adhere to their concept, while others do not. This is the same as what happened in the story of Baal of Peor. Some people [just] ate and drank, some people were whoring as well, and others also worshiped idols, as it is said: "While Israel was staying in Shittim, the men began to indulge in sexual immorality with Moabite women, who invited them to the sacrifices to their gods. The people ate the sacrificial meal and bowed down before these gods. So Israel yoked themselves to the Baal of Peor" (Num 25:1–3). The same also happened in the story of Achan, where it is said: "Israel has sinned; they have violated my covenant" (Josh 7:11) [even though only one man—Achan—has sinned]. Aaron could not find any other way to distinguish [between sinners and nonsinners] other than to comply with their demand, and also to build an altar and declare: "Tomorrow will be a festival to the LORD!" (Exod 32:5). This story is similar to the story of Jehu, who wanted to cleanse Israel of Baal's worship, as it is said: "Jehu was acting deceptively in order to destroy the servants of Baal" (2 Kgs 10:19). He could only have done so by encouraging people to worship Baal and by pretending to recognize it [Baal], as it is said: "Then Jehu brought all the people together and said to them, 'Ahab served Baal a little; Jehu will serve him much'" (10:18). He assembled Baal worshipers so that not one of them remained outside, as it is said: "Then he sent word throughout Israel, and all the servants of Baal came; not one stayed away" (10:21), and gave them as presents fancy suits, as it is said: "And Jehu said to the keeper of the wardrobe, 'Bring robes for all the servants of Baal'" (10:22). Jehu ordered to conduct a search and make sure that not one of God's believers is among them, as it is said: "Jehu

---

2. Unless otherwise indicated, all biblical translations are from the NLT.

said to the servants of Baal, 'Look around and see that no one who serves the Lord is here with you—only servants of Baal'" (10:23). He did not kill them until they prayed to Baal as it was customary to pray to him according to their religion, as it is said: "Jehu said, 'Call an assembly in honor of Baal.' So they proclaimed it" (10:20). They even offered sacrifices according to their custom, as it is said: "As soon as Jehu had finished making the burnt offering, he ordered the guards and officers, 'Go in and kill them'" (10:25). God was not angry with him for allowing them to worship Baal and offering sacrifices to him, but, on the contrary, he praised him for that, as we can see at the end of the story, where it is said: "you have done well in accomplishing what is right in my eyes" (10:30). The story of Aaron is no doubt similar to the story of Jehu, and what is said at the end of the story: "Moses saw that the people were running wild" (Exod 32:25) supports the notion that Aaron wanted to test them. If so, if the story of Aaron is similar to the story of Jehu, why was Aaron not praised like Jehu was, but rather we find that his act resulted in [God] being angry at him: "the LORD was angry enough with Aaron to destroy him" (Deut 9:20)? The reason is that Jehu smote them after the sacrifice while Aaron did not, but waited until Moses came down from the mountain, because he believed it to be the best course of action.

Discussion

Aaron's role in the story of the golden calf has been hard to understand for Bible readers all through the ages. How could the prophet Aaron, Moses's brother and the founder of the priestly dynasty, participate in the act of idol worship? Moreover, biblical narrative describes Aaron not only as a participant, but also as the key figure in creating the calf. This story was even more problematic for Jews in Sa'adia's time (tenth century CE) because they were influenced by the Islamic concept of "Infallibility of the Prophets" ('Iṣmat al-Anbiya), which means that prophets cannot commit a sin, at least not a major sin. Can one really consider the building of the calf a minor sin?!

Sa'adia was familiar with two explanations that tried to solve this problem. One is the traditional explanation found in rabbinic literature (Tanḥ. Ki Tisa' 19), according to which Aaron simply feared for his life. This explanation relies on the fact that Hur is mentioned as the leader of the people of Israel in Moses's absence, together with Aaron (Exod 24:14), but is not mentioned in the story of the golden calf. Where did he vanish to? According to the midrashic completion, which has no trace or mention in the biblical text, Hur was murdered by the people who demanded to build the calf, and Aaron was afraid that he would be murdered too, and therefore he complied with their demand and built the calf. Sa'adia rejected this explanation on the ground that Hur's murder is not mentioned anywhere in the Bible. It should be noted that Sa'adia respected rabbinic tradition, but he did not follow it blindly.

A second explanation was that Aaron did not mean to build a calf at all. He intended and started to build something else, but someone intervened in the middle of the building process and turned it into a calf. There are several versions of this explanation. One can be found in the Qur'an, which mentions that a certain Samaritan (Arab. *al-samiri*) built the calf (Q Ta-ha 20:93–87). According to another suggestion, reflected in [relatively late] rabbinic sources (Tanḥ. Ki Tisa' 19), Micah, the creator of Micah's idol (Judg 17:4), is the person who managed to turn Aaron's creation into a calf. A similar type of explanation is found in the work of the Karaite David ben Bo'az, a later contemporary of Sa'adia, who did not pinpoint a specific biblical figure, but rather suggested that it was the artisan who was in charge of the construction who shaped the object into a calf, not Aaron; he argued that this explains Aaron's specific wording, when explaining himself to Moses: "I simply threw it into the fire—and out came this calf!" (Exod 32:24).[3] Sa'adia presents this latter explanation in a manner that deliberately ridicules it and distorts it: "Some people say that this Aaron was not Moses' brother, but some goldsmith whose name was Aaron." Against these options and for his own part, Sa'adia insists that such an act like building the calf could only have been committed by the leader of the people, namely, by Aaron the brother of Moses himself. Sa'adia apparently believed that the people would never have dared to build it and worship it without Aaron's consent and active participation, so there is no point in arguing that the calf was shaped by someone else.

After Sa'adia rejects the existing explanations for Aaron's behavior, he has to come up with an explanation of his own in order to exonerate Aaron. However, he could not exonerate Aaron completely, because Moses (and according to Deut 9:20, also God) had clearly disapproved of Aaron's actions. Therefore, Sa'adia constructs an argument that consists of two parts: in the first part, he explains why Aaron's actions were intended

---

3. MS NY JTS 8916, F49522 in the Jewish National Library, 94b.

for the best; and in the second part, he explains why they were still a sin after all.

In order to demonstrate that Aaron had only good intentions at heart, Sa'adia turns to another biblical story, the story of Jehu and the worshipers of Baal. Jehu had called for a feast in Baal's honor and actually encouraged people to worship Baal by granting gifts and prizes (2 Kgs 10:19–22). He even offered a sacrifice during this feast, which was probably conducted according to customs of idol worshipers. There is no hint in the biblical narrative that Jehu was rebuked by the prophets for this behavior. Are Aaron's actions in building the calf really that different? According to Sa'adia, Jehu's intention was good: he wanted to assemble all Baal's worshippers in one place so they could be distinguished from God's believers and then be killed. Why can we not assume that Aaron's intention was similar? Sa'adia insists that even though the Bible says that "the people of Israel" wanted to build the calf, it does not necessarily mean that *all* the people of Israel supported this action. On the contrary: Sa'adia cites other biblical stories in which the text mentions that "the people have sinned," but the sin was actually committed by a few. Therefore, Aaron's action was intended as a way to distinguish between sinners and nonsinners and was not meant to provoke idol worship among the people.

The second part of Sa'adia's argument is meant to explain why Aaron's actions were still a sin after all. In this part he bases himself on the difference between the two stories, that of Jehu and that of Aaron. Jehu set his troops in motion even before the feast for Baal had begun, and the moment he was sure that only Baal's worshipers were in the hall, he sent his troops in to kill them. Aaron, on the other hand, has done nothing, but let the idol worshipers do as they please. Sa'adia explains that Aaron thought it best to wait until Moses had come down from the mountain. Why? Sa'adia does not mention any reason, because apparently there was no good reason. This was Aaron's sin. It is not a terrible sin, just a misguided tactical decision. Nevertheless, this decision had grave (and unfathomable) consequences, in as much as Aaron could foresee: Israel's camp was ruled by idol worshipers who practiced their rites, without anyone standing in their way.

Is this a convincing explanation for Aaron's behavior? Judging by the response of Sa'adia contemporaries, the answer is no. Qirqisānī and Yefet ben 'Eli, Karaite commentators from the tenth century as well, vehemently rejected Sa'adia's interpretation, and especially the first part of his argument.

Qirqisānī raises two arguments against this interpretation. First, if this was really the reason why Aaron built the calf, why did he not mention this when he tried to justify his actions to Moses (Exod 32:22–24)? Second, Aaron could see with his own eyes who were the people who came to him and demanded that the calf be built, and who were those who did not express this demand. Why did he need to devise tests and experiments?[4]

Yefet too raises two objections against Sa'adia's interpretation. First, there is a big difference between Jehu's actions and Aaron's actions. Jehu indeed declared that he wants to worship Baal, but did not actually worship it himself. Aaron, on the other hand, actually built an idol. Second, according to biblical law, a person who incites other persons to worship idols is condemned to death (Deut 13:7–12). If Aaron could claim that he only built the calf in order to test the people and see who would worship it, why can the inciter not do the same?[5]

The second part of Sa'adia's argument was received much more positively. Both Yefet and David ben Bo'az agreed that Aaron's sin was not the building of the calf. David ben Bo'az claimed that Aaron did not intend to build the calf, and Yefet claimed that Aaron was threatened by the idol worshipers and feared for his life. His sin was that he failed to organize the believers of God and fight the idol worshipers, as Moses did later.[6]

Sa'adia's interpretation of the calf story had better success in Samaritan circles. Ṣadaqa b. Munajja, a Samaritan commentator from the thirteenth century (quoted by Ghazal ben Abi Srur, a Samaritan commentator of the eighteenth century) presented the same arguments about Aaron and the calf that Sa'adia did. Ṣadaqa did not mention the story of Jehu, because the Samaritans sanctify the biblical books of the Pentateuch only; however, other than that his argument is the same. It should be noted, however, that this interpretation met resistance in other Samaritan circles. Ghazal ben Abi Srur, after mentioning Ṣadaqa's opinion, stated simply: "The honorable Ṣadaqa is mistaken on this issue."[7]

All in all, it seems that Sa'adia's contemporaries and later commentators felt that Sa'adia's interpretation was based on theological and apologetical considerations (that is, his will to defend Aaron) and not on a careful and close reading of the biblical text. Moreover, his defense is not even a suit-

---

4. MS SP RNL Yevr.-Arab. 1:4531, F58215 in JNL, 183b.
5. MS SP IOS B 220, F69212 in JNL, 59b-60b.
6. MS NY JTS 8916, F49522 in JNL, 94b; MS SP IOS B 220, F69212 in JNL, 61a.
7. MS Lon BL Add 19657, F8408 in JNl, 78a.

able defense for Aaron. Describing Aaron as caving in to pressure on the part of idol worshipers is bad enough; but describing Aaron as if he were plotting a grand scheme in order to flash out sinners, a plot that ended in nothing more than an orgy of sinful acts, is in many ways worse. Sa'adia's astute medieval readers clearly felt that it is better for Aaron to be blamed for caving under pressure than for intentionally instigating idol worship.

Bibliography

Ben-Shamai, Haggai. "The Tension between Literal Interpretation and Exegetical Freedom." Pages 33–50 in *Scripture and Pluralism: Reading the Bible in the Religiously Plural Worlds of the Middle Ages and Renaissance.* Edited by Thomas J. Heffernan and Thomas E. Burman. Leiden: Brill, 2003.

Berman, Samuel A., ed. *Midrash Tanhuma-Yelammedenu: An English Translation of Genesis and Exodus from the Printed Version.* Hoboken, NJ: Ktav, 1996, 598.

Brody, Robert. *Sa'adiyah Gaon.* Oxford: Litman Library of Jewish Civilization, 2013.

Friedländer, Michael. "Life and Works of Saadia." *JQR* 5 (1893): 177–99.

Malter, Henry. *Saadia Gaon, His Life and Works.* New York: Jewish Publication Society of America, 1929.

Ratzabi, Yehuda, ed. *Saadya: Rav Saadya's Commentary on Exodus* [Hebrew]. Jerusalem: Mosad harav Kook, 2013.

The Entry *g[a]d* in Al-Fāsī's Dictionary *Kitāb Jāmi'* *al-Alfāẓ*: Lexicography, Commentary, and Grammar

Esther Gamliel-Barak

Introduction

At the end of the ninth century CE and during the tenth, several dictionaries were written specifically for the Hebrew words of the Bible, introducing different methods of lexicography. The tenth-century Karaite David ben Abraham Alfāsī, the author of the dictionary *Kitāb Jāmi' al-Alfāẓ*, was innovative in the sphere of lexicography. In this essay I focus on the entry *gd* and show some of his innovations, such as presenting all the meanings of the entry and using many citations from the Bible which are connected to the word entry. Citations have a dual role: on the one hand, they prompt a certain meaning, whereas, on the other hand, they may support a meaning that has been established. Citations are also the basis for exegetical discussions, which are also characteristic of Alfāsī's dictionary work. From Alfāsī's exegetical discussions we can learn about the means by which he elucidated the biblical text. In the entry *gd*, Alfāsī uses two approaches: the context, and comparison to other Semitic languages. In many cases Alfāsī uses grammar as an exegetical tool; but, in this particular entry, he only discusses the change of vowels when using the radical root *gd* as a verb in the future tense. None of the entries in Alfāsī's dictionary are identical, neither in length nor in their extent of representing Alfāsī's semantic and exegetical methods. Each entry depends on the semantic and the exegetical difficulties that arise from the context of the biblical text, so there is no one entry which exactly embodies Alfāsī's semantic and exegetical methods. Nevertheless, the entry *gad* is one of the entries which most closely represents Alfāsī's methods. Below I will introduce Alfāsī's semantic and exegetical methods according to the entry *gd*.

Lexicographical Innovations

One of Alfāsī's lexicographical innovations is the presentation of all the meanings of an entry, including the metaphorical meanings. This is also seen in the entry *gd*. Alfāsī identified the different meanings of the word and decided that the definition will not be perfect without presenting them all to the dictionary user. The main meaning, although important, may not fit certain verses. Alfāsī wanted to give the dictionary user all the information that would help understand each word in every possible context. This method is an innovation: Saʿadia Gaon, in his *Ha-Agron*, usually presents only one common meaning.[1] Judah ibn Quraysh in his *Risāla* sometimes presents more than one meaning; but, unlike Alfāsī, whose purpose was to focus on a word and present all its meanings, ibn Quraysh's purpose was to distinguish between similar words that have different meanings.[2] For him, the meaning of a word as a principle was not a central issue. In Alfāsī's opinion, *gd* is a biradical root which, according to its occurrences in the Bible, has more than one meaning: (1) a horseman; (2) a knot; (3) coriander; (4) a cut or a wound; (5) speech; or (6) plenty of rainfall.

Another prominent characteristic in most of the entries is the expansive use of citations. This is also an innovation of Alfāsī: Saʿadia Gaon does not tend to bring in citations in *Ha-Agron*; and Menaḥem ben Saruq, although he brings in citations, in most cases does it without definitions, in other words, without generalization of meaning from several verses.[3] Citations have a double role: on the one hand, they prompt a certain meaning while, on the other hand, they may support a meaning that has already been established. The use of citations may also hint at Alfāsī's Karaite origin. Like other Karaite scripturalists who upheld the saying attributed to Anan ben David, "Search carefully in the Torah and do not rely on my opinion," Alfāsī's work is individualistic in nature. He introduces his own definitions, directs users to the relevant verses, and thus opens his work to discussion and learning. Obviously, Alfāsī did not intend to cite all the

---

1. See Nehemiah Allony, *The Agron of Rav Saʿadia Gaon: A Critical Edition with Introduction and Commentary* [Hebrew] (Jerusalem: Academy of Hebrew Language, 1969).

2. See Dan Becker, *The Risāla of Judah Ben Quraysh: A Critical Edition* [Hebrew] (Tel Aviv: Tel Aviv University Press, 1984).

3. Angel Sáenz-Badillos, *Menaḥem ben Saruq: Maḥberet* (Granada: Universidad de Granada, 1986).

occurrences of each word but only those which were relevant to other introduced meanings. This claim is strengthened by the fact that, in the second edition of his dictionary, Alfāsī reduced the amount of citations.

Citations are also the basis for exegetical discussions, which are also characteristic of Alfāsī's dictionary work. Alfāsī uses the meaning of the word *gad* as a horseman in Gen 30:11: "And Leah said, 'Good fortune!'[4] so she named him Gad" (Gen 30:11 NRSV). Alfāsī knew of (and introduced later) the other explanation of the word *gad* in this verse, which is "fortune" ("Good fortune has arrived"), but he discusses other verses at length to prove his explanation of *gad* as a horseman. In this discussion, Alfāsī mentions Jacob's blessing to his son Gad, which uses the verb form *yagud* (Gen 49:19) to show that the tribe of Gad will always be the defenders of the other Israelite tribes: they will be (at the front) or at the back against any enemy's attack—"but he shall raid at their heels."[5] Alfāsī also cites Moses's blessing of the Gad tribe ("lives like a lion," Deut 33:20) and Gad's description in the book of Chronicles ("whose faces were like the faces of lions," 1 Chr 12:9) to show that *gad* alludes to brave horsemen. He also uses the fact that the geographical dwelling place of the Gad tribe was Transjordan, which was separated from the dwellings of most of other Israelite tribes, to strengthen the characterization of the tribe of Gad as aggressive and courageous. Alfāsī adds that the Reuben and Manasseh tribes, who also lived in Transjordan, would not have been able to survive without having the tribe of Gad to defend them.

Alfāsī uses the meaning of the root *gd* as "cut" when explaining the word *yitgodad* in the verse, "there shall be no gashing [*yitgodad*], no shaving of the head for them" (Jer 16:6). Alfāsī asks an obvious question regarding this prophecy of Jeremiah: how could Jeremiah have proclaimed that there will be no gashing or shaving as punishment if gashing and shaving is in fact already forbidden in the Torah? Alfāsī's answer to this question is that, after the people of Israel commit their sins and the Lord punishes them by killing their young boys, they will not have the strength to continue committing these sins.

---

4. Gad (someone strong, a horseman) has arrived. All biblical translations are from the NRSV.

5. The NRSV translation is different from Alfāsī's explanation. According to the NRSV here, the tribe of Gad will attack the enemy from behind.

Exegetical Means

From Alfāsī's exegetical discussions we can learn about the means by which he elucidated the biblical text. In the entry *gd*, Alfāsī uses two methods: looking at the context, and comparison with other Semitic languages such as Aramaic.

Using the Context

When using the context, as opposed to when using analogy, verses are not elucidated through comparison with verses anywhere in the Bible, but only with neighboring verses. Alfāsī mentions this method in his introduction to the dictionary, where he notes that sometimes verses may be explained by their context.[6] One of the goals in using this method is to explain difficult words or *hapax legomena* (words that occur only once within the Bible). Yefet ben ʿEli, the greatest Karaite exegete who lived in the tenth century, also uses this method.[7]

To indicate that a particular interpretation is based on the context, Alfāsī uses several Arabic terms. The main ones are *min al-mujāwara* (= "from the vicinity") and *min al-qarīna* (= "from the immediate context"), which is also used with a pronominal suffix, *min iqrānihi lahu*, and rarely *min al-maʿnā tuʾḥaḍ* (= "the meaning is learned from the immediate context").[8] In our text, the expression used is *biqarīnatihi* (= "because of the immediate context").

As was already mentioned, Alfāsī argues that the meaning of the name that Lea gave to her son is "horseman." He also thinks that this meaning fits the verse "who set a table for *gad*" (Isa 65:11), but also introduces another meaning of *gad* as the name of a specific star. According to this explanation, the verse describes a situation of star-worship. Alfāsī notes that this meaning also exists in Arabic and Aramaic, but he prefers the former interpretation, since it reflects the immediate context of the verse (Arab. *biqarīnatihi*). The verse continues: "and fill cups of mixed wine for

---

6. Solomon L. Skoss, *Kitāb Jāmiʿ Al-Alfāẓ (Agron) of David Ben Abraham Al-Fāsī*, 2 vols. (New Haven: Yale University Press, 1936), 1:13, 2:265–69.

7. Yoram Erder, "Yefet b. ʿEli the Karaite on Morality Issues, in the Light of His Commentary on Exodus 3:21–22" [Hebrew], *Sefunot* 7.22 (1999): 313–34.

8. *min al-mujāwara*: Skoss, *Kitāb*, 2:124:38; *min al-qarīna*: Skoss, *Kitāb*, 2:126:82; *min iqrānihi lahu*: Skoss, *Kitāb*, 2:386:31; *min al-maʿnā tuʾḥaḍ*: Skoss, *Kitāb*, 1:106:347.

Destiny."[9] Alfāsī explains these as the vessels and the drink which were prepared for the horsemen.[10]

From Alfāsī's exegetical discussions we learn that he introduced other exegetes' opinions as an important part in the process of determining the actual meaning of the biblical text. Other Karaites in his era did the same without mentioning the name of the exegete they quoted. According to Khan, this practice derived from the will to legitimate an opinion not due to the person who said it, but according to its merit. It may also have been done for pedagogical purposes—to encourage the examination of multiple views and exercise individual judgement.[11]

Comparison with Other Languages

Alfāsī compares Semitic languages as a commentary technique. Comparison to other Semitic languages was used by other lexicographers and exegetes to explain Hebrew or Aramaic words in the Bible, especially rare words or *hapax legomena*. This technique is based on the principle that Hebrew, Arabic, and Aramaic are similar in grammar, lexicon, and aspects of spelling, pronunciation, and meaning. Judah ibn Quraysh indicates that the similarity derives from vicinity and genealogy, that is, the geographical vicinity of the peoples who spoke Hebrew, Arabic, and Aramaic; and the genealogical connection: the patriarchs, Abraham, Isaac, and Jacob, who spoke Hebrew; Yishma'el, Abraham's son, who spoke Arabic; and Terah, Abraham's father, who spoke Aramaic.[12] The comparison to other Semitic languages developed from literary and linguistic circumstances: the existence of Hebrew and Aramaic translations to the Bible, which emphasize the connection between Hebrew, Arabic, and Aramaic; the diglossia among Jews; and the use of Hebrew characters in Arabic writing.[13] In his comprehensive research *Comparative Semitic Phi-*

---

9. The word "destiny" is according to the NRSV translation. In the MT we read: "… for *gad*."

10. The meaning "vessel" for the word *mni* is perhaps derived from a comparison with Aramaic. See the next paragraph. Rashi, RaDak, Metsudat David, and 'Ibn Ezra interpreted the verse as meant to describe star-worship as well.

11. Geoffrey Khan, *The Early Karaite Tradition of Hebrew Grammatical Thought: Including a Critical Edition, Translation and Analysis of the Diqduq of 'bū Ya'qūb Yūsuf ibn Nūḥ on the Hagiographa* (Leiden: Brill, 2000), 17

12. Becker, *The Risāla*, 116–19.

13. David Téné, "Comparison of Languages and Language Knowledge (in the

lology in the Middle Ages from Saadiah Gaon to Ibn Barun (Tenth–Twelfth Centuries), Aaron Maman coins the terms "etymological synonym translation," that is, an equivalent translation that uses the same radical, and "non-etymological synonym translation," that is, an equivalent translation that uses a different radical. Maman also discusses comparisons with or without expressions of comparison in the works of different grammarians from the tenth to the twelfth centuries, and he suggests models for the various practices.[14]

In the *gd* entry, Alfāsī compares Hebrew to Aramaic and adds other meanings to the radical. One is the meaning "to cut," which he derives by comparing it to the meaning of the radical in the verse "Cut [*godu*] down the tree and chop off its branches" (Dan 4:14). The second meaning is "plenty of rainfall," which he derives by comparing a Hebrew word from the Bible to its parallel Aramaic translations (Deut 8:7).

Linguistic Discussions

Apart from the exegetical discussions, the entries occasionally include philosophical discussions but also many philological ones. In many cases Alfāsī uses grammar as an exegetical tool, but not in this particular entry. After Alfāsī introduces the last meaning of the radical *gd*, he adds that there is no difference between the words *yagid* and *yaged*, just as there is no difference between *yagel* and *yagil*; in other words, the difference in the vowels does not change the meaning of the word. It seems that Alfāsī does not want the user of his dictionary to think that the word has additional meanings. Another example of the same kind of comment is seen in Alfāsī's discussion of *yesh ha-yishkhem*.[15]

Appendix: A Translation of Alfāsī's Entry *Gad*

So she [Leah] named him Gad (Gen 30:11 NRSV).

Arabic-Speaking Region in the Tenth and Eleventh Centuries)" [Hebrew], in *Hebrew Language Studies: Presented to Professor Ze'ev Ben Hayyim*, ed. Moshe Bar-Asher et al. (Jerusalem: Magnes, 1983), 237–38, 249, 268.

14. Aaron Maman, "Comparative Semitic Philology in the Middle Ages from Saadiah Gaon to Ibn Barun (Tenth–Twelfth Centuries) [Hebrew] (PhD diss., Hebrew University of Jerusalem, 1985), 29–69.

15. Skoss, *Kitāb*, 1:80:194.

(1) A name derived from [the word] *gedud* as she said, *Ba' Gad*,[16] which means "here comes a horseman." And the meaning of *Gad gedud yegudenu*[17] (Gen 49:19) is that the tribe of Gad will have many squadrons, that is, the Israelite squadron will put Gad's fighters in front of them when they go [to battle] to meet their enemies. And when they come back from war, they [the Israelite squadron] will put them [Gad's horsemen] instead of them [the Israelite squadron]. They [the tribe of Gad] will always interpose between them and the enemy, fearing that the enemy will attack them. Also fearing the robbers at night, as it is written: "but he shall raid at their heels."[18] And you should know that, only because of the Gad tribe, the Reuben tribe and half of the Manasseh tribe dared to live there [in Transjordan]. And this is what the prophet Moses described in his blessing: "Blessed be the enlargement of Gad" (Deut 33:20), [which means] blessed be he who enlarged Gad [who enabled Gad to live in peace without fear], because he lives like a lion, he tears at arm and scalp. "Lives like a lion" is meant to describe his [Gad's] courage to live in the Transjordan, separated from the rest of his people. "Tears at arm" means [tear] the commanders and the soldiers; "and scalp" means the kings. And as he described them in Chronicles, when they devoted themselves to David, blessed be his memory: "From the Gadites there went over to David at the stronghold in the wilderness mighty and experienced warriors, expert with shield and spear, whose faces were like the faces of lions" (1 Chr 12:9). When David saw them, he feared and shook, and therefore he asked them: "If you have come to me in friendship to help me" (12:18). From this word is [what appears in the verse] "who set a table for Gad" (Isa 65:11): those who set a table for the horsemen, those who are willing to make preparations, in other words, the inviters. And others say that *Gad* is the name of a star, as it is said in the Mishnah: *gada tava*.[19] And in Arabic we say: "Someone's *jad*" to mean a star and a fortune. They [the other interpreters] understood [the verse] "who set a table for Gad" (Isa 65:11) as [the verse]: "to make cakes for the queen of heaven" (Jer 7:18). And they interpreted [the phrase] *ba' gad* (Gen 30:11) as if she [Leah] said: "Here comes the

---

16. I prefer to quote the MT here and not the NRSV ("Good fortune!") in order to remain closer to Alfāsī's idea and explanation.

17. As in n. 16. (NRSV: "Gad shall be raided by raiders.")

18. See n. 5.

19. This does not exist in the Mishnah but appears in the Targum Yerushalmi to Gen 30:11. Alfāsī's citations are not always accurate.

fortune," in other words, "Here I am fortunate!" The first [interpretation, a horseman] is more acceptable because of the context: "and fill cups of mixed wine"[20] (Isa 65:11)—that is, the vessels and the drink they prepared for them [the horsemen].

(2) The same [radical] is written in the verse: "They band together against the life of the righteous" (Ps 94:21): they agreed together against the righteous. And the same is: "and formed a single band" (2 Sam 2:25), one knot. In other instances: [as] "a bunch of hyssop" (Exod 12:22), a package of hyssop.

(3) And we have *gad* [with the meaning of], coriander [as in:] "like coriander seed, white" (Exod 16:31), "Now the manna was like coriander seed" (Num 11:7).

(4) And we have [another interpretation of] *gd* as a radical for the meaning of excision, cutting. Also for this meaning is the verse: "you must not lacerate yourselves" (Deut 14:1): do not wound or cut yourselves and do not harm yourselves, as non-Israelites do to themselves [in mourning] for their deceased. Similarly, "as their custom they cut themselves with swords and lances" (1 Kgs 18:28), "and their clothes torn, and their bodies gashed" (Jer 41:5), "on all the hands there are gashes" (Jer 48:37)—all are wounds and scratches. People may ask about the verse: "And no one shall lament for them; there shall be no gashing, no shaving of the head for them" (Jer 16:6), because if it is anyhow forbidden, how could the prophet have said that a time will come when "there shall be no gashing, no shaving of the head for them?" The answer to this is that it is a disgraceful action, for God has forbidden it according to the verse: "You must not lacerate yourselves" (Deut 14:1). But when they did it in disobedience to the Lord and against his command, then the prophet said to them that a time would come, and their beloved young men would die, and then they would not have the ability to carry on with their disobedience. This is as it is said: "Both great and small shall die in the land; they shall not be buried and no one shall lament for them; there shall be no gashing" (Jer 16:6), "No one shall break bread for the mourners ... nor shall anyone give them the cup of consolation" (16:7). In all these descriptions, there is an action which is obligatory, an action which is permitted; and another which is forbidden. From this it is said in Aramaic: "Cut down the tree and chop off its branches" (Dan 4:14): cut it down, demolish the tree. Some say that

---

20. NRSV: "and fill cups of mixed wine for destiny."

is similar to the phrase *hagidu venagidenu* (Jer 20:10), [which means] cut and we will cut him from the earth.[21] But I think that it is more correct to understand it as connected to the meaning of "talking," because of the context: "Perhaps he can be enticed, and we can prevail against him" (Jer 20:10).

(5) And we have *gd* as a radical meaning "talking" as in: "told them" (Jer 36:13), "he told us" (1 Sam 10:16), "it was told to your servants" (Josh 9:24); and all that is inflected from this word has the meaning of "talking." And there is no difference between *yaged* and *yagid*. This is similar to *yagel* (Ps 21:2) and *yagil* (Hab 1:15).[22]

(6) And we have *gd* as a radical to mean "plenty of rainfall," as in: "You water its furrows abundantly, settling its ridges" (Ps 65:10): wet its furrows abundantly, let the rain be poured out on earth. In Aramaic they also name the streams *nagdin demayin* [the Targum Yerushalmi to Isa 44:4]. And [similarly Onkelos] translated "flowing streams" (Deut 8:7) [by the words] *nagda naḥlan demayan*. The same [meaning of the radical is in Dan 7:10]: "A stream of fire issued and flowed out from his presence": falling down.

Bibliography

Allony, Nehemiah. *The Agron of Rav Saʿadia Gaon: A Critical Edition with Introduction and Commentary* [Hebrew]. Jerusalem: Academy of Hebrew Language, 1969.

Becker, Dan. *The Risāla of Judah Ben Quraysh: A Critical Edition* [Hebrew]. Tel Aviv: Tel Aviv University Press, 1984.

Erder, Yoram. "Yefet b. ʿEli the Karaite on Morality Issues, in the Light of His Commentary on Exodus 3:21–22" [Hebrew]. *Sefunot* 7.22 (1999): 313–34.

Khan, Geoffrey. *The Early Karaite Tradition of Hebrew Grammatical Thought: Including a Critical Edition, Translation and Analysis of the Diqduq of ʾbū Yaʿqūb Yūsuf ibn Nūḥ on the Hagiographa*. Leiden: Brill, 2000.

---

21. The NRSV translates: "Denounce him! Let us denounce him! All my close friends..." (Jer 20:10).

22. The NRSV translates *yagel*: "how greatly he exults!" The NRSV translates *yagil*: "so he rejoices and exults."

Maman, Aaron. "Comparative Semitic Philology in the Middle Ages from Saadia Gaon to Ibn Barun (Tenth–Twelfth Centuries)" [Hebrew]. PhD diss., Hebrew University of Jerusalem, 1985.

Sáenz-Badillos, Angel. *Menaḥem ben Saruq. Maḥberet*. Granada: Universidad de Granada, 1986.

Skoss, L. Solomon. *Kitāb Jāmiʿ Al-Alfāẓ (Agron) of David Ben Abraham Al-Fāsī*. 2 vols. New Haven: Yale University Press, 1936–1945.

Téné, David. "Comparison of Languages and Language Knowledge in the Arabic-Speaking Region in the Tenth and Eleventh Centuries" [Hebrew]. Pages 237–87 in *Hebrew Language Studies: Presented to Professor Zeʾev Ben Hayyim*. Edited by Moshe Bar-Asher, Aron Dotan, Gad Zarfati, and David Téné. Jerusalem: Magnes, 1983.

Yefet ben 'Eli on Leviticus 27:30–31
and Deuteronomy 26:12

Yoram Erder

In this essay I present Yefet ben 'Eli's translation and commentary on the theme of the tithe in Lev 27:30–31 and Deut 26:12. I also discuss some of his comments on other related verses such as Deut 14:28–29 and Deut 26:13–15. Yefet's work on these books has come down to us in various manuscripts, from which I chose two early ones. These were kept by the medieval Karaite community of Cairo and, due to the efforts of the famous Crimean Karaite collector Abraham Firkovich, were moved to Russia in the nineteenth century. They are now housed in the Russian National Library in Saint Petersburg (RNL Yevr.-Arab. 1:565. fols. 39a–42b [Leviticus]) and the Russian Institute of Oriental Studies in Moscow (IOS C72, fols. 8a–10a [Deuteronomy]). I will first cite the relevant biblical Hebrew verses, then the JPS (1985) English translation (with slight adaptations so as to follow the Hebrew as closely as possible), verse by verse. Then I provide my English translation of Yefet's Arabic rendering of these verses, followed by my translation of his Arabic commentary on the same verses. Finally, I offer a short discussion of Yefet's exegetical contribution to this complex biblical law. Within my translation of Yefet's commentary, references to Hebrew Bible verses are indicated in ordinary brackets; additions, clarifications, and at times Hebrew terms in transcription are enclosed in square brackets.

Leviticus 27:30–31

וכל־מעשר הארץ מזרע הארץ מפרי העץ ליהוה הוא קדש ליהוה
ואם־גאל יגאל איש ממעשרו חמשיתו יסף עליו

All tithes of the land, whether seed from the ground or fruit from
the tree, are the LORD's; they are holy to the LORD. If anyone wishes
to redeem any of his tithes, he must add one-fifth to them. (JPS)

Every tithe of the land of the seed of the land *and* of the fruit of the
tree is the Lord's: it is holy unto the Lord.[1] And if a man *chooses to*
redeem any of his tithes, he must add what is equal to a fifth.

As to the **Levites**, it [the text/author/editor] did not mention any privilege
they may deserve, except for the **tithe**.[2] For it says about them: "And to
the Levites I hereby give all the tithes in Israel as their share in return for
the services that they perform, the services of the Tent of Meeting" (Num
18:21). He did not mention concerning them anything else, and he did not
mention a **tithe** that might be taken by the **priests** from [the people of]
Israel. It is imperative that every tithe be for the **Levites**, and the Israelites
do not owe them (in other words, the Levites) anything besides it. Within
what is owed to the **Levites** he/it has already mentioned the right of the
sons of Aaron [in other words, the priests] which is a tenth of the **tithe**
(see Num 18:26). For this reason the **tithe** mentioned here [in Leviticus] is
for the **Levites** and not others.

It/he already mentioned in the pericope/chapter/unit/section (Num
18:8) "The LORD spoke further to Aaron: I hereby give you charge of My
gifts, all the sacred donations of the Israelites; I grant them to you and to
your sons as a perquisite" that the ḥerem is for the **priests** [Heb. *kohanim*].
For it is said: "Everything that has been proscribed in Israel shall be yours"
(Num 18:14). The priest also deserves the **first born of the fruit of the
womb** [Heb. *bekhor peter reḥem*], for it is said: "The first issue of the
womb of every being [which they bring unto the LORD]" (Num 18:15). All
these things are for the **priest**, but the **tithe** is for the **Levites**, as already

---

1. The only change Yefet enters in his Arabic rendering of v. 30 is the "and"
between "seed of the land" and "fruit of the tree." Yefet's rendering of v. 31 is more
explanative. I have indicated the changes in italics.

2.The term *tithe* appears in its biblical Hebrew form מעשר (*ma'aser*) throughout
the translation and commentary. Other unique terms such as "priests" (כהנים) or "Levites" (בני לוי) also appear in Hebrew form. I have indicated all these terms in bold script
within my translation in order to emphasize the common use of Hebrew words within
the Judeo-Arabic text of Yefet's commentary. Such usage underscores, in my view, the
linguistic mélange within his work and his usage of Arabic as a Jewish language, not
only in terms of its Hebrew script but also its semantics.

mentioned above. And it is said: "And all the tithe of the land" (Lev 27:30), and immediately afterwards he made clear that he means what grows in it [in the land], and not the land itself, for it may have been possible to understand [otherwise] that a tenth of the land belonged to them. [This is why he then] said, "of the seed of the land, of the fruit of the tree." And his saying, "of the seed of the land," includes all the grains and all the seeds and all the plants and vegetables. And anything of the land's produce—they have a tithe in it, that is, after setting aside what is [designated as] the right of the priests in the **first born** [Heb. *reshit*] and the rights of the **poor** [Heb. *'aniyim*], in respect of the **left-over** portions [Heb. *pe'ah, leqet, shikhechah, 'olelot* and *peret*]. These rights [of the priests and poor] take precedence over the **tithe** of the **Levites**....

He commanded yet another tithe, additional to that of the grain, [that is] wine and oil, which they should bring to the temple. If they come on a pilgrimage to the temple, then they should eat from it. If the pilgrim chooses to stay in Jerusalem for a while, he also can eat from it, as has been explained in the passage: "You shall truly tithe the increase of your seed" (Deut 14:22), and it is said: "You shall eat in the presence of the Lord the tithes of your new grain" (Deut 14:23). He forbade eating it anywhere but in Jerusalem, for it is said: "You may not eat in your settlements of the tithes of your new grain" (Deut 12:17).

The **tithe of the Levite** is tithed from the fruit of the grapes, nuts, sesame seeds, and olives which are without blemish. The **second tithe** [Heb. *ma'aser sheni*, in other words, which they should bring to the temple] is from the wine and oil. Yet he also commanded a **third tithe** [Heb. *ma'aser shelishi*], that is, the **tithe of the poor** [Heb. *ma'aser 'ani*], and he mentioned it in two passages. First: "At the end of three years you shall bring forth all the tithe of your increase" (Deut 14:28); and second: "When you have set aside in full the tenth part of your yield" (Deut 16:12). Yet this latter tithe (for the poor) is from the grains and the seeds alone, and one should not tithe it every year, unlike the other two tithes. It should be tithed once every three years, for it is said: "in the third year, the year of the tithe" (Deut 26:12). Hence, it should be tithed in the third and sixth year of a **six-year** cycle....[3] Now he said here (Lev 27:30) that the tithe is

---

3. In the next few lines, which I summarize here for the sake of brevity, Yefet goes on to explain that the tithe for the poor should be distributed by the owner of the produce to poor members of his household. This tithe is different from the Levites' tithe in two aspects. First, it is only from the grain (and not also from the fruit); and second,

holy [Heb. *qodesh*], and so he said with regard to the **tithe for the poor** [Heb. *ma'aser 'ani*]: "I have cleared out the consecrated portion from the house" (Deut 26:13). And there is no doubt that the **second tithe** is **holy** too, similarly, and that all three tithes are **holy tithes** [Heb. *ma'aserot qodesh*]....[4] We have mentioned here all there is to point out in regard to the matter of the three [types] of tithes [namely, those of the Levites, the priests, and the poor].

Deuteronomy 26:12

כי תכלה לעשר את־כל־מעשר תבואתך בשנה השלישת שנת המעשר
ונתתה ללוי לגר ליתום ולאלמנה ואכלו בשעריך ושבעו:

When you have set aside in full the tenth part of your yield—in the third year, the year of the tithe—and have given it to the Levite, the stranger, the fatherless, and the widow, that they may eat their fill in your settlements. (JPS)

Yefet's translation of this biblical verse is literal, similar to his version of Lev 27:30. The importance of his commentary on it lies, however, in the fact that it includes a systematic excurses on the topic, and survey of the three interpretive methods applied to it, as follows.

Before I commence commenting on this section, let me mention the methods of the scholars concerning it, which are three.

The first method is that of whoever contends that every year one should tithe three **tithes**. The first is the Levite tithe [in accordance with Lev 27:30 and Num 18:21, see above]; the text has taught us that this tithe is eaten by the Levites in all their places of dwelling and that this is their reward, as it is said (Num 18:31). On the second tithe it has been said

---

it is distributed in the home and not in the field/outdoors. From the moment the grain is hoarded in the house, the poor ought to receive from it once in a while. Yefet states that, in biblical times, there were agents responsible for this distribution in cases where grain was kept in large stocks within storage facilities, and that it was forbidden (for regular folk, not within the three mentioned tithe categories) to eat from the tithe. His references include Deut 14:28–29 and Deut 24:13–14.

4. Yefet continues to elaborate, in this passage, the various differences between the three types of tithes, such as who is allowed to eat them and where they can be eaten.

(Deut 14:22), and it/he has instructed, that it should be eaten only in Jeru-salem, nowhere else, as it is said (Deut 12:17–18). The third tithe is this one [in other words, the one described in Deut 26:12]. [He who upholds this method] and contends that three tithes are mentioned herein, is correct; yet, his claim that the **third tithe** should be tithed every year, similarly to the **first and second tithes**, has no proof [in the text], and no apparent explanation to lean on.

The second method claims that there are two tithes, namely, the **first tithe**, which is the **Levite tithe**, and the **second tithe**, which is to be eaten in Jerusalem. They believe that the tithe mentioned here (Deut 26:12) is [not a separate tithe but] related to the leftovers of the second tithe. Those who uphold this method have evidence in what is written in the Torah, as well as logical arguments. The evidence from the Torah includes where it is written: "you shall bring out [Heb. *totsi'*] the full tithe of your yield of that year" (Deut 14:28), and it is not written "tithe tithings" [Heb. *'asor ta'aser*], nor any other phrase like it. They also interpret "the full tithe" (Deut 14:28) as taking out from storage the leftovers of the last two years. They also cite "I have cleared out the consecrated portion from the house" (Deut 26:13) as proof, and claim that [the second tithe] is called **holy** [Heb. *qodesh*], since it is eaten in Jerusalem. As to their logical argumentation, they deduce this from the obligation to eat the **second tithe** during a pil-grimage. The sum of pilgrimage days every year is around fifteen days: the seven days of *matzah* [Passover], the day of *Bikkurim* [Firstfruits], and the seven days of the *sukkah* [Sukkoth], that is, altogether fifteen days. They say, at the most one should add to these fifteen days another five days, alto-gether twenty days. They claim, since the tithe is the tithe from crops, and the crops suffice for twelve months, this is much more than what is eaten in twenty days, and so it is logical that much of these crops still remains [uneaten]. And if there are leftovers, then there is no doubt that we should be told what is to be done with them, and so the Lord instructed to leave out the leftovers of the two years together with those of the third year and to donate them to the poor....[5]

We also have evidence, which we shall mention in its place, that strengthens the **third** method, upheld by most of the scholars, who claim this tithe (Deut 26:12) is the third tithe, yet it should be tithed every three years, once. [And see his commentary on Lev 27:30–31 above].

---

5. Here I have skipped some of the text in the manuscript between 9b and 10a.

Discussion

The main dispute between Karaite and Rabbanite Jews, from the Middle Ages until today, concerns the status of Jewish oral law, especially as reflected in the codified and sanctified compositions of the Mishnah and the Babylonian Talmud. While rabbinic Judaism venerated oral law as a main source for Jewish law, which complements the written Torah (in other words, mainly the Pentateuch, but also the Hebrew Bible in general), the Karaites of the tenth–twelfth centuries completely rejected it, designating it as "a commandment by men learned by rote" (see Isa 29:13; Heb. מצוות אנשים מלמדה). Yefet's discussion on the tithes from agricultural produce[6] reflects well, to my mind, the essential dispute between these two scholarly camps. Their basic disagreement is on the interpretation of the pentateuchal sources that teach about the different tithes. Even within the Karaite camp there was disagreement as to how we must understand these sources, which is not surprising when one considers the elliptical and opaque formulations of the tithe laws preserved in the Pentateuch, leading to further debate and disagreement over every aspect of them. Here I choose to concentrate on the debate concerning the *number* of tithes required according to biblical law, the *years* in which they have to be tithed, their *holiness*, and *what constitutes a tithe*.

The First and Second Tithes

Most of the Karaite thinkers, much like the ancient rabbis, thought the Pentateuch stipulates three types of tithes. A minority among the Karaites contended that there are only two tithes. What both groups accepted was that the first tithe belongs to the Levites, in accordance with Num 18:21–32. There it is mentioned that the Levites are given the tithe in return for their work in God's sanctuary (Heb. *'ohel mo'ed*; v. 21) and that a tenth of the tithe should be given by the Levite to the priest (Heb. *kohen*; vv. 25–28). The ancient rabbis designated this tenth part of the tithe by the Hebrew name *terumat ma'aser* (lit. "a donation from the tithe"). As to the first tithe, Yefet emphasizes in his commentary that the Levite alone is entitled to the full portion of this tithe. We know from rabbinic literature that, in Second Temple times, this tithe was given to the priests and not to the Levites (b.

---

6. Tithes from animals (see Lev 27:32–33).

Yevam. 86a–b; b. Sotah 47b–48a). The Karaites appear to have objected to this change. In respect of the second tithe, both groups among the Karaites agreed, on the basis of Deut 12:17–19 and 14:22–27, that the owner of the tithe is entitled to it, but he should eat it in Jerusalem. If he is far from the city he can sell it for money and then buy his food with this money when in Jerusalem, as stipulated in Deut 14:25–26.

The dispute between the ancient rabbis and the Karaites regarding the first tithe and the second one stems from their different understanding of Lev 27:30–31. While the ancient rabbis claimed it refers to the second tithe, the Karaites claimed it refers to the first tithe, which belongs to the Levites.

The Third Tithe

According to the ancient rabbis (and rabbinic tradition at large), the third tithe was intended for the poor and hence was called in Hebrew *ma'aser 'ani* ("the tithe for the poor"), and it was to be tithed in the third and sixth years of the seven-year reaping cycle known as *shemitah*. The sages stipulated that in the year of this third tithe, there is no second tithe (b. Rosh Hash. 12b). All Karaite groups rejected this understanding. From the expression *shanah shanah*, in other words, "year [after] year/every year" in Deut 14:22, the Karaites learned that the second tithe should be tithed every year. They understood the double mention of "year" in the biblical expression to mean always, every year.[7] Yefet presents two methods prevalent among the Karaites who uphold three types of tithes. The first method is that the third tithe be tithed every year. The second method is that it be tithed in the third year of the cycle. According to Qirqisānī, the Karaites who upheld that the third tithe (for the poor) was to be tithed every year claimed that in practice it should be stored in the homes and actually distributed to the poor in the third year. This they deduced from the wording of Deut 14:28–29: "At the end of three years thou shalt *bring out* (Heb. *totsi'*) all the tithe...."[8] Yefet did not accept this as proof, and he claimed the third tithe was required only every third year of the seven-year

---

7. See Yefet on Deut 12:22 (MS IOS C41 55b): "as to the second tithe—it, too, is compulsory in every year, as it is said here 'year year'..., which means, every year, always, and this is said regarding the second tithe."

8. See Qirqisānī's commentary on Deut 14:28–29 in MS RNL Yevr.-Arab. 1:4531, fol. 48a.

cycle. This year is what Deut 26:12 (see his commentary) calls "the year of tithing": "For the tithes in this year are additional to the two tithes, hence it is called *shenat ha-ma'aser* ["the year of tithing"], due to the addition of this [third] tithe [to the poor]." Yefet claims that this understanding was the more common among the majority of Karaite scholars.[9]

The Karaites who claimed that there are three tithes deduced the third tithe from Deut 14:28–29 and Deut 26:12–15. The ancient rabbis (and rabbinic tradition at large), however, used Deut 14:28–29 and Deut 26:12 as proof texts for the understanding that the tithe for the poor (known as the third tithe) is given once every three years, whereas Deut 26:13–15 they called "the tithe confession" (*viduy ma'aser*), which should be pronounced when the third tithe is completed. This created yet another dispute between the Karaites and rabbinic tradition: while the ancient rabbis considered the third tithe as a nonholy portion (*chol*) (Sifre Num. 122), the Karaites considered it as a holy or sacred portion, calling it *qodesh* (which is the Hebrew word used in Deut 26:13). Yefet also discusses the opinion of the minority among the Karaites who contended that there were only two tithes claimed and that Deut 14:28–29 and Deut 26:12–15 both relate to the second tithe. They interpreted the expression *qodesh* ("sacred portion") in Deut 26:13 as a reference to the second tithe. They also claimed that since Deut 14:28 does not use the (imperative) Hebrew wording *'aser te'aser* ("tithe a tithing"), but rather *totsi'* ("bring forth"), this is not a separate tithe but leftovers from the second tithe which are to be distributed to the poor. Their argument from logic was that since it was only possible to eat the second tithe during the pilgrimage days (which amounted to fifteen days annually), there would be much left over, and so the biblical text had to stipulate what to do with the remainder. The prohibition to eat the second tithe *outside* the days of pilgrimage formed yet another dispute between the Karaites and rabbinic tradition, which does not recognize this prohibition. Yefet dealt with the issue of the abundance of leftovers from the second tithe, in the two-tithe system upheld by some Karaites, by suggesting that the second tithe could have been eaten by its owner if he chose to stay longer in Jerusalem. In his commentary on Deut 26:12, Yefet explains that a longer stay in the city was used for study, in accordance with the ending of Deut 14:23: "You shall consume the tithes of your new grain and wine and oil, and the firstlings of your herds and

---

9. See Yefet's commentary on Deut 26:12 in MS IOS C72 fol. 10b.

flocks, in the presence of the LORD your God, in the place where He will choose to establish His name, so that you may learn to revere the LORD your God forever."

This second tithe, he claimed, was also intended for poor pilgrims, orphans, and widows, as well as for Levites who were able to cover travel to the city yet found it hard to sustain themselves during their stay in Jerusalem, and therefore not much was left over after all.[10]

As we have shown above, there existed much dispute between the Karaites and rabbinic tradition over the tithe laws, and even among the Karaites themselves. This reflects the vibrant interpretive discussions going on in the Islamic milieu, and the growing place and significance of "written Torah"—that is, the scriptural sources (in our case from Leviticus and Deuteronomy), and their specific wording, in defining the "right" interpretation of biblical law.

Bibliography

Baumgarten, Joseph M. "The First and Second Tithes in the Temple Scroll." Pages 5–15 in *Biblical and Related Studies Presented to Samuel Iwry*. Edited by A. Kort and S. Morschauer. Winona Lake, IN: Eisenbrauns, 1985.

Erder, Yoram. "First and Second Tithes in the Temple Scroll and in the Book of Jubilees according to Early Karaite Discourse" [Hebrew]. *Meghillot* 13 (2017): 231–67.

Henskhe, David. "On the History of Exegesis of the Pericopes concerning Tithes: From the Temple Scroll to the Sages" [Hebrew]. *Tarbiz* 72 (2003): 85–111.

Horowitz, Haym Saul, ed. *Sifre Numbers*. Jerusalem: Wahrmann, 1966.

Oppenheimer, A. *The ʿAm ha-Aretz: A Study in the Social History of the Jewish People in the Hellenistic-Roman Period*. Leiden: Brill, 1977.

Weinfeld, Moshe. "The Royal and Sacred Aspects of the Tithes in the Old Testament" [Hebrew]. *Beer-Sheva* 1 (1973): 122–31.

Wilfand, Yael. "From the School of Shammai to Rabbi Yehuda the Patriarch's Student: The Evolution of the Poor Man's Tithe." *Jewish Studies Quarterly* 22 (2015): 36–61.

---

10. See Yefet on Deut 26:12 (MS IOS 72, fols. 9b–10a).

A Prophet Warning Himself:
Yefet ben 'Eli's Dialogical Reading of Numbers 23–24

Sivan Nir

Introduction: Yefet ben 'Eli's Lessened Prognostic Exegesis, as Compared to Daniel al-Qūmisī

The most prominent exegete of the Karaite late medieval golden age, Yefet ben 'Eli (still active in 1005 CE) translated and interpreted the whole of the Hebrew Bible during the last thirty years of his life (960–990 CE).[1] Yefet's exegesis of the Bible demonstrates both typical Karaite approaches to the text, that is, a contextual linguistic approach and a prognostic symbolic approach mostly centered on the prophetic books and the Song of Songs.[2]

---

1. Lawrence Marwick, "The Order of the Books in Yefet's Bible Codex," *JQR* 33 (1943): 448–60. For a comprehensive survey of all of Yefet's published works, see Marzena Zawanowska, "Review of Scholarly Research on Yefet Ben 'Eli and His Works," *Revue des études juives* 173.1–2 (2014): 97–138. Concerning Yefet's exegetical methodology, see Meira Polliack, "Major Trends in Karaite Biblical Exegesis in the Tenth and Eleventh Centuries," in *Karaite Judaism: A Guide to Its History and Literary Sources*, ed. Meira Polliack, Handbuch der Orientalistik 73 (Leiden: Brill, 2003), 389–410; Michael G. Wechsler, *The Arabic Translation and Commentary of Yefet ben 'Eli the Karaite on the Book of Esther*, Karaite Texts and Studies 1 (Leiden: Brill, 2008), 13–40; Meira Polliack and Eliezer Schlossberg, *The Commentary of Yefet ben 'Eli the Karaite on the Book of Hosea* (Ramat Gan: Bar-Ilan University Press, 2009), 41–69; Miriam Goldstein, "'Arabic Composition 101' and the Early Development of Judeao–Arabic Bible Exegesis," *JSS* 55 (2010): 451–58.

2. By *prognostic*, I refer to a nonliteral reading of the Bible with strong eschatological tendencies. The exegete identifies an esoteric message referring to his time and place as the intended recipient of the biblical text in question. Such hermeneutics might be typical of sectarian circles in turmoil, even beyond the Dead Sea Scrolls and the Karaites. For prognostic interpretations as relating to Qumran, see Yoram Erder, *The Karaite Mourners of Zion and the Qumran Scrolls: On the History of an Alternative*

Yefet's predecessor, Daniel al-Qūmisī, identified two independent layers in prophetic biblical accounts, historical and prognostic.[3] In his interpretation of Hos 12:11, al-Qūmisī claims that God created man to receive punishment or reward and so the prophets' prerogative is to warn the Jews of their upcoming punishment for their bad deeds:

> and several aspects to tell and to show to Israel the vengeance of exile and the vengeance of sinners so that they know that [I = God] did not in vain create man and not in vain did I choose Israel but to demand of them as it is writ[ten], "You only have I known of all the families of the earth [and therefore I will punish you for all your iniquities"] (Amos 3:2 NRSV).[4]

Al-Qūmisī understands the words "multiplied visions" (Hos 12:10) as a divine declaration that God endowed certain prophecies with additional meaning, warning different people in different time periods. One such a meaning is a warning for the ancient Israelites, detailing their upcoming punishment should they not repent, whereas the other is a warning to the sinners of the future exile, that is, al-Qūmisī's generation and audience.[5]

Generally speaking, Yefet tones down al-Qūmisī's predictive readings. Throughout Yefet's commentary on Hosea, he stops relying on al-Qūmisī

---

to *Rabbinic Judaism* [Hebrew] (Tel Aviv: Sifriat Hillel Ben-Haim, Kibbutz Meuhad Press, 2004), 116–75, 378–93. For a different view, consult Meira Polliack, "Wherein Lies the Pesher? Re-questioning the Connection between the Medieval Karaite and Qumranic Modes of Biblical Interpretation," *JSIJ* 4 (2005): 181–200; Polliack, "Historicizing Prophetic Literature: Yefet ben 'Eli's Commentary on Hosea and Its Relationship to al-Qumisi's Pitron," in *Pesher Naḥum: Texts and Studies in Jewish History and Literature from Antiquity through the Middle Ages, Presented to Norman (Naḥum) Golb*, ed. Joel L. Kraemer and Michael G. Wechsler, with the participation of Fred Donner, Joshua Holo, and Dennis Pardee, Studies in Ancient Oriental Civilization 66 (Chicago: Oriental Institute of the University of Chicago, 2012), 152–56, 159–63, 175–80.

3. Polliack and Schlossberg, *Hosea*, 18–19. So, Yefet can treat the text as dual-layered, an approach not dissimilar to Jewish medieval exegetes' practice of noting a contextual linguistic interpretation and then a midrashic one, for the same verse.

4. Nehemia Gordon, "Does Scripture Really Only Have One Meaning? A Study of Daniel al-Qumisi's Exegetical Pitron Shneym 'Asar" [Hebrew], *Tarbiz* 76.3–4 (2007): 399.

5. Gordon, "Does Scripture," 399.

exactly when the latter starts to read things symbolically.[6] Yefet views the predictive role of prophecy as mainly educational, and he emphasizes that the continued value of prophecy to Israel in exile was in strengthening the belief of future salvation, more so than in prognostic elements.[7] Thus, Yefet's interpretation of Hos 12:11 (above) is not a reference to the multiple prognostic aspects of prophecy but a discussion about the different subgenres of prophecy.[8] Yefet prefers to discuss the immediate historic context of prophecy, seeing that this literature was foremost created for that specific historical audience.[9]

Accordingly, Yefet views some of Balaam's speeches as prophetic (Num 24:15 onwards; 23:24; 24:6–9) and preforms a kind of prognostic reading of the last speech, as well as identifying historical events from Israel's ancient history in others. However, Yefet's interpretation of Num 23:7 shows that he thought that not all of Balaam's parables contained prognostic information. Instead, some parables were literal and meant to answer the audience's concerns.[10]

Hence, the following English translation of a selection of Yefet's notes on Num 23–24 will highlight how Yefet preserves the two-tiered structure of a prognostic reading, while interpreting what he understands as the literal parts of Balaam's speeches.[11] Instead of interpreting the speeches as meant for

---

6. Polliack and Schlossberg, *Hosea*, 77–78.

7. Polliack and Schlossberg, *Hosea*, 16. Yefet preferred to preform actualizing readings of books and texts displaying messianic contents or an allegoric bent, such as in his commentaries on Daniel and the Song of Songs. For instance, comparing Yefet and al-Qūmisī on Hos 1–3 shows that while the latter devotes more than half of his comments to prognostic readings, Yefet does so only for several verses. Cf. Polliack and Schlossberg, *Hosea*, 20.

8. Polliack and Schlossberg, *Hosea*, 46–47.

9. Polliack and Schlossberg, *Hosea*, 22–23.

10. Erder, *Mourners of Zion*, 343. Al-Qūmisī does insist that a prognostic sense of a verse must always be derived from the literal sense. There is not one example in all of his writings where a symbolic message is based on a literal interpretation different from the one he supplies for that verse. See Gordon, "Does Scripture," 395.

11. The translation is mostly based on A-MS SP RNL Yevr.-Arab. 1:86 (53813), fols. 88–106, which is dated to the eleventh century CE, as well as Tzvi Avni's critical edition and translation into Hebrew of Yefet on Num 23–24, which relies on that manuscript. See Tzvi Avni, "Balaam's Poetic Verses in the Commentary of Yefet ben 'Eli the Karaite" [Hebrew], *Sefunot* 8 [23] (2003): 375–78. Avni also consulted several other manuscripts: MS BL Qr. 2475 Margoliouth 271 (6247), fols. 31–17, which was his first choice for completing lacunas; and other lesser, later manuscripts: MS

their historical audience and Yefet's generation, Yefet chooses to understand them as addressing two historical audiences at once: God spoke through Balaam to all present, but he also addressed Balaam and Balak personally.

The first part of this essay will show how Yefet accomplished his dialogic reading of Num 23–24, and the second part will focus on the hidden divine message to Balaam to convert to Judaism, which went unheeded, and why Yefet chose to understand the text thusly.

The Additional Recipients of Numbers 23–24:
A Prognostic Literal Reading

Verses Answering Other Verses

Yefet notes that certain verses spoken by Balaam are an argument against him and Balak, answering their future or past claims in specific verses. The most contextually apparent of these assertions is that God refuted Balak's hopes that Balaam could curse Israel against his wishes:

> In him saying: "How can I curse" (Num 23:8) there is an argument against Balaam who claimed that he could cause bad luck and good luck to whomever he wished; and when he said, "How can I curse whom God has not cursed?" he denied his own saying and in that there is also an answer to Balak saying, "for I know that whomsoever you bless is blessed" (Num 22:6).[12]

Balaam is referenced separately from the verse's speaker, showing that Yefet views God as refuting Balaam's claims and also answering Balak, who echoed these claims. Numbers 23:8 is an answer to Num 22:6 and probably to Num 23:3, in which Balaam still hopes for a better outcome.

A very similar interpretation is:

> … him [Balaam] saying, "How can I curse" (Num 23:8): God forced him to say to Balak by his own admission: "Balak, know that [with regards to]

IOS B365 (53544), fols. 63–33; MS SP RNL Yevr.-Arab. 1:23 (53809), fols. 18–6; MS SP RNL Yevr.-Arab. 1:171 (53822), fols. 426–405. Additionally, Avni used B-MS BNP 283 (4301), fols. 171–194, which is dated to Jerusalem 1399 CE, according to which I amend the text in a few instances. Square brackets denote a completion by the translator, while round brackets are purely explanatory additions.

12. Avni, "Balaam's Poetic Verses," 381, 422.

you saying to me 'whomsoever you curse is cursed' (Num 22:6) that was not of my doing but of God's doing, not as I used to claim[13] and not like [what] you and any who had heard of me[14] assumed."[15]

Yefet paraphrases Num 23:8, noting that God forced Balaam to refute past claims and give credit to God. However, Yefet also notes an instance wherein the divine message prefigures an answer to another of Balak and Balaam's future attempts to curse Israel:

> and God inspired Balaam that he was forced to say "or number the fourth part of Israel" (Num 23:10), in order to cancel Balak's hope that [he (Balaam)] could curse the part he saw from Bamoth-Baal … him saying "Let me die the death of the upright" (Num 23:10) is of the angel's forcing him to speak and he forced him to speak thus due to two matters, one of which is to rouse Balak's wrath by displaying his (God's?) love for Israel, for he (Balaam) does not wish to be like them (Israel) when he wishes them ill; the second (matter) is him notifying (Balak) that they (Israel) are a people whose end is good, so that Balak and Balaam as well should know that nothing that they wish will not befall [Israel]. And him saying "and let my end be like his!", he is referring so to the world to come. This saying also approves the religion of Israel as the right one and no other, and that is why he wishes that his end will be like the end of Israel.[16]

Yefet emphasizes that Num 23:10 is forced upon Balaam by God, thus treating it as a divine rebuke. First, the inability to count the fourth part is understood as an answer to Balak's request to curse only a part of Israel (Num 23:13), which shows that Balak did not heed this warning. The rest of the verse is propaganda for the religion of Israel voiced by God, since Balaam—who wishes Israel ill—would not desire an end like that for Israel. These claims are also meant to annoy Balak by displaying God's love, which is not what Balak expected. Another point is to emphasize that Israel's fate is

---

13. Simpler form according to B: claimed responsibility for it, *'id'ayahu*. See Joshua Blau, *A Dictionary of Mediaeval Judeo-Arabic Texts* [Hebrew] (Jerusalem: Israel Academy of Sciences and Humanities, 2006), 215.

14. Other versions: "him."

15. Avni, "Balaam's Poetic Verses," 382, 423–24. B: *musūkīn = maskūnīn?*, is likely erroneous, but perhaps influenced by the "naïve" (*miskīn*) who believed Balaam's claims (Blau, *Dictionary*, 303).

16. Avni, "Balaam's Poetic Verses," 384–85, 425–26.

good,[17] meaning that Balaam and Balak should stop their attempts to curse Israel as these attempts will fail and things will only end well for Israel.

Addresses to Balaam or Balak as Addressing Both

Another way for Yefet to find additional messages meant for Balaam or Balak is by understanding certain direct addresses to one of them as addressing them both simultaneously:

> (From Yefet's concentrated interpretation to the second speech) The beginning of his words was "Rise, Balak, and hear" (Num 23:18), "God is not a human being, that he should lie" (Num 23:19), "See, I received a command to bless" (Num 23:20), and these utterances even though he confronted Balak with them, they are actually addressed to them both, for they thought that by moving to the field of Zophim, the situation of Israel will change with the Master of the universe. The utterance "Rise, Balak, and hear" (Num 23:18), there have been said about it two opinions: One [opinion] is that Balak told Balaam, "What has the Lord said?" (Num 23:17), and that was[18] said of his part in a mocking fashion; and the angel made him (Balaam) speak to tell him "Rise Balak" in a fashion of mocking and rebuke, meaning: "rise to stand [on your feet] so that you hear these things, for they are the words of God and so do not make light of them![19] The second [opinion] is that it has been said that he meant by that: "Rise and take leave of these places and return to the situation you were in, as there is no room for you [to have] designs on this people.[20]

Numbers 23:18–20 contains rebuke addressed not only to Balak but also to Balaam,[21] as they both cooperate in the second attempt to curse Israel

---

17. See Abraham Ibn Ezra's comment on the verse, which notes an opinion that Balaam longed truly to end much like Israel in addition to voicing Israel's praise, since he knew he would die by the sword (H. Norman Strickman and Arthur M. Silver, trans., *Ibn Ezra's Commentary on the Pentateuch: Numbers* [New York: Menorah, 1999], 196). Ibn Ezra's cited opinion also assumes that Balaam is talking about two different things at once, Israel and himself. This doubled address he notes is then less sophisticated than Yefet's.

18. Up until this point, the translation is based on MS BL Qr. 2475 Margoliouth 271 (6247), as MS A is stained.

19. Num. Rab. *Balak* 20:20.

20. Avni, "Balaam's Poetic Verses," 392, 430–31.

21. See also Joseph Bekhor Shor on vv. 17–19 in Yehoshafat Nevo, *The Commen-*

without heeding the warnings delivered to them, thus thinking that God would change his mind. Yefet mentions two readings of "Rise, Balak, and hear" (Num 23:18). The first rebuke, for making light of God, is known from the Midrash.[22] The second option might mean that Yefet understands the call to leave as addressed both to Balak and to Balaam, as he notes this passage among those meant for both of them, a category he refers to as "these utterances."

Similarly, Yefet views Num 24:9 not only as a curse on Balaam for his attempt to curse Israel but also, indirectly, as a curse on Balak,[23] who is the instigator of the attempt to curse. This is attested by Balak's anger (Num 24:10) on hearing verse 9:

> Know that this blessing (Num 24:9: "Blessed is everyone who blesses you, and cursed is everyone who curses you"), God gave inspiration to Balaam to say it, to bless Israel, and he [Balaam] was not made happy by it and did not intend[24] to [do] that willingly and so he was not blessed, even if his saying[s] bless [them].[25] This saying had in it a curse on Balak, as he cursed Israel and so he (Balak) got angry this time.[26]

Negative Epithets

Yet another way in which Yefet understands the speeches as admonishing Balaam and Balak is by systematically interpreting the derogatory terms mentioned in the speeches as hinting at their personal idolatrous practices:

> He [Balaam following God's instructions] said: Indeed, I saw him [Israel] from the top of the rocky peaks and beheld him from the hills (based on Num 23:9) and I see him as a people living alone, not like the nations

---

tary of R. Joseph Bekhor Shor on the Torah [Hebrew] (Jerusalem: Mosad HaRav Kook, 2000), 285.

22. See for instance, Tanḥ. Balak 13. In this and all other references to Tanḥuma Balak, I am referring to sections according to the manuscript transcribed by the Historical Dictionary of the Hebrew Academy, as representative of the printed editions, being MS Cambridge University Library, Add. 1212, https://tinyurl.com/SBL6702a.

23. Bekhor Shor, for v. 9, notes that God insinuates that Balak was cursed, similarly to Yefet (Nevo, *Commentary of R. Joseph Bekhor Shor*, 287).

24. According to B: Judeo-Arabic: *qāṣada*; probably an instance of phonetic spelling of the Arabic *qaṣada*. Cf. Blau, *Dictionary*, 548.

25. Cf. Tanḥ. Balak 12.

26. Avni, "Balaam's Poetic Verses," 409, 445.

dwell with each other, as Midian lives with Moab; and he does not mingle with the nations, with their foods, with their feasts and with them in wedlock. And all these matters are included in "living alone." And him saying, "not reckoning itself among the nations," intends that the rest of the nations are considered together, since they return to one source as we shall explain in "their vine comes from the vine-stock of Sodom" (Deut 32:32), and that is in the sense that he who worships another beside God and does not follow in his teachings belongs to [the] one part, which is of a lie; and whoever worships God and follows in his teachings, certainly is [of the part of] truth. That is why he said "and not reckoning itself among the nations!" (Num 23:9). And in these sayings there is also an argument against Balaam and Balak for they are not apart from the nations but of their entity, and [they] all [are going] to destruction and doom and have no merit and no existence as he (Isaiah) said "Even the nations are like a drop from a bucket" et cetera (Isa 40:15); and he said "All the nations are as nothing before him" (Isa 40:17).[27]

Yefet paraphrases Num 23:9. By being apart from the nations in custom and religion, by "living alone," Israel is spared the fate of the nations and is "not reckoning itself among" them. Yefet also finds in this argument a personal message for Balaam and Balak, namely that their fate will be horrendous, as they are part of the nations.[28]

Yefet understands Num 23:21 in a similar fashion to his rendering of Num 23:9, meaning not only as praise for Israel when compared with the nations, but also as a hidden rebuke for Balaam and Balak due to their idolatry. They are the men of "misfortune" and "trouble" mentioned:

... him (Balaam) saying "He has not beheld misfortune in Jacob" (Num 23:21) means that the bad ways like apostasy in God and the worship of another apart from him—that is not found in the house of Israel. This saying teaches three things: the one, a claim against the nations

---

27. Avni, "Balaam's Poetic Verses," 383, 424. See Blau, *Dictionary*, 95–96, for C's use of *majmū'ūn* to describe the nations being in agreement instead of returning to one source. This is also evident in Sa'adia's commentary to Genesis.

28. In the world to come probably, see Yefet on 24:2 below. Al-Qūmisī raises a similar point about Mic 6:5. He claims that Balaam was forced to pronounce the fact that all the gentiles are sinful, as he was used by God as a mouthpiece to demonstrate God's and Israel's glory. See Isaac D. B. Markon, *Daniel Al-Qumisi, Pitron Shneym 'Asar (Commentary on the Twelve Prophets)* [Hebrew] (Jerusalem: Mekitzei Nirdamim, 1958), 46–47.

apart from them (from Israel), whose religious ways are misfortune and trouble (based on Num 23:21); and Balaam and Balak are men of misfortune and trouble and the argument is against them both.[29]

Furthermore, Num 23:23 similarly understands the negative epitaph "enchantment," which is not among Israel, as referring to Balaam's wrongful practices of divinations and omens,[30] which are attested elsewhere in the text:

> Afterwards he said, "Surely there is no enchantment among Jacob" (Num 23:23), which teaches that like there are no misfortune and trouble (Num 23:21), so there is no use of enchantment and divination among them. This is also an argument against Balaam who was a diviner as he said "the Israelites also put to the sword Balaam son of Beor, who practiced divination" (Josh 13:22) and would look for omens as he said "so he did not go, as at other times, to look for omens" (Num 24:1) and he (God) gave divination and omens the same rank as that of idolatry, for all of these are abhorrent to the Lord.[31]

The Unheeded Call to Repent

A Call to Convert

In his introduction to Hosea and prophecy at large, Yefet notes that admonishing is one of the major functions of biblical prophecy.[32] It is unsurprising, then, that having established Balaam and Balak as recipients of an additional divine message mostly noting their inequities, Yefet also identifies in the same text a call for Balaam to repent, which Balaam ignores. This strand appears in all of the addresses to Balaam and Balak we have seen above, thus unifying them.

> Num 23:14: So he took him to the field of Zophim, to the top of Pisgah. He built seven altars, and offered a bull and a ram on each altar. And

---

29. Avni, "Balaam's Poetic Verses," 393, 432.

30. Rashbam on Num 23:23 also understands the mention of enchantment and divination as hinting at Balaam and Balak but paraphrased as Balaam's willing message. See Martin L. Lockshin, trans., *Rashbam's Commentary on Leviticus and Numbers: An Annotated Translation*, BJS 330 (Providence: Brown University Press, 2001), 274.

31. Avni, "Balaam's Poetic Verses," 394–95, 434.

32. Polliack and Schlossberg, *Hosea*, 15, 141, 260.

he took him to the field of Zophim, to the top of Pisgah. And he built seven altars, and offered a bull and a ram on each altar. [This] teaches that Balaam went with him [Balak] because he longed [to do them (Israel) harm], as Balak longed; and also because he wanted to answer Balak's need and thus show him that he wished to do that if he could succeed.... him [the text/narrator] saying, "He built seven altars" (Num 23:14), teaches that Balaam continued as was his habit, with building the alters and offering the sacrifices, since the angel[33] did not deter him from that when he told him (the angel), "I have arranged the seven altars" (Num 23:4). Additionally, Balaam did not dwell on him saying "Let me die the death of the upright" (Num 23:10), for then he would have abandoned his [evil] way. All these things testify that he was continuing in his evil way while knowing that he is sinning. Woe to whoever respects Balaam's situation, while these verses make clear his sin and his evil and insolence.[34]

Had Balaam listened to God (Num 23:10), he should have ceased trying to curse Israel and wishing for the "death of the upright." Instead, Balaam longed to curse Israel and continued to set up altars, while knowing that he was continuing to sin against God. How precisely does Yefet think Balaam should have repented? By converting to Judaism:

24:2: Balaam looked up and saw Israel camping tribe by tribe. Then the spirit of God came upon him. Balaam looked up and saw Israel camping tribe by tribe. Then a divine spirit[35] came upon him [Balaam]. He explained that the tribes of Israel were dwelling in the desert and Balaam saw them. Him (the text/narrator) saying, "Then a divine spirit came upon him," intends that at that time, when he did not go in search of omens and the angel did not speak to him and all he [Balaam] said was divinely inspired, to teach that when he was going in search of omens the angel met him with a drawn sword (based on Num 22:23). And when he turned to the desert to look on their situation, a divine spirit came upon him and God did this to him, in order to change his mind, to leave his worthless religious way and to return to the religion of Israel in the

---

33. Yefet systemically changes "God" to "angel" in God's dealings with Balaam up to 24:2. This change is in line with Yefet's tendency to alter biblical anthropomorphisms, at times. See Marzena Zawanowska, "In the Border-Land of Literalism: Interpretative Scripture Alterations in Medieval Karaite Translations of the Bible into Arabic." *IHIW* 1 (2013): 179–80.

34. Avni, "Balaam's Poetic Verses," 387, 427–28.

35. Avni, "Balaam's Poetic Verses," 438 n. 446.

same manner he [God] did with Nebuchadnezzar, for Balaam and Nebuchadnezzar witnessed[36] the wonders of the Lord and his signs[37] and acknowledged that and admitted [the truth?] of his religion and did not leave their religious way and left the world being odious,[38] and there is no doubt that they shall be punished.[39]

At the start of Num 24, Balaam does not try to divine or to curse Israel, so he was directly inspired by God and not an angel. "God did this to him" as a great favor, meant to cause Balaam to convert. This is probably due to the actual experience of the divine.[40] Balaam's experience should be considered together with Yefet's conception of degrees of prophecy. Balaam's medium of revelation as described seems to be limited to sound and so might be superior to that of Abraham and similar to the high prophetic degree, which Yefet bestows on Samuel. Hence, Balaam should have converted when given such an undeserved honor.[41] Nevertheless Balaam, like Nebuchadnezzar, refuses to convert and thus shall be punished, possibly in accordance with his own warning about the fate of the nations (Yefet on Num 23:9).

---

36. Rendered according to B as a plural.

37. David S. Margoliouth, *A Commentary on the Book of Daniel by Jephet ibn Ali the Karaite* (London: Oxford University Press, 1889), 20. Thus, Nebuchadnezzar in his letters came to note God's signs and wonders: "Shewing that he believed in them, and did not reject them as the philosophers do."

38. A: "condemned." Here according to B and others, *madmūmīn*, as it has a correlate in Yefet's commentary to Daniel (Blau, *Dictionary*, 220).

39. B and others reflect a more difficult form, *mu'aqābīn* instead of *mu'āqabīn*, perhaps *ma'ikābīn*, "lowered," as a metonym of being spidery, but unlikely. See Edward W. Lane, *An Arabic-English Lexicon* (Beirut: Librairie du Liban, 1968), 2119, 2177. For the entire translation, see Avni, "Balaam's Poetic Verses," 400, 438.

40. Alternatively, God was trying to educate Balaam that cooperating with him has a beneficial outcome, as demonstrated by the removal of the forceful angel; but Balaam did not learn. See Avni, "Balaam's Poetic Verses," 376–77.

41. For a detailed discussion of Yefet's list of prophetic degrees, see Daniel J. Lasker, "The Prophecy of Abraham in Karaite Thought" [Hebrew], in *Jerusalem Studies in Jewish Thought: Joseph Baruch Sermoneta Memorial Volume*, vol. 15 of *From Rome to Jerusalem*, ed. A. Ravitzky (Jerusalem: Hebrew University of Jerusalem, 1998), 104–5. For a similar claim that in the Midrash Balaam was honored with prophecy not for his sake, see Tanḥ. Balak 1. For the possibility that a certain layer in the Tanḥuma Balak might have been influenced by Karaites or influenced them, see Israel Knohl, "The Acceptance of Sacrifices from Gentiles" [Hebrew], *Tarbiz* 48.3–4 (1979): 343–45.

Comparison with Nebuchadnezzar and Confessing Faith

While Yefet's assumption that Balaam should have converted might seem strange, it is rooted in his theological worldview, as Balaam was forced to acknowledge God's supremacy by confessing God's nature. This confession is the prime characteristic of gentile conversion at the end of days. According to Yefet's interpretation to Joel 3:5, at the end of days there shall remain in the world only Jews who call the name of the Lord. Among those Jews will probably be converted gentiles.[42] This fact is made more apparent in Yefet's comments on the Psalms. In his interpretation of Ps 53, Yefet notes that the remnants of Ishmael will enter the religion of Israel willingly at the end times.[43]

More importantly, in his interpretation of Ps 139, Yefet similarly notes that Muslims that will survive the judgment of the end of days would be those closest to admitting God's unity, especially the *Muʿtazilites*.[44] Hence, Balaam comes close to being as such a Muslim by having voiced God's nature (Num 23:19, for instance), and so should have naturally converted.

The comparison with Nebuchadnezzar strengthens this conclusion, as it hints at the genuine character of Balaam's admission of the divine. In Yefet's comments on Dan 2, Nebuchadnezzar undergoes a kind of conversion, resulting in his recognizing God as the God of gods.[45] Yefet also suggests that Nebuchadnezzar's continued worship of idols in subsequent narratives could be the result of political necessity: "if he proclaimed to the world that he adopted the religion of the Jews, their laws would be incumbent on him, and he would fall."[46]

Moreover, Yefet appreciates the candor of Nebuchadnezzar's conversion, even in spite of the idol worshiping in Dan 3. He, like the Israelites

---

42. Erder, *Mourners of Zion*, 412–14. The pseudo-Qūmisīan sermon might also reflect a more missionary approach to gentiles. See Leon Nemoy, "The Pseudo-Qūmisīan Sermon to the Karaites," *PAAJR* 43 (1976): 86. The author of the sermon notes that it is forbidden to say that gentile and Israel are alike in respect to all things. However, it is also forbidden to make distinctions between gentile and Israelite except where God alone has made such.

43. Yoram Erder, "The Attitude of the Karaite, Yefet ben Eli, to Islam in Light of His Interpretation of Psalms 14 and 53" [Hebrew], *Michael: On the History of the Jews in the Diaspora* 1 (1997): 47 and n. 95 there.

44. Erder, "The Attitude of the Karaite."

45. Margoliouth, *Daniel*, 15.

46. Margoliouth, *Daniel*, 21, for Yefet on Dan 4:5–6.

in the desert, could rationalize away the miracles that he had seen and abdicate a faith genuinely gained.[47] According to Yefet, Nebuchadnezzar admits that God was righteous in dealing with him. Daniel had warned him to no avail, until Nebuchadnezzar was punished for his abandoned faith by being turned into a beast.[48] Similarly, Balaam truthfully admitted God's power and righteousness (Yefet on Num 23:10, 18), but neither converted nor repented of his sorcery.

Yefet's disappointment with Balaam as "evil" merits further explanation, as he does not have ample narratives of repentance, such as Nebuchadnezzar's. However, according to Yefet's commentary on Num 20, a prophet cannot not err in relaying his divine message, although this may happen in other things between himself and God.[49] Hence, while Balaam is forced to voice God's exact message, God still needs to convince him to convert. Furthermore, Yefet held the unique position that God chose as prophets only people that would feel obliged, as his representatives, to be truthful to his intentions.[50] Yefet attributes a special role to the prophet's own psyche and choice. Hence, while Balaam was acting under duress, Yefet probably thought that Balaam had the potential to act willingly, else God would not have chosen to use him. However, this one prophet did not heed the warnings of his own prophecy.

Conclusions: A Literal, Contextual, Prognostic Reading

We have seen how Yefet's treatment of Balaam's poetic verses is unique in that Yefet understands them systematically as addressing both Balak and Balaam, while being spoken by the latter. I have argued that Yefet was inspired to this dual-audience interpretation by being familiar with and adept in prognostic readings, while understanding the verses as literal but divine. As literal parables, they are meant for a historical audience; but as divine, they might have an additional audience. Thus, Yefet reapplied the Qūmisīan model unto two historical audiences.

Having treated the parables as a kind of prophecy, Yefet was shown to have seen in the scattered addresses to Balaam a connecting missionary

---

47. Margoliouth, *Daniel*, 19.

48. Margoliouth, *Daniel*, 24.

49. Moshe Zucker. "The Problem of 'Iṣma—Prophetic Immunity to Sin and Error in Islamic and Jewish Literatures" [Hebrew], *Tarbiz* 35.2 (1965): 164–65.

50. Zucker, "Problem of 'Iṣma," 164–65.

strand, calling him to convert to Judaism. This emphasis on conversion was understood in light of Yefet's emphasis upon Balaam's genuine prophetic experience and genuine confession of faith, as hinted at by his comparison with Nebuchadnezzar.

It is my hope that further study of Yefet's corpus of exegesis of non-prophetic texts will produce similar examples of Yefet's highlighting the dialogic potential of biblical verses as an expansion of his understanding of biblical allusion.[51] For now I will point to Yefet's treatment of dialogue in biblical prose as the closest equivalent.[52]

Bibliography

Avni, Tzvi. "Balaam's Poetic Verses in the Commentary of Yefet ben ʿEli the Karaite" [Hebrew]. *Sefunot* 8 (2003): 371–428.

Blau, Joshua. *A Dictionary of Mediaeval Judeo-Arabic Texts* [Hebrew]. Jerusalem: Israel Academy of Sciences and Humanities, 2006.

Erder, Yoram. "The Attitude of the Karaite, Yefet ben Eli, to Islam in Light of His Interpretation of Psalms 14 and 53" [Hebrew]. *Michael: On the History of the Jews in the Diaspora* 1 (1997): 29–49.

———. *The Karaite Mourners of Zion and the Qumran Scrolls: On the History of an Alternative to Rabbinic Judaism* [Hebrew]. Tel Aviv: Sifriat Hillel Ben-Haim; Kibbutz Meuhad Press, 2004.

Goldstein, Miriam. "'Arabic Composition 101' and the Early Development of Judeao-Arabic Bible Exegesis." *JSS* 55 (2010): 451–78.

Gordon, Nehemia. "Does Scripture Really Only Have One Meaning? A Study of Daniel al-Qumisi's Exegetical Pitron Shneym ʿAsar" [Hebrew]. *Tarbiz* 76.3–4 (2007): 385–414.

Knohl, Israel. "The Acceptance of Sacrifices from Gentiles" [Hebrew]. *Tarbiz* 48.3–4 (1979): 341–45.

Lane, Edward W. *An Arabic-English Lexicon*. Beirut: Librairie du Liban, 1968.

---

51. Polliack, "Historicizing Prophetic Literature," 168–74.

52. Wherein Yefet highlights how certain verses are answers to others. See, for example, his treatment of Exod 3, where he emphasizes the dialogue between Moses and God (Zucker, "Problem of Işma," 157); or Naomi's manipulation of her daughters-in-law in Ruth 1 (Sivan Nir, "The Portrait of Ruth in Medieval Jewish Exegesis" [Hebrew] [Master's thesis, Tel Aviv University, 2013], 43–45).

Lasker, Daniel J. "The Prophecy of Abraham in Karaite Thought" [Hebrew]. Pages 103–11 in *Jerusalem Studies in Jewish Thought: Joseph Baruch Sermoneta Memorial Volume*. Vol. 15 of *From Rome to Jerusalem*. Edited by A. Ravitzky. Jerusalem: Hebrew University of Jerusalem, 1998.

Lockshin, Martin L., trans. *Rashbam's Commentary on Leviticus and Numbers: An Annotated Translation*. BJS 330. Providence: Brown University Press, 2001.

Margoliouth, David S. *A Commentary on the Book of Daniel by Jephet ibn Ali the Karaite*. London: Oxford University Press, 1889.

Markon, Isaac D. B., ed. *Daniel Al-Qumisi, Pitron Shneym 'Asar (Commentary on the Twelve Prophets)* [Hebrew]. Jerusalem: Mekitzei Nirdamim, 1958.

Marwick, Lawrence. "The Order of the Books in Yefet's Bible Codex." *JQR* 33 (1943): 445–60.

Nemoy, Leon. "The Pseudo-Qūmisīan Sermon to the Karaites." *PAAJR* 43 (1976): 49–105.

Nevo, Yehoshafat. *The Commentary of R. Joseph Bekhor Shor on the Torah* [Hebrew]. Jerusalem: Mosad HaRav Kook, 2000.

Nir, Sivan. "The Portrait of Ruth in Medieval Jewish Exegesis" [Hebrew]. Master's thesis, Tel Aviv University, 2013.

Polliack, Meira. "Historicizing Prophetic Literature: Yefet ben 'Eli's Commentary on Hosea and Its Relationship to al-Qumisi's Pitron" [Hebrew]. Pages 149–86 in *Pesher Naḥum: Texts and Studies in Jewish History and Literature from Antiquity through the Middle Ages, Presented to Norman (Naḥum) Golb*. Edited by Joel L. Kraemer and Michael G. Wechsler, with the participation of Fred Donner, Joshua Holo, and Dennis Pardee. Studies in Ancient Oriental Civilization 66. Chicago: Oriental Institute of the University of Chicago, 2012

———. "Major Trends in Karaite Biblical Exegesis in the Tenth and Eleventh Centuries." Pages 363–413 in *Karaite Judaism: A Guide to Its History and Literary Sources*. Edited by Meira Polliack. Handbuch der Orientalistik 73. Leiden: Brill, 2003.

———. "Wherein Lies the Pesher? Re-questioning the Connection between the Medieval Karaite and Qumranic Modes of Biblical Interpretation." *JSIJ* 4 (2005): 151–200.

Polliack, Meira, and Eliezer Schlossberg. *Commentary of Yefet ben 'Eli the Karaite on the Book of Hosea* [Hebrew]. Ramat Gan: Bar-Ilan University Press, 2009.

Strickman, H. Norman, and Arthur M. Silver, trans. *Ibn Ezra's Commentary on the Pentateuch: Numbers*. New York: Menorah, 1999.

Wechsler, Michael G. *The Arabic Translation and Commentary of Yefet ben ʿEli the Karaite on the Book of Esther*. Karaite Texts and Studies 1. Leiden: Brill, 2008.

Zawanowska, Marzena. "In the Border-Land of Literalism: Interpretative Scripture Alterations in Medieval Karaite Translations of the Bible into Arabic." *IHIW* 1 (2013): 179–202.

———. "Review of Scholarly Research on Yefet Ben ʿEli and His Works." *Revue des études juives* 173.1–2 (2014): 97–138.

Zucker, Moshe. "The Problem of ʿIṣma—Prophetic Immunity to Sin and Error in Islamic and Jewish Literatures" [Hebrew]. *Tarbiz* 35.2 (1965): 149–73.

On the Former and Latter Prophets

Yefet ben 'Eli on the Book of Joshua: A Selection

(Preface; 1:1; 1:8; 4:9; 6:3–5; 6:15; 9:27; 10:12–14; 23)

James T. Robinson

Yefet's commentary on Joshua is possibly the earliest commentary written on the book during the Middle Ages, and it is a rare specimen in Judeo-Arabic. There is evidence of notes on Joshua by Yefet's son Levi and discussion of verses from Joshua in nonexegetical books, such as Ya'qūb al-Qirqisānī's theological work *Kitāb al-Anwār* (*Book of Lights*) and David ben Abraham al-Fāsī's lexical work *Kitāb al-Alfāẓ*.[1] The next full Judeo-Arabic commentary I know of is not until the thirteenth century (by Tanḥum ben Joseph ha-Yerushalmi). Despite this lack of systematic treatment of the work, however, Yefet does not have a hard time finding sources of inspiration. The commentary on Joshua—as his other commentaries— is filled with references to earlier positions held by *'ulama*, Yefet's standard term for the rabbinic sages, and unidentified *mufassirun*, Yefet's standard term for other exegetes, usually Karaite.

Yefet's commentary on Joshua includes a short Hebrew exordium praising the Lord, followed by his Arabic translation of the verses, together with extended commentary. One of the most interesting things about the translation is the strong tendency to Arabize biblical place names, which has a double effect—decoding places from antiquity, on the one hand; and making current the ancient places in relation to the contemporary world the Karaites encountered in tenth-century Palestine. The commentary itself has many of the same features and tendencies found in Yefet's other commentaries: he surveys the opinions of others, as noted; he provides explanations of words in context; and he puts the emphasis on meaning.

---

1. See Esther Gamliel-Barak's essay in this volume, 129–38.

In Joshua the meaning comes out mainly through a very sensitive elaboration of the complicated narrative development of the book, filling in when necessary and expanding to complete the story.

The texts singled out below illustrate Yefet's rich treatment of Joshua from multiple perspectives. When commenting on Josh 1:1, we see his attempt to completely Arabize the story: Moses is presented as *Rasul 'Allah* (Arab. "God's messenger," referring in Islamic Arabic to the prophet Muhammad), and Joshua as his *Khalifa* (Arab. for Muhammad's successor) who rules the Israelite *'Ummah* (Arab. "nation"), based on his knowledge of Moses's (Musa's) *sira* (Arab. "way") as passed onto him. When commenting on Josh 1:8, Yefet continues and expands the use of this verse as a motto in Karaite ideology: one should meditate only on written law to the exclusion of all else, especially the oral law. The commentary on Josh 4:9 picks up on an apocalyptic theme, apparently from rabbinic sources, that the twelve stones represent a sign of the time to come, while at Josh 6:3–5 and 6:15 Yefet dismisses a polemical theme, found already in early Christian sources, that the seven circumambulations around Jericho on the seventh day took place on Shabbat. Yefet is at his best when explaining the logic of scriptural narrative, which comes out with special nuance in his treatment of the treaty with the Gibeonites in Josh 9:27. Yefet's explanation of the sun standing still at Gibeon shows his familiarity with contemporary astronomy, despite his overt criticism of studying the sciences. The last example given here is the entire commentary on one chapter in Joshua, chapter 23, giving a sense of how the commentary develops over several verses. In this case, Joshua's deathbed exhortation develops around the common theological *topos* of divine "promise and threat," one of the principle categories in *mu'tazilite* thought.

In the following, each biblical text is given in the JPS (1985) English translation, in italics, modified if necessary. It is followed by my translation into English, based on my recently published edition,[2] of Yefet's Arabic translation of the verse (in bold) and then commentary on the verse or a sequence of verses. Arabic terms used by Yefet in his commentary are given in the translation within square brackets, wherever deemed necessary, and so are clarifying additions. Where Yefet cites Hebrew words or phrases in his commentary, they are reproduced here in translation. When

---

2. James T. Robinson, *The Arabic Translation and Commentary of Yefet ben 'Eli the Karaite on the Book of Joshua* (Leiden: Brill, 2014).

a direct reference to the Hebrew word/term is needed, it is reproduced in a simple transliteration.

Exordium

In the name of the God of Israel, living and existing eternally and forever and ever, the faithful God, who keeps the covenant and grace with those who love him and keep his command- ments, and nothing has fallen from all his good message which he revealed through the hand of Moses his servant. May he and his name be blessed.[3]

Joshua 1:1

After the death of Moses the servant of the Lord, the Lord said to Joshua son of Nun, Moses' attendant.

After the death of Musa, Allah's servant, Allah spoke to Joshua the son of Nun, Musa's minister, saying,

His saying "after the death of Moses" has several meanings. One is that Allah had not chosen who would succeed Moses in the category of mes- sengerhood [Arab. *risāla*] during his lifetime, for he was the first of the prophets of the 'Ummah, and no one would succeed him during his life- time. The second is that Allah would not leave his 'Ummah without a leader to govern it, so when Moses, peace be with him, passed away, he set up someone else in his place. The third is that, a month or so after his [Moses's] departure, Allah commanded Joshua to cross the Jordan into the land, this because Allah had given judgment with respect to Musa that he not enter the land, thus so long as he remained alive it was not possible for Israel to violate this, yet when he had passed away he commanded them to cross over. When he says "Moses' attendant"—this has two meanings. The first is that Allah Most High established for them a student of the messenger [*al-rasūl*], peace be with him, that knew his way [*sira*] with them and was attached to him, as he says: "He laid his hands upon him" (Num 27:23). The second is that Allah chose him as his disciple and he

---

3. Originally written by Yefet in Hebrew.

became his *khalifa*, for so was his station [*manzila*] in Allah's view. Do you not see that after his saying, peace be with him: "Let the LORD, Source of the breath of all flesh, appoint someone" (Num 27:16), he added: "Single out Joshua son of Nun" (Num 27:18). Thus did Allah satisfy his promise [*wa'ad*] he had given to Musa.

Joshua 1:8

Let not this Book of the Torah cease from your lips, but recite it day and night, so that you may observe faithfully all that is written in it. Only then will you prosper in your undertakings and only then will you be successful.

The book of this law [Arab. *shari'ah*] shall not depart from your mouth; but you shall meditate upon it day and night, so that you may observe to do according to all that is written in it; for then you shall make your ways prosperous, and then you shall have right guidance.

He made it a requirement that one not refrain from taking guidance in reading Sefer Torah, and since it is not possible to read it all in one day, he made it necessary that one read every day, whatever is possible. He says: "observe faithfully all that is written in it"—this points to the fact that the precepts [Arab. *farā'iḍ*] are in textual form, written down, and if one were to do what is written one has done the will of Allah in a perfect sense; were what is written only part of the Will, one would not be worthy of what he promised him. When he says: "prosper in your undertakings, be successful" [Heb. *taskil, tasliah*], these are two things corresponding with two things, which are like [Heb. *chazaq we-'emats*] "be strong and resolute" (Josh 1:7) and "Let not this Book of the Torah cease from your lips" (Josh 1:8)—as if he had done the commandment [Arab. *wasiyya*] of Musa and accepted all of his commands [Arab. *umūr*], and if he were to do the rest of the precepts [Arab. *farā'iḍ*], then God will make his ways prosperous. The meaning of *taskil* [translated by Yefet as "and then you shall have right guidance"] is like "and David was successful in all his undertakings" (1 Sam 18:14), and this corresponds with everything he helps him with. From his statement—"Let not this Book of the Torah cease from your lips"—we learn that he (Joshua) had with him the copy of the Torah that Musa had written.

Joshua 4:9

Joshua also set up twelve stones in the middle of the Jordan, at the spot where the feet of the priests bearing the Ark of the Covenant had stood; and they have remained there to this day.

And Joshua set up twelve stones in the midst of the *Urdun*, in the place where the feet of the imams which bear the Ark of the Covenant stood; and they are there unto this day.

With this too, it is impossible Joshua did this based on his own opinion; rather, he did it with Allah's command, which is that they take twelve stones from the Jordan and put in their place twelve stones from the dry land; yet he did not mention why they did this. The religious scholars [Arab. *'ulama*] said about this that they [the stones] will remain there until they cross the Jordan in the future [Heb. *'atid la-vo'*]; that Allah will divide the Jordan for them; and that they should take these twelve stones as a sign also for the children, thus for this root were the first twelve stones sign for the past, while these are a sign for the future, thus at the beginning these stones are a sign like those.

Joshua 6:3–5

3. Let all your troops march around the city and complete one circuit of the city. Do this six days,

And you shall circle round the city, all men of war, and go round about the city one time; thus shall you do six days

4. with seven priests carrying seven ram's horns preceding the Ark. On the seventh day, march around the city seven times, with the priests blowing the horns.

And seven imams shall bear before the ark seven trumpets of rams' horns, and on the seventh day you shall circle round the city seven times, and the imams shall blow the trumpets.

5. And when a long blast is sounded on the horn—as soon as you hear that sound of the horn—all the people shall give a mighty shout.

Thereupon the city wall will collapse, and the people shall advance, every man straight ahead.

It shall come to pass, that when they make a long blast with the ram's horn, and when you hear the sound of the shofar, all the people shall shout with a great shout; then the walls of the city shall fall down in their place; and the people shall ascend up every one of them straight before him.

He made known that he conquered the city through what they did, which includes three things done by the men of war. The first is, they circled the city from every direction. The second, they carried the ark and circled with it. The third is, the *kohanim* [Heb. "priests"] and others blew the trumpets, as we will explain in what follows. Then he established that for six days the way they circled the city would be the same, one time around and then return to the camp; on the seventh day, in contrast, they should do two additional things. The first is that they circle the city seven times and the second is that they, while on the six days they do not shout, on the seventh day they do shout. Then he made known that when they shout after having circled the city seven times the walls of the city will fall in their place.

We say, in an approximate way, that he did this on the seventh day even though Allah was capable of doing something like it in the blink of an eye—this has several meanings. One is that their obedience [to God] become perfected through circling and blowing the trumpets; and moreover this makes public the report each day, meaning that the people of Jericho would go up on the walls and see how they are circling about and blowing the trumpets day after day without approaching the walls, from which they say that those people are madmen. They likewise grow fearful of us, that they cannot overcome us, and with this their desire to overcome them seems proper and their inclination for war strengthens, as he says: "the citizens of Jericho fought you" (Josh 24:11). It is possible that Allah made the walls fall every day, little by little, from below the earth, in light of his saying: "thereupon the city wall will collapse under itself" (Josh 6:5). When he says (therein): "and the people shall ascend up every one of them straight before him"—he made it necessary that everyone enter the city from whatever place he was at, for the troops were circling the city.

Joshua 6:15

On the seventh day, they rose at daybreak and marched around the city, in the same manner, seven times; that was the only day that they marched around the city seven times.

And it came to pass on the seventh day that they rose early with the dawning of the day, and circled the city after the same manner seven times, only on that day they circled the city seven times.

On each of the six days, the day would break upon them, then they would circle the city one time; in contrast, in order to circle it on the seventh day seven times, they needed to rise at the break of dawn. That he says "that was the only day that they marched around the city seven times" after having said "They did this six days" (6:14) has significance, which is that it was possible that "They did this six days" has the meaning of circling only, or the meaning of blowing the trumpets, without necessarily meaning "one time." Thus he made known that on the seventh day they made seven trips according to their custom (see 6:13): following the vanguard and the seven priests, bearers of the ark, and the rear guard, as we explained before in relation to his saying: "in the same manner" (6:15). Anyone who says they circled the city on Shabbat errs, for there is nothing that should lead them to this conclusion. Rather, they circled the city seven days during *yemey ḥol* [weekdays, and took the Shabbat off].

Joshua 9:27

That day Joshua made them [the Gibeonites] hewers of wood and drawers of water—as they still are—for the community and for the altar of the Lord, in the place that He would choose.

And Joshua made them that day hewers of wood and drawers of water for the congregation, and for the altar of the Master of the worlds, even unto this day, in the place which he should choose.

It was the *nesi'im* [Heb. "leaders," "princes"] who required them to be hewers of wood and drawers of water for the community. Then Joshua required them to be hewers of wood and drawers of water for the community for the altar of the Lord. It was then mentioned at the end of the chapter that he required of them both things together: for the community and for the altar of the Lord. As for the *ummah* ("nation"; i.e., the Israelites), they put them (i.e., the Gibeonites) into service as hewers of wood and drawers of water in order to make them serve and provide drink; and also wood for the altar, about which it is said: "A perpetual fire shall be kept burning on the altar, not to go out" (Lev 6:6). The water was also needed to wash the *qerev, kera'ayim,* and other sacrifices which were washed and purified of blood; they needed a good supply of water each and every day. When he says: "in the place that He would choose"—he means, to any place which "He would choose to establish His name" (Deut 14:24), meaning Gilgal, Shilo, Bethel, Nob, Gibeon, and Jerusalem.

The people differ regarding their being hewers of wood and drawers of water. One said that this is in place of taxation, and they had no other obligation; so they did this in Nob without having wages for it. One group said, in contrast, that they take their wages in what they do specifically for the community, but do not take wages for what is specific to the house of Allah. They sought to make them despicable because of this, as was already said: "Therefore, be accursed!" (Josh 9:23); and with those like them, he said: "(your children, your wives, even the stranger within your camp), from woodchopper to water drawer" (Deut 29:10).

Now that we have reached the end of the interpretation of this story, we return to elucidate what requires elucidation, which is that the Creator, great is his greatness, commanded the killing of seven nations (of Canaan). How then could this oath be canceled? Is there a difference between this and someone who takes an oath to eat bread when it had been made clear that it was pure but then it became clear to him afterwards that it was impure, forbidden [Arab. *ḥarām*], is it incumbent upon him to eat this bread or not? In fact, the law is established in its place, while the oath, in contrast, does not have binding force on him. So why did this not happen also with the affair of the Gibeonites?

The difference between them is that the word of Allah, "you shall not let a soul remain alive" (Deut 20:16), does not apply in every case, for he said after: "lest they lead you into doing all the abhorrent things" (Deut 20:18). Since he connected to the ruse of the Gibeonites their entry into the religion, then the oath stands. Likewise we say that, were all the seven nations [*shiv'a goyim*] to enter the religion before the sword, it would be obligatory to allow them to live, for the reason for destroying them is so they not teach us their beliefs. The same applies with the prohibition against marrying them (see Deut 7:4). What makes the case of the

Gibeonites fall with Israel is that they did not come to them out of fear (of their religious belief), and for this reason he said to them: "Therefore, be accursed!" (Josh 9:23).

If someone should now ask: if this principle were in fact sound, why did the community make an uproar against the *nesi'im*? We say they did not know how the story had unfolded between the *nesi'im* and them [the Gibeonites], so when this was disclosed by the princes, they were fine holding to it.

Joshua 10:12–14

12. *On that occasion, when the Lord routed the Amorites before the Israelites, Joshua addressed the Lord; he said in the presence of the Israelites: Stand still, O sun, at Gibeon, O moon, in the valley of Aijalon!"*

Then spoke Joshua with Allah in the day when Allah delivered up the Amorites before the children of Israel, and he said in their presence, "O sun, stand still from your cycle in Gibeon; and you, O moon, stand still in the valley of Ayalon."

13. *And the sun stood still and the moon halted, while a nation wreaked judgment on its foes—as is written in the Book of Jashar. Thus the sun halted in midheaven, and did not press on to set, for a whole day.*

So the sun stood still, and the moon stayed, until the people had avenged themselves upon their enemies. Is not this written in the Book of the Straight? And the sun stood still in half of the heaven, and hasted not to go down in a whole day.

Joshua did not refrain from killing them until the sun had reached the highest point in the heaven. Then he surveyed the camp's size and realized they would not succeed in killing them all on that day, which means that when the night would divide them, they would escape, and their burden would extend even longer.

He said: "Joshua addressed the LORD"—and then said after: "Stand still, O sun, at Gibeon." It is impossible that one speak to the Lord saying: "Stand still, O sun, at Gibeon," so what seems correct is that he asked Allah for the day to stop for him, knowing that Allah would grant him what he asked for in this matter; and in fact Allah did answer him with respect to this, but he said to him: "Speak directly to the Sun and Moon in the presence of the children of Israel (Arab. *Isra'il*) so that, when it does stand still, they will know that I am the one who made it stand still through your speech and for your sake."

By saying: "Stand still, O sun, at Gibeon"—he points to the fact that all the spheres continued to move other than the sphere of the sun and moon, which points to the fact that the sun and moon are together in one zodiacal constellation, and for this reason he mentioned sun and moon. When he says: "Stand still"—he means, stay firm from your movement, which points to the fact that when he said: "O sun, at Gibeon"—Joshua was in Gibeon before he had chased after them, while the sun was at the high point of the heaven, as he said: "Thus the sun halted in midheaven."

He says: "in the Book of Jashar" [Heb. *Sefer ha-Yashar*]—it has been said that he refers to Sefer Torah, namely, the saying: "and his offspring shall be plentiful enough for nations" (Gen 48:19). This refers to what was heard in the world with regard to what happened to him, for when the sun and moon stood still for him [Joshua], this was reported and people knew that the source of it was Joshua. It has also been said that the book of Joshua is *Sefer ha-Yashar*; and similarly it is said in (David's) dirge: "It is recorded in the Book of Jashar" (2 Sam 1:18), which alludes to the book of Samuel, which was called *Sefer ha-Yashar* on account of its establishing Israel's matters [Arab. *'aḥwāl*] according to their religion and all its other conditions [Arab. *'aḥwāl*]. The book of Judges and the book of Kings, in contrast, are not called *Sefer ha-Yashar* on account of the disorder of their matters and religion. It has also been said that they were in possession of a distinct book called *Sefer ha-Yashar*.

When he says: "and did not press on to set, for the whole day"—he made known that he made the sun stay where it was without moving for three-fourths of the day, which means that it stood still from its movement until one fourth of the day remained; it did not need to move through a full complete day; it was as if it moved the distance of a quarter day then stood still for three-quarters of the day. That is, if you were to combine together the hours of sunlight during that day, they would count thirty hours approximately, while the total hours of that day would be forty-two.

Then he made known that since Allah's creation of the world and as long as the world exists, there is nothing comparable to this day in terms of length or the standing still of a sphere without revolving, as he says:

14. *For the Lord fought for Israel. Neither before nor since has there ever been such a day, when the Lord acted on words spoken by a man.*

There was no day like that before it or after it, that Allah hearkened unto the voice of a prophet, for Allah fights for Israel.

When he says: "when the LORD acted on words spoken by a man"—this corresponds with what he already said, that a man asked Allah that he remove the conventional working of time from its order, as it was said: "If you could break My covenant with the day and My covenant with the night, so that day and night should not come at their proper time" (Jer 33:20). Then Allah received his word and changed it from its [natural] order. We will speak about the return of the sun in the time of Hezekiah in its place (see [our commentary on] 2 Kgs 20:8–11).

Joshua 23

1. *Much later, after the Lord had given Israel rest from all the enemies around them, and when Joshua was old and well advanced in years,*

It came to pass many days after Allah had given rest unto Israel from all their enemies round about, that Joshua waxed old and entered into days of old age.

2. *Joshua summoned all Israel, their elders and commanders, their magistrates and officials, and said to them: "I have grown old and am advanced in years."*

So Joshua called for all Israel, and for their elders, and for their heads, and for their judges, and for their officers, and said unto them, "I am old and have entered the days of old age."

3. *"You have seen all that the Lord your God has done to all those nations on your account, for it was the Lord your God who fought for you."*

"And you have seen what Allah your God has done unto these nations because of you; for Allah your God, he fights for you."

He says: "Much later, after"—what he means is, after many years when the death of Joshua approached, he called all of Israel from their places, including among them the children of Reuben, Gad, and Manasseh. When he says to them: "I have grown old and am advanced in years"—his purpose in this is [to indicate] that I, who persisted in your presence, am passing away from among you. So now consider how you will be after me with respect to obedience to Allah. If you are obedient to Allah, then he will obliterate these remaining nations and you will be at ease in your land and with your good things [Arab. *ni'am*]. Yet if you rebel against him you will be destroyed and eliminated from this land. This is the purpose of the chapter. When he says: "You have seen"—what he means is, you have witnessed what Allah did to your enemies who are greater in number and stronger than you. You know that Allah fights for you.

> 4. "*See, I have allotted to you, by your tribes, [the territory of] these nations that still remain, and that of all the nations that I have destroyed, from the Jordan to the Mediterranean Sea in the West.*"

"Behold, I have divided unto you by lot cities of these nations ['*umam*] that remain, to be an inheritance for your tribes, from the Urdun, **and the land of all the other nations [*Arab. 'ahzaab*] that I have cut off, even unto the great sea westward."**

> 5. "*The Lord your God Himself will thrust them out on your account and drive them out to make way for you, and you shall possess their land as the Lord your God promised you.*"

"And Allah, your God, he shall expel them from before you, and drive them from out of your sight; and you shall possess their land, as Allah, your God, has promised you.

His purpose in this verse is twofold. First, that Allah satisfied his promise and gave them the land of these nations. The second is moving them to obliterate what remains of the seven nations of Canaan [Heb. *shiv'a goyim*] so that they inherit the totality of the country with no one else remaining in it. When he says: "The LORD your God Himself will thrust them out on your account"—he means, if you take action in war against them, Allah will expel them from before you; at the time of war you will rout them. When he says: "and drive them out to make way for you"—that is, he will obliterate anyone remaining in the country, from old men to children and others.

6. *"But be most resolute to observe faithfully all that is written in the Book of the Teaching of Moses, without ever deviating from it to the right or to the left,"*

"Be you therefore very courageous to keep and to do all that is written in the composition [Arab. *diwaan*] of Moses, that you turn not aside therefrom to the right hand or to the left."

7. *"and without intermingling with these nations that are left among you. Do not utter the names of their gods or swear by them; do not serve them or bow down to them."*

"That you come not among these nations, these that remain among you; neither make mention of the name of their gods, nor cause to swear by them, neither serve them, nor bow yourselves unto them."

8. *"But hold fast to the Lord your God as you have done to this day."*

"But cleave unto Allah, your God, as you have done unto this day."

He commanded them to do all that Allah required of him in the book of the Torah of Moses and warned them strongly against entering into the seven nations (of Canaan), as he said: "and without intermingling"—that is, do not follow their beliefs, do not marry with them, and do not reside among them. When he says: "Do not utter the names (of their gods)"—he means, do not describe them with pleasant descriptions. When he says: "But hold fast to the LORD your God"—he means, cleave perpetually to obedience to him; do not remove yourself from that.

9. *"The Lord has driven out great, powerful nations on your account, and not a man has withstood you to this day."*

"Allah has driven out from before you great nations and strong; but as for you, no one has been able to stand before you unto this day."

10. *"A single man of you would put a thousand to flight, for the Lord your God Himself has been fighting for you, as He promised you."*

"One of you shall chase a thousand, for Allah, your God, he it is that fights for you, as he promised you."

He describes again Allah's ways with them since they had entered the land until this moment in order to exhort them not to allow the seven nations to survive and not to mix with them. He said: "A single man of you would put a thousand to flight"—yet there was no such previous guarantee to the fathers; rather, he guaranteed: "Five of you shall give chase to a hundred" (Lev 26:8). In this there are two meanings. One is that the guarantee was to your generations which remain obedient over the passing of time; the second is, that [guarantee] was said of the [Israelite] *Ummah* (Arab. "nation") as a whole, while this one for an individual.

11. *"For your own sakes, therefore, be most mindful to love the Lord your God."*

"Take good heed therefore unto yourselves, that you love Allah, your God."

He says: "be most mindful"—this needs some elaboration, which is: keep from being rebellious and from serving anything other than Allah, as it is said in the Torah: "For your own sake, therefore, be most careful—since you saw no shape" (Deut 4:15).

12. *"For should you turn away and attach yourselves to the remnants of those—to those that are left among you—and intermarry with them, you joining them you joining them and they joining you,"*

"Else if you do in any wise go back and cleave unto the remnant of these nations, even these that remain among you, and make marriages with them, and go in unto them, and they to you,"

13. *"Know for certain that the Lord your God will not continue to drive these nations out before you; they shall become a snare and a trap for you, a scourge to your sides and thorns in your eyes, until you perish from this good land that the Lord your God has given you."*

"Know for a certainty that Allah, your God, will no more drive out any of these nations from before you; but they shall become snares and traps unto you, and scourges in your sides, and thorns in your eyes, until you perish from off this good land which Allah, your God, hath given you."

He said: know that when you return from what Allah commanded you and mix with these nations and marry amongst them, Allah will withdraw from having providence over you and make the remainder of these nations "become snares and traps unto you, and scourges in your sides." As for snares and traps [Heb. *paḥ u-moqesh*]—these are used with reference to their joining in their religion and accepting their beliefs. As for: "and scourges in your sides" [Heb. *leshotet be-zideykhem*]—this refers to taking them and dividing them into two groups. As for them that reside in the villages separately, he likened them to "scourges" which beat them from behind, while those that reside with them in their villages are like the teeth of a spear that enters the eye. Moses, peace be with him, said something similar: "those whom you allow to remain shall be stings in your eyes and thorns in your sides" (Num 33:55).

14. *"I am now going the way of all the earth. Acknowledge with all your heart and soul that not one of the good things that the Lord your God promised you has failed to happen; they have all come true for you, not a single one has failed."*

"And behold, this day I am going the way of all the earth; for you know in all your heart and soul that not one promise has failed of all the good promises which Allah, your God, spoke concerning you; all are come to pass unto you, and not one word has failed thereof."

When he says: "I am now going the way of all the earth"—he means, I am passing away from you, and you are in the best state with respect to your life in this world and your religion; Allah has already completed for you his good promises in my days. When he says: "Acknowledge with all your heart"—he means, it is required that you affirm that Allah completed his promises for you and that not one thing of his promises fell away. Allah will take proof [Arab. *hujja*] from this with respect to you, that you stand firm in obedience to him so that his providence remain continuously upon you and his goodness over you.

> 15. *"But just as every good thing that the Lord your God promised you has been fulfilled for you, so the Lord can bring upon you every evil thing until He has wiped you off this good land that the Lord your God has given you."*

> **"Therefore it shall come to pass, that as all the good word comes upon you, which Allah <your God> said to you, so shall Allah bring upon you all the difficult threat [Arab. *al-wa'iid*] that he threatened you with, until he has destroyed you from off this good land which Allah your God has given you."**

> 16. *"If you break the covenant that the Lord your God enjoined upon you, and go and serve other gods and bow down to them, then the Lord's anger will burn against you, and you shall quickly perish from the good land that he has given you."*

> **"When you have transgressed the covenant of Allah your God, which he commanded you, and have gone <and served> other gods <and bowed yourselves to them>, then shall the anger of Allah be kindled against you, and you shall perish quickly from off the good land which he has given unto you."**

He said, if you transgress the covenant of Allah, your matters [Arab. *'aḥwāl*] will be upturned upon you, for just as he is capable of giving you good, so is he capable of destroying you and obliterating you from this land, exactly as he made as condition upon you. Know that "if you break the covenant that the LORD" (v. 16)—this is prior in action to "But just as every" (v. 15), for that is description of their action (v. 16) and this of their recompense (v. 15).

Bibliography

Robinson, James T. *The Arabic Translation and Commentary of Yefet ben 'Eli the Karaite on the Book of Joshua*. Leiden: Brill, 2014.

A Judeo-Arabic Manuscript by an Unnamed Author: A Story about King Solomon

Rachel Hasson

Introduction: The Manuscript

The manuscript under discussion, MS SP RNL Yevr.-Arab. 2:1484, is part of the Firkovitch Collection, held at the Russian National Library in Saint Petersburg, originally from a Karaite genizah in Cairo. The manuscript comprises a single page, and its author is not named; from the shape of the writing, it appears to date to the fifteenth century CE.[1] The script is a precise late Oriental hand. Arabic *shadda* (doubling sign over a consonant) and *tanwīn* (nunnation) signs appear here and there throughout the manuscript. The title הדה קצה סלימאן אבן דאוד ("This is the story of Solomon son of David") does not reveal which of the many stories about King Solomon appears in the text, but it may be a prologue to the "Story of the Ant" (see below). The initial words, הדה קצה ("this is the story"), are written in an enlarged square script, and the letters are decorated by a surrounding external line and foliation above them. The manuscript includes marginal notes correcting or complementing the text. Thus, the story appears to have undergone careful collation by the copyist (as the same script appears both in text and margins).[2]

---

1. My thanks to Ms. Tamar Leiter, from the Paleography Institute at the National Library of Israel, Jerusalem, who helped me date the manuscript.

2. Within the translation that follows, parentheses indicate additions or clarifications. Square brackets indicate marginal or interlinear notes in the manuscript. Hebrew Bible verses are found within the Judeo-Arabic text in Hebrew but are hereby translated into English as well.

Translation

/fol. 1a/ This is the story (*qiṣṣa*) of Solomon the son of David, may he rest in peace.

We have heard about Solomon the son of David, may he rest in peace, that nobody was better than him in the world's wisdom, as the Book (the Bible) indicates]three verses] by its saying: "He was wiser than anyone else," and so on.[3] And it is mentioned of him that he spoke with the plants, animals, and reptiles on the land, and he spoke with the fish of the sea like (the Bible) says: "He would speak of trees," and so on.[4] In accordance with that (Solomon),[5] may he rest in peace, (was occupied with) producing gold from its mines and silver and gems; and the buildings and the trees were well established (by him), like (the Bible) says: "I made great works; I built houses and planted vineyards for myself ";[6] and says: "I also gathered for myself silver and gold and the treasure of kings";[7] and (Solomon) also reprimanded the ignorant people, the brutal people who forgot to have authorization (for their actions), with a decisive reproach and made for them, concerning

/fol. 1b/ this matter, a fable, and said: Woe weak person, who speaks about his profit and cautionary measures[8] using what rescues him from God's punishment? Woe poor person, go to the ant, look at her manners and become wise! As (the Bible) says:

---

3. "He was wiser than anyone else, wiser than Ethan the Ezrahite, and Heman, Calcol, and Darda, children of Mahol; his fame spread throughout all the surrounding nations" (MT 1 Kgs 5:11, NRSV 4:31).

4. "He would speak of trees, from the cedar that is in the Lebanon to the hyssop that grows in the wall; he would speak of animals, and birds, and reptiles, and fish" (MT 1 Kgs 5:13, NRSV 4:33).

5. As far as I understand, the author of our text attributes the next verses he quotes (Qoh 2:4, 8) to King Solomon; he also does the same concerning the "Fable of the Ant" (Prov 6:6–8).

6. Qoh 2:4 NRSV.

7. "I also gathered for myself silver and gold and the treasure of kings and of the provinces; I got singers, both men and women, and delights of the flesh, and many concubines" (Qoh 2:8 NRSV).

8. Arab. *istiʿdād* (Joshua Blau, *A Dictionary of Mediaeval Judaeo-Arabic Texts* [Hebrew] [Jerusalem: Israel Academy of Sciences and Humanities, 2006], 425).

"Go to the ant, you lazybones," and so on.[9] She does not have a ruler[10] nor a consultant, and she does not have a someone to warn her nor an informer, (she has) just what God engages in her through the fineness of his wisdom, as (the Bible) says: "Without having any chief," and so on.[11] And look, woe to you, at what the ant does through (God's) fineness of creation and wisdom, (that despite) her lack of swiftness and power, she gathers during the summer her nutriment and accumulates at harvest time her food, as (the Bible) says: "It prepares its food in summer," and so on.[12] And she has many perfections apart from this, like good planning and civility, because (the Bible) says: "consider its ways" and not "its way," and hence that she first prepares a place where she (can) accumulate what she gathers to (be) a mark for her.

Comments

Biblical and midrashic stories—the genre to which our text belongs—are very popular in the Cairo Genizah. These stories were widespread due to the functions they fulfilled within the life of Jewish communities in Islamic lands. Some stories played a role in Jewish communal life outside formal prayers while others, apparently in most Jewish communities in the Islamic lands, had a role identical to the latter. Such a story is, for instance, *Qiṣṣat Ester* ("Story of Esther"), written in rhyming prose and telling the story of the Esther Scroll. *Qiṣṣat Ester* was apparently read on Shabbat *Zechor*, the Saturday before Purim. *Qiṣṣat Yūsuf* ("Story of Joseph") was read during Passover. *Qiṣṣat Ḥannah* ("Story of Hannah"), a lament for Hannah and her seven sons, and *Qiṣṣat Zechariah* ("Story of Zechariah"), a lament for the destruction of the Jerusalem temple, were read on the ninth day of the month Av, the commemorative day for the destruction.

Other stories too were intended to serve didactic purposes within the Jewish community. These were meant to teach stories from the Bible and the Midrash, to demonstrate God's miracles and the superiority of the Jewish faith. Such, for example, are the story of Abraham and Nimrod and

---

9. "Go to the ant, you lazybones; consider its ways, and be wise" (Prov 6:6 NRSV).

10. I.e., to instruct it what to do.

11. "Without having any chief or officer or ruler" (Prov 6:7 NRSV).

12. "It prepares its food in summer, and gathers its sustenance in harvest" (Prov 6:8 NRSV).

the stories about King Solomon deriving from the Midrash, which are the focus of this article. The Cairo Genizah contains a few dozen Judeo-Arabic manuscripts of stories about King Solomon, among them the "Story of King Solomon and Asmodeus," the "Story of King Solomon and the Queen of Sheba," the "Story of King Solomon's Throne," and the "Story of the Ant."[13]

The literature about biblical prophets is roughly equivalent to the genre called in Arabic *qiṣaṣ al-anbiyāʾ* ("Tales of the Prophets") or *al-isrāʾīliyyāt*. This genre comprises ancient tales about the children of Israel (*banū Isrāʾīl*) and folkloric material of Jewish origin, transmitted orally during the first generations of Islam. Already then storytellers who specialized in transmitting traditions about the Qurʾanic prophets appeared. Their tales included Christian and Jewish material and much content from the Midrash. Against this background, medieval popular tales about biblical prophets are usually characterized by intercultural influences. These influences reflect the close relations of the Jews with their surroundings.[14]

It should be noted that the term *qiṣṣa*, which appears in the title of our manuscript, is the popular term used in Judeo-Arabic popular stories that focus on biblical characters. The term was adapted by Jews from Islamic sources to indicate a narrative unit connected to the history and acts of a biblical character. This use of the term *qiṣṣa* is found in Judeo-Arabic exegesis to the Bible already from the ninth century CE.[15]

As for the text in our manuscript, it is filled with many biblical quotations and shows no direct Muslim influences. The biblical quotations are accompanied by partial or complete free translations or, sometimes, by paraphrases. The first page describes the virtues, power, and wisdom of King Solomon, interspersed with verses from 1 Kgs 5 and Qoh 2. On the second page the author begins telling the story that appears in Prov 6:6–8.

---

13. Rachel Hasson-Kenat, "New Manuscripts Written in Late Judaeo-Arabic from the Firkovitch Collection—Classification, Description and Sample Texts" [Hebrew] (PhD diss., Hebrew University of Jerusalem, 2016), 23–27.

14. Hasson-Kenat, "New Manuscripts," 29; Shlomo Dov Goitein, *Jews and Arabs: Their Contacts through the Ages*, 3rd ed. (New York: Schocken, 1974), 194–95; Marc S. Bernstein, *Stories of Joseph: Narrative Migrations between Judaism and Islam* (Detroit: Wayne State University Press, 2006).

15. Meira Polliack, "Conceptualization of the Biblical Narrative and Its Preparation to Written Form from Oral Traditions: From New Judaeo-Arabic Commentaries of Middle Ages" [Hebrew], *Bein ʿEver la-ʿArav: Contacts Between Arabic Literature and Jewish Literature in the Middle Ages and in Modern Times* 6 (2014): 113–14.

This may be part of the beginning of the "Story of the Ant," a section that includes the story's prologue. The "Story of the Ant" is quite popular in the Firkovitch Collection. So far seven manuscripts with this story have been found, all of them incomplete; those that contain the beginning of the text do not have a prologue such as appears in our manuscript. Although it is not at all certain that this manuscript is indeed part of the "Story of the Ant," it should be noted that this story is not Jewish in origin, and it is similar to medieval Arabic fantasy tales. To this we should add that the queen ant's warning to her soldiers to beware of King Solomon's spirits, which appears in the Qur'an (Al-Kahf 18:27), is mentioned in this story as well. It is also possible that this text is not the prologue to a specific story about King Solomon, but rather a collection of biblical verses that the author saw fit to connect to the king.

The author usually begins with the translation and only afterwards brings in the biblical text. A quotation begins with the Judeo-Arabic word וקאל ("and [the Book] says") or the abbreviations בקו׳ or בק׳ (בקולה, "as [the Book] says"). These words apparently relate to the Book, that is, the Bible; I conclude this from the words that appear before the first quotation in the text: כמא שהד אלכתאב ק׳ ("as the Book indicates by its saying").[16] The abbreviations וכו׳ (וכולי, "and so on") or וג׳ (וגומר, "to the end of the verse") appear after incomplete quotations.

The author of this manuscript translates the biblical text freely, according to his understanding of it and without relying on specific exegesis.[17] It may be assumed that the author/copyist (who also wrote down the footnotes) had an expert knowledge of the biblical text. Thus, for example, it was important for him to be precise at the beginning of the manuscript and to note that King Solomon's wisdom is mentioned in three verses (1 Kgs 5:11–13 MT, 4:31–33 NRSV), although just the beginning of the first (1 Kgs 5:11 MT, 4:31 NRSV) and end of the third (1 Kgs 5:13 MT, 4:33 NRSV) of these verses are quoted in the text.

---

16. However, one can claim that the abbreviations בקו׳ or בק׳ refer to the author/editor (*mudawwin*) of the Bible. The question of the *mudawwin*'s identity falls beyond the scope of this essay. For further discussion, see Ilana Sasson's essay (243–53).

17. I compared the verses quoted from Proverbs—which are probably the most important ones, if we have before us a prologue to the "Story of the Ant"—to the translations of Yefet ben 'Eli and the Tafsīr of Sa'adia Gaon. The verses in our manuscript are not identical with either.

The biblical quotations do not appear *in toto* and, in fact, only the beginnings of the verses are cited—in contrast to the paraphrase/translation, which can refer to the unquoted, subsequent part of the relevant biblical verse. For example, in the passage

> And it is mentioned of him that he spoke with the plants, animals, and reptiles on the land, and he spoke with the fishes of the sea like (the Bible) says: "He would speak of trees," and so on.

the translation also refers to parts of the verse that are not quoted: "He would speak of trees, from the cedar that is in the Lebanon to the hyssop that grows in the wall; he would speak of animals, and birds, and reptiles, and fish" (1 Kgs 5:13 MT, 4:33 NRSV). Furthermore, in this example we see that the author does not translate the words "from the cedar that is in the Lebanon to the hyssop that grows in the wall."

In the following passage the author combines, respectively, two verses from Qoheleth, 2:4 and 2:8:

> In accordance with that (Solomon), may he rest in peace, (was occupied with) producing gold from its mines and silver and gems; and the buildings and the trees were well established (by him), like (the Bible) says: "I made great works; I built houses and planted vineyards for myself," and says: "I also gathered for myself silver and gold and the treasure of kings."

However, the translation that precedes the quotation refers first to verse 8 and only then to verse 4. Furthermore, the author makes no reference to the second part of verse 8: "and the treasure of kings and of the provinces; I got singers, both men and women, and delights of the flesh, and many concubines."

The author uses paraphrases in his translation, such as "nobody was better than him in the world's wisdom" as a translation of "he was wiser than anyone else." It should be noted that the author does not quote this verse precisely, and allows himself to add Solomon's name to the biblical quotation: "as it is written: Solomon was wiser than anyone else." The translations are usually not close to the Hebrew original, thus the author uses the phrase "and become wise" as a translation for the word וחכם in the verse "consider her ways and be wise" (Prov 6:6)—rather than the verbs *aʿqala* or *taḥakkama* that could have replaced the Hebrew word exactly. As a translation for the phrase "without having any chief or officer or ruler"

(Prov 6:7), the author brings in a particularly long translation that does not follow the original closely: "She does not have a ruler nor a consultant, and she does not have a someone to warn her nor an informer, (she has) just what God engages in her through the fineness of his wisdom."

After the author finishes recounting the virtues of King Solomon (fol. 1a), he continues, as said, to a discussion and translation of the "Parable of the Ant," which appears in Prov 6:6–8 (fols. 1a–1b). This discussion starts with clarifying the background for why the Bible includes the "Parable of the Ant." The author explains that Solomon rebukes, with criticism and reproach, those who do not obey the law and still expect to escape punishment; in his opinion, the parable is aimed at these brutish ignoramuses. (The author is perhaps referring here, albeit obliquely, to King Solomon's juridical wisdom, as is shown in 1 Kgs 3:16–28, Solomon's judgment between the two women.) When the author finishes translating and quoting Prov 6:8, he repeats his emphasis that the ant has many virtues that the Bible does not note explicitly, since the lazy is told to consider the ant's *ways* (plural) and not its *way* (singular). This usage hints that the ant has many excellent methods of action related to planning beyond those mentioned in verses 6–8: for example, the ant will prepare storage space for food in advance.

It is possible that the author made use, in this text, of the midrash on Prov 6:

"Lazybones, go to the ant; study its ways and learn" (Prov 6:6)—R. Judah ben Pedaiah said: In the future the wicked will say to God, "Master of both worlds, allow us to do so, and we will offer penitence before You!"

God will reply to them saying, "O you consummate fools! The world you were [living] in resembles the eve of the Sabbath, whereas this [next] world [of Judgment] is like Sabbbath itself. If a person does not prepare [his Sabbath meal] on the eve of the Sabbath, what will he eat on Sabbath day? The world you were [living] in resembles dry land, whereas this world [of Judgment] is like the sea. If a person does not prepare [provisions] on dry land, what will he eat at sea? The world you were [living] in resembles a vestibule, whereas this world [of Judgment] is like a dining chamber. If a person does not arrange himself in the vestibule, how can he enter the dining chamber? The world you were [living] in resembles summer, whereas this world [of Judgment] is like winter. If a person does not plow and plant in summer, what will he eat in winter? Not only this, but should you not have learned [at least] from the ant?" Hence Scripture says, "Lazybones, go to the ant; study its ways and learn"

(Prov 6:6). What is its wisdom? "It lays up its stores in summer, gathers its food at the harvest" (Prov 6:8). ("Without leaders, officers, or rulers" [Prov 6:7]—R. Eleazar asked R. Joshua: "Master, what is the meaning of this verse?"

Rabbi Joshua replied, "My son, the ant has neither king, nor overseer, nor ruler to make her wise, rather her wisdom comes from within her.")

[God continued His rebuke, saying:] "And you wicked ones, should you not have learned from her? Yet you held on to your indolence and your foolishness and failed to repent!" Therefore Solomon said, "How long will you lie there, lazybones; When will you wake from your sleep" (Prov 6:9)?[18]

According to this midrash, the ant of the parable works hard in the present in order to achieve profit and advantage in the future, without having been taught this way of life. According to the midrash, this parable teaches us that wise action is to do something in the present in order to create a future advantage. In other words, one must repent in this world in order to merit the next world. Yet the "lazybones" are fools because they do not act in the present and are not concerned with the future. Our text may be hinting at this when it says that the ant has many wisdoms connected to its ability to plan ahead.

The way biblical verses are inserted into medieval folktales has not yet been studied properly. We have brought an example of a text, titled the "Story of Solomon Son of David," that includes many biblical verses. The text provides complete or incomplete translations of the verses it quotes. The translations are easily understood, combining paraphrase and exegesis. The author allows himself a great deal of freedom: his translations are not always close to the biblical text and may at times also ignore the order of the biblical verses. We have not found a medieval translation parallel to the biblical translation that appears in our text, which leads to the assumption that the anonymous author did not copy his translations and they are original to him. It may be that he was knowledgeable about the midrash and used it in his explanations to the biblical verses.

The text is didactic in character; the method of translation that the author uses indicates that the texts were aimed at broad audiences, particularly at the middle and lower/uneducated strata of medieval Jewish

---

18. Midrash Prov. 6:6 in Burton L. Visotzky, trans., *The Midrash on Proverbs* (New Haven: Yale University Press, 1992).

societies where the manuscript was copied. It appears that the aim of the manuscript's author was to narrate King Solomon's wisdom and activities in a simple manner, while teaching and explicating relevant biblical verses.

Bibliography

Bernstein, Marc S. *Stories of Joseph: Narrative Migrations between Judaism and Islam*. Detroit: Wayne State University Press, 2006.

Blau, Joshua. *A Dictionary of Mediaeval Judaeo-Arabic Texts* [Hebrew]. Jerusalem: Israel Academy of Sciences and Humanities, 2006.

Goitein, Shlomo Dov. *Jews and Arabs: Their Contacts through the Ages*. 3rd ed. New York: Schocken, 1974.

Hasson Kenat, Rachel. "New Manuscripts Written in Late Judaeo-Arabic from the Firkovitch Collection—Classification, Description and Sample Texts" [Hebrew]. PhD diss., Hebrew University of Jerusalem, 2016.

Polliack, Meira. "Conceptualization of the Biblical Narrative and Its Preparation to Written Form from Oral Traditions: From New Judaeo-Arabic Commentaries of Middle Ages" [Hebrew]. *Bein 'Ever la-'Arav: Contacts between Arabic Literature and Jewish Literature in the Middle Ages and in Modern Times* 6 (2014): 109–52.

Visotzky, Burton L., trans. *The Midrash on Proverbs*. New Haven: Yale University Press, 1992.

Sa'adia Gaon's Translation of the References to Jerusalem in Isaiah 1–2: A Case Study in Lexical Choices

Zafer Tayseer Mohammad

Introduction: The Meanings of Biblical Jerusalem in Sa'adia's Arabic Translation of Isaiah

The references to the holy city of Jerusalem permeate the Hebrew Bible, especially its prophetic, poetic, and historiographical books. The holy city, with its remarkable and splendid stature, impressively retains conspicuous prominence and presence throughout the numerous utterances about it in the diverse biblical sources.

Scholars point out that Sa'adia Gaon's Tafsīr (i.e., Arabic translation of the Pentateuch) was enormously "successful and it spread to the far corners of the Islamic world," while "displacing earlier Judeo-Arabic translations and joining the Masoretic Text and Onqelos in the trilingual versions of the Pentateuch."[1] Sa'adia was an acclaimed and prolific translator whose translations of the Hebrew Bible included the book of Isaiah.[2] It is likely that as he worked on the numerous references to the holy city of

---

1. Richard C. Steiner, *A Biblical Translation in the Making: The Evolution and Impact of Saadia Gaon's Tasfir* (Cambridge: Harvard University Press, 2010), 129.

2. Amir Ashur, Sivan Nir, and Meira Polliack argue: "It seems that Sa'adya produced separate self-contained translations of the Pentateuch, the Five Scrolls, and Isaiah. The fact that these books served in Synagogue worship further suggests that Sa'adya's practice of separating their tafsir from their commentary was functional, and motivated by the specific needs of a wider Jewish audience, who would be hearing or reading the self-contained translations on the Sabbath and Festivals, and who needed a rendition into Arabic that was straightforward and short—and yet accurate and attractive—which did not stray too much from the literal unless absolutely necessary." See Amir Ashur, Sivan Nir, and Meira Polliack, "Three Fragments of Sa'adya Gaon's Arabic Translation of Isaiah Copied by the Court Scribe Joseph ben Samuel (c.

Jerusalem in the book of Isaiah, his approach to their translation became highly charged, especially considering Isaiah's preoccupation with Zion's final destiny.[3]

One may then ask: How does Sa'adia express this concern in his translations of the different references to the holy city, either to its dire experiences in former times or its deliverance and restoration in future times, according to the book of Isaiah? This concern can be accompanied by acknowledging that the portrayals of Jerusalem in Isaiah serve to highlight its exceptional position and its prominence in the faith experience of biblical Israel and the Jewish people. Thus, an engagement with Sa'adia's translations of Isaiah, especially the references to Jerusalem, can serve as a legitimate reason for opening a whole array of reflections on the city's status. The translator lived during the medieval Islamic rule over the city; yet Jerusalem, as portrayed or envisioned in Isaiah, did not fulfil the prophetic hopes of deliverance when under Islamic dominion. So one may ask: How did Sa'adia embark on translating these references to Jerusalem, with all their political and theological significance, in light of the fact that during his time the city was under non-Jewish rule?[4] And how did he, in his translations, grapple with the theological significance of Jerusalem in light of the important place the holy city holds in Islamic thinking? In

---

1181–1209)," in *Senses of Scripture, Treasures of Tradition: The Bible in Arabic among Jews, Christians and Muslims*, ed. Miriam Lindgren Hjälm (Leiden: Brill, 2017), 488.

3. On this topic, see modern commentators such as Christopher R. Seitz, *Zion's Final Destiny: The Development of the Book of Isaiah: A Reassessment of Isaiah 36-39* (Minneapolis: Fortress, 1991), x. On the Judeo-Arabic translation of the Bible, see, for example, Meira Polliack, "Bible Translations: Judeo-Arabic (Ninth to the Thirteenth Centuries)," *EJIW* 1:464–69; Polliack, "Arabic Bible Translations in the Cairo Genizah Collections," in *Jewish Studies in a New Europe: Proceedings of the Fifth Congress of Jewish Studies in Copenhagen 1994*, ed. Ulf Haxen, Hanne Trautner-Kromann, and Karen Lisa Goldschmidt-Salamon (Copenhagen: C. A. Reitzel, 1998), 595–620; and Sidney H. Griffith, *The Bible in Arabic: The Scriptures of the People of the Book in the Language of Islam* (Princeton: Princeton University Press, 2013).

4. On the relationship between Sa'adia and Christianity and Islam and the Jews in Islamic Countries in the Middle Ages, see Daniel J. Lasker, "Saadya Gaon on Christianity and Islam," in *The Jews of Medieval Islam: Community, Society, and Identity*, ed. Daniel Frank (Leiden: Brill, 1995), 165–77; Shelomo Dov Goitein, *A Mediterranean Society: The Jewish Communities of the Arab World as Portrayed in the Documents of the Cairo Geniza*, 2 vols. (Berkeley: University of California Press, 1967); and Moshe Gil, *Jews in Islamic Countries in the Middle Ages*, trans. David Strassler (Leiden: Brill, 2004).

other words, can his choice of words reveal certain aspects of his theological attitude as well as the religious and ideological thinking of the Jews of his time toward their special holy city?

Sa'adia encountered not only the reality of the Islamic dominion but also the different theological perspectives held by other Jewish groups. In this regard, scholars have shown that Sa'adia titled his translation and commentary on Isaiah, as he did with all his exegetical works, with a thematic name, thus emphasizing its primary subject or purpose in his thinking: *The Book of Perfecting Obedience to God*.[5] Further, these scholars highlight that this epitaph concurs with Sa'adia's view of prophecy as mainly educational in its function and mission, whereas "its predicative dimension is limited to the historical horizon of the prophets themselves."[6] Moreover, they point out that his approach appears to "have been fueled by his anti-Karaite polemic, since the Karaite movement emphasized the messianic aspects of biblical prophecy as the fulfillment of prophetic visions concerning the people's return to Jerusalem at the end of times."[7] An additional formative influence on Sa'adia's translations of the Hebrew Bible, as pointed out by various scholars, is his response to the spiritual, literary, and scientific awakening of Islam, and his desire to reinforce traditional (that is, rabbinic) Judaism. The city of Jerusalem occupied a prominent and central position in Jewish thinking. One may then question how and in what way, in his Judeo-Arabic translations, did Sa'adia express and convey the prominent position of Jerusalem and its obvious significance, as he perceived it, in a nonbiblical language, Arabic.

To further illustrate this point: Sa'adia's theological perspective on Jerusalem evidently appears as he translated, for example, Isa 14:32a, "For the Lord will establish [MT: *yissad*] Zion" (NRSV: "The Lord has founded Zion"). In his commentary, he mentioned that he did not translate the Hebrew *yissad* as "erect" because Zion has already been erected.[8] In this text, he evidently expressed his theological stance regarding the physical existence of Jerusalem, while engaging in his Judeo-Arabic rendering. A thorough examination of his translations of other Isaian

---

5. Ashur, Nir, and Polliack, "Three Fragments," 498.

6. Ashur, Nir, and Polliack, "Three Fragments," 499.

7. Ashur, Nir, and Polliack, "Three Fragments," 499.

8. See Sadok Masliyah, "Saadia Gaon's Arabic Versions of the Book of Isaiah," *Hebrew Studies* 20–21 (1979–1980): 82.

references to Jerusalem may provide new theological perspectives and insights concerning its significance in Jewish thinking during the Middle Ages, and the reception history of Isaiah among Jews during the Abbasid Caliphate.

It is worth noting here that, until recently, Isaian scholarship has not critically dealt with the book's Arabic versions and their variations, especially the Jewish translations and the semantic choices in them. Therefore, such critical examination can be a valuable addition and indeed an indispensable contribution to the understanding of Isaiah, while at the same time dealing with an important translation milieu that shows how medieval Jews, living in an Islamic context, read Isaiah and other biblical books in Judeo-Arabic.

Choices of Arabic words traverse new meanings and open new gates to reflect on the texts within new contexts, and with new lenses. The purpose of this essay is to examine the references to Jerusalem, with a particular focus on analyzing the Arabic words that convey Jerusalem's deliverance and its stature in Sa'adia's translations of Isa 1–3. I will particularly investigate his lexical choices, which are unique to his translation of the Jerusalem references, in order to highlight their purport and interpretation of Jerusalem, with special emphasis on the city's deliverance and theological significance in Isa 1:26 and chapters 2 and 3. It is my hope that this essay will encourage further study of other references to Jerusalem in Sa'adia's Isaiah and other Bible translations, in order to understand its significance and stature in Jewish religious thought, as manifested in those Arabic translations:

Isaiah 1:26

Sa'adia's translation:[9] *Wa-'aruddu qaḍatak ka-al-'ula wa-ḥukamak kal-'ibtida' ba'd dhalika tud'in balad al-'adl al-qarya al-'amina*

English translation of Sa'adia's text: And I will restore your judges as at the first, and your wise people as at the beginning. Afterward you shall be called the country of justice, the faithful/genuine village.

---

9. See the critical edition by Yehuda Ratzaby, *Saadya's Translation and Commentary on Isaiah: Collected, Edited with Translation and Notes* (Kiriat Ono: Makhon Moshe, 1993), 5.

NRSV: And I will restore your judges as at the first, and your counselors as at the beginning. Afterward you shall be called the city of righteousness, the faithful city.[10]

In this verse, Jerusalem in the time of its future restoration is promised by Yahweh to have a new system of governance based on justice and righteousness. This is clearly manifested by the restoration of judges and counselors in Zion as at the beginning. In the MT Jerusalem is called the "city of justice" (Heb. *'ir ha-tzedeq*) and the "faithful city" (Heb. *qiryah ne'emanah*). These names, bestowed upon the restored Jerusalem, can be theologically and thematically connected to its unique status as Yahweh's dwelling place on earth; as such, the holy city bears the characteristics of its master or ruler, Yahweh. In short, Yahweh in this verse proclaims the restoration of Jerusalem to its former original and authentic times of glory.

Sa'adia's Judeo-Arabic translation of this verse begins with the verb *'aruddu*, derived from the root *rdd* (here in the verb form IV, first-person, future) which has diverse meanings. It can simply mean "restore" or "return"; yet it also has legal and moral connotations, which are primarily connected to "restoring" respect after a verdict, "restoring" dignity or civil rights; and the abolition of punishment. In the Qur'an, the root *rdd* is sometimes used to refer to nonbelievers in God who seek to turn true believers from the true path of faith. This meaning is quite evident in Q Al-Baqarah 2:109: "Many of the People of the Book (i.e., Jews and Christians), after the truth has become manifest to them would desire out of sheer envy generated by their minds that, after you have believed, they could *turn you* [*yaruddunakum*] into disbelievers."[11]

In addition, the Arabic noun *ridda* ("apostasy"), which is derived from the same root *rdd*, can mean "the abandonment of one's religious beliefs or principles." In Islamic history, the Ridda Wars (Arab. *ḥurub al-ridda*), are the "Wars of Apostasy," relating to a series of military campaigns launched by the Caliph Abu Bakr against the rebel Arabian tribes during 632–633 CE, immediately after the death of Prophet Mohammad. These movements have been described politically and theologically as separatist movements from the Medina central authority, founded by Prophet Mohammad and the Abu Bakr's leadership. Moreover, the root *rdd* also conveys the theme

---

10. All English Bible translations in this essay are based on the NRSV.

11. See Muhammad Zafrulla Khan, *The Quran, Arabic Text with a New Translation*, rev. ed. (London: Curzon, 1981), 19 (with slight changes).

of transformation and change: to "change or transform from one condition/state to another."[12]

Having examined the different connotations of the verb 'aruddu in Arabic and other related forms, one may argue that Sa'adia's use of this form in translating the Hebrew we-ashiva (Isa 1:26) eloquently highlights a theological aspect of God's promised restoration of Jerusalem at the very outset of Isaiah. The translation focuses the Arabic-speaking reader on God's response to Jerusalem's bleak former times and his means of intervention, especially his redemptive role in the history of the holy city (Isa 3:1), after judging it so harshly. In the Arabic version, Yahweh resolutely acts not only to *return* the city to its former status but to *transform* and *restore* it to its original glory and to deliver the people of Israel by transforming former times into new, hopeful, promising ones. Thus the Arabic verb chosen by Sa'adia captures a strong theme underlying the book of Isaiah, which is related to restoring respect, fame, glory, and dignity for Jerusalem and her people, as well as to the abolition of a divine punishment. It highlights the theme, in the prophet's thought, of the turning around and coming full circle for the divine verdict that had initially caused the city's destruction and the exile of its people (Isa 3:1; 54:6–7).

Another point concerning the verb 'aruddu is that it accurately reflects the verbal Hebrew form we-ashiva (first-person singular, yiqtol), with Yahweh as speaker. Retaining the first-person singular in Arabic appears to assert Yahweh's forceful involvement in history as the restorer of Jerusalem's glory and its miraculous future transformation. The verb emphasizes Yahweh as judge, and Jerusalem as the judged city (also elsewhere in Isa 3:26; 40:1–2). It also shows Yahweh's profound capability to accomplish the transformation of Jerusalem's former times and install a new system of governance based on justice and righteousness. Though Sa'adia could have chosen not to retain the first-person pronoun in Arabic, he does so, I believe, in order to emphasize the divine commitment to the city and her people. Thus he connects Isa 1:26 to the wider theme of the active divine restoration of Zion that underlies the book. For instance, in Isa 40:2 ("Speak tenderly to Jerusalem, and cry to her that she has served her term, that her penalty is paid, that she has received from the LORD's hand double for all her sins"), Yahweh the judge tangibly and influentially intervenes in

---

12. Ibraheem Mustafa et al., *Al-Mo'jamam Al-Wasset*, 2 vols. (Istanbul: Islamic Library, 1972), 338.

the unfolding history of his people and city. Yahweh changes his former verdict, so that the judged/punished city of Jerusalem is forgiven, and then graciously given a new life full of hope, peace, optimism, and glory.

In summary, the choice of the Arabic verb *'aruddu* for translating *we-ashiva* in Isa 1:26 eloquently captures the Isaian theme of Zion's/Jerusalem's restoration, its transformation, and its return to the original status of glory and fame as Yahweh's unique dwelling place on earth, including his direct involvement in the whole process of its deliverance. This is all happening in the aftermath of its past demise and destruction and the exile of its people.

Interestingly, the Karaite translator, Yefet ben 'Eli, also uses the Arabic verb *'aruddu* for translating *we-ashiva* in Isa 26:1,[13] while other medieval and modern Christian Arabic versions use the Arabic root *'yn* (verb form II) instead of the root *rdd* for translating *we-ashiva*. The form *'aruddu* stresses the accomplishment of an action or mission. Sa'adia's choice clearly focuses, therefore, on the priority God will give to restoring Jerusalem to its original state.

Moreover, in Arabic, verbs are also connected to certain contexts or specific (extra-linguistic) environments. The verb *'aruddu* can be related to a "desert" context (*şahrai*), whereas the verb *'ayyan*—with its soft pronunciation—can be related to an "urban" context. One can presume then that Sa'adia was influenced by a desert context, not an urban one, here and used the Arabic *'aruddu* to emphasize the accomplishment of a mission and the tangible transformation which would be happening in Jerusalem, also affecting its exiled people. Thus he was affording this mission a note of noble accomplishment and making tangible the deliverance of Jerusalem by Yahweh within a real historical context. The Christian versions reflect a verb which denotes the mere issuing of a decree or order for the appointment of judges or leaders in Jerusalem.

Another Arabic term Sa'adia also uses in translating Hebrew *ke-bar-ishona* in Isa 26:1 is *kal-'ibtida'*, which means "as at the first." The noun is derived from the Arabic root *bd'* ("begin/start," verb form VIII) especially in the sense of doing things before others, advancing a mission or task as a priority, or initiating something.[14] It also means to found and create.[15] In the Qur'an, the verb *bada'a* (verb form I) is used in connec-

---

13. See MS SP RNL Yevr.-Arab. 1:568 27a (F35623 at the IMHM).

14. Mustafa, *Al-Mo'jamam Al-Wasset*, 42.

15. Mustafa, *Al-Mo'jamam Al-Wasset*, 42.

tion to creation by God.[16] (Q Al-Rum 30:27: "He it is Who originates/
begins (*yabda'u*) creation and then repeats it, and it is most easy for
Him.")[17]

In addition, the nominal *'ibtida'* is used to refer to the appearance of
a new tooth after fallout, especially for children.[18] It also means to "resort
to the first road," which one has come from.[19] Further, the definite form
al-'ibtida' is also used as a technical term to commonly refer to one of the
famous rules in the recitation of the Qur'an, meaning the reinitiation of
reading after a pause, stopping, or cutting off.

Reflecting on the diverse meanings of the nominal *'ibtida'* and the
verb *'ibtida'a*, one may conclude that Sa'adia's choice of this term also has
a theological undertone: Yahweh, who deserted Jerusalem, causing the
collapse of its system and life (Isa 3:1), will initiate a change. The city's
bleak and distressful condition will be marvelously altered when Yahweh
will renew his role in history as the redeemer of Jerusalem and its people;
and he will be giving high priority to accomplishing this mission. Thus,
the term highlights Yahweh's active role in the restoration and rebuilding
that would follow Jerusalem's catastrophe, by which his temporary absence
(pause or absence) from the holy city will cease. Yahweh will embark on a
new marvelous mission to restore the city as at the beginning: to its former
glory, fame, and prominence.

Further in Isa 1:26, Sa'adia translates the phrase *'ir ha-tzedeq qiryah
ne'emanah* (Heb. "city of justice, the faithful city") as Arabic *balad al-'adl
al-qarya al-'amina* ("country of justice, the faithful village"). The translation of *'ir [ha-tzedeq]* as *balad* stands out, since in Arabic this means
"country," not "city" (only *baldah* means "town"). Moreover, the medieval
and modern Christian Arabic versions use the expression *madinat al-'adl*
("city of justice"), as does the Karaite translator, Yefet ben 'Eli.[20] One may
curiously ask: Why does Sa'adia use *balad* ("country") instead of the obvious *madina* ("city")? A study of the references to *balad* in the Qur'an may
provide a plausible answer.

16. Muhammad Ibn Mukarram Ibn 'Alī ibn Ahmad Ibn Manzūr, *Lisān Al-'Arab*,
20 vols. (Beirut: Dar Ehya Al-Tourah Al Arabi, 1986), 1:334.

17. Khan, *The Quran*, 398 (with slight changes).

18. Mustafa, *Al-Mo'jamam Al-Wasset*, 42.

19. Majd Al-Din Muhammad Ibn Yaqub Al-Fayruzabadi, *Al-Qamoos Al-Muheet*
(Beirut: Dar Al Fikr, 1995), 33.

20. See MS SP RNL Yevr.-Arab. 1:568 27a (F35623 at the IMHM)

Noticeably, the Qur'an refers to Mecca as *balad*; and Muslim theologians say it was the first name given to it by the prophet Abraham (Q Ibraheem 14:35: "When Abraham said: My Lord, make this country [*hadha al-balad*, Mecca] inviolate, and keep me and my children away from the worship of idols").[21] Further, Al-Balad is the ninetieth chapter of the Qur'an, with twenty verses all lashing out a severe attack against the people of Mecca, who opposed the prophet Mohammad and strongly rejected his claims to prophecy. Most Muslim exegetes agree that *balad* is an idiosyncratic reference to the holy city of Mecca.

In Arabic *balad* also refers to a large portion of land.[22] Thus, Sa'adia's choice of this lexeme as a signifier for Jerusalem may be a deliberate polemical indication that Jerusalem—not Mecca—is the real and true *balad* ("country") and the center of earth, because Yahweh resides in Jerusalem, which is his favorite and chosen dwelling on earth (Isa 8:18; 28:16). In addition, even if Sa'adia's usage of the term *balad* is not an allusion to the association with Mecca (as an anti-Muslim polemic), it seems that in Sa'adia's theological thinking Jerusalem is not a mere city (*madina*), but an entire country (*balad*) or kingdom. By choosing this word, he highlights Jerusalem's special status for the Jews as a holy location (which can be extended to the land of Zion/Israel in general; *ziyyon* being mentioned immediately after, in v. 27). Sa'adia's choice of *balad* here is meaningful in several ways and certainly expresses the strong attachment to Jerusalem as the center of faith in Yahweh and of the historical experience of the Israelites, as well as the Jews, through the generations.

In translating the second part of the *'ir ha-tzedeq // qiryah ne'emanah* parallelism, Sa'adia uses the Arabic expression *al-qarya al-'amina*, "the faithful/genuine/authentic village." The Arabic adjective *'amin* usually means "known to be true or genuine, trustworthy" and "reliable," and, in some contexts, "safe." When used to describe a person, it means "fair and just in character or behavior," "not cheating or stealing," "free of deceit and untruthfulness," and "sincere." Considering all these denotations and connotations, the description of the city of Jerusalem as *al-'amina* perfectly fits its unique status as Yahweh's dwelling place on earth, for theologically it is meant to mirror his values.

---

21. Zaffrulla Khan, *The Quran*, 241 (with slight changes).
22. Mustafa, *Al-Mo'jamam Al-Wasset*, 68.

Sa'adia also uses the word *al-qarya* (Arab. "village"). The noun *al-qarya* appears fifty-six times in the Qur'an, and in many cases it is an obvious reference to Mecca (Q An-Nahl 16:112; Muhammad 47:3; An-Nisa' 4:75). Similar to the use of the term *balad*, Sa'adia seems to stress here, in a subversive polemical reference, the theological superiority of Jerusalem over Mecca. He does so by installing in the reader's mind the notion that this term is used to refer to the city of Jerusalem as Yahweh's faithful or genuine city on earth.

Several other observations about Isa 1:26 seem appropriate. The verse begins with the prefix *we*, generally known in Biblical Hebrew as the *waw* consecutive. Its Arabic cognate is termed *waw al-'atf* ("conjunction *wa*"). Indeed, one of the functions of the *waw* consecutive in Biblical Hebrew is to link together two or more elements in the text. Its function in Isa 1:26 is probably to create a link with the preceding verse, Isa 1:25: "I will turn my hand against you; I will smelt away your dross as with lye and remove all your alloy." This link shows that Jerusalem's purging will be followed by the restoration of its system of governance and that she will be given new (respectable) names.[23] Theologically, Yahweh works according to a determined plan and his actions have a meaningful purpose in human history; accordingly, his purging and cleansing of the city and the exile of its people (Isa 1:21–23; 3:1) will eventually culminate in the reemergence of her past glory (Isa 1:21), her restoration, and deliverance.

Sa'adia translates the Hebrew temporal conjunction *'aharey khen* (Isa 1:26) with Arabic *ba'da dhalika* ("after that"). This expression serves to connect the clauses in Isa 1:26. This connection manifests the timeframe of Yahweh's plan concerning Jerusalem's deliverance in Isa 1:25–26: the purging of the city will be followed by restoring the judges and counselors. After this, Jerusalem's names will also be restored, and she will be renamed "city of justice/faithfulness." Thus, the reflection of the Hebrew conjunctions (*waw* and *'aharey khen*) in the Arabic translation evidently expresses

---

23. The Hebrew term *qiryah ne'emanah* is also found in Isa 1:21, though in reference to the city having become an "(unfaithful) whore" (Heb. *zonah*), hence the emphasis in v. 26 is on her reclaiming of the title *ne'emanah* ("faithful"). Note that while Sa'adia's translation of *qiryah ne'emanah* in v. 21 is consistent with v. 26 (Arab. *kayfa ṣarat tagiya al-qarya al-'amina*): "how has the faithful city erred to idol worship," he does not render the Hebrew *zonah* literally here, most likely due to apologetic reasons.

the smooth and systematic stages of Yahweh's plan concerning the future of Jerusalem and its exiled people.

To sum up, in the translation of Isa 1:26, Sa'adia's use of the Arabic verb 'aruddu (with Yahweh as its subject) in rendering Hebrew we-ashiva, and his use of the passive Arabic verb tud'inu ("she will be named") in rendering Hebrew yiqqare' lakh ("you will be named"), seems to stress a strong theological undertone of the prophetic text, namely, that Yahweh is the sole power behind the restoration of Jerusalem's judges and counselors, and that this is his foremost priority. For any reader who might infer that the nations, or even the people of Israel, are the initiators of this change, the translation makes doubly clear that only God can perpetrate it. He will be the one who will call Jerusalem by its new and astounding names. The semantics of the translated text underlines the systematic interaction and compatibility between Yahweh's past response and future plan concerning Zion, and the positive human response to it. Yahweh's actions to alter Jerusalem's grim condition and desolate past become tangible to the reader: real occurrences in human history, not mere promises or decrees. Yahweh does not act in a vacuum devoid of actual historical contexts; the divine declaration will be fulfilled and realized in an actual historical reality, and it will be acknowledged and appreciated by the peoples of the earth as well as the people of Israel.

Isaiah 2:2

Sa'adia's translation:[24] *Fa-yakun fi 'akhir al-zaman 'an yakun jabal bayt 'allah muhiyan 'ala ru'us al-jibal wa-saniyan[25] min al-yafa' wa-yuqbil 'ilayhi jumu' al-'umam.[26]*

English translation of Sa'adia's text: In the last of time, the mountain of the Lord's house will be established on the heads of the mountains, and raised above the hill, and the masses of nations shall head to it.

---

24. Ratzaby, *Saadya's Translation and Commentary on Isaiah*, 6.

25. The *an* at the end of *muhiyan* and *saniyan* signifies a *tanwin* ending, which in classical Judeo-Arabic is transliterated by the Hebrew letters *yod* and *aleph*.

26. Isaiah 2:2–4 has an almost verbatim parallel in Mic 4:1–3. Since only a few excerpts of Sa'adia's translation are extant for the Minor Prophets, no comparison is possible for this text.

NRSV: In days to come the mountain of the LORD's house shall be established as the highest of the mountains, and shall be raised above the hills; all the nations shall stream to it.

The verse highlights the value of Yahweh's house, or his temple in Jerusalem, which shall be established as the highest of mountains. The verse likely asserts the insignificance of other temples when compared with the great prominence and stark importance of Mount Zion, Yahweh's dwelling. Thus, Jerusalem is a city that attracts the conspicuous attention of the whole world, as the masses of peoples stream to it to be in Yahweh's vicinity.

In examining Saʿadia's translation of this verse, there are some points that are worth highlighting. Saʿadia translates the Hebrew idiom *aharit ha-yamim* quite literally by the Arabic *'akhir al-zaman* (lit. "last of time"), and so does the Karaite translator Yefet ben ʿEli;[27] whereas the medieval and modern Christian Arabic versions use the more comprehensible expression, *al-'ayam al-'akhirah* ("the last days"). Is there special theological significance in Saʿadia's usage of *'akhir al-zaman*? As shown in our discussion, he seems to be relying on the idiom's specific Islamic connotations. In Muslim theology the expression *'akhir al-zaman* ("last time") refers to eschatology, a branch of Islamic thought concerned with the end of the world or the termination of life on earth and the occurrence of the "day of resurrection" (Arab. *yawm al-qiyama*). In Islamic literature, the expressions *al-yawm al-'akhir* ("last day") or *al-'akhira* ("end of time") denote the day of judgment and the day of resurrection.

In the Qur'an, *al-'akhira* means "afterlife," as evident in Q Al-Aʿla 87:16–17: "But you prefer the hither life, whereas the Hereafter [*al-'akhira*] is better and more lasting."[28] It is obvious that Saʿadia uses a term embedded in Islamic theology, but the theological rendition is quite different in his translation and within the context of the verse. In contrast to the Islamic expression, which is concerned with the annihilation of all forms of life, followed by the resurrection of dead and the judgment by Allah, Saʿadia's *'akhir al-zaman* ("last time") primarily concentrates on the restoration of Yahweh's house in Jerusalem, sitting on the highest of the mountains, with the massive voluntarily streaming of many peoples to learn of Yahweh's teachings and abide by his instructions (Isa 2:3). Saʿadia employs the

---

27. See MS SP RNL Yevr.-Arab. 1:568 30a (F35623 at the IMHM).
28. Khan, *The Quran*, 615.

expression within a new context to highlight the centrality of Jerusalem: Yahweh will not be sitting in judgment in the "last time" in Jerusalem; rather, he will be spreading his teachings and light, thus embracing the people of Israel and entire humanity. This "last time" is not the end but actually a new beginning. Here we witness a new resurrection anchored in Yahweh's redemptive intervention and graceful deeds in human history. Yahweh's actions in Zion are indeed rooted here in a theology of life, happening within a reconciliatory atmosphere, which celebrates Jerusalem's religious prominence, glamorous status, and theological significance.

Therefore, Sa'adia seems to transform the purport of the expression 'akhir al-zaman from its Islamic theological milieu—a dreadful time replete with fear, punishment, and anxiety—to a new time of joy, new life, acceptance, and celebration: the future encounter with Yahweh in Jerusalem is located within a new redemptive, hopeful, and inclusive context.

Moreover, in this verse Sa'adia uses two Classical Arabic words to capture the lofty position of the temple in Jerusalem. The participle (Arab. root hy', verb form IV) used to translate the Hebrew nakhon means "good looking/shapely." In our context it can also mean "regaining good shape" in the aftermath of reparation, or suffering damage.[29] The participle (Arab. root sny, verb form I) used to translate the Hebrew nissa' means "high, sublime" and "exalted." The Arabic root is also used to describe "increasing light" or "flames of fire."[30] It may refer to gaining reputation, fame, glory, and prominence.[31] The noun sana' denotes flashes of light produced by thunder.[32]

So we see how both Arabic words chosen by Sa'adia show concreteness and focus the reader on a visualization of the Temple Mount and on the actual accomplishment of the restoration of Yahweh's house in Zion. The two words also appear to stress that the existence of the Jerusalem temple is tangible, visible, magnificent, and lofty. Interestingly, the medieval and modern Christian Arabic versions use the word zahiran ("visible") to convey a similar idea; and Yefet ben 'Eli uses two words—murattab ("arranged/set up"; participle, verb form II) for Hebrew nakhon, and wa-yatasana ("will be sublime," similar to Sa'adia's choice) for the Hebrew nissa'.[33] Sa'adia, how-

---

29. Ibn Manzūr, Lisān Al-ʿArab, 15:170.

30. Mustafa, Al-Moʾjamam Al-Wasset, 456.

31. Mustafa, Al-Moʾjamam Al-Wasset, 456.

32. Mustafa, Al-Moʾjamam Al-Wasset, 1116.

33. See MS SP RNL Yevr.-Arab. I:568 30a (F35623 at the IMHM).

ever, employs two more distinctively Classical Arabic participles in order to thicken this lofty visibility and magnitude of Yahweh's house, which acquires an actual, physical existence through his word choice.

Sa'adia uses the Arabic lexeme *al-yafa'* (in the singular: "hill overlooking land") to translate the Hebrew *geva'ot* (in the plural). The plural of *al-yafa'* is *yufu'*; yet, Sa'adia seems to deliberately refrain from using it.[34] Sometimes *al-yafa'* is used to refer to all high places, including high mountains.[35] The verbal *yafa'a* means "to become lofty" or "high" and may also convey a meaning related to beauty. The medieval and modern Christian Arabic versions translate *geva'ot* literally by the more regular and plural Arabic noun *tilal* ("hills"), and the Karaite translator Yefet ben 'Eli uses another common noun, *al-ruwabi* ("hills"), also in the plural.[36]

Sa'adia's insistence on the unusual noun *al-yafa'*, in the singular, appears to refer to a specific house, raised from a particular hill, not just raised above all the hills. In his translation the house of Yahweh in Jerusalem is raised from a specific hill (*yafa'*) overlooking the land. His usage stresses the Jerusalem temple as having a defined location, on a conspicuously visible hill overlooking the land, which has a beautiful shape. No wonder, then, that all the peoples have interest in it and can easily find it when they stream to Zion. This may also hint that Yahweh, in his Jerusalem dwelling, would be very accessible and approachable because no hindrances would impede the direct encounter between him and humans at his holy and beautiful abode, the temple, which can be visible above the heads of other mountains and is situated remarkably on a specific hill. In this translation, this alluring place in Zion is quite known and has a definitive address, since no earthly power will be able to conceal its physical presence.

Isaiah 2:3

Sa'adia's translation:[37] *wa-yantaliqu al-shu'ub al-kathirun wa-yaqulun ta'alu nas'ad 'ila jabal 'allah wa-'ila bayt 'ilah ya'qub yadulluna min sayarihi ma nasir bihi fi turuqihi li'anna al-tawrah*

---

34. Mustafa, *Al-Mo'jamam Al-Wasset*, 1064.

35. Ibn Manẓūr, *Lisān Al-'Arab*, 15:425, where the word is said to denote "anything that is elevated."

36. See MS SP RNL Yevr.-Arab. 1:568 30a (F35623 at the IMHM).

37. This translation is cited from Ratzaby, *Saadya's Translation and Commentary on Isaiah*.

takhruj min ziyyon (Heb.) *wa-kalam 'allah min yerushalayim* [the name of the city follows its Heb. pronunciation]

English translation of Saʿadia's text: Numerous peoples are proceeding, and say: come to ascend to the mountain of the Lord and to the house of the Lord of Jacob, in order to guide us in his ways and how to walk in his paths, because the Torah goes out from Zion, and the words of the Lord from Jerusalem.

NRSV: Many peoples shall come and say, "Come, let us go up to the mountain of the LORD, to the house of the God of Jacob; that he may teach us his ways and that we may walk in his paths." For out of Zion shall go forth instruction, and the word of the LORD from Jerusalem.

Isaiah 2:3e describes many peoples who will stream to Jerusalem at the end of days (continuing v. 2), thus underscoring the prophetic message that Yahweh will indeed restore his holy city to its former glory and fame. These peoples shall go to Zion for a good purpose: to learn Yahweh's teachings and his words that go forth from Jerusalem. This portrayal of the willingness to journey to Jerusalem reflects an optimistic attitude toward people in general: they are willing to come closer to Yahweh in order to learn his ways in Zion. In theological terms, this portrayal reflects the positive spirit of this future age of Zion's transformation, as Yahweh reconciles with all peoples in Jerusalem, when it becomes the center of world attention and worship.

Saʿadia's Arabic version opens with the verb *'inṭalaqa* (Arab. root *ṭlq*, verb form VII), which usually means "move" or "run" rapidly or quickly,[38] and also "move rapidly after being freed from chains." In general, the verb connotes moving in order to gain freedom and, subsequently, become unrestrained. As such, it is a rather loaded translation of the Heb. *wehalkhu* (lit. "they will walk"). The Arabic verb reflects accurately the present continuous/future tense of the Hebrew, yet it clearly intensifies the picture of peoples' rapid and continuous movement from all corners of the earth, with great enthusiasm, to embrace the belief in Yahweh in his dwelling place, Zion. Through the choice of the Arabic root *ṭlq*, these peoples are

---

38. Mustafa, *Al-Mo'jamam Al-Wasset*, 562.

described as gaining a new freedom as they make their rapid journey to Jerusalem, which will further nourish their theological and spiritual experiences and transform their previous aggressive behavior (2:4). Elsewhere in Isaiah we also find that, for the people of Israel, the journey to Zion is the attainment of a new freedom, terminating the long and painful years of exile and deportation (Isa 26; 40).

When translating the Hebrew *'amim* ("peoples"), Sa'adia uses the Arabic plural *al-shu'ub* (singular *sha'b*): again an interesting choice, since it often refers to a large group of persons, larger than a tribe, sharing one father and speaking one language.[39] The use of this particular word seems to highlight that the many peoples who shall stream to Jerusalem will contain many large groups sharing identity and culture. This may indicate that, within this special unity of peoples streaming to Jerusalem, there is also tremendous diversity. Sa'adia's translation of the Hebrew *we-amru* ("and they will say") is literal (Arab. *wa-yaqulun*). The act of "saying" seems to stress that Jerusalem, in its new times of deliverance, would have regained its universal appeal and global attention, so that people encourage other people to come to worship Yahweh in it. Yahweh promises Jerusalem glory and fame; Zion's glory would be spread through word of mouth by all the peoples of the earth.

In rendering the Hebrew *na'aleh* ("we shall ascend"), Sa'adia uses the Arabic root *ṣ'd* (in the verb form I).[40] In the Qur'an, this verb also means "ascend (to God)" (Q Saba' 35:10: "To Him ascend [*yaṣ'adu*] good words, and righteous conduct exalts them")[41] This verb is often used in the qur'anic context in relation to God, whose dwelling and throne are in heaven. Sa'adia's choice of it seems to be influenced by the qur'anic meaning and setting since, in the case of Jerusalem, ascending to the mountain of Yahweh aims at coming closer to God and encountering his presence at his dwelling place in Zion.

Sa'adia translates the Hebrew phrase *yoreynu mi-derakhav* ("that he may teach [or "show"] us his ways") into Arabic *yadulluna min sayarihi* ("guide us in his ways"). The Arabic root *dll* (verb form I) means "guide," "show the right way."[42] Interestingly, the medieval and modern Christian

---

39. Mustafa, *Al-Mo'jamam Al-Wasset*, 482.

40. So does also Yefet ben 'Eli; see MS SP RNL Yevr.-Arab. 1:568 30b (F35623 at the IMHM).

41. Khan, *The Quran*, 428.

42. Mustafa, *Al-Mo'jamam Al-Wasset*, 294.

versions use the common Arabic root 'lm ("teach," verb form II), and Yefet ben 'Eli uses the verb rashada ("teach/instruct"), which often has a religious sense of "following the right path."[43] Sa'adia's translation again intensifies the high expectations and emotions of the peoples streaming to Jerusalem. They anticipate receiving divine guidance from God in order to know and follow the right path to Yahweh: the journey made by these peoples has a moral and thoughtful purpose, to be fulfilled while they seek and find divine guidance in Zion/Jerusalem.

This understanding is strengthened by the word sayarihi, Arabic for "ways/paths," with a particular semantic focus on learning about histories, legacy, actions, speeches, proverbs, and so on.[44] Thus, these nations stream to Jerusalem to learn about Jacob's history and legacy and to follow his path. Jacob, whose Arabized qur'anic name Ya'qub is used by Sa'adia, is recognized in Islam as a prophet guided by God (Q Al-An'am 6:84). One can find certain connections between the prophet Ya'qub (Jacob) and the theme of guidance in qur'anic understanding. The use of the Arabized form Ya'qub in Sa'adia's translation (and so he does with regard to other Hebrew names like Musa [for Moshe, Moses], etc.) creates a connection with the Islamic tradition of the revered Israelite prophets. Unlike this translation of a proper Hebrew personal name, when it comes to the proper Hebrew place name, Sa'adia prefers to retain the Hebrew name of Jerusalem, Yerushalayim, in his Judeo-Arabic text. He could have applied well-known medieval Arabic names of the city, such as al-Quds or Bayt al-Maqdis. By retaining Yerushalayim he appears to stress the ancient Hebraic origin of the city's name, hence what might be deemed the Jewishness of the city, or the Jews' historical connection to it. The fact that he does not do so with regard to Jacob or Moses suggests to me that his choice of Yerushalayim here might be polemical, so as to completely distance it from Islamic contexts or claims, of which he is undoubtedly well aware.[45]

---

43. See MS SP RNL Yevr.-Arab. 1:568 30b (F35623 at the IMHM).

44. Mustafa, Al-Mo'jamam Al-Wasset, 467.

45. Yefet ben 'Eli also uses the Hebrew forms of Jacob, Zion, and Jerusalem, as a general practice. See Meira Polliack, The Karaite Tradition of Arabic Bible Translation: A Linguistic and Exegetical Study of the Karaite Translations of the Pentateuch from the Tenth and Eleventh Centuries C.E. (Leiden: Brill, 1997), 200–208. Note, however, that Yefet translates torah in Isa 2:3 by the Arabic shari'ah (a distinctive Islamic term for law); see MS SP RNL Yevr.-Arab. 1:568 30b (F35623 at the IMHM).

Further in the verse Sa'adia uses the Arabic verb *kharaja* ("go forth" and "separate"; verb form I), in the present continuous/future, in rendering the Hebrew *tetse'* ("will come forth").[46] Most dictionaries emphasize that the verb *kharaja* is the opposite of the verb *dakhala*, Arabic for "enter."[47] Thus, *takhruj* can be juxtaposed with *yantaliqu*, examined above, to consider that the verse captures two different and complementary movements to Jerusalem: entering Jerusalem, and departing from it. As the peoples of the earth rapidly stream to come *into* Jerusalem, the words of Yahweh and his teachings (Heb. *torah*) go forth *from* Zion, without interruption. This ongoing movement highlights the significance of Jerusalem as an active religious center of global attention and interest, wholeheartedly welcoming worshipers and spreading the words of Yahweh who resides amongst his holy people in Zion.

Jerusalem's magnificence is further intensified in Sa'adia's translation as he translates the Hebrew phrase *devar Yahweh* ("word" or "saying" of Yahweh, in the singular) by the Arabic *kalam Allah*. Arabic *kalam* is the plural of the singular noun *kalima*. This is in line with the Islamic theological use of the Arabic phrase, since the Qur'an is described by Muslims as *kalam Allah* ("words of Allah"). The medieval Christian Arabic versions use the term *kalimat al-rab* ("word [in the singular] of the Lord"). The use of the plural amplifies the significance of Yahweh's words that go forth from Zion, thus asserting that Yahweh in his magnificence has *many words* originating from his holy abode in Zion, not only *one word*. Moreover, this use again reflects Sa'adia's subtle polemical stance, brilliantly imbued in the Arabic lexicon of his translation. It is as if he is saying to his Jewish but possibly also Muslim readers: what the Muslims call the "words of Allah," which is the name of their Holy Qur'an, is actually what the ancient Hebrew prophets called *devar Yahweh*. The biblical Jacob is your Jacob, and so on. Does this mean that Jerusalem also should be more like its biblical depiction at the end of days, as found in Isaiah?

Conclusions

Haggai Ben-Shammai points out that Sa'adia was faced with the task of rendering the sacred text of Judaism into a language that had become the

---

46. Mustafa, *Al-Mo'jamam Al-Wasset*, 224.
47. Al-Murtaḍá al-Husaynī Al-Zabīdī, *Tāj Al-'Arūs*, 5 vols (Kuwait: Arabic Heritage, 1969), 5:508.

vehicle for a new, expanding religion with imperial backing.[48] His task could be seen as being both an attempt to Judaize the Arabic language and to Arabize Judaism. The observations in this essay have shown that Sa'adia's translations of the references to Jerusalem in Isaiah evidence his creativity and innovation, since he does not adhere to a style of a word-to-word literal translation. He interacts with the target language to provide new interpretative insights and meanings, so that the significance of Jerusalem, as he understands it, within the biblical source text, is powerfully expressed in Arabic and within a new non-biblical linguistic setting.

These observations also show that Sa'adia had great familiarity with and knowledge of Islamic theological and literary concepts and themes; yet, he employs them to serve his exegetical purpose, which is to draw attention to the importance and magnificence of Jerusalem as a leading holy city in biblical thought and in its Jewish understanding, and to differentiate between certain Islamic notions and Jewish ones. Indeed, he employs the Islamic terms within a biblical context, while retaining and enriching the distinctive character and spirit of the biblical text.

Sa'adia's Arabic is of a high register, and his word choice clearly manifests his depth of knowledge in the Arabic lexicon and qur'anic terminology. He eloquently crafts his translation to capture subtle theological meanings concerning Zion, thus benefiting from the wealth of Arabic vocabulary, creating a lively and powerful engagement with the biblical text and more venues for further reflection and interpretation. He invites the reader versed in the Arabic language to interact with the biblical text in each reading, and to have a thoughtful and continuous dialogue with its words.

Sa'adia's Arabic word choice for describing Jerusalem's deliverance shows he is not so much concerned with the actual fulfillment of the predictive dimension of biblical prophecy, but rather with the historical horizon of the biblical prophets themselves. The hopes and desires for Jerusalem's deliverance are kept alive, as expressed in his choice of words, while the aspirations for preserving Zion's glory cannot be limited to one historical reality or time setting. Each generation can experience Jerusalem's pivotal significance and its fascinating centrality in new, creative, inspiring, and innovative terms. Sa'adia successfully managed to assert that the stream-

---

48. Haggai Ben-Shammai, *A Leader's Project: Studies in the Philosophical and Exegetical Works of Saadya Gaon* [Hebrew] (Jerusalem: Bialik Institute, 2015), 145.

ing of peoples to Jerusalem is a continuous action, an unhindered process of imperishable desire. Perhaps he had this desire, too. His attachment to Jerusalem is quite evident through his word choice. This attests to his awareness of Zion's everlasting and enduring theological stature, which cannot be tied merely to messianic expectations. In short, his translation succeeds not only in retaining the emotive aspects of the biblical text about Jerusalem but also in enriching it, augmenting the enduring presence of Jerusalem by using a nonbiblical language—Arabic, the sacred language of the Qur'an. The reader of his text in Arabic truly enjoys each word Sa'adia diligently and eloquently crafted, and is irresistibly invited to traverse the abundant meanings of Jerusalem's deliverance and its marvelous transformation.

Bibliography

Al-Fayruzabadi, Majd Al-Din Muhammad Ibn Yaqub. *Al-Qamoos Al-Muheet.* Beirut: Dar Al Fikr, 1995.

Al-Zabīdī, Al-Murtaḍá al-Husaynī. *Tāj Al-ʿArūs.* 5 vols. Kuwait: Arabic Heritage, 1969.

Ashur, Amir, Sivan Nir, and Meira Polliack. "Three Fragments of Sa'adya Gaon's Arabic Translation of Isaiah Copied by the Court Scribe Joseph ben Samuel (c. 1181–1209). Pages 487–508 in *Senses of Scripture, Treasures of Tradition: The Bible in Arabic among Jews, Christians and Muslims.* Edited by Miriam Lindgren Hjälm. Leiden: Brill, 2017.

Ben-Shammai, Haggai. *A Leader's Project: Studies in the Philosophical and Exegetical Works of Saadya Gaon.* Jerusalem: Bialik Institute, 2015.

Gil, Moshe. *Jews in Islamic Countries in the Middle Ages.* Translated by David Strassler. Leiden: Brill, 2004.

Goitein, Shelomo Dov. *A Mediterranean Society: The Jewish Communities of the Arab World as Portrayed in the Documents of the Cairo Geniza.* 2 vols. Berkeley: University of California Press, 1967.

Griffith, Sidney H. *The Bible in Arabic: The Scriptures of the People of the Book in the Language of Islam.* Princeton: Princeton University Press, 2013.

Ibn Manzūr, Muhammad Ibn Mukarram Ibn ʿAlī ibn Ahmad. *Lisān Al-ʿArab.* 20 vols. Beirut: Dar Ehya Al-Tourath Al Arabi, 1986.

Khan, Muhammad Zafrulla. *The Quran, Arabic Text with a New Translation.* rev. ed. London: Curzon, 1981.

Lasker, Daniel J. "Saadya Gaon on Christianity and Islam." Pages 165–77 in *The Jews of Medieval Islam: Community, Society, and Identity*. Edited by Daniel Frank. Leiden: Brill, 1995.

Masliyah, Sadok. "Saadia Gaon's Arabic Versions of the Book of Isaiah." *Hebrew Studies* 20–21 (1979–1980): 80–87.

Mustafa, Ibraheem, et al., eds. *Al-Mo'jamam Al-Wasset*. 2 vols. Istanbul: Islamic Library, 1972.

Polliack, Meira. "Arabic Bible Translations in the Cairo Genizah Collections." Pages 595–620 in *Jewish Studies in a New Europe: Proceedings of the Fifth Congress of Jewish Studies in Copenhagen 1994*. Edited by Ulf Haxen, Hanne Trautner-Kromann, and Karen Lisa Goldschmidt-Salamon. Copenhagen: C. A. Reitzel, 1998.

———. "Bible Translations: Judeo-Arabic (Ninth to the Thirteenth Centuries)." *EJIW* 1:464–69.

———. *The Karaite Tradition of Arabic Bible Translation: A Linguistic and Exegetical Study of the Karaite Translations of the Pentateuch from the Tenth to the Eleventh Centuries CE*. Leiden: Brill, 1997.

Ratzaby, Yehuda. *Saadya's Translation and Commentary on Isaiah: Collected, Edited with Translation and Notes*. Kiriat Ono: Makhon Moshe, 1993.

Seitz, Christopher. *Zion's Final Destiny: The Development of the Book of Isaiah: A Reassessment of Isaiah 36–39*. Minneapolis: Fortress, 1991.

Steiner, Richard C. *A Biblical Translation in the Making: The Evolution and Impact of Saadia Gaon's Tasfir*. Cambridge: Harvard University Press, 2010.

A Ninth-Century Text of Questions and Answers on Biblical Contradictions

David Sklare

The *genizot* of Cairo have preserved fragments of two Judeo-Arabic texts consisting of questions and answers on issues of consistency and apparent contradictions between biblical texts. In both texts, the authors are responding to questions asked by someone else. Both texts are anonymous, but internal indications allow us to date them tentatively to the middle of the ninth century CE. The two texts are similar in style and exegetical approach and may have been composed by the same author, although this cannot be established with any certainty. A few passages in the texts reflect a Christian cultural environment. This, together with the detailed knowledge of Armenia demonstrated in one of the texts, suggests that these texts were written in the area of northern Mesopotamia known by the Arabs as *al-Jazirah*. These texts and their cultural context are discussed in detail in my 2017 article.[1] An overview of the Judeo-Arabic genre of biblical questions and answers may be found in my earlier work (2007).[2] Selections from one text, which I call Text B, are presented here. Fragments of this text have been preserved in two manuscripts: SP RNL Yevr.-Arab. 1:3292; and BL Or. 12299, fols. 26–27.

---

1. David Sklare, "Ninth-Century Judeo-Arabic Texts of Biblical Questions and Answers," in *Senses of Scriptures, Treasures of Tradition: The Bible in Arabic among Jews, Christians and Muslims*, ed. Miriam Lindgren Hjälm, Biblia Arabica 5 (Leiden: Brill, 2017), 104–24. The complete text from which the present selection is taken will be published in the future with a critical edition of the Judeo-Arabic text, together with an annotated English translation.

2. David Sklare, "Scriptural Questions: Early Texts in Judaeo-Arabic" [Hebrew], in *A Word Fitly Spoken: Studies in Mediaeval Exegesis of the Hebrew Bible and the Qur'an Presented to Haggai Ben-Shammai*, ed. Meir Bar-Asher, Simon Hopkins, Sarah Stroumsa, and Bruno Chiesa (Jerusalem: Ben Zvi Institute, 2007), 205–31.

Most of the questions addressed by our author are concerned with apparent contradictions on historical matters between different books of Scripture. The author's exegetical approach is rationalistic, almost scientific. This can be discerned in his answers and in the methodological statement found in his answer to Question 25 (given below). He is clearly a Rabbanite as he recommends studying Mishnah, Talmud, the Mekhiltot, Sifre, and Halakhot Pesuqot as preparation to dealing with questions of the sort he responds to in this text (evidently to sharpen one's mind). Nevertheless, he is critical of Aggadah and Midrash, an attitude found typically among the Geonim of the tenth century CE, from Sa'adia Gaon through Hayya Gaon.[3] Indeed, our author makes very little use of rabbinic exegesis when addressing the questions raised by the interlocutor.

In addition to his original solutions to exegetical problems, our author evidently had an unconventional approach to the redaction of the biblical text. In his response to Question 25, he appears to take the position that Ezra the scribe edited Scripture, interpolating editorial comments. While rabbinic tradition attributes to Ezra an important role in reestablishing the Torah after the Babylonian exile and even in comparing manuscripts and indicating doubtful words with dots, our author goes several steps further.[4] He may have been influenced by the Christian tradition that saw Ezra as the restorer and editor of all of Scripture, a tradition stemming from the story in 4 Ezra 14, in which Scripture is divinely revealed to Ezra. This image of Ezra may be found, for example, in Origen and Eusebius.[5] It would seem that our author's view of Ezra as editor is related to the idea of the *mudawwin* (compiler/editor) used by Jewish exegetes in the tenth and eleventh centuries CE.[6]

---

3. For the approach of the later Geonim to Aggadah, see David Sklare, *Samuel ben Hofni Gaon and His Cultural World: Texts and Studies* (Leiden: Brill, 1996), 39, 42–47.

4. Richard Steiner ("A Jewish Theory of Biblical Redaction from Byzantium: Its Rabbinic Roots, Its Diffusion and Its Encounter with the Muslim Doctrine of Falsification," *JSIJ* 2 [2003]: 123–67) discusses a number of the rabbinic traditions. Hava Lazarus-Yafeh (in ch. 3 of *Intertwined Worlds: Medieval Islam and Bible Criticism* [Princeton: Princeton University Press, 1992]) discusses the polemical use of Ezra as editor in Muslim literature.

5. See Yonatan Moss, "Disorder in the Bible: Rabbinic Responses and Responsibilities," *JSQ* 19 (2012): 108 n. 7; and Moss, "Noblest Obelus: Rabbinic Appropriations of Late Ancient Literary Criticism," in *Homer and the Bible in the Eyes of Ancient Interpreters*, ed. Maren R. Niehoff (Leiden: Brill, 2012), 252 n. 29.

6. See Haggai Ben-Shammai, "On the *Mudawwin*, the Redactor of the Hebrew

Our author and his readers assumed that the books of Scripture are to be read together as a unified text and that there should be no contradictions between different texts. While this assumption also underlies much midrashic exegesis, it may have found new emphasis in this period due to the understanding that Scripture had undergone an editing process by Ezra the priest. This is quite different from the approach of modern exegetes, who see the biblical texts as having been written by different authors in disparate historical contexts. This work, written in the early, nascent period of Judeo-Arabic culture, provides us with a small, limited window into the sorts of exegetical issues that occupied Jewish students of Scripture in the ninth century and how they sought to resolve them.[7]

Translation of Selected Passages

Different Measures: 2,000 Bat [Kings] or 3,000 Bat [Chronicles]?

12. You inquired about what it says in Kings, "It was a handbreadth thick, and its brim was made like that of a cup, like the petals of a lily. Its capacity was 2,000 *bat*" (1 Kgs 7:26); whereas in Chronicles it says, "It was a handbreadth thick, and its brim was made like that of a cup, like the petals of a lily. It held 3,000 *bat*" (2 Chr 4:5). [When it says] 2,000 *bat*, this is with a large measure, and when it says 3,000, this is with a small measure. We might possibly say today that a thing weighs three *raṭls* using the Baghdadi *raṭl*, but when using the Kufi *raṭl* it weighs something like two *raṭls*. Indeed, you see that pepper and saffron and similar things are measured with a *raṭl* whose weight is 260 (*dirhems*). There are (also those who) use a *raṭl* of 400 (*dirhems*). Oil is weighed using a *raṭl* of 130 (*dirhems*) and with a *raṭl* of 300. It may be weighed with a *raṭl* of 165[8] (*dirhems*). Since

---

Bible in Judaeo-Arabic Bible Exegesis" [Hebrew], in *From Sages to Savants: Studies Presented to Avraham Grossman*, ed. Joseph R. Hacker, Yosef Kaplan, and B. Z. Kedar (Jerusalem: Zalman Shazar Center for Jewish History, 2010), 73–110.

7. In the translations below, round parentheses indicate additions made by the translator in order to clarify the meaning of the text. Square brackets indicate text missing in the manuscripts due to holes and tears. Translation of biblical citations is from the Jewish Publication Society (JPS 1985), although altered at times to fit the author's intention. Titles have been added at the beginning of each question/answer so that the content will be clear to the reader.

8. The Judeo-Arabic text has ק'ה' ס. This may be an unusual way of indicating the number 165 or an abbreviation, a technique that the scribe uses in the next sentence.

this (use of different measurements) existed in the days of King Solomon, in this way (a vessel) of two thousand *bat* may also have held three (thousand) *bat*. Therefore, the matter is such that it can include all, fitting what is in Kings and what is said in Chronicles.[9]

Who Carried the Ark—The Priests [Kings] or the Levites [Chronicles]?

13. You inquired about what it says, "When all the elders of Israel had come, the priests lifted the Ark" (1 Kgs 8:3); whereas it says in Chronicles, "When all the elders of Israel had come, the Levites carried the Ark" (2 Chr 5:4). There it says "priests" and here it says "Levites" and you consider this contradictory. It is (however) not as you think, for the priests are called "sons of Levi." They would carry (with) the sons of Kehat,[10] as it says, "Do this with them, that they may live and not die when they approach the most sacred objects: let Aaron and his sons go in and assign each of them to his duties and to his porterage" (Num 4:19). The priests carried the ark of the Lord at the [crossing of the Jordan River, as it says,] "When the feet of the priests bearing the Ark of the Lord, the Sovereign of all the earth, come to rest in the waters of the Jordan, the waters of the Jordan ... will be cut off and will stand in a single heap" (Josh 3:13). In a similar manner, the Levites carried it until they came to the *devir* sanctuary, for they were not permitted to enter into the temple of the Lord. The table and the menorah and the incense altar were not placed in the *devir* of the temple. It (therefore) describes the Levites as carrying it up to the place permitted to them and then the priests carried it to the place where others are not permitted to carry it, and they brought it into the *devir* of the temple, all this in one day. The narrative here does not describe for us all of the procedure (in detail). It says, "Aaron and his sons shall go in and take down the screening curtain and cover the Ark of the Pact with it" (Num 4:5). (Further on) it says, "When Aaron and his sons have finished covering the sacred objects and all the furnishings of the sacred objects at the breaking of camp, only then shall the sons of Kehat come and lift

---

9. Rabbinic literature has different answers to this problem. One answer, based on the difference between dry and liquid measurements, is found in Tosefta Kelim 5:2; Sifre Num. 42; Num. Rab. 11:7; b. Eruv. 14b has yet another approach.

10. The sons of Kehat are those Levites whose job it was to carry the holiest elements of the tabernacle, after the priests had covered them, lest the Levites perish from seeing the holiest things uncovered. See Num 4:1–20.

them, so that they do not come in contact with the sacred objects and die" (Num 4:15). If they (the sons of Aaron) carried for just one step, then Scripture would prove to be true.[11] How much more (did the priests carry the ark) as it describes the *devir* of the temple as being twenty cubits long and twenty cubits wide (1 Kgs 6:20).[12]

Was Solomon's Sukkot Celebration Seven or Eight Days? Kings versus Chronicles

14. You inquired about what it says in Kings, "On the eighth day he let the people go. They bade the king good-bye and went to their tents" (1 Kgs 8:66); whereas it says in Chronicles, "On the twenty-third day of the seventh month he let the people return to their tents..." (2 Chr 7:10).[13] The idea here is that when Israel came on pilgrimage to celebrate a feast, they had tents with them in which to dwell around the city. He (Solomon) enjoined them to stand around the altar and pray until the burnt offering was completely consumed. Hezekiah, king of Judah, acted similarly as it says, "All the congregation prostrated themselves, the song was sung and the trumpets were blown—all this until the end of the burnt offering. When the offering was finished, the king and all who were there with him knelt and prostrated themselves" (2 Chr 29:28–29). On the eighth day, he sent them to their tents that were around the city and on the twenty-third (of the month) he sent them to their villages. For on the eighth day it would not have been permissible for them to carry their baggage and travel on the eighth day as it is a holy convocation (מקרא קודש). Villages can be called "tents," as it says, "The Judahites were routed by Israel, and each person fled to his tent (אהלו)" (2 Kgs 14:12), but they actually fled to their villages. *'Ohalim* (אוהלים) are (also) called tents, as it says, "Now Dathan and Abiram had come out and they stood at the entrance of their

---

11. That is, if the priests carried the various objects just one step in the process of covering them and getting them ready for the sons of Kehat.

12. That is, if the priests carried the tabernacle utensils to place them on the sons of Kehat, and that was considered carrying if only for one step—certainly when the priests carried the ark into the *devir*, which is twenty cubits in length, it should be understood as carrying the ark.

13. The issue here is that the eighth day of the Feast of Tabernacles falls on the twenty-second day of the month. On which day did King Solomon release the people to their tents (or homes), on the twenty-second or the twenty-third?

tents (אהליהם)" (Num 16:27); and as it says, "Move away from the tents of these wicked men" (Num 16:26). The word for a tent is *'ohel* and the word for a village can (also be) *'ohel*.[14]

Where Did Aaron Die? Numbers versus Deuteronomy

15. You inquired about what Scripture says, "From Be'erot-benei-Ya'akan, the Israelites marched to Moserah. Aaron died there and was buried there" (Deut 10:6); whereas (elsewhere) it says, "They set out from Kadesh and encamped at Hor Ha-Har, on the edge of the land of Edom. Aaron the priest ascended Hor ha-Har at the command of the Lord and died there" (Num 33:37–38). The idea here is that one name can refer to fifty villages, more or less. It could be that Hor ha-Har was one of the villages in Moserah. This is similar to what can be said about Armenia. It has a number of cities and many settlements which together are called Armenia, [such as ...] and al-Adin[15] and Shakhi and Gakit and Guakh and K[...]shut and Shuranim and al-Harakh and Khagrund and al-Kunyah [... and] these places are many, being approximately one thousand places. All of them (together) are called Armenia and each also has its own name. This is true also of Syria and Byzantium, Khurasan, Khazaria, Sind, India, Ethiopia, Nubia, the Maghreb, and the land of the Sambation River. In each of these lands there are cities, villages, and fortresses that cannot be counted quickly. It is thus reasonable (to suggest) that Moserah was the name of the entire region and Hor ha-Har was within it, or Hor ha-Har was the name of the region and Moserah was within it. It is impossible to refute this explanation. It thus comes about that there is one meaning for the two verses.[16]

King Ahaziah's Death in Kings and Chronicles: A Contradiction?

16. You inquired about what it says in Chronicles, "He sent in search of Ahaziah, who was caught hiding in Samaria, was brought to Jehu, and

---

14. For the rabbinic response to this issue, see Gen. Rab. 35:3. A different approach is found in b. Mo'ed 9a and Tanḥ. Bereshit 13.

15. The transliterations of the place names are only conjectures. Some experts on Armenian toponyms have tried to identify these places, without much success. The spaces in the text [...] here and elsewhere indicate lacunae in the manuscript.

16. The rabbinic response to this problem was to add some extra travels for the Israelites. See y. Yoma 1:1; Tanḥ. Huqqat 18, and parallel sources.

put to death. He was given a burial..." (2 Chr 22:9); whereas it says in Kings, "On seeing this, King Ahaziah of Judah fled along the road to Beth-haggan. Jehu pursued him and said, 'Shoot him down too!' (And they shot him) in his chariot at the ascent of Gur, which is near Ibleam. He fled to Megiddo and died there" (2 Kgs 9:27). You consider these two verses to be contradictory, but it is not as you think. For it says, "He fled to Megiddo and died there," and when a man flees, it is reasonable that his journey [...] was the name of the city and name of the [...] it was called "the mountains of Gilead" and the Gilead has many villages. Similarly, in the mountains of Samaria there were numerous villages and Megiddo was (one of) these in the district of Samaria. It is possible, however, that among the villages of Israel there were many small villages named Megiddo, just as you know that that there are two Zarephaths. Therefore, God said to the prophet, "Go at once to Zarephath of Sidon" (1 Kgs 17:9).[17] Similarly, many villages with the same name are mentioned in Joshua. In Israel there was a city named Shomrom different from the city built by Omri, as it says in Joshua: "So King Adoni-zedek of Jerusalem sent this message to King Hoham of Hebron (Josh 10:3) and to the king of Shimron-meron" (Josh 12:20).[18] The proof that the name of the mountain is Shomron (is in the verse) since it says, "Then he (Omri) bought the mountain of Samaria from Shemer for two talents of silver; he built [a town] on the mountain and named the town which he built after Shemer, the owner of the mountain" (1 Kgs 16:24). So the name of the mountain was Shomron and Ahaziah fled (there) and hid in a village named Megiddo, one of the villages on the mountain known as Shomron. They killed him in Megiddo and it is sound [...] one is the name of the entire country [and the other is the name] of the village which is part of the country, as I have explained.

Which Tribes Remained Loyal to the House of David, Judah or also Benjamin?

18. You inquired about what it says, "However, I will not tear away the whole kingdom, I will give your son one tribe, for the sake of My servant

---

17. The name Zarephath also appears in Obad 20. The author quotes only the verse referring to Zarephath of Sidon, understanding that the words "of Sidon" were added in order to distinguish this Zarephath from the other one.

18. The author has evidently put two different verses together, perhaps due to a faulty memory. The MT has *Shimron*, while our author has *Shomron*.

David and for the sake of Jerusalem which I have chosen" (1 Kgs 11:13). Moreover, it says, "But one tribe shall remain his..." (1 Kgs 11:32). And again it says, "Only the tribe of Judah remained loyal to the House of David" (1 Kgs 12:20). (On the other hand) in Chronicles it has, "... thus Judah and Benjamin were his" (2 Chr 11:12). There, (in Kings it says) "but one tribe" and here (in Chronicles) it counts two tribes. You therefore consider this to be contradictory. There is, however, no inconsistency here. For God had already related to the prophet that he would give Rehoboam one tribe at one time and two tribes after that, as it says, "Ahijah took hold of the new robe he was wearing and tore it into twelve pieces" (1 Kgs 11:30). Then it says, "'Take ten pieces,' he said to Jeroboam. 'For thus said the Lord, the God of Israel: I am about to tear the kingdom out of Solomon's hands, and I will give you ten tribes'" (1 Kgs 11:31). Does this not indicate that two pieces are for Rehoboam? At the time, [the tribe of Benjamin] did not follow Rehoboam, as it says, "Only the tribe of Judah remained loyal to the House of David" (1 Kgs 12:20). The tribe of Benjamin, however, joined him later, as it says, "Take ten pieces" (1 Kgs 11:31). We have shown that Rehoboam would be given another tribe other than Judah, for Judah were followers of the house of David. Jeroboam had ten tribes and the remaining ones were therefore for Rehoboam, in a manner similar to David who first ruled over Judah and then later ruled over Israel and Judah. Thus, at first the tribe of Judah followed Rehoboam and then Benjamin joined it later on. The verse "I will give your son one tribe" (1 Kgs 11:13) indicates that he will give him another tribe, other than the tribe of Judah, as they were (already) the followers of his house. There is a clear proof in the verse "I will give you the ten tribes" (1 Kgs 11:35) that he promised to give ten tribes to Jeroboam and it is correct and he will give to Rehoboam two tribes and it is correct. There is no element of error in this, so understand and be rightly guided.

Saul and Ish-bosheth

25. Concerning what you inquired about, that it says, "Saul was a year old when he became king, and he reigned over Israel two years" (1 Sam 13:1);[19] and then it says, "Ish-bosheth son of Saul was forty years old when he

---

19. Modern biblical scholarship considers this verse to have a lacuna. For example, the JPS translation has "Saul was ... years old" with the following note: "The number is lacking in the Hebrew Text; also, the precise context of the 'two years' is uncertain. The verse is lacking in the Septuagint."

became King of Israel and he reigned two years" (2 Sam 2:10). From this verse itself (it would seem) that Ish-bosheth was older than his father by thirty-eight years.[20] This is even more astonishing than the story of Ahaziah and Jehoram his father,[21] for that concerned two years and this is thirty-eight. It is an amazing wonder. The question may (also) be asked in this manner. It could be said that Saul is described as having three sons, two daughters and his wife. There is no mention of Ish-bosheth among them and no [...] name by a name as were the three that were named in (the book of) Samuel during the time of his reign. They were the ones who were killed in the battle with their father Saul, as it says, "Thus Saul and his three sons and his arms-bearer, as well as all his men, died together on that day" (1 Sam 31:6).

The greatly abbreviated answer is that these forty years of Ish-bosheth relate to an event[22] that occurred to him during these years. The intention is to a certain issue that took place in the tenth year of Saul's life.[23] Saul fathered Ish-bosheth during this time period. He was the oldest and the reason that he is not mentioned in (the book of) Samuel is that he was not born by Ahinoam. Only her children were mentioned, as it says, "Saul's sons were: Jonathan, Ishvi, and Malchishua: and the names of his two daughters were Merab, the older, and Michal, the younger" (1 Sam 14:49); but it does not say, "All of Saul's sons were..." Moreover, they are mentioned because of what will happen to them, that they will be killed on one occasion. Knowledge of this prepares us for what will happen to them. Ish-bosheth is not mentioned [here] because nothing of what befell them will happen to him.

Furthermore, every story that is not completed in one of these five books—Genesis, Deuteronomy, Joshua, Samuel, Kings, and Ezra—is completed and explicated in Chronicles. Deuteronomy, however, does not mention anything that is in Chronicles, except for a few matters, such as the number of the sixty cities.[24] Since not all of the details of Saul's affairs were treated fully in Samuel, they were completed in Chronicles.

---

20. Ish-bosheth reigned immediately after Saul.

21. A previous question dealt with a similar textual problem, where the biblical text seems to say that Ahaziah was two years older than his father.

22. Evidently, the event of Ish-Bosheth being made king.

23. The meaning of the Judeo-Arabic text is not very clear here, perhaps due to the author's brevity. It is also possible that there is a textual problem in the manuscript.

24. See Deut 3:4 and 1 Chr 2:23.

It describes Ish-bosheth and explains his affairs completely, except that it exchanged (the ending of his name) *sheth* with *'al*, such as Yeruba'al instead of Yeru*boshet*, as in the verse, "Ner begot Kish, Kish begot Saul, Saul begot Jonathan, Malchishua, Abinadab, and Eshba'al" (1 Chr 8:33).

Similarly, in Genesis there is the narrative from Adam up through Jacob and his children, and Chronicles begins with this. (In the book of) Joshua, all of the allotments of land are mentioned in the same way as in Chronicles. Similarly, in Samuel and Kings there are the stories of the battles and the kings (that are also described in Chronicles). From Ezra, Chronicles describes those who settled in the land and the ranks of the priests, the Levites, the singers, the gatekeepers and the rest of the matters. […] In Ezra, it says, "But the Levite heads of clans are listed in the book of the chronicles to the time of Johanan son of Eliashib" (Neh 12:23),[25] and they are mentioned (in Chronicles) in the vicinity of the verse, "And Phinehas son of Eleazar was the chief officer over them in time past, and so on" (1 Chr 9:20). I do not mean the story of Asaf and the rest of the (men) whom David ranked,[26] but rather those who settled in Jerusalem (in the time) of the second temple.[27] As for Isaiah, only a little of it is mentioned in Chronicles, such as the story of Rezin king of Aram and Ahaz and the story of Hezekiah. As for the Psalms, there is very little of it, such as the verse "Praise the Lord; call on His name" (Ps 105:1; and see 1 Chr 16:8). As for (the book of) Ruth, there is only the narrative of David's family lineage.

Therefore, if you have a difficulty with some matter, or seek to comprehend the foundations of the questions concerning the historical traditions, examine all these books, contemplate carefully, and you will then gain broad knowledge and you will understand the matter. This is particularly true if you wear yourself out studying the Mishnah, the Talmud, the Mekhiltot, Halakhot Pesuqot, and Torat Kohanim (the Sifra), for they are the foundations. As for things like the Aggadah and Piyyut and similar things, do not decide on the basis of them at all. For they have been collected from interpretations (אלתאוליאת); and they contain some things which are true and some things that are not, all according to the breadth of the knowledge of the person who composed them.

---

25. Ezra and Nehemiah were usually considered to be one book.
26. See 1 Chr 16:1–7; 25:1–31.
27. See 1 Chr 8:28, 32; 9:34, 38.

We consider these other passages[28] to be from Ezra the priest, except that the names of the scholars have been exchanged.[29] In this manner (we are to understand) what it says, "And the sun stood still and the moon halted, while a nation wreaked judgment on its foes—as it is written in the Book of Yashar" (Josh 10:13). This refers back to (the verse) "Yet his younger brother shall be greater than he, and his offspring shall be plentiful enough for nations" (Gen 48:19).[30] In the same manner, (the verse) "He ordered the Judahites (בני יהודה) to be taught the bow. It is recorded in the Book of Yashar" (2 Sam 1:18), refers back to (the verse) "You, O Judah, your brothers shall praise; Your hand shall be on the nape of your foes" (Gen 49:8).[31] Likewise, the verse "Ish-bosheth son of Saul was forty years old when he became king of Israel, and he reigned two years" (2 Sam 2:10) is to inform us how old he was (as a son of) Saul[32] when he became king. He was forty years old, as it says "Ish-bosheth son of Saul was forty years old" and so on.[33]

---

28. Referring to verses, or parts of verses, which seem to be later additions. He may be referring to passages he had mentioned above, such as the genealogy of David at the end of Ruth.

29. The intention of this last phrase is not clear. The two manuscripts vary here and the text has probably not been preserved accurately, as indicated by the problematic syntax.

30. The author (and rabbinic tradition) interpreted the verse in Joshua to be the fulfillment of Jacob's prophecy for Ephraim, in that the halting of the sun and moon were witnessed by all the nations. This connection is found in a number of rabbinic sources which also understand "the Book of Yashar" as referring to Genesis, the book of Abraham, Isaac, and Jacob (who were known as *yesharim*, "upright"), strengthening the connection between these two verses. See b. Avod. Zar. 25a; Gen. Rab. 6; Aggadat Bereshit 5, ד"ה הבן יקיר, as well as later midrashic collections such as Lekah Tov. Our author evidently took the verse in Josh 10:13 to be an editorial addition by Ezra the priest.

31. This second example of a reference to *Sefer ha-Yashar* is also found in b. Avod. Zar. 25a. The verse in 2 Samuel says that the descendants of Judah knew how to use the bow. The verse from Genesis implies this by saying that Judah's hand will be on his enemies' nape, hinting at the use of the bow in which the archer's hand is drawn back close to the nape of the neck.

32. The Judeo-Arabic text has: ליפידנא בן כם כאן לשאול פי וקת מלך. The mention of Saul here may be a scribal error. The sentence would flow better if it read: ליפידנא בן כם כאן לאיש בשת פי וקת מלך.

33. Our author evidently also sees this verse as an editorial interpolation by Ezra the priest.

If you were to ask what is the meaning of the verse "Saul was a year old when he became king, and he reigned over Israel two years" (1 Sam 13:1), I would give three answers. The first (answer) is that it means to say that he was like a one-year-old, with the goodness of an infant who has no sin.[34] [The text of the second answer is too fragmentary in the manuscript to translate.] The third answer is that it refers to the year in which the king was anointed (with oil) and that his state (of being anointed) would not be protracted like it was for David. He remained anointed for two years until he became king over Judah and seven years until he became king over all of Israel, for after David became king of Judah, Israel remained without a king for five years. It said about David, "The Philistine officers asked, 'Who are those Hebrews?' 'Why, that's David, the servant of King Saul of Israel,' Achish answered the Philistine officers. 'He has been with me for a year or more...'" (1 Sam 29:3).[35] It is for this reason that it has "Saul was a year old when he became king" and so on, that is, from the time of his anointment.

I have instructed you and have explained this question and its ramifications to you with a clear explanation. So give generous consideration to it. It comprises seven (sub-)issues that have been clarified in our answer. Moreover, I have shown to you and informed you about the obscure stories in the twenty-four books. In the same manner, for that passage whose explication is not completed at the end of Kings, it is completed at the end of Jeremiah. The remaining part of the obscure narrative about the nations of the world is explained in Ezekiel and some in Isaiah and the Minor Prophets. That which is not clarified in the four books is explained in the fifth book. With all that you have studied in Scripture, the difficult matters will become easy for you, as it says, "...and giving the sense; so they understood the scriptures" (Neh 8:8).

Bibliography

Ben-Shammai, Haggai. "On the *Mudawwin*, the Redactor of the Hebrew Bible in Judaeo-Arabic Bible Exegesis" [Hebrew]. Pages 73–110 in *From Sages to Savants: Studies Presented to Avraham Grossman*. Edited

---

34. This is the answer given in rabbinic literature. See b. Yoma 22b; y. Bik. 3:6; Pes. Rab., First Addition, *piska* 1.

35. Our author quotes this verse to demonstrate that, at the time David was serving in the army of Achish the Philistine, more than a year had passed since he was anointed by Samuel (1 Sam 16:13), and it would still be more time until David reigned as king.

by Joseph R. Hacker, Yosef Kaplan, and B. Z. Kedar. Jerusalem: Zalman Shazar Center for Jewish History, 2010.

Lazarus-Yafeh, Hava. *Intertwined Worlds: Medieval Islam and Bible Criticism*. Princeton: Princeton University Press, 1992.

Moss, Yonatan. "Disorder in the Bible: Rabbinic Responses and Responsibilities." *JSQ* 19 (2012): 104–28.

———. "Noblest Obelus: Rabbinic Appropriations of Late Ancient Literary Criticism." Pages 245–67 in *Homer and the Bible in the Eyes of Ancient Interpreters*. Edited by Maren R. Niehoff. Leiden: Brill, 2012.

Sklare, David. "Ninth-Century Judeo-Arabic Texts of Biblical Questions and Answers." Pages 104–24 in *Senses of Scriptures, Treasures of Tradition: The Bible in Arabic among Jews, Christians and Muslims*. Edited by Miriam Lindgren Hjälm. Biblia Arabica 5. Leiden: Brill, 2017.

———. *Samuel ben Hofni Gaon and His Cultural World: Texts and Studies*. Leiden: Brill, 1996.

———. "Scriptural Questions: Early Texts in Judaeo-Arabic" [Hebrew]. Pages 205–31 in *A Word Fitly Spoken: Studies in Mediaeval Exegesis of the Hebrew Bible and the Qur'an Presented to Haggai Ben-Shammai*. Edited by Meir Bar-Asher, Simon Hopkins, Sarah Stroumsa, and Bruno Chiesa. Jerusalem: Ben Zvi Institute, 2007.

Steiner, Richard. "A Jewish Theory of Biblical Redaction from Byzantium: Its Rabbinic Roots, Its Diffusion and Its Encounter with the Muslim Doctrine of Falsification." *JSIJ* 2 (2003): 123–67.

The Meaning of "The Great House" and "The Little House" in Medieval Jewish Exegesis

Meirav Nadler-Akirav

The terms "the great house" and "the little house" appear in Amos 6:11:

כי־הנה יהוה מצוה והכה הבית הגדול רסיסים והבית הקטן בקעים

For behold, the LORD commands, and the *great house* shall be smitten into fragments and the *little house* into bits. (RSV, emphasis added)

The prophet Amos turns to the sinful people, those who pursue pleasure and put trust in their power, describes their harsh sins, and then declares that terrible calamities are expected to come upon them. As part of these disasters, the prophet claims in verse 11 that the great house and the little house will be smashed into fragments and bits.

The question is: What are those two houses, which are differentiated by size and the type of "smiting" that will come upon them and destroy them? A study of medieval exegesis raises various possibilities for understanding these expressions. The notion common to all is that it is indeed a description of part of the punishment that will be given to the people for their sins.

This paper focuses on the different approaches of understanding the meaning of the terms "the great house" and "the little house" as it is reflected in several medieval Jewish thinkers' exegesis, both Karaites and rabbinical, such as Sa'adia Gaon, Daniel al-Qūmisī, David ben Abraham Alfāsī, Yefet ben 'Eli, Ibn Ezra, R. David Kimchi, and Rashi.[1]

---

1. For a review of medieval Jewish thinkers who translated the books of the Minor Prophets into Arabic, see Meira Polliack and Meirav Nadler-Akirav, "Minor Prophets: Primary Translations: Arabic Translations," in *Pentateuch, Former and Latter Prophets,*

Two Houses—Two Kingdoms

We first find the interpretation of the two houses as two kingdoms in Targum Pseudo-Jonathan (the accepted and earliest Jewish Bible translation into Aramaic) and in Yefet ben 'Eli's exegesis.

Targum Pseudo-Jonathan explains: ארי הא יי מפקיד וימחי מלכו רבא מחא תקיפא ומלכו זעירא מחא חלשא, meaning: "God will destroy the great kingdom with a great blow and the little kingdom with a small blow." Even though it is not clear who the "great kingdom" and the "little kingdom" are, we can assume that Targum Pseudo-Jonathan refers to the kingdoms of Israel and Judah.[2] Rashi cites the targum and explains: "According to its importance, so will the blow be," but we cannot infer from that as to the purpose of Targum Pseudo-Jonathan. Joseph ben Simeon Kara' (France/ Germany, eleventh–twelfth century), who was one of Rashi's pupils, quotes the targum and explains: "He calls the ten tribes 'the big house'; and he calls the tribes of Judea and Benjamin 'the little house,' because the ten tribes are more than the tribes of Judea and Benjamin, as Ezekiel says: 'And your elder sister is Samaria ... and your younger sister' (Ezek 16:46 RSV)."[3]

The possibility that the two houses should be identified, according to their relative size, as the kingdoms of Israel and Judah, appears also in Yefet ben 'Eli's commentary on the book of Amos.[4] Yefet explains that "the

---

vol. 1 B of *The Hebrew Bible*, ed. Armin Lange and Emanuel Tov, Textual History of the Bible (Leiden: Brill, 2015), 652–59.

2. See also the interpretation of *Mezudat David* (seventeenth century) to the book of Amos.

3. Menachem Cohen, ed., *Mikra'ot Gedolot 'Haketer': The Twelve Prophets* [Hebrew] (Ramat-Gan: Bar-Ilan University Press, 2012), 129, 131.

4. For discussion of the metaphorical interpretation of the Bible, and especially in the book of Amos, see Meirav Nadler-Akirav, "The Literary-Historical Approach of Yefet Ben 'Eli in His Commentary of the Book of Amos," *European Journal of Jewish Studies* 10.2 (2016): 175–93; Nadler-Akirav, "Yefet Ben 'Eli's Commentary on the Book of Amos: A Critical Edition of Chapters 1–4 with Hebrew Translation, Introduction, and Notes" (PhD diss., Bar-Ilan University, 2009), 5–57 (written under the guidance of Prof. Eliezer Schlossberg and Prof. David Doron). On Yefet's exegesis and approaches, see Meira Polliack and Eliezer Schlossberg, *Yefet Ben'Eli's Commentary on Hoshea— Annotated Edition, Hebrew Translation and Introduction* [Hebrew] (Ramat-Gan: Bar-Ilan University Press, 2009), 17–40; Polliack, "Major Trends in Karaite Biblical Exegesis in the Tenth and Eleventh Centuries," in *Karaite Judaism: A Guide to Its History and Literary Sources*, ed. Meira Polliack (Leiden: Brill, 2003), 393–98; Michael G. Wechsler, *The Arabic Translation and Commentary of Yefet Ben 'Eli the Karaite on the Book of*

great house" and "the little house" are a metaphor for Israel and Judah, respectively, that they will be exiled by the kings of Assyria, like Nebuchadnezzar, who did so on four occasions. Here is the first example, in English translation:

> Saying: "And the great house shall be struck down into fragments," he is referring to the kingdom of the Ten Tribes, which is the house of Israel. Saying "the little house," he is referring to the kingdom of Judah. He likened them to a house that is struck relentlessly by heavy rains and with no one to rebuild it, so it is destroyed. Thus the kings of Assyria went to the land of Israel time after time and exiled the people until the kingdom came to an end and the land was destroyed. And he likened the kings of Assyria to a flood and hail, saying: "Behold, the Lord has one who is mighty and strong; like a storm of hail, a destroying tempest, like a storm of mighty, overflowing waters" (Isa 28:2 RSV). And he likened the destruction of the house of Judah to the crevices found in the wall of the house and in its ceiling, and there is no one who can build it and so it becomes ruined. Like this Nebuchadnezzar came to them four times and every time he had a great influence on them like the crevices in the wall of a house until the kingdom of Judah was destroyed.[5]

This example emphasizes the importance of history as a means for proving the precision of Yefet's interpretations. Yefet's exegesis of the Bible reveals two main exegetical approaches. The first is the contemporary-symbolic approach, by which it is understood that the text alludes symbolically to the past and present history, as well as the future, of the Karaite movement and its destiny.[6] The second approach is the literary approach, which is

---

Esther, Karaite Texts and Studies 1, Études sur le judaïsme médiéval 36 (Leiden: Brill, 2008), 13–40; Marzena Zawanowska, *The Arabic Translation and Commentary of Yefet Ben ʿEli the Karaite on the Abraham Narratives (Genesis 11:10–25:18)* (Leiden: Brill, 2012), 111–88.

5. Translated from MS SP RNL Library Yevr.-Arab. 1:298 (433) (IMHM 54886), 112b–113a.

6. Meira Polliack and Eliezer Schlossberg, "Historical-Literary, Rhetorical and Redactional Methods of Interpretation in Yefet Ben ʿEli's Introduction to the Minor Prophets," in *Exegesis and Grammar in Medieval Karaite Texts*, ed. Geoffrey Khan, JSSSup 13 (Oxford: Oxford University Press, 2001), 6; Polliack and Schlossberg, *Yefet ben ʿEli's Commentary on Hoshea*, 20; Naphtali Wieder, *The Judean Scrolls and Karaism* (London: East and West Library, 1962), 53–67; Wieder, "The Dead Sea Scrolls Type of Biblical Exegesis among the Karaites," in *Between East and West* (London: East

the more common method applied in Yefet's commentary on the Prophets. This method can be divided into two types: the linguistic-contextual method and the historical method.[7] Both types are on biblical evidence taken from references to other biblical texts.

Later on, in his commentary on Amos 6:11, Yefet explains the shards and cracks mentioned in this verse by way of a metaphor: the rain fell on the house constantly, so that no one could rebuild and repair it. We find a similar explanation in David ben Abraham Alfāsī's dictionary:

> And from that, the cracking of the walls and ramparts and striking the large house into splinters [רסיסים] and the little house into fragments [בקעים] are cracks in the wall. Splinters are the rainfall that comes into these cracks and easily topples them.[8]

And he adds:

> "And striking the great house with splinters [רסיסים]" means that rain will strike it and enter the cracks and this [is the meaning] when later on he says "crevices [בקעים]," referring to the two houses at once: when he says about the one "splinters" it necessitates the other; and when he says about the other one "crevices" it necessitates the first, meaning if the [walls] of the houses are fissured, rain will enter and they will be destroyed.[9]

---

and West Library, 1958), 75–76; Rina Drory, *The Emergence of Jewish-Arabic Literary Contacts at the Beginning of the Tenth Century* [Hebrew] (Tel Aviv: Ha-Kibbutz Hameuhad, 1988), 106–10.

7. On historicizing as a primary tool in Yefet's biblical commentaries, see Meira Polliack, "Historicizing Prophetic Literature: Yefet Ben 'Eli's Commentary on Hosea and Its Relationship to al-Qūmisī's Pitron," in *Pesher Naḥum: Texts and Studies in Jewish History and Literature from Antiquity through the Middle Ages, Presented to Norman (Naḥum) Golb*, ed. Joel L. Kraemer and Michael G. Wechsler, with the participation of Fred Donner, Joshua Holo, and Dennis Pardee, Studies in Ancient Oriental Civilization 66 (Chicago: Oriental Institute of the University of Chicago, 2012), 149–86; Polliack and Schlossberg, "Historical Literary, Rhetorical and Redactional Methods," 1–39; Polliack and Schlossberg, *Yefet Ben 'Eli's Commentary on Hoshea*, 21–25.

8. I. D. Markon, *Pitron Shneym 'Asar, perush l-itrey 'asar hibro Daniel al-qumisi* [Hebrew] (Jerusalem: Meqitsei Nirdamin, 1957), 1:263.

9. S. L. Skoss, *Kitab Jami' Al-Alfāz of David Ben Abraham Al-Fasi*, 2 vols. (New Haven: Yale University Press, 1936–1945), 2:614. David ben Abraham al-Fāsī was a lexicographer, grammarian, and commentator active in the tenth century; he wrote an

Later on, Yefet explains that the rain is a metaphor for the kings of Assyria, who are likened to hail in Isa 28:2:

הנה חזק ואמץ לאדני כזרם ברד שער קטב כזרם מים כבירים שטפים

See, the Lord has one who is mighty and strong; like a storm of hail, a destroying tempest, like a storm of mighty, overflowing waters. (NRSV)

Here, Yefet elaborates upon the metaphor:

> And he mentioned three things: a storm of hail, a destroying tempest, a storm of mighty, overflowing waters [זרם ברד שער קטב כזרם מים שטפים]. And these three things are an image of the three exiles. The first exile is of the two tribes by Pul and Tiglath. This, he likened to "a storm of hail" because of the strength of their deeds. And the second exile is the exile of Zebulun and Naphtali by Tiglath in the period of Pekah ben Remalyahu. This, he likened to a "destroying tempest," because his deed was even more powerful than that of Pul. The third exile is the exile of Samaria. This, he likened to "a storm of mighty, overflowing waters" because he exiled all of the Ten Tribes. [10]

Sa'adia Gaon, in his commentary on Isa 28:2, also explains the verse by way of metaphor. In his commentary, though, the water destruction is not a metaphor for Assyria but, rather, for the harsh decrees and calamities that will be brought by God.[11] Even so, we cannot conclude from Sa'adia's exegesis to Isaiah that this is also his interpretation of Amos 6:11. Neither can we determine whether he understands "the great house" and "the small house" as a metaphor of the ten tribes and two tribes kingdoms or for the destruction of the First and Second Jerusalem Temples, or as a general description of punishment. This difference highlights Yefet's literary-historical approach, which searches in the Bible for the precise events alluded to by the verses under discussion.

Arabic dictionary of biblical grammar called *Kitāb jāmi' al-Alfāẓ*. For more details, see Skoss's introduction to *Kitab Jami' al-Alfaz* (*Jāmi'*, 1:xxxii–xl).

10. Translated from MS BL 280a (IMHM 6274), 4b.

11. Yehuda Ratzaby, *Saadya's Translation and Commentary on Isaiah, Collected, Edited with Translation and Notes by Yehuda Ratzaby* [Hebrew] (Kiriat Ono: Mekhon Mishnat ha-Rambam, 1993), 55.

Two Houses—The First Temple and the Second Temple

Similar to the Targum Pseudo-Jonathan and to Yefet ben ʿEli, we find a contemporary-symbolic interpretation in the exegesis of the Kara-ite Daniel al-Qūmisī (tenth century). In his book *Pitrōn Shneim ʾAsar*, which includes a commentary on the Minor Prophets, Daniel al-Qūmisī too explains Amos 6:11 as a metaphor; however, according to him the metaphor refers to the destruction of the First and Second Temples. He indicates that the First Temple will be destroyed easily and that, in con-trast to the Second Temple, the latter would require a severe blow to be destroyed:

> The first house, in a slight blow, as [Heb.] *rəsîsîm*, [Arab.] *rashāsh*, a little from the measly (part) of the land and it will soon be built; and the second house in a great blow, as water flows and as *mêmê bəqîʿîm* [Heb., "overflowing waters"], cruel enemies.[12]

Two Houses—A Metaphor for Two Different Sins

We also find interpretations of the "houses" as a metaphor for different kinds of people who commit different kinds of sins. Abraham Ibn Ezra divides the people into two types accordingly to the size of their houses: "big" and "small"—which probably means rich people and poor people, or privileged people and ordinary people. Ibn Ezra explains: "And it is like a parable, meaning: the big [people] committed more sins, the sins that the small [people] did not commit,"[13] meaning, the sins of the leaders and the rich are greater than those of the common people. He also brings an anon-ymous interpretation that refers to "the minister and his people."[14] Rabbi Eliezer of Beaugency (France, twelfth century CE) similarly explains: "The king's house and the ministers' houses."[15]

---

12. Markon, *Pitron Shneym ʾAsar*, 37.
13. Uriel Simon, *Hoshea, Joel, Amos*, vol. 1 of *Abraham Ibn Ezra's Two Commen-taries on the Minor Prophets: An Annotated Critical Edition* [Hebrew] (Ramat-Gan: Bar-Ilan University Press, 1989), 309–10.
14. Simon, *Abraham Ibn Ezra*, 241.
15. Cohen, *Mikraʾot Gedolot ʿHaketerʾ: The Twelve Prophets*, 129.

The Word "House" in Amos 3:15

The word "house" is also mentioned in Amos 3:15:

והכיתי בית־החרף על־בית הקיץ ואבדו בתי השן וספו בתים רבים נאם־יהוה

"I will smite the winter house with the summer house; and the houses of ivory shall perish, and the great houses shall come to an end," says the LORD. (RSV)

Rabbi David Kimhi (RaDak, twelfth–thirteenth century CE) finds a connection between Amos 6:11 and Amos 3:15; he claims that the destruction of "the great house" and "the little house" is similar to the fall of the houses mentioned in the latter and that both of them are symbolic of the similar disasters to come.[16] In his exegesis to Amos 3:15, Kimhi explains that it was the custom of kings to build special seasonal homes, either winter or summer, an explanation that is not found in his own exegesis to Amos 6.[17]

According to Kimhi's interpretation of both verses, we can assume that he means that a big disaster will come in the future, one that will crush all the houses, even the biggest and greatest one.

Yefet ben 'Eli, in his commentary on Amos 3:15, also refers to different kinds of houses, but he does not make a connection between the two verses. While in his commentary to Amos 6 he declares that the houses are a metaphor of the fall of the two kingdoms, here—in his commentary on Amos 3—he produces a literal interpretation, in which the verse refers to the peoples' houses and homes. He even forecasts how their houses will be destroyed: the enemy will destroy the houses at a time they will still live in them, or the enemy will exile the people and then destroy their houses:

> He refers to those houses, and divides them into four (types of) houses: some of them are winter houses … some summer houses … some houses of marble … and some palaces … those houses will be destroyed in two ways: either the enemy will destroy them, or they will be destroyed when their inhabitants will be exiled from them; and they will remain so year after year, with no one left to rebuild them and (full of) rain and flood waters.[18]

---

16. Cohen, *Mikra'ot Gedolot 'Haketer': The Twelve Prophets*, 129–30.
17. Cohen, *Mikra'ot Gedolot 'Haketer': The Twelve Prophets*, 113.
18. Translation made from MS SP RNL Yevr.-Arab. 1:298 (433) (IMHM 54886),

This is in contrast to Daniel al-Qūmisī, who presents a metaphorical explanation for both verses (Amos 6:11 and 3:15). But, while in Amos 6 al-Qūmisī refers to the fall of the temples, in 3:15 he presents an allegorical interpretation with an implied reference to his own time. According to him, the text implies the punishment that will befall the people in exile in general and the people of the Babylonian exile in particular:

כבוד מלכים הראשונים וגם כל עושר וכל כבוד אנשי גלות... ואף כי אוי
לכם יא עשירי גלות ועשירי ישראל בבבל נוטעי גנות ופרדסים... ותשכחו
תורתה ואבל ירושלם.[19]

The honor of the first kings, and also all wealth and all respect of the people of exile.... Woe unto you, the rich people of the exile, and the rich people of Israel, who plant gardens and orchards.... Forgetting his Torah and the mourning for Jerusalem.[19]

Summary

The word combinations "the great house" and the little house are examples of expressions that are interpreted in different ways but are understood metaphorically within a context of destruction. They are read as denoting a disaster that is about to come in the near or distant future. Among medieval thinkers, there are three main approaches to understanding the metaphorical function of these expressions within their biblical (Amos and Isaiah) contexts.

The first approach is represented by the Aramaic targum (Targum Pseudo-Jonathan), where the two houses are explained as a metaphor for *two kingdoms*. Later Jewish thinkers, like Rashi and Josef ben Simeon Kara', suggest that Targum Pseudo-Jonathan points to the biblical First Temple period kingdom of Israel and the kingdom of Judah. A similar interpretation appears in the commentary of Yefet ben 'Eli on the book of Amos. Yefet explains in detail how the kings of Assyria and Nebuchadnezzar acted again and again until the kingdoms of Israel and Judah were destroyed.

98a. The ellipsis here and in the next excerpt indicates a skip in the translation for the sake of brevity.

19. Markon, *Pitron Shneym 'Asar*, 34.

The second approach is found in the commentary by Daniel al-Qūmisī. In his interpretation, the destruction of the houses is a metaphor for the destruction of the *First and Second Temples.*

According to the third approach, which is found among commentators like Abraham ibn Ezra and Eliezer of Beaugency, we can infer from the difference between the sizes of the houses about the type of people dwelling in them and the type of punishment they would receive. This means that the *size* of the house indicates the status of the person living in it: rich people such as the elite live in the big houses, whereas simple people live in small houses. Sin and its punishment are in direct proportion to the status of the house inhabitant and the house size: the richer the person, the greater the sin and punishment. Rabbi David Kimhi even refers to the custom of some people to build different houses for each season and finds a connection between Amos 6:11 and 3:15.

To sum up, even when there is almost a consensus that a particular verse, phrase, or term in the Bible has a metaphorical denotation, we can still find that the metaphor is interpreted as having multiple meanings.

Bibliography

Cohen, Menachem, ed. *Mikraʾot Gedolot 'Haketer': The Twelve Prophets* [Hebrew]. Ramat-Gan: Bar-Ilan University Press, 2012.

Drory, Rina. *The Emergence of Jewish-Arabic Literary Contacts at the Beginning of the Tenth Century* [Hebrew]. Tel Aviv: Ha-Kibbutz Ha-meuhad, 1988.

Kraemer, Joel L., and Michael G. Wechsler, eds., with the participation of Fred Donner, Joshua Holo, and Dennis Pardee. *Pesher Naḥum: Texts and Studies in Jewish History and Literature from Antiquity through the Middle Ages, Presented to Norman (Naḥum) Golb.* Studies in Ancient Oriental Civilization 66. Chicago: Oriental Institute of the University of Chicago, 2012

Markon, I. D. *Pitron Shneym 'Asar, perush l-itrey 'asar hibro Daniel al-qumisi* [Hebrew]. Jerusalem: Meqitsei Nirdamin, 1957.

Nadler-Akirav, Meirav. "A Comparative Discussion of Prophetic Vision in Jeremiah and Amos" [Hebrew]. *Ginzei Qedem* 10 (2014): 129–55.

———. "The Literary-Historical Approach of Yefet Ben 'Eli the Karaite in His Commentary of the Book of Amos." *European Journal of Jewish Studies* 10.2 (2016): 171–200.

————. "Yefet Ben 'Eli's Commentary on the Book of Amos: A Critical edition of Chapters 1–4 with Hebrew Translation, Introduction, and Notes" [Hebrew]. PhD diss., Bar-Ilan University, 2009.

Polliack, Meira. "Historicizing Prophetic Literature: Yefet Ben 'Eli's Commentary on Hosea and Its Relationship to al-Qūmisī's Pitron." Pages 149–86 in *Pesher Nahum: Texts and Studies in Jewish History and Literature from Antiquity through the Middle Ages, Presented to Norman (Nahum) Golb*. Edited by Joel L. Kraemer and Michael G. Wechsler, with the participation of Fred Donner, Joshua Holo, and Dennis Pardee. Studies in Ancient Oriental Civilization 66. Chicago: Oriental Institute of the University of Chicago, 2012.

————. "Major Trends in Karaite Biblical Exegesis in the Tenth and Eleventh Centuries." Pages 363–413 in *Karaite Judaism: A Guide to Its History and Literary Sources*. Edited by Meira Polliack. Leiden: Brill, 2003.

Polliack, Meira, and Meirav Nadler-Akirav. "Minor Prophets: Primary Translations: Arabic Translations." Pages 652–59 in *Pentateuch, Former and Latter Prophets*. Vol. 1B of *The Hebrew Bible*. Edited by Armin Lange and Emanuel Tov. Textual History of the Bible. Leiden: Brill, 2015.

Polliack, Meira, and Eliezer Schlossberg. "Historical-Literary, Rhetorical and Redactional Methods of Interpretation in Yefet Ben 'Eli's Introduction to the Minor Prophets." Pages 1–39 in *Exegesis and Grammar in Medieval Karaite Texts*. Edited by Geoffrey Khan. JSSSup 13. Oxford: Oxford University Press, 2001.

————. *Yefet ben 'Eli's Commentary on Hoshea—Annotated Edition, Hebrew Translation and Introduction* [Hebrew]. Ramat-Gan: Bar-Ilan University Press, 2009.

Ratzaby, Yehuda. *Saadya's Translation and Commentary on Isaiah, Collected, Edited with Translation and Notes by Yehuda Ratzaby* [Hebrew]. Kiryat Ono: Mekhon Mishnat ha-Rambam, 1993.

Simon, Uriel. *Hoshea, Joel, Amos*. Vol. 1 of *Abraham Ibn Ezra's Two Commentaries on the Minor Prophets: An Annotated Critical Edition* [Hebrew]. Ramat-Gan: Bar-Ilan University Press, 1989.

Skoss, S. L. *Kitab Jami' Al-Alfaz of David Ben Abraham Al-Fasi*. 2 vols. New Haven: Yale University Press, 1936–1945.

Wechsler, Michael G. *The Arabic Translation and Commentary of Yefet Ben 'Eli the Karaite on the Book of Esther*. Karaite Texts and Studies 1. Études sur le judaïsme médiéval 36. Leiden: Brill, 2008.

Wieder, Naphtali. "The Dead Sea Scrolls Type of Biblical Exegesis among the Karaites." Pages 75–106 in *Between East and West: Essays Dedicated to the Memory of Bela Horovitz*. Edited by Alexander Altman. London: East and West Library, 1958.

———. *The Judean Scrolls and Karaism*. London: East and West Library, 1962.

Zawanowska, Marzena. *The Arabic Translation and Commentary of Yefet Ben ʿEli the Karaite on the Abraham Narratives (Genesis 11:10–25:18)*. Leiden: Brill, 2012.

On the Writings

Yefet Ben 'Eli on Proverbs 30:1–6

Ilana Sasson

Introduction

Yefet ben 'Eli, the tenth-century CE Karaite exegete who lived and worked in Jerusalem, translated the Bible into Arabic and wrote a commentary on the entire Bible in the same language. A critical edition of his translation and commentary on the book of Proverbs was published recently.[1] The edition was prepared according to fifteen manuscripts, the oldest of which was copied in Arabic script in the eleventh century CE (BL Or 2553). Others were copied in the fifteen, seventeen, and nineteen centuries, and were written in Hebrew script. The edition is diplomatic, based primarily on this BL Or 2553 manuscript. However, because this manuscript contains only about half the text, the rest was taken from a fifteenth-century manuscript at the British Library that contains almost the entire text.[2] The rest was taken from a seventeenth-century manuscript that contains the entire corpus.[3] All other manuscripts are represented in the apparatus. As a result, and in order to best reflect the manuscripts, the critical edition is presented in a combination of Arabic and Hebrew script.

The corpus of Yefet's work on Proverbs is enormous. It would have been impractical to publish Yefet's edition in addition to an introduction and a translation of his work into English all in one volume. It was therefore

---

Ilana Sasson completed this article shortly before she passed away. On her work and on the dedication of this volume to her blessed memory, see the acknowledgments. .ת.נ.צ.ב.ה.

1. Ilana Sasson, *The Arabic Translation and Commentary of Yefet ben Eli on the Book of Proverbs*, vol. 1 (Leiden: Brill, 2016).

2. BL Or 2506 and BL Or 2507.

3. Adler 3356 and Adler 3357, in the library of the Jewish Theological Seminary, NY.

decided to publish the edition together with an introduction in the first volume and the English translation in a second volume.[4]

The process of preparing a critical edition necessitates some deliberation and decision making. For example, one of the questions I was faced with was how to translate Yefet's Arabic translation of the biblical text into English. Yefet's translation is extremely imitative and purposely wooden or stiff, following the Hebrew text very closely. For Yefet, it is not about the Arabic. It is about representing the Hebrew as accurately as possible. The English translation must reflect this feature even if the final product comes across as wooden and stiff as well. In addition, the book of Proverbs includes many terms that recur often such as "wise," "righteous," "wicked," "fool," and so on. It is important to be consistent in the translation with regard to such terms. Yet, one has to take into account the degree of consistency found in Yefet's translation, as well as the level of consistency found among the different manuscripts. While Yefet is fairly consistent with some of the terms, we see that there is a discrepancy among the different manuscripts with regard to certain terms.[5]

One other feature of Yefet's translation is the expansion of meaning. When a Hebrew word is polysemic or homonymic and must be translated by different Arabic words according to their context, Yefet chooses one of the Arabic words and consistently translates the Hebrew word with that one regardless of the context. Thus he expands the meaning of the Arabic word in light of the semantic field of the Hebrew word. This is a known feature of Yefet's translation, and has already been described by other scholars.[6] Clearly, it was not possible to imitate Yefet's expansion in the English translation: it is therefore important to reflect this feature by other means, such as footnotes and the use of parenthesis.

One feature of Yefet's writing style is the abundance of Hebrew words and terms embedded in his Arabic commentary. On the one hand, it would

---

4. Editor's note: Sasson prepared substantial parts of the second volume, containing the English translation of this work, with which she entrusted Meira Polliack and Michael G. Wechsler, for the purpose of its future completion and publication.

5. For example, the rendition of the word kəsil ("fool") in BL Or 2553 is almost always jāhil, whereas it is rendered as aḥmaq in most other manuscripts.

6. Joshua Blau and Simon Hopkins, "The Beginning of Judaeo-Arabic Bible Exegesis according to an Old Glossary to the Book of Psalms" [Hebrew], in *A Word Fitly Spoken: Studies in Medieval Exegesis of the Hebrew Bible and the Qur'an Presented to Haggai Ben-Shammai*, ed. Meir M. Bar-Asher et al. (Jerusalem: Ben-Zvi Institute, 2007), 249–51.

be important for the reader to see this feature; but on the other, it would be very cumbersome to include the terms in Hebrew and add their translation into English in parenthesis, as it would disturb the reading flow. I therefore chose not to reflect this feature on a regular basis in the English version, except for cases in which it is essential for the point that Yefet conveys. One other consideration was how to represent the name of God, *Allah*. Should it be transliterated into English, or should one use a different term?[7] In the current edition I have decided to use "the Lord" to present the Arabic *Allah*, which stands for the Hebrew *Yhwh*, and "God" to present the Arabic *Ilāha*, which stands for the Hebrew *Elohim*. The editors of other editions chose to represent the name of God in different ways.[8]

An essential feature of a critical edition is the apparatus. In the case of my edition, the body of the text is written in Arabic. As mentioned above, some of it is written in Arabic script and some in Hebrew script, whereas the introduction is written in English. Therefore questions arise: In what language should the apparatus be written? Should it be in agreement with the body of the text, meaning in Arabic? Or should it be in agreement with the introduction, meaning in English? Or should it be in agreement of the Hebrew script, meaning in Hebrew? When looking at previous publications in the same series (Brill's Karaite Texts and Studies), we see that the apparatuses of the Esther edition, the Genesis edition, and the Ecclesiastes/Qoheleth editions are written in Hebrew.[9] In the edition at hand, I have decided to present the apparatus in English in order for it to be in agreement with the introduction and the paratext of this publication.

The following is an excerpt from Yefet's translation and commentary on Proverbs. Yefet uses Prov 30:1–6 as a polemical platform in which he attacks the study of secular sciences, cosmology in particular.[10] He con-

7. See, for example, James T. Robinson, *Asceticism, Eschatology, Opposition to Philosophy: The Arabic Translation and Commentary of Salmon ben Yeroham on Qohelet (Ecclesiastes)*, Karaite Texts and Studies 5, Études sur le judaïsme médiéval 45 (Leiden: Brill, 2012). See also Michael Wechsler, ed., *The Arabic Translation and Commentary of Yefet ben'Eli the Karaite on the Book of Esther*, Karaite Texts and Studies 1, Études sur le judaïsme médiéval 36 (Leiden: Brill, 2008).

8. See, for example, Wechsler, *Esther*; and Robinson, *Asceticism*.

9. Wechsler, *Esther*; Marzena Zawanowska, *The Arabic Translation and Commentary of Yefet ben 'Eli the Karaite on the Abraham Narratives (Genesis 11:10–25:18)*, Karaite Texts and Studies 4, Études sur le judaïsme médiéval 46 (Leiden: Brill, 2012); Robinson, *Asceticism*.

10. For a detailed discussion of this passage in Hebrew, see Haggai Ben-Shammai,

demns those who pursue foreign books (Arab. *al-kutub al-barrāniyya*)
and foreign knowledge, the kind that stands in contradiction to Scripture. Yefet suggests that there is some superfluous knowledge that God
bestows on special individuals, such as King Solomon. Solomon did not
learn this knowledge from books or from teachers; he received it directly
from God. In fact, this, according to Yefet, is proof of the existence of God.
This knowledge is not for anyone to possess, but only for those special
individuals whom God chooses. God created the world for the sake of the
Law (Arab. *al-šarīa*), by which he means: the Torah. Since the Torah is perfect, we are prohibited from adding anything to or subtracting anything
from it. He explains that any addition, including knowledge pertaining
to the wonders of creation, which is beyond human comprehension, is
prohibited and its pursuance will not go unpunished.[11] He warns the aver-
age aspirant not to look for this type of knowledge because of the risks
involved. He urges people to adhere to the Torah, saying that the knowledge it contains is all one needs in order to live well in this world, and to
gain reward in the world to come.

Yefet's Translation of Proverbs 30:1–6

In the ensuing I shall present the Hebrew text of Prov 30:1–6, verse by
verse, together with an English rendering of Yefet's Arabic translation.[12]

1 דברי אגור בן־יקה המשא נאם הגבר לאיתיאל לאיתיאל ואכל
The exhortation of *al-majmūʿ son of al-mutaqayyiʾ* (literally: "the
poised one, son of the one who spews") is a story, at the outset of
which the man proclaims, "Regarding the existence of the Omnipotent, regarding the existence of the Omnipotent, I am capable."

"The Doctrines of Religious Thought of Abû Yûsuf Yaʿqûb a-Qirqisânî and Yefet ben
ʿElî" [Hebrew], 2 vols. (PhD diss., Hebrew University of Jerusalem, 1977), 1:102–5;
2:274–78.

11. Lists of curriculums compiled by later Karaites suggest that the opposition
to the study of secular sciences was eased after a while. Such lists include the study of
mathematics, astronomy, and philosophy, among others; see Simcha Assaf and Samuel
Glick, eds., *Mekorot le-toldhot ha-Hinukh be-Yisrael* [Hebrew], 2 vols. (New York:
Jewish Theological Seminary of America, 2001), 2:609–10, 619–20. See also Sasson,
Proverbs, 119–20.

12. For the text in Arabic, see Sasson, *Proverbs*, 497–501.

2 כי בער אנכי מאיש ולא־בינת אדם לי

I have been ignorant among people, and I have no human understanding.

3 ולא־למדתי חכמה ודעת קדשים אדע

I have not learned wisdom, but I have known the knowledge of
the distinguished natures.

4 מי עלה־שמים וירד מי אסף־רוח בחפניו מי צרר־מים בשמלה מי הקים
כל־אפסי־ארץ מה־שמו ומה־שם־בנו כי תדע

Who ascended to the heavens and came down, who gathered the
wind in his palms, who collected water in a garment, who established the ends of the earth, what is the person's name, and his
son's name, so that you know.

5 כל־אמרת אלוה צרופה מגן הוא לחסים בו

All divine words are pure, he is like a shield to all who humble
themselves before him.

6 אל־תוסף על־דבריו פן־יוכיח בך ונכזבת

Do not add to his exhortation lest he rebuke you and you be severed by his hand.

Yefet's Commentary on Proverbs 30:1–6

(on v. 1) His saying, "the words of Agur" end with "the words of Lemuel."
"Agur" is Solomon, who has five names, and they are: Solomon, Jedidiah,
Agur, Lemuel, and Qoheleth (Ecclesiastes).[13] Each one of these five
names has a meaning. He names him Solomon in light of the idea, "And
I will give peace and quiet to Israel in his time" (1 Chr 22:9). He names
him Jedidiah for the Lord loved him, as per the saying, "And the Lord
loved him" (2 Sam 12:24). He names him Agur for he is like a collection
of certain things in one place. It is derived from the idiom "collecting it in
the time of the harvest" (Prov 6:8). It is as if he obtains secular knowledge
and religious knowledge of every matter. He names him this name here,

---

13. Clarifications, biblical references, and additions are contained in round
parentheses.

I mean Agur, for it is befitting this chapter. He names him Lemuel for he is "the substitute of the Lord on earth,"[14] as we shall explain in its place. He names him Qoheleth because he gathers all the wise and the learned around him in order that they listen to his wisdom, as we shall explain in the introduction to Qoheleth with the help of the Lord, exalted.[15] He says, "son of Jakeh," perhaps pointing to David, peace upon him, for he also was wise and used to compose psalms by the "holy spirit," meaning by divine inspiration. Solomon fits this description too. He says, "son of Jakeh," comparing him with someone who spews the contents of his guts when his stomach is too full. So too, knowledge increases in his heart and he utters it, cooing it like the coo of a dove. He says, *ha-maśśa*', this term indicates prophecy, and since he conveys laws (inspired) by the divine spirit, he says, *ha-maśśa*'. It is also possible to interpret *ha-maśśa*' as "story," similarly to "the story (*maśśa*') that his mother taught him" (Prov 31:1). He says, *divrey Agur* ("the exhortation of Agur"), asserting that it is a story he authored after "the proverbs of Solomon" (Prov 1:1; 10:1; and 25:1). His saying "*Ne'um ha-gever*" ("the exhortation of the man") points to the aforementioned Agur. By his saying *le-Ithiel* ("to Ithiel"), he asserts that this exhortation deals with matters pertaining to the existence of the Creator.

He repeats "to Ithiel" twice. The first is related to the existence of the Creator alone, for he is the Preexistent (Arab. *al-qadīm*) by his essence. He was never in a state of nonexistence, and none precedes him, for everything else is created, not preexisting. The second "to Ithiel" points to his existence after the existence of the universe, for he will never expire. With regard to this attribute ("Preexistent"), none of the theologians who discuss the Creator differ, for they all profess his (eternal) existence. They might, however, disagree with regard to his (other attributes such as) the Wise, the Omnipotent. Hence the wise one (= Solomon) mentions (here)

---

14. Yefet uses the Arabic expression *khalīfat Allah fi al-arḍ*, which is a well-known theological definition of the leader in Islamic literature. See also Patricia Crone and Martin Hinds, *God's Caliph: Religious Authority in the First Centuries of Islam* (Cambridge: Cambridge University Press, 1986).

15. This commentary about the five names of Solomon is also found in a very similar version in the commentary of Salmon b. Yerūḥam the Karaite on Qoh 1:1; see Robinson, *Asceticism*, 96, 174–77. See also Moshe I. Riese, "The Arabic Commentary of Solomon ben Yeruham the Karaite on Ecclesiastes" (PhD diss., Yeshiva University, 1973), 111.

an attribute which none of the monotheists (Arab. *al-mu'ahhadīn*) deny, rather they all confirm.

He says, *"ve-ukhal"* (Yefet: "I am capable"), meaning "I can establish evidence and proof for his existence." He had already mentioned evidence for that, saying (on vv. 2–3), "I have been ignorant among people," meaning that I know this (evidence) from my own situation. I was ignorant of both the hidden and revealed sciences yesterday, but today I have become knowledgeable of all. Yet I have not learned from a teacher, nor from a book, and I have not done it by myself. This is something people have noticed and do not deny, for (I was) young in years and full of knowledge. Every philosopher and every learned person who had already read (the writings) of the sages, and who had already studied the hidden sciences such as the arrangement of the spheres, the qualities of gemstones, the plants, and the animals, and the rest of the refined sciences, came to me in order to listen to me and to learn from my speech. This is proof for me and for them that there is an acting (force) that is not created. It has already been put forth in the book of Kings, "God gave Solomon very great wisdom" (1 Kgs 5:9). It is also said about him, "He was wiser than anyone else…. He composed three thousand proverbs…. He would speak of trees…. People came from all the nations to hear the wisdom of Solomon" (1 Kgs 5:11–14 MT). It is (further) said about him, "All the kings of the earth sought the presence of Solomon" (2 Chr 9:23). He shows that they wanted to see him and hear his words because they were amazed at the stories they had heard about him. (Solomon) says: "That I see myself full of wisdom and knowledge after not knowing a thing, not learning from anyone, and not reading any scholar's book, is one of the proofs of the existence of the Lord."

The saying *"ve-da'at qedoshim eda'"* (Yefet: I have known the knowledge of the distinguished natures) points to the knowledge of the Creator, who is *"elohim qedoshim"* (a holy God, Josh 24:19). He means by it additional knowledge, not (a result of) inference, as this could (potentially) include errors. After he presents proof for the existence of the Creator from his own condition, he, likewise, compares it to (the condition) of the rest of people and animals, upon whom the Lord bestowed wisdom, which they did not acquire through anyone else, as was explained earlier.

He then says, "Who ascended to the heavens and came down?" (v. 4). He mentions four things: heavens, wind, water, and earth. He asks, "Who has ascended the heavens and came down?" (v. 4)—not, "Who created the heavens?" Likewise, with regard to the wind (he asks a similar question): "Who gathered the wind?" About the water he asks, "Who collected water in a garment?"—not, "Who created it"; for his purpose is twofold: first, he wants to respond to those who are engrossed in knowledge[16] not mentioned by Solomon, peace upon him. These are some of the scholars of the nations who disclose measurements and capacities which are wrong and unfounded. He asks, "Who has ascended the heavens and came back down to communicate the measurements of the spheres? Who lifted them up in order to say that the measurement of this sphere is such and such, and the distance between this sphere and the one above it is so and so," and so on? He asserts that the statements of such people are invalid, for the Lord did not impart this information to them. None of them ascended and measured the spheres to inform and teach people of their measurements and distances. Likewise, (he asks,) "Who gathered the wind in the palm of their hands to assess its capacity?" Similarly, (he asks) "Who collected water in a garment?" In like fashion, (he asks,) "Who established the ends of the earth and cast its foundations, who lifted it to know its depth, (who) informed people so they know the quantity and quality of the winds and the water, the heights of the sphere, and the depths of the earth?" (This is in accordance with) what the other prophet said, "If the heavens above can be measured, and the foundations of the earth below can be explored," and so on (Jer 31:37). He asserts that this is not possible. He says that if no mortal ascended to the spheres and came down, nor gathered the wind, nor collected the waters, nor set the foundations or the directions of the earth—how can they know and profess (such information)?[17] He then says, "What is the person's name, and his son's name?"—meaning, that if there were one who professed doing so, his name should have been mentioned and well known. Who is the son of this person to whom he transmitted (this knowledge), (a son who would say,) "I have seen my father, or heard him say, 'I ascended to the heavens, gathered winds, collected the water, and established the earth' "? He says, "tell (us) if you know

---

16. Significantly, the Arabic word denoting English "knowledge" and "science" is the same ('ilm). This is also etymologically true for the Latin root of the English word "science" (scientia).

17. Cf. the words attributed to R. Simeon b. Yoḥay (Gen. Rab. 6:8), who claims that no one knows or is able to find out how the luminaries travel when they are not seen in the sky: "R. Simeon b. Yoḥay said: we do not know whether they fly through the air, glide in the heaven, or travel in their usual manner. It is an exceedingly difficult matter, and no person can fathom it." See Harry Freedman and Maurice Simon, eds., Midrash Rabbah, 10 vols., 3rd ed. (London: Soncino, 1983), 1:47.

(such a person)," by which he means that no one can say this or impart such information. Therefore, the statements of the one who claims that he knows the measurements of the sphere and the earth, the capacity of the wind, the waters, and the earth, are invalid, and he engrosses himself with what he does not know.

(The second purpose:) After he establishes the (existence) of the Creator, and nullifies the argument of those who say that they know the measurements of the world and (other) hidden things, which are only known to the one who created them, he mentions the Law (Arab. al-šarīʿa) for which the world was created. He says (v. 5), "All divine words are pure," meaning that there is neither a deceit nor a flaw in it. Likewise, the words of David, peace upon him, "This God—his way is perfect" (2 Sam 22:31 = Ps 18:31). He mentions the Law after he mentions monotheism (Arab. al-tawḥīd), because anyone who believes in monotheism must also accept the Law. Similarly, David says, "The heavens are telling the glory of God" (Ps 19:2), in order to mention the proof for the existence of the Creator; he then says, "The teaching of the Lord is perfect," and so on (Ps 19:8).

He then says, "He is like a shield to all who humble themselves before him." So, too, David says, "The word of the Lord is pure. He is a shield to all who take refuge in him" (2 Sam 22:31 = Ps 18:31). He means to say here that the Lord protects his followers and servants, who find refuge in him and depend upon him. He points by it to the day of judgment (yom ha-din), on which the Lord will punish the wicked and reward the righteous.

He then says, "Do not add to his exhortation" (v. 6), meaning, "Do not add to what he has written in his Law," for it entails "great and marvelous things" (Job 9:10) "(which are) beyond human (comprehension)" (Joel 1:12). This (prohibition) also includes "do not add to the commandments," as per "you must neither add anything to what I command you" (Deut 4:2). However, he omits (the prohibition to) subtract (from Scripture), yet it is said in the exalted Torah "nor take away anything from it" (Deut 4:2), for they add, as we mentioned before.

Thus he includes in this section the mention of monotheism (al-tawḥīd), the Law (al-šarīʿa), and the day of judgment, which encompasses reward and punishment. He says about the reward, "He is like a shield to all who humble themselves before him"; and about the punishment, "Lest he rebuke you and you be severed by his hand." Thus he shows that the Lord holds responsible the one who adds upon his words and who makes assertions which he cannot support with evidence. Such a person will be proven wrong,[18] and after that punishment will follow, no doubt.

Bibliography

Assaf, Simcha, and Samuel Glick, eds. *Mekorot le-toldhot ha-Hinukh be-Yisrael* [Hebrew]. 2 vols. New York: Jewish Theological Seminary of America, 2001.

Ben-Shammai, Haggai. "The Doctrines of Religious Thought of Abû Yûsuf Ya'qûb a-Qirqisânî and Yefet ben 'Elî." 2 vols. PhD diss., Hebrew University of Jerusalem, 1977.

Blau, Joshua. *A Dictionary of Mediaeval Judaeo-Arabic Texts* [Hebrew]. Jerusalem: Israel Academy of Sciences and Humanities, 2006.

Blau, Joshua, and Simon Hopkins. "The Beginning of Judaeo-Arabic Bible Exegesis according to an Old Glossary to the Book of Psalms" [Hebrew]. Pages 234–84 in *A Word Fitly Spoken: Studies in Medieval Exegesis of the Hebrew Bible and the Qur'an Presented to Haggai Ben-Shammai*. Edited by Meir M. Bar-Asher, Simon Hopkins, Sarah Stroumsa, and Bruno Cheisa. Jerusalem: Ben-Zvi Institute, 2007.

Crone, Patricia, and Martin Hinds. *God's Caliph: Religious Authority in the First Centuries of Islam*. Cambridge: Cambridge University Press, 1986.

Freedman, H., and Maurice Simon, eds. *Midrash Rabbah*. 10 vols. 3rd ed. London: Soncino, 1983.

Riese, Moshe I. "The Arabic Commentary of Solomon ben Yeruham the Karaite on Ecclesiastes." PhD diss., Yeshiva University, 1973.

Robinson, James T. *Asceticism, Eschatology, Opposition to Philosophy: The Arabic Translation and Commentary of Salmon ben Yeroham on Qohelet (Ecclesiastes)* Karaite Texts and Studies 5. Études sur le judaïsme médiéval 45. Leiden: Brill, 2012.

Sasson, Ilana. *The Arabic Translation and Commentary of Yefet ben Eli on the Book of Proverbs*. Vol. 1. Leiden: Brill, 2016.

Wechsler, Michael, ed. *The Arabic Translation and Commentary of Yefet ben 'Eli the Karaite on the Book of Esther*. Karaite Texts and Studies 1. Études sur le judaïsme médiéval 36. Leiden: Brill, 2008.

---

18. See Joshua Blau, *A Dictionary of Mediaeval Judaeo-Arabic Texts* [Hebrew] (Jerusalem: Israel Academy of Sciences and Humanities, 2006), 554, for the meanings of ינקטע and אלאנקטאע.

Zawanowska, Marzena. *The Arabic Translation and Commentary of Yefet ben 'Eli the Karaite on the Abraham Narratives (Genesis 11:10–25:18).* Karaite Texts and Studies 4. Études sur le judaïsme médiéval 46. Leiden: Brill, 2012.

Psalm 121 from Medieval Jewish Exegesis to Contemporary Israeli Culture: Some Reflections

Ora Brison

Introduction

During the last decades, reciting psalms has become a noticeably widespread phenomenon in contemporary Israel. This trend has a most significant presence in Israeli Jewish cultural life in both the private and the public spheres. The reciting of psalms is practiced by men and women, young and old, nonreligious and ultraorthodox, as part of their daily spiritual routine, regardless of the formal practice of Jewish prayer. An examination of this phenomenon indicates that the importance assigned to biblical psalms as personal prayers in modern Israel is, perhaps, much more similar to the medieval Karaite liturgical culture than to that of the Rabbanites. To demonstrate this "old-new" widespread cultural phenomenon of reciting psalms I have chosen Ps 121 ("I lift up my eyes to the hills"), one of the Songs of Ascents (Pss 120–134), as a case study.[1] In this essay I will present a short comparison between the exegetical approaches of the medieval exegetes Sa'adia Gaon, Yefet ben 'Eli, and Salmon ben Yerūḥīm on the book of Psalms, focusing on Ps 121. I shall also propose a modern commentary on Ps 121, examining its prayer and cultural reception in various Jewish communities of contemporary Israel.

This article is expanded from a paper originally presented at the international conference of the *Biblia Arabica* project, Tel Aviv University, November 2017. I am grateful to mentors and colleagues who participated in the conference for their helpful comments, which have contributed to this paper.

1. Unless otherwise noted, I quote from the NRSV.

Medieval Rabbanite and Karaite Exegesis of the Book of Psalms

To state the obvious: Saʿadia Gaon and the Karaite commentators, Salmon ben Yerūḥīm and Yefet ben ʿEli, differ in their exegetical approaches to the book of Psalms.[2]

Saʿadia's complex perception of the Psalms is expressed in his three introductions and commentaries to the book of Psalms.[3] Saʿadia equates Psalms' educative potential to that of the Torah.[4] However, he denies that Psalms has any literary uniqueness within the biblical canon. He does not agree with the talmudic statement that "David wrote the book of Psalms with ten elders" (b. B. Bat. 14b). According to Saʿadia, Psalms, the "Book of Praise" (*Kitāb al-tasābiḥ*), was a second Torah given by God to David and composed solely by him: "[The book of Psalms] was revealed to the best of kings, the prophet David, peace be upon him, the chosen [of God]."[5] While the sages regarded the Psalms as authentic prayers, he asserts that psalms as formal prayers were intended only for the Levites' prayer recitation during the time of the temple. He argues that, in the diaspora, the book functions as a theological-ethical book of direction and guidance. Saʿadia was opposed to the Karaite belief that the book was the prophetic mandatory prayer book (*diwan al-ṣala*) of the Jewish people throughout the generations. However, he recognizes Psalms' secondary role in the synagogue liturgy. This is likely why he does not oppose the inclusion of psalms in the prayer book, as long as it is understood that individual psalms were not prayers by themselves but additions to the actual mandatory prayers.[6]

---

2. On Karaite tradition of Arabic Bible translations, see Meira Polliack, *The Karaite Tradition of Arabic Bible Translation: A Linguistic and Exegetical Study of Karaite Translations of the Pentateuch from the Tenth and Eleventh Centuries C.E.* (Leiden: Brill, 1997); Polliack, "Major Trends in Karaite Biblical Exegesis in the Tenth and Eleventh Centuries," in *Karaite Judaism: A Guide to Its History and Literary Sources*, ed. Meira Polliack, Handbuch der Orientalistik 73 (Leiden: Brill, 2003), 389–410.

3. Yosef Kafiḥ, *Psalms with the Translation and Commentary of Saadiah Gaon* [Hebrew] (Jerusalem: "Hathia" Publishing, 1966).

4. Moshe Sokolow, "Saadiah Gaon's Prolegomenon to Psalms," *Proceedings of the American Academy for Jewish Research* 51 (1984): 131.

5. See Kafiḥ, *Psalms*, 27 (English translation here and elsewhere is mine); for the commentary section on this translation, see Uriel Simon, *Four Approaches to the Book of Psalms: From Saadiah Gaon to Abraham Ibn Ezra*, trans. Lenn J. Schramm (Albany: State University of New York Press, 1991), 5–6.

6. Simon, *Four Approaches*, 25–28.

Salmon ben Yerūḥīm compares the book of Psalms to the Torah, and he discusses the parallels between the two. In his polemic with Saʻadia Gaon he expresses the Karaite conception regarding the purpose of the Psalms. However, while both of them subscribe to the same literary model, Salmon's comparison focuses on the content; in that he differs from Saʻadia, who deals mainly with the rhetoric and style of the Psalms.

Unlike Saʻadia, Salmon considers the book of Psalms as unique within the biblical canon. For Salmon, Psalms is not only a book of directions and guidance, but it is designated to serve as the source for Jewish prayer in all times, for the generations prior to the building of the temple as well as for the exilic eras. For him, reciting psalms as prayers was not limited to Jerusalem or to any particular geographical area. His purpose was to show the important status of the psalms and their close relationship with the Torah and prophecy.[7] According to Salmon, although the book is named after King David, some psalms were composed by other prophets.[8] He argues that there is a thematic link between each psalm and the one preceding it, and that the psalms are prophecies and are therefore arranged in a certain order. In his introduction to the book, Salmon emphasizes the use of the imperative form in many verbs that express the various aspects of prayer—such as pleading, crying, begging, and appealing—as well as directives to thank the Lord, sing to him, exalt and glorify him, and more.[9] All these, for Salmon, were proof of the very nature of the Psalms: not only as prayers, but also as including within their text detailed instructions about their character and practice.

Yefet ben ʻEli also maintains that the book has a number of prophetic authors besides David, among them Moses (Ps 90), Solomon (72; 127), and others like Asaph (76; 82), Jeduthun (62; 77) and the Sons of Korah (85; 87). Moreover, in his commentary on Ps 1 he also acknowledges that the authorship of some psalms is unknown.[10] These prophetic authors

---

7. Simon, *Four Approaches*, 61.

8. The Karaites made an effort to give meaning to the prophecies of redemption not only in the books of the Prophets. The Torah, the book of Psalms, Daniel, and the Song of Songs were also seen as prophecies for the future. See Yoram Erder, "The Attitude of the Karaite Yefet ben ʻEli to Islam in Light of His Interpretation of Psalms 14 and 53" [Hebrew], *Michael: On the History of the Jews in the Diaspora* 14 (1997): 30–31.

9. Joseph Shunary, "Salmon ben Yeruham's Commentary on the Book of Psalms," *JQR* NS 73 (1982–1983): 159, 169–70.

10. Simon, *Four Approaches*, 76–79.

recorded the prayers as a book of instruction (for generations to come) on how to pray.[11] Yefet divides the psalms into twelve different categories, or "gates" (*abwab*), representing the different stages of biblical historiography.[12] He also classifies several thematic categories within the book such as songs of praise, petition, thanksgiving, and more.[13]

Yefet argues against Sa'adia's claim that Psalms constitutes a "book of edification," that the psalms are "closed" prophecies, and that the hymnal character of the book is simply an external rhetorical form. He maintains that Psalms is a prayer book in content, style, and form, and that the prophetic prayers are imposed upon the worshipers of all generations.[14]

Sa'adia, Salmon, Yefet, and other medieval Rabbanite and Karaite translators of the Bible from Hebrew to Arabic try to emulate the Hebrew source language, including content and context, as well as lexical and syntactic characteristics. However, their different approaches and perspectives are also expressed in their methods of translation and exegesis. In her work on the Karaite translations of the Pentateuch, Meira Polliack writes that a major difference between the Karaite Judeo-Arabic translations and that of Sa'adia's is demonstrated in the aspect of the use of alternative translations within the translated text.[15] Ilana Sasson adds: "Saadiah strives to present his audience with an independent final product and with a closed self-contained version."[16] This distinction is reflected also in their commentaries on the Psalms.

The Songs of Ascents

The Songs of Ascents collection includes fifteen psalms (120–134) that have the superscription *šîr hamma'ălôt*, "Song of Ascents," with the excep-

---

11. Shunary, "Salmon ben Yeruham," 159.

12. Sokolow, "Saadiah Gaon's Prolegomenon," 137–49.

13. Ilana Sasson, "Psalms: Primary Translations: Arabic Translations," in *Writings*, vol. 1C of *The Hebrew Bible*, ed. Armin Lange and Emanuel Tov, Textual History of the Bible (Leiden: Brill, 2017), 112.

14. Simon, *Four Approaches*, 75.

15. For a comprehensive comparison between these exegetes and their methods of translation see Polliack, *Karaite Tradition*, 242–77, esp. 268; Polliack, "Medieval Karaite Methods of Translating Biblical Narrative into Arabic," *VT* 45 (1998): 375–98.

16. Ilana Sasson, "The Book of Proverbs between Saadia and Yefet," *IHIW* 1 (2013): 167.

tion of Ps 121, which is entitled *šîr lammaʿălôt*.[17] These psalms are widely recognized as a subdivision within the book: not just because of their common superscriptions, but, mainly, because of the thematic, stylistic, and syntactic similarities they share and the parallel phrases that appear in them. According to Berhardus Eerdmans, the collection is a "suite" of songs to be read in succession.[18]

"Ascents" (*maʿălôt*, מעלות) is the plural form of the singular noun מעלה (*maʿălâ*): "step, stair" (from the root *ʿlh*, עלה: "go up, ascend, climb").[19] The two most commonly accepted interpretations of the Songs of Ascents are either as "pilgrim songs," referring to traveling to Jerusalem for one of the three annual festivals (Deut 16:16; also Ezra 7:9 and Ps 24:3), or as referring to the exiles returning from Babylon as they ascended the mountains to Jerusalem (Ezra 2:1; 7:7).[20] In the Mishnah (m. Sukkah 5:4; m. Mid. 2:5), the "ascents," מעלות (*maʿălôt*) are explained as the fifteen stairs of the temple upon which the Levites used to stand, ascend, sing, and play these psalms.[21] When comparing the works of Saʿadia and the Karaite

---

17. The meaning of the superscription "Song of Ascents" is unclear, and the word "ascents" (*maʿalôt*) has several interpretations: temple stairs (as in Ezek 40:6, 49; 1 Chr 17:17); altar stairs (as in Exod 20:26; Ezra 43:17); Solomon's throne stairs (as in 2 Kgs 10:19–20; 2 Chr 9:18–19); the enthronement of Yehu (as in 2 Kgs 9:13) (BDB "מַעֲלָה," s.v.); in Neh 9:4 the *maʿalôt* are the stairs of the Levites. In the Septuagint and the Vulgate the collection is numbered as Ps 119–133. The form of the superscription, "to or for Ascents" (למעלות, *lammaʿălôt*) in Ps 121 is a little different from that of the other psalms in the collection (*hammaʿălôt*, המעלות). In the Dead Sea Psalms Scroll, Ps 121 has the superscription *šîr hammaʿălôt*, the same as the other fourteen psalms of the collection. See James A. Sanders, *The Dead Sea Psalms Scroll* (Ithaca, NY: Cornell University Press, 1967), 38–39.

18. Loren D. Crow, *The Songs of Ascents (Psalms 120–134): Their Place in Israelite History and Religion* (Atlanta: Scholars Press, 1996), 16–17. See also Claus Westermann, *The Psalms: Structure, Content and Message*, trans. Ralph D. Gehrke (Minneapolis: Augsburg, 1980), 100; Bernardus D. Eerdmans, *The Hebrew Book of Psalms* (Leiden: Brill, 1947), 548–71.

19. The singular noun מעלה is also interpreted as "good quality/virtue." See BDB "עָלָה," s.v. See also John Day, *Psalms* (Sheffield: Sheffield Academic, 1990), 61–64.

20. Westermann (*The Psalms*, 100) points out that "in the western world the Songs of Ascents became the most important sources for travelers' songs."

21. Rashi, in his commentary to Ps 120, explains the title *hammaʿălôt* as referring to the fifteen steps that descend from the general court to that of the women's court. Rashi also finds in it an allusion to the heavenly stairs, intended for the righteous. The book of Psalms is highly significant for the Christian and the Islamic worlds. Fathers of the church, including Origen (ca. 185–253 CE) and Jerome (342–420 CE), interpreted

commentators, we see that Yefet and Salmon interpreted the Songs of Ascents as prayers recited by the Levites in the temple, whereas Saʿadia explains the term "ascents" as a musical term (ascending musical keys). His interpretation relies on the root *ʿlh* in 1 Sam 5:12 and Jer 14:2, there describing the raising of one's voice.[22] Saʿadia interprets both superscriptions (*hammaʿălôt* and *lammaʿălôt*) as being identical in meaning, and he considers them musical directives for playing or for singing Ps 1.[23]

Psalm 121

In the first part of Ps 121, the psalmist describes his distress and asks an indirect question, a rhetorical request for help, which he then answers with a statement of trust.[24] In the second part, another speaker tries to support the psalmist with depictions of God's power and greatness (vv. 3–4). The second speaker seeks to encourage and assure the psalmist of God's protection by continually repeating words with the root *šmr qal* (שמר, "keep, guard"). This root appears in the psalm six times, almost as part of an apotropaic formula, a mystic mantra: "he who *keeps* you" (v. 3); "he who *keeps* Israel" (v. 4); "the LORD is your *keeper*" (v. 5); "the LORD will *keep* you…; he will *keep* your life" (v. 7); "the LORD will *keep* your going" (v. 8).[25] In the third part of the psalm the psalmist turns back directly to God.

---

the meaning of the Songs of Ascents in relation to spiritual steps/ascents taken by the believers. See Rowan A. Greer, "Prologue to the Commentary on the Song of Songs," in *Origen: An Exhortation to Martyrdom, Prayer, and Selected Works*, trans. Rowan A. Greer, Classics of Western Spirituality (New York: Paulist, 1979), 239; *The Homilies of Saint Jerome, Volume I (1–59 On the Psalms)*, trans. Marie Liguori Ewald, FC 48 (Washington, DC: Catholic University of America Press, 1964). Augustine of Hippo (354–430 CE) interpreted these Psalms allegorically as portraying the soul's spiritual pilgrimage to God. See the translation by A. Cleveland Coxe in NPNF 1/8:589, 593. In the Qur'an God gives the Psalms (known as *zabūr*) to David (Q Al-Nisa' 4:163; Al-Isra' 17:55; Al-Anbiya' 21:79; 105).

22. Kafih, *Psalms*, 31; Simon, *Four Approaches*, 17.

23. Abraham ibn Ezra understood the change in the title of Ps 121 as designating a different melody from that of the other Songs of Ascents. See Simon, *Four Approaches*, 249.

24. See Julius Morgenstern, "Psalm 121," *JBL* 58 (1939): 311–23; Mitchell Dahood, S.J., *Psalms III, 101–150: Introduction, Translation, and Notes*, AB (Garden City, NY: Doubleday, 1970), 199; Crow, *The Songs*, 38–43.

25. This could be a reference to Gen 28:15: "Know that I am with you and will keep you wherever you go, and will bring you back to this land."

When comparing the translations of this psalm by Sa'adia, Yefet, and Salmon, it is important to consider the different methodologies they use and the different purposes that their translations are meant to serve.[26]

Whereas Sa'adia's interpretation of Ps 121 is free of alternative translation suggestions or interbiblical textual references, Yefet's approach to the Psalms and to prophecy is characterized by allusions to other texts.[27] Yefet suggests that the speaker's voice here is a prophet's voice.[28] In his interpretation of verse 1, "I lift up my eyes to the hills," he identifies the "hills" as the mountains of Jerusalem, and he inserts a comment referring the reader to verses from Isaiah and Nahum. Yefet quotes the following verses:

> Isa 40:9 O Zion, you who bring good tidings, get you up to a high mountain O Zion, herald of good tidings; lift up your voice with strength, O Jerusalem, herald of good tidings, lift it up, do not fear; say to the cities of Judah, "Here is your God!"

> Isa 52:7 How beautiful upon the mountains are the feet of the messenger who announces peace, who brings good news, who announces salvation, who says to Zion, Your God reigns.

> Nah 1:15 Look! On the mountains the feet of one who brings good tidings, who proclaims peace!

These innerbiblical allusions seem to reflect Yefet's view that some of the psalms also function as prophecies of the exile and of future redemption and and thus have relevance to the Karaites' eschatological-messianic aspirations.[29] Psalm 121 also reflects Yefet's assumption that the personal psalms

---

26. All quotes are from one manuscript of Yefet's commentary on Ps 121, MS BNP Héb. 286–289, dated 1612–1614; and from one manuscript of Salmon ben Yerūḥīm, MS Firkovich 556 Héb, dated 1519.

27. See Polliack, *The Karaite Tradition*, 267–68. On Yefet's approach to prophecy in his translation and commentary, see Meira Polliack and Eliezer Schlossberg, *Commentary of Yefet ben 'Eli the Karaite on the Book of Hosea* [Hebrew] (Ramat Gan: Bar-Ilan University Press, 2009), 10–70.

28. "Yefet's commentary on Psalm 137 exemplifies how far, in his view, the prophetic power of a Psalm can go," says Simon, *Four Approaches*, 110 n. 87.

29. On the messianic interpretations of Sa'adia Gaon, Salmon ben Yerūḥīm, and Yefet ben 'Eli of Isa 52:13–53:12, see Joseph Alobaidi, *The Messiah in Isaiah 53: The Commentaries of Saadia Gaon, Salmon ben Yeruham, and Yefet ben 'Eli on Is. 52:13–53:12*, La Bible dans l'histoire (Bern: Lang, 1998).

also have a national aspect and are meant to be used as future prayers for the whole exiled Jewish community. As articulated by Uriel Simon, for the Karaites,

> This is the force and authority of prophetic prayer. Its capacity to break through the mists of the future and match the needs and situation of a distant generation comes from its prophetic nature, while its eternal authority as obligatory prayer is entailed by its inclusion in Scripture.[30]

The multiple use of the verb *šmr qal* ("keep, guard") reminds the modern reader of the priestly blessing in Num 6:24–26: "The LORD bless you and keep you; the LORD make his face shine upon you, and be gracious to you; the LORD lift up his countenance upon you, and give you peace."

It is worth noting in this regard that Liebreich argues that the fifteen psalms in the Songs of Ascents collection were chosen for inclusion in the book in accordance with the fifteen words of the priestly blessing in Num 6:24–26. He notes that the four key phrases of the priestly bless-ing—[May the LORD] bless you; keep you; be gracious to you, and give you peace—occur throughout the Songs of Ascents (121:3–5, 7–8; 122:6–7, 15; 128:5), and those psalms are, in fact, commentaries on these priestly bless-ing expressions.[31]

Although this allusion to the priestly blessing might have been noticed by many rabbinic medieval commentators, they rarely mention it in their interpretations.[32] Neither does Sa'adia. Notably, he rarely includes Ps 121 in his prayer book (known as *Siddur Rasag*). In contrast with Sa'adia, Salmon, in his Arabic translation and commentary, inserts a comment referring to these verses, including the keywords and the relation to the thematic verb "keep, guard" in Ps 121, to the priestly blessing in Numbers.[33] This addition might have a didactic purpose, suggesting to the worshiper the

---

30. Simon, *Four Approaches*, 97.

31. Leon J. Liebreich, "The Songs of Ascents and the Priestly Blessing," *JBL* 74 (1955): 33–36. Three of the psalms—124, 126, and 131—do not contain one of the key words. Liebreich suggests that the original collection had only twelve psalms and that these three were added to bring the number up to fifteen, to correspond with the number of words in the blessing. See Crow, *The Songs*, 20–21.

32. The Sifre to Numbers in the commentary (144) on Num 6:24, "keep you," quotes Ps 121. On the history of the priestly blessing, see Ismar Elbogen, *Jewish Liturgy: A Comprehensive History* (Philadelphia: Jewish Publication Society, 1993), 62–66.

33. The priestly blessing is celebrated today at the Western Wall during the

precise biblical background of this specific text.[34] This biblical intertextual reference also strengthens Salmon's argument about the status of the book as a prayer book. So also, interestingly, Liebreich, who suggests that the allusion expressed in some verses of Ps 121 to the priestly blessing contributes to its sacred status and its universal appeal.[35] And it is worth mentioning that in prayer books of different Jewish communities, Ps 121 is most frequently recited after the priestly blessing.

The main themes in this psalm are those that Yefet classifies as the main themes of the whole book. One is God's greatness as manifested in the creation and his control of the cosmos and of time (vv. 2, 6, 8). A second theme depicts God as the guardian and protector of Israel (v. 4) and all his believers, as expressed in the repetition of the verb "keep." The third theme is the message of faith—"My help comes from the LORD ..." (v. 2)—followed by a blessing for the individual believer and the community: "The LORD will keep your going out and your coming in from this time on and forevermore" (v. 6).

Meir Weiss asserts that the uniqueness of the book of Psalms is that, while many biblical books transmit theological and religious messages through human historiography with a view from God to man, Psalms expresses the relationship between God and man with a view from man to God.[36] This statement by Weiss beautifully sums up the Karaite belief and assertion that the psalms are prayers, both personal and communal.

The Songs of Ascents and Psalm 121 in the Jewish Prayer Books

Throughout Jewish history the texts of the Jewish prayer book, the Siddur, have had several traditional basic liturgical formulas. It includes many biblical verses as well as newly composed liturgical poems, added according to the different religious customs of different communities.

Sukkot (Feast of Tabernacles) and Pesach (Passover) holidays, with many thousands of participants.

34. On Yefet's didactic style see Meira Polliack, "The Medieval Karaite Tradition of Translating the Hebrew Bible into Arabic: Its Sources, Characteristics and Historical Background," *Journal of the Royal Asiatic Society* 3/6.2 (1996): 191–92.

35. Liebreich, "The Songs of Ascents," 33–36.

36. Meir Weiss, *Ideas and Beliefs in the Book of Psalms* [Hebrew] (Jerusalem: Bialik Institute, 2001), 14.

Psalms are an integral liturgical part of the Jewish prayer books and are included in prayer books of all the different Jewish communities around the world; they have a special and significant status and are recited daily.[37] Nowadays, Ps 121 is one of the most frequently recited psalms among the Songs of Ascents collection. It is read every weekday in the afternoon prayer, and is among the psalms recited before the *pesukei de-zimra* (a collection of verses of hymns and songs recited before the main prayers) in the morning prayers of Shabbat and Holy Days. In many communities it is customary to incorporate it also into the Sabbat afternoon and evening prayers. In some Ashkenazi communities it is recited only on the *Shabbat ha-gaddol*, the Saturday before Passover. According to Sephardic communities and several Hasidic communities, it is recited in the evening prayers of each weekday, before "We must praise," one of the Eighteen Blessings. In the Yemenite community, in the morning prayers, verses from Pss 19, 30, 33, 34, 47, 48, 90, 91, and 103 are read and sometimes followed by Pss 98, 121, 123, and others. In the Yemenite engagement blessings, 121:3–8 are recited among some other biblical verses followed by the priestly blessing. Verse 4, "He who keeps Israel will neither slumber nor sleep," is part of the bedtime Shema.[38] Many recite this verse in the Traveler's Prayer (*Tefilat ha-derekh*), and in some communities it is recited in the Sanctification of [the new] Moon service (*Kiddush ha-levana*). Additionally, Ps 121 (at times, just some of its verses) is recited on religious liturgical occasions accompanying the Jewish individual from cradle to grave: it is recited during the Circumcision and First-Born Redemption (*pidyon ha-ben*) ceremonies, and often also in funerals and memorial services.[39]

---

37. On the Songs of Ascents in the Jewish prayer book, see Naphtali Wieder, "The Fifteen 'Songs of the Ascents' and Psalm 119—The Division of their Reading for the Seven Days of the Week (in the Prayer Customs of the Karaites and in Rabbinic Judaism" [Hebrew], in *The Formation of Jewish Liturgy in the East and in the West*, vol. 1 (Jerusalem: Ben-Zvi Institute, 1998), 352–57.

38. Verse 4 appears in many fragments of prayer books in the Shema prayer in Judeo-Arabic found in the Cairo Genizah. They suggest that this verse is probably the source of inspiration for the signature of the prayer in which the Lord is called, "He will keep his people keep Israel forever," which is attributed to the Geonim period in Babylon. See Shimon Fogel and Uri Ehrlich, "On the History of the Ancient Version of the '*Ha'shkivenu*' Blessing" [Hebrew], *Tarbitz* 84.1–2 (2016): 78–94.

39. See also Sung-Soo Kim, "Reading the Songs of Ascents (Psalms 120–134) in Context" (PhD diss., Luther Seminary, 2003), 95.

Sa'adia Gaon's Prayer Book (*Siddur Rasag*)

One of the earliest codifications of the Jewish prayer book was drawn up by Sa'adia Gaon. His prayer book was composed in an attempt to present a uniform version of a prayer book that would be a compromise between the various versions of prayers and customs in the Jewish communities in the Middle East (Egypt, Palestine, and Babylon). It includes a translation into Arabic and a commentary, and it also contains liturgical poetry composed by Sa'adia himself and by others. He explains that the purpose of his prayer book is "for learning and understanding" and that, from the outset, it is not intended to be used for prayer but to teach the rules and customs of the prayers. He himself did not call his work by the well-known Hebrew name Siddur, but rather "a composition" of mandatory prayers and of blessings (*Kitāb jāmi' al-ṣalawāt wal-tasābiḥ*). It should be noted that he added some psalms to his prayer book as additions to the mandatory prayers and that the prayer instructions (rubrics) are also in Judeo-Arabic.

However, although popular during the Middle Ages, his prayer book has rarely been in use for the last five hundred years.

The Reception of the Songs of Ascents and Psalm 121 in the Karaite Prayer Book

The early Karaites insisted that formal prayer should mainly consist of recitations from the Psalms and quotations from other biblical books. However, similar to what happened with the rabbinic prayer book, a process of inserting some personal prayers composed by "wise and understanding" individuals into the Karaites' prayer book continued throughout the generations.

The early Karaites avoided rabbinic liturgical and poetic works, and they insisted that formal prayer should consist exclusively of recitations from the Psalms and quotations from other biblical books. However, some individuals, if they were "wise and understanding," were permitted to insert their personal prayers into the liturgy. This led to Karaite experimentation with poetic works patterned after rabbinic models, and by the thirteenth century CE the Karaite prayer book compiled by Aaron ben Joseph included numerous traditional-typed *piyyutim* written mostly by Karaites and some by Rabbanites as well.[40] The proto-Karaite author,

---

40. Leon J. Weinberger, "A Note on Karaite Adaptations of Rabbinic Prayers," *JQR*

Anan ben David, whom the Karaites consider as founder of their movement, assigned a special place in his prayer book for the Songs of Ascents,
together with other psalms. Since we have only a few passages from Anan's
prayer book, it seems that his intention was to divide the Songs of Ascents
(together with Ps 119) so that two hymns will be recited on each weekday and three on the Shabbat. This custom was practiced by the Karaites
who lived in Jerusalem, who recited psalms in this manner not only in the
morning prayers, but also in the evening prayers. On Yom Kippur all the
Songs of Ascents were read, as well as near the end of the Sabbath on the
seven Sabbath days between Pesach (Passover) and Shavu'ot (Pentecost).

Interestingly, the combined recitation of the Songs of Ascents together
with Ps 119, and their distribution throughout the week's daily prayers,
was adopted in rabbinic circles. This practice was also found in later periods and in different geographic regions, but with a change: it was removed
from the synagogue, transferred to the private home, and attached to the
bedtime Shema prayer. A trace of this custom is preserved in the Sephardi-
style prayer book. In the *pesukei de-zimra*, four Songs of Ascents were
included, Pss 121–124. This is apparently one of the Karaite traditional
prayer customs, preserved to this day.[41]

Tentative Conclusions

Regardless of the specific biblical and historical cultic/liturgical background and the *original* context of the psalms, their comforting, hopeful
messages are suitable for reading and praying at different events and in
various circumstances, joyful and optimistic as well as frightening and distressful—then and now.

Psalm 121 is a good example of this phenomenon. It is an important
example, not only of the different translation and interpretive approaches
of medieval Jewish commentators, but also of their viewpoints and ideolo-
gies concerning the book of Psalms in Jewish liturgy.

NS 74 (1984): 267. See also Leon Nemoy, *Karaite Anthology* (New Haven: Yale University Press, 1952), 273–74. Yet see the recent article by Riikka Tuori, "'More Didactic
than Lyrical': Modern Views on Karaite Hebrew Poetry," *Studia Orientalia* 111 (2011):
343–64, who argues against the idea of adaptation.

41. For Karaite and Rabbanite sources on the subject, see Wieder, "The Fifteen
'Songs of the Ascents,'" 352–56.

Saʿadia Gaon's exegetical approach to the Psalms, as being suitable for prayer mainly at the times of the temple, is well demonstrated by his commentary on Ps 121. Yefet ben ʿEli and Salmon ben Yerūḥīm present the Karaite tradition of literal interpretation, on the one hand, and the Karaite belief that Psalms is actually a prayer book, on the other. The exegesis by Karaites, enlisting the priestly blessing and the "redemptive voice on the hills," demonstrates their belief that some of the psalms are prophecies of past/present exile and of future salvation. Their perception and approach to the Psalms is that the book is an important part of the Jewish biblical canon and includes forms of prayer that embody eschatological and mystic elements for the individual believer as well as for the community.

Research shows that the acceptance of the book of Psalms (and Ps 121 in particular) into Jewish liturgy during the decades since the Karaite/Rabbanite polemics took place indicates that the Karaite approach had greater impact than usually imagined. I found that, in almost all the Jewish communities around the world, the Karaite liturgical recitation of psalms was in fact accepted and became dominant in the wider Jewish-rabbinic prayers, even if not in the rabbinic prayer book.

I would carefully add that, from what I have learned, it would seem that the Karaite approach to the Psalms is the one that dominates the personal and public spheres in contemporary Israel. This is perhaps both surprising and unsurprising, when one thinks of Jewish history, on the one hand, and personal prayer and nonliturgical devotion, on the other hand.

Bibliography

Alobaidi, Joseph. *The Messiah in Isaiah 53: The Commentaries of Saadia Gaon, Salmon ben Yeruham, and Yefet ben ʿEli on Is. 52:13–53:1.* La Bible dans l'histoire. Bern: Lang, 1998.

Crow, Loren D. *The Songs of Ascents (Psalms 120–134): Their Place in Israelite History and Religion.* Atlanta: Scholars Press, 1996.

Dahood, Mitchell, S.J. *Psalms III, 101–150: Introduction, Translation, and Notes.* AB 17A. Garden City, NY: Doubleday, 1970.

Day, John. *Psalms.* Sheffield: Sheffield Academic, 1990.

Elbogen, Ismar. *Jewish Liturgy, A Comprehensive History.* Philadelphia: Jewish Publication Society, 1993.

Erder, Yoram. "The Attitude of the Karaite, Yefet ben ʿEli, to Islam in Light of his Interpretation of Psalms 14 and 53" [Hebrew]. *Michael: On the History of the Jews in the Diaspora* 14 (1997): 29–49.

Eerdmans, Bernardus D. *The Hebrew Book of Psalms*. Leiden: Brill, 1947.

Fogel, Shimon, and Uri Ehrlich. "On the History of the Ancient Version of the '*Ha'shkivenu*' Blessing" [Hebrew]. *Tarbitz* 84.1–2 (2016): 72–101.

Greer, Rowan A. "Prologue to the Commentary on the Song of Songs." Pages 217–79 in *Origen: An Exhortation to Martyrdom, Prayer, and Selected Works*. Translated by Rowan A. Greer. Classics of Western Spirituality. New York: Paulist, 1979.

Jerome, Saint. *The Homilies of Saint Jerome, Volume I (1–59 On the Psalms)*. Translated by Marie Liguori Ewald. FC 48. Washington, DC: Catholic University of America Press, 1964.

Kafiḥ, Yosef. *Psalms with the Translation and Commentary of Saadiah Gaon* [Hebrew]. Jerusalem: "Hathia" Publishing, 1966.

Kim, Sung-Soo. "Reading the Songs of Ascents (Psalms 120–134) in Context." PhD diss., Luther Seminary, 2003.

Liebreich, Leon J. "The Songs of Ascents and the Priestly Blessing." *JBL* 74 (1955): 33–36.

Morgenstern, Julius. "Psalm 121." *JBL* 58 (1939): 311–23.

Nemoy, Leon. *Karaite Anthology: Excerpts from the Early Literature*. New Haven: Yale University Press, 1952.

Polliack, Meira. *The Karaite Tradition of Arabic Bible Translation–A Linguistic and Exegetical Study of Karaite Translations of the Pentateuch from the Tenth and Eleventh Centuries C.E.* Leiden: Brill, 1997.

———. "Major Trends in Karaite Biblical Exegesis in the Tenth and Eleventh Centuries." Pages 363–413 in *Karaite Judaism: A Guide to Its History and Literary Sources*. Edited by Meira Polliack. Handbuch der Orientalistik 73. Leiden: Brill, 2003.

———. "Medieval Karaite Methods of Translating Biblical Narrative into Arabic." *VT* 45 (1998): 375–98.

———. "The Medieval Karaite Tradition of Translating the Hebrew Bible into Arabic: Its Sources, Characteristics and Historical Background." *Journal of the Royal Asiatic Society* 3/6.2 (1996): 189–96.

Polliack, Meira, and Eliezer Schlossberg. *The Commentary of Yefet ben ʿEli the Karaite on the Book of Hosea* [Hebrew]. Ramat Gan: Bar-Ilan University Press, 2009.

Sanders, James A. *The Dead Sea Psalms Scroll*. Ithaca, NY: Cornell University Press, 1967.

Sasson, Ilana. "The Book of Proverbs between Saadia and Yefet." *IHIW* 1 (2013): 159–78.

————. "Psalms: Primary Translations: Arabic Translations." Pages 110–14 in *Writings*, vol. 1C of *The Hebrew Bible*. Edited by Armin Lange and Emanuel Tov. Textual History of the Bible. Leiden: Brill, 2017.

Shunary, Joseph. "Salmon ben Yeruham's Commentary on the Book of Psalms." *Essays in Honor of Leon Nemoy. JQR* NS 73 (1982–1983): 155–75.

Simon, Uriel. *Four Approaches to the Book of Psalms: From Saadiah Gaon to Abraham Ibn Ezra*. Translated by Lenn J. Schramm. Albany: State University of New York Press, 1991.

Sokolow, Moshe. "Saadiah Gaon's Prolegomenon to Psalms." *Proceedings of the American Academy for Jewish Research* 51 (1984): 131–74.

Tuori, Riikka. "'More Didactic than Lyrical': Modern Views on Karaite Hebrew Poetry." *Studia Orientalia* 111 (2011): 343–64.

Weinberger, Leon J. "A Note on Karaite Adaptations of Rabbinic Prayers." *JQR* NS 74 (1984): 267–79.

Weiss, Meir. *Ideas and Beliefs in the Book of Psalms* [Hebrew]. Jerusalem: Bialik Institute, 2001.

Westermann, Claus. *The Psalms: Structure, Content and Message*. Translated by Ralph D. Gehrke. Minneapolis: Augsburg,1980.

Wieder, Naphtali. "The Fifteen 'Songs of the Ascents' and Psalm 119—The Division of Their Reading for the Seven Days of the Week (in the Prayer Customs of the Karaites and in Rabbinic Judaism)" [Hebrew]. Pages 352–57 in *The Formation of Jewish Liturgy in the East and the West: A Collection of Essays*. Vol. 1. Jerusalem: Ben-Zvi Institute, 1998.

On the Advantages of Studying the Book of Job as Outlined in Yefet ben 'Eli's Commentary

Arik Sadan

The Text

This is a translation of the second part of Yefet ben 'Eli's introduction to his commentary on the book of Job, followed by a short discussion. The translation is my own work, from my book on Yefet's commentary.[1] The translation is based on the following manuscripts: BL Or. 2510 (IMHM 6284); JTS MS 3354, ENA 100 (IMHM 32039); SP RNL Yevr.-Arab. 1:247 (IMHM 53850); SP RNL Yevr.-Arab. 1:248 (IMHM 54035); and SP RNL Yevr.-Arab. 1:304 (IMHM 53876).[2]

Translation

And when I introduced what is incumbent to introduce in the matter of this great man [that is, Job], may peace be upon him, I consider it right to gather the main issues of this book and its benefits before I begin its commentary, in order that the learner would be aware of its benefits and wish to teach and obtain them. And from the giver of wisdom [that is, God] I ask to guide me in the right path toward the true success, and from him I seek aid.

The first [issue] that we learn from this book is that there had been a group of believers in the unity of God[3] and people of knowledge not from

---

1. Arik Sadan, *The Arabic Translation and Commentary of Yefet ben 'Eli the Karaite on the Book of Job*, Karaite Texts and Studies 12 (Leiden: Brill, 2019).

2. Clarifications and additions within the translation are in square brackets; references to biblical verses are in round brackets.

3. This is the translation of מוחדין, a word that also occurs later (n. 5 below).

our nation, because Job and his friends were not of the antecedents of Jacob. And he taught us that those who believe in the unity of God and the believers have always been in the world, but they are not many among the nations of the world. Neither a nation nor most of it were believers except for our nation.

The second is his instructing us that the believers have always joined one another, as we will explain in what follows: each one of Job's friends was of a [different] city and [a different] family, as he said: "each of them set out from his home" (Job 2:11).[4] And he makes us desire to join and to become near one another, as faith makes incumbent.

The third is that the believers had places in which they gathered on a certain day in order to worship [God] and to discuss the religion of God, as we will explain in [the matter of] "one day the heavenly beings came to present themselves before the Lord" (Job 1:6). And he encourages us to be like them, especially on Saturdays and at the beginning of months and feasts.

The fourth is what we learn from the story of the Satan: that there was in the past someone who wandered in the land, called the people to the religion, and watched [them] on behalf of God Almighty; and that no one was neglected in the world without a caller [to his religion] or watcher [for God]. As it was said about the ancient generations, "At that time people began to invoke the name of the Lord" (Gen 4:26). And he informed of the reasons for the destruction of our nation when it lacked it (that is, who invites the people to God), as he said, "Run to and fro through the streets of Jerusalem, look around and take note! Search its squares" (Jer 5:1); and he destroyed the land and most of them died by his "four deadly acts of judgment" (Ezek 14:21).

The fifth is what he instructed us of the religion of Job, his being pious and his good deeds, in order that we follow his path and footsteps and act like him, even though he is not of our nation.

The sixth is his [Job's] holding on to his religion and his endurance at the trial that befell him, which had not happened to any of the righteous but him. And in that there is a lesson for us to hold on to the religion of God despite the conditions of the diaspora and the magnitude of our

---

According to another version that appears in several manuscripts, מזהירין ("warners"), Yefet here refers to the Karaites, as this is one of the names by which they referred to themselves.

4. The translation of this biblical verse, as of all others, is that of the NRSV.

disasters; as he said, "All this has come upon us, yet we have not forgotten you, or been false to your covenant" (Ps 44:18). However, the calamities of Job did not injure him because of sins, whereas our disasters are due to weighty sins; and it is therefore more appropriate for us to endure the disasters that injure us.

The seventh is the return of God to him [Job] and removing his anger, which he described to us, since his fortune returned to him doubled, his body recovered from the disease, and he surpasses the people of his time in power and rank. And we also hope for a relief, the removal of disasters away from us and our return to what is better than [our situation] in ancient times. Job was sure that God would return to him, even if he [that is, God] did not notify him of that. It is therefore more appropriate that we be confident of all God's promises, which every prophet mentioned, especially [those mentioned] with pacts and treaties, and then we would find comfort in them and endure the conditions of the bitter diaspora.

The eighth is that everyone was slandering Job's way and compared it to every abhorrent thing, such as what happens to us especially from Ishmael; and he [Job] endured that until God revealed his proof and it was obvious for the people that it is the right way, as God said to Elifaz, "My wrath is kindled against you and against your two friends; for you have not spoken of me what is right, as my servant Job has" (Job 42:7).

The ninth is that he taught us the way of his [Job's] friends and their way of speech [that is, their way of argumentation, their methodology in speech] in order that we would know what they were thinking before God revealed to them the truth, in order that we would know that the disagreement was among the ancient ones, although they believed in the unity of God[5] and believers, and that God made them be in need of deepening in the discussion; sometimes they go into it [that is, discussion] in the right way; sometimes they reach the truth, and sometimes not. And in it there is a response to the way of whoever considers the tradition right and rejects the discussion, because he can be wrong or right, and that is the way of the traditionalism like al-Fayyūmī [Sa'adia Gaon] and those who follow him and the traditionalism of every nation.

The tenth is that we learn from them [the friends] the good ways of study and discussion, because each [of them] waited patiently for his friend to finish his words and stop [talking], and kept in his heart all that

---

5. This is the translation of מוחדין, a word that also appeared before, according to several manuscripts (see n. 3 above).

he would say, and then spoke in his turn and responded to the words of his friend in what he considered as the [right] belief. We, too, will do like them in our discussion; and whoever deviates from this way is one of little knowledge, no manners and condemned.

The eleventh is that speech ensued from them three times, although Job was confident of the truth of his way and they were confident of the truth of their way. Neither he conceded to them nor they conceded to him, and then they stopped talking to him. This shows that people of study can differ in their view, without one of them conceding to his friend, and there is no doubt that the truth is with one of them. In the end the truth will appear from God, as he said on the Remainder:[6] "he who vindicates me is near. Who will contend with me? Let us stand up together. Who are my adversaries? Let them confront me" (Isa 50:8).

The twelfth is that in this book there is a mention of God's braveries and his wonders. Eliphaz mentioned some of them, Job and Elihu elaborated, and God said more than all. We therefore know from them [from all the dialogues] many of God's wonders.

The thirteenth is that God Almighty constructed the story of Job for us in order that it would be for the generations to come, so that he would be remembered for the good and not forgotten among the scholars and the righteous. And such are the stories of the righteous and learned,[7] as it was said, "Let this be recorded for a generation to come" (Ps 102:19).

And these matters that I mentioned—we learn them from this book besides what we learn from many things that were said in their [the friends'] discussions. The benefits of this book thus became clear, and it is incumbent upon the people to desire to realize the knowledge in it. Hereby I begin to interpret verse by verse, and to mention its matters according to what we heard and what seems appropriate to us. I will mention in all of them which way is closer [to the truth], since many scholars directed the words of Job not toward their goal and aim; and Job was then condemned in some way. God Almighty testified for him at the beginning of his book that he is "blameless and upright, one who feared God and turned away from evil" (Job 1:1); and at the end of his book, he said, "for you have not spoken of me what is right, as my servant Job has" (Job 42:7). By these texts

---

6. This is the translation of שארית, a term that the Karaites used to refer to themselves. See also the next note.

7. This is the translation of משכילים, a term that the Karaites used to refer to themselves. See also the previous note.

it is obligatory that we make this a principle, and point all the words of Job on a way which corresponds to this principle. We will also interpret every verse whose interpretation is difficult in its place, God willing in his grace and honor.

Short Discussion

Yefet ben ʿEli's translation of and commentary on the book of Job contains an introduction, which can be divided into two parts. Whereas the first part discusses the various creations of God and their divisions and connects them to the book of Job, the text of the second part, brought here in its English translation, details the thirteen advantages that make it worthwhile to study the book well.

Yefet begins the list of these advantages with the general perspective of the book, and he emphasizes that Job was a righteous man who was not a member of the sons of Israel's community. Despite that, as Yefet claims and shows, the sons of Israel should learn from Job and his ways. Job is a role model for any believer, Jew or non-Jew, and therefore his story and the issues it raises ought to be studied. Yefet then moves on to the more specific advantages of the book and its dialogical nature, from which one should learn the importance of discussions and conversations, as well as the importance of performing them in a civilized manner, such as showing respect to people of various opinions even when they greatly differ from one's own opinion. Yefet uses some of the advantages he discusses in order to show that the way of the Karaites is the right way, since they aim at seriously discussing matters rather than just accepting them. In the ninth advantage Yefet even explicitly mentions al-Fayyūmī (Saʿadia Gaon) and those who follow him as an example for those who oppose discussions and thus should be condemned.

Bibliography

Ben-Shammai, Haggai. "The Arabic Commentary of Yefet Ben ʿEli to Job 1–5" [Hebrew]. M.A. thesis. Hebrew University of Jerusalem, 1969.

Goodman, L. E. *The Book of Theodicy: Translation and Commentary on the Book of Job by Saadia Ben Joseph al-Fayyūmī.* Yale Judaica Series 25. New Haven: Yale University Press, 1998.

Hussain, Haidar Abbas. "Yefet ben Ali's Commentary on the Hebrew Text of the Book of Job I–X." Ph.D. diss. University of St. Andrews, 1986.

Qafiḥ, Yosef D. *Saʿadya Gaon's Translation and Commentary of the Book of Job* [Hebrew]. Jerusalem: Ha-Makor, 1973.

Sadan, Arik. "Islamic Terminology, the Epithets and Names Used for God and Proper Nouns in Yefet Ben ʿEli's Translation of the Book of Job in Judeo-Arabic." Pages 436–47 in *Senses of Scripture, Treasures of Tradition: The Bible in Arabic among Jews, Christians and Muslims*. Edited by Miriam L. Hjälm. Biblia Arabica 5. Leiden: Brill, 2017.

———. *The Arabic Translation and Commentary of Yefet ben ʿEli the Karaite on the Book of Job*. Karaite Texts and Studies 12. Leiden: Brill, 2019.

Salmon ben Yerūḥīm on Lamentations 1:12

Jessica Andruss

Salmon ben Yerūḥīm was a leading Bible scholar among the Jerusalem Karaites. In the middle of the tenth century CE, he authored Arabic commentaries on at least six biblical books—Psalms, Song of Songs, Lamentations, Qoheleth (Ecclesiastes), Esther, and Ruth—and composed a now-lost linguistic treatise in Arabic about the "interchangeable letters" of biblical Hebrew (*Kitāb al-Ibdāl, Book of Substitution*). Salmon's exegetical method is informed by his Karaite sensibilities: he translates Hebrew verses into Arabic, begins his comments with linguistic observations, justifies his interpretations with parallel biblical passages, and writes his excursuses in a homiletical style in which he chastises and consoles, exhorting readers to greater piety and penitence.

The passage below comes from Salmon's commentary on Lamentations.[1] This biblical book was central to the liturgy and communal identity of the Jerusalem Karaites. It describes the anguish experienced by the people of Jerusalem when the city fell to the Babylonians in 586 BCE and most of the population was sent into exile. The themes of Lamentations—sin and punishment, exile and loss—resonated with the spiritual and social concerns of Salmon's community, who referred to themselves as "mourners for Zion" to emphasize their return to the holy city and their program of grieving over its ruins and the sins that had caused its downfall.

The homiletical thrust of Salmon's commentary reflects his understanding of Lamentations. Like most traditional Jewish interpreters,

---

1. Salmon's text can be found in Mohammed Abdul-Latif Abdul-Karim, "Commentary of Salmon Ben Yeruham on Lamentations" (PhD diss., University of St. Andrews, 1976), 48–49. The NRSV translation of the Hebrew text of Lam 1:12 is reproduced in italics, followed by Salmon's translation of the verse into Arabic and then his commentary.

Salmon identifies the prophet Jeremiah as the book's author. Yet for Salmon, Lamentations is not merely Jeremiah's poetic lament for the fallen city. It is, rather, the prophet's "instruction for Israel," a guidebook that teaches Jews to recognize and repent for their sins during times of exile. The book's cries of woe and images of devastation are intended to rouse the exiles to a sincere and radical repentance that will ultimately lead to redemption. Within the commentary, Salmon amplifies the homiletical message that he ascribes to Jeremiah with his own homilies that draw on Karaite rhetoric, rabbinic models, and oratorical techniques from the Arabic-Islamic sphere. Further, to each chapter of Lamentations Salmon assigns a biblical verse that justifies Israel's suffering as punishment for the people's sins, and he uses this verse as a refrain at the end of his comment on each verse of Lamentations.

Salmon's homiletical hermeneutic is apparent in his comment on Lam 1:12, cited below. The biblical verse demands,

Look and see if there is any sorrow like my sorrow (NRSV),

which Salmon expands with a short, self-contained homily that leaves no doubt about what Israel has lost:

There is no community in the world [to whom] God communicated or to whom he revealed prophets except for Israel! Or for whom he revealed divine glory and celestial fire and signs and wonders, except for Israel!

These exclamations—which may be borrowed from an actual Karaite sermon—intensify the emotional force of the biblical passage by forging an implicit contrast between Israel's ancestral glory and the degraded conditions of exile.

This homily—as well as Salmon's approach to Lamentations more generally—is rooted in comparison, and Salmon uses Lam 1:12 as a prooftext to justify his comparative hermeneutic. For Salmon, Jeremiah's command to "look and see if there is any sorrow like my sorrow" is not a rhetorical plea but an exegetical imperative for readers of Scripture. Salmon himself practices this comparative method throughout the commentary. In the introduction to his commentary, he systematically compares the sufferings of Israel and the sufferings of Job, concluding that the former far outweigh the latter and declaring unequivocally that:

There is no calamity that is greater than our calamity, and no pain that is greater than our pain.

He reaffirms this assessment in his comment to Lam 1:12 with the addition of verses from Daniel and Ezekiel that note the singularity of Jerusalem's punishment.

At this point, however, Salmon's comparative inquiry takes an unexpected turn. He compares the punishments of Israel with those of Egypt and Canaan and, whereas the previous comparisons highlight the severity of Israel's suffering, this comparison reveals instead the exceptional degree of divine mercy toward Israel. For while the enemies of Israel were completely annihilated—so argues Salmon—the Israelites were merely sent into exile. God did not "make a full end" (Heb. *kālāh*; Jer 30:11) of Israel, as God did with the other nations.

Salmon makes the case for this interpretation on the basis of two lines of reasoning, both drawing on Isa 27:7–8. This biblical passage juxtaposes the punishments of Israel and Israel's enemies, concluding with the assertion that,

By measure [בסאסאה, *bəsaʾssəʾâ*], by expulsion [בשלחה, *bəšalḥāh*], you did contend with them.

Salmon first addresses the passage from a linguistic point of view, defining the *hapax legomenon bəsaʾssəʾâ* as "to a certain extent," which he interprets in apposition to expulsion (*bəšalḥāh*). Thus, exile is a restrained, measured punishment, in contradistinction to the full, horrific effects of unbridled divine wrath that afflicted Israel's enemies.

To this explanation, Salmon appends a figurative interpretation of the verse inspired by paranomasia, a typically midrashic technique. Here he presents the expulsion (*šalḥāh*) as an allusion to the branches (*šəlūḥôt*) of a tree. Just as the destruction of a tree's branches is far less severe than the fatal destruction of a tree's roots, so the punishment of exile that Israel endures is far gentler than the punishment of complete annihilation which brought the peoples of Egypt and Canaan to a violent end.

Salmon's exegesis of Isa 27:7–8 constitutes a "commentary within a commentary" that enables him to read Lam 1:12 against the grain, and, indeed, in contrast to the interpretation that he initially advocates. In Salmon's double-reading, exile signifies both the unprecedented severity of God's punishment and the unequaled mercy of God's protection. The complexity of this message accords well with Salmon's homiletical goals. Exile—so familiar to the lived experience of Salmon's readership—proves that Israel has sinned and also promises that Israel will be redeemed. In Salmon's homiletical interpretation, the suffering to which Jeremiah refers is nothing less than exile, which continues to punish and preserve the Jewish community in his own time, and which persuades perceptive readers of the Bible of the need to repent.

Translation—Salmon on Lamentations 1:12

Is it nothing to you, all you who pass by? Look and see if there is any sorrow like my sorrow, which was brought upon me, which the Lord inflicted on the day of his fierce anger.

"Is it nothing to you?" I call[2] to all you who pass by. "Look and see if there is any sorrow like my sorrow which was brought upon me, which the LORD inflicted on the day of his fierce anger."

I translated *lô' 'alêkem*[3] as "Is it nothing to you?" because often for us *lô'* (the negative) has the meaning of *ha-lô'* (the negative interrogative), as in "before their eyes, will they not [*lô'*] stone us?" (Exod 8:26); and similarly, "for now the slaughter among the Philistines—was it not [*lô'*] great?" (1 Sam 14:30). The meanings of *ha-lô'* are many. They have also translated *lô' 'alêkem* to mean, "Heaven forbid that what befell me should befall you!"[4] However, the first rendering is more proper and more plausible.

He [Jeremiah] says, "Is it nothing to you? I call to all who pass by the road: Reflect on my condition, and see! Did you witness what happened to me—the sorrow and the magnitude of the calamities that happened to me and to my life?"

There is no community in the world [to whom] God communicated or for whom he revealed prophets except for Israel! Or for whom he revealed divine glory and celestial fire and signs and wonders, except for Israel!

---

2. Salmon has added the verb "I call" in his Arabic translation.

3. Hebrew: לוא אליכם.

4. This reading is advanced by the rabbis; see, e.g., the paraphrase offered in Lamentations Rabbah: "The Community of Israel says to the nations of the world: 'May there not come upon you what has come upon me!'" (see A. Cohen, trans., *Midrash Rabbah: Lamentations*, 3rd ed. [London: Soncino, 1983], 117).

For this reason, he says, "if there is any sorrow like my sorrow," just as I explained in the introduction to this book, regarding the calamities that troubled the tried one—that is Job, peace be upon him. The calamities of Israel are far greater, as I have explained. Daniel said, "by bringing upon us a great calamity; for under the whole heaven there has not been done the like of what has been done against Jerusalem" (Dan 9:12). And God said through Ezekiel, "I will do with you what I have never yet done, and the like of which I will never do again" (Ezek 5:9).

"Which was brought upon me" means "that which was done to me" and this is like the verse, "with whom have you dealt thus?" (Lam 2:20).

"Which the LORD inflicted" means that he expelled Israel from their country and their temple, as it is said, "I will drive them out of my house" (Hos 9:15); and likewise as it is said, "He removed them with his fierce blast in the day of the east wind" (Isa 27:8). Its meaning is [expressed] in the beginning of the verse, "Has he smitten them as he smote those who smote them?" (Isa 27:7a). This [verse indicates] God's benevolence to this community, since he spared it and did not destroy it on account of the evilness of its deeds, as I have explained in the introduction to this book. He said, "See my grace: is the smiting of the one who smote him like the smiting of the Lord of the worlds?" The smiter alluded to in this verse is Pharaoh and his people; when they exceeded all bounds, God destroyed them completely.

"Or have they been slain as their slayers were slain?" (Isa 27:7b)—"or have they been killed as their killers were killed?" This means the Canaanites. God commanded that they be killed, and Israel killed them. Was Israel in its entirety killed, like them? That is to say, the way that God destroyed Israel was not like the destruction of Pharaoh and his people, and it was not like [the destruction of] the Canaanites, as he says, "The whole land shall be a desolation; yet I will not make a full end" (Jer 4:27). In what follows, he also says, "I will make a full end of all the nations" (Jer 30:11).

Then it is said, "By measure [bəsaʾssəʾâ], by expulsion [bəšalḥāh], you did contend with them" (Isa 27:8). This means that their destruction only resembled the destruction of their enemies to a certain extent, because the expression bəsaʾssəʾa means "by the measure," as in "for every measure [səʾôn]" (Isa 9:4/5) and "a measure [səʾâ] of fine meal" (2 Kgs 7:18). The meaning of "by the measure" is, in other words, "to a certain extent." It is not in the root because "by expulsion [bəšalḥāh]" is like, "Its shoots [šəlūḥôtehā] spread about and passed over the sea" (Isa 16:8). "By expulsion you did contend with them" (Isa 27:8) is a statement about its branches; he means to compare Israel to a tree. He says that the destruction that happened to them was in their branches and not in their root, because expulsion [bəšalḥāh] is like "its shoots [šəlūḥôtehā] spread abroad" (Isa 16:8). He says of its branches that he disputes with them, which is to say, he punishes them.

"He removed them with his fierce blast in the day of the east wind" (Isa 27:8) means that in his mercy he did not destroy them completely; rather, a large gathering of them remained. He drove them out into the exile by the hand of the enemy, which is compared to an east wind, as it is said, "the east wind, the wind of the LORD, shall come" (Hos 13:15).

"On the day of his fierce anger." Because the exile was the day of the LORD's anger—as he had established through Moses, peace be upon him, when he said, "then my anger will be kindled against them in that day, and I will forsake them" (Deut 31:17)—all of this overtook them when they increased their rebellions, as it is said, "who is the man so wise that he can understand this? Why is the land ruined and laid waste like a wilderness, so that no one passes through? And the LORD says: 'Because they have forsaken my law which I set before them, and have not obeyed my voice, or walked in accord with it'" (Jer 9:12–13).

Bibliography

Abdul-Karim, Mohammed Abdul-Latif. "Commentary of Salmon Ben Yeruham on Lamentations." PhD diss., University of St. Andrews, 1976.

Andruss, Jessica Hope. "Exegesis, Homily, and Historical Reflection in the Arabic Commentary on Lamentations by Salmon ben Yerūḥīm, Tenth-Century Karaite of Jerusalem." PhD diss., University of Chicago, 2015.

Ben-Shammai, Haggai. "Poetic Works and Lamentations of Qaraite 'Mourners of Zion'—Structure and Contents" [Hebrew]. Pages 191–234 in Kenesset Israel: Literature and Life in the Synagogue: Studies Presented to Ezra Fleischer. Edited by Shulamit Elitsur, Mosheh David Herr, Avigdor Shinan, and Gershon Shaked. Jerusalem: Ben Zvi, 1994.

Cohen, A., trans. Midrash Rabbah: Lamentations. 3rd ed. London: Soncino, 1983.

Frank, Daniel. Search Scripture Well: Karaite Exegesis and the Origins of the Jewish Bible Commentary in the Islamic East. Études sur le Judaïsme Médiéval 29. Leiden: Brill, 2004.

Robinson, James T. Asceticism, Eschatology, Opposition to Philosophy: The Arabic Translation and Commentary of Salmon ben Yeroham on Qohelet (Ecclesiastes). Karaite Texts and Studies 5. Leiden: Brill, 2012.

Salmon ben Yerūḥīm on Qoheleth:
A Selection (Preface; 1:1–4; 4:17; 7:16; 12:12)

James T. Robinson

Salmon ben Yerūḥīm is the earliest of the Jerusalem Karaites to leave us a substantial corpus of commentaries written in Arabic. The commentary on Qoheleth was completed in the 950s CE. Typical of the Jerusalem tradition, it begins with a systematic introduction, in which Salmon singles out the five main themes of Qoheleth. A very full commentary follows, in which Salmon discusses each verse at great length, providing a complete Arabic translation with detailed exposition. Although Salmon is very eager to get at the proper linguistic sense of every word in context, what truly motivates him are the historical context, setting Qoheleth's teaching properly within the life of Solomon, and philosophy, bringing out the sober otherworldly ascetic teachings he finds Qoheleth to be teaching in this book of wisdom. This gives Salmon's commentary a strongly homiletical character, sometimes even poetic, in its call to the reader to follow the lessons taught by Solomon.

The samples given below provide illustrations of Salmon's homiletical method. The commentary on the first verses works hard to establish the wisdom credentials of Solomon and all the knowledge the book points toward. Here as elsewhere, Salmon's Qoheleth is constantly pushing the reader away from this world and toward the other, to a life of prayer, learning, and contemplation of the divine. The commentary on Qoh 4:17 shows Salmon's creative exegetical faculties serving his homiletical ideals, as he reads *regel* (Heb., lit. "foot") euphemistically in relation to the male pudendum, thus understanding the verse as a whole as warning against sexual impropriety. The commentaries on Qoh 7:16 and 12:12 establish the foundations for a polemic against "foreign wisdom," which will become typical of the Jerusalem Karaite school in general.

Salmon's commentary was edited with Hebrew translation in Moshe Riese's unpublished doctoral dissertation.[1] Selections were published with French translation by Georges Vajda.[2] Most recently, I published the complete text with an annotated English translation and introduction.[3] The following translations are based on my edition and translation.

In this essay, beyond Salmon's preface to his commentary (only in an English translation of the original Judeo-Arabic), the selected biblical verses are presented, in most cases and without extra markings, in the English rendering of the JPS (1985) translation, slightly modified at places (in italics); at times, when the NRSV is more precise or bears a greater similarity to Salmon's rendering, it is reproduced instead (and marked as such). The next step is an English rendering of Salmon's translation of the relevant verses (in boldface) and, finally, his commentary on them. Hebrew and Arabic words will be given in transliteration, and additional matters in parentheses.

Salmon's Preface

In the name of YHWH the eternal God (Gen 21:33), let his name and his memory be exalted.

Let Allah the Deity of Israel be blessed, let his memory be exalted: the One; the Primordial, Eternal, Everlasting Truth; the Everlasting, All-Powerful, Creating Truth. In all he created he has no equal [Arab. *nidd*]; in all his kingdom he has no contrary [Arab. *ḍidd*]; nor has he partner or opponent. Let him be praised, as is worthy him and as he justly deserves, for ever and ever.

The commentator, his memory for a blessing, said: The learned ought to know that the meanings of Qoheleth, peace be with him, are according to their external sense [Arab. *ẓāhir*] and are not proverbs [Arab. *amthāl*], for Sulaymān [Solomon] the sage, peace be with him, had already collected

---

1. Moshe Riese, "The Arabic Commentary of Solomon ben Yeruham the Karaite on Ecclesiastes," PhD diss., Yeshiva University, 1973.

2. Georges Vajda, *Deux commentaires karaïtes sur l'Ecclésiastes* (Leiden: Brill, 1971).

3. James T. Robinson, *Asceticism, Eschatology, Opposition to Philosophy: The Arabic Translation and Commentary of Salmon ben Yeroham on Qohelet (Ecclesiastes)*, Karaite Texts and Studies 5, Études sur le judaïsme médiéval 45 (Leiden: Brill, 2012).

proverbs in the book of Proverbs, on account of which he opened with its very first word saying: "The proverbs of Solomon son of David" (Prov 1:1). Yet when he decided he would write this noble book [Qoheleth] he opened with its very first word saying: "The words of Qoheleth" (Qoh 1:1), intending thereby to explain that it ought to be understood according to its external sense. He likewise said: "The words of Agur son of Jakeh" (Prov 30:1), and "The words of Lemuel" (Prov 31:1)—according to what we explained in the preface to Proverbs.

The reason I begin this way is because I have learned of people who interpreted the book improperly, saying, for example, that with the verse: "the sun rises and the sun goes down" (Qoh 1:5), he refers to the kingdom's appearance and disappearance, as it is said: "her sun went down while it was yet day; she has been shamed and disgraced" (Jer 15:9). They likewise explained: "in the day when the guards of the house tremble" (Qoh 12:3) with reference to bet ha-Miqdash [the (Jerusalem) temple], with the guards [Heb. shomrim] as priests and Levites [Heb. kohanim u-leviyim]. The book as a whole [they understood] in this same way. The one who first introduced these meanings was Benjamin al-Nahāwandī, may Allah have mercy on him. Yet the intention is not at all what Benjamin and others besides him thought, for in contrast to what Solomon, peace be with him, intended in this book has five foundations [Arab. khamsa uṣūl]—his book and his discourse are built upon them. It is them that he points to with all his intentions.

The first is to make known to the students that all things of this world are "dust" and that man was not created to perdure in it. He bases this proof on empirical evidence, as he says: "A generation goes, and a generation comes" (Qoh 1:4). The second is his describing to the people of the world the many slaves he acquired and great wealth he amassed and the great size and number of his houses and his various plants, gardens, orchards, pools of water, many cattle, and peculiar treasures of kings (see Qoh 2:4–8)—that all of this passes away and disappears and does not persist. He arouses them to the fact that they ought not to suppose they can attain what he attained, and because of this they should not desire this world; rather should they renounce it, for true shelter is in the Abode of Perdurance. The third is the difference between wisdom and ignorance. He exhorts the people to acquire wisdom and remove themselves from ignorance, as he says: "Then I saw that wisdom excels folly as light excels darkness" (Qoh 2:13). The fourth is the final aim, searching after one's deeds, as Allah commanded over the created beings: this consists of fearing Allah and keeping his commandments, as he says: "Fear god" (Qoh 12:13). The fifth is to make known to those who serve [him] that Allah has an abode other than this world in which he rewards the righteous and punishes the wicked, as he says: "I said in my heart, God will judge the righteous and the wicked" (Qoh 3:17). This being so, it is required to renounce this world and abandon it and despise its lower corporeal matters, as man must suppress his bestial desire for it and despise any excess derived from it. He ought to take of it only what is required, what he cannot do without, such that he can reach obedience to his Lord as is incumbent upon him, as he says: "There is nothing better for mortals than to eat and drink, and find enjoyment in their toil" (Qoh 2:24).

Now that I have introduced in general the sage's intentions in this book, I begin to explain its words and summarize its meanings. From Allah I ask assistance in leading us to this [goal] by his grace and favor and generosity and with his abundant kindness and beneficence.

Qoheleth 1:1–4

1. *The words of Qoheleth son of David, king in Jerusalem.*

The words of Qoheleth, son of Dāwūd, <u>the</u> king in Jerusalem.

We have already made known, in what we wrote as preface, the meaning of "words," and that what the sage aims to teach with this term is that this book is [written] according to its external sense. As for his saying "Qoheleth"—it alludes to Solomon, as he says: "Qoheleth son of David." And Qoheleth is derived from *qehillah* [community].

Solomon has five names, all of them possessing in their derivation noble significations. The name *Shelomo* (Solomon) is derived from *shalom*, as it is said: "Solomon will be his name and I shall confer peace and quiet on Israel in his time" (1 Chr 22:9). *Yedidya* (2 Sam 12:25) is derived from *yedidut* (Heb., "friendship"), with the sense: "friend of the Eternal." These two names were given him by Allah. As for Agur (Prov 30:1), it is derived from *'agra* (Prov 6:8), *'oger* (Prov 10:5) [from the Hebrew root *'a-g-r*, "collect"], meaning that he has wisdom collected in him. *Lemuel* (Prov 31:1) is derived from [the Hebrew root] *m-w-l*, that is, he in his wisdom was equal to all the people of the world or even superior to them, as it is said: "he was the wisest of all men" (1 Kgs 5:11), and: "Solomon's wisdom greater ..." (1 Kgs 5:10). As for *Qoheleth*, it is derived from *q-h-l*, that is, insofar as Allah collected in him the wisdom of this world and the wisdom of the hereafter.

Regarding the wisdom of this world it is said: "He was the wisest of all men" (1 Kgs 5:11), and: "He discoursed about trees, from the cedar in Lebanon" (1 Kgs 5:13). He indicated moreover that Allah—great and exalted—inspired him to acquire this wisdom, as it is said: "God endowed Solomon with wisdom" (1 Kgs 5:9). Thus he discoursed on the species of plants and all the trees, large and small, as it is said: "from the cedar in Lebanon" (1 Kgs 5:13). He taught the people the properties of all the trees and their utilities—every single one—and which ones are dangerous; and likewise the utilities of shrubs and seeds and herbs—which ones are useful and which dangerous, which can be used as nutrition and which can lead to poisoning and cause death, which ones mix and which combine. And by knowing this science he was able to know all human illnesses and diseases, both external and internal. He thus classified the various elixirs, theriacs, and digestifs, and all things people require of the various types of remedies. He was the master of every sage and philosopher. And because of him everyone was helped by the wisdom of the "Book of Plants" to its end. All people of the world accept the authority of Sulaymān [Solomon].

He likewise taught the people the utilities of the beasts and gave instruction regarding their harmful properties: which is domesticated with cloven foot and chews its cud; which has cloven foot but does not chew its cud; which chews its cud but does not have cloven foot; which has hoofs and which has claws, whether large or small, as it is said: "and he discoursed about beasts" (1 Kgs 5:13). He taught first their characters and their natures and what utility their limbs have [when treating] illnesses, diseases, and sicknesses, chronic and otherwise, external as well as concealed and internal. So too did he discourse on the natures of the various types of feathered fowl and water fowl and their utilities and harmful properties and characters and what can be used of each of them, as it is said: "and on birds" (1 Kgs 5:13). So he discoursed on the natures of the various types of creeping things including those that crawl, such as the viper and asp, those that walk on four legs, such as the dung beetle and ant, as well as those that have many legs, such as scorpions, as it is said: "on creeping things" (1 Kgs 5:13). He likewise discoursed on the natures of the fish of the sea with their many genera and species and individuals, as it is said: "with its creatures beyond number" (Ps 104:25). He taught the people their utilities and harmful properties and characters, as it is said: "on fish" (1 Kgs 5:13).

So, too, did he know the nature of all the various types of soil and had complete grasp of the science of minerals, the various species of gems, the divisions of the winds and cause of the different types of water, including bitter, salty, sulfurous, sweet, and toxic, as it is said: "but the water is bad and the land causes bereavement" (2 Kgs 2:19). Likewise did he know the fine points of the sciences of geometry and arithmetic and the movement of the stars, so well that the great kings were forced to seek his advice, even coming to Jerusalem to learn from him; they recorded these sciences, which they would study, as it is said: "All the world came to pay homage to Solomon" (1 Kgs 10:24); "and each one would bring his tribute" (1 Kgs 10:25). So too did the Queen of Sheba come to him with questions, and he answered everything she asked him. He had no difficulty whatsoever in answering whatever she asked so that she submitted [to him] and acknowledged the wisdom of Sulaymān, peace be with him. And what she witnessed was far greater than what is connected with her.

As for the wisdom of the Torah, Allah—great and exalted—said to him in a dream: "Ask, what shall I grant you" (1 Kgs 3:5), and he said: "Grant, then, your servant an understanding mind to judge your people" (1 Kgs 3:9), to which Allah replied: "I now do as you have spoken; I grant you a wise and discerning mind; there has never been anyone like you before" (1 Kgs 3:12). He also said: "And all Israel heard the decision that the king had rendered" (1 Kgs 3:28). Then when all the different areas of wisdom were collected in him he was called *Qoheleth*; and likewise when prophecy and wisdom and kingship and anointedness and lineage and beauty and love from Allah and peace and security and wealth and good memory and fear and the collection of warriors and ministers and the building of the temple and marital alliance with kings were collected in Solomon, peace be with him—with the collecting of all of these states and their like he was called *Qoheleth*.

The term *Qoheleth* is feminine, as he said [using the third-person grammatical feminine form]: "said Qoheleth" (Heb. *'amrah*, Qoh 7:27). What this means is that, just as a woman gives birth and raises children, so Qoheleth draws out wisdom and organizes it according to its types and classifies it in divisions. Some have suggested that [the feminine verb] *'amrah* ([she] said, at Qoh 7:27) refers back to the Holy Spirit, for it had already been said [here, using the masculine]: *'amar* ([he] said, Qoh 1:2), which refers back to him.

He says: "son of David"—this makes known his lineage, indicating that he hails from the sons of Perez, son of Judah, son of Jacob our father, peace be with him; and Perez was the one fit for kingship since he was the eldest son, as it was said: "and out came his brother" (Gen 38:29), while of Zerah it was said: "Afterward his brother came out, on whose hand was the crimson thread" (Gen 38:30). He said "son of David" also in order to honor him, for he is a prophet son of a prophet, an anointed one son of an anointed one, a chosen one son of a chosen one, a king son of a king. Yet another reason he said "son of David" is that prophecies and writings were written for David, so Qoheleth had prophecies and writings, including [the books of] Proverbs and the Song of Songs and Qoheleth.

He says: "king"—that is, these words were spoken by Sulaymān the king. They are not like other sayings produced by someone without a settled heart. For this reason he said: "Listen, for I speak noble things" (Prov 8:6). He says: "in Jerusalem"—that is, he is the chosen king of the chosen people in the chosen place. Jerusalem itself had already been called "the throne of YHWH," as it is said: "Solomon successfully took over the throne of YHWH as king instead of his father David, and all went well with him" (1 Chr 29:23). And it is said: "By that time they shall call Jerusalem the throne of YHWH" (Jer 3:17).

2. *Vanity of vanities, said Qoheleth, vanity of vanities, all is vanity!*

Dust of dust, said Qoheleth, dust of dust. All is dust.

The sage, peace be with him, intended in this dictum to teach the people of the world that all things of this world and what people occupy themselves with in terms of toil and work and building and planting and the amassing of numerous supplies and property—all of it is dust and of no value; not a thing in it persists for man. And since it is dust, one ought to renounce it and turn oneself to something other than it, to that which should be sought after. For this reason he said: *havel havalim*—that is, the things of this world are at the utmost of what is dust, of no value, lacking persistence; there should be no desire for it, for it will become as if it never was.

He says: "all is dust, הבל (*hevel*)"—that is, what I said, namely, *havel havalim*, I did not say in the sense that part is הבל and part is not הבל, but rather all is הבל. For he will be annihilated and destroyed and pass away and be cut off, while the only thing that will last are good works, as it is said: "Your Vindicator shall march before you" (Isa 58:8).

As for the meaning of the sage's dictum, "all is dust"—he does not refer to created beings, for everything Allah created is wisdom, as it is said: "You have made them all with wisdom" (Ps 104:24), which has the same meaning as: "YHWH made everything for a purpose" (Prov 16:4). Since this is so, he said "everything is *hevel*" only with reference to excess, as in: "mere *hevel* is his hustle and bustle" (Ps 39:7). What is condemnable with respect to the things of this world is being completely preoccupied with desire for them and with increase in accumulating them and being distracted by passion for them and grasping at their trifles and having exaggerated love for them and gaining pleasure from them, for when a man keeps at these things constantly he loses his hereafter and remains among those that are lost. Nor does anything of what he labored over in the things of this world perdure, for there is no escape from privation and passing away, as is clear from this world's betrayal of its people. For there is no joy without sorrow in its train; no beneficence without poverty close behind; no majesty without humility as its consequence; no happiness without sorrow following after. While it is good to him, lo it will take from him; while it controls him, lo it will make him a slave; while it clothes him, lo it will strip him naked; while it feeds him, lo it will make him hungry; while it makes him happy, lo it will make him seek happiness. Thus everything in it, every one of these aspects, is "vanity." It is for this reason that he said: *havel havalim ha-kol hevel* (הבל הבלים הכל הבל).

3. *What value is there for a man in all the gains he makes under the sun?*

What profit has a person in all his work that he works under the sun?

He says: "What profit has a person"—that is, there is no profit for him in the acquiring of things of this world, not in the effort he puts into serving it or his work in building houses and planting gardens or his efforts to settle it, employing workers and servants and amassing property. We witness people exerting themselves in this matter and killing each other for it, yet when they die they leave it and pass away, as it is said: "for when he dies he cannot take all of it" (Ps 49:18). Nor will he know to whom it will pass, as it is said: "amassing and not knowing who will gather in" (Ps 39:7b). And nothing remains for a man of all he has amassed, nor does he take any pleasure in it, which is why he said: "What profit has a person in all his work that he works."

However, works relating to divine obedience—what a man does in connection with what Allah commanded him—this is what perdures for a man and what he benefits from in the hereafter, as it is said: "The righteous man finds security in his death" (Prov 14:32). His saying "under the sun" proves that he is referring to the works man does under the sun; the works of Torah, in contrast, are not under the sun, for it is said of the Torah: "I spoke to you from the very heavens" (Exod 20:22 [Eng. 20:20]). [Nor does this relate to the works of the righteous,] for the righteous, with their works, elevate their nature such that they reside among the angels, as it is said: "I will permit you to move about among these attendants" (Zech 3:7).

Now, if someone should say that Sulaymān in this dictum has prohibited us from settling this world, we would respond: He did not prohibit what cannot be avoided; rather, what he prohibited was greed and excess, as he says: "I have also noted that all labor" (Qoh 4:4); and he praised contentment, as when saying: "Better is a handful of gratification than two fistfuls of labor which is pursuit of wind" (Qoh 4:6).

Should someone say, on the other hand, that the prophets did accumulate property, we respond as follows: But they were collecting it in order to spend it properly, in the way that David, peace be with him, accumulated much property and spent it on building Jerusalem, and as Solomon collected it and stored it away in the house of the Lord for the benefit of the people. As for the other [prophets], you know the matter of Elijah: "with a leather belt tied round his waist" (2 Kgs 1:8); and he [God] said: "I have designated a widow there to feed you" (1 Kgs 17:9). And likewise it was said of Elisha: "A man came from Baal-shalishah and he brought the man of God some bread of the first reaping" (2 Kgs 4:42). It is the same with the sons of the prophets about whom it is said: "So one of them went out into the fields to gather sprouts. He came across a wild vine and picked from it wild gourds, as many as his garment would hold" (2 Kgs 4:39). He thought it was eggplant but was instead colocynth.

All of this points to two things: One is their limited occupation with this contemptible world, and that they did not elevate its affairs in any way. The second makes known the beauty of their contentment with little sustenance, their trust in what they knew they would have before their Lord. Do not suppose that had they sought wealth they could not have gotten it. Know that Naaman carried to Elisha, peace be with him, ten talents of silver, six thousand *dinār*, and ten robes of the finest raiment (see 2 Kgs 5:5), yet he [Elisha] did not take any of it at all and kept himself from it.

4. One generation goes, another comes, but the earth remains the same forever.

A generation goes, and a generation comes, and the earth forever abides.

Having said *havel havalim ha-kol hevel* (Qoh 1:2), he establishes now proof for this from empirical evidence, saying: "a generation goes, and a generation comes"—this refers to annihilation and corruption and dissolution, that is, the decomposition of the man's body and its departure from this world after having passed from state to state. At first it was a fetid drop, as it is said: "You poured me out like milk." And then it congeals as milk congeals, as it is said: "Congealed me like cheese" (Job 10:10). Then bones are formed and veins and nerves covered by flesh with skin above, as in: "You clothed me with skin and flesh" (Job 10:11). Then he—great and exalted—commands and he is brought out from the narrow place into this world with great force, as it is said: "you drew me from the womb" (Ps 22:10a). Then when coming out he provides him with food, as it is said: "made me secure at my mother's breast" (Ps 22:10b). Then he leads him from weaning to childhood to youth to young adulthood to maturity to old age to hoary old age to death, which means the decomposition of his parts and separation of soul from body, as it is said: "His breath departs, he returns to the dust" (Ps 146:4). Every state changes in him without his choice; rather his Creator governs him and leads him, makes him live and makes him die, as it is said: "YHWH deals death and gives life" (1 Sam 2:6). And as the first ones said: "For despite your wishes were you formed, despite your wishes were you born, despite your wishes do you live, despite your wishes do you die, and despite your wishes are you going to give a full accounting before the King of kings of kings, the Holy One, blessed be He." [m. Avot 4:29, Neusner's translation].

When saying: "a generation goes, and a generation comes"—Sulaymān drew attention to the works of the Creator—great and exalted—indicating that man was not created to perdure in this world; and seeing that he will not perdure, all the more so his accumulation [of wealth] and labor [over it] will not perdure. Thus one ought to reflect and be content with the nourishment one gets in this world, as Solomon, peace be with him, said: "provide me with my daily bread" (Prov 30:8); and our master Moses, peace be with him, said: "befriend the stranger, providing him with food and clothing" (Deut 10:18).

This verse contains a reflection [Arab. *i'tibār*] that a man ought to have his attention drawn to, for when he describes him—great and exalted—as having mercy on the stranger and loving him and governing him by providing food—which is the means he cannot live without, as it is said: "providing him with food and clothing" (Deut 10:18), and as Jacob our father, peace be with him, said: "and gives me bread to eat and clothing to wear" (Gen 28:20)—all of this indicates that greed has no utility for man. His seeking to increase the wealth of this world only damages him, which is why Solomon, peace be with him, said: "Do not toil to gain wealth" (Prov 23:4); and: "You see it, then it is gone" (Prov 23:5); and: "A miserly man runs after wealth" (Prov 28:22)—as I explained these matters in the commentary on Proverbs.

I say, moreover, that no man who is intent on accumulating wealth can possibly escape from wrongdoing in his speech, in weights, in accounting, or during his negotiations; and even then he might bequeath to someone who may be a wicked fool who will spend it not to obey Allah but on acts of disobedience and offensive behavior and the committing of sins, which means his accumulating of wealth is in fact for the purpose of strengthening the wicked in acting rebelliously. We might say this even of someone exceedingly cautious, all the more of someone with passion for this world and little thought for what is permitted or prohibited, who has no fear of Allah, great and exalted. For this reason did the sage Sulaymān designate this book to arouse the people to renunciation of this world.

He makes reference to death when saying: "a generation goes." And when he says "a generation comes," he alludes to the perfection of the world from the six days of creation, drawing attention to empirical evidence of creation, for creation refers to something that was not, then was. When he says "and a generation comes" this is precisely the notion he intends. It is not as the fools think, namely, that Sulaymān aims to refer with this to the idea that the world, as it is, will never pass away. How is it possible for any rational person to think this? And indeed already in this book he says: "I realized, too, that whatever God has brought to pass will recur evermore" (Qoh 3:14); while in another book he said: "YHWH founded the earth by wisdom" (Prov 3:19).

When he says: "and the earth forever abides"—he does not mean that the earth abides forever, for the term "forever" [Heb. *le-'olam*] is used in different senses. One is for a specific time, as in the statement of our master Moses, peace be with him: "and he shall remain his slave *le-'olam*" (Exod

21:6). One is the length of a man's life, as in: "he must remain there *ad 'olam* (1 Sam 1:22). It is the same as when he said of the earth and heavens: "they shall perish but you shall endure" (Ps 102:27). Thus we learn that "and the earth forever abides" alludes to the moment that Allah had set for it. And when the life of this [world] comes to an end, that is, the time span of this world, its Creator will annihilate it and create another, as it is said: "For behold! I am creating a new heaven and a new earth" (Isa 65:17). I already explained these matters sufficiently in the commentary on: "A prayer of the lowly man when he is faint" (Ps 102:1).

Qoheleth 4:17

Mind your feet [foot] when you go to the House of God: more accept-able is obedience than the offering of fools, for they know nothing [but] to do wrong.

Control your pudendum <u>always</u>, as <u>at the time</u> when you go to the house of Allah; and coming close to hear <u>is better</u> than the ignorant giving sacrifices, for they know not the doing of evil.

After teaching that the wisdom of the world and its affairs are "dust," Salmon begins now with an exhortation to follow the will of Allah, to observe the commandments, and to work for the affairs of the hereafter, taking provisions in this world—which passes away—for the abode of everlasting life.

So he says: "mind your feet" [in the plural, following the written con-sonantal form, the *ketiv*], which is read: "your foot" [in the singular, as in the recited version according to Masoretic pointing, the *qere*]. He implores us to keep our pudenda [Arab. *furūj*] from committing sexual offence with forbidden women. When he says: "Keep thy foot" [*shamor raglekha*], it resembles the dictum: "he had not taken care of his feet" (2 Sam 19:25 NRSV), the translation of which is: [Arab.] *faraj*.

He says: "when you go to the house of God"—that is, someone who goes on pilgrimage to the house of Allah ought to be pure, free of iniquity and rebellious behavior, as our father Jacob, peace be with him, said: "Rid yourselves of the alien gods in your midst, purify yourselves, and change your clothes. Come, let us go up to Bethel" (Gen 35:2–3). Here he obligates man to be pure, free of all disobedient acts always as when he goes to the House of Allah.

"Better than the ignorant giving sacrifices"—getting close to hearken to the word of Allah is better than fools giving sacrifices; that is, accepting obedience to Allah and observing what he commanded and prohibited is better in Allah's view than fools giving sacrifices, as in the statement of master Samuel, peace be with him: "obedience is better than sacrifice" (1 Sam 15:22). And he said: "The sacrifice of the wicked is an abomination" (Prov 21:27).

He says: "For they know nothing to do wrong"—this refers to the righteous that he mentioned at the beginning of the verse. He says that those who come close to the hearkening of the word of Allah, who keep his ways, will not know the doing of evil, meaning that they have already become accustomed to doing good and thus know not how to do evil. Another exegete said, in contrast, that his dictum: "For they know nothing to do wrong"—is connected to the "fools," since they in their foolishness do not know the measure of the doing of evil they approached, and Allah demands retribution of them first of all for their abandoning of wisdom and knowledge with respect to what Allah commanded. Yet another exegete said: "For they know nothing to do wrong"—that is, they know only to do evil; that is, for the fools understand nothing but the doing of evil deeds, as it is said: "They are clever at doing wrong" (Jer 4:22).

Qoheleth 7:16

Do not be too righteous, and do not be too wise; why should you destroy yourself? (NRSV)

Be not righteous over much; neither make yourself over wise. Why should you become desolate <u>and destroy yourself</u>?

Sulaymān said that Allah—great and exalted—forces man into servitude and imposes upon him what he knows he can do. He does not impose upon him what he cannot do, for the imposition of something one cannot do is oppressive and lacking in justice, as the prophet Micah, peace be on him, said: "My people! What wrong have I done you? What hardship have I caused you" (Mic 6:3). And since commands and prohibitions are given according to the measure of ability, he established stipulations lest a transgressor overstep the boundaries, adding or removing, as he said: "You shall not add anything to what I command you" (Deut 4:2).

What he says here (in Qoh 7:16) is similar: "Do not be too righteous"—that is, do not do what Allah has not commanded, that is, do not fast so much that it makes you weak; do not say: "This year I will not eat bread, I will eat vegetables only." Perhaps you will attack your body, weaken it, and kill yourself. Nor ought you to engage in monastic isolation in the mountains and deserts thinking that in this way you are coming near to Allah. Perhaps you will be led astray and kill yourself. And in any event this is not something Allah has required of you. Or sometimes you might consider as follows: that charity is a noble act might lead you to distribute everything you own; as a result you yourself will become a mendicant requiring charity. Yet Allah did not make it incumbent upon you to give all your wealth as charity. On the contrary, it is said: "Honor YHWH with your wealth" (Prov 3:9), and: "for he gives his bread to the poor" (Prov 22:9). It was not said: "all his bread." Likewise Job, peace be with him, said: "By eating my food alone, the fatherless not eating of it also" (Job 31:17). Nor ought a man to say that he will not allow himself to engage in a profession since it is impossible to free oneself from false speech and the fixing of scales—as a result of which he cuts himself off from a livelihood. And it is possible that in a time of hunger he will need to steal or will take a vow upon himself to fast forever, yet sometimes an illness will supervene which will lead him to break the vow. There are innumerable similar examples. Because of this he said: "Do not be too righteous"—that is, do not impose upon yourself that which you cannot do. Know that the One that requires service—great and exalted—judges and sees the service you do. Blessed is he who exerts himself working constantly in what he commands, as is said: "happy are those who keep the law" (Prov 29:18 NRSV).

"Do not act too wise"—that is, just as he commanded you not to add upon yourself to what he commanded and prohibited, so he commands that you not be over wise, that is, saying: "I will study the sciences of this world," as a result of which he abandons the wisdom of Torah. He explained this at the end of the book, saying: "Of anything beyond these, my child, beware. Of making many books there is no end" (Qoh 12:12 NRSV). All the more so someone who has no worry or toil but rather wanders around in the cities and markets seeking foreign books such as the books of the philosophers and the books of Ibn al-Rāwandī and the books of Ibn Suwayd which lead to unbelief with respect to Allah and his prophets and his book. Allah takes vengeance against them who have deeds and ways like these; it is what leads people such as these to eternal existence in *Jahannam* [Arab. "hell"], especially someone who takes money from the poor and orphans and widows and spends it on books such as these and fears not nor submits piously to the Merciful. When it is said to them that such action is prohibited, they consider him who reproaches them a fool and ridicule him. As they withdraw amongst themselves, they diminish only themselves, not Allah and his book. Allah will surely take vengeance against them and remove their veil within the community and not give them any rank or knowledge and will make them as those about whom it is said: "My hand will be against the prophets who prophesy falsehood" (Ezek 13:9)—they and their helpers and their friends and benefactors along with those who rise up against God's fearful servants, and those who advise ill against them; Amen, Amen. [The last sentence was written originally in Hebrew.]

He says: "do not act too wise" after having said: "Do not be too righteous." He means: do not question the meanings of Allah's book, saying: "Why did he command this and why not this or that?"—as did Hiwi al-Balkhi, may Allah curse him. He [Hiwi] said: "Why did he [God] command sacrifices if he requires no nourishment?" "Why did he command the shewbread if he does not eat it?" "Why did he command lamps if he requires no illumination?" Already the sages, may their memory be for a blessing, responded to him and rebuked him. They said to him: O fool, how can he be nourished from the sacrifices? Does not the fire consume part of them whereas the other part is eaten by the priests? How can he eat the shewbread when the priests eat it, as it is said: "It shall belong to Aaron and his sons, who shall eat it in a sacred precinct" (Lev 24:9)? How could he need illumination? Is he not the creator of fire and light, as it is said: "God said, 'Let there be light;' and there was light" (Gen 1:3), and the prophet Isaiah, peace be with him, said: "I form light and create darkness" (Isa 45:7). He—great and exalted—is above these attributes and has been cleansed of them, as it is said: "Do I eat the flesh of bulls?" (Ps 50:13). He teaches, moreover, that he—great and exalted—did not command this; rather it is for the utility of man and his success, as it is said: "Sacrifice a thank offering to God" (Ps 50:14), "Call upon Me in time of trouble" (Ps 50:15). This is why he says here: "Do not act too wise"—that is, do not question Allah, thinking that your knowledge is stronger and deeper; rather ought you to trust in Allah and receive all that he commands you, as it is said: "Trust in the LORD and do good" (Ps 37:3); "Trust in the LORD with all your heart" (Prov 3:5).

He says: "Why should you destroy yourself" [Heb. *lama tishomem*]—that is, as soon as you abandon study of the book and occupy yourself with something other than it or question Allah with respect to what he commanded and prohibited, you will become bereft of knowing what you ought to know. He speaks like Uzziah, about whom it was said: "And his mind was elevated" (2 Chr 17:6), and: "When he was strong, he grew so arrogant" (2 Chr 26:16). And his affair continued until: "he trespassed against his God by entering the Temple of YHWH" (v. 16), "When the chief priest Azariah and all the other priests looked at him" (2 Chr 26:20)—continuing to the end of the story.

Qoheleth 12:12

Of anything beyond these, my son, beware. Of making many books there is no end, and much study is a weariness of the flesh. (NRSV)

And more than these, O my son, be warned: the making of many books has no end; and much devotion [to them] is labor and toil for the flesh.

Sulaymān the sage adds here a warning and threat regarding the desire for foreign books, saying: "Of anything beyond these, my son, beware"—that is, beware lest you come to desire books other than the revealed holy books, for when someone has desire for something other than them he acquires ignorance and what is lacking in wisdom, as it is said: "they rejected the word of YHWH so their wisdom amounts to nothing" (Jer 8:9).

He says: "My son, beware"—that is, he who desires the holy books is a student of the prophets and a student of Qoheleth, and still more than this a student of his Creator, as it is said: "I am the LORD your God, who teaches you for your own good" (Isa 48:17 NRSV), and "He engirded him, watched over him" (Deut 32:10). In contrast, he who desires the wisdom of strangers has become a student of the unbelievers and the heretics and the materialists and the dualists and the trinitarians; of them that discourse on natural science; of the Brahmins who deny prophecy; of them that discourse on prime matter; of them that believe in worshiping fire and water; and all the other sages of the various false sects about whom it is said in general: "for the laws of the nations are *hevel*" (Jer 10:3), and: "to you nations shall come from the ends of the earth" (Jer 16:19). Were there in the world any [other] book which has utility or benefit, why would he say exclusively of the Torah of Moses: "but recite it day and night" (Josh 1:8)?! Rather would he have said: "[recite it] and external, nonbiblical books" [Heb. *sefarim ḥitsoniyim*].

Since he specifically designated this enjoinder (i.e., Josh 1:8) for this Torah—along with the other words of prophecy, as it is said: "to seal (both) vision and prophet" (Dan 9:24 NRSV), and indeed it is made obligatory in the Torah of Moses itself, "the man of God" (Deut 33:1), peace be with him, to accept the word of the prophets, as it is said: "a prophet from among your own people like myself" (Deut 18:15)—we learn that any speculation in and occupation with any book other than the books of the prophets is forbidden [Arab. *ḥarām*] for Israel, for it leads to the beliefs of the gentiles. As for him that renounces the book of Allah and desires the books of the gentiles, Allah testifies regarding him that he is a renouncer of the Creator. Allah will make judgment of anyone who leads the people to desire the books of the gentiles and leads them to renounce the book of Allah.

He says: "Of making many books there is no end"—that is, there is no end to foreign books. One ought to direct oneself to the books of the prophets for which Allah has already made a limit and measure, and with respect to which he commanded not to add to them or diminish therefrom, as he says: "Do not add to His words, lest He indicts you and you be proved a liar" (Prov 30:6).

He says: "and much study is a weariness of flesh"—he means that much devotion to anything other than the book of Allah will weary the body and cause grave sin. For he has already obligated us to meditate upon the book of Allah day and night, as it is said: "recite it day and night" (Josh 1:8), thus anytime you are occupied with any other book besides the book of Allah you have already violated this commandment and perverted the straight. Our master Moses, peace be with him, said: "these instructions with which I charge you" (Deut 6:6); "recite them to your sons" (Deut 6:7 adapted from NRSV; NRSV and JPS: "children").

Already the first ones said: "And these are the ones who have no portion in the world to come ... He who reads in heretical [= external, nonbiblical] books" (m. Sanh. 10:1, Neusner's translation). Our Book and our Way and our Guidance is sufficient for us, as it is said: "Your word is a lamp to my feet" (Ps 119:105); and: "the unfolding of your words gives light" (Ps 119:130 NRSV); and: "For the commandment is a lamp" (Prov 6:23). In contrast to this, he said of foreign books: "All who go to her cannot return" (Prov 2:19).

Bibliography

Riese, Moshe. "The Arabic Commentary of Solomon ben Yeruham the Karaite on Ecclesiastes." PhD diss., Yeshiva University, 1973.

Robinson, James T. *Asceticism, Eschatology, Opposition to Philosophy: The Arabic Translation and Commentary of Salmon ben Yeroham on Qohelet (Ecclesiastes)*. Karaite Texts and Studies 5. Études sur le judaïsme médiéval 45. Leiden: Brill, 2012.

Vajda, Georges. *Deux commentaires karaïtes sur l'Ecclésiastes*. Leiden: Brill, 1971.

Yefet ben 'Eli: A Selection from the Commentary on Qoheleth (Preface; 1:1–4; 1:8; 1:12; 4:17; 5:1; 6:6; 12:12)

James T. Robinson

Yefet ben 'Eli was the most prolific of the Karaite exegetes, producing a complete translation and commentary on the entire Hebrew Bible. The work on Qoheleth was likely written in the 990s. It is very characteristic of his work as a whole. In terms of general form it includes a short exordium in Hebrew, followed by an Arabic translation of each verse with a commentary, sometimes lengthy and detailed. The commentary itself varies throughout, but there are common tendencies, for instance an obsession with the literary context—every verse needs to fit into its place in the book, following logically from the section before and setting up the verse that follows. Yefet also identifies a general structure for the book as a whole, identifying different literary units as he moves along. He surveys earlier explications critically, introduced by "some commentators said," "they said," or simply "it has been said," before presenting his own preferred interpretation. This gives the commentary a strongly anthological feel, although Yefet's commentarial voice is always strongly present. Although there is ample discussion of grammar and lexicon in the commentary, for the most part Yefet is interested in meaning in context, Arabic *ma'na*.

The samples singled out below reflect all of these tendencies and relate to some of the key themes motivating his commentary. In the commentary on Qoh 1:1 and continuing through 1:3, Yefet introduces the main subjects of Qoheleth and the purpose of its author. He also differentiates between the work of a later editor or redactor of the work, Arabic *mudawwin*, responsible for the first few verses, from the work of Solomon himself. The discussion of the work of the *mudawwin* is found also at Qoh 1:12, where Yefet works to explain the problematic past perfect in that verse: "I, Qoheleth, had been king in Jerusalem." At Qoh 1:8 and 5:1, Yefet emphasizes the limitations of human knowledge and the need for humans to submit piously to divine will. This focus on pious adherence to divine law and Scripture is found also in Yefet's polemic against "foreign books" at Qoh 12:12, a topos found already in Salmon's commentary. As for the relation to Salmon in general, Qoh 4:17 provides a nice contrast, while Qoh 6:6, against the rabbinic idea that Elijah was occulted, shows the existence of a continuous tradition of reading throughout the Karaite tradition.

The first six chapters of Yefet's commentary on Qoheleth were edited with English translation by Richard Bland in his unpublished doctoral dissertation.[1] Selections were published with French translation by Georges Vajda.[2] The translations here of Qoh 1:1–4; 1:8; 1:12; 4:17; 5:1; and 6:6 are based on Bland's edition and English translation. The translation of 12:12 is based on my forthcoming edition and translation of the entire commentary.

In this essay, after the Exordium (only in an English translation of the original Hebrew), the selected biblical verses are presented (in italics), in most cases and without extra markings, in the English rendering of the JPS (1985) translation, slightly modified at places; at times, when the NRSV is more precise, or bears a greater similarity to Yefet's rendering, it is reproduced instead (and marked as such). The next step is an English rendering of Yefet's translation of the relevant verses (in boldface) and, finally, his commentary on them. Hebrew and Arabic words will be given in simple transliteration, and additional matters in parentheses.

Exordium (originally in Hebrew)

In the name of YHWH we shall commence and succeed

In the name of YHWH the living and eternal God, first and last, who creates all and sustains the life of all, governs all and carries out his will in all, and there is no deliverance from his hand, who performs kindness [Heb. ḥesed] and judgment and justice in his world, and who will tell him: You have done wrong? He who understands human thoughts because he creates their heart together, who knows the mysteries of the heart, who teaches humans to know him,

---

1. Richard Bland, "The Arabic Commentary of Yephet ben ʿAli on the Book of Ecclesiastes, Chapters 1–6" (PhD diss., University of California, 1966).

2. Georges Vajda, *Deux commentaires karaïtes sur l'Ecclésiastes* (Leiden: Brill, 1971).

because he is their creator and treats each one of them as deserved, in his wisdom and sagacity. And this [divine] knowledge is beyond humans, awe-inspiring, they cannot handle it. And if the wise [man] would try to know, he cannot find [it]. And therefore he [Qoheleth] said: "and deep, deep down, who can discover it?" *(Qoh 7:24). And a foolish man [Heb. kesil] says: Why is this? And for what is this? And he [God] sees all created creatures, that one is not similar to the other and that one is different from the other. And a person [Heb. ben 'adam, "son of man"] should think in his heart that he who created all did not create the world for his own needs, but to inform his creatures of his competence and wisdom, as it is written:* "to make His mighty acts known among men" *(Ps 145:12). And the poet [David] said:* "How great are Your works, O Lord" *(Ps 92:6). And he said:* "How many are the things You have made, O Lord; You have made them all with wisdom," *and so on (Ps 104:24),* "A brutish man cannot know, a fool cannot understand this" *(Ps 96:7). And the wise person will understand YHWH's deeds and his wonders, and will praise YHWH, as it is written:* "I praise You, for I am awesomely, wondrously made; Your work is wonderful; I know it very well" *(Ps 139:14).*

Qoheleth 1:1–4

1. *The words of Qoheleth son of David, king in Jerusalem.*

The <u>discourse</u> [Arab. *kalaam*] of Qoheleth, son of David, king in Jerusalem.

In the preface to Song of Songs we already discussed the purpose of each of the books of Solomon, namely, Proverbs, Song of Songs, and Qoheleth. We say that the purpose of this book revolves about two things. One is that the works of man, many though they may be, fall into only two categories: the first consists of this-worldly actions that will neither benefit him for the Abode of Perdurance nor prejudice him, they being indifferent actions, as we will explain at: "what real value is there for a man" (Qoh 1:3). The second consists of actions having to do with command and prohibition for which one will be rewarded or punished. It is with these that he concluded his book: "The end of the matter; all has been heard. Fear God, and keep his commandments; for that is the whole duty of everyone" (Qoh 12:13 NRSV).

The second includes three things: first, the urging of the people to renounce excess with respect to accumulating wealth and overindulgence with respect to food and drink, and at the same time condemning those who withdraw completely, refusing to enjoy the worldly pleasures that Allah Most High has created for man; second, exhorting the people to obedience while teaching them proper guidance in the Abode of this World; third, prohibiting the people from being occupied with *sifre ḥitsonim* ["external books"], as we will explain at: "my son, be warned! The making of many books is without limit" (Qoh 12:12). He himself had gained wide knowledge of the various types of indifferent actions, and he made known that they will be of no utility for the Abode of Perdurance in order to exhort men toward what will be of benefit to them in the Abode of Perdurance.

The book bears the title "The Words of Qoheleth" for one of three possible reasons: (1) because it is speech [Arab. *kalaam*] in the literal sense, following narrative form [Arab. *rasm al-qiṣaṣ*] rather than the form of song [Heb. *shir*] or proverbs [Heb. *meshalim*]; or (2) because among the contents of this book are accounts [Arab. *akhbaar*] concerning himself, as in: "The words of Jeremiah" (Jer 1:1), peace be upon him, in which he explained the events [Arab. *qiṣaṣ*] that happened to him; and: "The words of Amos" (Amos 1:1), discussing in his book what befell him at the hands of Amaziah, priest of Bethel (Amos 7:10); or (3) because he intended to attach this book to Proverbs. That is to say, in the book of Proverbs he used the phrase "proverbs of Solomon" three times: first, in the beginning of the book (Prov 1:1); second, in: "The proverbs of Solomon: a wise son brings joy to his father" (Prov 10:1); third, in: "These too are the proverbs of Solomon" (Prov 25:1). Then he said further on: "The words of Agur son of Jakeh" (Prov 30:1), and secondly: "The words of Lemuel, king ..." (Prov 31:1). To these latter two he then joined: "the words of Qoheleth," with the result that there are three sections [Arab. *fuṣuul*] of "proverbs of" and likewise three sections [Arab. *dufaʿāt*] of "words of."

He named him Qoheleth rather than Solomon in accordance with his design [Arab. *rasm*]; that is, wherever he used the phrase "proverbs of" he called him Solomon, and whenever he used "words of" he used another name, as in: words of Agur, words of Lemuel, and likewise here: words of Qoheleth.

The simple meaning of Qoheleth is: "she who gathers" [Arab. *jāmiʿah*], from the lexical class [Arab. *min lugha*] q/h/l. We have found many terms for gathering: [Heb.] *qebitsah, asifah,* and *kenisah* are used with human beings as well as furnishings, silver, gold, and the like; [Heb.] *agirah*, in contrast, we have not found with reference to human beings and animals, while [Heb.] *qehillah* we find used only with humans. Thus Solomon was called Agur because of the various disciplines of wisdom [Arab. *aṣnāf al-hokhmot*] combined in him, and he was called Qoheleth for one of two reasons: either because he gathers [Arab. *jāmi'*] in this book all classes [Arab. *tabaqaat*] of men, for he did not pass over even one without mentioning it in this book; or because he gathers [*jāmi'*] all the kings of the earth by his wisdom, as it is said: "and all the kings of the earth came to pay homage to Solomon" (2 Chr 9:23). Thus, by virtue of his wisdom, he made them assemble about him at some place. He ascribed the activity to his wisdom [Heb. *hokhmah*, a feminine noun] and for that reason put Qoheleth in the feminine gender [Heb. *leshon neqevah*]; when he said *'amrah* [feminine verb, "said"] Qoheleth (at Qoh 7:27), it was *hokhmah* speaking.

He says: "king in Jerusalem"—this makes known to us that he was indeed Solomon, for it might be that David had a son named Qoheleth other than Solomon, but we know from his saying "king in Jerusalem" that he was Solomon, for David had no other son who was king in Jerusalem. The reason [Arab. *al-ma'na*] for making this known to us is that when people would read its title and realize that it is a discourse [*kalaam*] of Solomon, they would study it and set their minds on his discourse, for it is the discourse of a sage rich in ideas [Arab. *ghaziir al-ma'aani*].

Know that *qoheleth* is similar in form to *shoma'at* [Heb. "who hears"]. Its imperative [Arab. *amr*] is *qehal*, as with *shema'*. The translation/meaning [*tafsiir*] of *qehal* is "assemble" [Arab. *ajma'*], as with *haqhel* [*hiphil*]. Both have the same meaning [*tafsiir*], just as *keroth* and *hakhret* [Heb. "cut"], both have the same meaning [*tafsiir*]; likewise *shelaḥ* and *hashlaḥ* [Heb. "cast," "send"].

2. *Vanity of vanities!—said Qoheleth—Vanity of vanities! All is vanity!*[3]

O man affected by a multiplicity of loss, said Qoheleth, O man affected by a multiplicity of loss, all is loss—a term that may also be interpreted "dust."

---

3. The enigmatic Heb. text *havel havalim … hevel* is largely understood as "futility," "vanity," "dust," "breath," etc. Yefet understands it as "loss" and understands *havel* as a person possessed of loss, as he explains in his commentary.

In their opinion, it is generally thought that *havel* is a term for a ray of sunlight in which something like dust [Arab. *jabaar*] becomes visible. You stretch out your hand and grasp it, but there is nothing in your hand. *Havel* is in the grammatical form [Arab. *wazn*] of: *halebh goyim* ("milk of nations," Isa 60:16) and is a substantial noun [Arab. *ism jism*].

Know that he said: *dibhrey qoheleth* (Qoh 1:1) and then went on to clarify that the words of Qoheleth are concerned with the subject of *havel havalim*, since the expression *dibhrey* [Heb. "words" and also "things"] could refer to a variety of subjects. Know also that *havel* is a term for an individual [Arab. *insaan*] who has exhausted himself and become wretched in things that do not last for him, just as one is called *rash* [Heb, "poor"] because of poverty which has befallen him. He puts *havalim* in the plural [Heb. *leshon rabbim*] in view of the fact that *havalim* of various kinds mentioned in this book affect him.

Know also that in this book there are two types of *hevel*. Some are *hevel* in the sense that they do not last for their owner, though they may be useful in the Abode of this World, for example, estates, plantations, money, and similar things that serve man in this world of his. They are *havalim*, however, in view of the fact that he will leave them behind and they will become the property of others, as it is said: "for when he dies he can take none of it along" (Ps 49:18). The other type of *havalim* is not only not beneficial, but obviously harmful, as in: "Even if a man should beget a hundred (children)" (Qoh 6:3)—as we will explain, each in its proper place. For this reason he said *havel havalim* twice. As for his saying: *ha-kol havel*—this implies that this phrase applies to both of these categories inasmuch as none of these things remains his possession because he is separated from them.

These two verses were added by the editor [Arab. *mudawwin*] and do not belong to the "words of Qoheleth." However, he wanted to begin with a statement on the aim of the book similar to what he said in Proverbs, from the verse: "for learning wisdom and discipline" (Prov 1:2), to the end of that section in which he explained the aim of that book and its utilities.

3. *What gain*[4] *is there for a man from all the toil which he toils under the sun* (NRSV, modified).

---

4. Heb.: *mah yitron* …

Nothing is left to man from all his labor or his toil that he labors under the sun.

This verse is the beginning proper of the "words of Qoheleth." In our language [i.e., Hebrew] the particle [Arab. *lafẓa*] *mah* ["how," "why," "what"] can be used for both negation and affirmation, and one determines whether it is negative or affirmative from its context [Arab. *ma'na*]. It is affirmative in: "How lovely, how beautiful they shall be" (Zech 9:17); "how [*mah*] sweet is your love" (Song 4:10); and in many other places in Scripture. It is negative in: "what [*mah*] does he care about the fate of his family" (Job 21:21). It is also used in an interrogative sense, as in: "whatever [*mah*] you want" (1 Sam 20:4), and for disapprobation, as in: "why [*mah*] are you here" (1 Kgs 19:9, 13; Isa 22:16), and: "how [*mah*] dare you crush my people" (Isa 3:15). In *mah yitron* it is negative, with the meaning: a man has no *yitron*.

Yitron stands for *ytr*, the translation [Arab. *tafsiir*] of which is remainder [Arab. *bāqiya*] or merit [Arab. *faḍīla*], that is, *yitron* has two possible interpretations/translations [Arab. pl. *tafsiirayn*]. It may be interpreted as "merit," as in "wisdom is superior to folly" (Qoh 2:13), but it cannot be so interpreted here, since it is inevitable that there be some sort of merit or benefit. Do you not see, he did not say what is beneficial for a man, but rather *mah yitron la-'adam*, meaning that when he dies, not a single thing will remain in his possession. Instead: "and leave their wealth to others" (Ps 49:11 NRSV).

The phrase "for a man" has both a general and a specific sense. In its general sense it refers to the ruler and to those under him down to the lowest ranking of the people, the believer and the unbeliever alike. In its specific sense, responsible people capable of discernment are not included in it.

"From all his toil"—this also has a general and a specific sense. In its general sense it applies to every type of variety of earthly works, but in its specific sense the doing of *mitsvot YHWH* (God's commandments) is not included in it, since this is of eternal benefit to man, as it is written: "by the pursuit of which man shall live" (Lev 18:5).

Know that when he says "in all" [Heb. *be-kol*] he does not intend the prescribed actions themselves, like the *mitsvot* that consist of prescribed acts. He has in mind, rather, completed activities and things which he acquired, such as a building, plantations, furnishings, jewelry, and the like. He said "in all his toil that he toils" only because of the fact that among men's actions are some that are actions and nothing else; and he declared that his assertion in those actions until that thing is done will not be of eternal benefit to him. There is no difference between the things in which he himself engages and those things which he uses and for which he spends his money or toils his mind. It is all his labor, as he will say later: "I hated all my toils" (Qoh 2:18 NRSV), though the craftsman did the work.

The expressions "under the sun," "on earth," and "under heaven" are all used in a specific way in this book. In one place he says "under heaven" and in another "done on earth." They serve the same purpose, but "under heaven" is a more general expression than "under the sun," since what is done at night is "under heaven" but not "under the sun." Likewise, "under the sun" is more general than "on earth" for those sailing on the sea are not "on earth." He probably says "under heaven" because "heaven" encompasses the earth and everything on it, and there is no activity of man anywhere that is not "under heaven." He says "under the sun" because Allah made the daylight for men to carry on worldly activities and to pursue their livelihoods, and he made the night as a time of rest for men and for the prowling of the beasts of prey, as it is written: "You make darkness … the young lions roar.…When the sun rises … people go out for their work …" (Ps 104:20–23 NRSV). Moreover, all of men's labor can be done in the daylight, but there are many activities that are not done in the daylight. He says "on earth" because it is their habitation, as it is written: "but the earth He gave over to men" (Ps 115:16).

Another teaching [Arab. *qawl akhar*] in "under the sun" is that the sun rather than any star separates the days, and each day man performs the labor in which they are engaged. Therefore he says: "that he toils under the sun."

4. *One generation goes, another comes, and the earth remains the same forever.*

A generation goes and a generation comes, and the earth persists <u>to eternity</u>.

Know that he began with: "What gain [Heb. *yitron*] is there for a man" (Qoh 1:3) but he did not follow this with the toil of men. Instead he took up another subject [Arab. *ma'na*] from: "A generation goes" (Qoh 1:4) through "I, Qoheleth" (Qoh 1:12). We will explain the reason for this after the interpretation [Arab. *tafsiir*] of the verse is completed.

He says: "A generation [Heb. *dor*] goes"—this does not refer to the lifespan of an individual person, though this may be called according to the view of some of the exegetes with respect to Hezekiah's statement: "My age is departed and is removed" (Isa 38:12 KJV). Rather, he refers to the generation of every age, whether their lifetimes be long or short, a son following after the father, as it is written in Job: "four generations" (Job 42:16); and similarly: "blameless in his generation" (Gen 6:9 NRSV; תמים היה). It is also said that a *dor* is [the period of time] in which the people propagate themselves, one coming immediately after the other. Similarly, they immediately turn away from the commandments, as it is written about the fathers: "this evil generation" (Deut 1:35); "Forty years I was provoked by this generation" (Ps 95:10). The same is true for: "A generation goes."

He says: "A generation goes"—this refers to the passing from the surface of the earth to the grave, similar to the statement further on in this book: "but man sets out to his eternal abode" (Qoh 12:5); the saying of Job: "And I shall go the way of no return" (Job 16:22); and those of David: "I shall go to him" (2 Sam 12:23); and: "I am going the way of all earth" (1 Kgs 2:2).

He says: "and a generation comes"—this means: comes to the world after them. He says "comes" [Heb. *ba'*] rather than "arise" [Heb. *qam*] as in: "and another generation arose" (Judg 2:10); "He had raised up their sons" (Josh 5:7); "and rise up and tell their sons" (Ps 78:6 NRSV modified). He does this in order to use a term comparable to "goes" as if to say: "a generation goes from the world and a generation comes into the world," so that the world is not left uninhabited. He said "goes" and "comes" rather than "will go" and "will come," the difference being that "comes" indicates something happening every day. It is well-known that "comes" is prior in time to "goes." [The reason that he put "goes" first is that] had he put "come" before "goes," he would have depicted one generation only which will come into the world and go from the world. Hence he put "goes" first in order to mention two generations, one passing away and another that will come. Another possibility is that he spoke first about the existing generation and then continued with the one that will come after it.

By placing "and the earth remains the same forever" before "a generation comes, and a generation goes," he points to the difference between man and the earth, that is, the earth is man's habitation and could not possibly come to an end with the passing away of each and every generation. Furthermore, the earth is an element [Arab. *'unṣur*], unlike mankind which is not elemental, but rather comes to be like the plants. Another meaning is that the earth remains after him for the possession of others, so that even if men do possess some part of it, they will pass away from it, but it stays on after those who pass away from it.

Now that we have given the interpretation of this verse, let us discuss his reason [Arab. *ma'na*] for having this verse follow "what gain [*yitron*] is there for a man" (Qoh 1:3). We maintain that he is furnishing proof of the validity of his teaching, that is, man is not permanent, but rather passes away, and anything of the earth that he possesses—and this is the most important of his possessions—remains behind him, and someone else will come after him and take it over. Thus his statement that "what gain is there for a man in all his toil" is confirmed. As for *mitsvot YHWH*, they endure for him and because of him.

Qoheleth 1:8

All [such] things are wearisome: no man can ever state them; the eye never has enough of seeing, nor the ear enough of hearing.

All things are wearisome, <u>one</u> is not able to speak; the eye is not satisfied with seeing, nor the ear filled with hearing.

He says: "all things"—it is possible this refers to all existing things, for we have *debharim* which are interpreted as "things," as in: "so that you do not forget the things that you saw with your own eyes," and so on (Deut 4:9). He would not have said "which your eyes have seen" about "words" [the same in Hebrew as "things"]. So also it is possible that "all things are wearisome" alludes to all the created beings which he has not already mentioned in this preface.

He makes known that men grow weary in them—he means they discuss them but never cover them completely. Yet their lives are dependent upon them and they want to understand them, so they weary themselves but do not succeed because these things are so many, as he says: "the eye never has enough of seeing"—because it does not see all of them. There are things on land and in the sea and in the heavens to which men have never attained so that they might exhaust seeing them.

Similarly: "the ear [never] has enough of hearing"—for every day a man hears new things, and even if he should live a great number of years, he would still not hear everything about YHWH's deeds and his wonders, as it is written: "How great are your works, oh Lord" (Ps 92:6). This refers not to men's talk and reports, but to the works of Allah, exalted be he.

If we were to say that the interpretation [Arab. *tafsiir*] of *kol ha-deb-harim* is "all the words," then it would refer to all the words which men use in speaking about *ma'aseh YHWH*. [Heb., "God's deed"]. These are words in which they grow weary.

Qoheleth's purpose in this verse is to show that these created things are innumerable and incomprehensible, so that if an individual should desire to busy himself with them until he understands them, he will not succeed for two reasons: first, because of their great numbers; second, because among them are hidden things—*gedolot ve-nifla'ot* [Heb., "great and miraculous things"]—and though men burden themselves with speaking about them, they will never fully understand them. In a similar sense, Elihu son of Barachel, the Buzite, said: "See, God is greater than we can know" (Job 36:26); "He works wonders that we cannot understand" (Job 37:5); and David said: "I do not aspire to great things or to what is beyond me" (Ps 131:1).

These texts forbid man's engaging in discussion about this subject, but the lying foreign magicians do discourse about it, that is, having abandoned the knowledge of the religious laws [Arab. *'ilm al-sharā'i*], they have created for themselves a substitute and entered into discussion about these *nifla'ot* [Heb. "miraculous things"] so that they may have a theological system [Arab. *kalaam*] and science [Arab. *'ilm*] in accordance with which they may present their point of view. They have corrupted a great number of people by it, and even some of Israel have become occupied with their books and been ruined by them and had their faith [Arab. *'aqīda*] corrupted with respect to the foundations of their beliefs. Woe to anyone who is distracted by them from *Torat YHWH* ["the Torah of God"]!

Thus: "the eye never has enough of seeing, nor the ear enough of hearing"—points out their extensiveness. The eye is not satisfied because of his knowledge that there are things which he has not seen, nor is the ear filled because of his knowledge that there are things that he has not heard. The reason for that is that the world is far-reaching and in this clime and country are things that exist nowhere else, so every people knows something about animals, herbs, and the like that no one else knows. Therefore he says: "the eye never has enough of seeing, nor the ear enough of hearing."

It is best, however, to minimize the study of such things, since they are not among the things that are beneficial for life in the world to come. It is more important to devote oneself to God's Torah and his prophets' words, since these are the things that are profitable for the life in the world to come, as it is written: "Happy is the man who has not followed

the counsel of the wicked … rather, the teaching of the LORD is his delight
…" (Ps 1:1–2).

Qoheleth 1:12

I, Qoheleth, was king in Jerusalem over Israel.

I Qoheleth was king over Israel in Jerusalem.

He begins with: "I, Qoheleth"—this is because he intends to relate from
his own experience everything to which he refers in what follows. "I,
Qoheleth"—this shows that just as the editor [*al-mudawwin*] called him
Qoheleth, so also he called himself Qoheleth. It is likely that it was he who
first called himself Qoheleth, the editor following his example. He says: "I,
Qoheleth, was"—without mentioning the name of his father, for if he had
said son of David, it would have meant that his father had a part in some
of the things he mentions. Or else he may have omitted it for the sake of
brevity, relying upon the editor to supply it.

There is significance [Arab. *ma'na*] in his saying "I, Qoheleth, was
king" rather than "I, Qoheleth, king of Israel," which is that he was king
over Israel from the very start. In other words, its meaning is that from the
time I became king over Israel, in Jerusalem I ruled—since he never ruled
anywhere else, unlike David who ruled first in Hebron, then in Jerusalem.
Supporting this interpretation, namely, "ever since the time I became king
over Israel in Jerusalem," is: "I set my mind to study and to probe with
wisdom" (Qoh 1:13). Then his statement "I … was king" is a preface [Arab.
muqaddima] to: "I set my mind" (Qoh 1:13).

In addition, it seems likely that he [Solomon] made this statement
after Allah's word had reached him concerning the removal of the *'aseret
shebatim* [Heb. "Ten Tribes"] from his authority, Allah being upset
with him because of the *nashim nokhriyot* [Heb. "foreign women"]. He
felt remorse at that and began to practice abstention [Arab. *zuhd*] from
worldly affairs and from power. It is as though he were relating to us the
things he had been doing when he ruled by virtue of this strength and
courage and his firm grasp of the kingship. He mentioned himself, the
country over which he ruled, and the city in which he ruled; he was the
one who was chosen from the sons of David, as it is written: "He chose
my son Solomon to sit on the throne of the kingdom of the Lord" (1
Chr 28:5); "you shall be My treasured possession among all the peoples"

(Exod 19:5; Deut 7:6; 14:2); and Jerusalem is chosen "more than all the dwellings of Jacob" (Ps 87:2). He mentioned this in order to show that he was the most excellent of all men in station and had arrived at circumstances at which no one else had arrived. Nevertheless he turned his back on this world [Arab. *al-dunya*]. He gained nothing from it and remained full of remorse over the things in which he wearied himself, as he will make clear in what follows.

Qoheleth 4:17

Mind your steps [Heb. lit. *watch your foot*, according to the *qere*] *when you go to the house of God; to draw near to listen is better than the sacrifice offered by fools; for they do not know how to keep from doing evil.* [NRSV 5:1]

Guard your foot as when you go to the house of the Deity, and being near <u>to accept</u> [is better] than the fool's offering of a sacrifice; for they do not know [how] to do what is <u>forbidden</u>.

Know that Qoheleth, peace be upon him, did not keep this book entirely free from mention of the Law [Arab. *al-shar'*]. He mentioned it in three places. The first is here; the second is: "Go, eat your bread with gladness" (Qoh 9:7); and the third is at the end of the book. He did this in order to arouse the people to observe the Law [*al-shar'*] and hold fast to it. He mentioned this passage because it is similar to the preceding idea. That is to say, after he mentioned the disparity in the circumstances of people at different times—one time they may be in goodness and joy and another time in tribulation and sorrow—he then said: "Mind your steps when you go."

There are two points [Arab. *ma'nayn*] here. One is that he strongly warns the people against changing their religions even though their circumstances may have changed. Remember that in the case of Job, peace be upon him, his circumstances changed, but his faith in his religion did not change, as Scripture bears witness: "and he still keeps his integrity" (Job 2:3). The reason for this is that this world is not the Abode of Recompense, and we must not allow our devotions to change with a change in circumstances. The second idea is that the servant may derive help in improving his circumstances and his integrity by acts of devotion and vows, and as it is written: "call on me in the day of trouble and so on" (Ps 50:15 NRSV), following the verse: "And pay your vows to the Most High" (Ps 50:14); also: "[vows] that my lips pronounced, that my mouth uttered in my distress" (Ps 66:14). For this reason he started this section immediately after the discourse which preceded it.

He says: "Watch your foot," not: "watch yourself [your *nephesh*]" as it is written elsewhere: "and watch yourselves scrupulously" (Deut 4:9), because he meant the foot by which a man is enabled to engage in travels, in the going and coming in pursuit of his livelihood, and in the rest of his affairs. Therefore he said: "watch your foot," and not "watch yourself." The meaning of "watch your foot" is that you should not walk in what Allah has forbidden, as it is written: "do not walk on the way of evil men" (Prov 4:14); "keep your feet from evil" (Prov 4:27), and the like.

He says: "when you go to the house of God"—this means, be continually on guard against sins just as you take precautions in the times when you go to the house of Allah, in times of pilgrimage [Arab. *al-ḥajj*], or in times required by obligation of sacrifices or vows. The meaning of this saying is that it is the nature of the righteous to examine thoroughly his affairs when it is time for him to go to the house of Allah. He does not go when he knows that there is some sin upon him, but only when he has no fault or guilt so that when he comes to the house of Allah and prays and calls upon him, Allah will accept him and fulfill his needs. Therefore he said: "when you go to the house of God."

He says: "and draw near to listen" [Heb. *ve-qarobh lishmo'a*]—this means that Allah will be near to you in accepting your supplication, as it is written: "The Lord is near to all who call on Him and so on" (Ps 145:18).

He says: "sacrifice offered by fools [Heb. *kesilim*]"—he means that Allah accepts your request and supplication without sacrifice, but he does not accept the sacrifice of the fools, as he says: "(is better than) sacrifice offered by fools."

Then he says: "for they do not know"—making known the reason why Allah does not accept their sacrifice, even if it is satisfactory in its provisions. He said that Allah does not accept their sacrifice because they do not know what makes them pleasing in the sight of Allah. On the contrary, they are diligent in doing what is forbidden and shameful. This verse is like Jer 4:22, where it is said: "For my people are foolish." There they are called 'evilim [Heb. "fools"] just as they are here called *kesilim*; there, he said: "they do not know me," and here: "they do not know"; there, he said: "they are skilled in doing evil," here: "to do evil" (all translations for this verse NRSV).

This "evil" includes every area of activity that Allah has forbidden, as it is written concerning the fathers who were coming to the house of Allah to offer their sacrifices and pray to him: "Will you steal and murder and commit adultery and swear falsely, and sacrifice to Baal" (Jer 7:9) and "then come and stand before Me in this House," and so on (Jer 7:10). To them the Lord said: "Add your burnt offerings to your other sacrifices and eat the meat!" (Jer 7:21); and similarly: "Hear the word of the Lord, the chieftains of Sodom," and so on (Isa 1:10), "What need have I of all your sacrifices" (Isa 1:11), continuing to the end of that text [Arab. *qissa*].

Know that: "they do not know"—this means they are not learned and do not know [their] duty toward Allah, since they disregarded instruction and busied themselves without wisdom. For this reason they are continually doing what is forbidden.

In this verse the sage called attention to two things: first, that it is the duty of the people to be on guard against sins; second, that they acquire learning so that they may know their duty toward Allah, and that they not be like the fools who busy themselves apart from learning with the result that they carry on forbidden activities.

Qoheleth 5:1

Do not be rash [Heb. 'al tebhahel] with your mouth, and let not your heart be quick [Heb. 'al yemaher] to bring forth speech before God. For God is in heaven and you are on earth; that is why your words should be few [Heb. me'atim].

Do not be hasty with your mouth, and let not your heart be hasty to utter a word before the Deity, for the Deity <u>possesses this world</u>, and you are on the earth; therefore <u>it is necessary</u> that your words be few <u>and brief</u>.

I have explained 'al tebhahel as "do not make haste," as in: "and God has commanded me to hurry" (2 Chr 35:21 NRSV), "and hurriedly brought Haman" (Esth 6:14). It may also be translated as *dohsha* [Arab. "amazement," "perplexity"], as in: "a speedy riddance of all" (Zeph 1:18 KJV). Its meaning here is the same as 'al yemaher [Heb. "let him not hurry"], but since 'al tebhahel means the same thing as 'al yemaher, and since he intended to mention two things (using the same idea), he said concerning the one 'al tebhahel and concerning the other 'al yemaher because it

is not proper for him to repeat the same word when it is ambiguous in
the language.

He says: "Do not be rash with your mouth"—he means that if you are
pondering something of those works of Allah which he causes to vary in
his world as he wills, and if you do not understand the reason behind it,
and if there should pass through your mind anything by way of questioning
Allah concerning his works, take care that you not speak it lest you be held
accountable for the thought and the word. This is similar to the verse: "if
you have been a schemer, then clap your hand to your mouth" (Prov 30:32).

He says: "let not your heart be quick to bring out speech"—this follows:
"do not be rash with your mouth," though its intent is the same, for one of
two reasons: either because the first phrase concerns the general works of
Allah in which that person and others partake, and the second concerns
what happens specifically to that person by way of trials and tribulations,
and Qoheleth forbids his saying a word, his statement referring to either
case; or else the first may concern vicissitudes that occur from time to time
in some of that person's affairs such as a loss or decrease in prestige or an
objective or the death of a son, while the second applies to tribulations that
pile up all at once on the order of what happened to Job. Therefore he said:
If you see that your affairs have taken a turn against you, take care that you
do not let your heart be hasty with a word which you may speak before
Allah, lest he become displeased with you.

He says: "For God is in heaven"—this means he rules over [Heb.
ba-] the heavens. Qoheleth wanted to mention the heavens because they
encompass the earth and everything in it. Hence, the sense in this phrase
is that Allah rules everything, his dominion is over everything: "and his
kingdom rules over all" (Ps 103:19 NRSV); "you have dominion over all"
(1 Chr 29:12). Therefore the greatest of the created things and the least are
under his dominion.

He says: "and you are on earth"—this means that you are small and
insignificant among his creations, since mankind itself is hardly mention-
able in comparison with the multitude of his creations, as it is written:
"What is man that you have been mindful of him" (Ps 8:5). How much less
is a single individual among all the millions and myriads! Furthermore,
you are on the earth, along with the created things and do not belong to
the category of the exalted angels who have been endowed with a wisdom
with which you have not been endowed. For this reason it is necessary
that your words be few and brief. So do not question Allah concerning his
works, but know your station and do not discuss things that are bigger and

too wonderous for you [Heb. *gedolot ve-niflaot mimekha*]. The explanation of this idea has already been discussed above.

He says *me'atim* rather than *qetanim* [Heb. "few" rather than "small"] in order to inform us that it is expedient for a person to say less than he knows about something so that he does little speaking. If, however, he says more than he knows, then it is not well. Hence the sage warned that a man ought not to think about those things which are beyond his ken, for Allah did not create him for that and it is not among his activities, but if the thought should pass through his mind, he ought not to speak it.

Qoheleth 6:6

Even though he should live a thousand years twice over, yet enjoy [lit. *see*] *no good—do not all go to one place?* (NRSV)

Were a man to live a thousand years twice over, but good he does not see—is it not to one place that all go?

He has already said: "and live many years—no matter how many the days of his years may come to" (Qoh 6:3), a time span which is possible for people to live. Then he said: "even if he lived a thousand years twice." This is a span which is not possible for people to live, though Elijah, peace be upon him, has lived more than a thousand years twice over in the opinion of some scholars. That, however, does not belong in such contexts as this. He said: "a thousand years twice," though it would have been possible for him to say two thousand, because the first ten generations came close to a thousand years, as did Methuselah, but none of them exceeded a thousand years. Therefore he said: "a thousand years twice," meaning that if a man lived a thousand years, as did others, and then added a like number to them and still did not see good in any of them, he and the stillborn would be in the same situation.

Note that he said: "and his gullet is not sated through his wealth" (Qoh 6:3) and: "enjoy no good," in order to show that people should be satisfied by the good whenever they are set in the midst of it and see it. It is also possible that: "and his gullet is not sated through his wealth" (Qoh 6:3) may refer to the amenities of this world, while "enjoyed no good" refers to good works.

Then he said: "do not all go to one place"—which is similar to: "all turn to dust again" (Qoh 3:20 NRSV), though the latter is applied to both

man and beast while the former is applied to the stillborn and the rest of
mankind. Thus he declared that whoever has reached the age of responsibility under the commandment ought to live comfortably in the Abode
of this World in the measure that the Creator has bestowed upon him,
and do good works. If he does not do this, there would be no difference
between him and the stillborn, for the stillborn did not find pleasure and
this person did not find pleasure. The stillborn, however, is better off than
he, as previously discussed.

Qoheleth 12:12

*A further word against them my son, be warned! The making of
many books is without limit. And much study [Heb. lahag harbeh]
is a wearying of the flesh.*

**And more than these, O my son, beware: the making of many
books has no limit <u>or end</u>, and much occupation is a burden to
the body.**

Having mentioned his and the other prophets' books, making known that
they, all of them, are "pleasing words" and "words of truth plainly" (Qoh
12:10 NRSV) and were received "by one shepherd" (Qoh 12:11), he now
warns the people against any other books possessed by the world, namely,
books of the philosophers and others in which the truth is thought to
reside, when in fact they are filled with nothing but propaganda relating to
and discourse about what no human should be drawn to. We already mentioned something of this at the book's beginning when speaking about the
verse: "I do not aspire to great things or to what is beyond me" (Ps 131:1).
Yet nevertheless the people do occupy themselves with their books. Thus
the sage, peace be with him, warned against being occupied with them or
laboring over them, as he says: "making books."

There are two things [in the verse, that is, two proscriptions]. The first
is "making books"—it refers to being occupied with what they [the books]
say, for they are contrary to Torah; the second is "much study" [Heb. *lahag
harbeh*]—which refers to reading them and wasting one's time with them.
He also says "without limit" since their books have no end or limit, perhaps because there are so many. Yet he adds an extra statement which
also teaches they are many; he says: "much, many" [Heb. *harbeh*]. Thus
the reason he says "without limit" is to teach that foreign books [Arab. *al-*

kutub al-barāniyya] have no end, that is, each one of them differs from the other without end, and likewise each teaches a science the end of which cannot be reached, for the works of the Creator, great and exalted is his mention, are too great to be encompassed, as we explained at: "no one can find out what is happening (Qoh 8:17 NRSV). This is why he says "without limit."

He then says "much study is a wearying of the flesh." The sage, peace be with him, teaches that occupation with them and wasting one's time with them burdens and weakens the body; nor does one even gain any benefit from it whatsoever in terms of rewards in this world or the hereafter. In contrast, "making books" with YHWH's words is something with benefit in this world and the next, as it is said: "recite it day and night, so that you may observe faithfully" (Josh 1:8). Since he commanded to read them and to labor over what is in them, he says: "only then you will prosper in your undertaking" (Josh 1:8). Thus the word of Allah, great and exalted, has benefit for anyone who is occupied with it and labors over what is in it. Wasting time with anything else has no benefit, as he says: "wearying of the flesh."

Solomon, peace be with him, mentions that they cause harm, as in the verse: "Do not add to His words, lest He indict you and you be proved a liar" (Prov 30:6). With this he alludes to those that discourse on the surface of the land and seas when they are certainly ignorant of it, as in the dictum: "Have you surveyed the expanses of the earth?" (Job 38:18); and as he says: "Have you penetrated the sources of the sea?" (Job 38:16). Even more significant is their discoursing on the spheres, saying that between each sphere is such and such, relating to hidden things that no one knows except their Creator, may his mention be exalted. It is incumbent upon us to reach only what is below him through his books in which his prophets give report. We ought not to discourse on anything contrary to or external to them lest we join those liable for punishment, as in the verse: "lest He indict you and you be proved a liar" (Prov 30:6). Now there is no doubt that the philosophers, as those among our *Ummah* [Arab. "nation"] that follow their words, are subject to punishment.

Woe to them that are distracted from the books of Allah, great and exalted, and his sayings, [led astray] by those which are other than them. About them he said [as can be read in Prov 9:14–18] "Woman Folly," and so on.

What he makes known is that the wise men of the foreign nations resemble the foolish whore who sits in the paths and, as the fools pass,

brings them into her. She has sweet and seductive speech, at least according to its external appearance, while the ignorant masses fail to grasp her
true intent. She is: "Stolen waters are sweet" (Prov 9:17), after which he
said: "he does not know that the shades [Heb. *repha'im*] are there" (Prov
9:18). He teaches that anyone caught there is already caught in hell [*Gehen-
nam*], as he says: "her guests are in the depth of Sheol" (Prov 9:18).

Qoheleth, peace be with him, has collected in these verses everything
one needs to labor in, which is that the man ought to burden his soul in
words of the wise, which derive from one source. Be warned against occupation with external books and occupation in reading them. One should
not labor in what is in them or believe them. This is why he says "and much
study" after "making many books."

> *Happy are those whose way is blameless…. Happy are those who
> observe His decrees.* (Ps 119:1–2)

Bibliography

Bland, Richard. "The Arabic Commentary of Yephet ben 'Ali on the Book
of Ecclesiastes, Chapters 1–6." PhD diss., University of California,
1966.

Vajda, Georges. *Deux commentaires karaïtes sur l'Ecclésiastes.* Leiden: Brill,
1971.

Sa'adia Gaon on Esther's Invitation of Haman:
A Case Study in Exegetical Innovation and Influence

Michael G. Wechsler

Introduction

While the seminal position of Sa'adia Gaon (882–942) in the history of Jewish Bible exegesis has long been affirmed in the subsequent scholarly tradition, medieval and modern alike, our understanding of the precise nature and scope of his contribution continues to grow with the ongoing publication of his works—both *editiones principes* and revised editions—and the many scholarly studies that they engender. Recently I had the privilege of contributing to the former corpus with the publication of Sa'adia's commentary on the book of Esther, reconstructed and edited from a total of sixty-three extant, separately-catalogued witnesses representing twenty-three distinct manuscripts. This commentary, which consists of a Judeo-Arabic translation (the first-known Arabic translation of the Hebrew text of Esther) and commentary proper, is entitled by him *Kitāb al-īnās bi-'l-jalwa* ("The Book of Conviviality in Exile") and appears to have been one of his latter works, composed circa 933–934.[1]

Like Sa'adia's other biblical commentaries and monographic works, *Kitāb al-īnās* is immediately distinguished by its innovative compositional structure. Following Arabic and Greco-Arabic compositional models, Sa'adia opens his commentary with a methical introduction in which,

---

1. As I discuss in the edition (Michael G. Wechsler, *The Book of Conviviality in Exile* [*Kitāb al-īnās bi-'l-jalwa*]: *The Judaeo-Arabic Translation and Commentary of Saadia Gaon on the Book of Esther*, Biblia Arabica 1 [Leiden: Brill, 2015], 3 n. 4), this title is intended by Sa'adia for the *combined* work of the biblical text (albeit in Arabic translation) and his commentary thereon. On the reasoning concerning this date of composition, see Wechsler, *Conviviality*, 4–5.

after an opening doxology, he discusses foundational themes in the book
and the literary organization of these themes in the biblical text, and
he also resolves certain theological cruxes. Following the introduction,
Sa'adia arranges his commentary proper in seven sections corresponding to the thematic-literary structure outlined in his introduction. Within
each section, moreover, Sa'adia organizes his commentary by pericope,
first giving his Arabic translation of the pericope and then following this
with his commentary thereon. Grammatical and lexical issues reflected in
his translation are typically discussed by him—when he feels the need to
do so—at the outset of his commentary on each pericope. Sa'adia's strongly
didactic intent is clearly borne out at the end of each section, which he
concludes with a concise enumeration of that section's "derivative points"
(*shu'ab* or *furū'*, suggesting the terminology of Islamic *uṣūl al-fiqh*).[2] The
personalized stamp of Sa'adia is also reflected throughout the commentary
in his use of first-person forms (both singular and plural). This personalized
and programmatic Graeco-Arabic compositional model—which Sa'adia is
the first-known Jewish exegete to adopt (and adapt) for a commentary on
Esther[3]—would have served his purpose well as the self-perceived stew-
ard of his people's intellectual and spiritual welfare (as he elaborates in
Sēfer ha-Gālūy, his *apologia pro vita sua*)[4] by (1) helping to acclimate and

---

2. I.e., the theoretical bases of Islamic law, in which the synonymous terms *shu'ab*
and *furū'* (lit. "branches/limbs") signify the rules or principles that, while not themselves explicitly revealed in scriptural texts (*nuṣūṣ*), are derived from such by jurists in
various ways including personal reasoning (*ijtihād*) and analogy (*qiyās*). See further
Wechsler, *Conviviality*, 225 n. 166, and, on the influence of *uṣūl al-fiqh* on the Geonim
generally, G. Libson, *Jewish and Islamic Law: A Comparative Study of Custom during
the Geonic Period*, Harvard Series in Islamic Law 1 (Cambridge, MA: Islamic Legal
Studies Program, Harvard Law School, 2003).

3. Previous exegetical treatments of Esther, following the standard rabbinic-
midrashic model, are *impersonal* in that they are anonymous compilations of named
or unnamed rabbinic authorities (whose comments are often decontextualized and
digressive), and they are *nonprogrammatic* in that they are typically organized around
successive biblical lemmata rather than around a multilayered, literary-thematic plan,
with subsidiary thematic pericopes informing one central theme (notwithstanding, in
a few of these sources, the inclusion of theological proem intended to set the venue
of coming affliction counterbalanced by God's faithful solicitude for Israel—as in
Midrash Esther Rabbah).

4. See A. E. (A. Ya.) Harkavy, ed. "The Surviving Remnants of R. Saadia's *Sēfer
hā-Gālūy*" [Hebrew], in *Leben und Werke des Saadjah Gaon (Said al-Fajjumi, 892–
942), Rectors der Talmudischen Akademie in Sora*, part 5 of *Studien und Mittheilungen*

so facilitate the interaction and "convivializing" of his Jewish readership with their Islamicate literary and intellectual culture, and (2) providing his Rabbanite readership with a viable intellectual counterpart to the similar, competing literary models being adopted by Karaite exegetes.

Beyond these noteworthy aspects of compositional innovation, Sa'adia's commentary on Esther exhibits a wealth of content attesting not only to his originality and creativity as an exegete, but also to his influence upon subsequent Jewish exegesis of this vastly popular biblical book.[5] In addition to the few initial steps that have recently been taken in exploring this wealth of content,[6] let me ask the reader now to join in taking one more as we consider three specific facets of innovation and influence centered in Sa'adia's comment concerning Esther's invitation of Haman to her two banquets (Esth 5:4–8).

---

aus der Kaiserlichen Oeffentlichen Bibliothek zu St. Petersburg (Saint Petersburg: Tipo-Litografiya Bermana i Rabinovicha, 1891), 154; Michael G. Wechsler, "Saadia's Seven Guidelines for 'Conviviality in Exile' (from His Commentary on Esther)," *Intellectual History of the Islamicate World* 1 (2013): 205.

5. Vastly popular, that is, in Jewish tradition: cf. B. D. Walfish, *Esther in Medieval Garb: Jewish Interpretation of the Book of Esther in the Middle Ages* (Albany: State University of New York Press, 1993); A. Koller, *Esther in Ancient Jewish Thought* (Cambridge: Cambridge University Press, 2014); and the diachronic survey of Esther in Judaism contained in the articles found in *EBR* 8:13–30. In Christian tradition, generally speaking, the attitude toward this book is far more reserved: see E. Horowitz, "Esther (Book and Person): III.A. Christianity: Patristics and Western Christianity," *EBR* 8:30–34; and Michael G. Wechsler, "Esther (Book and Person): III.B. Christianity: Near-Eastern Christianity," *EBR* 8:34–38.

6. See, in addition to our introductory discussion in *Conviviality*, 6–29, and the discursive material in our footnotes to the English translation (*Conviviality*, 93–416), Michael G. Wechsler, "Ten Newly Identified Fragments of Saadia's Commentary on Esther: Introduction and Translation," in *Pesher Naḥum: Texts and Studies in Jewish History and Literature from Antiquity through the Middle Ages, Presented to Norman (Naḥum) Golb*, ed. Joel L. Kraemer and Michael G. Wechsler, with the participation of Fred Donner, Joshua Holo, and Dennis Pardee, Studies in Ancient Oriental Civilization 66 (Chicago: Oriental Institute of the University of Chicago, 2012), 240–43; Wechsler, "Guidelines"; Wechsler, "New Data from Saadia bearing on the Relocation of the Palestinian Yeshiva to Jerusalem." *Jewish Studies, an Internet Journal* 12 (2013):1–9; and my unpublished paper "Innovative Aspects of Saadia Gaon's Judaeo-Arabic Translation and Commentary on the Book of Esther" (paper presented at the Annual Meeting of the Society of Biblical Literature, Atlanta, 21 November 2015).

On Esther's Invitation of Haman (from Sa'adia's Commentary on Esther)

The following excerpt is taken from Sa'adia's larger comment on Esth 5:1–14 and, except for a few slight changes, is identical to my translation in *Conviviality*, pages 296–302.

Now, among those things for which a reason must be sought is Esther's invitation of Haman, for insofar as she had in mind the deliverance of her people, then why did she invite their enemy to her reception? For this we can discern in fact several possible reasons, (1) the first of which was so that she might augment (Haman's) standing[7] and treat him as an equal of the king, in order that such might become the cause of his demise—for in the case of anyone who attains perfection, there is nothing left thereafter except for his decline—consistent with the sense of (the statement) משגיא לגוים ויאבדם (Job 12:23), which may possibly be interpreted, "Who causes (the nations) to become a multitude and then destroys them."[8] And (Haman) himself was, in fact, beguiled by this, for so he says: *Moreover, Queen Esther invited no one else along with the king to the reception,* etc. (5:12), and in his view this was equivalent to[9] *the magnitude of his wealth and the multitude of his sons* (5:11), since he singles it out with its own special statement.[10] (2) Another possible reason[11] was to show

---

7. Or "(self-)importance" (Arab. *miqdār*, on which see Joshau Blau, *A Dictionary of Mediaeval Judaeo-Arabic Texts* [Hebrew] (Jerusalem: Israel Academy of Sciences and Humanities, 2006), 531a.

8. Sa'adia's tentative qualification of this interpretation (Arab. *yumkinu an yufassaru*) is consistent with the fact that he construes the Hebrew clause in Job differently in his translation of that book—i.e.: "The one who displaces tribes and then destroys them" (Sa'adia, *Job*, 87), in which he connects משגיא to the root סוג (which he also renders by another root *ad* Pss 53:4; 80:19, albeit in his *Egrōn*, s.v. זאיל:סג), rather than, as in the present instance, to the root ס/שׂגה (as in his *Egrōn*, s.v. סגיא: כתיר). See also the citation of this verse with reference to Haman's rise and fall in Esth. Rab. 7:2 (*ad* Esth 3:1).

9. "Equivalent to"—Arab. *maqām*, on this sense of which see Blau, *Dictionary*, 576b.

10. "He singles ... statement"—or, more literally: "set apart for it a statement of its own" (Arab. *farrada lahu qawlᵃⁿ ʿalā ḥaddihi*; cf. Blau, *Dictionary*, 494b); i.e., Esther's invitation of Haman with the king is the sole focus of the two clauses in v. 12, whereas "*the magnitude of his wealth and the multitude of his sons*" is presented by him as one in a series of items (i.e., direct objects introduced by את) in the single clause comprising v. 11.

11. "Another possible reason"—so, in the interest of clarity, for Arab. *thumma* (lit. "moreover," "furthermore"), as also when introducing the remaining possibili-

him kindness and to treat him honorably, for so long as one treats his enemy honorably, he is like one who strews coals of fire on his head by comparison [...], as it says, (*If thine enemy be hungry, give him bread to eat*, etc.;) *for thou wilt heap coals of fire upon his head* (Prov 25:21–22). (3) Another possible reason was to keep him planted close to her lest she (appear to) be averse to him and he [...][12] wealth and power, and he thereby appeal (to others) for help and rebel against Ahasuerus, and so depart and slip out of her hand and out of the king's hand. (4) Another possible reason was to augment her self-abasement so that God would regard her as being just as subdued as one who was distressed and had suffered harm, as (borne out by her) acting subserviently to[13] (Haman) and treating him jointly just like the king. (5) Another possible reason was so that he might not discern that she was a Jew, for such is the practice of those who are perspicacious[14] among the people to remove what they wish to conceal far away from (the rest of) the people.[15] (6) Another possible reason was to make the sons of Israel despair of her in the event that they had come to place their confidence in her, that she, to the exclusion of their Lord, was the one attending to their situation. Hence, rather than being delivered, when they heard that she had invited (Haman) to her reception they would have said, "Our eyes have been fixed upon this person, yet since she has shown herself to be favorably inclined towards our enemy with her own personal charity, there is nothing left for us but to turn to the Lord and put our confidence in Him alone." (7) Another reason, possibly, was so that the king might come to suspect that she and Haman had devised a plot against him, whereupon they would be

---

ties below (albeit for the seventh, we have rendered it simply "another reason," since Sa'adia there adds explicitly *fī 'l-imkān*).

12. Notwithstanding this lacuna, Sa'adia's point is clear from what follows—viz., that were Haman not preoccupied by the queen's receptions, he might discern the queen's intention and so make use of his power and wealth to secure protection and foment rebellion (cf. the third reason in the excerpt from b. Meg. 15b below).

13. Or "humbling/humiliating herself before" (Arab. *mustakhdhiya ʿindahu*, on which cf. Ibn Manẓūr, *Lisān al-ʿarab*, 20 vols. in 10 (Cairo [Būlāq]: Al-Matbaʿat al-Kubrā al-Mīriyya bi-Būlāq, 1882–1891), 18:246. Her humiliation/subservience lay in the fact that, by inviting Haman to the feast that *she* had prepared (see 5:4, 8, 12; 6:14), she was effectively according him the treatment due only to her superior, the king.

14. Or, perhaps, "meticulous" (Arab. *ḥudhdhāq*).

15. Sa'adia's point here, apparently, is that Esther "removed" far away from herself any evidence of the anxiety and grief that she felt on behalf of her people (from which Haman might infer her Jewishness) by focusing her actions on doing that which would give the opposite impression (cf. also the eighth reason given in the Byzantine Karaite Compilation cited below).

executed together and the decree would be annulled, though she did not have in mind the annulment of the[16] [...]. (8) Another possible reason was because the king was fickle and she wanted to be sure that he would respond positively to her [...], whereupon (the king) would demand of him [...], and so she ensured that (Haman) was present so that the blow might fall upon him at the same time that the king gave the order.

Such is what has come to our mind of the possible reasons for Esther's invitation of Haman, and it may be that it was for some of these, or for all of them—and (ultimately) for that which would prove most fitting—that Esther deemed it right to invite Haman. Indeed, it is one of those commonly-understood things that a person may undertake an action and it be deemed right by him for many reasons, as (in the case of) one who says, "I consider it right that I go forth to Jerusalem[17] in order that I might acquire merit,[18] and that I might meet the scholars, and that I might [...], and that I might amass[19] its sweet fruits, and that I might exhibit my reliance on God to keep me safe during the journey, and that I might be absented for a time from those who annoy me; and so too, (that) if I should die, then I will be buried there"—and for whatever else he might add to these exemplary reasons and others like them.

Discussion

Repackaging Rabbinic Tradition

Sa'adia's attitude toward rabbinic tradition, as well noted elsewhere, is a nuanced one.[20] On the one hand, toward halakhic tradition (that is, the

---

16. "Though she ... the"—a tentative translation vis-à-vis the following lacuna.

17. Arabic *bayt al-maqdis* (probably abbreviated from *madīnat bayt al-maqdis*, "the city of the temple"). On this common designation of Jerusalem see, among others, M. Gil, *A History of Palestine, 634–1099*, trans. E. Broido (Cambridge: Cambridge University Press, 1992), 114 (§125) and his full note thereto, as well as the rich collection of sources supplied by M. A. Friedman, *Jewish Polygyny in the Middle Ages: New Documents from the Cairo Geniza* [Hebrew] (Jerusalem: Mosad Bialik, 1986), 25–53 n. 28.

18. I.e., merit in God's eyes for making the pilgrimage.

19. "That I might amass"—Arab. *li-astakthira min*, on which see R. Dozy, *Supplément aux dictionnaires arabes*, 2nd ed., 2 vols. (Leiden: Brill; Paris: Maisonneuve frères, 1927), 2:445a; as well as Sa'adia's translation of Prov 22:16a, עשק דל להרבות לו, construed as a protasis: "Whosoever wrongfully takes from a poor man to amass (more) for himself"; see Sa'adia, *Proverbs*, 173.

20. See, among others, Haggai Ben-Shammai, "The Rabbinic Literature in Se'adyā's Exegesis: Between Tradition and Innovation" [Hebrew], in *Heritage and*

oral law) he maintains an unquestioning allegiance, rooted in the rabbinic dogma of the oral law as an extrabiblical corpus of reliable tradition, faithfully handed down from the prophets who received it from God.[21] Hence, in the extant text of his commentary on Esther we find eight direct halakhic citations (three from the Mishnah, four from the Babylonian Talmud, and one from the Jerusalem Talmud),[22] all presented by Saʿadia as prescriptive and consistent with the positive behavior of the Jewish protagonists in the biblical text. Toward aggadic-midrashic tradition, on the other hand, Saʿadia exhibits a critical and independently analytical attitude, according to which a given interpretation might, vis-à-vis the perceived constraints of reason, be rejected or endorsed with varying degrees of reservation. A clear example of this latter attitude is afforded by the following excerpt, the bulk of which consists of a reworked paraphrase of the following aggadic-midrashic exegetical tradition in b. Meg. 15b:[23]

Innovation in Medieval Judaeo-Arabic Culture: Proceedings of the Sixth Conference of the Society for Judaeo-Arabic Studies, ed. J. Blau and D. Doron (Ramat-Gan: Bar-Ilan University Press, 2000), 33–69; R. Brody, *The Geonim of Babylonia and the Shaping of Medieval Jewish Culture* (New Haven: Yale University Press, 1998), 312–15; Brody, *Saʾadyah Gaon*, trans. B. Rosenberg (Oxford: Littman Library of Jewish Civilization, 2013), 73–78; Wechsler, *Conviviality*, 11–20; M. Zucker, ed., *Saadya's Commentary on Genesis* [Hebrew] (New York: Jewish Theological Seminary of America, 1984), 13–18.

21. See m. Avot 1:1, the *locus classicus* for this dogma, as well as the following statement from Saʿadia's polemic work *Taḥṣīl al-qiyās fī ʾl-sharāʾiʿ al-samʿiyya* (per Zucker, *Genesis*, xiii n. 9): "This (following) discussion [i.e., the second part of *Taḥṣīl al-qiyās*] is intended to affirm the transmitted tradition ... known (to us) from the Mishnah and the Talmud: To begin, I aver that the fundamentals of the law have come to us in the same way that they came to our forebears (who saw the deeds and heard the words of the prophets)—by way of sense perception (Arab. *al-ḥiss*)—and they in turn handed them down to us. It is in this same way that the (specific) laws prescribed (from these fundamentals) came to us: based on the knowledge acquired by our forefathers by means of sense perception. And insofar as there is no need for us in this book to explain sense perception, since it is self-evident, ... so too, therefore, is there no need for us to explain how (halakhic) tradition came about, since it is self-evident."

22. This last, brief citation, concerning the "the twenty-four (benedictions) of fasts" (see y. Ber. 4:3 [33b]; y. Taʿan. 2:2 [9b]) and found at the end of his comment on 4:1–4, bears out Saʿadia's additionally innovative role as the first of the Geonim to cite the Jerusalem Talmud as a source of halakhic authority (see further Brody, *Geonim*, 166–69, 240–41).

23. Here given per the translation in M. Simon, "Megillah: Translated into English with Notes, Glossary and Indices," in *The Babylonian Talmud: Seder Moʿed*, ed. I. Epstein (London: Soncino, n.d.), 4:92–93 (with some slight adjustments).

Our Rabbis taught: What was Esther's reason for inviting Haman? (1) R. Eleazar said: She set a trap for him, as it says, *Let their table before them become a snare* (Ps 69:23). (2) R. Joshua said: She learnt to do so from her father's house, as it says, *If thine enemy be hungry give him bread to eat*, etc. (Prov 25:21–22). (3) R. Meir said: So that he should not form a conspiracy and rebel. (4) R. Judah said: So that they should not discover that she was a Jewess. (5) R. Nehemiah said: So that Israel should not say, "We have a sister in the palace," and so should neglect (to pray for) mercy. (6) R. Jose said: So that he should always be at hand for her. (7) R. Simeon b. Menassiah said: (She thought), "Perhaps the Omnipresent will notice and do a miracle for us." (8) R. Joshua b. Korḥa said: (She thought), "I will encourage him so that he may be killed, both he and I." (9) Rabban Gamaliel said: (She thought), "Ahasuerus is a changeable king." (10) Said R. Gamaliel: We still require the Modean, as it has been taught: R. Eliezer of Modiʿim says: She made the king jealous of him and she made the princes jealous of him. (11) Rabbah said: (She thought), "*Pride goeth before destruction*" (Prov 16:18). Abaye and Raba gave the same reason, saying: (She thought), "*With their poison I will prepare their feast*" (Jer 51:39).

Rabbah b. Abbuha came across Elijah and said to him: Which of these reasons prompted Esther to act as she did? He replied: (All) the reasons given by all the Tannaim and all the Amoraim.

When one compares this talmudic passage to the reasons enumerated by Saʿadia in his comment, it becomes apparent that, beyond simply paraphrasing the former, Saʿadia also takes the liberty to make more substantive *editorial* changes: he omits any mention of the rabbinic authorities associated with each reason and he also reorganizes the reasons, slightly changing their order and combining a few closely-related pairs into one. This reorganization may be summarily illustrated by the following table, in which the reasons as presented by Saʿadia are juxtaposed with the corresponding reasons in b. Meg. 15b (per our parenthetical enumeration of the reasons in each excerpt above):

Saʿadia	b. Meg.
1	1(?)/11
2	2
3	3
4	7
5	4
6	5

7   8/10
8   6/9

By making these more substantive editorial changes to the rabbinic tradition, as well as by presenting such through the medium of vernacular Arabic
paraphrase, Sa'adia is able to disassociate the tradition from its canonically-
imbued expression in the Talmud. This critical, noncitative "repackaging"
of aggadic-midrashic tradition is characteristic of Sa'adia's exegetical writing and bears out—beyond the more general accretive-communal nature of
medieval Judeo-Arabic exegesis[24]—two interrelated concerns that qualify
almost the entirety of Sa'adia's literary activity: (1) refuting and forestall-
ing, as far as possible, Karaite criticism of rabbinic-Rabbanite tradition *qua*
rabbinic tradition (regardless of any rational or scriptural merit); and (2)
reestablishing the Bible's preeminent position within the literary-canonical
hierarchy of Judaism (in which, by Sa'adia's day, it had become relegated to
the practical periphery).[25] In keeping with the former concern, the critically
modified content of the aggadic-midrashic tradition is presented squarely
on its own terms, rather than by association to a canonical rabbinic source
or individual rabbinic authorities, as a rationally valid explanation—and
one which is in this case further corroborated, as Sa'adia points out in the
latter part of his comment, by both psychological truism ("Indeed, it is one
of those commonly-understood things ...") and social *realia* ("as [in the
case of] one who says ..."). Any potential (or actual) Karaite criticism of the
reworked tradition *qua* a rabbinic tradition—even if Karaite scholars were
able to discern the basis for Sa'adia's comment in the traditional source
material—is thus largely neutralized. And, in keeping with the latter concern, Sa'adia's presentation of the reworked tradition through the medium
of vernacular Arabic paraphrase serves not only to disassociate that tradition from its canonically-imbued talmudic/rabbinic expression in Hebrew

---

24. See, among others, I. Goldziher, *Studien über Tanchûm Jerûschalmi* (Leipzig:
List & Franke, 1870), 3–4, as well as our more extended discussion of this "accretive-
communal" (certainly not "plagiaristic" in the modern/unethical sense) approach to
exegesis in the commentaries of Sa'adia's devotee Tanḥum ha-Yerushalmi (d. 1291), in
Michael G. Wechsler, *Strangers in the Land: The Judaeo-Arabic Exegesis of Tanḥum ha-
Yerushalmi on the Books of Ruth and Esther*, Magnes Bible Studies (Jerusalem: Magnes,
2010), 54–66.

25. See Brody, *Geonim*, 241–42; Brody, *Sa'adyah*, 58–73; R. Drory, *The Emergence
of Jewish-Arabic Literary Contacts at the Beginning of the Tenth Century* [Hebrew], Literature, Meaning, Culture 17 (Tel Aviv: Hakibbutz hame'uchad, 1988), 156–64.

and Aramaic, but also to emphasize and augment the contrasting presence and authoritative position of any scriptural prooftexts, which, unlike the nonscriptural textual elements of the tradition, are consistently retained by Saʿadia in their precise canonical (Hebrew) form (notwithstanding that in the present example only one of the four scriptural prooftexts given by Saʿadia is carried over from the talmudic source—i.e., Prov 25:21–22—and even then Saʿadia cites the latter rather than the former part of the biblical prooftext, perhaps to further disassociate his comment from its aggadic-midrashic source).

As a Source of Contemporary Realia and Social History

At various points throughout his commentary on Esther, Saʿadia draws upon contemporary *realia* to further elucidate and/or substantiate the meaning of the biblical text.[26] Hence, whether citing the contemporary dissimulation of Jews and Christians in the service of Muslims to illustrate the prudence of Esther's initial dissimulation in the palace,[27] or the worship of the Khazarian Khaqan by his people as well as of ʿAlī b. Abī Ṭālib by certain Muslims in the Maghrib to illustrate the plausibility of Haman also being intended as an object of worship (3:2),[28] Saʿadia presents the reader with information relevant not only for the study of exegetical history, but also for the study of social history.

---

26. The discussion in this section represents an abridged and updated version of Wechsler, "New Data."

27. From his comment on 2:16–20 (Wechsler, *Conviviality*, 206–7): "The juxtaposition of (the clause) *Mordecai was sitting in the king's gate* (v. 19b) with *Esther would not make known her kindred* means to say that, even though Esther had provided Mordecai with an official position in the ruler's household, she still did not reveal the identity of her people. Indeed, she conducted herself just like many Jews and Christians (in our time) whom we see devoting themselves to the service of Muslims; it is thus that one must view her."

28. From his comment on 3:1–5 (Wechsler, *Conviviality*, 218–19): "It may then be asked: Was it truly among the customs of the people to set up for themselves a man whom they would worship? And we would respond by saying this: Before the man of the best qualities among them they do indeed prostrate themselves and worship him, and call him by the name Khaqān—notwithstanding that they set up another one (in his place) as time goes on. It has also been said that in the Maghrib is a region whose people have been worshipping Abbāʾ ʿĀfir [= Abū Turāb, a soubriquet for ʿAlī] and his progeny over the course of time. The situation regarding Haman may thus have transpired in much the same fashion."

So also in the present excerpt: to underscore the general plausibility of Esther having multiple reasons for her invitation as expressed in the reworked aggadic-midrashic tradition, he appeals first to a psychological truism ("it is one of those commonly-understood things that a person may undertake an action and it be deemed right by him for many reasons"); and then follows this with the specific (albeit hypothetical) example, ostensibly drawn from the *realia* of contemporary Jewish social life, of the multiple reasons that a Jewish man in Sa'adia's day might have for making a pilgrimage to Jerusalem, designated by Sa'adia in Arabic as *bayt al-maqdis*.[29] In describing this scenario, significantly, Sa'adia provides information which may in turn contribute to a more refined understanding of the time at which the Palestinian *yeshiva* was relocated (either from Ramla or Tiberias) to Jerusalem, the *terminus ad quem* of which event has previously been placed at circa 960 CE.[30]

The information in question hinges specifically on two expressions, the first of which is *bayt al-maqdis*, an Arabic calque of the Hebrew expression *bēt ha-miqdāsh*. Though this former phrase is also attested in medieval sources as a designation of the contemporary temple mount as well as of Palestine in general, its usual reference is either to the biblical temple or to Jerusalem.[31] This is certainly so in Sa'adia's usage: in particu-

---

29. On this phrase, see n. 17 above.

30. This being the approximate date when the letter of King Joseph of Khazaria to Ḥasday ibn Shaprūṭ was composed, in which express reference is made to "the yeshiva that is in Jerusalem" (הישיבה שבירושלם); see Gil, *Palestine*, 499–500 (§738), positing a relocation from Tiberius. The relocation from Ramla, on the other hand, is entailed by the proposals of J. Mann (*The Jews in Egypt and in Palestine under the Fāṭimid Caliphs: A Contribution to Their Political and Communal History Based Chiefly on Genizah Material Hitherto Unpublished* [repr., New York: Ktav, 1970], 1:59, 65) and B. Z. Kedar ("When Did the Palestinian Yeshiva Leave Tiberias?," in *Pesher Naḥum: Texts and Studies in Jewish History and Literature from Antiquity through the Middle Ages, Presented to Norman [Naḥum] Golb*, ed. Joel L. Kraemer and Michael G. Wechsler, with the participation of Fred Donner, Joshua Holo, and Dennis Pardee, Studies in Ancient Oriental Civilization 66 [Chicago: Oriental Institute of the University of Chicago, 2012], 117–20), who place the *yeshiva* there in the late ninth or early tenth century (though neither scholar addresses the bearing of King Joseph's reference upon a subsequent relocation to Jerusalem).

31. See the richly documented discussion of Gil, *Palestine*, 114 (§125) and n. 38. One point of his, however, we would call into question (which he reiterates on p. 788 [§924])—viz., that the Karaite Sahl ben Maṣliaḥ "evidently means Palestine" when, in his letter to Sa'adia's disciple Jacob ben Samuel, he says "I have come from *bēt*

lar, as regards the present passage, of the ten other occurrences of this phrase in the extant text of his commentary on Esther, *all* of them are clearly delineated by context as references either to the biblical temple[32] or to Jerusalem.[33] Consistent with this observation, *bayt al-maqdis* in the present passage is best understood as a designation of contemporaneous Jerusalem (certainly not the temple mount, which would hardly constitute an expected venue at which to "meet the scholars").

The second key expression is *al-ʿulamāʾ* ("the scholars/sages"), by which Saʿadia typically designates the collective intellectual authorities of the time.[34] Since he uses the term here without further qualification— other than that they are to be met with in *bayt al-maqdis* (= Jerusalem)—it seems to us most reasonable to construe this as a reference to the collective scholars of the *yeshiva*. Indeed, in Saʿadia's usage the unqualified, definite honorific *al-ʿulamāʾ* is semantically equivalent to Hebrew *ha-ḥăkhāmīm*, by which latter he typically designates the collective of authorized scholars of the *yeshivot*.[35]

---

ha-miqdāsh to issue a warning ..." (see S. Pinsker, *Lickute Kadmoniot: Zur Geschichte des Karaismus und der karäischen Literatur* [Hebrew] [Vienna: Adalbert della Torre, 1860], 2:30 [second par.], as earlier on p. 27 [last par.]). In fact it would make eminent sense that he means Jerusalem (so J. Mann, *Karaitica*, vol. 2 of *Texts and Studies* [Philadelphia: Hebrew Press of the Jewish Publication Society of America, 1935], 22), which was his primary residence and where he was active within the prominent Karaite circle of "the teachers of the émigrés to Jerusalem" (Arab. *muʿallimu ʾl-maqādisa*). Cf. also Friedman, *Polygyny*, 252–53 n. 28.

32. E.g., in his commentary on 3:6–15 (Wechsler, *Conviviality*, 241): "In Tishri their kingdom was revitalized by the consecration of the Temple (*bayt al-maqdis*) in the time of Solomon, as it says, *Then Solomon assembled the elders of Israel*, (etc.) (1 Kgs 8:1)." The other uses of this phrase as a designation of the temple are found in his commentary on 1:3–4 (once); 3:1–5 (once); and 3:6–15 (once). The phrase also occurs once each in his commentary on 8:1–14 and on 9:1–19, where it may refer either to the temple or to Jerusalem—though certainly not to Palestine.

33. E.g., in his commentary on 1:3–4 (Wechsler, *Conviviality*, 137): "The starting date (of the 70-year exile) was at the end of (Nebuchadnezzar's) conquest of Jerusalem (*bayt al-maqdis*)—consistent with what Daniel says, *to accomplish the desolations of Jerusalem, seventy years*, etc. [Dan 9:2]"). The other uses of this phrase as a designation of Jerusalem are likewise found in his commentary on 1:3–4 (five times), in addition to the two ambiguous uses remarked in the previous note.

34. I.e., of his or any previous time; cf., e.g., Saʿadia, *Proverbs*, 244 (on Prov 30:1). For the collective authorities of bygone ages—except for those of his own (i.e., the geonic) age—Saʿadia also uses, apparently interchangeably, the terms *awāʾil/awwalūn*.

35. See Saʿadia, *Egrōn*, 223; and H. L. Bornstein, "The Controversy between Rabbi

Hence, if our reasoning is correct, Sa'adia's exegetically oriented anecdote offers us historical evidence of the *yeshiva*'s existence in Jerusalem by at least September 942, when Sa'adia died. If, moreover, Sa'adia's *Sēfer ha-Gālūy* was indeed his last work, the final version of which was composed between 935 and 936,[36] then the *terminus ad quem* of our evidence from his commentary on Esther—which was composed before his commentary on Daniel[37]—may be reasonably pushed back to 933/934. Though this revised date point certainly does not preclude the possibility of a prior relocation to Ramla (per the theories of Jacob Mann and Benjamin Kedar),[38] it does lead us to wonder whether, if the *yeshiva* did in fact relocate to Ramla toward the turn of the century, it was intended only as a *transitional* relocation before the final move to Jerusalem—the desirability of which destination is at any rate clearly expressed by the Gaon of the Palestinian *yeshiva* himself, Aaron b. Meir, in a letter written around the time of his calendar dispute with Sa'adia, ca. 921/922: "The glory of Israel is naught but Jerusalem, the Holy City, and the Great Sanhedrin therein, for so our sages of blessed memory have taught: 'He who has never beheld the joy of the Bēt ha-Shō'ēvā has never beheld joy in his life (m. Sukkah 5.1).'"[39]

Sa'adia Gaon and Ben Meir" [Hebrew], in *Sefer ha-Yovel le-Nahum Sokolov* (Warsaw: Shuldberg, 1903–1904), 75, lines 10–15. Though unlikely in my view, the possibility cannot be absolutely dismissed that Sa'adia is referring to a nonspecific collective of scholars in Jerusalem.

36. See Harkavy, "Surviving Remnants," 147; H. Malter, *Saadia Gaon—His Life and Works*, The Morris Loeb Series 1 (Philadelphia: Jewish Publication Society of America, 1942), 269; E. Schlossberg, "Concepts and Methods in the Commentary of R. Saadia Gaon on the Book of Daniel" [Hebrew] (PhD diss., Bar-Ilan University, 1988), 45, 65 n. 1.

37. See Sa'adia, *Daniel*, 57 (on Dan 2:46); p. 140 (on Dan 7:17–18); p. 163 (on Dan 9:2–3); and again there.

38. See above.

39. Bornstein, "Controversy," 62, lines 1–3. The reference by Sahl ben Matsliaḥ, writing in the second half of the tenth century to "the students of the Rabbanites on the Holy Mountain and in Ramla" (Pinsker, *Kadmoniot*, 2:33, second par., line 1)—if indeed a reference to yeshiva students (so Mann, *Palestine*, 65) and not Rabbanites in general (so, apparently, Gil, *Palestine*, 802, n. 15 [§931], 811 [§937])—may attest to a small holdover of the *yeshiva*'s presence in Ramla, following its relocation *magnam partem* to Jerusalem (not dissimilar, perhaps, from the scenario of a present-day college's main campus, where the administration and most of its facilities are situated, and its much smaller extension site in another location).

Influence on Later Karaite Exegesis

As regards the literary interplay between Saʻadia and the Karaites, scholars have tended to focus on the polemical aspect, and understandably so,
given that refuting the Karaite threat was a central concern for Saʻadia; and
that the degree to which he addressed this threat in his writing—contra the
sparse attention paid to the Ananite-Karaite conglomerate by the preceding Geonim[40]—secured his status as a favored literary opponent of Karaite
polemicists for many generations thereafter. In view of the scholarly focus
on this often fierce polemical interplay, one might well conclude that the
Karaites would have found little value in anything that Saʻadia wrote; yet
this would be a mistake. Just as in our day, so too in that of Saʻadia, a
scholar might engage in strongly polemical literary language with another
scholar on points of deep disagreement, yet elsewhere cite the work of
that same scholar with approbation where they agree. And, indeed, my
nearly two decades of research on Judeo-Arabic and Karaite exegesis of the
book of Esther has borne out that this is precisely the case with regard to
Karaite engagement with Saʻadia's commentary, various aspects of which
are incorporated (usually noncitatively) not only as viable exegetical
options, but even endorsed ones. One of Saʻadia's fiercest Karaite literary
opponents, Salmon ben Yerūḥim (mid-tenth century), in fact admits at
one point in his own commentary on Esther (*ad* 5:14), after citing—albeit
without express attribution—Saʻadia's application of Ps 7:16 to the scenario
in Esther (found at the end of Saʻadia's comment on 5:1–14), that "in his
commentary there is indeed benefit for those who are educated."[41]

With reference to the present excerpt, there is nothing we can see in the
Judeo-Arabic commentaries of subsequent Karaite exegetes in the tenth–
eleventh centuries that would indicate *express* influence by or borrowing
from Saʻadia—though the latter's commentary on Esther was available and

---

40. At least per the extant sources, according to which the only certain polemical
references were made by Naṭrūnai ben Hillai (Gaon of Sura, 853–861) and Hayy ben
David (Gaon of Pumbedita, 889–896); see David E. Sklare, *Samuel ben Ḥofni Gaon
and His Cultural World: Texts and Studies*, Études sur le judaïsme médiéval 18 (Leiden:
Brill, 1996), 76–77 (on the range of their gaonates see M. Gil, ed., *In the Kingdom of
Ishmael* [Hebrew], 4 vols., Publications of the Diaspora Research Institute 117–120
[Tel Aviv: Mosad Bialik, 1997], 1:319–22, 336–37 [§§197–98, 206]).

41. For both the text and translation of the fuller comment see Wechsler, *Conviviality*, 304 n. 131.

known to these Karaite exegetes and undoubtedly contributed, if only in a general accretive sense, to the intellectual backdrop against which they coalesced and formed their own personalized views on the point in question. Hence—and unsurprisingly given the Karaite rationalist aversion to exegetical polysemy (even though the issue is specifically one of multiple *reasons* for what the text describes rather than multiple *meanings* of the text itself)—the two known Karaite exegetes of this period, from whom we have an extant comment on this passage, advance only a single reason for Esther's invitation of Haman. Thus Salmon ben Yerūḥim, presenting the combined equivalent of Sa'adia's third and eighth reasons:

> As to her summoning Haman and inviting him along with the king—(this was) in order that he not elude her, her specific intention thereby being that he not escape. Yet had she spoken (of this) to the sovereign in his royal court, someone may possibly have interceded for (Haman) or helped him to escape, whereas her keeping him close at hand was to ensure that the matter not be delayed and that, when the king's anger flared up, the blow would fall quickly upon (Haman).[42]

And Yefet ben 'Eli (late tenth century), presenting a more concise equivalent of Sa'adia's third reason: "She invited Haman in order to keep him close to her, for had he not been present with her he might have been able to slip out of her hand."[43]

Moving on to the realm of Hebrew Karaite exegesis in Byzantium, on the other hand, we find clear evidence of the profound degree to which Sa'adia's exegesis was valued and incorporated into the Karaite exegetical tradition. This evidence, which derives from the earliest, formative period of Byzantine Karaism (eleventh–twelfth centuries), is found in an as-yet unpublished anonymous commentary on Esther, replete with Byzantine Greek glosses, which (as has already been recognized concerning the commentary on Ruth in the same manuscript) is clearly the source epitomized by the Karaite scholar Jacob ben Reuben (late eleventh–early twelfth cen-

---

42. Per MS SP RNL Yevr.-Arab. 2:110, fol. 6r (*ad* Esth 5:5), cited in Wechsler, *Conviviality*, 300.

43. See Michael G. Wechsler, ed., *The Arabic Translation and Commentary of Yefet ben 'Eli the Karaite on the Book of Esther: Edition, Translation, and Introduction*, Karaite Texts and Studies 1, Études sur le judaïsme médiéval 36 (Leiden: Brill, 2008), 44*/271. For a preliminary assessment of Sa'adia's influence on Yefet's Esther commentary, and more definitive examples, see there, 66–71.

tury) for his much briefer commentary on the book in *Sēfer hā-ʿōsher*.[44] In this anonymous Hebrew commentary on Esther—which is in fact an exegetical compilation of translated selections drawn primarily from the Arabic commentaries of Salmon ben Yerūḥim, Yefet ben ʿEli, and, *to an even greater degree*, Saʿadia—we find, loosely translated into Hebrew, what is unmistakably the Gaon's reworked Arabic version of the aggadic-midrashic exegetical tradition, cited above, concerning the reasons for Esther's invitation of Haman, enumerating the same eight reasons, and in the same order (excepting Saʿadia's fifth reason, which is presented last):

> (Scripture) indicates that Esther prepared (another) banquet and (again) invited Haman together with the king. Now, as to (her reasons for doing) this, there are eight explanations: (1) First, to make him seem equal to the king—as if to say, "Should I invite the king and not also invite you?!"—which situation would then become the end and demise of his eminence, for though she honored him up to heaven, (the Lord) would cast him down to the earth; yet this fool, being gullible, said, *Moreover, (Queen Esther) invited no one else*, etc. (5:12)—which matter we have already explained. (2) Second, because this feast was a cause for rejoicing to Haman, and Esther was therefore treating him in a manner consistent with what Scripture says, *for thou wilt heap coals of fire*, etc. (Prov 25: 22). (3) Third, to exhibit to him (the sentiment) "I favor you" so as not to reveal to him her enmity, since the king did not (yet) know, for she had not (yet) told him anything about Haman so that no one (would find out and) inform Haman and he consider (it) and flee and escape out her hands, for he was a powerful man. (4) Fourth, because, while they would be eating, drinking, and rejoicing, she would be in distress, grief, and despair, and perhaps God would take account of this. (5) Fifth, that Israel might trust in the Lord and pray fervently and not trust in Esther, and so she exhibited to them (the sentiment) "I favor (Haman) greatly and am not worried about you"—(to which,) perhaps, Israel would despair

---

44. The printed portion of *Sēfer hā-ʿōsher*, included under the rubric of Aaron ben Joseph's *Mibḥar yĕshārīm*, is now freely accessible on the National Library of Israel website: http://rosetta.nli.org.il/delivery/DeliveryManagerServlet?dps_pid=IE13020860 (the commentary on Esther is on pp. 17a–b of the pagination beginning with Proverbs). On the commentary on Ruth and Jacob's epitome thereof, see Z. Ankori, *Karaites in Byzantium: The Formative Years, 970–1100*, Columbia Studies in the Social Sciences 597 (New York: Columbia University Press, 1959), 197 n. 105. On the extant witnesses to the anonymous Byzantine commentary, see Wechsler, *Yefet*, 133, to which should also be added MS RSL 182:403, fols. 37v–46r (a modern copy of SP RNL Yevr.-Arab. 1:583, fols. 22r–35r).

greatly and call out passionately to the Lord. (6) Sixth, to sow jealousy in the king's heart, insofar as the king would have thought, "Perhaps they are planning to kill me," whereupon he would execute both Haman and Esther and the decree would be annulled. (7) Seventh, in order to draw Haman under the king's direct control, so as to execute him quickly, for she knew that the king was fickle and might relent (of his execution); hence she confined Haman with herself and with (the king) in the same room. (8) Eighth, that he might not discern that she was a Jew and anxious about Israel; hence she prepared a banquet in order to show that she was joyful.[45]

Although this particular passage is not epitomized by Jacob ben Reuben in his *Sēfer hā-ʿōsher*,[46] its presence in this anonymous compilation—especially when considered together with the many other loosely translated excerpts from Saʿadia's commentary found therein[47]—attests to a far greater degree of penetration by Rabbanite-rabbinic exegesis into early Byzantine Karaite exegetical thought than one might have expected, given the polemical focus and undertone of previous scholarship on the interplay between Rabbanites and Karaites during this period. Indeed, that the Rabbanite exegesis in question is specifically that of the Karaites' arch-polemical opponent Saʿadia Gaon (albeit noncitatively presented), and that it is found in a work clearly deriving from the *communally-oriented* literature of the early Byzantine Karaite community,[48] only reinforces one's impression of the intellectual receptivity to and breadth of this penetration. A fuller assessment of this multilayered—that is, Rabbanite-Karaite as well as Islamicate-Byzantine—intellectual and literary "conviviality" (to borrow the apropos rubric by which Saʿadia himself sums up the theme of Esther), and the extent to which it characterizes

---

45. Per MS SP RNL Yevr.-Arab. 2:A 78, fol. 22v (cited also in Wechsler, *Conviviality*, 299 n. 114).

46. Nor have we found any evidence of this passage in the anonymous compilation being directly referenced in the later Karaite Hebrew commentaries on Esther by Abraham ben Judah (fifteenth century; in his complete Bible commentary ספר יסוד מקרא, per MS RU Or. 4739 [Warn. 1], fols. 234r–35r) or Moses ben Judah Meşşorodi (d. 1637; in his Esther commentary משאת משה, per MS SP IOS B 238, fols. 106r–228v).

47. For a preliminary enumeration of these see the index in Wechsler, *Conviviality*, 494–95 (under "A Byzantine Karaite exegetical compilation on Esther").

48. For a discussion of this literature, representing the so-called "Byzantine Karaite Literary Project," and of which the anonymous compilation under discussion bears all the main hallmarks, see Ankori, *Byzantium*, 415–44.

later Karaite exegesis of other biblical books, are matters that remain to be explored in future scholarship.

Bibliography

Allony, N., ed. *Haʾegron / Kitāb ʾuṣūl al-shiʿr al-ʿibrānī by Rav Sĕʿadya Gaʾon* [Hebrew]. Texts and Studies 8. Jerusalem: Academy of the Hebrew Language, 1969.

Ankori, Z. *Karaites in Byzantium: The Formative Years, 970–1100*. Columbia Studies in the Social Sciences 597. New York: Columbia University Press, 1959.

Ben-Shammai, Haggai. "The Rabbinic Literature in Seʿadyāʾs Exegesis: Between Tradition and Innovation" [Hebrew]. Pages 33–69 in *Heritage and Innovation in Medieval Judaeo-Arabic Culture: Proceedings of the Sixth Conference of the Society for Judaeo-Arabic Studies*. Edited by J. Blau and D. Doron. Ramat-Gan: Bar-Ilan University Press, 2000.

Blau, Joshau. *A Dictionary of Mediaeval Judaeo-Arabic Texts* [Hebrew]. Jerusalem: Israel Academy of Sciences and Humanities, 2006.

Bornstein, H. L. "The Controversy between Rabbi Saʿadia Gaon and Ben Meir" [Hebrew]. Pages 19–189 in *Sefer ha-Yovel le-Nahum Sokolov*. Warsaw: Shuldberg, 1903–1904.

Brody, R. *The Geonim of Babylonia and the Shaping of Medieval Jewish Culture*. New Haven: Yale University Press, 1998.

———. *Saʿadyah Gaon*. Translated by B. Rosenberg. Oxford: Littman Library of Jewish Civilization, 2013.

Dozy, R. *Supplément aux dictionnaires arabes*. 2nd ed. 2 vols. Leiden: Brill; Paris: Maisonneuve frères, 1927.

Drory, R. *The Emergence of Jewish-Arabic Literary Contacts at the Beginning of the Tenth Century* [Hebrew]. Literature, Meaning, Culture 17. Tel Aviv: Hakibbutz hameʾuchad, 1988.

Friedman, M. A. *Jewish Polygyny in the Middle Ages: New Documents from the Cairo Geniza* [Hebrew]. Jerusalem: Mosad Bialik, 1986.

Gil, M. *A History of Palestine, 634–1099*. Translated by E. Broido. Cambridge: Cambridge University Press, 1992. Revised translation of the first volume of *The Land of Israel in the First Islamic Period (634–1099)* [Hebrew]. Tel Aviv: Tel Aviv University Press, 1983.

———, ed. *In the Kingdom of Ishmael* [Hebrew]. 4 vols. Publications of the Diaspora Research Institute 117–120. Tel Aviv: Mosad Bialik, 1997.

Goldziher, I. *Studien über Tanchûm Jerûschalmi.* Leipzig: List & Franke, 1870.

Harkavy, A.E. (A.Ya.), ed. "The Surviving Remnants of R. Saadia's *Sēfer hā-Gālūy*" [werbeH]. Pages 133–238 in *Leben und Werke des Saadjah Gaon (Said al-Fajjumi, 892–942), Rectors der Talmudischen Akademie in Sora,* part 5 of *Studien und Mittheilungen aus der Kaiserlichen Oeffentlichen Bibliothek zu St. Petersburg.* Saint Petersburg: Tipo-Litografiya Bermana i Rabinovicha, 1891.

Horowitz, E. "Esther (Book and Person): III.A. Christianity: Patristics and Western Christianity." *EBR* 8:30–34.

Ibn Manẓūr, Muḥammad b. Mukarram. *Lisān al-ʿarab.* [Arabic]. 20 vols. in 10. Cairo (Būlāq): Al-Maṭbaʿat al-Kubrā al-Mīriyya bi-Būlāq, 1882–1891.

Kedar, B. Z. "When Did the Palestinian Yeshiva Leave Tiberias?" Pages 117–20 in *Pesher Naḥum: Texts and Studies in Jewish History and Literature from Antiquity through the Middle Ages, Presented to Norman (Naḥum) Golb.* Edited by Joel L. Kraemer and Michael G. Wechsler, with the participation of Fred Donner, Joshua Holo, and Dennis Pardee. Studies in Ancient Oriental Civilization 66. Chicago: Oriental Institute of the University of Chicago, 2012.

Koller, A. *Esther in Ancient Jewish Thought.* Cambridge: Cambridge University Press, 2014.

Libson, G. *Jewish and Islamic Law: A Comparative Study of Custom during the Geonic Period.* Harvard Series in Islamic Law 1. Cambridge, MA: Islamic Legal Studies Program, Harvard Law School, 2003.

Malter, H. *Saadia Gaon—His Life and Works.* Morris Loeb Series 1. Philadelphia: Jewish Publication Society of America, 1942.

Mann, J. *The Jews in Egypt and in Palestine under the Fātimid Caliphs: A Contribution to Their Political and Communal History Based Chiefly on Genizah Material Hitherto Unpublished.* 2 vols. Repr., New York: Ktav, 1970.

———. *Karaitica.* Vol. 2 of *Texts and Studies.* Philadelphia: Hebrew Press of the Jewish Publication Society of America, 1935.

Pinsker, S. *Lickute Kadmoniot: Zur Geschichte des Karaismus und der karäischen Literatur* [Hebrew]. Vienna: Adalbert della Torre, 1860.

Qafiḥ, Y., ed. *The Book of Beliefs and Opinions by Saʿadia ben Joseph Fayyūmī* [Hebrew]. 4th ed. Jerusalem: Mĕkhōn Mishnat ha-Rambam, 1995.

————, ed. *Proverbs, with the Translation and Commentary of the Gaon R. Saʿadia ben Joseph Fayyūmī* [Hebrew]. 2nd ed. Kiryat-Ono: Měkhōn Mishnat ha-Rambam, 1994.

Schlossberg, E. "Concepts and Methods in the Commentary of R. Saadia Gaon on the Book of Daniel" [Hebrew]. PhD diss., Bar-Ilan University, 1988.

Simon, M. "Megillah: Translated into English with Notes, Glossary and Indices." Pages 55–232 in vol. 4 of *The Babylonian Talmud: Seder Moʿed*. Edited by I. Epstein. London: Soncino, n.d.

Sklare, David E. *Samuel ben Ḥofni Gaon and His Cultural World: Texts and Studies*. Études sur le judaïsme médiéval 18. Leiden: Brill, 1996.

Walfish, B. D. *Esther in Medieval Garb: Jewish Interpretation of the Book of Esther in the Middle Ages*. Albany: State University of New York Press, 1993.

Wechsler, Michael G., ed. *The Arabic Translation and Commentary of Yefet ben ʿEli the Karaite on the Book of Esther: Edition, Translation, and Introduction*. Karaite Texts and Studies 1. Études sur le judaïsme médiéval 36. Leiden: Brill, 2008.

————. *The Book of Conviviality in Exile (Kitāb al-īnās bi-ʾl-jalwa): The Judaeo-Arabic Translation and Commentary of Saadia Gaon on the Book of Esther*. Biblia Arabica 1. Leiden: Brill, 2015.

————. "Esther (Book and Person): III.B. Christianity: Near-Eastern Christianity." *EBR* 8:34–38.

————. "Innovative Aspects of Saadia Gaon's Judaeo-Arabic Translation and Commentary on the Book of Esther." Paper presented at the Annual Meeting of the Society of Biblical Literature. Atlanta, 21 November 2015.

————. "New Data from Saadia Bearing on the Relocation of the Palestinian Yeshiva to Jerusalem." *Jewish Studies, an Internet Journal* 12 (2013): 1–9.

————. "Saadia's Seven Guidelines for 'Conviviality in Exile' (from His Commentary on Esther)." *Intellectual History of the Islamicate World* 1 (2013): 203–33.

————. *Strangers in the Land: The Judaeo-Arabic Exegesis of Tanḥum ha-Yerushalmi on the Books of Ruth and Esther*. Magnes Bible Studies. Jerusalem: Magnes, 2010.

————. "Ten Newly Identified Fragments of Saadia's Commentary on Esther: Introduction and Translation." Pages 237–91 in *Pesher Naḥum: Texts and Studies in Jewish History and Literature from Antiquity through the Middle Ages, Presented to Norman (Naḥum) Golb*. Edited by Joel L. Kraemer and Michael G. Wechsler, with the participation of Fred Donner, Joshua Holo, and Dennis Pardee. Studies in Ancient Oriental Civilization 66. Chicago: Oriental Institute of the University of Chicago, 2012.

Zucker, M. *Rav Saadya Gaon's Commentary on Genesis* [Hebrew]. New York: Jewish Theological Seminary of America, 1984.

Contributors

Jessica Andruss is assistant professor of religious studies at the University of Virginia. Her research focuses on medieval Jewish biblical exegesis, literature, and intellectual history in the Islamic world. She wrote her doctoral dissertation (University of Chicago, 2015) on Salmon ben Yerūḥīm's Judeo-Arabic translation and commentary on Lamentations, exploring the development of Arabic models of exegesis, homily, and historiography in Karaite writings. Her article "Wisdom and the Pedagogy of Parables in Abraham ibn Ḥasday's *Book of the Prince and the Ascetic*" is forthcoming in *Knowledge and Education in Classical Islam* (ed. Sebastian Guenther; Leiden: Brill).

Nabih Bashir is adjunct lecturer at the Master's Program in Israeli studies, Center for Advanced Studies, Birzeit University, Palestine, and post-doctoral fellow at the Triangle Regional Research and Development Center, Israel Ministry of Science and Technology. His fields of interest include medieval Jewish philosophy, Judeo-Arabic literature, and Bible exegesis. He wrote his doctoral dissertation (Ben Gurion University of the Negev, 2015) on Saʿadia Gaon's conception of the role of angels and humans in God's creation. On this topic he wrote the article "A Reexamination of Saadya Gaon's Dictum 'Humankind is More Sublime Than Angels'" [Hebrew], *Ginzei Qedem* 14 (2018): 9–54. A major endeavor is his initiation of publications for bringing classical medieval Jewish literature to a wide Arabic reading audience. Such is his influential edition in Arabic script of Judah Halevi's famous Judeo-Arabic polemical treatise, known as *Ha-Kuzari* (*Yehuda Halevi, The Kuzari—In Defense of the Despised Faith* [Arabic] [Beirut: Al-Kamel Verlag, 2012]).

Athalya Brenner-Idan is professor emerita of the Hebrew Bible/Old Testament chair at the Universiteit van Amsterdam, and she served as professor in the Department of Biblical Studies, Tel Aviv University. She also taught in Hong Kong and in the United States (Brite Divinity School, Fort Worth, TX), was extraordinary professor at Stellenbosch University, South Africa, and is currently also affiliated as research associate with the Orange Free State University, South Africa. She received an honorary PhD from the University of Bonn in 2002, and was president of the Society of Biblical Literature in 2015. Her publications include twenty edited volumes in the series A Feminist Companion to the Bible (Sheffield Academic and T&T Clark/Bloomsbury, 1993–2015), six edited volumes (with Archie C. C. Lee and Gale Yee) in the Texts@Contexts series (Fortress and T&T Clark/ Bloomsbury, 2010–2017), and her book *The Israelite Woman: Social Role and Literary Type in Biblical Narrative* (English: Sheffield Academic and Bloomsbury, 1985, 2014; Hebrew: Tel Aviv University Press, 2018).

Ora Brison is an independent scholar. Her research interests focus on contextual readings of biblical and ancient Near Eastern texts and on the reception of biblical texts, particularly the book of Psalms, in contemporary Israeli Jewish societies. She devoted her doctoral dissertation to the study of female heroines as intermediaries between the human and divine spheres in biblical and ancient Near Eastern literature (Tel Aviv University, 2015). Her recent publications include "Women's Banquets and Gatherings in Text and Context: The Queens' Banquets in Esther and Contemporary Women-Only Israeli/Jewish Ceremonies," in *The Five Scrolls*, ed. Athalya Brenner-Idan, Gale A. Yee, and Archie C. C. Lee, Texts@Contexts (London: Bloomsbury T&T Clark, 2018), 189–209; "The Medium of En-dor (אשת בעלת אוב) and the Phenomenon of Divination in Twenty-First Century Israel," in vol. 1 of *Samuel, Kings and Chronicles*, ed. Athalya Brenner-Idan and Archie Lee, Texts@Contexts (London: Bloomsbury T&T Clark, 2017), 124–47; "Judith: A Pious Widow Turned Femme Fatale, or More?," in *A Feminist Companion to Tobit and Judith*, ed. Athalya Brenner-Idan and Helen Efthimiadis-Keith, Feminist Companion to the Bible (Second Series) (London: Bloomsbury T&T Clark, 2015), 175–99.

Yoram Erder is a retired professor of Jewish history, Tel Aviv University. He specializes in legal and exegetical texts and the relationship between medieval Karaite works and the literature and legal notions of ancient Jewish sects (especially the Qumran sect). In his many articles, he has traced intricate halakhic (i.e., legal) interpretive methods and analogies which these literatures appear to have in common. Examples include his articles "The Observance of the Commandments in the Diaspora on the Eve of Redemption in the Doctrine of the Karaite Mourners of Zion," *Hen* 19 (1997): 175–202; and "Understanding the Qumran Sect in View of Early Karaite Halakhah from the Geonic Period," *RevQ* 26 (2014): 403–23. Erder also studies the complex relationship between Shiʿite Islamic sources and proto-Karaite and Karaite (scriptural and messianic) texts, as in his article "The Doctrine of Abú Isá al-Isfahání and Its Sources," *JSAI* 20 (1996): 162–99. His comprehensive English monograph on these topics and others has recently been published under the title *The Karaite Mourners of Zion and the Qumran Scrolls: On the History of an Alternative to Rabbinic Judaism* (Turnhout: Brepols, 2017).

Esther Gamliel-Barak is an independent scholar. She worked at the Israeli Ministry of Education for thirty-six years as a teacher of Arabic and Hebrew, served in other capacities at the Israeli education system, and taught several subjects in Ashkelon, Achva, and Levinsky Colleges (Israel). Her areas of interest include medieval Hebrew and Arabic language, linguistics and lexicography, and Karaite and Rabbanite exegesis. She wrote her doctoral dissertation (Bar Ilan University, 2010) on the tenth-century David ben Abraham Alfāsī and the methods of biblical interpretation in his Hebrew-Arabic biblical dictionary, known as *Kitāb Jāmiʿ Al-ʾAlfāẓ*. She has also published a lengthy article on this work, entitled "Exegesis Methods of the Bible in the Dictionary of the Karaite David Ben Abraham Alfāsī, ʿKitāb Jāmiʿ al-Alfāẓʾ " [Hebrew], *Beit Mikra* 59.2 (2014): 76–128.

Rachel Hasson is associate lecturer at the Department of Middle Eastern Studies, Ben Gurion University of the Negev. She wrote her doctoral dissertation (Hebrew University of Jerusalem, 2016) on popular (folk) Judeo-Arabic literature, based on hitherto unknown and unclassified manuscripts from the Cairo Genizah. Her research includes Judeo-Arabic language, literature, and culture; pre-modern Arabic dialects; and medieval Arabic. Her publications include "The story of Zayd and Kaḥlāʾ: A Folk Story in a Judaeo-Arabic Manuscript," in *Middle Arabic and Mixed Arabic*, ed. Liesbeth Zack and Arie Schippers (Leiden: Brill, 2012), 145–56; and two forthcoming essays: "Two Judaeo-Arabic Popular Stories from the Genizah" [Hebrew], *Massorot* 19; and "Late Judaeo-Arabic Manuscripts of Popular Literature from the Firkovitch Collection" [Hebrew], *Ginzei Qedem* 15.

Zafer Tayseer Mohammad teaches ancient history at An-Najah National University in Nablus, Palestine. He studied English language and literature (at An-Najah), international peace studies (at the University of Notre Dame), and biblical studies (at the Catholic Theological Union, Chicago). He wrote his doctoral dissertation (University of Zurich, 2016) on Zion theology in the book of Isaiah, concentrating especially on the dismal depictions of Jerusalem and her transformation. His current research analyzes the references to the city of Jerusalem in medieval and modern Arabic, Jewish, and Christian versions of the book of Isaiah, comparing them with the ancient versions (Targum, Septuagint, and Vulgate). A recent publication is "Jeremiah: The Prophet and the Concept: A Response to Reinhard G. Kratz," in *Jeremiah's Scriptures: Production, Reception, Interaction, and Transformation*, ed. Hindy Najman and Konrad Schmid, JSJSup 173 (Leiden: Brill, 2016), 225–27.

Meirav Nadler-Akirav is lecturer at the Department of Arabic, Bar-Ilan University. She wrote her doctoral dissertation (Bar-Ilan University, 2010) on Yefet ben ʿEli's commentary on the book of Amos, including a critical annotated edition of chapters 1–4 and an extensive analytical introduction. Her research focuses on medieval Judeo-Arabic translations and commentaries on the Bible, especially the Prophets. Currently she is completing a critical edition with English translation of Yefet's commentary on the books of Haggai and Malachi (to be published by Brill). Her recent publications are "The Meaning and the Translation of the Biblical Adverb ʾūlay (Perhaps) among Medieval Jewish Thinkers," *JSS* 68 (2017): 78–96; "The Biographical Stories of the Prophets in the Writing of Yefet Ben ʿEli," in *Senses of Scripture, Treasures of Tradition*, ed. Miriam Lindgren Hjälm (Leiden: Brill, 2017), 182–97; and "The Literary-Historical Approach of Yefet Ben ʿEli in his Commentary of the Book of Amos," *EJJS* 10 (2016): 171–200.

Sivan Nir has a PhD in biblical studies (Tel Aviv University, 2019). In his doctoral dissertation he analyzes the late midrashic and medieval conceptions of biblical characters and their characterization (focusing on Balaam, Esther, and Jeremiah). He also served as an instructor at the Department of Biblical Studies therein. His MA thesis (2013) was devoted to the characterization of Ruth in medieval Jewish exegesis, including Yefet's commentary on Ruth. His research interests include the transition from midrash to systematic Bible exegesis, as well as the interaction of these genres with Islamic and Christian sources. He has also published (with Amir Ashur and Meira Polliack) "Three Fragments of Sa'adya Gaon's Arabic Translation of Isaiah copied by the Court Scribe Joseph ben Samuel (c. 1181–1209)," in *Senses of Scripture, Treasures of Tradition*, ed. Miriam Lindgren Hjälm (Leiden: Brill, 2017), 485–508.

Meira Polliack is professor of Bible at Tel Aviv University and former head of the Department of Biblical Studies therein. Her areas of expertise include Arabic Bible exegesis and translation among the Jews of the Islamic world, literary approaches to the Bible, and Judeo-Arabic literature. Her MPhil (1989) and PhD (1993), both from the University of Cambridge, analyzed Cairo Genizah sources in connection to the Hebrew Bible, focusing on the Karaite tradition of Arabic Bible translation in comparison with Sa'adianic, Samaritan, and Christian Arabic sources. On these see her monograph *The Karaite Tradition of Arabic Bible Translation: A Linguistic and Exegetical Study of the Karaite Translations of the Pentateuch from the Tenth to the Eleventh Centuries C.E.* (Leiden: Brill, 1997). She has published extensively on medieval Judeo-Arabic Bible exegesis and its Islamic context. During 2012–2018 she served as one of the principal researchers of the internationally-led *Biblia Arabica: The Bible in Arabic among Jews, Christians and Muslims* research project.

James T. Robinson, MPhil (Oxford University), MA, PhD (Harvard University), is Caroline E. Haskell Professor of the History of Judaism, Islamic Studies, and the History of Religions at the Divinity School, University of Chicago. His research focuses on medieval Jewish intellectual history, philosophy, and biblical exegesis in the Islamic world and Christian Europe; and the interactions between the Jewish, Islamic, and Christian intellectual traditions. He has published extensively on medieval Jewish philosophy and exegesis, including *Samuel Ibn Tibbon's Commentary on Ecclesiastes, The Book of the Soul of Man* (Tübingen: Mohr Siebeck, 2007); *The Cultures of Maimonideanism: New Approaches to the History of Jewish Thought* (Leiden: Brill, 2009); *Asceticism, Eschatology, Opposition to Philosophy: The Arabic Translation and Commentary of Salmon b. Yeroham on Qohelet (Ecclesiastes): A Critical Edition of the Judaeo-Arabic Text with Annotated English Translation and Introduction* (Leiden: Brill, 2012); and *The Arabic Translation and Commentary of Yefet b. 'Eli the Karaite on the Book of Joshua* (Leiden: Brill, 2014).

Arik Sadan is senior lecturer in Shalem College, Jerusalem, and also teaches at the Hebrew University of Jerusalem. He holds a BA in linguistics and Arabic language and literature (2001) and an MA (2004) and PhD (2010) in Arabic language and literature, all from the Hebrew University of Jerusalem. His research fields are Arabic grammatical thought; Arab grammarians; Judeo-Arabic, classical, modern, and colloquial Arabic linguistics; manuscripts in Arabic grammar; and other fields. Two of the three books he published so far are *The Subjunctive Mood in Arabic Grammatical Thought* (Leiden: Brill, 2012), which is a revised English version of his PhD dissertation; and, together with Almog Kasher, *A Critical Edition of the Grammatical Treatise Mīzān al-ʿarabiyya by Ibn al-ʾAnbārī* (d. 577/1181) (Wiesbaden: Harrassowitz, 2018).

Ilana Sasson Z"L (11 June 1954–15 October 2017) received her BSc in Biology (1977) and MSc in Genetics (1980) from the Hebrew University of Jerusalem. After her marriage to Professor Ron Prywes (of Columbia University), she moved to the United States, where she first devoted herself to raising their two sons, Noam and Eden, and also became much involved in the Jewish community. She began studying biblical and ancient Near Eastern literature at Columbia University (1998) and received her MPhil (2007) and PhD (2010) in Bible and ancient Semitic languages from the Jewish Theological Seminary, New York. She was a postdoctoral fellow at Tel Aviv University, Department of Biblical Studies (2012–2014), and affiliated with the *Biblia Arabica* research project until 2017. She taught courses on comparative religions, Hebrew Bible, and women in the Bible at Sacred Heart University in Fairfield, CT; and a Judeo-Arabic course at the Jewish Theological Seminary. Her doctoral dissertation, on Yefet ben ʿEli's commentary on the book of Proverbs, was ultimately expanded into an annotated critical edition with a detailed introduction in her book *The Arabic Translation and Commentary of Yefet b. ʿEli on the Book of Proverbs. Volume 1: Edition and Introduction* (Leiden: Brill, 2016). She also prepared substantial parts of the second volume, containing the English translation of this work, which she entrusted with Meira Polliack and Michael G. Wechsler, for the purpose of its future completion and publication.

David Sklare (PhD, Harvard University, 1992) served as director of the Center for the Study of Judeo-Arabic Culture and Literature of the Ben-Zvi Institute in Israel (1995–2015) and is currently a research associate at the Hebrew University of Jerusalem. His fields of interest are Judeo-Arabic literature and culture, including legal literature and theory, theology, philosophy, biblical exegesis, and Jewish-Muslim polemics. His publications include *Samuel ben Hofni Gaon and His Cultural World: Texts and Studies* (Leiden: Brill, 1996); "Hayya Rosh ha-Yeshivah and the Karaites" [Hebrew], in *Yad Moshe: Studies in the History of the Jews in Islamic Countries in Memory of Moshe Gil*, ed. Yoram Erder, Elinoar Bareket, and Meira Polliack, Te'uda 29 (Tel Aviv: Tel Aviv University Press, 2018), 87–103; and "Mu'tazilî Trends in Jewish Theology–A Brief Survey," *Islâmî Ilimler Dergisi* [*Journal of Islamic Sciences*] 24 (2017): 145–78.

Yosef Yuval Tobi is professor emeritus of medieval Hebrew poetry at the University of Haifa and former head of the Department of Hebrew Literature therein. Currently he heads the Department of Hebrew Language and Literature in Al-Qasemi Academy, Baqa al-Gharbiyya (Israel). His main scholarly fields are the spiritual, cultural, and historical affinities between Judaism and Islam during the Middle Ages and modern time. His main recent publications include *The Jews of Yemen under the Shade of Islam since Its Advent to Nowadays* [Hebrew], Misgav Yerushalayim, The Hebrew University (Jerusalem: Abraham Stern Press, 2018); editor of the journal *Ben 'Ever la-'Arav: Contacts between Arabic Literature and Jewish Literature in the Middle Ages and Modern Times* 9 (2017); and (coauthored with his wife Tzivia Tobi), *Judeo-Arabic Literature in Tunisia, 1850–1950* (Detroit: Wayne State University Press, 2014).

Ronny Vollandt (PhD, University of Cambridge, 2011) is professor of Judaic studies at the Ludwig-Maximilians-Universität, Munich. His research focuses on the Arabic versions of the Bible and biblical exegesis in the Arabic language, and more broadly on medieval Christian and Judeo-Arabic literature. Two recent publications are *Arabic Versions of the Pentateuch: A Comparative Study of Jewish, Christian, and Muslim Sources* (Leiden: Brill, 2015); and "The Status Quaestionis of Research on the Arabic Bible," in *Studies in Semitic Linguistics and Manuscripts: A Liber Discipulorum in Honour of Professor Geoffrey Khan*, ed. Judith Olszowy-Schlanger, Nadia Vidro, Ronny Vollandt, and Miriam Wagner (Uppsala: Acta Universitatis Upsaliensis, 2018), 242–67.

Michael G. Wechsler (PhD, University of Chicago, 2006) is professor of Bible at the Moody Bible Institute, Chicago. His current areas of interest include biblical exegesis, Near Eastern exegetical literature (Jewish and Christian), and the intercommunal interplay of ideas reflected in that literature. He is coeditor, with Meira Polliack (Tel Aviv University), of Brill's Karaite Texts and Studies series (2008–) and has published a variety of articles and books, including *The Book of Conviviality in Exile (Kitāb al-īnās bi-ʾl-jalwa): The Judaeo-Arabic Translation and Commentary of Saadia Gaon on the Book of Esther* (Leiden: Brill, 2015); and *Strangers in the Land: The Judaeo-Arabic Exegesis of Tanḥum ha-Yerushalmi on the Books of Ruth and Esther* (Jerusalem: Magnes, 2010).

Doron Yaʿakov is senior lecturer in Hebrew language at Herzog College and a lecturer in Hebrew language at the Hebrew University of Jerusalem. He served as scientific secretary at the Academy of the Hebrew Language in Jerusalem (2007–2015). He is currently involved in the Academy's Historical Dictionary Project, and he is academic supervisor of the collection of Jewish community traditions, founded by Prof. Shlomo Morag. He researches the ancient reading traditions of the Bible and rabbinic literature and the Hebrew language of medieval literature, focusing on traditions of Yemenite Jews in Hebrew, Aramaic, and Arabic. His PhD dissertation (Hebrew University of Jerusalem, 2012) was on the language traditions of the Jews of Southern Yemen. Among his recent publications are "The Relation between Maimonides and the Yemenite Tradition in Mishnaic Hebrew," in *Studies in Mishnaic Hebrew and Related Fields: Proceedings of the Yale Symposium on Mishnaic Hebrew, May 2014*, ed. Elitzur Bar-Asher Siegal and Aaron Koller (Jerusalem: Magnes, 2017), 396–409; and "Remarks on a Verbal Form in the Yemenite Tradition of Mishnaic Hebrew" [Hebrew], *Language Studies* 17–18 (2017): 337–46.

Marzena Zawanowska is assistant professor at the Faculty of History, University of Warsaw, and Curator of Manuscripts in the Emanuel Ringelblum Jewish Historical Institute of Warsaw. Her dissertation (PhD, University of Warsaw in cooperation with Tel Aviv University, 2008) was devoted to Yefet ben Eli's commentary on the Abraham cycle in Genesis and was significantly expanded in her book *The Arabic Translation and Commentary of Yefet ben ʿEli the Karaite on the Abraham Narratives (Genesis 11:10–25:18)* (Leiden: Brill, 2012). Her research focuses on medieval Bible exegesis, Hebrew literature, and Jewish philosophy. She was head of a major publishing project of Chayyim Nachman Bialik's complete poetry oeuvre in bilingual Polish-Hebrew and Polish-Yiddish editions (Warsaw, 2012). Recent relevant publications are "Reading Divine Attributes into the Scriptural Text in Medieval Karaite Bible Translations," in *Senses of Scripture, Treasures of Tradition: The Bible in Arabic among Jews, Christians and Muslims*, ed. Miriam Lindgren Hjälm (Leiden: Brill, 2017), 153–81; "The Bible Read through the Prism of Theology: The Rendering of Explicit Anthropomorphisms in the Medieval Karaite Tradition of Arabic Bible Translation," *JJTP* 24 (2016): 1–66; and "'Where the Plain Meaning Is Obscure or Unacceptable …': The Treatment of Implicit Anthropomorphisms in the Medieval Karaite Tradition of Arabic Bible Translation," *EJJS* 10 (2016): 1–49.

Arye Zoref is postdoctoral fellow at the Department of Biblical Studies, Tel Aviv University. His PhD dissertation was on "Tanchum ha-Yerushalmi's Commentary on Canticles: Studies in Its Tendencies and Its Jewish, Sufi-Islamic and Christian Sources, with a Critical Edition" (Hebrew University of Jerusalem, 2013). He specializes in Judeo-Arabic literature and interreligious discussions. Selected recent publications include "The Influence of Syriac Bible Commentaries on Judeo-Arabic Commentaries: Demonstrated by Several Studies from the Book of Genesis," *Studies in Christian-Jewish Relations* 11 (2016): 1–16; and "The Journeys for God in Sufi and Judeo-Arabic Literature," *PaRDeS: Zeitschrift der Vereinigung für Jüdische Stadiën* 22 (2016): 109–19.

Index of Ancient Sources

Index of Judeo-Arabic Commentators

LIVECELL

LIVECELL

A NOVEL BY

ERIC GREEN

Printed in the United States of America

Copyright © 2011 by Eric Green

Library of Congress Control Number: 2011938312

ISBN 9781937644031 (pbk)
ISBN 9781937644048 (eBook)

Cover design by Amanda Green, all art by Eric Green
Interior design by Janet Robbins, North Wind Design
& Production, www.nwdpbooks.com

Cadent Publishing
9 Gleason Street
Thomaston, ME 04861
www.cadentpublishing.com

For Amanda

AUTHOR'S NOTE

The first draft of *LiveCell* was begun in 2001 and finished about a year later. I continued to work on the novel intermittently over the next ten years, but the world I initially envisioned was locked into the early part of the new century, and I decided to leave it that way. I felt that keeping the earlier time period lends the book an interesting mix of retro and new. Hopefully readers will find the blend intriguing as well.

ACKNOWLEDGMENTS

Over the ten years I worked on *LiveCell*, the book made some friends. These mean a great deal to a writer because it's not always easy to maintain faith in a project over extended periods of time. Therefore I wish to thank the following people: Ben Taylor, Ben Duffy who never flagged for an instant, Margo and Jay Davis, Sterling Watson who early on showed me three major mistakes I was making with my prose, Susan Kelly, Rick Russo, Carl Hays, Pete Llanso who mailed me the largest hunk of coal anyone has ever received for Christmas, Nina Young, R. D. Eno, Kathy McCarty Thornberry, Jake MacKenzie who is vaguely related to Mary, Elisabeth Green to whom I so wish I could hand the paperback, Barbara Verbrick, Helen H. Clark whose enthusiasm generated quite a following for the novel in an assisted living residence in upstate NY, Buck Sawyer, Marsea Ryan, Tris Coburn, Jon Eaton, Kathrin Seitz, Lionel Tardif, and my wife Amanda who transformed my writing, tenderly, patiently, and edited the book so many times she probably knows the thing better than I do. Without her efforts there wouldn't be a *LiveCell*.

That a life will be spent gaining inches,

When this distance is read in miles.

—Kelly Harris

PROLOGUE

Occasionally something that changes our world is discovered quietly, without reporters or cameras, without showing up on the Internet or in a newspaper, without being witnessed. The invention is even missed by the usual corporate radar and remains hidden for some time because the inventor isn't willing to share it. The inventor wants complete control.

Jay Chevalier glanced around the room though no one else was working this late. His lone companions were the mechanical churn of one bioreactor, an intermittently flickering fluorescent tube, and a cat with a missing ear, a feral stray that normally would never have been allowed into the lab. Outside was only the humid chaos of the city, Wilmington, Delaware, a place that had remained alien for Jay during the eight years he'd been employed at DuPont. When the bioreactor coasted to a halt, he meticulously transferred the inert gray cell structure to the holding vessel and set the timer for the final incubation interval. There was nothing to do now but wait.

He settled on a metal chair. "Inside," he said to the cat, his voice hollow in the cavernous room, the animal arching its back in response. "I'm always inside. Working." He reached down to stroke the neglected fur, praying that the fundamentals of his life might soon change.

His eyes focused uncertainly on the impenetrable blackness beyond the glass-brick windows, the future, but his mind slid into the past and the purity of the wilderness. Hadn't he always sought the refuge of the

wilderness when his life became desperate or untenable? Even with the precise warmth of the controlled laboratory air, for an instant he shivered as if from cold. Ten years ago he'd left New York City. Ten years ago his life had reached a nadir of emptiness and despair. And what had he done? Though he hadn't realized it at the time, this instinct to return to Maine was what had been so crucial to everything that followed.

Like a wing-damaged carrier pigeon, he had homed north, not knowing where else to go. With a bitter wind coming off the Hudson River, he stood in the breakdown lane next to the highway, the collar of his jacket turned up, one sore hand stuffed into a pocket, the other with thumb out, a duffel bag at his feet. Dried bodies of dead leaves leapt in a spiral when trucks roared past. He felt about like those leaves; he had been close to so few people in his life, and he'd lost yet another.

A week before, his boxing trainer Pete had grabbed his arm and slumped to the gym floor. Jay had sat in the hospital waiting room for nine hours, but his friend never regained consciousness. At the age of twenty-six, Jay had begun to understand that we rarely get second chances; he'd never gotten the opportunity to tell Pete how he felt about him, or even to thank him for his kindness. After the funeral, he'd returned to the gym for one last workout and unloaded his frustration into the rough weave of the heavy bag.

Jay had earned a living for two years in New York as a sparring partner and by working in the gym, but with Pete gone that was over. Pete's brother, in a moment of sentiment at the funeral, had asked Jay to stay, but he couldn't—they'd never gotten along that well anyway. So he'd left the city and hitchhiked home to northern Maine.

The driver of a massive logging truck dropped him off between distant towns before turning farther north into the great tracts of forest owned by the paper mills, the grumble of diesel stacks gradually absorbed by the stillness of the woods. It had been so many years since he'd heard real quiet. Mount Katahdin was above the deep reach of pine, its remembered shape like a forgotten lullaby, its bald crown already beginning to luminesce with snow. He drew the icy air into his lungs as if it were an antidote for despair. Finally toward late afternoon a Canadian motorist stopped and took him the last stretch.

Using up the little money he'd saved from New York, he ate in the same diner every day, the narrow restaurant with its hand-painted *Cafe* and rough wooden booths so different from the rampant electricity, mas-

sive steel and mirrored glass of the city. One of the waitresses was friendly—lank black hair, bad skin, middle-aged, always cheerful. He felt awkward around someone so content, and at first he couldn't talk to her, but one afternoon when the diner was empty, she brought over a mug of coffee.

"Okay if I sit down?" she said.

He nodded.

"You're not from around here, are you?"

"I was born here."

"Madawaska?" She examined his face. "What's your name?"

"Jay Chevalier."

She shook her head. "I don't know any Chevaliers, and I know just about everyone around here."

"I grew up in the boys' home."

"That explains it," she said.

On his arrival into town he'd located the building first thing, pathetic in the early dusk, all the windows smashed, his childhood home so obviously abandoned. He'd sat on the curb until dark, his mind stumbling through the past, a slide show run amok.

"I was sent there as a kid when my mom died."

"And your dad?"

"He wasn't from around here. I never knew him."

"So why'd you come back then?"

He thought a moment. "I think I came to see my mother's grave."

That had taken him some time to locate. She was buried in a section of Saint David's Cemetery across the road from the Catholic church. Of course it made sense that her legal name was on the cross, but it took him a couple hours of roaming between the headstones to remember that. The weather had caught a last caress of warmth, the sky incongruously blue compared to the somberness of his mood. When he finally found her grave, he kneeled on the thick mat of damp leaves and scrubbed his fingers over the small iron cross, loosening the rusty scale until some of the black metal showed through, her name and 1934–1966. He cleared the leaves from around the grave as well, but when he stood, the isolated patch of grass looked so lonely and separate that he brushed them all back.

"What was her name?" the waitress said.

"What?"

"Your mother's name, her family's name."

"Oh . . . Madeline Katliin."

"She was Micmac?"

He nodded and her eyes lit.

It turned out the waitress was Micmac as well. She offered him a place to sleep, but he refused though he'd been stretching out on burlap sacks in a deserted potato barn. He had this fear that if he gave in to any human kindness, he might shatter. Two days later she told him his grandfather might still be alive.

"There's a cabin in the woods," she said, "just under the border by the Beaulieu. Be real careful approaching is what I heard."

Within the hour Jay walked north out of Madawaska toward the cabin. The sky had a dull sheen like raw metal, and he could already imagine the coming snow. As he made his way through dense second-growth woods, he realized how much better he felt in the wilderness even though he had some trouble staying on the vague dirt path.

The cabin was chained to a white pine to keep it from toppling, wood smoke a drifting smudge from a stovepipe chimney. An old man in a wool shirt and knitted cap was outside splitting firewood in the cleared yard. He was strong; Jay could see that by the way he swung the maul in a hard clean arc. As Jay approached, his heart started to pound. The man looked up from his work, and Jay searched the face under the dirty orange tuque for resemblance.

"What do you want?" the man said.

"I'm Jay Chevalier."

"So?"

"I'm Madeline's kid."

The old man didn't say a word, just leaned the maul against the pile of split birch and went into his cabin. Jay waited ten minutes, maybe longer, stood there as it began to snow, the woods fading to a chalky monochrome, disappointment choking him. He was about to walk off when a head stuck out of the cabin door and said, "Are you coming in or not?"

There was a wood stove with chinks in the iron drum revealing hot ember, a dry sink with a galvanized pail of river water next to it, a yellow enameled breakfast table and two rusted chrome chairs with most of the rubber feet missing, a half-loft with a steep ladder and a mattress. A Pyrex pot steamed on the table. The old man poured the hot liquid into two thick mugs, gestured for Jay to take a seat, picked up a mug and blew across it to cool the tea, a bitter concoction of dried Labrador leaves and spruce shavings as it turned out.

Then he said, "Are you angry with me?"

The question surprised Jay. "Why would I be angry?"

"You should not be, but you might be. If you did not understand." He examined Jay for what seemed like a couple minutes. "I did not take you in after Madeline died. I knew they could take better care of you, those state people. I liked to drink then and was not willing to raise a young kid. I never let them know I existed. I'm glad you are not angry with me."

And so Jay moved in with his grandfather. They extended the loft with scrap lumber so there would be an extra place to sleep. He slept on blankets, telling his grandfather he was too young to need a mattress. It was luxury after the potato barn. From the first day, they seemed to get along as if they'd always lived together, Jay willing to fit himself to his grandfather's routine.

One day his grandfather said, "I named you. When you were being born I was waiting outside in the yard, letting the women be. A large blue jay flew on a birch limb, looked at me for a long time, said nothing. They usually come in pairs, but this one was alone. Just so you know."

His grandfather had not stopped drinking. Not in the least. He made his own liquor using a wood-fired pot still, and though hesitant at first, he began to teach Jay his secrets. The moonshine itself was straight forward, mostly a potato mash with some corn thrown in. What made it remarkable was the inclusion of *Amanita muscaria* mushrooms.

"Most people will tell you they are poisonous," he said, holding Jay for a moment with his deadpan stare. "They are, but I know a few things."

The mushrooms grew in a certain part of the woods among the birches near the river. Jay and his grandfather harvested them as the veil ruptured and the gills began to open. They carefully cleaned the cap of nubs, trimmed the root, and hung the mushrooms upside down from the cabin's rafters with bits of string. Once dried, the fungus was simmered in river water for hours, creating a rust-colored tea, his grandfather very attentive as he stirred the pot. To this cold tea they added measured amounts of raw moonshine, along with an essence boiled from black birch buds and fresh shoots of red spruce; herbs—dock, saxifrage, bettony, and wild sage; and roots of young borage and elecampane. The mixture sat for several months in white-oak barrels and once ready was strained into clean quart beer bottles and stoppered with whittled-down wine corks. It was an ancient recipe and one that his grandfather adhered to like an

alchemist. He was precise about this one aspect of his life and nothing else.

They made enough extra liquor to sell to a few customers so they could buy shells for the .30-30, his grandfather's Bull Durham or Bugler, and the few things they couldn't shoot, trap, forage or grow—salt, flour, sugar, and yeast. They drank almost every evening. Did nothing but hunt, fish the Lower Beaulieu, garden some, distill, chop wood, and drink. It was quite a change for Jay who had never drunk anything stronger than a little wine. After all the years he'd spent studying and working indoors, or training as a boxer, he was finally back in the wilderness, and as he continued to live with his grandfather, something began to gather inside him.

There was an old sweat lodge down near the river. It hadn't been used in many years, and Jay asked his grandfather about it, wanted to rebuild it. His grandfather resisted. "Why mess with the past? Let it rest where it died. Most Micmacs are Catholic now anyway. They made sure of that. Never understood why Madeline gave in. I guess after she got sick, she weakened. It is difficult to be strong when you are sick." But after a few weeks of Jay's prodding, they dug a new fire pit, cleared and deepened the earthen hollow inside the lodge, cut young alder and black ash and repaired the canvas canopy, spread cedar boughs inside. They started to take sweats.

They heated rocks in the pit. Jay shoveled the glowing stone into the hole in the center of the lodge. Both of them inside, the door flap pulled closed, they poured water on the rocks and added sweetgrass. His grandfather told him, "What matters in the sweat is the heat of the rocks. Let the rock bring the smell of the earth into your lungs. Let the steam bring you out through your pores. Know you are nothing. Then you can start to become something. You can bring questions into the sweat. Many times they are answered."

Jay had a question.

One night he took a long sweat alone. When he finally crawled from the heat, he stretched out against the cold ground, steam pouring off him as if his skin were smoldering. He could feel the entire enormous mass of the earth against his naked back, the curve of the planet as it moved through space. He stared up at the sky, at the infinite heavens, got that incredible understanding of distance, where everything is so close and so far away in the same instant. A meteor cut an acid-green pathway across the sky, the woods springing alive in a flare of radiance. And then there was a voice inside his mind. At first he did his utmost

to ignore it, to shut it out with the boundaries of logic, but soon he knew it was real, and though it didn't speak in clear words, he sensed exactly what it was saying.

The next morning he packed his duffel bag. He explained his decision to his grandfather and thanked him. The old man listened, barely nodding his head, his face expressionless. Jay waited. He gave it a few minutes, then simply shook the callused hand one last time and walked off down the dirt path after two years in the woods.

The timer signaled the end of the final incubation interval, and Jay's thoughts returned to the laboratory, the cat having long since asked to rejoin the outside world. As dawn began to blue the glass-brick windows, he noticed something he'd never seen before or ever expected to see. The structure in the holding vessel seemed to be pulsing, not from movement but with shifting color. A prismatic rainbow beauty not unlike the wet skin of a trout just pulled from the Beaulieu. He almost turned, half-expecting to see his grandfather standing behind him. Instead he reached down and touched the cell aggregate with his fingertips.

What happened next changed his life and many lives forever, like a fresh channel of rushing water broken free from a river that can never be held back again.

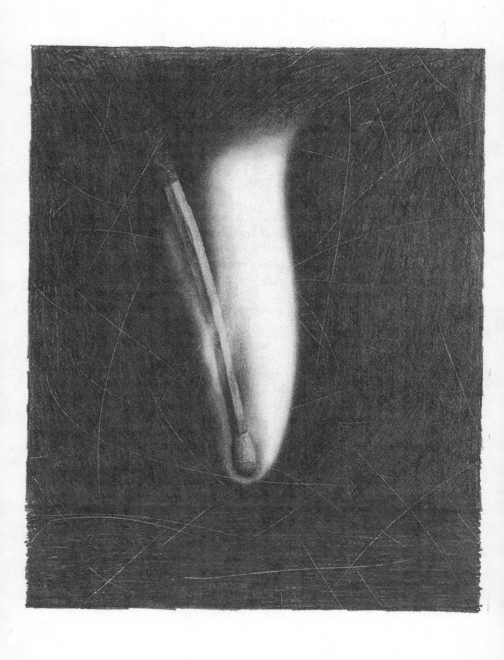

TWO YEARS LATER

ONE

Mary hated her new car. As she waited in a crawling line of traffic over the Bay Bridge, her mind veered into the same annoying quicksand that had mired it for a week—anemic engine, buzzing speakers, and worse, a wheel vibration so evil the car needed an exorcism. Even the horn had laryngitis. What was she doing in this twenty-year-old Fiesta? The car had become a symbol, and she couldn't seem to stop obsessing about it or transferring her other frustrated emotions to the pathetic thing.

Part of her resentment came from the loss of her Porsche convertible. Unable to manage the payments, she'd been forced to hand over the keys at the dealership, the same salesman who'd always beamed kilowatts suddenly treating her with bored condescension. Forget him, she told herself, but she wanted to be back in the silver Porsche, rocketing up the steep streets around San Francisco, through morning fog, that gentle moisture misting her face from over the windshield, then sunlight warming her skin. Instead she hobbled along in the lime-green Fiesta, feeling robbed.

Two weeks ago she'd asked her boss what he planned to do with the company, and though everyone in management had been strung along for months, he'd refused to tell her anything. This morning, in less than an hour, he was finally going to reveal their future, and she was worried. At a stop sign onto Market Street, she waited again, tapping her fingernails impatiently, the van in front of her eventually pulling forward. But then,

inexplicably, it stopped and its backup lights flared. She pounded her horn to alert the driver, got only the feeble bleat, and the van rammed her car with a sickening crunch, her forehead almost hitting the steering wheel. At least the Fiesta didn't have an airbag.

For a moment she couldn't seem to move, her heart pounding, the whole miserable month cloaking her like a rotting cape. "Great," she muttered. "What next?" She got out her cell phone, pressed 9-1-1 and gave the dispatcher the location of the accident through a jumble of poor reception. Then she rang her office.

"Clicksave, marketing your internet future, may I help you?"

"Deirdre, it's Mary MacKensie." She attempted to control her voice. "Something unexpected's come up, and I'm going to be late. If anyone asks, tell them I'll be there by nine for the meeting." She wasn't about to explain. The other execs had already made enough stupid jokes about the Fiesta. "That thing's not a lemon, it's a lime." Well, they'd be delighted; now it was juiced.

The van's door opened, and the driver stepped out and walked toward her. He placed his hands on top of her car and leaned in—eyes unfocused, his skin like wet saltines, spinnaker-sized sweat suit bulging in unpleasant places. "What the fuck's wrong with you, tailing me like that?"

His breath pushed her back like a filthy hand. For the moment she was too startled to be scared. "Bitch, you hear me?"

Suddenly he slammed his massive fist down on the Fiesta's roof. Mary jumped and edged farther away, wondering if she should roll up the window and lock the door or try to get out the other side. She was maneuvering toward the passenger door when she heard a voice behind her.

"Wasn't enough to smash up the car, you gotta pound in the roof?"

Mary turned. Just behind her, a small guy in a cowboy hat was leaning against a muddy pickup. Not a dude, she decided, this one looked like the real thing, like a worker, though these days with bankers and brokers wearing five-hundred-dollar tattered ranch outfits, who knew. Whatever he was, she was relieved he was there. He spit a stream of chew onto the street and walked up to her, ignoring the big guy.

"You okay?" he said.

She nodded.

"That was quite a bump. Your neck all right?"

"Whaddaya think *you*'re doing?" It was the big guy again.

The cowboy looked up at him. "Haven't you caused enough trouble?" His voice was easy, melodious, but there was something hard under-

neath. "What the hell is it with you anyway?" He spit next to his boot. "Vet can't get your medication right?"

"This ain't none of your business, dickwad."

The cowboy continued to stand calmly—if anything, he seemed amused—as the other guy glared and tightened his fists. Then a police car arrived, siren strangling into silence, and the big guy headed back to his van. The cop said something to him, and soon the ball hitch complained with a metallic groan as it released the Fiesta's radiator, the car bleeding its paint color, antifreeze still spreading, a rivulet nosing into the gutter.

Mary curbed the Fiesta, and the cowboy moved his truck. Although hesitant to admit it, she was mildly intrigued by him. He had an unpretentious confidence though he seemed younger than her by at least a few years, probably mid-twenties. She was reminded of farm kids back home, something she realized she missed after being in the city for so long.

The cop arrived to collect her license and registration. The cowboy stepped forward.

"Sir, name is Hank McKeen from Likely. That's up near Alturas." He extended his hand. "Modoc County," he added as if it would make a difference.

The cop glanced at the hand. "What do you want?"

"Saw the whole thing. Saw the smash, him pound her roof. All of it." His grin spread.

"If I need to, I'll talk to you in a minute." He walked off to his cruiser.

Mary opened the door and went to examine the front of the Fiesta. It wasn't terminal, despite the sprung radiator, but it wasn't drivable. She glanced at her watch—she had to get to the office.

"You know about cars?"

There he was again. "Some," she said. "My mother taught me."

"Name's Hank, Hank McKeen." He started to lift his hand, hesitated. "Well, actually . . . it's Garland McKeen, but I'm known as Hank. 'Cause of Hank Williams, the singer. Senior, not the son. Big favorite of mine. You need to get somewhere? Got the truck right there." He pointed to his pickup.

She continued to study him. "Okay," she said. "I really need a ride to work." She was willing to take the gamble that he was safe even if he wasn't clean because at this point she couldn't take a chance at finding a cab. She circled the puddle to the cruiser. The cop told her that from the

antifreeze trail he could tell what had happened, asked if she wanted to file a charge of criminal mischief over the damaged roof. She shook her head; the meeting was the only thing that mattered right now. The officer handed her the accident report and wished her a better day. She took it as a positive sign.

Hank McKeen maneuvered his pickup along Market Street and couldn't think of a thing to say. Nobody had ever done this to him before; he always had something to say. While she'd talked with the cop, he'd frantically tidied up his truck. He'd found the cleanest towel and spread it over the dirty vinyl of the bench seat, wiping the seat back with another rag. Everything else: assorted tools and rope, stained styrofoam coffee cups, a Rainier pounder with the bag twisted around the neck, and his spit can, he tossed into the bed. He dug his chew out with his finger and rinsed his mouth with some water left in his canteen. He even wet back his hair in the rearview mirror before remounting his hat. Maybe Pa had a point after all—the right woman could civilize you.

She broke the silence: "Garland, what are you doing in San Francisco?"

"Cousin's in the hospital. Cancer. Came down to see her."

"Is she going to be okay?"

"Nope."

"I'm sorry," she said.

He glanced over at her for a second; his eyes returned to the road. Goddang, there was a mad herd of traffic in this city. He didn't want to depress her about his cousin. He also didn't tell her how much she reminded him of Patsy—way she used to look when she was living at the ranch. Same smooth whitish skin with the round face, same mouth just like you'd draw one, and those stern sun-bleached eyes seeing everything, but with the glitter of wildness.

He'd been with Patsy all night in that stuffy room, trying not to reflect in his face what he saw on the bed. Every time he truly focused on her it hurt him, but there was nothing he could do. Something in him wanted to bundle her up and get her out of there, take her up to the ranch, make her a warm spot on the porch glider with blankets where she could look out over the fields and feel the late-summer breeze. But he knew it wouldn't do a lick of good. Patsy had asked to hear some stories during their vigil, begging him to stay with her, and he tried desperately to recall some of their best times together from when they were teenagers

and later on before she left. He got her laughing a few times, at least a little. As the hospital room slowly sharpened with daylight, she'd been able to fall asleep. He got out of his chair and kissed her forehead. Then he took the stairs down two at a time—unable to wait for the elevators—and located his truck. He'd been so upset he'd needed to drive around, and that's when he'd pulled up behind the Fiesta.

Reaching up now and feeling his chin, he wished again that he'd shaved. He kept his left hand positioned on the steering wheel so she wouldn't notice the missing joints of his index finger, and for the first time in his life he worried about the appearance of his hands. Their size and strength were good for ranching, but he wasn't so sure how a woman like Mary would feel about them.

"Buy ya breakfast?" he said after contemplating the appropriateness of the question.

"No thank you, Garland. I just need to get to the office. You'll want to turn left here."

"Okay." A pause. "What's in the box?"

"A pool cue."

"What for?"

"To shoot pool with?"

Ouch. Was he only going to say dumb things? First all that stuff about Hank Williams, now this. She'd also called him Garland, again. This wasn't going so good. "I mean—you the player?"

She told him she was. He was about to ask more when she said, "Anywhere up here on the right is fine." As they drew up to the office building he panicked. What should he say to her? Can I see you again? Ask for her phone number? Yet when he ground to a stop in front of the big glass doors, all he managed was a grin. She thanked him, hopped down from his truck, and with a walk that broke his heart, pool cue on one side, briefcase on the other, she entered the building and was gone.

Hank sat and stared at the closed doors for maybe two or three minutes as if he half-expected her to return. Finding a pencil stub with some difficulty, and frustrating himself further by having to sharpen it with his Buck knife, he wrote down the address of the Harcourt Building. Behind him someone started honking. He almost shot the cabby the finger, but instead looked back and waved. Then he eased the Chevy forward, back toward the hospital and his sick cousin.

TWO

Mary greeted Manuel at the front desk—that ever-present whiff of cologne or hair oil—and walked across the polished marble to the elevators. Once again she tried to ignore the huge tangle of modern sculpture in the lobby. It wasn't easy. She stood waiting for an elevator but changed her mind and returned to Manuel. Handing him the cue case, she asked if he would look after it until that evening. No one at the office knew about her other life, and she wanted to avoid explanations. Manuel confirmed her hunch.

"Oh my, a musical instrument?"

"Kind of. Let's hope it plays sweetly tonight."

"Sweetness is good, dear."

As she approached the elevators a second time, a bell dinged, doors whispered open, and she entered without breaking stride. Maybe she was back on track? Pressing the button for the fifth floor, she glanced at her watch. Eleven minutes until Wendell's declaration.

She figured Wendell Alden III had never experienced a bad moment. Until recently. He'd come to San Francisco from Connecticut and started Clicksave.com a little over six years ago. The company provided internet marketing, and with the strong financial backing he'd brought with him from the East, Clicksave had grown rapidly. As he liked to tell everyone, he'd outperformed his peers since prep school. His education and business decisions were guided by his father, an investment banker, and

everything had gone exactly according to the family's plan. She had to admit, he possessed the height, the build, and the self-assurance of the archetype. If he lacked anything, maybe it was heart. But what use had Boy Wonder, as she privately called him, with such a thing? This wasn't the *Wizard of Oz*. About a year ago, an Alden family friend at Goldman Sachs had overseen the release of Clicksave's initial public stock offering, and the IPO had performed miraculously. The Aldens were heavily invested, and everything had run perfectly.

Until now.

Mary had a theory about what destroyed Clicksave.com. When the IPO was launched, the stock price doubled the first day, then leveled, fluctuating but generally climbing. After months of this pattern, it surged unexpectedly. While everyone at the office celebrated, she researched online and found some revealing traces. She suspected their main competitor, Buynow.com, of purchasing large blocks of stock using surrogate investors to veil the transactions, then salting internet chat rooms with false prophesy about Clicksave's potential earnings. She told Wendell and a few coworkers, but they dismissed her fears, said she worried too much, but if she hadn't been obligated by her lockup agreement, she would have sold all her stock. While everyone else in the office was still grinning, Buynow yanked the stopper, selling all their Clicksave holdings. The same henchmen peppered the Internet with predictions of doom. Clicksave's stock plummeted.

With his family holding sixty percent of the company, Wendell stepped in and bought back shares, but the other stockholders panicked. Wendell insisted publicly, "Clicksave is a sound company. It's growing daily. The stock will rebound." It didn't. In the past weeks, a rumor that Buynow would be investigated by the Securities and Exchange Commission circulated around the office, and her theory suddenly had credibility.

On the fifth floor of the Harcourt Building, a narrow room next to the elaborate grid of work cubicles was designated as a lounge. A few molting sofas, a pink wicker rocker, two kinds of coffee makers, a small fridge, a standing lamp with a dented shade, sea-green walls with some Edward Hopper prints—Mary considered the room a subtle, or not so subtle, dig at Wendell, who had sent an office memo requiring that the door always be kept closed. The rest of the floor, and those above and below it, reflected Wendell's taste: off-white walls, chromed chairs, pickled hardwood floors, brushed metal desks, recessed fluorescent ceiling

lighting, and *the* paintings. She stepped into the lounge and closed the door.

"Why are you so late?" It was Duncan; otherwise the lounge was empty. Duncan hated to sit in the boardroom waiting for meetings to start. "You want some coffee?"

She nodded. His espresso with foamed milk balanced out some of his other traits. Duncan had trouble meeting her eyes and blushed if she caught him staring at her breasts, made comments behind her back about Vermont dairy farms not just producing great milk. Obsessed with the fact that she'd grown up on a farm, he repeatedly questioned her about it, as if being a farm girl might mean something unusual sexually. "Do cows do it the same as horses?" "Cows don't *do* it, Duncan." She knew he didn't have a social life, but she wanted him to stop hoping for one with her. Then one night she dreamed she was milking him, squatting naked on a three-legged stool, liquid ringing the metal pail beneath her hands until she awoke horrified. After that—blessedly—he'd stayed out of her subconscious.

Duncan was the only one who'd taken her Buynow subterfuge theory seriously, but when Wendell had asked his opinion, he hadn't spoken up. He was far too shrewd for that, realizing no one ever wanted the truth of failure when they could have the illusion of success. He'd never be shot for being the messenger. Yet if Clicksave was restructured, he might be let go. With his quirky personality, unsavory humor, and sloppy appearance, he probably wouldn't impress new owners.

"So, any brilliant insights?" said Duncan. "What's your old dowsing rod say?"

"I think you should consider a new career . . . dairy farming. You could milk cows every day." She regretted the comment immediately, and it triggered his self-conscious giggle, belly shaking uncontrollably. She noticed he'd trimmed his goatee and was wearing a new suit. Though the fabric was expensive, it still looked grabbed off the rack, reminding her of a kid dressed by a grandparent, and she felt a ripple of tenderness and pity. Did he buy the suit to impress new owners? Where had he gotten the money? Actually, he probably saved every dime he'd ever made; after all, he still lived with his mother in Santa Rosa. Mary wished again that she'd saved. No one in upper management had been paid in months, and she'd maxed out her cards. Wendell had begged them to "fight along with him" as he deferred their checks, promising he would make it right in the end. Today they should be paid their back wages, hopefully with a nice

bonus. She could finally pay off some of her debt. Otherwise she'd simply have to win the pool tournament tonight.

When Mary and Duncan walked into the boardroom, the other senior executives were already inside, most seated. She greeted a few and nodded to the others. Chet Simmons had his electronic notebook lined up exactly with the table edge, his glass of water exactly in front of that. Cliff Thompson looked like a cadaver, probably hung over, and who could blame him considering the stress they'd been living under. Nancy, the only other female, was as usual stationed next to Wendell's chair. She certainly didn't have on jeans. For the third time that morning, Mary questioned her decision to wear jeans to the office. She wanted them for the pool tournament—she played best in them, a superstition—but they'd bug the hell out of Wendell. Something had made her wear them anyway. To hell with Wendell's dress code.

The boardroom continued the bleached Clicksave look; it certainly had the worst paintings. To avoid them, she took a seat facing the picture windows, preferring the middle floors of other buildings and the pinch of bay in the distance. The conference table, a massive slab of oiled cherry beginning to crack at one of its glue joints, floated on spindly legs in the center of the room. She rather liked it—at least it was raw wood. By now, everyone had taken one of the chrome and black leatherette chairs. Duncan, who read Wendell's habits like a weathervane, always took his seat moments before he appeared, a door between Wendell's office and the boardroom reserved for this.

First thing she noticed about Wendell was that his hair, as on every Monday, sported the same expensive haircut, and though it looked great, it annoyed her. She couldn't remember the last time she'd had her hair done. He greeted everyone solemnly, allowing Nancy his secret little glance even today, and opened the meeting.

After the usual formalities, he clasped his hands together and said, "This is not a pleasant day for me. You have all worked very, very, hard. All of you. And I thank you for that. Clicksave is a viable concept. I know that. You know that. It's a great company, and what has happened, should not have happened. But it did. And if there had been any other way out of this, I would have taken it, believe me. I am not happy with the way things have turned out. Know that. We all deserved better." He scanned their faces. "I have sold my family's sixty percent of the company."

He took a long sip of water.

"My suspicion is that Buynow is the purchaser, though the on-paper

name is LiveCell. My lawyers have been unable to ascertain the identity of this *Live-Cell* or what they do. LiveCell doesn't seem to exist. Therefore, it must be Buynow using another name. We certainly know how dirty they can be."

Something is not right, she thought. Something false in his face.

Wendell reached up and touched the knot of his tie. "All financial responsibility will be absorbed by the new owners."

A grumble ricocheted around the table. Feeling as if she'd been run over, not merely backed into, she realized he wasn't going to pay their back salaries or leave them with any kind of severance. Her devalued stock was to be the sole legacy of four years of constant work. Duncan looked wilted. Chet Simmons, exhumed. Cliff Thompson and Randy Dyer had been with Wendell from the beginning; they looked outraged. Jack Wingham and Wendell golfed together at The Presidio every weekend. Jack looked ready to kill. Even Nancy's cover-girl serenity was majorly disturbed. No one was on the inside. Everyone had gotten screwed.

But before anyone could confront Wendell, the boardroom door opened, and a stranger walked in. The pursuing receptionist, Deirdre, a big surfer girl, said, "Sir! You can't like, *go* in there. *Sir!* . . . I'm so sorry, Mr. Alden, he just won't listen."

Wendell seemed relieved to have their attention diverted, and Mary wondered if the disturbance was a set up.

In a faded blue T-shirt, jeans, worn loafers, his skin pallid and pocked along the temples, the stranger contrasted with the tanned and suited group around the table. Though of ordinary height, his body was proportioned like a gymnast's, his arms and shoulders the kind that would normally have a few tattoos. Mary's impression was that he'd just gotten out of jail and might be dangerous. She couldn't stop staring at him, though something self-protective in her wanted to turn away. As if he sensed this, his eyes found hers. And she—Mary of the cool gray gaze—looked down.

Wendell was by now in front of the stranger. Cliff Thompson and Jack Wingham were on their feet.

"What're you doing in my boardroom?" said Wendell.

The stranger's voice was calm and straightforward, without emotion. "Are you sure it's your boardroom?"

Wendell hesitated but only for an instant. "I want you out of here immediately."

The stranger didn't move.

Mary glanced at the others. Cliff said, "Who is that guy?" Duncan, still seated, shrugged.

"Did you hear me? I want you out of here," said Wendell again.

"Mr. Alden, it's you who're leaving."

"Should I, like, go get security?" said Deirdre halfheartedly.

The stranger answered though she'd been talking to Wendell. "There's no need. Mr. Alden will go quietly."

"Who the hell are you?" said Wendell, his face slack.

"Jay Chevalier." He pronounced it Cheval-*yer*, something guttural yet sensual in his tone. Likely a New England voice, thought Mary, though she couldn't quite place it.

"And that's supposed to mean something to me?"

"It's not your company any more."

"How the hell do you know that?"

"Because I own half."

"*You?*"

The interest in Jay Chevalier magnified. Even the lanky Deirdre straightened her posture. Some of the executives moved toward the new owner, wanting to be introduced. Others got up from the table.

"You're going to believe him?" said Wendell, his face contorted. "Look at him."

"Mr. Chevalier, I'm Cliff, Cliff Thompson, head of investor relations. This is . . ." and he started to introduce the others who clustered around Jay.

Mary remained seated. She was still reeling from her financial ruin. At least now there was some hope, but there was something about Jay Chevalier that bothered her. She realized she was attracted to him and resented it. He'd looked at her as if he could see right into her, as if he knew her secrets. She didn't want to introduce herself.

Wendell pushed into the group. "What are you people doing? Cliff, come on . . . You don't know who this guy is. He could be some nut."

Jay Chevalier faced him again. "Mr. Alden, I purchased your half of Clicksave. Now, please, if you would," and he gestured toward the door. "I'm sorry, but there's nothing more for you to do here." He grasped him by the arm the way an orderly would assist someone confused or hurt, and he guided him firmly out the boardroom door. From there, Wendell Alden seemed to exit their lives.

Mary figured it wasn't completely his fault. After all, she'd worked

four years for him, and knew he was spoiled, but not a total bastard. She had a strange intuition that there was more to the failure of Clicksave than anyone realized, even Wendell. Why hadn't the father stepped in and helped? With his power and money he probably could have, yet he'd let his son and the company fail. She'd met the man once and he'd truly frightened her. Unlike Wendell, he was of common stature and ordinary handsomeness, scrupulously polite, generally bland in manner, almost bored. But under that unassuming manner, she had sensed evil. At the time she'd dispelled the reaction, but now she wondered. Wendell had even told her once: failure wasn't tolerated in his family. Maybe the father had wanted to prove something to someone, perhaps Wendell's mother? It made her almost feel sorry for Wendell, even if she never wanted to see him again.

When Jay Chevalier returned, everyone in the room quieted. He sat down in Wendell's chair and fanned out his hands, his palms against the tabletop. Then he closed his eyes. Mary questioned what he was doing. This was her new boss? With his eyes closed, just sitting there, his fingers splayed in that odd arrangement as if he were trying to read some divine message through the wood. She could finally study his face: the uneven brow, slightly crooked nose, jaw like a fist. Graceful hands with long fingers. She imagined those hands touching her, caressing her, and was startled by the intensity of the thought. She glanced at Nancy to see if she was affected, but she only seemed moody and unsure; maybe the new boss hadn't appropriately acknowledged her charms yet. Mary wondered if the stunning blue of his eyes was from colored contacts. It was an eye color she'd never seen before, bordering on violet, but she doubted he'd wear tinted lenses.

Finally, Duncan, "Mr. Chevalier? May I ask you a few questions, sir?" Jay shook his head.

Duncan was sweating. Mary could almost hear his mind grinding, trying to work this all out. He was also probably lamenting his new suit as a wasted investment. Her jeans had been the right choice after all.

The silence started ticking again.

This time, Nancy, "Mr. Chevalier,"—in her sweetest voice—"maybe you'd like a hot coffee, or a mineral water, or something . . . I could get it for you." He glanced abruptly at her, frowned slightly, and shook his head. She continued to watch him, as if expecting more of a reaction, but he ignored her. Soon a chair sighed, high heels snapped on hardwood,

and the door closed. She must've had second thoughts and went to find Wendell, decided Mary. After all, he was still very rich.

Jay's eyes closed again, and the silent waiting folded in like a fog of claustrophobia. Everyone was looking at each other, raising eyebrows, mouthing comments. Then—

"Your lives are about to change. More than you ever thought possible. That is if you stay with me."

He opened his eyes and they were slightly wet. She hadn't considered that. He must have a tender side, or at least an emotional one.

He continued, "If you stay with me, you will also make a great deal of money. But after a while that won't matter to you. Other things will become more important. What you must ask yourselves right now is: Do I want to stay? Does it feel right? Rely on your intuition. If you stay, I will hope for a high level of commitment from each of you. I want you to decide in the next ten minutes."

Some of the execs started to complain. He raised his hand. "I will pay your back salaries, stay or not. I also offer anyone who wants to leave a fifty-thousand-dollar settlement for doing so. However, your stock in the company will transfer to me with the acceptance of this offer. Please discuss it among yourselves." He glanced pointedly at Mary and walked out of the room.

As everyone else started to discuss the situation, she wondered why he'd looked at her like that again, as if he knew her or knew something intimate about her. She had never experienced a look like his before. There was something magnetically compelling about him, and she couldn't decide if it was just sexual attractiveness or something more. It scared her.

Then her mind flickered to her car problem. She decided to dump the Fiesta and get a rental for the time being. Should she still enter the pool tournament?

Duncan cut into her thoughts: "Mary . . . What are you going to do?"

The group stopped talking.

"Stay. Why wouldn't I?"

This triggered more discussion. Who was he? Was he crazy? Did it matter? What did he plan for the company? Should they grab the fifty thousand and run? Their stock options weren't worth anything now anyway. Did you see him handle Wendell?

"One good thing," said Cliff Thompson, "at least we won't have to worry about a dress code." This raised a few grins.

"Hey, Duncan," said Mary. "Intuitive move with the new suit by the way. Armani?" Everyone started laughing. That was when Jay Chevalier returned.

And he smiled; it softened his face, gave it an odd innocence. He walks into a room of strangers laughing, and he smiles, she thought. Not a nervous smile, not a questioning smile, doesn't look down at himself to see if he's untucked or unzipped, just seems pleased they're laughing. This time he carried a briefcase. One of those old-fashioned leather brief-cases with the double handles and the accordion effect on the ends, the corners tipped in brass, the flanks worn to a polish like the skin of a fallen chestnut. He sat back down, set the briefcase beside him, looked up and made the circuit of their faces. "Well . . . what are your decisions?"

Duncan spoke first. "Mr. Chevalier, you haven't explained what you expect out of us, or told us if our salaries will remain the same, or defined our job descriptions. Everyone, I'm sure, is very relieved that you've res-cued the company and are willing to pay us to date, but this entire morn-ing has been a bit confusing."

"Linden—"

"Duncan."

"Sorry. Duncan. I want you to make your decision intuitively. With-out facts. Now, if you would."

Duncan looked away, at Mary, Cliff, back at Jay. He was sweating heavily, and his hesitation bugged her. Why didn't he take off his suit jacket if he was so warm? His boss was in a T-shirt.

"Duncan?" said Jay again.

"You mean make my decision right now?"

Jay nodded.

"For how long? Do we have to sign a contract?"

Jay waited.

"Okay. *Okay*. I'll stay."

"Thank you." Turning to Myron Banks, next in line, "Well?"

"I'll take the money. I'd need to know more to make an informed decision."

"Then please leave."

"Right *now*?"

"Anyone who is leaving should go now."

"When will we be paid?" said Myron.

"I'll need three weeks to a month. Again, anyone not staying, please leave."

Everyone churned with unanswered questions, and they hesitated, but eventually four of the executives stood. The four, including Myron Banks and Jack Wingham, waited by their chairs. Someone asked a question. No response from Jay. Eventually there was nothing for them to do but walk out.

Jay said, "You know very little about me, yet you have stayed. Your motives in staying are important to me. Everything about you is important to me. But allow me to tell you a little about myself.

"I am not a businessman and I have never run a company before. I'm an inventor." He reached down and unclasped his briefcase. From it he drew a dull gray object approximately the size of an enlarged deck of playing cards and placed it in front of him. The surface began to shimmer, reminding Mary of an early season brook trout lifted from a stream. Then it went dull again. She looked up, wondering if a fluorescent tube was flickering.

Jay picked up the object and whacked it on the edge of the table. A startled cry escaped from Chet Simmons who'd barely moved since he'd aligned his electronic notebook. Now his eyes jumped between Jay and the object. An obvious dent was in the gray surface. As it oscillated between dull and glowing, she had the peculiar notion that it was upset from being whacked. The dent gradually filled in and the object recovered its former round-edged shape.

"Is it some kind of new packing foam?" said Cliff Thompson, sounding unimpressed.

"Patience," said Jay.

Reaching into the briefcase again, he extracted a small black box fitted with two thin polished-metal prongs. He attached this to the gray object by pressing the prongs imprecisely into one end, the gray material yielding and aligning itself slowly. From the pulsing glow against his hands, she realized that the iridescence was inherent.

"Cliff? Do you have an answering machine?" said Jay. Cliff nodded. "Your phone number please?" He gave the ten digits. Jay whispered *okay* to the object and handed it to Cliff. "Place it against your ear." He did, looking foolishly around at the group, clowning a little. Mary worried for the first time that Jay might actually be a nut.

Cliff leapt to his feet and dropped the object as if it had shocked his hand.

"Jesus Christ, how in the hell did you do that?"

"Do what?"

"*How* did you do that trick?"

"It's not a trick."

"What happened?" said Duncan.

Cliff glared at the object as if it were possessed.

"Come on, Cliff—*tell*," said Duncan again.

"I heard my outgoing message through that *thing*."

"Maybe there's a tape inside?"

"No. You don't understand, you don't understand at all." He shook his head back and forth, looking ill. "I heard it inside my head. Like a thought. Like thoughts. Like there was a speaker, or voice, inside my brain somewhere. Damn it, *what* is going on here?"

"It's a new telephone," said Jay.

"A *telephone*?"

"Yes. I've created a new kind of telephone. Allow me to show you." He reached over and took the object.

"Mary, what's your cell phone number?" She gave it to him. Had she told him her name? She didn't think so. His attention was on her now, the length of table between them. "Please turn on your cell phone," he said. She took it out of her briefcase and did. He whispered *okay* to the gray object in his hand and her phone started to ring. She answered it, feeling silly. He started talking to her through the gently pulsing object, explaining about his invention, his voice through her cell phone even more sensual than in person. Those incredible eyes on her eyes. His look pouring into her. She clutched her phone, feeling very self-conscious. Her heartbeat and breathing quickened. She began to sense a warmth between her thighs. She wished her legs weren't crossed, yet she was incapable of moving them, wished that her jeans weren't pressing her just there. He kept staring at her, talking about something. She couldn't understand his words, couldn't turn away. It was almost like being hypnotized but wasn't. It was something else. She had never felt anything like this, this level of pure attraction. And then she felt something more, the confusion and fear that she might orgasm.

Mary rose blindly from her chair almost knocking it over and half-ran from the boardroom. She didn't know what else to do.

THREE

The day finally over, the lounge empty, Mary was settled on one of the tattered sofas when she opened her briefcase and glanced at the new phone. Toward the end of the afternoon, Jay had given one to each of the remaining executives. Hers rested against the red lining, dull gray now, inert. It seemed to luminesce only when touched. She ignored it for the moment and picked up a folded letter. Though she'd read it four times since she received it last week, she read it again:

Cage Dairy Farm, Monkton, Vermont
*August 7, 200_*

Dear Mary,

Your letter upset me deeply because I hate to hear you're not happy and that you're lonely. Not that we can be fulfilled all the time, but having someone to share things with helps. Life doesn't work out that great for most people, and it's wicked hard to accept this. We have all these dreams when we're young, and few of them ever make it. Of course some of us barely even have the dreams. As you requested, I've kept everything in your letter confidential from your parents.

When I moved into the old trailer, before you were born, Patty had just died and I was desperately alone. Boy do I know about loneliness! What you don't know is that the reason your father brought me back to Vermont with him is he was worried I wouldn't make it. He was right. When I told you I had been a pool hustler in New York, I told you that because I didn't want to be a bad example. The truth is that I was a junkie. I shot pool to make money for dope. Patty helped me get straight—not that anyone can ever really do that—and we went to Wisconsin together after she got sick. Now you realize why your mother never liked me so much, and worried about our friendship. I don't blame her. She can't understand someone who would throw his life away like that. Of course, she's never done junk. (Just kidding.) I know I should have told you sooner, I just couldn't. I pray that you will be able to accept this part of my past.

You say you don't have a life except work, and I know how you long ago decided to save yourself for that one perfect guy. You wanted to share yourself with only one man, one love, forever. It's a noble idea but a rougher reality. But then I wonder, if you gave up your dreams, if you would be pleased with that. I remember you learning pool and how if you missed a shot, you would keep practicing the same shot over and over until you had it cold. Your determination never to be weak in the same way twice always impressed me. If only life were as fair as a level pool table. If only gravity and time were what decided winners—

She stopped reading for a moment and skipped to the end.

The dogs are fine, but I'm sure Pilgrim misses you terribly. Will you visit soon? We all miss you. I want to see that massé in action.

My love to you,

Kelly

P. S. I had a visit a few months ago from someone I knew in New York. A secretive fellow, but brilliant.

She read the postscript twice, refolded the letter, placed it back in her briefcase. Then she thought of Jay—his face, his voice, his hands.

After running to the bathroom and sitting in a stall until she calmed down, she'd patted her face with cold water, touched up her mascara.

She'd never been so affected by anyone in her life, and it made her uncertain and nervous. She didn't like the feeling. On reentering the boardroom, she'd apologized to Jay for leaving, explaining she'd not felt well. With a concerned look, he said it was a trying day for everyone. Glancing around at the table of faces, she figured no one had noticed. Then they had all gotten down to work.

Some of the executives questioned Jay about the new phone: How did it work? What comprised its unusual structure? Who had previously manufactured it? He said, "I don't think the phones' secrets are decipherable." He remained deadpan, not giving the group anything further. She decided he wasn't very forthcoming, but why should he be? Then he said, "All I can tell you is I discovered the cell aggregate while working in the forgotten laboratory for DuPont. Now, there is more pressing business to address first.

"We're to become manufacturer, marketer, and retailer of the phone. We need an ad campaign and press releases, phone-marketing and public-relations strategies, packaging and shipping. The pronged black boxes need to be farmed out. They send radio waves, carry the battery and charging system, allowing our phones compatibility with all conventional systems. Our phone must be licensed and agreements must be established for the use of existing telecommunication pathways. Your job descriptions and salaries must be settled, and a new board of directors chosen. One of my stipulations for purchase was that I could appoint a new board. With my sixty-percent ownership, the stock holders' approval should be a formality."

He may not have had any experience in running a company, but he seemed to know exactly what he wanted and how to achieve it. He asked her to design a new web site, which he wanted compelling and informative in a completely fresh way. My God, she thought, he only wants the future.

Mary looked at her watch: if she was going to this tournament she'd better get moving. For a moment she considered skipping it, but her fifty-dollar greens fee was mailed in, and she was too wound up to be stuck at home. Nine-ball might provide a good distraction. Besides, she hated to ask Jay for an advance and reveal her finances. The thousand-dollar first prize, if she won, would be heaven-sent.

Finally she reached for the new phone. So much was riding on it that she'd been nervous to examine it before now. As she picked it up, the surface started to pulse with that eerie phosphorescence. The texture surprised her—something like skin, though cool to the touch, more firm and

almost but not molding itself to her hand, so sensual and appealing that she wanted to keep holding it. She told it the numbers of Manuel's desk phone, feeling slightly foolish. Said okay. Within a moment, Manuel's voice spoke inside her mind, just as Cliff had described it, saying he still had her instrument case, and for some reason she knew he'd looked at her cue. She asked him to get her a cab and ended the call, giggling with excitement. And Jay had been so modest about it: "I've never owned a company, I'm only an inventor." My God, they were going to make a fortune, an absolute fortune. Nokia, Motorola, and Samsung, look out. Gathering her things, she headed for the elevator. From the cab she'd reserve a rental at the airport for later on. Right now she was headed directly to Jake's poolroom. She needed a sandwich and a cold beer.

When she collected her cue from Manuel, he said with a conspiratorial wink, "Have a lovely *concert*, dear."

Outside, the sun gilded the tops of the tallest buildings, the sky a vibrating cerulean, the air with that faint brininess of the sea. She walked toward the cab, noticing a police cruiser across the street. Oh Christ, it couldn't be. She recognized the truck—the worst-looking one in San Francisco. She was tempted to hop quickly into the cab, but with a sigh she asked the cabby to please wait and headed across the street.

"Garland, what's going on?"

His smile spread as he sat calmly on the bench seat.

"Do you know this man?" said the officer standing by Garland. The other cop was still in the cruiser, talking on the radio.

"Yes," she said, reluctantly. "What's he done?"

"He refuses to move, and he's about to get a citation. Or we may haul him in."

"Officer, could I speak to you for a minute? In private, please." She used her eyes. A curt nod. They walked to the tailgate. He scowled down at her. She introduced herself. "And you are?"

"Sergeant Boronski."

"Thanks, Sergeant, for talking with me. Garland's cousin is—"

"Who's Garland?"

She pointed.

"He said his name is Hank."

"Hank's his nickname. He's from Likely—"

"Believe me, we know. Likely, near Alturas. Moduck County. He told us about six damn times."

She smiled, hoping to lighten him up, wondering why she was doing

this. "Garland's cousin is dying of cancer. He's been with her in the hospital for days. He might not be himself."

"That's no excuse for ignoring a police officer."

"No. No, of course not. But I'm sure I can get him to move."

"Believe me—*we* can get him to move."

They were interrupted by a blast from the cabby's horn, the driver signaling impatiently. The cop frowned and went back to the front of the pickup. She followed.

"Hank, are you going to move now?" he said.

"Yep. Sure will."

"You might get away with this kind of behavior up there in Likely, but not here, Hank. Okay?" Garland nodded. "You behave yourself while you're in San Francisco."

"Yes, sir, sure will."

Now the sergeant turned to her. "Good luck," he said, smiling.

She suddenly realized the cop had been toying with her, had been amused by Garland all along, had probably heard about that morning and expected her to get into his truck. Oh, what the hell, after all this, Garland could at least provide another ride. She waved off the taxi, the cabby muttering and shaking his head, tires squawking.

When she circled around the hood, Garland leapt across the bench seat to open the door for her. She settled onto the tan vinyl, quite a bit cleaner than that morning. Garland was sporting a new shirt, his boots shined, and a shave.

"Garland—"

"Wish you'd call me Hank."

"I like Garland."

"You do?"

She nodded.

"Well, all right then." The grin. Getting the truck rolling. Waving to the cops. Was he always this cheerful?

"What are you doing here, anyway?" she said.

"Waiting."

"*Waiting?*"

"Thought ya might need a lift."

"How long have you been waiting?"

"Since three."

"Three? That's two and a half hours."

"Didn't wanna miss ya. Thought I mighta though. Guy inside your

building kept getting up and peering out at me. He musta called the cops."

"That was probably Manuel."

"The guy with the big hair, looks like a fag."

Mary turned to stare at him, decided to let it go. "*Garland*, you shouldn't be waiting for people you don't know."

"Can't help it."

His cheeks went red through the tan. *Oh, great*. She told him to turn right on 16th Street and head over to Dolores.

"How's your cousin?"

"Maybe just some better. She et something." A silence. "You going that pool tourney?"

"Jake's Billiards, on Van Ness. If you wouldn't mind dropping me off?"

"Anything. Just ask." A pause, and he blurted out, "I know a lot about ranching. If you wanna know something."

"So you know a lot about ranching?" she said.

"Yes, ma'am. Been ranching since I had memory. Pa too. Mean, Pa ranched from when he was a kid. My family's always ranched, came over from Wyoming." He swallowed nervously. "We run three hundred head of Black Angus."

"The Cage farm milks thirty head of Jersey and Holstein."

He slowed the truck for a red light, stopped, people walking in front of the hood.

"*You?* That your last name?"

"I grew up on a dairy farm. Monkton, Vermont. That's near Lake Champlain. Addison County."

The loud hoot made her jump, along with a few pedestrians. "God-dang! Just knew it. I just knew it." He pounded the steering wheel, the horn going off.

"*Garland*, for Christsakes, calm down."

"Sorry. Can't help it."

They drove together through the soft evening light, Garland asking questions, telling a couple of stories, angling his hat back, his confidence seeming to grow each time he made her laugh. Mary knew she shouldn't encourage him but got swept along. He told her about playing shortstop as a teenager and how a stray bull had wandered into the game. The bull was about to charge the first baseman when Garland beaned it with a hard throw right between the eyes, and the animal had bellowed angrily but

loped away. He told her about how happy his cousin had been at the ranch.

They pulled up outside the pool hall. Thanking him for the ride, she jumped down, slammed the rusty door, and he drove off. She was finally rid of him, yet for the first time wasn't so sure she wanted to be.

She climbed the dark stairwell over the Chinese dry cleaner, the chemical smell assaulting her until she reached the entrance, then the familiar rhythm of colliding pool balls, the din of voices, jukebox thump, the nervous energy of everyone practicing for the event. Jake's was an older billiard room, in business long before the pool craze glossed the game and hundreds of thousands of dollars funded new designer pool palaces. Jake's was no-frills. It offered twenty-two level regulation tables with worn cloth, good sandwiches and cold beer, and held the best regional tournaments in the area. Mary favored Jake's as a nod to Kelly Harris who had grown up in such places. In many ways she would have preferred the luxurious trappings of the new rooms, the designer carpet instead of crumbling linoleum, incandescent lighting instead of fluorescent, better air, but she remained loyal to Jake's and Kelly Harris. Besides, she liked the bartender, Sammy, and the owner, Nick Brignolia, even if he was a bit dour.

At the bar, she asked Sammy for a Weinhard's draft and a crabmeat roll and passed him her briefcase to stash. She imagined the wrong person stealing it and finding the phone, but knew it was safe with Sammy. As she stared blankly at the enormous oak beer cooler with all its fogged glass doors, he set down her draft, the frozen base inching fractionally along the Formica. Now that she was finally at rest, she was suddenly exhausted; it had been quite a day.

"Not seen you 'round much," he said.

"Work, too much work."

"How that Porsche runnin'? Nice you take me out that day. I still think on that." He slid her a saltshaker.

"Gone." She shook a few grains into her beer, a habit copied from her dad.

Sammy looked concerned. "Accident?"

"No." She took a long sip. "Repo."

"Damn, girl, this recession gettin' *ugly*—everybody juss losing and losing. I shoulda listen to you. Or stuck with my horses. Odds be a hell of a lot better, and you get something pretty to view while they takin' your money. Crab be right out." Sammy turned, his huge shoulders mov-

ing under a vintage mint-green bowling shirt, though she knew he did-n't bowl. But he always wore the shirts—he must collect them. Against his skin color the bright green looked great, a tone that would've only made her appear sickly.

She was on her second beer and halfway through her crab roll when someone took the stool beside her. She couldn't believe it.

"Took a bit to find parking. Goddang, lot of people live down here." He signaled Sammy, who sauntered over, looked curiously at the two of them.

"He with you?" he asked her.

"I suppose so," she said. "We met during a car accident." She introduced them.

"Hey there, Sammy,"—Garland standing up, extending his hand—"Hank McKeen from Likely, that's up near Alturas, Mo—"

"Garland," she said, "you don't have to announce to everyone you meet *exactly* where you're from, they already know, believe me."

He looked confused, then his grin spread. He shook hands with Sammy. "Worked with a black guy on our ranch one year, great big fella. Real good worker. Looked like you. Lemay Jefferson. Maybe you know him?"

"*Garland*," she said. "Why don't you have a beer or something?"

Sammy took the whole thing in, seemed barely to keep from crack-ing up.

Garland ordered the same as Mary. "Glad you're not drinking that micro stuff. Tried one the other day. Just asked for a draft and that's what they give me. I tell you what, I gave it right back to 'em."

Sammy placed a beer in front of Garland. He drained it in one pull, thumped the glass down on the Formica. "This city stuff makes me thirsty. Again, Mary too."

"Not for me." She took out her wallet.

"Mary . . ." he said, "I got it."

"What're you saying?"

"I'm paying. Goes without saying."

"I can't let you do that."

"Just let me. Look, I know I ain't no good at all this kinda stuff, but let me just pay supper. *Please*."

What was she getting herself into? She would have to have a talk with Garland, though now wasn't the moment. What she needed now was some table time.

Armed with a plastic tray of balls, she walked toward table fourteen as the fluorescent light flickered on above it. Endlessly coached by Kelly Harris that a smooth and consistent stroke was the foundation of the game, she always began a practice session with table-length straight shots. Her forearm hung straight down from the elbow, moving like a pendulum, till the whole arm followed through. She was surprised to be in stroke. Maybe days like this were good for her game?

As she practiced, Nick Brignolia walked over. He wore his uniform: shiny black wing tips, pressed black slacks, starched white shirt with the top button closed. It made him look like a stocky Sicilian waiter. He watched her shooting long shots off the rail for a few minutes before speaking.

"You know what I nickname you after that shot in the semi-final last month?" His voice was gruff. "Mary Massé."

"You saw it?"

"Saw it? Course I saw it. What's wrong with you, *saw it*? You know I saw it." He was already getting angry. Nick was always getting pissed off about something.

"I still lost in the final."

"Mary." He paused, peering at her through his thick glasses, the heavy black frames contrasting with his papery skin. "What do I keep telling you? *Safety*. You gotta play safe. You, you shoot at anything, so what happen, you miss. Safety, you get the table back. But you won't listen to Nick."

"I just love making the crazy ones."

"Make them when you not play for money. Money, you gotta play smart. I'm telling you, you got the nerves, the heart. That's what it takes. All in the head." Nick tapped his white hair with his index finger. "And the stroke. But you, you make that massé, but you make Nick mad." And he walked off.

All around her women were practicing, the clicks and taps of varied shots ringing in the big room, the jukebox still thumping. She glanced over at the bar; Garland had Sammy laughing. She sensed that he was taking his cousin's illness very hard, yet outwardly he still managed to be so cheerful, so positive. He seemed to accept things as they were and go on from there. Maybe that was the secret? She sighted down the row of support columns that bisected the room, the same two-tone as the wainscoting and the walls, a dingy green with a cream above, and wondered if Nick's North End room in Boston had been painted in the same com-

bination. She would have to ask him, but you could never tell what would make him mad. Most questions about his past in Boston upset him. Even her cue irritated him. "What you need all that inlay for? That don't make a stick play better. And that fancy box. You waste your money, Mary." And as if he'd heard her thoughts, there he was ringing the bell signaling the start of the tournament.

She drew Karen Valdez as her opponent for the first round and won the coin toss. Mary shattered the rack, holing the three ball and the seven. Break patterns, like most things in nature, are never the same, each with its own quirky perfection. She examined the lie of the seven remaining balls as she rubbed her cue tip with the edge of a chalk cube. As the balls lay, she couldn't quite *see* the one. She considered calling a *push-out* or playing a safety. Instead, checking quickly to see if Nick was watching, she lifted the butt of her cue so that the whole stick was at a forty-five degree angle to the cloth; then she stroked in a downward motion onto the top of the cue ball. It curved in a gentle arc around the six and pocketed the one, Karen Valdez tapping her cue on the linoleum in recognition of the shot. "Another massé for you, Nick," she said under her breath. "Maybe I am Mary Massé." She ran out the remaining balls. As the nine ball fell into the pocket, she heard a hoot. Actually, everyone in the entire poolroom heard a hoot. He stood by the bar, draft in hand, mouthing Sorry, and she had to smile. He gave her a thumbs up and walked over.

"You didn't miss," he said in a whisper. She was waiting for Karen to rack the balls.

"Isn't that the idea?"—though secretly pleased.

"And that curving thing was frigging unbelievable."

"Massé shot. The guy who invented the leather tip, Mingaud, discovered the shot while in prison because there was so little room in his cell. The more you lift the butt of your cue, the more the ball will curve. I love them, but they're inconsistent."

"Something special to see. You mind me watching from here?"

"Are you going to hoot every time I win?"

He blushed again. "Couldn't help it. Never seen them all run out like that."

"It happens a lot around here. It's stringing the runs together that's tough. The best I've run is a four pack, but only once during a tournament."

"Four pack?"

"Four in a row."

"You ran out four games in a row? . . . No misses?"

She nodded and walked over to check the tightness of Karen's rack. A loose rack could lose a match. Another Kelly Harris admonition.

The match with Karen went to Mary, Garland only letting out a chirp when she dropped the last nine ball into the pocket. As she played out the set, Jay kept intruding into her thoughts. Each time she waited for her opponent to rack, he was there again. Only when she was shooting did her thoughts of him recede.

Late now, a settled quiet blanketed the poolroom. A crowd of beaten players and stragglers watched from the shadows, slumped in chairs or leaning on nearby tables, all the other table lights turned off, the one rectangle of chalky green everyone's focus; Sammy was out from behind the bar, the kitchen long closed, the jukebox mute. There was an intimacy to the moment, a closeness that a group of people can encounter when they are all concentrating on the same thing, sharing the same momentary obsession.

Mary was in the finals with Laura Sedgewick, who, as she insisted on telling everyone, had played snooker in England for two years. Tall and blonde and snobbish Laura Sedgewick. Mary had wanted to crush her quickly and collect her money, yet after sixteen games they were both *on the hill*. Mary had missed a few crazy ones and let Laura back in, Nick frowning at her from the duskiness at the edge of the audience. She just wished she wasn't so tired.

As fate would have it, the final game hinged on her decision between a safety shot and a nearly impossible ninety-degree cut down the rail, the bank shot blocked. She didn't want to find Nick's eyes. She did see Garland smiling confidently at her, looking certain she couldn't miss, no matter the difficulty. If she fired the cue ball with full left English into the cushion just behind the two, the cue could kick off the bank at enough of an angle to clip the ball down the rail and into the pocket. About to attempt this shot, she inadvertently caught Nick's expression.

She stood back up. Looking the table over again, she played a perfect safety, delicately touching the two and trapping the cue ball behind the seven. Nick smiled. At least for Nick it was a smile. No one else would have noticed, but she did.

Laura rose from her stool and addressed the table. For her even to touch the two was unlikely, and if she missed, Mary would have ball in

hand and a likely win—the one large. Laura, her arrogance finally looking ruffled, stared at the lie of balls. She was stuck. *Snookered.* Her only
chance was a three-rail hit, but with all the other balls on the table in the
way, the shot had slim odds. She had to try it. Laura stroked smoothly
and the cue ball bounded off one rail, then two, whispered by the eight
ball, cleared the six by a wish, off the final cushion to contact the two perfectly, running it down the rail and into the pocket. A unified shout from
the shadows. The crowd quieted and Laura, back to her cocky blonde self,
carefully ran out the remaining balls. Mary congratulated her with a firm
handshake.

As she was unscrewing her cue Garland walked up.

"You were great," he said.

"Thanks."

"Never seen no one play like you."

"As my dad says, God loves a trier."

Garland thought a moment. "I like that. *God loves a trier.* That is dang
good." Garland nodding his head, looking serious, then brightening.
"Hey, you hungry or thirsty or anything?"

"I just need a ride to the airport."

"You flying somewhere?"—sounding concerned.

"I've got a rental waiting."

"You don't need no rental. Drive you anywhere you wanna go."

"Just the airport. *Okay?*" She looked at him, hoping he would read
her expression. She was too exhausted for anything else.

When she collected her five hundred for second place from Nick, he
wouldn't meet her eyes. He handed her the envelope full of bills. As she
turned to leave—

"Mary."

She stopped.

"You play the right shot. You lose the match, but you play the right
shot. Over time you win. Believe me. No one beat the odds. You play the
right shot. I feel this."

She glanced down at him, studying him for a moment. "Thanks,
Nick. Thanks for caring about me."

The old pool player looked up at her, and if he'd ever smiled in the
last twenty years, now was that time.

FOUR

Friday morning she awoke before her alarm went off and lay there tired. Last night, that dream again. For months now, about every dozen days, the dream returned. It always ended with his head on her chest, Mary crying as she gently stroked his brow with her fingers. Now she believed *he* might be Jay Chevalier.

Her hand appeared out of the sheets, and she switched off the alarm, turned on the radio. ". . . stupid and contagious," she heard, "here we are now, entertain us," and the band exploded into electric fury. God, Nirvana had such a sense of dynamics—building tension by withholding. Such a simple concept, though like many simple things, they only seem simple after you understand them. But to think of them first, that's the difficult part, she thought, and got out of bed.

She walked into the kitchen naked, still a little sweaty from her night of dreams. Adhering to her workday ritual, she filled and switched on her coffee grinder, that irritating whine. She shut off the machine and lifted it to her nose, the reassuring aroma of French Roast beans. It seemed like the first casual thing she'd done in four days. She poured boiling water over the coffee and watched it drip for a moment, then walked to the window. Outside, as dawn began its slow focus, early-morning mist wreathed the few eucalyptus trees that bordered her un-mown yard. She gazed idly at the fog and shivered, her eyes no longer seeing anything.

Jay Chevalier had more energy than anyone she'd ever been around,

and if there'd been a clue on Monday what her week would be like, she would've forgone the pool tournament and headed to bed early. Entering the Harcourt Building on Tuesday morning—punctually and without incident—there was the smell of paint in the elevator. Jay had painters redoing the walls, each floor a different color. A soft rust on four where reception was, a gray-mauve surrounding the computer cubicles on five, and for the executive offices, a muted sage-green similar to the old lounge color, though to her eye a more refined hue. The lounge itself he left alone. The new colors, along with the removal of *the* paintings, transformed the place. It was now LiveCell.

At Tuesday morning's meeting, Jay insisted she head up the entire advertising department, though she argued for hiring an outside professional firm. From head web-designer to advertising manager seemed like too much of a jump. "We'll try it and see how it goes," he said. So she not only had this new web site to design, but ads to formulate: print, newspaper, radio, TV, bus cards; there were people to interview and hire, drawing from inside the firm if she could. She'd never had so much responsibility. On Wednesday, he handed her an envelope and said, "Get the Porsche back if you want." How had he known about her Porsche? But she didn't have time to think about leasing a new car. On Thursday she told him she wasn't sure she could handle the job. "I have faith in you, please have faith in me," was his reply. Not knowing quite what he meant, she went back to work.

Now on Friday morning, waiting in line for the Bay Bridge toll, she listened to the radio again. With her FasTrak renewed, the wait was brief this early—nice to have money again. Her rental car had clear speakers and an emphatic horn. As she scanned through different radio stations, she heard something, and her finger locked it in:

" . . . and in financial news today, the new firm LiveCell, which recently acquired Clicksave.com, says it has a new telephone that it's bringing to the market place. The new phone apparently works on a completely new technology, and allows for hand-held, static-free communication."—she recognized some of the copy, pleased that *new* was repeated four times—"I hear it utilizes paper cups and kite string but might lead to severe ear infections . . . and now stay tuned for your Bay Area forecast." The last line was slipped in by the announcer using a different tone of voice. A damn sarcastic tone.

On reaching the garage, she jerked the rental into her space and went directly to Jay's office, the only room painted a burnt orange. She wasn't

sure about the color. His door was open, it was always kept open, and there he sat behind a large thirties-style battered oak desk that he'd had hauled in. Sentimental, he explained it. She knocked on the doorframe.

"Jay?"

He looked up and waved her in.

"Did you hear the news on the radio? From the press release?" she said.

"Duncan called me. He's up early too."

"Jay, I did *not* write that copy. About the cups and string."

"Kind of funny," he said. "Mary, sit down. Don't look so worried."

She chose one of the mismatched chairs. Where had he unearthed all these relics? She had to admit she preferred them to Wendell's chrome and white world, but there must be something in-between. She looked at Jay, able to look him in the eyes now. As the days passed, she'd been too busy working to contemplate other kinds of thoughts. They were still there nonetheless.

"We can only expect this kind of thing," he said. "There will be ridicule; there will be controversy; there will be sabotage. To be expected. We have a new product and it must prove itself."

"Do you think the radio announcer ad-libbed, or did someone write that copy?"

"Does it matter?"

"Doesn't it?"

"Not to me."

She wasn't even sure now why it had bothered her, but on hearing it, she'd had a disquieting premonition.

"Are you okay?" he said.

She didn't answer.

"Do you need to take the day off?"

She shook her head.

"This evening, where would be a good place to get a drink?"

"You drink?" Somehow she didn't think he did.

"Sometimes wine."

"You want a wine bar?"

"Where do you go?"

"Usually Jake's. It's a poolroom. I don't think they have much wine."

"We'll go there then. Okay?"

"Jay, I don't know anything about you. I shouldn't tell you this, but Duncan has spent a few nights online trying to find out about you. He's

usually incredible at hacking information, but even he couldn't find much."

"What did he find?"

"You were born in Madawaska, Maine, in nineteen-sixty. You went to Harvard at seventeen, went from undergrad to finish your doctorate in biochemistry in a record seven years. Then you seem to have disappeared."

"And?"

"Is it so wrong to want to know something about your boss?"

"What do you want to know?" His eyes moved to the window. They appeared to focus on the one slice of blue bay between the buildings, or maybe she imagined it since that's where she usually looked. He leaned back in his chair and folded his arms across his T-shirt. He always wears blue, she thought, wondering if maybe he did have some vanity.

"You don't mind my asking?" she said. "I know I should get to work."

"Why did you come in so early?"

"Well, . . . I thought you might be here." *He knows.*

"So let's have our talk."

"You really don't mind?"

"What do you think?"

She searched him for a second. "I don't understand where all the money's coming from. Duncan couldn't find any indication that you're wealthy yourself. You don't act rich, but then it can be hard to tell. Duncan thought you must have financial backing from somewhere. Is that true?"

"I recently sold a patent to Swatch in Switzerland."

"One of the patents for the phone?"

"No. I didn't patent the phone."

"What? Why *not*?" His words brought her out of her chair. *Everything* rested on patents for the phone as far as she could tell.

"The phone's cell makeup is not its only secret."

"It isn't?" She stood there, stunned. "Then what is?"

He didn't answer.

"Whatever it is, it needs to be patented. All its innovations need to be patented. Believe me, otherwise it will be stolen and we'll be out of business. Someone will be making it overseas for half the price in no time. Jay, I can't believe this. We have to hire a patent attorney immediately."

"It's not possible. Please, sit down."

She found her chair again. "I can't help being upset. Patents for new inventions are imperative. You must know that."

He held her with his calm look and she quieted outwardly, but it lessened none of her uneasiness. How could he leave himself so unprotected? It was crazy, insane. There was that fear again.

He continued to study her. "You'll have to trust me."

She nodded and looked away, trying to calm herself. Her entire future, all her financial dreams, rested on LiveCell's success.

"Can you tell me about the Swiss patent?"

"I invented a new way to indicate time."

"And?" she said, using his technique.

For a moment he seemed to listen to the silence of the empty offices. Then, in an almost bored tone, "My watch utilizes colored light to indicate time. Three colored fiber-optic dots move in the same orbit at the perimeter of the watch face. Blue for the hour, red for the minutes, yellow for the seconds. It runs off of a single LED and has the advantage of being visible in all conditions, even under water. People with poor eyesight will be able to use the watch. It also keeps the center of the watch face free for other uses, such as digital readouts, or three-dimensional designs. As a clock, in a steeple for instance, time can be read from much farther away. It's also visually appealing—at least I think so—because as the dots of light pass each other the color blends for an instant. Kids could learn about mixing color from the watch. When all three primaries meet you see white light for that split second."

So simple when you understood, but to think of it first—

Every time she started to worry about him, he amazed her again. But the phones still needed patents; she didn't care what he thought.

"Other questions?" he said.

He always sensed when she was frustrated with him and gave her just enough. She nodded, and he continued.

"I was born to a single mom in northern Maine. She told me my father was French and Finnish. He was a *voyageur*, a trapper, one of the last of the breed. From the other side of the Saint Lawrence River, the north side. Though they didn't marry, she still took his name. My mom died when I was still fairly young, and I never knew him. I became a ward of the state, and as Duncan found out, got myself an education. Then I searched for meaning for a few years, changed course again and started working as a neurobiologist for DuPont in Delaware."

"The lost laboratory?"

"You remembered. What a place. A big thirties building with those ochre-colored bricks. You know the kind?" She nodded. "The entrance

was curved glass-brick shaped like a bell, rather appealing. I think the lab was basically a tax write-off for DuPont. They also used the publicity. We all worked exclusively for environmental causes, and in my case they'd employed a Micmac, probably filling some quota. All the neurobiologists and biochemists worked pretty much separately—they barely spoke to me—and all DuPont required was a progress report every six months. They were generous with equipment, and I liked the feeling of being forgotten, liked the old building though I didn't care for Wilmington."

He glanced away as if deciding something.

"I was originally convinced that the right combination of cells could feed on varied air impurities—or what the human body considers impurities—similar to how plants feed on carbon dioxide. Over the years it led me to experiment with a diversity of cells, but I always ran up against the same problem. I could support cell life, but the extraction of impurities was so minute as to be meaningless in cleaning the air. So I was forced to accept a new vision. I searched for combinations of cells that would replicate with unusual intensity, yet also be able to stabilize and maintain a specific solidity at a desired proportion. This I achieved."

He stopped talking for a moment, and Mary wondered if that was it.

"Then I made a breakthrough. No one had ever managed to reproduce mature brain cells. I found that certain cultured neuronal cells could be mutagenized to alter their genetic makeup by infecting them with a viral DNA. These mutant neurons once triggered by a variety of differentiation factors had the exceptional capacity to form unusually high numbers of axonal processes with similar electrophysiological properties to the human brain. They acted almost like a silicon chip. The trouble was that they were completely unstable. So I amalgamated these cells with other more stable aggregates, and added the cells that would support the matrix by absorption of impurities. Basically I combined the knowledge of all three kinds of cells I had worked with over the years. At first I thought I was on to a novel kind of computer biochip, vastly superior to silicon in storage capacity and speed. And then I made a discovery that startled me. Terrified me at the time." He pulled on his ear for a moment.

"I realized instantly that I wasn't willing to share the discovery with DuPont, or anyone for that matter. People who had not spoken to me in years sensed it, began nosing around, unnerving after being ignored for so long. I was suddenly not so lost. I quit. Disappeared so I could finish the work. Was fortunate to sell the watch patent, borrowed money from

a Swiss bank against future royalties to fund my project. Bought Click-save to market the phone, and here we are."

She sat for quite a while in silence, processing it all. He didn't inter-rupt her. Though she hadn't understood all his words, she still sensed what he meant, that he'd cloned the phones out of a mixture of cells, including brain cells. "Where did you get these, *cells*?" She hesitated to say *brain*.

"You mean the brain cells?" he said.

She nodded. Sometimes she felt he really could read her thoughts.

"Initially I worked with stem cells." He paused. "I discovered I needed fresh brain cells. I knew a surgeon at a nearby hospital, and I used my own." He watched her carefully. "It was only a limited series of very minute extractions, everything was reproduced from those. It was the extraction from my pineal gland that really changed things."

"You used your own brain cells to make the phones?"—knowing the answer but not wanting to believe it.

He nodded.

She didn't say anything for some moments. She couldn't.

"You okay?" he said.

"What was this discovery that you didn't want to share?" She was apprehensive, but too curious not to ask.

But he said, "Let's get to work now, okay? We have a lot to do," and stopped her with his look. Was he concerned that he'd revealed too much? Not that she thought it was too much. Maybe he's worried that I think it's strange? But it *is* strange!

"You won't tell me?" she said.

"No. Not yet. We have other things to concentrate on first."

She would have to be patient. She moved her mind reluctantly back to the morning's business. "So you don't want me to follow up on that?" He didn't understand her at first. "The radio press release?"

"Leave it, it's meaningless. Nothing at all to be worried about. Some-one goofing around. We have much better things to do."

Mary retreated to her office. For the first fifteen minutes or so she couldn't get to work. She still had so many questions: what did he do dur-ing those missing years? where did he live now? how did the phone work? what was the discovery he wouldn't share? why no patent? did DuPont know about the invention? would they sue? and why did he buy Clicksave?

She thought about him having his own cells extracted to seed the LiveCell phones, and it bothered her, even made her queasy. But maybe

it was like some things on the farm—they were strange until you got used to them. She could only hope. She imagined him working year after year in that forgotten laboratory by himself, carrying his worn leather briefcase past the glass brick every morning, making his discoveries, accepting his defeats, continuing on because he believed in himself, in his vision. He had followed his intuitions and decided to have his own brain cells extracted. She kept coming back to that. Could having certain brain cells removed affect a person, change him? What if you removed the wrong cells? And this was the man she was *so* attracted to? With part of his brain missing?

Her coworkers started to arrive, and her attention was required for advertising LiveCell phones, not worrying about her boss's peculiarities. Duncan, one of the first to arrive, looked annoyed that she was already there; he was probably worried she'd been alone with Jay and found out things he hadn't. And as usual, he was correct. He seemed even more stressed since Jay had taken over the company, if that were possible.

Mary spent the morning writing a radio ad, then devised a unique way to navigate the new web site and met with her programmers, took the usual flotilla of phone calls. A short lunch and an equally busy afternoon. At five-thirty people started to leave for the weekend. At six she wandered down the corridor and looked in on Jay. He glanced up at her. "Are you ready?" she said. His face remained blank. "To go out for a drink? . . . the poolroom?" That got a response.

They took his car to Jake's. It made her Fiesta seem like an indulgence. An avocado-green mid-seventies Cutlass with the driver's side badly scarred. "Came that way," he said. When he opened the mildly blemished passenger door for her, it complained loudly. She slid onto the bench seat, and something hiding in the ripped cover spiked her. She winced, yet managed not to cry out. Jesus, she muttered, *quite* the ride.

"How did you know I had a Porsche?" she said, as he followed her directions to the poolroom.

"I just heard about it." There was something odd in his tone, but she let it go. Being around him you had to let go of a lot of things, but then he was her boss after all.

Driving along the same route with Jay reminded her of the evening in Garland's pickup. She wondered how Garland was, how his cousin was doing, and decided to call or write him to find out. She still carried the slip of paper he'd given her with such seriousness. *Call me for any reasin* was written across the top with the address of the ranch carefully penciled below the phone number.

"We're already getting inquiries about the phone," she said. "That banner ad I placed, and some of the radio releases. We had over ten-thousand unique users today alone. Have you decided where to price it?"

He glanced at her. "Mary, no more work. Tell me about Porsches. Or about something else."

She did, and soon they pulled up near the poolroom and parked.

Sammy set down her draft as they approached the bar.

"Hey girl, twice in one week. Now that *is* nice. Where's the cue?"

"Sammy, this is Jay Chevalier, my new boss."

At the introduction they shook hands, nodding cautiously to each other, looking as if they might be checking the other's grip. Probably both alpha males. She knew men had all these odd rituals to show their masculinity, though she wouldn't have thought Jay was that way.

Sammy turned to her. "Where you working now?"

"Same building, new boss, new name. LiveCell."

"LiveCell? 'Nother dot com?"

"We're going to sell phones. A new kind of telephone."

"H-m." Sammy slowly moved his focus to Jay. "Man, what you want to drink?" He was never in a hurry, and with his size why should he be? He was wearing another one of his bowling shirts, orange with navy blue stripes.

"You have any Chianti?" said Jay.

Sammy started to chuckle in his low almost soundless way. "No one ever ask for wine. Man, I sure don't recommend it. The house red's ugly. Sure ain't no *Chian*-ti. Come in a plastic cup."

Jay decided on a draft and Sammy turned to pull it, set it beside hers. No one else was sitting at the bar. One or two players drifted up for drinks and sandwiches, or to cash out table time, and Sammy took care of them. As Mary sipped her beer, she watched Jay looking around the poolroom. Over half the tables were full of Friday night players, a less serious crowd than on other evenings. A group of Asians ganged around two adjoining tables, laughing and yelling excitedly when someone missed an easy shot or pocketed a good one. She had seen them every Friday night she'd been there. Nick was sequestered in his office, a glow of diffused light visible through the opaque glass of the door, the transom window angled. Nick practically lived at his poolroom, always there; she was pretty sure he didn't have a family.

"So, tell me about this *new* telephone?" said Sammy, when he was free of other customers.

"Jay?" She looked to him.

"You have yours?"

She dug it out of her purse and laid it on the bar top. Was about to explain it when she noticed a slight negation in Jay's expression.

"This? A phone?" Sammy reached for it. The minute he touched it, the surface started to shimmer. "*Hey.* This damn thing's glowing. Feel all funny. What kinda plastic's this?" He looked it all over, the phone pearlescent for only an instant, then abruptly turning dull gray. "This one funny ass telephone. No screen, no buttons, no nothing, juss this funny little box sticking out."—with a perplexed expression now as if he'd eaten something strange.

"It shut itself off," said Jay, "because it doesn't know you."

They both stared at him.

"Each phone gets to know its owner, and when it does, no one can use your phone unless you tell it okay."

"Man, you joking me, right?"

"You dial it by speaking the number to the phone; it does the rest. You can even tell it to keep dialing a busy number."

Sammy incredulous.

"Try it if you like. Call someone." He asked Mary to release her phone. She did and it began to pulse again in Sammy's hand. He didn't drop it; he glared at it as if it were alive.

She turned to Jay. "No one could steal someone else's phone?"

"It wouldn't do them much good."

"So, they can't be stolen *or* damaged?"

"What you talking about, can't be damaged?" said Sammy.

She took her phone from Sammy and whacked it on the bar edge hard enough to make a fair-sized dent. As it healed Sammy started to chuckle.

"Man, what is this crazy shit? Damn! Where'd you get this thing?"

"He invented it," she said, "and LiveCell will manufacture and market it—Jay's company."

"You got to be fucking with me."

"Try it."

Sammy did, hesitating before he told the phone his home number in Oakland, addressing it as if he knew they were playing a practical joke on him and there was no way he was going to fall for it, maintaining full cool. This cool, however, completely deserted him when his wife answered. He tried to explain to Jolene about how he had called her,

about the new phone, about her voice sounding as if it were inside his head. She told him to get out of Felix's Lounge right that instant. "And *you* should be at work," she said. "And you sober your ass up before you come home to me and the kids or you got *some*thing else coming."

Mary watched the usually calm and cool Sammy.

"This the most amazing fucking thing I ever seen." He held it out in front of him as if it were a divine object. "Damn." He stood there shaking his head, placed the phone carefully in front of Mary again. He turned and walked over to the tap and drew himself a beer, came back to them. "Jolene thinks I been drinking anyhow." He lifted his glass to Mary. Then to Jay.

"Man, you some kind of motherfucker." He downed his drink in a long swallow, hummed his approval. "Okay, tell me more."

"Hey?" said a new voice, "Can I get a hot dog?"

Sammy turned to the teenager, not saying anything. The kid looked nervously over his shoulder at his friends and then down at his sneakers as if the solution might be there. Then Sammy broke into a grin and went off to fix the kid a hot dog.

"Is there anything that's not incredible about your phone?" she said.

"You don't know all of it yet."

"Well? . . ."

He said nothing.

"How do you expect me to market these things if I don't know everything about them?"

"You're doing fine. You hungry?"

"Why did you want Sammy to know about the phone?"

"You certainly are perceptive, aren't you?"

"And are you always this forthcoming?"

It took him a moment to answer. "I've lived alone most of my life. Worked alone. Maybe it makes me too careful, a bit withdrawn with people."

"I shouldn't have said that. It was rude."

"Let's eat something. And another beer. I think I like beer. Then we'll have a game of pool."

"You shoot?"

"No, but I want to watch you."

"I'm not any good," she said, and he smiled slightly. Maybe he does have a sense of humor even if he always acts serious? He was so hard to read.

Sammy took their dinner order and poured three more drafts, refilling his own glass though Nick didn't like him to drink on the job. Soon he brought out two cheeseburgers crowded by chips and nudged by a few pickle spears. He waited while they ate, sipping his beer this time, looking as if he was trying to be patient, but soon—

"Man, you gotta tell me more about this telephone."

Jay wiped his mouth with a paper napkin. "I think a lot of people don't realize one thing about the phones. They're alive."

Sammy dropped his glass of beer and Mary choked on a potato chip. Four eyes stared at him: *Alive?*

"All the cells are maintained in a sleep-like state when not in use. Some of the aggregate feeds on air impurities to sustain the neurons and the substrate. That's how they heal, they're genetically coded to have memory of their shape, same as they remember their owners. When you use the phone, or while it heals, it phosphoresces at its core as kinetic energy floods it, similar to a firefly."

He examined Mary. "You going to be okay?" She was still choking a little. She nodded, though she wondered. "I thought you realized that this morning," he said to her.

Sammy broke in, "This thing is *living*? That the wildest shit I ever heard! Man, oh, man . . ." He chuckled, slapping his thighs. "Everybody going to want this here phone. *Everybody*. Be like having a pet, much as owning a phone. How long they last? How much they gonna cost?"

"As far as how long they will last, that I don't know. But feeding off air impurities they should last many years—we have a lot of impurities. As far as cost, how much would you pay for one?"

"Are you joking me? I'd pay next to anything for one a these things. Man, that is just the coolest kind of shit."

"Give me a figure. What would you *like* to pay?"

"What I like to pay." Sammy thought a minute. "Hundred and a half, two bills, anyway. And that would be cheap. I never heard a telephone that clear. And the way you talk to the thing and the way those things heal up. Damn, man, that *is* some very outrageous shit." Sammy shook his head back and forth again, still chuckling. "Mary, I tell you girl, you bring some crazy people in here. Monday that cowboy, now this cat. I tell you . . . can I invest in this?"

"LVC," said Jay.

"That the ticker symbol? I'm down with that. Monday, I'm buying."

She had stopped coughing, her dinner left unfinished. Why hadn't she realized they were living? But why would she?

Sammy went to get a bar rag to clean up the spilled beer.

She looked at Jay. "You really are something. I mean it all makes sense now, if you can call it that. Do you realize your brain is living in all those phones?"

"Does it bother you?"

"I don't know. Growing up I got used to some strange things. I suppose I'll get used to this. Sammy seems to have no problem with it being alive. I wonder if anyone else at LiveCell has any idea."

Sammy straightened up, the cracked beer glass in his hand. He started questioning Jay about the stock again. Moved over and dropped the glass in the trash as he talked.

"Sammy, no stock is foolproof," she said, annoyed *that* was what he was concentrating on.

"I got a hunch with this one, girl. Big hunch. Jay is the man."

"Where do you work out?" said Jay. He always gets uncomfortable with praise, she noticed.

"Cyclone Gym. Over in Oakland on Ninety-eighth and Edes. Southeast of the Coliseum. You looking for a place?"

Jay nodded.

"This mainly a boxing gym. But we got all the free weights you want. You box?"

He nodded again.

"Man, I thought so. You got the nose and scar tissue. You also shake hands like a boxer. Tough guys always wanna break your fucking hand, show you how damn tough they are. Boxer always shakes soft 'cause his hands sore lot of the time."

"So you boxed?" she asked Jay.

"Yeah. Those missing years I did a lot of stuff."

"Is there anything you don't do?"

"I be at the gym tomorrow," Sammy broke in. "You wanna come? I show you round. Best you go with me, first time."

They arranged to meet in front of the gym at ten o'clock. Sammy explained that the Cyclone looked like an abandoned storefront from the street, there was a small sign. "Anybody try an bother you, you juss mention my name, Samuel Holmes." Then some customers pulled him away.

"He really likes you," she said.

"I like him."

"I shouldn't have said that about your not being forthcoming."

"There's truth in it."

"People seem so drawn to you. I bet you could get along with anyone."

"Not anyone." His eyes shifted. She wanted to but didn't ask. He broke the silence. "That was a good hamburger."

"Except the cheese. I've asked Nick to buy a Vermont cheddar, or even a jack, but he always gets that same rubbery provolone."

"I guess you would know about cheese."

"What do you mean?"

"Didn't you grow up on a dairy farm?"

How did he know that? Maybe Duncan told him, or maybe Jay had been asking about her. "How do you know these things about me?" she said.

"Let's play pool."

He is a very closed person, she thought again. But then, she knew she was as well. But in a way he wasn't closed—it was confusing. She wanted to find a way to get to him, yet had no idea how. He was so straightforward about everything, so honest, so directed. She wondered if he ever joked around or just acted silly.

She went to retrieve a tray of balls from Sammy, but didn't ask for her usual table because there were too many noisy players on the adjacent tables; he must have kept it open for her. Slightly guilty, she asked for a different table. She wanted quiet, and certainly wasn't concerned about the cloth's action tonight. Sammy reached for the switch, and they both watched the fluorescent flicker on in the far corner, the cloth turning a vivid green. The sight always stirred her.

"Sammy?" she said, and he leaned across the counter to her, his shoulders pulling the bowling shirt taut. "There is something about him, isn't there?"

"Girl, I never met the likes."

Jay and Mary played a few games of eight-ball. She considered shooting one-handed, hoping to make their games more competitive, yet hesitated to show off in front of him. She attempted more questions about the phone, but he refused, so she tried to relax and just shoot pool. He played pretty poorly, and she considered giving him a few pointers but rejected the idea. She eased back her game and watched his arm muscles move as he stretched for certain shots. Then, as she sank her third eight ball in as many games, he said something that stopped her.

"Your stroke is like Kelly's."

She straightened.

"I know I should have told you sooner. I was worried you might leave the company if you knew. I was so relieved when you decided to stay that first day, and I didn't want you to change your mind."

She didn't respond.

"I'm sorry," he said. "I wanted to tell you sooner, but it's so important to me that you stay. I couldn't risk it."

It took her a moment more before she spoke. "Why?"

"Why what?"

"Why is it so important?"

"I need someone I can trust."

"And Kelly told you that."

"Yes. I went to see him. Actually, at first I thought he might be the one to help me, then he told me about you, and I knew. Difficult fellow to find. We'd been out of touch for many years. Though Kelly had been an addict, even drugs couldn't destroy what he has inside him."

"Can we sit down?"

They moved over to the wood bleacher seats against the wall. Neither of them said anything, the noisy room filling up more now as it neared nine o'clock. She broke their silence.

"I'm very confused by all this. Kelly wrote me and said he'd had a visitor. It was you."

"I asked him not to say anything, but in his affection for you he probably wanted to."

"Where did you meet?"

"New York. Twenty years ago."

"Jay? What's this all about?"

"I need someone I can trust completely. After I received the patent money from Swatch, I could proceed with the phone, but wasn't sure how to go about it, it was all new to me. I decided to find Kelly. I had a premonition that he might be able to help. When I found him, he told me about you, and then I knew. I checked into Clicksave and it looked okay."

"I still don't understand?"

"I bought Clicksave to get you."

She leaned back against the darkened seat.

This was all getting stranger and stranger.

FIVE

Cage Dairy Farm, Monkton, Vermont

*November 2, 200_*

Dear Mary,

It was great to talk. When Jay gave me the phone, he said you'd call one day, and there you were. The way they don't ring but you hear the call is something.

    I felt that you should meet Jay, and I'm glad it's worked out. You asked, so here's what I remember. In the city, he was in two worlds. He had the physical with the boxing and the fitness, but when he wasn't in the gym, he was in the Bowery. With all the druggies and drunks. He'd help out the sick, but wouldn't lay out for smack or booze. Some days he'd arrive with these stuffed grocery bags and make everyone sandwiches. It was funny because we only ate the sandwiches to please him. All we wanted was junk! What the hell did we want bologna for? He couldn't seem to understand that (or maybe he did). I guess he just wanted to do something good for others. His street name was Boxer, but actually, as a boxer he sucked. No killer instinct. If he had an opponent in trouble, he'd back off. Drove his trainer crazy. I went to a cou-

ple of his fights, and he could've won both. He'd go with me when I hustled pool. Once, he knocked down two guys who'd attacked me in this hellhole, but he never liked to hurt people. Actually, he was embarrassed when he knocked the two guys down, and you should've seen them! I don't know what obsessed him to be a boxer.

It means a lot to me that you've accepted my past. I was worried about it. Your father said tell her. Your mother was against. I'm just glad it's out in the open.

It's great to know you and Jay are going well. And again, I don't need any money. I'd just use it for junk. (Kidding!) Your mom, though, was delighted by your gift, and your dad walks around floating on air, talking you up to everybody. Everyone is buying a phone. People around here say, "You got your Live one yet?" Old Vermonters jabbering on those crazy glowing phones. It's a strange world. You must be making the fortune you always wanted.

My love to you,

Kelly

Mary thought about the letter again as her newly leased Porsche carved through another corner; the pewter sky echoed in the macadam, the monochrome of the weather the antithesis of her emotions. The windshield wipers removed a slowly gathering mist every four or five seconds with one quick sweep. A new Porsche has a smell like no other car, she thought, breathing it in. More than just the scent of leather, it had a quality she couldn't quite define. And the roar of the engine behind her, vibration like pleasure.

Before leaving Berkeley that morning, she'd examined the brooding sky to the north and reluctantly left the top up. She'd headed down the narrow driveway, her last days in the apartment. Most of her belongings were boxed and lined up near the front door ready for the movers, and she'd taken one small overnight bag. Two weeks ago she'd rented a house north of San Francisco—modern with lots of open space, light, clean lines, a huge kitchen with noble materials, large redwood deck, garage underneath, and most importantly, a fantastic view of the Pacific.

After about half an hour on the 101, she exited at Cotati in the direction of the coast and was soon pointed north up Route 1. The highway was empty, maybe because it was Saturday morning or maybe just

the gloomy November day. At the end of a tree-lined straightaway, the taillights of a logging truck appeared, and she rapidly closed the gap. She shifted down one gear, and with a brisk thrill of acceleration, the rear tires biting into the damp pavement, passed the truck as quickly as the thought. She surprised herself by letting out a little shout. It was a shout describing not only being in a Porsche again but the last few weeks as well.

Then a single headlight grew in her rearview mirror, and she negotiated a few corners faster than she normally would have, wanting to outrun the light. "Get used to the car before driving it hard," the salesman at the dealership had told her. "Break it in carefully. This is much more powerful than your other one. It handles differently." She ignored the advice, the headlight remaining annoyingly in her mirrors even with the increased speed. Entering a long straight section, she stamped the accelerator and the car twitched on the greasy surface as it shot out of the corner. Both her hands tightened on the wheel, the tachometer and speedometer needles blurred, her right hand darted down for the shift. The mist changed to a light rain and she adjusted the wipers. The power of the car scared her, and maybe because it scared her, she repeated this severe acceleration twice more, braking late and violently for the corners. She searched her mirrors and the headlight wasn't there. Though she knew she was acting foolish, she couldn't suppress a grin and looked again to make sure it was truly gone. It was this second scan for the motorcycle that was her mistake.

Her foot dove for the brake pedal, but her car was already at the corner. A yellow highway sign read CAUTION 35; she was traveling nearly three times the speed. Wrenching the steering wheel toward the curve and jamming the brakes, she felt the rear tires break loose, the car slide. *Fuck!* The car snapped around on the wet road, careening backwards. A telephone pole darted toward her like the dark ax of an executioner. Something intuitive made her accelerate. Anything not to hit the pole, anything to get away from it. The car spun one more half-revolution and lurched to a stop a few feet from the pole. Tire smoke shrouded the car, and an eerie silence pulsed.

The motorcycle passed her, the rider slowing. He turned and came back as she restarted her car, pulling it parallel to the shoulder to clear the lane. He got off his bike and walked up, stood a moment beside her window until she lowered it. "You okay?" he said. She nodded. "You're some lucky. If a vehicle had been coming the other way . . ." He waited

as a logging truck roared by, the one she'd passed earlier. "I was just entering the straight when I saw your brake lights vanish, headlights appear, and I thought, *Oh, shit*."

She couldn't say anything.

"Well, I'm glad you're okay. And I think the car is fine. You're lucky Porsches don't usually roll."

He was holding some kind of old helmet with canvas earflaps, wore a leather jacket soaked black by the drizzle, had pushed his goggles into his hair, a drop of rain hanging from his nose.

"You just get this?"

"Yeah," she finally managed.

"You should take it a bit easy at first. You were driving too fast for the conditions. Porsches have a hammer effect when they break loose."

"You were hardly going slow yourself."—annoyed by his didactic attitude.

"I know the road. I practice here all the time."

"What are you, a racer?"

"Naw—writer, a novelist. The bike helps clear my head. Allows me to see my characters better." He examined her again.

"I've owned a Porsche before," she said, wondering why she needed to explain herself to him.

Two campers passed, their tires hissing as they rounded the corner. His face turned to watch them, if he was even watching.

"Well, take care," he said.

She was intentionally silent this time.

He walked back to his bike, strapped on his helmet, pulled on gloves, and turned his machine around by lifting and pivoting it, the weight of the motorcycle balanced on its kickstand. She watched him without wanting to. He fired up his Ducati—she read the name on the tank—and without a backward glance slowly accelerated the big twin down the glistening road as if he were making a point, the low growl absorbed by the rainy fog. She pressed the button to raise the window, pressed it much harder than she needed to.

She continued north more slowly. Maybe the bike rider had a point after all. The near-accident disturbed her. Fate was like a jack-in-the-box thrusting up its cackling head just when you were your most content. She'd felt so on track that morning, felt as if her run of luck couldn't be touched, and then she'd almost been split in two by a pole. How could such a perfect moment be shattered? Was this a balance within nature? Must every-

thing always be balanced by its opposite? She wondered if Jay knew.

That morning when she'd dressed, she couldn't decide on her under-wear. She'd rejected black silk as too stark, red seemed suggestive, white didn't set off her skin enough. Eventually she'd chosen a powder-blue bra and panties. Over these she wore a plaid skirt and cashmere sweater in a soft gray-green. It did the most for her eyes. She'd inherited her father's eyes, her irises an even paler gray than her dad's, delicately flecked with yellow at the rim of each pupil. Her russet hair, which she biannually con-templated dyeing redder though never did, was pulled back with a bow. Maybe she should've gone with braids? *No*, she didn't want to look like a Catholic schoolgirl. She giggled, checked her face quickly in the rearview mirror. It was too round, she thought, and lacked the high cheekbones and full lips that everyone seemed obsessed with these days. "At least I have nice skin," she muttered. It had an almost luminous purity, one ben-efit of all her years spent inside studying and working.

As she drove farther north, her thoughts began to overrun her enjoy-ment of the new car. The emotions of the near-crash allied with the somber weather and turned her mind ever more inward. All the years growing up on the farm tumbled in on her: getting up at dawn, the same chores, the same concerns and worries with every passing season. The University of Vermont had been much the same kind of life, commuting back and forth from Monkton every day, continuing to help out with farm chores, working diligently at her classes, having virtually no time for her-self. Her whole life had been about discipline and patience, about trying to progress toward the things she craved. Her parents had always lived modestly, the farm barely sustaining itself, the debt increasing with each unlucky season. There was never money for extras, let alone extravagance. Nevertheless, her family had refused the many offers from developers, and though selling would've garnered significant capital, she understood what the homestead meant, particularly to her mother and her grand-parents. Her father, having grown up in a mill town in New Hampshire, had never wanted to be a farmer, yet he consistently made the best of it. The house and barns might not be much, everything old and worn, but the land was exceptional, the Adirondacks visible from the higher fields.

Even as a teenager she'd wanted to get away. It wasn't that she did-n't love the place and love her family. Those gentle hills and weathered structures, her unassuming father, strong-willed mother, the reclusive Kelly Harris, and her stoic grandparents—they were the foundation of all she believed was good. It was just that the world beyond the farm had beckoned with such promise, like a child's vision of a carnival's fluores-

cent whirl from across a dark field. She would move away, earn the things she wanted, get the high-paying job, a modern house against the ocean, and her life would be perfect. She would pay off her student loans and send money home so her parents wouldn't have to worry anymore. She would find the perfect guy, have a family of her own.

But what was it about desires that, once you achieved them, they could tarnish in mere weeks? Or in a matter of seconds. There was something in that motorcycle rider's manner that unsettled her more than she liked to admit. He hadn't been impressed by her at all. To him she was just a self-indulgent rich girl who didn't know the limits of her new toy. It simply wasn't true, quite the opposite, and it made her wonder all the more why his opinion bothered her. Maybe she was just hungry. She decided to look for a restaurant.

There was a roadside diner near the Oregon border, its half-lit neon winking in what was now heavy rain. She almost didn't park the Porsche out front, not wanting anyone to notice her car, an inclination new to her. When she entered the warmth of the diner, five or six patrons at the counter turned. Ignoring them, she picked up a Portland paper from the stack resting near the door and chose a booth. She looked out at her car curbed under the window, the rain beaded evenly across the silver paint. It looked so lovely that her self-assurance began to return.

With the paper open, a coffee in front of her and a BLT on order, she scanned the headlines. On page two she found:

New Phone Merits Confidence

A new cell phone design has been selling in unprecedented numbers, outselling every other phone on the West Coast in only its third month. LiveCell phones also rate an unusually high 97% in Consumer confidence. The phone has become a cult phenomenon in California and has spread to the East Coast as well. LiveCell is at the moment targeting only the US, but many international sales have been confirmed. A mail-order-only product, the phone offers a five-year unconditional guarantee. The two-month predicted waiting time for the phones has generated black-market sales of three times the retail price. LiveCell's stock price has reflected the craze for the new phone, investors scrambling to buy shares. Dr. Jay Chevalier, majority owner and CEO of the new firm LiveCell, has refused all attempts to be interviewed by—

She set the paper aside as her sandwich arrived. The *doctor* tag bugged Jay. She wasn't sure why the media insisted on using it; they must have gotten it from his Harvard records. She had tried to erase its use with repeated requests but without avail. She ate her sandwich. It matched her coffee, warm and tasteless, though she was too hungry to care.

The waitress, a woman about her age, cleared the plate. "That yours?"

"Excuse me?"

"That your car?"

She nodded.

"That thing is *so* awesome. Is it new?"

"Just got it."

"Wow. What is it?"

"A Porsche Carrera."

"God, would I love to have one of those. That is *such* a cool car. You are *so* lucky."

Mary smiled up at her, though it wasn't a smile she felt. The waitress envying her or admiring her only because of something she owned made her slightly queasy for the first time.

"You want more coffee, some dessert?" the waitress asked.

She shook her head. "Just a check please."

After a few more hours north, she glanced down at the written directions on the seat beside her. Darkness tinted thick fog, the gray shifted to a cold blue. The turn had to be around here somewhere, though in this weather she might have missed it. Finally, OLD SIUSLAW ROAD was visible on a canted signpost, the words blistered. The transmission whined in the stillness as she backed up. She headed along a paved road that soon changed to gravel toward what might be the Pacific; the map had indicated that it must be close. She rolled down the window to try to see better, and yes, heard a rolling swell pounding a rocky coast. Fog laced with salt and wet pine chilled her face but still felt wonderful, the heater automatically adjusting to the brisk air, fan humming. After a few more miles the car's fog lights picked out a mailbox with *Raymond Madsen* lettered across it. She pulled into the drive, a soaked matting of pine needles and some exposed roots of scrub pine. Stopping, she examined her hair and mascara in the lighted vanity mirror under the sun visor, took a few deep breaths, smelling the ocean, trying to calm herself.

His house on that November evening was an image painted from a lost Herman Melville manuscript, a painting hung in a dim hallway of a forgotten hotel, varnish darkening, its surface obscured by a smudged

patina of endless neglect. Surrounded by porches, graced by multiple dormers, covered in weathered shingles, the structure had never been finished—the uncompleted wing like the skeleton of a failed hundred-year-old dream. Scrub pine grew so close to the walls it seemed as if the trees were cupping the building in a giant verdant hand, silver shimmers of ocean through the outer fingers.

She parked near the one light, a porch light, a yellow nimbus in the ultramarine, and got out, the waves louder, coming from below on the far side of the mansion. As she climbed the rotten porch steps, there was another sound, so peculiar she questioned her hearing. It was a muffled train whistle, the lonesome cry of a locomotive. But how could it be? She hadn't crossed any railroad tracks, and beyond the house was only the Pacific.

There was no bell, just a knocker corroded into silence, so she tapped on the oak door with her knuckles. She waited and then tapped a second time. She pounded with her fist, heard only the dirge of the waves. A gust of cold fog brought a shiver, and her hand moved to the doorknob. She cracked the door open and called. As she stepped into the dark foyer, a train whistle cried out again, louder this time, and a tiny light approached her. Above it roiled a plume of ghostlike smoke. The diamond-ring-sized headlight gradually illuminated its surroundings and she realized the hall-way was crossed by miniature railroad tracks. She waited, astounded, as a toy passenger train roared past just in front of her, the engine chuffing realistically, smoking, the many passenger cars filled with two-inch people relaxing in well-lit interiors.

"Jay?" She stepped over the tracks and followed them into a cav-ernous room, a snapping fire in a fieldstone fireplace brushing light over the dusky interior, over pine-paneled walls. And there he sat, his hands at the controls of a black Bakelite transformer.

On noticing her he hopped up, slowing and stopping two trains in the process, silence expanding after the clatter and chuff. One hand wiped quickly across his eyes, but not so quickly that she didn't notice.

"You made it," he said. "Any trouble finding me?"

"Your directions were perfect."

He walked over to her, extending his hand. They shook awkwardly, and she wondered if he ever hugged anyone.

"Hungry?" he said. "Or can I get you a beverage? I bought some beer for you."

"A beer would be good. I had a sandwich at the border." She looked around. "This is some place."

"It's the first house I've ever owned."

"Kind of matches your Cutlass." She regretted the words immediately. "Are you going to fix it up?"

"Why?"

"Well, I just thought you might . . ."

"Let me get you a beer."

She followed him into the kitchen, watched those arms pull two beers out of a fifties icebox, the ivory enamel discolored by rust. She took in the peeling wallpaper, the worn floor, a double slate sink on cast-iron legs, a wood-burning cook stove accented in chrome, a galvanized bucket collecting a roof leak.

"This place is something. Looks completely original," she said, trying to be positive.

"I don't think much has been done to it since it was built. Glass?"

She nodded and he retrieved a glass from a built-in oak cupboard.

"Do you have running water?" *And hopefully a working bathroom.*

"Of course. I installed a generator and got the pump working again. Plenty of fresh well water."

"When did you buy this place?"

"When I left DuPont, I searched the coast for a remote location. I wanted to get as far away from the East as I could. Something about this place got to me. I loved the fog and the ocean being so close. It wasn't even listed when I found it. When I started negotiating for Clicksave, I realized it was too far from San Francisco and got my room at the Y. This place was very reasonably priced."

No wonder. "Had anyone been living here? I mean before you."

"An elderly lady died here about twenty years ago. It's been empty since then. I guess potential buyers saw it as too much work or too far from anywhere."

"Is that her husband's name on the mailbox?"

"I wrote that on the box." He started pouring the beer. "I bought this house under that name. You are the only person who can connect me to this place. That's one reason I wanted you to visit, so you would know how to find it. It's our secret."

She shivered. The wind had come up from the ocean and was ignoring the walls. After the warmth of her car, it was an abrupt change, and she wished she'd brought her jacket in with her. She looked out through a bank of small-paned windows, trying to see the ocean, but it was too dark now for anything except the rain streaming down, some beading on the inside of the mullions, seeping through cracked glass.

"Come back by the fire." He handed her the beer, and they headed into the parlor. "I wish I had a brandy or something for you."

"It would certainly fit this place. Or some whisky. My dad drinks Scotch. He likes this one from some island over there. Jay—maybe we could just turn up the heat?"

"Fireplaces are the heat. Don't worry, I've laid a fire in your bedroom." *Separate bedrooms?*

A dark shape shifted in the shadows of the hall. "Jay, something is moving over there." She pointed anxiously.

"The cats. They get spooked by the trains." He made a kissing sound and three motley looking cats, one even missing an ear, surrounded him, rubbing against his legs, arching up to brush their half-open mouths on his jeans.

She reached down to pet one, but it shied away from her. She knew animals well enough not to persist. Holding their drinks, they moved near the fire. She set hers on the mantle so she could wring her hands over the flames.

"Are these your childhood trains?" The second she asked she knew it couldn't be true. All these months around him and he still made her nervous. And he was always so calm it was infuriating.

"I always wanted trains as a kid. Any kind of trains. Used to spend hours studying train catalogs, and every Christmas I put in my plea at the orphanage. I guess trains were too expensive. When I finished the first phone, I bought these to celebrate."

"Did you work on the phone here?"

"I set up a simple lab, mostly dismantled now. Just a UV culture hood and basic bioreactor. It was difficult—"

"A bioreactor?"

"It's an apparatus that slowly spins the developing cells so they can form three-dimensional shapes. Running all the stuff off the one generator and maintaining temperature was difficult. And contamination was a problem. While the phones are forming they're delicate, fragile. Once they've matured they're completely stable. Kind of strange, but nature is strange. I had a firm in San Francisco fashion a few black boxes. An electrophysicist I knew from Harvard designed the conversion device that translates brain waves to digital sound waves. But all the real work was done before I left DuPont."

He drained his beer. "The final modification of the cell aggregate was with me when I left. I destroyed all the others. That one was all I needed, but it was indispensible. I drove across the country with it packed in a

sterile beer cooler like a harvested organ. Kind of funny. I was so nervous something would happen to it or someone would stop me. I took secondary roads the whole way west, only that yellow tomcat for company."

"In the Cutlass?"

He nodded. "I bought it just before I left Delaware." He reached down for a log and placed it on the fire. He added another. "You should warm up soon in here. Please, Mary, sit down."

She told him she was okay, she was warm. Actually the fire felt wonderful, the storm now increasing outside, the wind rattling the loose windows. She settled into the sofa facing the fireplace. He moved to an easy chair that looked a week away from a dump run, and she glanced for an instant at the empty section of sofa beside her. Here she'd finally found the one person she was completely attracted to and he seemed *completely* unaffected by her in that way. Why had he asked her to come here then? "Can we run the trains?" she said.

He leaned over and slowly rotated the transformer handles, and the trains came to life. The two trains departed and reentered the living room as whistles cried out echoing in the hall and the far room of darkness. Bells sang, smoke curled madly from the stacks, passenger car lights illuminated the floor like great ethereal centipedes.

She took a chance. "Jay, were you crying when I arrived?"

He slowed the trains and they came to a rest, all the tiny lights blinking out. She studied his face in the resonating silence but couldn't read it. Did he ever open up?

"The trains allow me to remember," he said finally.

"I thought you said you'd never had them before?"—almost angry.

"To remember about people, about what they want, about their desires, their needs. When I watch the trains I imagine people riding in them, and I think how they are all going towards or away from something—maybe a lover, their family, a home, their work, even their hopes and dreams." The firelight exaggerated his face as he paused, tough looking but still so gentle. "We seem to believe there must be something more to life than mere sustenance and procreation. We all have an emptiness inside us that yearns to be filled. We find different ways to try to fill this emptiness."

"You get all that from these trains?"

He grinned.

At least she'd made him smile. She knew he was trying to tell her something, but all she could think about was her *emptiness* for him. "What do *you* want?"

"I have everything I want."

She searched him again and worried it might be true. "Then why do you work so hard, why are you making all this money?"

"I work because it's what I believe in. I believe in the process of working. It helps fill the emptiness for me. When I said I don't want anything, I should have said, for myself. There are things I want for humanity."

"But aren't there things you want *just* for yourself?"

He didn't answer her this time, and she felt foolish for asking again. She always felt so unwise when she was with him. The flames twisted around the logs; they appeared to her like creatures with too much desire. What was she supposed to do with her desire? The storm slapped the house and the drip in the kitchen struck the rain-filled bucket like a slow metronome.

Eventually she said, "What did Kelly tell you?"

"You mean why did I purchase a company just to get you to work for me?"

She nodded.

"He told me about your dog."

"My *dog*? Pilgrim?"

"About the dog that disappeared when you were sixteen. Kelly told me how you knew something was wrong right away. Everyone on the farm assured you the dog would return soon—it had run off many times before, especially during deer season—but you insisted on going to look. When you found it, the poor animal had been shot in the leg and was dragging itself home. Kelly told me you led him almost directly to the dog. He said it terrified him that you were so intuitive, that sometimes you could sense things before they happened. He also told me you could be trusted with anything."

"He told you all that?"

"You saved the dog's life."

"She lost the leg but she's still alive though very old."

The fire snapped, a glowing cinder striking the hearth.

"You can do it too," she said. "Can't you?"

"Sometimes."

She wanted to go to him, to touch him, hold him. Instead she did nothing, started feeling uncomfortable, wondering if he knew what she was thinking.

"Are you hungry?" he said finally. "I'm afraid all I have are chicken pot pies and some russet potatoes. We can bake those. Let me get the stove in the kitchen going." He got out of his chair, gathered an armful

of kindling and newspaper, went to fire the stove, leaving her on the sofa.

Was this why he'd chosen her? She didn't want to tell him that since coming west five years ago, her ability—she wasn't sure what to call it—was probably gone. She was uncertain about it now. It was hard to tell if it was still an ability or if she just happened to guess correctly sometimes. She had never been able to do it on demand, but occasionally she'd simply known things, as with Pilgrim.

She continued to stare into the flames, wondering what she was going to do about these feelings for him. She wanted to touch him, have him touch her, but he was so remote towards her as if none of that could ever be a possibility. Was it from being an orphan? Or maybe he was gay? Had he been close to anyone in his life? Was he simply not attracted to her? Was this her punishment for turning down other men? She'd had such hopes driving up to see him today.

Since their first talk that one Friday morning he'd been shut tight—as if he'd decided he'd shared enough and that was the end of it. He was all work, work, work, from then on. Maybe if she could just hold him once. But he never touched anyone. He was such a loner. Here he had millions and he still drove that horrible junker, had that room at the YMCA, and now this place. Out of politeness, she hesitated to call it a dump. At least he'd bought the toy trains. Somehow that seemed like a good sign. But why had he wanted her to drive all the way up here if not for sex? It couldn't be only to show her his house and trains. It didn't make sense.

She moved from the sofa and stood close to the fire, absently wringing her hands near the flames again, waiting until her whole body was warm. Then she walked into the kitchen to be with him.

SIX

Deirdre Holly didn't understand why some authors used foreign phrases in their writing. Like we all spoke Latin? or even French? And some writers didn't even offer the English translation. She understood that by doing so they were exhibiting a class thing, showing up the rest of us. She'd learned recently that a lot of things in life are about class snobbery. Deirdre had only come to reading fiction in the last few years. In her twenty-eight years she'd come to many things late. As she put it, "I came to the bad things way early, the good things a little late."

She had left home at fifteen, left Monrovia and the San Fernando Valley and headed up the coast to Santa Cruz. Surfing had changed her life, her awkward body finding balance and confidence as her ability grew, her strong shoulders finally an asset. But surfing hadn't changed her life as much as Jay Chevalier was changing it now. It had only been slightly over six months since she'd followed him into what had then been Wendell Alden's boardroom, yet it seemed like years.

Jay had interviewed everyone in the company during the first month and a half of his takeover. Her interview, about two weeks after the famous Monday, stunned her. First thing he said when she walked into his office was, "Hey Deirdre, how are you? Thanks for not calling security." She realized he wanted her to know he'd remembered. Then he asked her a lot of questions about herself. Wanted to know all about her. *Like everything*. And she felt comfortable around him, which hadn't hap-

pened with most men. She had never had a boss treat her this way. A week later, he dropped the bomb.

Jay asked her to be in charge of the LiveCell manufacturing facility. "I've only had two years of community college. I have no background in any of this," she reminded him. His response was, "You are the one I want—it has nothing to do with formal education or previous experience."

She ended her relationship with Cathy, a decision that was long overdue, and moved into her own place. A really nice place too, south of Market. If only she still communicated with her family, something in her wanted to show it off to them, wanted to make them envious. Yet she knew better: like how many blows to the head do you have to take till you wise up? It hadn't really started until her father was injured on the job, but then he'd been home all the time, her mother working, and with nothing to do but drink and smoke pot, that's when the real trouble started. But when she finally rebelled after a year, her mother took his side, believed him not her, almost seemed to blame her, and Deirdre had fled and tried hard never to look back.

LiveCell needed a factory to fabricate the phones, though the phone's cell aggregates were replicated rather than fabricated. This required a unique environment providing sterility and a precise control of temperature and humidity—a *clean room*. The delicate cultures of cloned neurons, which had been seeded from Jay's initial pineal gland extraction, were added to the collagen and proteoglycans used as a supportive matrix. This mixture grew best at 37° C in a carbon-dioxide oxygen blend, and a clean room would provide this environment.

So Jay and Deirdre had the interior of an old warehouse renovated during an intense three weeks, the place saturated twenty-four hours a day with builders and contractors. She watched the transformation with a conflict of emotions, eager and nervous to begin her new job. Eventually they were finished: the floors gleaming white tile, the main room full of perfectly aligned stainless-steel lab tables canopied with multiple culture hoods and growth-inducing apparatuses, the lighting as bright as an operating room. She even had an office, a small unrestored room to the right of the double front doors, across the hall from the changing cubicle for the workers' sterile gear. She told Jay that she preferred the rough warehouse flooring and the old plaster walls, sensing that would please him and not wanting him to spend extra money just for her. After every-

thing was completed, the building from the outside matched her office; it offered no clues to the high-tech facility that was now inside.

While the factory was being renovated, and with Jay assisting her, she hired two dozen workers. Sharing the factory-hiring process with him, she better understood the method by which he'd hired her. It was by believing in something he must have sensed—it sure wasn't on her resume. That was how he hired everyone. She had to admit some of the choices simply baffled her. *Like made no sense at all.* He even hired a few Santa Cruz gang members, and they really looked like gang members, too. His print ads in the newspapers attracted all kinds of strange applicants. Too many applicants. Who didn't want to work for LiveCell? The pay and the benefits were unrivaled. And in a barren job market, everyone showed up to interview for the two dozen positions. Deirdre was exhausted and impatient by the end, Jay unaffected. Did anything ever get to him?

So LiveCell began production with this collection of carefully chosen misfits, Deirdre applying herself to her new job with the same big-boned intensity she'd used to master the waves. As the weeks passed she came to respect Jay's hiring decisions, even the few that had really surprised her, but she was learning not to be overly surprised by anything having to do with Jay Chevalier. As the workers adjusted to their jobs, LiveCell gradually increased output to around five-thousand phones a day. The procedure wasn't as complicated as she'd first thought. It was almost like baking bread or something. You just had to be really precise and thorough. It was simply amazing watching the cells replicate and then solidify as they achieved maturity. She never tired of watching the process, knowing she was creating something important.

It took about a week to make a phone. The basic cell aggregate first grew in bioreactors, the quick-replicating cells turning and rotating until they reached the phone's basic dimensions. Jay had developed an improved bioreactor that could form a long cylinder of cell matter, creating dozens of phones with one unit. As this fragile mixture multiplied, feeding on the substrate host, the stainless culture hoods that supplied the perfect air mixture and the UV-irradiation to prevent contamination were lowered. On the fourth day, the hoods were lifted, and the young phones could be disassociated from the host by proteolysis, carefully segmented and cradled in phone-sized plastic vessels where they matured and reached full structural density. Before they finished curing, she oversaw the injection by pipette of viral DNA into the center of each young

phone. Over the next two days, the virus spread through the cells and modified the neurons, elongating and intensifying their electrophysiological capacity.

Every evening, after the work crew had gone for the day, Jay would stop by to check the finished phones. She staggered the replicating process so that a new batch of phones would reach maturity at the end of each day. The warehouse would be empty, the day's freshly finished phones ready, laid out in an exact grid on the polished metal tables, thousands of them, missing only their pronged black boxes. She always waited for him, though he told her many times that she worked too much.

"Don't wait for me, there is no need," he'd say.

And she would answer, "I just want to be sure that everything was done right."

It was a point of inflexibility between them. Jay, however, insisted she not watch him do whatever he did in the clean room with the phones. Made her promise. He was adamant about it, asking her to wait in her office. It made her very curious, particularly since he always looked changed somehow after he was finished. Each time he went in there, he turned off all the rows of fluorescent lights, so she began to leave it that way for him. But like what can you *check* in the dark?

This was the routine through the fall and the winter, production increasing with each season, until LiveCell was outputting over ten-thousand phones a day. It was in early spring that she came to appreciate fully Jay's choice in workers.

One morning two men in ill-fitting dark suits and bland ties sauntered arrogantly into her office. She came out from behind her desk and politely asked if she could help them. They flashed IDs and said they were from the FCC, were there to investigate the premises. She ignored their bluster, explaining that no public access was permitted, to *anyone*. Like what would the Federal Communications Commission want with Live-Cell? She knew the licensing and all the permits were in order because the company lawyers had gone over everything carefully. Jay had been very thorough. And even if there was a problem, would this be the way the FCC would address it?

They argued with her, demanded admittance, became increasingly rude as she held ground, she more and more convinced they weren't FCC. "*Miss* Holly, do you realize the ramifications of obstructing a government investigation?" said the burlier of the suits. Like this was a government investigation? She didn't answer. She'd already told them to

contact Jay Chevalier, made it repeatedly clear that only a search warrant would get them through the clean-room door. Like why waste more words? But the burly suit suddenly shoved her out of the way, her body banging into the doorframe with a painful thud, and the two men headed down the hallway toward the clean room.

Jimmy Hakken was one of the Santa Cruz gang members whom Deirdre hadn't wanted to hire—she'd heard about his reputation over the years—until Jay insisted. He was changing into his sterile gear when she called out for help. In black chinos and sleeveless T-shirt, six-two, shaved head and fully tattooed arms, he charged out of the cubicle. The suits froze at the sight of him. Hakken stopped a few feet in front of the two men, blocking access to the clean room. He said nothing, his posture erect, his body dead still. His look said everything. It almost projected an eagerness for the suits to make a move, but his expression was too neutral for that, too unreadable. She decided there was something about absolute willingness that was really scary. Three other workers emerged from the clean room and blocked the doorway. She figured it was overkill.

The suits muttered a few more threats, backed up and left. She thanked her crew. "No problem, Dree," said Hakken with a quick nod. The others smiled, everyone going back to work as if nothing had happened. She returned to her office, livecelled Jay and told him what had happened.

"So you're okay? Everyone is okay?" he said.

She reassured him.

"Did you get a look at their IDs?"

"They were weird about showing them. Just flipped them like, and wouldn't let me examine them. Made me suspicious right away. Classic suit cop types, you know? Really forceful, in-your-face kind of bullshit."

"You did great."

"You should've seen Jimmy. He like really turned the tide. He comes blazing out and one of the suits like yelps. This little squeak. *Really* funny." Now that the tension had passed, she started to giggle. Her mind flashed to when she'd pursued Jay into Wendell Alden's boardroom trying to stop him. How different it was to work for Jay.

"This won't be the end of it," he said.

"You think they really were FCC?"

"We've been fully cleared with the FCC. And they would have contacted our legal department in writing if there was a problem."

"That's exactly what I thought." She wasn't laughing now, worried

again. "It just seemed *too* weird. They were somebody with power. Real cocky, you know?"

"I don't want you or anyone to get hurt."

"You should have seen the crew—they were ready."

"Not the point."

"I'm just saying—they're loyal. *Really* loyal."

"Deirdre, you have great people. I know that."

"I mean, you chose them, but they're really like my crew now. I can't tell you how good that feels." She paused. "They talk about you. You know what they say?"

He was silent.

"Because of Jimmy Hakken they think you're some kind of knight now or something. That's why he calls you *The* Chevalier and doesn't use Jay. Like you're from the Round Table or something. 'He's a knight, Dree—Chevalier suits him,' he says. Like just *Jay* isn't cool enough. And now he thinks he's this *yeo*man or something, that's what he calls himself. He takes it serious, too. I shouldn't have loaned him those books to read, but I told him I was trying to educate myself more, and he was all into the idea. He said he'd read a bit as a kid but then stopped. I think Dumas really fired him up, and now he's got everyone at the factory into it. He's really a natural leader, you know." *God*, these phones were so intimate. Like she could almost feel him, she understood him better, he got inside her somehow. Not that she could hear his thoughts unless he spoke or anything like that. "Jay?"

He answered.

"You know how much all this means to me, like what you've done for me and the rest of the crew, right?" Silence. "You there?"

"Shall we all go eat Mexican tonight? I'll invite everyone."

"You got to stop this."

"Dos Reales?"

"You're too generous, it's ridiculous. You don't need to do this."

"You like Dos Reales, don't you?"

"That's *not* the point."

"Think of that cactus salad."

"Cut it out."

"Those flautas?"

"*Jay!*"

"Mole Poblano?"

"Okay, what time?" She was laughing again. He could talk her into anything, always made her feel better about everything.

"I have to tend to the phones, then I'll meet you. You get everyone started. Tell them it's on me—they've earned it."

"I'll send them ahead and wait for you here."

"You don't need to."

"I know."

That evening when Jay arrived at the warehouse, Deirdre's sixties Dodge wagon was alone on the lot near the front entrance, illuminated by one of the two security lights. Then he noticed a black late-model sedan parked along the darkest side of the building, March twilight almost hiding the car.

He parked the Cutlass next to her wagon and got out, irritated that his door squawked so loudly when he opened it. He left it that way and quickly climbed the steps to the front doors. He rotated the steel knob slowly, pulled on it gently. Locked. It was unlikely it would have been Deirdre; she always kept it open for his arrival.

He leapt down the steps and sprinted to the far side of the building, his passkey in his hand by the time he reached the emergency exit. He unlocked the metal door, jerked it open, and was in the factory. All the banks of fluorescent lights were on. Normally they would have been off. He moved between the laboratory tables, the bioreactor apparatus humming. At the doors leading into the front hall, he cracked one, stood for a few seconds and listened. Muffled sounds were coming from the half-open door to Deirdre's office. As he entered the hall he heard her yell, "Fuck you," obviously terrified. There was a hard slap.

She was trapped awkwardly in her office chair, hands taped behind the chair's back, ankles taped to the rungs, her cheeks marked by red welts, mouth bleeding, eyes bleary with tears.

"Leave her alone," he said.

The two men in front of Deirdre turned to face him, a hulk in a rumpled suit and a smaller one with almost no forehead lazily pointing an automatic in his direction.

"Doctor Chevalier, I presume," said the one with the gun, a bored smile barely changing his expressionless face.

Jay moved straight at the voice and threw a right uppercut into the jawbone so hard it almost lifted the guy off his feet. The body slumped

heavily against the desk and pitched loudly to the floor, the gun clattering across the unpainted floorboards.

The large guy stared in disbelief at his downed partner. "What the fuck?" he said, grabbing inside his suit jacket. He fumbled a few seconds, and there was the black glint of a snub-nosed revolver. Jay stepped toward it, trying to get inside the gun's reach before the angle of the barrel found him. Using his left arm to deflect the weapon, he drove a straight right into the guy's lower ribcage. He heard the explosion but didn't feel the bullet or suspect that he'd been shot; the pain would come later. The impact spun him off balance and back a few feet. Deirdre screamed.

The guy swayed, bent over, wheezing painfully, the gun smoking in his hand. There was a second report and a dull thud, the bullet lodging into one of the thick planks inches from Jay's shoe. Jay recovered as his assailant began to straighten. He stepped in and started to throw a left hook when he realized his arm wasn't reacting. A spike of nausea jabbed him in the gut, flashing him back to his days in the ring. The same sensation as when he'd been stunned by a punch, but now covering up wasn't going to save him. The gun rose slowly and inexorably toward his head. Someone cried out. With the gasping face before him, the leaden cruelty of the eyes, he swung a brutal roundhouse right, his fist contacting the soft tissue and arteries at the side of the gunman's neck. The third shot remained unfired.

"Jay, Jay, Jay, . . ." he heard her saying between sobs.

Shocked by the violence of his punch, he looked down at the two splayed men and worried that he might have killed the second one. He'd never throw a blow that fierce in the ring, but there was nothing he could do about it now. Though he figured he didn't need to, he still kicked the two guns into a corner of the room. His left arm was numb, covered in blood. Blood was dripping freely from his hand as he attempted to wriggle his fingers, testing the damage. Nausea hit him again, and for a moment he thought he might go down. Supporting himself by grabbing the desk with his good arm, he could vaguely hear Deirdre saying something. He waited and his head started to clear.

"Jay, you're shot!"

"I think I'm okay. Just some blood."

"You need a doctor."

"We better call an ambulance."

"I can drive you. It would be faster."

He found a serrated plastic knife among her papers, guided himself

along the desk's edge to her chair, and with a sawing motion cut through the duct tape. "I mean for these two."

"You're the one who needs a hospital. To hell with those fuckers." She lifted herself clumsily out of the chair, rubbing her wrists.

"All I need is a flauta," he said, and winked at her. "And maybe a beer."

Slowly, the smile appeared.

It was almost eleven o'clock when they finally sat on the tattered bench seat of the Cutlass headed to Dos Reales. She called the restaurant as Jay drove. Her Dodge was left on the lot; it was not a night to be alone. Ricky, the owner, explained that a few of Deirdre's crew were still hanging around drinking beer and he would be glad to stay open for her and Jay. "Food? No problem. I make whatever you guys want." They were both hungry, and she'd never craved a vodka rocks more than at that moment. Like who wouldn't?

"How's the arm?" she said.

"Fine," he said, but she knew it wasn't. She'd cleaned and bound his flesh wound, which was similar to some of the worst surfboard cuts she'd seen, except for the ugly powder burn. She'd sterilized and butterfly sutured the gash in his bicep, using a first-aid kit from the factory. It still needed stitches, more than a few, but at least the bullet hadn't done as much damage as it could have. She'd urged him to let one of the paramedics examine his arm, but you couldn't get him to do something he didn't want to do. Like *way* stubborn.

"How can you say fine?" she said. "It must hurt like crazy. That thing is nasty." As the streetlights washed over his face, he appeared even paler than normal. Like a ghost. A real stubborn one.

"The trouble with complaining," he said, "is once you start you can't stop."

They drove awhile, both locked in their own thoughts.

She broke the silence: "The cops acted a little weird, don't you think? Like they didn't really believe you. Like you couldn't possibly have taken out those two guys with guns. Or maybe the whole thing didn't make sense to them either. But that one detective seemed to like you. Otega? Something like that. The Puerto Rican looking one. The others though . . . This whole thing is really *too* weird." She looked over at him, waiting for him to say something. "I thought we would never get out of there. Took for*ever*. They sure had enough cops and paramedics running

around. Like the whole force. I still can't believe you wouldn't let a medic look at your arm. You can be pretty weird, you know? And you sure won't talk to the press. Like not at all."

He still didn't say anything. She didn't care. He probably realized she just needed to talk. It made her feel better. Her face had even stopped stinging so painfully, though the inside of her mouth was still raw and getting itchy. The vodka would help that. She'd told the police that one of them was the same guy who'd visited the factory that morning insisting he was from the FCC. She'd never seen the other, the one who looked like a rat. He'd questioned and beat her. He was the one she hated.

What she didn't know was that Jay had quietly noted the serial number from the .38 before the police arrived. It told him something that the gun still had its number, belonging to the hulk. The one on the automatic had been filed off. She also didn't know that as he drove he kept replaying the event, realizing it had probably been a setup. He still had the mushy collapsing sensation of the guy's neck in his memory and was sickened by the violence. If they were after something in the factory, wouldn't they have entered at night? And why involve Deirdre? It was obvious to him now that they'd been waiting for him, using Deirdre as bait, had half-hidden their car so he could spot it. Were they testing him? Trying to scare him? Kill him? No, there were much easier ways to kill him if—

"Jay?" she said.

He moved his eyes from the street to her. "You okay now?"

To Deirdre he looked drawn and tired. She realized with a pang that he was vulnerable, that he had weakness. She wanted to bring her hand across the seat fabric to touch him.

"Thanks," she said instead.

He smiled at her, and she could tell he was mustering his energy.

"I wish I could fight like you. Then those assholes couldn't have pushed me around. They were all over me with their bullshit questions about you and the phones, and I'm all *yeah right*, like I'm going to tell you fuckheads anything. Maybe I should've locked the door, but I figured you'd be coming any minute, and I never lock the door until we leave. That gun really scared me. I hate guns. Seen too many horrible things happen with guns."

She looked out at the shadowed facades of city buildings, a small late-night grocery, closed shops, a brightly lit gas station as it flashed by in a fluorescent blur. Absently these images flickered across her consciousness as the fight dominated her mind.

"Jesus you can sure throw a punch," she said. "You lifted that one guy right into the air. That was *so* amazing. The rumor is you used to fight in the ring. It's true, isn't it?"

"What I did wasn't good. There was nothing good about it. I should have known better . . . but they hurt one of my family, and I overreacted."

That stopped her. "You feel that way about me?"

He nodded.

She glanced out the window again, not seeing anything this time.

Soon, there was the Dos Reales neon in the distance. He took his good arm off the wheel to reach across and flip on the blinker.

"I could have driven you know," she said. "Your arm must be killing you."

"We're here."

Jimmy Hakken listened without moving as Deirdre described what had happened. Only Hakken and Ramon had waited for them in the big padded booth. In the parking lot, Jay had asked Deirdre not to mention the incident, but she'd convinced him otherwise. She told him it was their workplace, she was their boss, and they had a right to know. Besides, he was bleeding through his bandage, like what was she supposed to tell them? Jay cut himself shaving? And how about the newspapers tomorrow? She continued to be put out that he wouldn't go to the hospital. His wound needed stitches. Tape wasn't going to hold the skin together long enough for it to heal. He was even paler, dabbing at the leaking blood with a paper napkin. But food was on its way, she'd already downed one of her signature vodkas, the second on order. Jay worked at a can of beer.

Jimmy Hakken sat immobile after she'd finished the story. He rarely spoke, and he was difficult if not impossible to read. He was the tall silent type, who just happened to be covered in too many medieval tattoos and have a shaved head with reddish sideburns. The ugliness of his face was almost handsome because of his eyes, the lightest of blue like a Nordic sled dog.

"Chevalier," he finally said. "Anything like this ever happens again, say the word, and my guys are there."

Jay took a sip. "Jimmy, we're not about violence. We make phones so people can communicate better."

"They fucked with you and Dree, man. That burns my ass. All I'm saying is, you need us, we're there. I don't give a fuck who they are."

"Let's hope this is the end of it."

Hakken examined his beer can, shook his head back and forth for

what seemed an eternity. "Man, you know it ain't over. Look—understand—it would be a fucking honor to move on this. You gave me a chance. No one else would've. I don't forget. Ever."

"I have your work. You do great work. That's all I need."

Hakken paused again, staring at Jay as if he were trying to memorize everything about him, scowling slightly. "Chevalier, you know I dig you. You know I respect your ass. But *no one* can go it alone." He crushed his beer can, dropped it, slid out of the booth and stood. He held out his hand to Jay with intense seriousness. They shook and released. "Take care of the wing," he said. He nodded to Ramon, blinked quickly with both eyes at Deirdre, and lumbered out of the restaurant.

SEVEN

Her curiosity was simply too much for her. And she was worried about him. That was how she rationalized it.

The day after the shooting, he came by as usual to check on the phones. When he walked into her office at the factory, he was so pale she thought he was about to faint. Again she urged him to see a doctor, said she would drive and go in with him, but he refused. Maybe that was why she broke her word. Her anger and concern made her disregard everything else.

Deirdre watched, spied on him from behind the hallway doors, her foot holding one cracked about an inch. The room looked so dark with the multiple banks of overhead fluorescent lights off, only a vague haze entering through the windows of the hallway doors, the few emergency exit signs glowing red. Thousands of newly matured phones cradled in their plastic vessels lay symmetrically arranged on the polished laboratory tables. She could faintly hear the electric motors in the bioreactors as younger phones replicated, the tissue culture hoods exhaling their air mixture and UV-irradiation onto the cells. Jay, in his usual blue T-shirt, didn't wear the sterility gear of the other workers. He'd explained to her that once the cells reached their final shape and solidified, they were immune to contamination. She still worried about the younger phones under the hoods, but you couldn't argue with him. Like about anything.

There he kneeled, his back half-turned to her, his face in three-quarter profile rimmed by the eerie light. His muscular arms were stretched out in front of him, the one with the bandaged bicep quivering slightly. She couldn't quite tell but thought his eyes were closed and his lips were moving.

He didn't seem to be doing anything else, so what was all the exclusion fuss about? She kept watching anyway, *Like who wouldn't?* But what was he up to, just kneeling there like that in the dark as if he were blessing the phones or something? And why no lights? It didn't make much sense unless he used some kind of instrument that required darkness, some kind of laser or something. He never carried anything in with him though—she'd checked. When you only wore T-shirts and jeans, it was hard to conceal things. Now she realized he wasn't checking anything.

He became completely still after a few minutes, his arms relaxed, his lips quiet, and that was when she first noticed a humming inside her brain, the way a nasty headache starts. The humming increased, an inexplicable nervousness enclosed her, and she felt as if something terrible was about to happen. She considered retreating to her office but couldn't seem to move. The sensation in her brain got worse and she fought against it, blinked rapidly, rubbed her temples; everything only seemed to intensify the pain. Maybe Jay had a good reason for demanding she didn't watch? But all he was doing was kneeling there.

And then he collapsed. Fell over on his side as if he'd passed out. The pain in her head subsided almost at once.

She pushed the door open. "Jay? . . . Jay, are you all right?" Called out again but there was still no response. Something must be very wrong, and she ran to him. Kneeled down beside him and shook him by the shoulder. Nothing. His wounded arm was crushed under his torso and she carefully rolled him on his back, straightening it. Was he breathing? She felt for a pulse. Found none. The panic started choking her. Knowing some CPR from her years of surfing, she leaned over him and placed her mouth on his, forced her breath into him, figuring it was the only thing to do. He can't die, she screamed to herself. Don't let him die. *Please.* She straightened, placed her hands on his chest and pressed down hard three or four times, then switched back again. As she inhaled and exhaled, her mouth on his with each arduous out-breath, an upsetting, confusing thought crossed her mind—that since her father's unwanted kisses, Jay's lips were the first male lips that had touched hers.

And he opened his eyes.

"Deirdre," he said.

There was a long intense moment—Deirdre hovering over him, Jay breathing strangely beneath her, their bodies touching as if they were lovers—and then she started to cry. Silently, but the tears kept coming.

"Deirdre. Please," he said.

He struggled out from under her into a sitting position, his face ashen, the pock marks on one of his temples accentuated by the light of an exit sign, his wound bleeding a little through the bandage, the blood black in the reddish glow. He reached out with his good arm and took her hand in his. After a long silence her tears stopped and he released it. She got to her feet awkwardly and looked down at him. It was only then, noticing something greenish-yellow in the periphery of her vision, that she turned and saw with a sudden gasp that all the phones had begun silently pulsing in their vessels.

It took him over half an hour to quiet her. They drove to a nearby tavern in his Cutlass because he felt she needed a change of scene; she had eyed the luminous pulsing phones with terror. In the darkened clean room, the thousands of phones were like a sea of undulating phosphorescence. For Jay they were always a vision of great beauty, yet he understood she had seen them differently at that moment. With one vodka rocks in her and a second in front of her, color was returning to her freckled skin, her spiked blonde hair a turmoiled crown above tear-marked eyes.

"Are you feeling better?" he said.

"Jay, I'm so, so, sorry I watched. I was just really worried about you. You always look so strange after you come out of there, and you looked totally sick going in today. I know I promised to never watch." Her face begged forgiveness. "What happened to you anyway? Did you like, *die* for a minute?"

"When I'm already tired, sometimes the infusing can be exhausting."

"I took your pulse. There was none. *Jay!* No pulse—none."

"Maybe my heart stopped for an instant. Actually I haven't had a problem in a long time."

She looked into her drink. "You got to be *really* careful."

There was a lull and she wouldn't look at him.

"I'm wondering if your touching me didn't help break the bond," he said, wanting to reassure and console her.

"What bond?"

"Between the phones and me."

She took a sip of her drink. "I had this sick feeling come over me. Not sick maybe, but real *freaky*, uneasy, you know? Like my brain felt weird and then I just knew something terrible was going to happen."

"I worried it wouldn't be good." He didn't tell her that she probably had something to do with his collapse, that somehow her resistance and fear had contributed to his blackout. He was fairly certain it had been her anxiety along with his exhaustion that had complicated the infusion. They usually went smoothly.

"No one else knows?" she said.

He shook his head. "I'm sorry you saw it, that it upset you so much."

"I'm okay now. I'm cool."—Jay studying her—"Really. I'm okay. But you got to admit, this whole thing you're doing is totally strange. I mean—my God . . . What were you really *doing* anyway? I know you said infusing, but what's *that*?"

"Will it be our secret?"

She paused to look at him. Studying *him* now. Her expression saying to him, Like there is anything I wouldn't do for you?

Jay looked around the bar. They sat in a back booth where he'd led them, so she could have some privacy until she calmed down. The tavern was almost empty, everyone home for supper. Though she had been over-wrought, she had just as quickly returned to her usual composure. She never stopped impressing him.

"I was programming the phones," he said. "I do it by channeling energy through my brain. My neurons in the phones respond to my brain waves. I'm wondering if what you felt, what you called freaky, might not have been your brain fighting against mine."

"Oh my God. Brain waves?"

"That's how they work. The phone becomes a medium and allows brain waves to be passed."

"Passed?"

"From a LiveCell to a human brain. Though brain waves had never been sent any distance, I discovered they could be, that my cell combination was capable of it once infused by my brain. LiveCell phones have identical cloned structures to each other, something that has never existed before, since no one had figured out how to replicate mature brain cells."

Her face twisted in a confusion of emotions. Awe won out.

"That is simply so amazing. I mean, my God. That is just *so* cool." She hesitated again. "I asked everyone. No one has any idea how they work. I was nervous to ask you."

"Believe me, a lot of people ask."

"Even if you told them, I don't know if they'd believe it. Jay, this is just *so* incredible."

"I'm used to it now, though it was strange at first."

"How do the phones remember what you tell them, or think at them, or whatever?"

"The neuron progenitor cells in the structure have become so elongated that they're sensitive to low-frequency impulses. So this particular aggregate is capable of absorbing and transmitting brain waves over the short distance we hold the phones from our brains."

"I thought maybe the black boxes carried all the electric stuff and the living part was like a special speaker or something."

"No, the cell tissue is what matters. It activates the number sequence in the black box to send the call and then translates the voice into a conventional digital code. The infusing is similar to downloading information into a computer. Imagine condensing human memory and filling a brain with a year's learned information in a couple minutes. That's what I do every evening at the factory. Once the phones are programmed, infused by the energy passing through me, they actually acquire an intelligence. This allows the phone's owner to program it by speaking to it. Just like a brain, the phone remembers, but unlike a brain, it never forgets. Better diet and no booze, I suppose." He winked at her.

He watched her face as it all sank in. "Another secret is that you don't have to speak out loud to the phones. Just think the instructions and the phone will usually respond if your thoughts are clear enough. Of course when you talk to another person through the phone, you must speak out loud for them to hear you, or for their brain to hear you. It's only the phone that can sometimes translate your thoughts without speaking. I figured people wouldn't be ready to accept something that unusual yet, so we pretend you must speak to the phones to get them to work—it's simpler."

"How did you discover all this?"

"By chance, I guess. Following my hunches. I was lucky, though sometimes I felt as if I was almost guided." He paused. "I suppose it's all possible within the randomness of life . . . though I keep wondering about randomness."

"You think everything happens to us for a reason?"

"Probably not. I don't think we're that important. Though overall, within the infinite balance of everything, I'm not so sure if some occurrences aren't calculable probabilities, even the future."

She took another pull on her drink, looking confused.

"In other words, if I pick a number between one and a hundred, and if you were to allow yourself, it is more likely for you to pick that number than any other, only because it *is* the number I thought of, because it exists. The future is the same, because it actually *is* going to happen. The problem is believing that you can do it, and then emptying yourself of everything else." She stared at him, and he liked her more than ever. "Of course, in a way, it will always be a guess. But sometimes it just might be the right one."

"That is *so* fucking cool."

"I wonder."—almost to himself.

"What do you mean?"

"I wonder how the whole thing will turn out, if I'll have enough time. Time can be misleading."

He studied her, hoping she was okay. It had been two rather intense evenings in a row for them. Everything always seems to come at once.

EIGHT

Jay Chevalier was hunched over his battered desk on the sixth floor of the Harcourt Building. He looked worse than usual. Though he was reluctant to admit it, Deirdre had been correct about his arm—it wasn't healing correctly. He straightened and picked up his LiveCell phone, sensing he had a call.

"Chevalier, Hakken."

They exchanged minimal greetings. *Very* minimal, it being Jimmy Hakken. "Listen, this new woman, something's not right."

"What do you mean?"

"Dree ain't herself."

"Jimmy, could you clarify that a little more please?"

"Chevalier, I'm telling you man, this new one is working Dree."

"How?"

A long pause. "Look, I said enough."

"Are you referring to Wendy Smith?"

Hakken grunted.

"I'm sure Deirdre can handle it."

"Chevalier . . . Would I rat on Dree if I thought she could?"

"Have you discussed this with Deirdre?"

"Some."

"Why not talk to her again? I'm sure she would listen."

A longer pause. "Chevalier. I never had your advantages."

"What do you mean?"

"Fancy schools, Harvard, all that shit. That's what I heard told."

"So?"

"Look—you know I dig you."

"It's not about how you talk or your background, it's about who you are now."

Hakken was silent again. Then he grunted and ended the call.

Jay sat for a while, his eyes traveling to the rectangle of bay out the window, which on this spring afternoon was horizonless with dense fog. This was about the only nature he got these days, this pathetic view from a window, this minor scrape of weather. He longed for the wilderness, for the northern Maine of his childhood, for the days he'd spent with his grandfather. So many years he'd been inside, and every one of them was a splinter under the skin. His phone signaled him again.

"Jay, Sammy. How you hanging?"

"Fine. You?"

"Fine too, *real* fine. We miss your ass over at the gym. Three Saturdays, still no Jay. Reggie call you the mighty Frenchman now, though you don't look any too French to me."—Sammy chuckling in his throaty almost silent way—"'Where that mighty Frenchman at?' he say. 'Man use to be in twice a week.'"

"I should have called you."

"No sweat. I juss wanna make sure everything cool." He paused. "I read about that bullshit stickup in the paper. That all true?"

"More or less."

"They make it sound like a publicity stunt by LiveCell in *The Chronicle*, but I know you better than that."

"It was an ugly thing. It shouldn't have happened."

"You know who was behind it?"

"Not certain yet."

"You got an idea?"

He was silent.

Sammy continued. "A bunch of us is in now. The stock make a wiggle, they *all* ask me, they *all* wanna know what's goin' down. These people can't afford to lose—you know what I'm sayin'?" He paused. "So we cool?"

"I don't watch it."

"Jay. I make a lot already, and I thank you. Man, my children thank

you, my wife, she *really* thank your ass. I only ask for the others that got in late. I mean, all the brothers is in now, whole neighborhoods. They all listen to me. They ask me to ask you."

"I don't pay attention to it."

Sammy didn't answer right away. "All right man, that's cool. You comin' our way this Saturday?"

"Maybe. I'll see how it goes."

"How's Mary?"

"Are you going to be bartending at the poolroom tonight?"

"Man, you know, with all the *long* bread I make I think a quitting, and I talk to Nick. He look at me like I his son saying I's going off to war, so yeah, I be there all week. Every week till who knows."

"We'll be over."

"All right, that excellent news. . . . Jay?"

He answered.

"Man, sorry to ask about that other shit."

"Sammy, I truly don't follow it. All I can tell you is that everyone should put their money in what they believe in, that's what matters."

No sooner had they concluded the call than he had another. It was Jimmy Hakken again. He took it reluctantly.

"Chevalier. You ever read this book *Count of Monte Cristo*?"

"A long time ago."

"Dree gave it to me. It's good."

Another Hakken pause. "You didn't grow up rich?"

"I became a ward of the state at age seven."

Another. "No shit. Later, Chevalier."

Mary walked to Jay's office and peered in the open door. He waved her in, and by the time he put his phone down she'd seated herself.

"Finally talking to the press?"

"Jimmy Hakken."

"Oh, *him*."

"You don't like him?"

"He's a little scary, isn't he?"

"How's that?"

"Well, to put it politely, he's hardly a wizard at communicating. He stares at me and I get shivers."

"I'm thinking of putting him in charge of the old factory when Deirdre moves to the new one."

"Jimmy *Hakken?*"

"Yes."

She glanced away, found the only picture he had on his walls. She'd examined it before and asked him about it. Ryder's *The Toilers of the Sea*, a small boat at the crest of a wave careening toward a full moon. She focused back on Jay. Sometimes she couldn't figure out what he was up to, but this was completely ridiculous. He wanted a former gang leader to run a high-tech factory?

"Did you read the latest?" she said.

"I don't read that stuff."

"Well, the headline was something like, Do They Clone Phones or Death-metal Fans? There was a photo of Hakken and another worker leaving the factory."

"Kind of funny. What's death metal?"

"It evolved out of heavy metal. It's sort of Gothic and dark. Like Black Sabbath on amphetamines."

"Oh," he said, sounding as if he didn't have a clue.

"Why are we getting so much bad publicity? I'm trying my best, but something's not right. As a matter of fact, something is wrong."

"Let's not worry about it."

"How can we not worry about it? For the first time our stock price has dipped. We're selling more phones than ever and our stock price goes down."

"The stock price is not what's important."

"What is then?"

"People are communicating better."

"You don't care about the stock price?"

"No."

She stared at him. And actually saw him this time, realizing he was grumpy today. *Really* grumpy. Maybe he wasn't feeling well. "Are you okay?"

"I'm fine."

"Jay, have you been eating, sleeping, taking care of yourself at all? You look feverish."

"Sammy asked about you. He called this morning. He's worried about the stock price too. He tells me a lot of people in Oakland have invested."

"Isn't that the main reason you showed Sammy the phone?"

He stared at her now.

"Have you ever eaten sushi?" she said.

He shook his head.

"Would you let me take you out tonight?"

"I told Sammy we might stop by. We haven't been at the poolroom for over two months."

"You don't need a greasy burger, you need some raw fish." She giggled. "My grandfather would growl at me if he ever heard me say that." She paused. "How's your arm? *Fine?*" she said before he could answer. He turned his head to glance out the window, and she followed his eyes. Fog drifted up the bay toward the Golden Gate Bridge, the distant shoreline barely visible.

"Do you want me to start talking to the press?" he said, facing her again. "Maybe that will fix our stock price. That seems to be the only thing anyone cares about."

She'd never heard him so sarcastic, but she ignored it. "The problem runs deeper than that. I think we're being sabotaged. I don't know what to do about it. Did you hear from Duncan?"

"Yes."

"And?"

"The gun was government issue registered to an address in Brooklyn."

"How does Duncan hack into that stuff? He's really remarkable at finding out things, isn't he? Does the address lead to anyone?"

"According to the police both men were using fake IDs, so we can't be sure. Besides, the guy who lived there moved out two weeks ago—Michael Pegonis."

"So?"

"He worked security for Alden Stone Associates four years ago."

"*Jesus.* Is that Wendell's father?"

"I doubt it has anything to do with the father. The more I've thought over the whole incident, I think it was Wendell getting even with me, hoping I might get intimidated, or at least beat up. After all, we didn't like each other on first sight, and then I humiliated him, intentionally or not."

He reached with his good arm and rubbed his ear. "Wendell probably knew Pegonis when he worked for his father and hired him. When they came to the factory that morning pretending to be FCC, Deirdre told me one of the men was frightened by Hakken."—*who wouldn't be?* she thought—"Pegonis, or whoever, must have replaced him by that

evening with the small guy who slapped Deirdre around. Maybe Pegonis got more than he bargained for with this new man, and things turned
messy. I haven't told you, but the father, or Alden Stone Associates, has
been trying to buy us, or buy me out. Maybe Wendell thought he might
expedite the negotiations for his father if I were scared or hurt, I can't
imagine he wanted me shot. That might have been his rationale for sending those men."

"The father's been trying to buy you out? Why don't you tell me
these things?"

"I just did."

She almost shook her head in frustration. "So *they*'re the ones dump-
ing the stock. I figured they had been buying it. And why wouldn't they?
They're not fools. But what *bastards*. God, I'm so glad I don't work for
him anymore. Are you thinking of selling?"

"That's not what this is about."

"I wish you would tell me what it *is* about."

"I have. It's about people communicating."

She sat there quietly though what she actually wanted was to go to
him, place her hands on his shoulders, stroke his pale face; he really
looked sick. Instead she said, "Jay, we need to hire more people. We need
a good PR person who does only that, who knows the business. This press
issue is hurting us, and I can't seem to straighten it out."

"Your work is superlative. You've been everything I hoped you'd be."

Did he really think that? "I need to know what you want so I can do
my job. You don't run a company like any I've been associated with. It
makes it a bit difficult sometimes. I wish you would at least hire a secretary."

"Are you working too hard? Do you want to take some time off?"

"Yeah," she said, and watched him suppress his surprise and distress.

"When? How much time would you like?"

She paused as if considering, letting him suffer, but relented since he
felt terrible anyway. "A few hours. Tonight. Please let me take you out for
sushi." *Wow*, a little smile.

"Okay," he said, "but allow me to treat you."

"No, *I* would like to pay for once; you're always so generous. And we
take my car. You haven't even ridden in it yet."—*and* it doesn't have a
bench seat with springs that jab and that's covered in cat hair. "Okay?"

He nodded.

She stayed in her chair, examining him, then stood slowly, adjusted her skirt, and headed toward the door. She wanted to know if he was watching her walk away, hoped he was, yet wasn't willing to turn around and check. God, he still made her nervous.

Jay knew he'd missed a few calls during his discussion with Mary. His phone remembered. For the moment he ignored the two from project managers renovating the new manufacturing facility. With the one from Deirdre he thought *dial* and she immediately answered.

"Deirdre. Jay."

"Hey," she said. "You know that kind of rhymes—Jay-*hey*. I know I called you, but can I call you back? Wendy needs me right now, if that's okay?"

"Of course." The call ended. He received another almost immediately.

"Mr. Chevalier?"

"Yes."

"Detective Artega. From the armed assault on March twenty-eighth."

"Right. I remember."

"I'd think you would. Mr. Chevalier, this is not an official call, but I noticed you're not pressing charges."

"That's right."

"May I ask you why?"

"May I ask your interest?"

"Off the record?"

"Sure."

"A lot of money was thrown at cleaning this thing up. And I mean a *lot*. I wondered if you'd been threatened in some way not to press charges. We can protect you if that's the case."

"Detective, I appreciate your concern. My reasons for not pressing charges have nothing to do with fear."

A silence as Jay wondered about the true intent of the call.

"I'll say good-bye then," said the cop.

"Detective Artega?"

"Yeah?"

"Thanks for calling."

Both listening, saying nothing. Then Artega said, "You make a great phone. Say hey to Sammy. We used to box together as kids, before he got so damn big," and he rung off.

So that was it: Sammy had called Artega.

He rotated out of his oak swivel chair and headed down the hall to Mary's office. Most of the office doors on the sixth floor were left open now though he'd never mentioned or recommended it. He glanced through her doorway—no one—greeted a few coworkers on his way to the elevators. He could've found her with his LiveCell yet rejected the idea, and rejected the elevator as well, passed by and entered the stairwell. Something in him wanted to be with her, just to feel her presence.

On the landing between the two floors, he stopped and gazed out the window. Though all but a sliver of bay was denied him, he could still tell that most of the fog had dissipated. He turned away from the view and threw maybe two dozen quick punches, shadowboxing fiercely for perhaps half a minute until the pain in his left arm and a rising nausea forced him to stop. Frustration flooded him. There was still so much to do. And he was sick, worn-out, impatient, angry. Some part of him wanted to desert all his goals and just disappear. If only he could be back in the wilderness with his grandfather. If only for a week. One week of the sweat lodge, the woods, the elixir! How he missed those days.

He descended the stairs and walked into the lounge, that door kept open now as well.

"I thought I might find you here," he said.

"You want a cup?"

"Okay." He took a seat in the wicker rocker.

"Did you go to my office?"

He nodded, but she missed it.

"Did you notice that new print ad layout on my screen?"

This time she saw him shake his head.

"It has the headline, 'Is your two-year-old using your cell phone as a hammer again? Not a problem if it's a LiveCell.' I'm trying to show that our phones are safe even for babies, along with, of course, their healing properties, and I figured a little humor wouldn't hurt. I suppose the signal boxes could be damaged though if a baby hammered on them. I'll have to think about that. We need a third supplier for those by the way. At over eighteen thousand phones a day now, it makes Chet Simmons too nervous with only the two suppliers. He told me our Mexican supplier's been repeatedly late in shipping us product over the last few months. I know it's overkill, but he'd like to have three."

"He can tell me these things, can't he?"

"Chet's still a little shy around you."

"Shy?"

"Well, scared I guess."

"I'll talk to him."

She brought the coffee, and he reached up to take one of the mugs from her, thanking her. She sat beside him on the leather sofa, took a sip of hers. "It's a little strong."

"It's fine," he said. She was examining him again, always watching everything. So aware.

"Jay? Are you sure you're okay?"

He nodded.

"I don't think you'd ask for help if you needed it. Would you?"

A pause, his nose pointed into the steam. "Wendy Smith. Do you know her?"

"I've met her a few times. Deirdre promoted her to personal assistant. Did you know that?"

"She told me."

"I don't think it was Deirdre's idea. What do you want to know about Wendy Smith?"

"Your intuition."

"The truth, no politics?"

He nodded again.

"She's very ambitious. I don't really trust her though I've no reason not to, and I wonder if her beauty doesn't make people envious and react differently than they might otherwise. She seems cold though, unemotional, controlling. Very directed. She's after something, and I think she's dangerous for LiveCell. I'm not sure about any of this; I'm only giving you my gut reaction. That enough?"

"Yes. Thanks."

"Jay?"

"Yeah?"

"Does Deirdre know how the phones work?"

"A lot of it."

"Does anyone else know?"

"I don't think so."

She hesitated. "Are you ever going to tell me?"

"I've planned to all along. There is a lot to tell you."

A silence had spread between them when she said, "Can we leave early for just once? It's almost five now. The sushi bar will be open by the time we get there. It's best when it's empty and the chefs aren't too busy."

He took a single sip from his coffee, his hands cradling the warm mug. "Sure," he said finally. "Let's go."

As they left the lounge he said he wanted to get something from his office, and they took the elevator up together. When they entered the orange room, he walked over to a standing coat rack and retrieved a jacket she hadn't seen before. *Actually* a sports coat. He shrugged it on over his sweatshirt.

"Where did you get *this*?" she said, feeling the material of the sleeve. "This is a really nice jacket. What is it, silk? Let me see the label."

He showed her.

"I can't believe it. She's a hot designer. What's happened to you? When did you buy it?"

"Deirdre gave it to me."

She was silent, not telling him how handsome he looked in it. Deirdre seemed to be everywhere these days. She just wished she'd thought to give it to him, but he'd always seemed so uninterested in clothes.

"Why did she give it to you?"

"I guess she wanted to thank me."

Even with his new jacket on, he didn't look any healthier in the Porsche. She retracted the cloth top so he could admire the full effect of the car, but he ignored even his seat belt, merely settled into the leather bucket and stared up at the sky as they drove through San Francisco. The day was clear now, a perfect late April afternoon, the sun on buildings and pavement and trees crystalline as fresh lacquer. She told herself not to drive too fast, but he seemed completely oblivious to the speed. He took out his phone.

"Duncan, Jay. . . . Fine, and you? . . . What I need is some information on a Wendy Smith. . . . You did? And? . . ." He listened for a while. "H-n. . . . Thanks. . . . No, it's all right that you did."

He put his phone away.

"Well?" she said.

"Well, what?"

She slowed for a red light, shifting down through two gears, not getting her usual pleasure from the sound of the engine.

"What did Duncan find out?"

"Wendy Smith doesn't exist. There are lots of Wendy Smiths of course; none matches ours. Duncan is sure it's an alias, probably chosen

because it's such a common name, but he couldn't uncover a link, as he called it. He doesn't know who she is."

"What are you going to do?"

"Nothing."

"*Nothing?*"

"Nothing."

"How about Deirdre?"

"I trust Deirdre."

"Are you going to warn her about Wendy?"

"No."

"Isn't that a lot to risk? Aren't we both thinking the same thing, that this woman is probably an industrial spy trying to get our secrets through Deirdre? Not that I understand everything about it, but it sure seems that way."

He glanced at her. "It's a lot to risk, that's true. I still trust Deirdre. That's what trust is."

"Without a patent? And Deirdre knowing how the phone works? What's going to keep other companies from stealing the secret? You know how strongly I feel about this."

The light turned green and she eased the car forward.

"Soon you will know why I can't patent the phone."

She could tell he'd ended the conversation, and she accelerated, not caring what he thought of her driving.

As she'd anticipated, the sushi bar was empty except for three chefs in crisp white jackets. They were seated by the equally immaculate Japanese hostess, the chefs greeting Mary by name and nodding to Jay. No sooner had they sat down at the polished wooden bar than a smiling waitress offered them a hot cloth dangling from a pair of bamboo tongs. Mary ordered a couple bottles of Japanese beer and a plate of mixed pickles. She tried to put the Deirdre thing behind her. It wasn't easy.

Jay looked up at the chef who bowed a few inches in response. Jay bowed, and the chef bowed again. Jay was starting to bow a second time when she came to the rescue.

"We'll start with sashimi, please." She turned to Jay. "Iso will give us what he feels is best today."

With a quick practiced motion, the chef slid open a glass door at the back of one of the refrigerated cases and selected three different rectangles of glistening fish, examining each for a second before slapping them

down on his cutting board. One piece he tossed back and exchanged for another. He picked up his knife.

The beer and pickles arrived.

"These are pickles?" said Jay. "What unusual colors."

She poured soy sauce into both saucers and separated her chopsticks. "Some people rub their sticks together thinking they're removing splinters. These sticks are high quality, and by trying to build a fire you show you haven't noticed. It would be an insult."

She ate a few pickles and took a long pull on her glass of beer. This was one of her favorite places, he was finally here, and now she was in a lousy mood and worried he wouldn't like it.

Iso reached behind him and selected a large sea-blue plate. On it he mounded three hillocks of finely shredded radish against which he arranged the slices of fish he'd cut. He added some pickled ginger. "*Toro, hamachi, katsuo,*" he said as he handed the plate to her. "*Katsuo* for spring time season. Very good." Iso grunted when she thanked him, reaching over quickly to toss a dot of *wasabi* onto the plate. It landed perfectly and she wondered again if he practiced the move. She turned to Jay.

"Add a little *wasabi* to your fish if you want with the tip of your chop stick. Don't mix it in your soy sauce. The Japanese believe any cloudiness in soy sauce is an indication of the impurity of the soul." Was she wasting her time explaining these things to him? She wondered why everyone tried to impress when they came to a sushi bar, herself included.

He stared at the raw fish in front of him for a long minute. Then struggling with his chopsticks, the fish slipping away twice, he dipped the edge into the soy sauce—following her admonition not to soak it—and levered it into his mouth, almost dropping it. He chewed thoughtfully, swallowed. Her concern increased as she waited.

"This is actually delicious. I'm surprised it's even fish. Almost melts on your tongue. What did I just eat?"

"That was a rare belly cut of tuna. Try the next one."

Iso was observing them without watching them.

"How do you know so much about Japanese food?" Jay asked her.

"I eat here a lot and I ask questions. This food gives me energy, and I find eating here relaxing."

He nodded to Iso. "This is delicious," he said across the fish case, Iso bowing. "Mary, thanks for this."

"I've wanted to take you here for a long time," she said, the beer, the food, and his appreciation improving her spirits.

Toward the end of their meal, she on her fourth beer as he finished his first, she ordered another round, asking the waitress to bring a beer for Iso as well. They had eaten a variety of sushi, bisecting the meal with a hot miso soup swimming with seaweed. Jay had liked most of it, particularly the raw shrimp where the heads are deep-fried and served separately. He hadn't been so sure about *ika-natto*—squid and fermented soybeans topped by a fresh quail egg yolk all stirred together into a strange porridge. She said it might be an acquired taste. She hadn't been so keen the first time either but hadn't had the heart to tell Iso what she really thought. She was relieved it grew on her.

As they dined, the restaurant and bar progressively filled so that now there was a clatter and murmur of many people around them, lending something intimate and private to their being together. Iso no longer concentrated his efforts on them; he rapidly assembled platter after platter of sushi for different tables, whisked away by the waitresses. Maybe from the beer, or maybe from being embarrassed that she'd gotten so jealous and worried, she suddenly felt an unusual openness toward him.

"You've never been to my new place," she said. "I look out over the entire Pacific, it's really something. Of course you have a similar view in Oregon. Have you been back up to the Siuslaw place?"

"Only once. I really haven't had time, though it breaks my heart. I love it up there."

"You bring those cats every time?"

He nodded.

"You don't know this, but I almost died the day I went up to see you."—her skin felt flushed, her eyes slightly unfocused—"It really frightened me. I guess I was too happy. Everything was so perfect that day. I was so excited to be visiting you, and I drove too fast. This guy on a motorcycle saw me spin and stopped. He treated me as if I were a careless rich idiot, and it bugged me."

"How come you didn't tell me?"

She shrugged and wet her lips. "Can I tell you something?" He nodded. "I'm always a little nervous around you."

He continued to look at her.

"I shouldn't have told you that." She glanced down for a second, wondering if she was getting drunk. He didn't say anything. "Will you tell me about yourself? You never do that. Most men, all they talk about is themselves until you think you're going to scream, but you . . ."

"What do you want to know?"

"You really don't mind?"

He shook his head, and she wondered again how much he'd shared with Deirdre.

"The boxing," she said. "It doesn't make any sense to me."

He took a sip of his beer. "You want the long or the short version?"

"Long." Though she was sure he sensed what she wanted.

He picked up a last pickle with his hand, a purple one, and examined it before tossing it into his mouth.

"I scored well on tests as a kid and was pushed into more and more schooling. I had this obligation to perform, to live up to the opportunities that were offered me. After all, other people were paying for it and I owed them. I was the orphan Indian kid from northern Maine who made it through Harvard. But when I finished there, I felt like I didn't exist. As if I wasn't anything—just all this learned information. You can only live the way other people expect you to for so long."

She knew how that was. Now he picked up a chopstick and started to toy with it, watching his hand as he played with the stick. She was relieved that he didn't drum with it as some men insisted on doing.

"I hitchhiked from Cambridge to Manhattan, not telling anyone I was leaving. Basically I disappeared, knowing it was the only way out. I got a room at the Y and wandered around for a couple of weeks. I remember looking at all the bricks in all the buildings, so many bricks, and thinking that each one had been placed by a human hand. That seemed incredible. One day I walked into a boxing gym. I watched for a while, and the owner and I got to talking. I knew right then I wanted to box. He tried to talk me out of it. 'You're too old to start boxing,' he said, and he was right. I had no illusions, no desire to become a great fighter. I didn't care about that. I just liked Pete. He'd been in the fight game a lot of years and was a terrific trainer. He wasted his time on me though. Until then I'd never had the opportunity to use my body much, but I found out I was naturally strong. My father must have been a very strong man. He might still be alive. Somewhere."

Maybe his father was the reason he didn't want the publicity? She took another drink. She really liked Japanese beer.

"I didn't mind getting hit. Actually, I liked it. I also loved the hard workouts, craved them. Boxing cleared up my complexion. So that's the story—I wasn't much of a boxer."

"Not what I heard."

"That should never have happened."

Iso at this moment reached over and set a plate in front of them with *yamagobo* and *umekyu*. "Good for finish," he said and returned to cutting fish.

"Tell me about these." He pointed at the new plate.

She looked down at the sushi. "They're good for digestion. The burdock root you eat fat end first and the other is full of pickled plum paste. So that's when you met Kelly?"

"About a year after I started boxing."

"He told me you made sandwiches for all the bums."

"He told you that?"

"Said they all ate the sandwiches only to please you."

He looked at her solemnly, and she worried she shouldn't have revealed that, but then he smiled.

"You want another beer?" she said, knowing she shouldn't have another but not caring. He declined. As their waitress passed she ordered it and some tea for them both.

There were so many things she wanted to share, yet she didn't know how to approach him, how to get close. She was used to men always coming at her, wanting her, and she knew how to respond to that, how to handle them. But with Jay, she felt off balance, careening toward him. Just like that boat toward the moon in the painting he had in his office.

She waited for him to speak, but he said nothing more. Was he going to clam up again? "Do you miss your mother?"

"Yes." He reached for another piece of *maki*. "Do you miss yours? You don't talk about her much."

"Did you meet her when you went to the farm?"

"Briefly."

"She's a strong woman. My grandparents are the same way. Solid Vermont Yankee stock is what she calls it. Mother can be tough to be around but everyone respects her. She never took to Kelly much. She was always strange around him, as if she watched him out of the corner of her eye. Did Kelly tell you about any of it?"

"In the city he used to talk about growing up with your dad in, wasn't it northern New Hampshire?"

She nodded. "Irving."

"At the farm I met your dad. Kelly told about how your father rescued him after Patricia died. They came back east together and Kelly moved into the abandoned trailer on the farm."

"My mom wasn't so keen on it, let me tell you. They used to fight

about it. Made me really mad because of how I felt about Kelly. Kelly sure liked my mom though. I've always wondered if he didn't have a crush on her. Maybe that's where the tension came from."

The waitress arrived with the tea and beer.

She filled her glass and took a long sip. "Jay, what are you really up to with the phones?"

"Besides people communicating?"

"I'm starting to believe it has nothing to do with money."

"Is this Jay-tells-all-his-secrets night?"

"So will you tell me?"

He looked around at the other diners, reached for his tea, sipped. "The world has always been manipulated by basically the same type of person. This self-professed *aristocracy* do whatever they want—they lie and deceive, they embezzle and steal, they murder and start wars—and so many lives are destroyed, and the rest of us sadly never seem to know what's going on, and it's this ignorance that keeps this group in power. This elect group, they—"

"You're after *them*?"

He paused. "My hope is that our phones will increase intuitiveness over time. People will become aware through using LiveCell phones, and collectively know how they are being manipulated and what to do about it. It won't happen with everyone, but it should affect enough—"

"I never thought of that," she said almost in a whisper. "They do increase intuitiveness, don't they?" She saw so much of it finally. It made sense and it excited her. She reached for her beer to be doing something with her hands. Being with him was always so complex.

"Did I answer your question?" he said.

It took her a minute. "Jay, wouldn't that make an incredible new ad slogan: Change The World, Use LiveCell Phones."

A grimace. "Maybe we better leave that alone for now."

"It's what you always insisted, people communicating better," she said, the feeling between them overwhelming her. Just ask him, she told herself. If you don't ask him nothing will ever happen.

"Jay," she said softy. "You want to come see my place tonight?"

He said nothing.

She tried again: "Maybe you could explain the phone to me if you came over?" God, she was sounding like a slut. This was ridiculous. *Here he tells me about changing the world, and all I want is him.*

"Actually I still have to stop by the factory," he said. "What time is it?"

In confusion she checked her wrist and told him it was twenty to eight. He never wore a watch. "So, are you coming over?" she said, taking another long swallow of beer, feeling really stupid, blushing again.

"I need to stop by the factory. I'm a bit late as it is."

"What's at the factory?"

"I need to do something."

"You go there every damn night. Why?"

"You want to come with me?" he said quietly.

"Precious *Deir*dre won't mind?" Why did she blurt out these things? The sad smile that came to his face made her doubly regret what she'd said.

"I'll show you. I'll call Deirdre, and if she's still there, I'll ask her to go home. Okay?"

She reached out and touched his shoulder.

NINE

Mary looked out across the endless reach of the Pacific. After a few minutes her glance shifted, focused on the scattered pile of mail on her dining room table. She spotted the corner of a postcard she hadn't noticed earlier. The face of the card was a main-street view of Alturas, California. She turned it over. It had been forwarded from her address in Berkeley.

Dear Mary, it started.

Hows everything going? I'm doing OK. Was sad about Patsy but I'm OK now. Been ranching alot which helps. Lot of work in the Springtime as you know. Hows the pool playing going? I read about you and your company in the paper. Wow you are something! I bought one. If you ever need anything you know where I am. Anything!!!

Sincerely,

Garland McKeen (Hank)

His signature was in an elaborate script. Mary wondered if she still had the slip of paper with his address; she knew she hadn't thrown it out. It seemed so long ago. She'd meant to call him and ask about his cousin.

She would write him a card of condolence. Thinking of Garland reminded her of the tournament, and her hands yearned to hold a cue again. Too much time had passed since she'd last played.

Today she finally had a Saturday all to herself—a day off. And all she could think about was Jay. She imagined preparing dinner for him, something special to usher in the summer season; she'd have it all ready to serve, then take a long bath, put on her new outfit—she had bought so many new clothes, yet he never seemed to notice any of them—and wait for him to arrive. They could share a bottle of champagne. Lately she'd been ordering it by the case. Though she still liked beer, she was amazed at how good really fine champagne tasted. Her house was already tidy as her maid cleaned Fridays. Would he come if she invited him?

While she was rinsing her hair in the bathtub, her phone signaled. The thought that it might be Jay and that she was naked excited her. But when the phone was close enough, she knew it wasn't him.

"Hello?" she said.

"Hey Mary, it's Duncan."

"*Oh*, hi, Duncan."

"Did I get you at a bad time?"

"Actually, could I call you back?"

"Will it be soon? I need to talk to you." A slight pause. "What're you doing, washing dishes?"

"I'll call you back in a little while, okay?"

"Okay," he said, and she ended the call.

Drying herself, she wandered over to one of the huge windows overlooking the ocean. Her thoughts ran to Jay again.

On the sushi night, she'd watched him minister to the phones for the first time. They'd pulled into the empty parking lot, Deirdre gone as promised. He unlocked the factory, turned on the hallway lights, but left the clean room in darkness, only the metal edges of the lab tables highlighted in red from the exit signs. She didn't comment. He turned to her, seeming nervous. "If you feel strange in any way, stop me. Any way at all." She wasn't sure what he meant by strange; she already felt strange, and his unusual nervousness was infectious. She couldn't remember him being even mildly nervous before.

He kneeled in front of the phones with his arms held out. She stood close beside him, no idea what he was doing, a thrill of anticipation mixing with the beer and her general excitation. His arms dropped and a stillness settled over everything, almost as if there was no time. A humming

started in her brain; was that what he meant by strange? After a few more minutes the humming moved lower between her legs. Unlike in the boardroom, she wasn't afraid. Quite the opposite. Strange or not, there was no way she was going to stop him! With a sharp thrill, maybe because she was allowing herself a newfound freedom, she knew she wanted it and wondered if he would notice, if she could do it soundlessly. She bit her bottom lip, feeling her orgasm rising, but just as it was about to happen, the phones began to throb with their eerie iridescence.

Afterwards, he'd questioned her. How had she felt? Had watching the infusion bothered her at all? She couldn't tell him the truth, not yet anyway, but wondered if he'd guessed, or if there was something else he was after. What did he mean by saying that humility was the beginning of salvation? Why had he said that? It was so hard to tell with him.

She stopped looking out the window and picked up the fallen towel. As she walked into the bedroom she brought her hand to her nose and smelled herself, rubbing the silky wetness between her fingers and thumb. She dressed slowly and decided to stop thinking about him, to contemplate her options for the day instead. Maybe she should head to the poolroom, say hello to Sammy and Nick, run a few racks, find that part of her life again? But her longing for Jay continued, much as she suppressed it. She made a deal with herself: "If he calls me, I'll ask him to dinner, I'll insist he come." She concentrated, attempting to will him into calling her.

And her LiveCell told her there was a call. She reached for it eagerly. It was Duncan again.

"I was just about to call you, what's up?"

"Mary, I'm sorry to bug you on your day off," he said with his tense giggle.

"What's on your mind?"

"It's this Wendy Smith thing. I've been making some headway. I think she's a fucking spy. My guess was that she's working for a cell phone manufacturer. But the weird thing is, her phone records show that she's made two calls to New York. Alden Stone Associates. Is that a weird coincidence or what? And you know I don't believe in weird coincidences."

"Have you told Jay?"

"That's just it, Jay doesn't seem to care. I've told him, and he just says things will take their course, for me to leave it alone. I mean, what the hell is that? Doesn't he realize how important this is? He runs this company like a—" He hesitated. "Do you know Wendy Smith is moving in with Deirdre?"

"When did that happen?"

"They just announced it. What a fucking company. What a *lovely* group. I go over there to warn *Miss* Deirdre Holly about Wendy Smith and you know what she does? She tells me to mind my own business. Then that tattooed totem pole Hakken shows up and stands there glaring at me. I mean, why is he working at the factory? He's like the grim reaper in a B movie. A real wacko. Put him in some satanic rock band, but keep him away from me and LiveCell. Hopefully Jay will fire him when they move to the new factory next week."

She didn't tell him that Jimmy Hakken might soon be running the old factory. Instead she said, "Duncan, you should worry about doing your work and let everyone else do theirs."

His voice jumped an octave. "We have a chance to make a fucking fortune here. Don't you realize that? But if we don't play smart, we're *fucked*. You know what else really bothers me?" He didn't wait for her reply. "I can't find *any* patents on the phones. Not a one. Nothing pending. *Nothing*, nada. And I still don't even understand how the fucking things work. I've analyzed the boxes. They're basic electromagnetic senders and receivers, standard to every cell phone, have the same battery and charging system. The inexplicable thing is that they're missing the central processing unit, the brain chip."—*he doesn't realize how close he is*—"And on top of that there's an analog preamp that translates digital code connected to the prongs, but why the signal even translates to the cell structure I can't figure out. Those prongs are highly sensitive, low-frequency electrodes, but beyond them are just cells. I've cut a few phones apart, but there aren't any other electronics or chips inside. And let me tell you, you cut into a LiveCell phone—it dies. Fast. Darkens a little and that's it. You can whack them, nick them, but don't cut them open. I'm there with this razorblade, and right after my first slice the phone starts blinking like crazy, like it's going insane. My second deep slice and it turns dull and hard. Thing wouldn't work at all. Does Deirdre know how the phones work?"

She sensed he was trying to sneak the question in.

"No," she said.

"Are you sure?"

"Yes."

"I don't think you're telling me the truth. I think you and her both know. You must because you and Jay are like—" He stopped again.

There was a long silence.

"Are you going to report this conversation to Jay?" he said. Again he didn't wait for her answer. "I'm only trying to look out for the good of the company. Here we might have a spy getting our secrets from Deirdre and no one listens to me. An industrial spy and no patents. What a *great* combination. I mean, we have the best fucking product since the silicon chip and he runs the company like— Oh, the hell with it. And everyone treats him like a goddamn saint. I know you think he's perfect." Tears crept into his voice. A brilliant guy but what an emotional wreck.

"Duncan."

"*What?*"

"Have you been taking any time off?"

"I'm just a little worried about the future. Our stock price slipped again last week."

"Only a fraction."

"Yeah, but it should be going through the roof."

"Everything is down. Besides we've already both made a lot of money."

"It depends what you call *a lot*."

"You can't tell me you need more."

"Listen, do you rent or own?"

"It isn't any of your business."

"My point. Mary, we could all become *really* rich. Super rich. Have anything we wanted."

Her eyes went out to the horizon. So clear this morning. The blue above blue like the tone of two harmonizing bells.

"And last week he brings the price of the phones down again. It looks bad, as if there's not enough demand, and here we are months behind in filling orders. At a hundred a phone we were giving them away, but now—

"Duncan, I've got to get going."

"You do? Where are you going?"

"Good-*bye*, Duncan."

"Okay. Listen, thanks for talking to me. And Mary?"

"Yeah."

"Talk to Jay. We need to get rid of Wendy Smith. We need to raise the price of the phones. *And* find out where the patents are. He'll listen to you." He terminated the call before she could reply.

Duncan had depressed her, and she longed to talk to Jay more than

ever. What she really wanted was for him to call her. She knew she had
to stop chasing him.

She reached for her phone, thought a number, waited.

"Hey Kelly."

"*Mary*, what's going on?"

"You have a minute?"

"Sure. Just came in from mending fences. Was about to fix myself
something to eat."

"It's Saturday. Why aren't you eating with the family?"

"Tonight I will."

"I got your letter. Thanks."

They were both quiet. She realized again how amazing the phones
were. Sometimes you didn't have to say anything.

"Was Jay changed when you saw him again?"

"Fifteen years is bound to change someone."

"How was he different?"

"Well, in New York, he was unsure of himself. Seemed lost. When I
saw him in Vermont he was at peace, seemed to know exactly what he
wanted."

"He's hard to read."

"Doesn't talk much about himself."

"I *guess!*"

"Mary, are you okay?"

A silence. "I just keep thinking about him too much. And I still don't
really understand him. I mean, I understand some things, but there's
something I'm not getting. Here he is the CEO of this company and he
doesn't want any kind of publicity for himself. I keep wondering if there's
some reason, if there's something in his past. I've had to take a lot of the
press responsibility, and I get asked about him all the time. I never know
what to say. And he's always so calm about everything, like nothing could
ever go wrong."

"Is that what's bothering you?"

"Maybe. Maybe it's that he has so much confidence in me. The
responsibility can be overwhelming. What if I let him down?"

He didn't reply.

"Jay never really tires," she said. "Even when he was shot he just kept
working. He almost had blood poisoning and had to be hospitalized, but
he worked the whole time. He's so disciplined it makes me feel I have to

perform at his level. Sometimes I can't, and he's eleven years older. He never even gets angry with anyone if he likes them, no matter what they do. He's hired some very strange people, and there are all these problems in the company because of it, but he doesn't intercede. He just has faith that people will do the right thing. If he likes you, he trusts you, and that's the end of it."

"Is it that you *sense* something is going to go wrong?"

They were silent again. Then she said, "I get the feeling he sort of knows everything, like he has this master plan and everything is just as it should be, so what do I know." She paused. "Kelly, why did Jay go find you?"

He didn't answer.

"You have it too, don't you?" she said.

"I did. The drugs dulled most of it."

"That's why you were so upset about me finding Pilgrim, wasn't it? You knew I had it and thought I'd fall apart like you did."

"I had it so bad as a teen, I couldn't stand it. I foresaw my father's death. I knew he was going to die in the mill. I'd seen the red pulp-water. No one believed me, I *begged* him." He paused. "After he died, Addison took me in, and I lived on a cot in the back of the poolroom, cleaned up and racked balls all day. No one except Addison and your father gave a rat's ass about me. I did every downer I could get my hands on. They helped. Smack was even better. That slowed things down. For me it was a huge relief."

"You asked Jay not to say anything. He knew you had the ability when you were together in New York."

"Yeah. He sensed it and I told him. I foresaw his boxing trainer's death. Sucked because of course it didn't make any difference."

"Do you still?"

"Rarely."

"You could have told me."

"I was too scared to reveal it. I wasn't even sure about telling Jay about you."

"It got him off your back."

He was silent.

"Sorry," she said. "I don't mean to be so bitchy, don't know what's wrong with me." A pause. "Since we're being so honest. Did he ever have any lovers, male or female?"

"I don't know."

She waited.

"That's the truth." Another lull. "He's the one, isn't he?"

"Yes." She could sense Kelly's emotion overwhelming him and his need to change the subject.

"What are you going to do today?" he said.

"I think I'll head to the poolroom and practice. I haven't been on a table in months. I need to do something."

"Get out of your head for a while. Pool might work."

"Instead of drugs, you mean." She meant it as a joke but realized it sounded cruel.

"Too bad we couldn't run a few racks together. We had some good afternoons, didn't we?"

"We did . . . You're about the only person I can really talk to." Her throat was tight. She told him she had to go, and they ended the call. She went to get her cue.

For once the traffic on the Golden Gate Bridge was moving briskly. With the top down and the sounds of a CD sailing just above the noise of the car, she glanced out past the sienna-red fencing to the flashing blue of the water. Her glance was habit instead of the yearning it had once been. " . . . a fire, these dreams that pass me by, this salvation and desire, keeps getting me down . . ." The sensuality of the singer's voice stirred up thoughts of Jay again. At least she was doing something besides waiting. Maybe Nick would shoot a few racks; she'd even play him straight pool if he wanted.

Once on Van Ness, she parked near the familiar sign, the neon *Jake's* script unlit and sad-looking. She battened the top, bleeped the locks, and walked toward the poolroom, her cue case gently nudging her thigh. As she climbed the stairs, nostalgia for the place increased with each step. The door was open but the room empty, the jukebox mute, and there was that almost brittle smell of old wood, chalk and wax. Four sconces were lit behind the bar, the cavernous room so dark and silent, the few window shades muddy green against the sunshine, a slice or two of dusty daylight angling to the floor. She set down her cue case on the bar, sat at one of the aligned stools, and stared at the beer cooler lost in thought. Nick's office door opened and he peered out through his thick glasses.

"Can I help you?" he said as he walked over. "—*Mary!* How nice, you come and see Nick."

She greeted him.

"You wanna cup of coffee or something?"

"Sure. That would be great."

"You wanna espresso? We got a new machine."

"Just regular would be fine."

"Okay. I put on the pot."

As he filled the coffee maker with water, she realized she didn't know anything about him. It was strange how you could feel close to someone without that knowledge, or how you could have a close relationship with someone on just one level. The machine gurgled and the aroma lent a freshness to the stale air.

Nick brought her a steaming cup along with a small plastic container of half-and-half and two packets of sugar. She ignored the sugar.

"You no take sugar?" he said.

She shook her head.

"Espresso I take sugar, no milk," he said.

"You're not going to have one?"

"One in the morning is good. Two is no good."

She took a sip of her coffee.

"How you been? You not practicing no more?" he said.

"I've been too busy, Nick."

"Yes, I know. I read about you and your special telephone in the papers. Sammy, he makes lotsa money."

"Do you invest in the market?"

"What do I need the worry for? Too many people lose lotsa money in that place. I have all I need anyway."

"Nick? Can I ask you something?"

"Sure, you go ahead."

"What do you do when you're not here?"

"I'm at home. I have a small apartment, a very nice neighborhood. I have a garden, some roses, some vegetables. I like opera. I listen to opera and I cook sometimes. I read books. My brother, he send me books in Italian, send me whatever I need. No TV. I don't like TV."

"You have a brother?"

"In Boston. He come over before me. He is different from me. He is a very important businessman, very powerful, many people work for him."

"You ever see him?"

"No."

"Why not?"

He didn't answer. He glanced toward a vibrating sliver of sunlight on one of the pool tables.

"Sorry, Nick. I didn't mean to pry."

"It's okay. Boston make me sad. I don't go back there."

"I'm sorry, Nick. I didn't mean to upset you."

"It's okay."

"You want to shoot some straight?"

It took him a little while to answer. He gave her one of his cryptic smiles. "Sure. Let's play some straight pool. We shoot some straight."

They played a couple of seventy-five point games, Mary running forty-two balls in the second game. Nick still won both games, yet only by a few points, and she wondered if she really wanted to beat him. There was such beauty in his careful, gentle stick-work, in the way he controlled the cue ball using mostly topspin, in his cautious safety play. No wonder he had been New England champion. They didn't talk, except to communicate about the game, and that was seldom. She relished it, this mid-day stillness of the old room with just the melody of clicking balls, the *k-nock* of successful shots striking wooden bottoms of leather pockets, Nick chalking his unadorned cue and slowly circling the table, examining the lie of balls through his glasses, then calculating his score and sliding the wooden beads into position on the overhead wire with his cue shaft.

On their third game, the poolroom began to fill, and Nick was intermittently pulled away to help customers. They decided to forgo the match.

She practiced for about an hour and kept making deals with herself—if I can run two tables of nine-ball in a row he'll call me, if I can make three massé shots in a row he'll call me—but kept missing, so she boxed her cue and went to the bar for a beer. She'd have to wait until Sammy arrived at four to order a sandwich though she could almost taste the crabmeat roll. She felt a little guilty being inside when outside such a perfect spring day waited. The poolroom languor and sipping drafts in the afternoon reminded her of being naughty as a child. Those times when she knew she was doing something she shouldn't, but the knowledge intensified the pleasure, just as it made her uneasy. Such a seductive decadence.

Twice she was offered nine-ball games, but she didn't feel up to playing for money. Then, half an hour early, Sammy walked in.

"Hey girl. How's things?"

"Okay. You?"

"I'm good, *real* good. Attended a workout with my man Jay. Good to see his ass after so many months. And now you back, makes it all doubly fine."

He sat down beside her. *So that's where Jay was.* She was relieved she hadn't called him. His arm must finally be better.

Sammy continued, "That boy got hisself some kinda punch . . . Hey, that thing yours?"

"What thing?"

"That silver bolt-a-lightning parked on Van Ness?"

She grinned.

"Goddamn girl, you gotta give me a ride."

"Anytime."

"I got me something German now too."

"What'd you get?"

"Mercedes, convertible."

"New?"

"Girl, I got a big family. Two-eighty SL—she used, but she smooth and silver too."

They grinned at each other.

"It's good to see you, Sammy."

"It fine to see you. Always fine to see you. Glad to see you got your cue."

"I shot some straight with Nick."

"How'd you do?"

"He beat me two games."

"You ease up on him?"

"I'm not sure. Just watching him play is kind of mesmerizing."

"He still a beautiful shooter, no doubt about that."

"What's between him and his brother? I asked a question about his brother and he went all sad on me—wouldn't say a thing."

Sammy glanced around him. "He don't talk to me none about that neither, and you know how close we are. I find out about it though. You cool right?"

She waited.

The smile. "This the story I hear." He leaned toward her and lowered his voice. "The poolroom Nick run in Boston, his brother own. Or brother and his *associates*. The brother a real big deal now, *real* big. Took over the whole fucking thing from these associates from what I hear. Anyhow, back then, I'm not so sure Nick know everything his brother

involved in. They use the poolroom for certain things, meetings in the back, drug deals, shit like that. Maybe Nick juss turn the blind eye, maybe he not hip, but he probably know—it his brother after all, right?"

Sammy glanced around again. "Then everything go south for a time, and there these shootings. Usual shit, retaliation over territory, like that. No big deal. Except—Nick's wife and son get gunned down. It some stupid fucking mistake. A *mistake*, can you believe that shit? Nick lost it, really fall apart. He in and out of an asylum out there. The end of his pool career as a stick, he all nerves now. Eventually, his brother buy him this joint, and he take care of everything. This place don't take in all that much, and the rent real steep in this neighborhood, so the brother juss send checks. I suppose he feel responsible. That the word I got anyway."

"Jesus."

"Sucks, don't it?"

They were both quiet.

"Like some months ago, I tell Nick I wanna quit, and you shoulda seen his face. He *still* ain't over that, and it musta been twenty years ago."

"I knew he didn't have a family, but I had no idea."

"Yeah, more you learn about other people, more you know we *all* carrying something around."

"Was Jake his son's name?"

Sammy nodded and looked at his watch—a new one. "I got to get working. You want a crab roll, 'nother beer?"

She didn't respond right away, but after a few moments she said, "Sure, why not?"

TEN

Deirdre Holly was relieved that she didn't have to look at the bullet hole in the floor of her old office any longer. The bullet hole in the wall had been patched, but the one in the wood floor, though the police had dug out the slug, remained, reminding her of a poorly healed wound. She'd felt chills every time she walked over the spot. Not the same chills as when Wendy's fingertips brushed along her naked body, but chills nonetheless. She missed Jimmy Hakken though—even if he'd been a bit icy towards her over the last few months. Let him be cold: *Hey*, she wasn't going to explain the situation to him. When she'd first come to Santa Cruz she'd heard rumors about Jimmy Hakken, but moving in different worlds—he was hardly a surfer-type—they hadn't run into each other until he'd applied for the job with LiveCell. Then she'd been so against hiring him, and now he was running the old factory. It showed her how presumption could mess you up. He wasn't a yeoman anymore; he'd become a knight. At least in his mind. In hers he was more of a Visigoth.

Wendy Smith had helped decorate her office in the new factory. Jay told Deirdre, "It's your office, do whatever you want," but Wendy had been uncompromising, insisting on white walls. Maybe because of this, Deirdre chose a muted copper similar to the orange of Jay's office. Wendy hated the color and had refused to help with the painting. That the color irked her, secretly pleased Deirdre. Perhaps to make amends she accepted

Wendy's preference in furniture: modern, blonde satin-finished maple; "simple but elegant" was how Wendy phrased it. Deirdre also agreed to hang framed vintage movie posters on the walls. They were an extravagance, like way too expensive, but she could afford it now. The one of Mary Pickford was Wendy's favorite, Deirdre quietly noting that her own appearance was nothing like the star's. She preferred the poster of Veronica Lake, who at least looked somewhat like Wendy.

With her new lifestyle, Deirdre had decided to see a therapist, choosing a name out of the Yellow Pages. She didn't know how else to go about it. Just as she never spoke about her family to anyone, she wasn't willing to mention this either. During the seventh session, the therapist had asked if she'd considered that her lesbianism might be a defense mechanism fostered by a fear of physical contact with men. She told the therapist, "I was gay before my father ever touched me, if that's what you're driving at." The therapist must have gotten her diploma from Walmart. Deirdre rejected the idea of further therapy, wondering why she'd entertained the notion in the first place. She supposed her impulse for help was some kind of media conditioning: like, get rich, get therapy. Wendy Smith's beautiful body was the kind of therapy she wanted. She'd deal with the pain from her past in her own way.

Deirdre headed for work in her Dodge wagon, no surfboards riding in back for almost a year. LiveCell and Wendy took all her time now. Wendy had stayed home that morning, saying she wasn't feeling well, and since Deirdre was alone and early for work—for once not having had to wait for Wendy to get out of the bathroom—she considered swinging by the old factory and attempting to patch things up with Jimmy Hakken. But just before the turnoff, she vetoed the idea. She'd be seeing him later on at the department heads meeting anyway. Her thoughts wandered back to when Jay had offered Hakken the job, asking him to run the old factory. Hakken had just stared. Then, without a word, he'd walked out of the office, leaving them both standing there. They'd looked at each other, not sure what was going on. When Hakken returned about four or five minutes later, he stood in front of them. "Chevalier, you will never regret this."

Jimmy Hakken metamorphosed her old office into what reminded her of a medieval dungeon. On the walls he hung an authentic hangman's noose with thirteen knots—he proudly pointed this out to her—three sets of crossed swords and some ancient axes with two blades; he even set out a human skull on the desk. She didn't check to see if it was

real. He probably prized the bullet hole in the floor. Deirdre had taken many of the original crew with her to the new complex, and Hakken filled the vacancies with some of his old gang, the Druids. She had to admit though, all the gang members he hired worked hard. He ran the factory with intense almost military seriousness. She didn't ask Jay if Hakken knew about infusing the phones. She doubted it. Jimmy Hakken would never break his word by spying as she had—he lived to keep his word. She wondered if Mary MacKensie knew.

With the station wagon's windows rolled down, a July breeze trifling with her hair—she was letting it grow out—she pulled in and parked in the empty lot; no one had a reserved space. Jay had unearthed another solid though dilapidated warehouse to hold the new facility, and again the exterior of the building hid the technologically sophisticated interior. As she unlocked the front doors, Luke, exactly fifteen minutes early as usual, rode up on his Panhead, the straight pipes barking, making a racket. He barely fit on the motorcycle, and it was a *large* bike. Jimmy Hakken had insisted she take one of his people for security, and he'd sent Luke Delamar. Jay okayed it; though as he stipulated with all the gang members, Luke wasn't to carry a gun. She didn't think he needed a gun. When she greeted him, he grunted. Jimmy Hakken was verbose compared to Luke.

She activated the voice lock and opened the inner doors, Luke following like a giant black bear. He began turning on lights and checking the humidity, temperature, and carbon-level of the clean room from the set of gauges in the hallway; soon he'd be preparing coffee. She'd explained to him many times that he didn't *have* to do those things, but he'd only stared at her. The one time she'd intentionally stared back and waited, he'd said, "Okay, so what? So God beat me with his ugly stick," and stomped off. She hadn't meant *that* at all. Since his beard and hair covered most of his face, it was impossible to tell what he actually looked like anyway, besides the large nose that reminded her of a rutabaga. After the staring confrontation he even cleaned up around her office and took out the factory's trash at the end of each day. She couldn't figure him out, so she just attempted to get along with him as best she could.

Walking into her office, she closed the door and settled in behind her desk. She pressed PLAY on her answering machine and began listening to messages—there were forty-seven. Every morning it was like that. Once she identified a person, she usually skipped the message, returning to it later. One message she listened to all the way through. It was from Chet Simmons, left at 10:21 last night. He *would* use her answering machine

instead of her LiveCell. In his nervous apologetic voice he explained that he was still having trouble filling the orders for the electromagnetic boxes. Those damn black boxes. First the long wait for FCC approval, now their latest supplier raising the price every month. LiveCell had been forced to give up on the Mexican firm, and the one in Korea was about to—

A knock. "Come in," she said.

It was Luke with a mug of coffee. He set it down carefully on her desk, grunted when she thanked him, and left. She'd given up explaining she could get her own coffee. What she hadn't been able to tell him was that she would *prefer* to get her own coffee. She went back to work.

There was a message from Mary's secretary reminding her of the one-thirty meeting. The majority of calls were from unauthorized retailers insisting their orders be filled. On a few of the messages they sounded irate, and that pleased her. LiveCell was a direct-order-only business. By ordering online, by phone, or by mail, a customer received a phone based on when the order came in. Simple. Until a secondary market mushroomed that resold LiveCell phones. These vendors ordered large quantities of phones, then resold them for double the price. Since LiveCell orders were backlogged for months, many consumers paid the higher price rather than wait. It bothered Deirdre—*Like what greedy pricks these phony retailers were*—but Jay told her not to worry about it for the time being. "As long as people are talking on our phones, that's what matters," he'd said. She still tried to fill small orders before the really large ones even though it was against company policy. The last message on her machine was from Wendy. She didn't return the call.

As workers entered the factory and changed into their sterile gear, she checked the inventory of black boxes. They had only enough for less than a week of production. Something had to be done immediately. Should she call Jay and tell him? But he probably knew about the problem though who could tell with Chet Simmons—he was still so nervous around Jay. She decided to wait until the meeting.

Her day proceeded through its normal pattern: she checked with shipping to see how the new ecological shipping-carton insert was working out; she reviewed a bundle of invoices before sending them to Randy Dyer in financial; she answered a few questions from the lab techs; she forced herself to do Wendy's job and returned ten calls to unauthorized retailers, trying hard to be polite—*Like it's not your company*, she reminded herself. She attempted to reach Chet Simmons. Was he hiding?

Twice she almost called Wendy, and twice put the phone back on her desk.

At noon she heard Luke kick-starting his big bike. It finally caught, reached the main road, shifted up through three gears, and the exhaust's bellow receded to silence. She thought of ordering out for a hot sandwich and chips, but she was trying to diet, so she reluctantly retrieved a yogurt from the fridge, added some fresh fruit, and ate outside on the back steps in the sun. As she finished her lunch she heard Luke return, and this prompted her to get ready for the meeting; he was always precisely on time. She went back inside, gathered her briefcase and headed for her wagon, figuring no matter what traffic was like it couldn't take her more than a half-hour to get to the Harcourt Building.

When she entered the elevator there, she was tempted to hit the fourth floor button and walk past her old reception desk, then take the stairs up to the boardroom. "Like what am I today? Miss Nos*talgia*," she said to herself and pressed six.

Jay was the only one in the boardroom, wearing one of his blue T-shirts again. Jay always in blue, Jimmy Hakken always in black, Mary liked silver—she wondered if she shouldn't appoint herself a color but had no clue what to choose.

"Hey, Deirdre," he said. "How are you?"

"I'm really great." When he asked the question she felt as if he really wanted to know. "Am I early?"

"A couple minutes."

The ugly red scar across his bicep made her wince. Though the wound was completely healed, some part of her still felt responsible. "Not much traffic today. You been outside? It's *so* beautiful."

"Not yet."

"You know, you really do work too much."

This slowed their conversation, and during the pause, other department heads arrived.

Mary arrived in the boardroom, her hair pulled back with a diamond clip, her face and neck radiant paleness. She greeted Jay and Deirdre. Duncan walked in next, no longer last as in the Wendell Alden days. He still wore a dark suit, but with an open collar on his dress shirt, no tie. Once a rumpled misfit among impeccably dressed men, now he was the only one in conservative clothes, an indication of how much things had changed. Mary had joked with Deirdre that there was no way Duncan wasn't going

to get full use out of those expensive suits once he'd spent the money. Chet Simmons, also in a jacket, a sports coat similar to the one Deirdre had bought Jay, greeted no one and went straight to his seat. He looked a bit strange, and Mary wondered what was up with him. Randy Dyer, who had worn suits all his adult life, was in khakis and a wildly floral sport shirt. He stopped to chat with Mary, Jay, Deirdre, and Cliff Thompson.

Eventually, they all took their places around the table. The crack where the glue joint was failing had lengthened by a few inches, and Clicksave's modern chrome chairs had been exchanged for some darkened oak ones. During the year, each person's seat choice had become an unspoken agreement developed over the five bimonthly meetings. It was when everyone was settled that Jimmy Hakken lumbered in. This was his first department heads meeting, required now that he was running the old factory.

He lifted his hand at the wrist to Jay and flicked his fingers horizontally in a kind of cutting motion, walked to the far end of the table, settled into an empty chair. He slumped back, his long legs awkwardly clamped under the rungs, the tattooed arms sticking out of a fringed black leather vest. Duncan turned his head away abruptly after a cursory glance. Mary figured any glimpse of Jimmy Hakken was too much for Duncan. She was amused by how much he detested him.

Jay opened the meeting in his usual way and welcomed Jimmy Hakken to the boardroom. Hakken nodded solemnly.

"It's been about a year since you joined me," said Jay. "I hope you're as satisfied with being here as I'm satisfied with each of you. We still have a lot of work to do, but LiveCell is making progress and that's what matters. As you see from the agenda, today each of you will update the rest of us about your department. Feel free to suggest changes, anything that concerns you, any problems you might have or foresee." Jay asked Randy Dyer, the CFO, to start.

Randy passed out copies of the financial report and went over each item carefully. LiveCell had sold around two million phones and generated over fifty million in net profits its first year. As he spoke, Duncan tapped quietly at his calculator. When he finished his report, Duncan's head came up, and his mouth twitched a little.

"By my estimation there's about three and a half million dollars unaccounted for."

There was a silence. Randy glanced at Jay, and Jay nodded vaguely.

"Some money has been moved to another account," Randy said.

"*Some* money?" said Duncan. "Three and a half million is *some money?*"

"Well . . ." he said, looking embarrassed.

"I asked him to do it," said Jay.

"You can't tell us what this is about?" said Duncan.

"No. Let's proceed—"

"Jay. Wait a minute, I think you owe us an explanation."

A long etched arm pointed at Duncan. "You heard the man. He said no."

Duncan rolled his eyes.

"Duncan," said Jay.

"What?"

"It was a charitable contribution."

"Oh yeah, which one?"

Jay hesitated. "Orphanages." A silence. "Can we move along now? . . . Cliff, are you ready?"

Cliff Thompson, head of investor relations, addressed the drop in the stock price. He explained that compared to the rest of the market, Live-Cell was holding and had only slipped marginally.

"I mean, we've gone from a low of eight cents to a high of twenty-seven and a half dollars a share in one year. The fact that we've eased back to the high nineteens recently is not a cause for alarm; instead we should be celebrating." He paused, then grinned. "I don't mean celebrating that we've eased back but celebrating that our stock is selling for a hundred and fifty times its former value. There, I think I have it right this time.

"What is interesting is that by my most recent calculations, institutional buyers make up only twenty-one percent of our investors, which is remarkably low. It used to be much higher. I think many of our new investors simply bought our phones, believed in them, and decided we were a company they wanted to support. Personally, I find that very gratifying."

"My boys are all in," said Jimmy Hakken, winking at him.

Cliff smiled back hesitantly. Mary figured that Deirdre Holly as a company director had probably been unusual enough for Cliff, but Jimmy Hakken? Cliff hadn't been the same since Jay had handed him the untried LiveCell phone nearly a year ago.

"I read in this article," said Deirdre, "that lots of lower-income people who have never even thought of being in the market or anything are

investing in LiveCell. They're using the money they used to spend on lottery tickets."

"Where did you read that?" said Mary. "Was it online?"

"Just one of the small local papers. They had like a whole thing on it. I'll save it for you."

"Please do."

"Chet, you okay?" Jay said, studying him across the table.

He nodded vaguely.

"Would you care to go next?"

"Maybe if I could excuse myself for a second first?" He jerked to his feet and left the boardroom.

"What's with Chet?"

"He left a message for me at ten o'clock last night," said Deirdre. "I think he's like, not got the best ever news to report." She waited. "Don't you know about it?"

"How can I know if I don't know?"

Mary cut in. "I was hoping he'd talked to you, Jay. I guess he didn't."

"What's this all about?" said Jay.

"I'll go get him," said Cliff just as Chet returned. A pasty perspiring Chet. He stood by his chair and faced Jay.

"Mr. Chevalier, I'm sorry. I should have alerted you to this sooner. It was just that I thought I could resolve the problem in time, before today's meeting, but I simply can't. I don't understand how it went so wrong. If you so wish . . . I will tender my resignation as manager of purchasing."

"Chet, please, sit down. Maybe you could tell me what you're so upset about?"

He stood frozen. Then in a rush of words, "I simply can't get anyone to supply us with the sender-receiver any longer. Mr. Chevalier, it is simply inexplicable. First I had trouble with our Mexican supplier, as you know, then with our Korean supplier. As problems mounted with Korea, I started to investigate other firms. I shook hands on the deal with the Chinese only four weeks ago, and I truly believed our problems were behind us. I mean, we had *a deal*. Now they have declined to fill our orders, and I can't even get the principals on the phone. I've never been treated this way. You know what I went through trying to get them made here. The few companies that *could* fabricate them felt they were undermining their relationships with larger clients by supplying us. I did not see the possibility of this occurring in China. I still don't. I thought with the world economy the way it is, they would be delighted to have the

work. This refusal we've just received from the last Asian manufacturer has completely floored me. I keep asking myself if it's my fault, if someone else could have done better, but believe me, sir, I tried."—he was near tears, and Mary wished she could think of something to say—"I understand that our phones are useless without the black boxes. Now in retrospect I realize I should have built up a larger inventory, but at the time I didn't want to tie up capital needlessly. I should have told you sooner. I just—"

"Chet, please. Sit down."

"Chevalier." It was Hakken.

Jay looked across at him.

"Fuck them all. My boys can make them. Get me the parts, we can put them together. They can't be that hard."

Jay ignored this and asked Chet, again, to please sit down. Finally, he did.

"LiveCell," said Jay, "is a young company without allies, and we have a product that is encroaching on the market share of some powerful corporations. I believe this is our difficulty with finding a supplier for the black boxes. Chet, please, from now on, come to me with these problems. Do not suffer like this on your own. We are in this together, and in the coming months things may get much more difficult. We need to stick together. We are a team. You are all here because I believe in you."

Mary noticed that Jimmy Hakken nodded at the end of each of Jay's sentences, his concentration such that he probably wasn't aware his head was moving.

"In the past month," said Jay, "I've had another offer for my share of LiveCell. I will not sell this company. Your jobs are secure, and no one will ever be fired when they are doing their best. And that means you, Chet."

Chet Simmons thanked him. He had four kids.

"There is nothing to thank me for. I know I demand a lot from all of you." A pause. "Don't worry about the black boxes."

"But Jay," said Deirdre, "I've only got enough boxes for like, less than one week of production. Then we're out of business."

"Same at my plant," said Jimmy Hakken.

"Duncan?" said Jay. "Have you done any snooping on this? I know how good you are at finding things out."

"You mean have I researched the unwillingness of these Asian manufactures to supply us?"

"Precisely."

"Actually, I have been online some since I knew Chet was experiencing problems."—Chet's head snapped around toward Duncan—"Jay, I believe your supposition is correct. I think in every case the companies have been offered more money not to produce the boxes for us."

Jay thanked him, and oddly enough he looked almost pleased.

He leaned back in his chair, placed his hands behind his neck, searched the ceiling. It reminded Mary of the first day, that endless lull when he seemed to be listening to the table wood. Today it seemed to be the ceiling that held the message.

"Mary," he said suddenly. "Set up a radio interview for me as soon as possible. Choose a program that we can trust, public radio please, and select a competent interviewer with a liberal bent. I am sure you would anyway, but this is important. I don't want to be censored."

She stared at Jay. An interview? Publicity? Even Jimmy Hakken exhibited a modicum of uncertainty.

Duncan broke the silence: "What are you going to say?"

"You'll have to tune in. Mary will tell you when."

"Do you think this interview will affect our stock price?" said Cliff Thompson.

Jay smiled. "Definitely."

"Which way?" said Duncan, the pitch of his voice revealing his emotion.

"Who knows."

"I think we need to know! . . . Jay?" He waited for an answer, his face turning red. "Jay? . . . This is ridiculous. You have to tell us. It's our money too."

"Drop it," said Jimmy Hakken.

Duncan swiveled violently in his chair. "I've had about enough out of you, you—"

Hakken calmly fixed his eyes on Duncan and said quietly, "Don't even go there."

"Duncan." It was Jay. "Let's have your report. I've made reservations for this evening at Dos Reales for everyone, and I don't want to have to carry anyone on a stretcher."

He's getting a sense of humor, she thought. And well timed, too. In a flash of insight, she saw how tense the year must have been for him, how much he'd agonized over the creation of LiveCell, and how as the company blossomed he was finally achieving success. This change in him

excited her. Maybe it would lead to other changes in him? She couldn't help hoping.

Duncan shuffled his papers. He flipped open his notepad and started to read his report.

"As director of order operations," he said, "I've installed new software allowing for easier secure online purchasing. These improvements should precipitate a trend toward online buying and will allow us to reduce our staff of order takers by at least half."

Jay cut in. "Don't let anyone go yet."

Duncan, after a muted grumble, continued. "LiveCell must create an electronic customer-service answering system to facilitate a reduction of personnel in that area as well."

"We'll keep things as they are."

"But Jay, you haven't even looked at the figures. Look at the potential savings of my plan."

"When someone calls LiveCell, I want them to hear a human voice immediately."

Duncan swallowed and moved on. "This new secondary retail market is selling every phone they can get their hands on for two-hundred dollars and up. We have to price our phones accordingly. I mean, why not? The demand is certainly there and we can *double* our profits."

"I have to admit," said Deirdre, "This thing is really annoying me too. Can't we sue them or something?"

"I could check with legal," said Duncan, looking surprised that she was agreeing with him, "but I doubt there is any possibility of litigation. We don't have a contractual agreement with our purchasers, so they can do whatever they want with the phones once they own them."

"I just feel people should be able to get our phones at the best possible price. Like why assist these greedy . . . ? People are being cheated. They may not realize they can get our phones for like half the cost directly from us. And these huge orders force everyone else to wait for their phones."

"That hardly seems to be the point," said Duncan with a frown. "If we raise our phone price, we won't care who has them or sells them afterwards because the out-of-company profit margin will evaporate. No one is going to be able to resell a two-hundred-dollar phone for twice the money."

"Why have we reduced the price of our phones anyway?" said Cliff Thompson. "I've been wondering if it isn't one of the reasons our stock

price has dipped slightly. It signals weakness to the Street."

Everyone looked to Jay. He rubbed his ear and glanced out the window. "I appreciate all your suggestions, but LiveCell is making a fair profit at our current price. It will stay where it is. As far as the outside retailers, we will limit all purchases to six phones once every year."

"But Jay," said Duncan, "that is absolutely ri—" He stopped.

Jay waited for him to continue, and when he didn't, he nodded to Mary.

Mary could see that Duncan was having difficulty containing himself. As she made her report, quickly updated now that Jay was willing to do an interview, she watched Duncan peripherally. Could his brain grasp Jay's reasoning? It was based on things only she knew, or things she assumed he'd told only to her. She wondered if Jay grasped Duncan's. Duncan's priorities were based purely on mercenary gain. Was that something Jay could comprehend?

As she continued with her report, she suggested that LiveCell reduce its advertising budget since the demand for the phones was so high. Jay agreed. She finished her report with the news that she'd managed to get LiveCell phones into a new movie with Mark Wahlberg. The actor had really taken to the phones. Everyone else was excited, but Jay disappointed her by asking who Mark Wahlberg was. Even when he finally said, "Oh, sure, *him,*" she didn't think he had a clue. Where had he been all his life?

After Deirdre and Jimmy Hakken had given their factory reports—Hakken's of course rather terse—Jay looked around the table. "So, is there any other business?"

When he first took over the company, he'd told them if they had a grievance, any kind of issue, they should air it at the end of these meetings. "Get it out in the open so we can get rid of it."

Duncan spoke first: "*Miss* Holly. Perhaps you might inform us about your *assistant*, Wendy Smith?"—a sarcastic smirk. Mary knew that smirk. What was he up to?

"What do you want to know?" Deirdre said hesitantly.

"Maybe you could start by telling us her name?"

"What do you *mean*, tell you her name? You know her name."

"So you think Wendy Smith is her real name?" he said smugly.

"What are you talking about?"

"Just what I said—Is Wendy Smith her given name?"

"Where are you going with this, *Duncan*?" Her anger apparent.

"Will you just answer my question?"

"This is really dumb. I don't have to answer your questions. What are you, a prosecuting attorney?"

Everyone in the room studied her, waiting for her answer. She glanced at Jay as if hoping for support. There was none. Obviously everyone was concerned.

"No." She spit the word at Duncan.

"No, what?" he said.

"*No*, I don't think *Wendy Smith* is her real name."

"You don't?" he said without quite the same confidence. "Well, can you tell us her name then?"

"It's Jennifer Stoddard."

"How the hell did you find that out?"—his voice up an octave again.

"Like everyone has a *mother*."

"What's *that* supposed to mean?"

"Simple. She writes her mother and a piece of paper underneath picked up the imprint. She was careful, but when you live with someone they're bound to make a mistake eventually."

She turned to Jay, ignoring Duncan. "Wendy, or Jennifer, what*ever* you want to call her is working as a spy for someone. She's like, *very* eager to find out how our phones work. Anyway, I knew Wendy was after our secrets, but I'm all, what are you going to do for me? I'm just a dumb surfer chick who runs the factory, and they aren't paying me enough. I figured two could play the game and I doubted she would suspect me. So I've been pretending like I might be willing to sell the phone's secret— not that *I* know it—and she's real close to making me an offer. Like days. Then I'll know who's behind it." She paused, glared at Duncan. "I *so* wanted it to be a surprise."

There was a silence. Then Jay started to laugh. No one had heard him really laugh before and the sound was strange, but then Mary joined him and almost immediately, Deirdre, and soon everyone was laughing, even Jimmy Hakken, if what he was doing could be called laughing. All except Duncan. He just sat there looking bitter.

ELEVEN

Mary wanted to drive Jay to the radio station in her car, but he insisted on going alone in his scarred wreck. "That will certainly make an impression," she said to herself. In fact, she wasn't particularly concerned about how he got there as long as he was still willing to do the interview once he arrived; he wasn't exactly headed for the public radio station he'd requested. She had tried to convince him of a televised interview, sensing how well he would come across on TV and knowing there was no better form of exposure, but he'd insisted on radio, so radio it was. Her choice of station though. That was why she wanted to drive him.

Jay pulled up in front of the *KBAY* building, towing a long plume of blue smoke. Twice he compared the street address to the one on Mary's typed directions, then parked the Cutlass in one of the visitor's slots out front. He rammed shut the groaning door, his eyes bumping along the dented body. Maybe it was time to get something else after all? The car had barely passed the smog test when he'd first registered it in California, and with the impurities this thing was putting out, it could feed a million LiveCell phones for a year. He would talk to Mary about buying another car; that would please her.

In the lobby of the radio station, lurid oversized headshots of radio celebrities smirked from the walls. A large three-dimensional aqua-blue

and silver THE BAY hung behind a young woman at the reception desk. She looked like a fashion model. He glanced around in confusion. Every-thing looked wrong. "I'm here for an interview, I think—Jay Chevalyer."

"*Doctor* Chevalier, oh my God—you're here," she said, her very white teeth surrounded by a violent lipstick.

"Jay is fine."

The smile widening.

"This isn't public radio, is it?" he said.

"Heavens *no*."—as if such an inference was unthinkable. "We're num-ber one in the Bay Area."

"And this is where I'm to be interviewed?"

"Keith Radmond's doing it," she said as if that would explain every-thing. "You must listen to his show?"—surprise touching her voice by degrees as he remained blank. "*What Gets Heard?* The highest-rated talk show in central Cal?" Jay shook his head. "You really haven't heard of him?" She pouted for an instant, but brightened immediately. "I have two of your phones, you know. I just *love* them. Jay, they are *so* amazing. I saw that ad with the baby and I bought my first one." She paused. "You're not at all like I imagined you." The white smile again. "Let me ring Keith for you, he's really eager to meet you. Just one moment, please." As she spoke into the receiver, she kept smiling at him. "Keith, Doctor *Jay* Chevalier is out front."

In just moments Keith Radmond walked into the room and extended his arm. "Doctor Chevalier, this is *certainly* a pleasure and an honor, sir." His voice had the archetypical ingratiating cadence and confidence. The short, balding radio-show host obviously knew exactly what the interview could mean to him. Everyone seemed to know exactly what was going on except Jay. Radmond's goatee was carefully manicured, and what was left of his hair hung to the shoulders of a new designer shirt. They shook and Jay offered his first name again. "Jay? Great, super. Would you care for a coffee, a latté, or maybe a spring water?" Jay declined. "Okay then. Please, follow me and we'll get set up. We have about—" He glanced quickly at his wrist. "—seven minutes until show time."

When they entered the sound studio, a producer and technician, both positioned behind a large plate-glass window in an adjoining room, waved and smiled. Jay returned a nod of greeting. As soon as he was seated on one of the padded stools, another dazzling young woman fit-ted him with headphones and adjusted a microphone to a precise angle to his mouth. "So you don't pop your Ps," explained Keith Radmond.

They were each asked to speak a few words, and the tech behind the glass set the sound levels and gave them the thumbs up. Everything seemed ready.

"Keith?" said Jay.

"Yes Jay, what's up? Do you need to use the men's room? I should have asked you sooner. We don't actually have the time for that at the moment."

"I'm fine."

"Great, super." Keith watched the producer as he signaled through the window by forming a cupped C with his hand. "Thirty seconds," said Keith, his eyes returning to Jay.

"I was just wondering if you use a delay?"

"We have one—a six-second digital delay—but we rarely use it. If people swear, no big deal, we mostly just leave it, so there's nothing to worry about. You okay, all set?"

Jay nodded. Over the headphones he could hear the top-of-the-hour jingle. Then, with an emphatic downward hand motion, the producer pointed at Keith through the glass.

"Good afternoon and welcome," Keith said, exaggerating the low officious sing-song voice, "to a very special edition of *What Gets Heard* on *K-B-A-Y*, ninety-eight-point-five FM, where what *you* want to hear gets heard first. I'm your host, Keith *Rad*mond, and today I'm talking with Doctor Jay Chevalier, CEO of LiveCell and the inventor of a new cellular telephone that's taken the West Coast by storm. Jay—up until today you've avoided all press coverage. You've been called The Man of Mystery. What made you decide to talk to *What Gets Heard* today?"

"My advertising head—*Mary MacKensie*—set it up." He said it so Mary would get the message as she listened.

"Jay, I mean, why have you decided to break the long silence, why have you finally decided to be interviewed?"

"There's something I'd like people to know about our phones."

"We'll talk about your amazing phones in just a moment, but I'm sure our listeners are eager to hear all about you first. Today we want to remove the mask of mystery and get to the man underneath. Can you tell us a little bit about your background?"

"Background?" said Jay.

"You know, your childhood, growing up, who was Jay as a boy?"

Jay paused. "I'd prefer to discuss our phones."

"Jay, we will shortly. But right now I think our listeners would be fas-

cinated to learn more about *you*, about the inner person that makes up the Man of Mystery."

Jay said nothing.

"Were you always interested in science?"

"Pretty much."

"Could you tell us about how and when you became interested in telecommunications?"

"Actually, I discovered the phone more or less by accident."

"By accident? That sounds remarkable. Please tell us the story."

"There is not that much to tell. I'd been genetically modifying organic structures in my lab when I realized that one of them had some unusual properties. I was originally working with cells that were intended to absorb air impurities, but that proved to be a bit of a dead end. I began concentrating on alternate problems, combining a variety of cells into my matrix, and eventually arrived at a mixture of cells that had certain unusual capabilities." He glanced over at the technician behind the large window.

"And these capabilities?"

"That became our phone."

"Can you tell us more than that?"

"I'm afraid some things need to remain secret."

Keith Radmond hesitated, but only for an instant.

"You are listening to *K-B-A-Y*, The *Bay*, ninety-eight-point-five. Call us at one eight-hundred the-*K*-Bay. Our guest this afternoon is Doctor *Jay* Chevalier. Jay, as an inventor, did you have any idea as to the magnitude of your invention at first? Did you realize that the phones would be so successful?"

"I thought they would be a good way for people to communicate."

"Can you elaborate on that a little?"

"They allow people to communicate in a new way."

"Tell me a little more about that."

"With the use of our phones some people's intuitive abilities seem to intensify over time, allowing people to communicate more fully. It doesn't happen with everyone." He reached up to readjust the headphones.

"That is simply awesome, Jay, just *super*. I've heard people say that, that they can almost sense what another person is feeling when they're on LiveCell phones. It's great to hear it from the phone's inventor. How do your phones do that, Jay?"

"It's within the nature of the communication."

"Can you elaborate?"

"Our phones are clear, the communication is precise, it allows people to concentrate on what is important."

"Yes, true, but how do the phones do that?"

"It's simply within their nature."

Keith hesitated again, but only fractionally.

"Jay, I was reading an article in the *Chronicle* on how telemarketers are complaining that they have a much higher failure rate with potential customers who are speaking on LiveCell phones. Some telemarketers are now determining what kind of phone they've called and are rejecting LiveCell users. There has even been some talk of a ban on your phones. How do you feel about that?"

"I don't concern myself. We attempt to manufacture the best product for the fairest price. We can't control people's response to our product."

Keith Radmond examined the computer screen in front of him and signaled his producer. "Jay, we're going to take a few calls now."

"Calls? What calls?"

"Many of our listeners are very eager to talk with you. As a matter of fact, our switchboard is receiving a record number of calls at the moment. You are a very popular man, Jay. Our first caller is Jesse from Santa Cruz. Jesse, you're on the air."

"Am I on?" she said.

There was a high-pitched quavering.

"Jesse, turn down your radio, please."

"My radio?"

"Yes, Jesse, the volume on your radio. Please turn it down."

The quavering stopped.

"Am I on the air?"

"Yes, Jesse, you're on the air."

"*Oh.* Hello Keith."

"Hello, Jesse."

"Doctor Chevalier?"

Jay nodded, rubbed his knee through his jeans, forcing himself calm.

"He's right here. Go ahead Jesse."

"Doctor Chevalier, I just want to thank you for what you've done for me and my family. My daughter hadn't spoken to me for three years, which felt like forever. We had this bad fight because of this awful, awful boy she was seeing who was just no damn good, and I told her that—"

"Jesse, tell us about the phone, please," cut in Keith Radmond.

"*Oh*. Well, as I was saying, my daughter and I hadn't spoken for three years because of this awful boy, and then I got one of your phones because all the wonderful things people were saying about them. I liked it so much I sent one in the mail to my daughter as a present just praying, hey, you never know, right? And then I called her and I said hello dear, and she said Mom? and then we just listened to each other for a while saying nothing, and then we just started bawling. Both of us! Doctor, you're right in what you say. You feel other people on them phones and you feel what's in their hearts. I'm a believer. You have a wonderful phone and you brought our family back together and may God bless you."

Jay was silent and even more uncomfortable.

"Thank you, Jesse," said Keith. "I'm sure we're all happy you're reunited with your daughter. That *is* a lovely story, isn't it, Jay?"

"Jesse," he said.

"Yes, Doctor Chevalier."

"Jesse, I appreciate your kind words, but you have nothing to thank me for. I did not do anything for your family. You did it yourselves. Our phones allow only for the possibility of better communication, but it's you who must communicate."

"Okay, let's take another caller," said Keith Radmond. "Bob from Hillsborough, go ahead Bob."

"Jay, the name is Bob Reikhart, and I'd like to tell you a little story that might just happen to interest you." He chuckled in a self-satisfied way. "I was fly fishing with my nine-year-old son in Wyoming on the Snake River. We always have our LiveCell phone with us in case Mother needs to call; she worries of course." He chuckled again. "The old-fashioned cell phones just don't have the reception of a LiveCell phone, particularly out there in the wilderness. Somehow, while wading up the stream, my phone must have fallen out of my fishing vest. I had no idea where or when it fell out. Well, to make a long story short, my son Jamie found the phone. But not by looking. He swears to this day that he just knew where the phone was, as though the phone were calling to him. Now is that something or what?"

There was nothing for Jay to do but answer. "The same way our phones allow you to sense when you have a call, your son must have sensed the location of the dropped phone. He might have a psychic predisposition. If you empty yourself of all anxious desire to find something, you can sometimes simply know where it is."

"That's very interesting, Jay," said Keith Radmond. "Sounds a little like Eastern philosophy. Are you a doctor of that as well?"

"No. I've never studied philosophy."

"But you do have a doctorate in biochemistry from Harvard. Can you tell us a little about your time there?"

"I studied a lot."

"Can you tell us a little more?"

"There really isn't all that much more to tell."

Keith Radmond studied his screen and signaled his producer again. "Do you miss the East Coast? I understand you're originally from Maine."

"I think we all have feelings about where we were born. I miss the change of seasons. I remember the stillness sometimes in winter on a clear night. I miss that."

"Jay, we have another caller. Roger from Marin County, you're on the air."

"Doc Jay—I just want to know why your phones can't take messages?"

"They aren't programmed for that. They allow you to sense any unanswered calls, but they don't record messages."

"Ain't that like a big drawback?"

The producer signaled Keith Radmond again, this time with a raised rapidly circling finger.

"Yes, I suppose it is," said Jay, "but there are many devices capable of that. It's simply not what our phones are about."

"Well, I think it sucks and it's—"

"You're listening to *What Gets Heard* on *K-B-A-Y*, ninety-eight-point-five on your FM dial, and I'm Keith *Rad*mond, your host. Call me at one eight-hundred the-*K*-Bay and talk with The Man of Mystery, Doctor Jay Chevalier, CEO of LiveCell. We're going to take a sixty-second commercial break, please stay with us."

Keith pulled off his headphones and smiled at Jay.

"Jay, you're doing great. You seemed a little surprised about the callers. Didn't Mary tell you?"

"Not a word."

"I guess you don't know the format of the show."

"I'm afraid not."

"I would've called and briefed you, but Mary said she thought it would work best this way."

"Oh, definitely."

"Yeah, no doubt." Keith nodded in agreement. "You're doing great, super, really great. The continued mystery thing is super. At first I thought it was a little bumpy, but I'm digging the dynamics of it now. I like that you're going with your first name, feels right, opens up the folk hero bit, and we already have plenty of doctors on the air. The whole interview is working super—you're burning up the phones."

The producer held up the cupped-hand signal.

"At some point," said Jay, "I would like to present something about our phones. It's really why I'm here."

"Let's save it for the end of the half-hour if that's okay. How long will it take?"

"Just a few minutes."

"Okay, I'll leave enough time."

They went back on the air and continued to take callers. There were people raving about the effect the phones had on their lives, there were calls about the stock price, people wanting to know how the phones worked, one call from someone who had lost her LiveCell phone and wanted to know if Jamie, the nine-year-old, could find it for her.

Finally, Keith Radmond said, "Jay, we only have a few minutes left. I understand there's something special you'd like to share with our audience? You are hearing it here, live, on *What Gets Heard*, K-B-A-Y, where what *you* want to hear gets heard first. Jay?"

Jay waited for an instant. He imagined Mary and everyone at Live-Cell listening to him, wondering nervously what he was going to tell the world. He hadn't given much to Keith Radmond. He hadn't intended to until now.

"On every LiveCell phone there is a small black metal box pressed into the end. This box allows our phones to communicate with all conventional telephone systems. As all LiveCell owners know, it requires a battery and must be recharged, same as any other cell phone. The box makes our phones similar to all other telephones, similar to the old technology. LiveCell phones are actually more radically different than that." He paused, feeling annoyed that his heart was racing involuntarily. He so wanted to say this intelligently. He had waited a long time for this moment.

"Our phones can be modified so they become the future. I want to let all LiveCell owners know, that if they wish, they can remove the black boxes simply by pulling the pronged end out of the rest of their phone.

The two holes will heal rapidly. Once you do this, you will be able to communicate with any other LiveCell phone anywhere in the world perfectly, and you will have the same LiveCell quality of communication. However, you will only be able to communicate with LiveCell phones. If you wish to call a conventional phone, simply reattach the black box." He paused again.

"A naked LiveCell allows you a few benefits. First, it will no longer be necessary to charge up your phone as it won't require a battery to work. Second—your calls will be completely safe. Without the black boxes, LiveCell phones cannot be bugged, no one can ever listen in on any of your conversations again. Third—all your calls will be absolutely free no matter the distance you call or the length of time you spend communicating. No more phone bills with a LiveCell . . ."

It was early afternoon when Jay got back to the Harcourt Building. Manuel turned off some salsa music and came out from behind the front desk.

"Jay! Say it is really true."

"What's that, Manuel?"

"I can call my mother and sisters in Mexico City and talk as long as we want and it will be free, no charge at all?"

"If they have a LiveCell phone."

"I'm going to kiss you!"

Jay grimaced and Manuel laughed.

"Okay, no kiss if you insist. But I'm going to send them one tomorrow. I can't believe this, it's just *too* fantastic. You know how much money I'm going to save? People are going to *love* you."

"Not everyone."

Manuel thought a second. "I guess you have a point—not everyone. You're going to piss off Ma Bell and her sisters very very much."

Mary was waiting with the others when Jay reached the sixth floor. Everyone clapped as he got off the elevator, and she was certain he blushed. He really *was* changing. She was so proud of him her throat tightened and at first she couldn't say anything. After everyone was finished congratulating him and he'd answered their questions, she was finally alone with him in his office, the two of them standing near his desk. He seemed riveted by the Ryder image on the wall; then he turned to face her, scowling. With each second, her elation diminished by another degree.

"What is it, Jay? What's wrong?"

"That was hardly a public radio station."

"I guess it wasn't. The Bay is the most—"

"Yes, believe me, I know. *K-B-A-Y*, the *Bay*, where *you* hear what *you* want to hear," he imitated Keith Radmond.

"Jay, the ratings were fantastic. I just got off the phone with them. And I haven't even told you the best news yet. I asked everyone to keep it a surprise."

"Well, I have a surprise for you."

"You do?"

He was still frowning and her stomach clamped.

"You're fired," he said.

Her mouth opened as if she'd been slapped.

"Mary, I'm just teasing you," he said immediately. She hung her head. "Please, don't look so upset. I'm not good at teasing. I didn't realize . . ." She tried to recover. "Mary, please. Don't cry—please. I'm so sorry."

She lifted her face. "You're not mad at me?"

"Of course not."

"I'm not fired?"

"Of course not."

She embraced him. The first time. Fully. His body stiffened, her tears against his neck. She felt him slowly relax as she held him, and gradually his arms came around her, one hand rubbing the small of her back. She breathed in his smell and liked it. After perhaps a few minutes, he took hold of her shoulders and moved her away.

"Shall we go out for sushi tonight?" he said. "I was going to invite everyone out to eat, but maybe you prefer we go alone."

"I would love to." She wiped her eyes. "I'm sorry I got so emotional. I'm not usually like this. I guess my New England ancestry deserted me."

"I shouldn't have teased you."

"Was doing the interview so terrible? It sounded so good. It really did."

"I expected a more sedate atmosphere. All these people called in. It was embarrassing. Why didn't you warn me?"

"Would you have gone?"

He thought a moment. "I suppose not."

"See! You wanted exposure. This was the best exposure I could get you outside of television. I know Keith Radmond seems a little commercial, but you have to admit he did a great job. I knew he would."

"We needed to get used to each other. Though you should have seen his face when I made my announcement."

"The only time I've heard dead air on his show."

"He looked at his producer and signaled a cut-off-his-head sign with a question mark drawn in the air."

"He did that?"

"His producer shook his head, and you heard the rest."

"I'm surprised Keith did that. What a wimp. Or maybe he owns a boatload of AT&T stock. I would have killed him if they'd cut you off. Maybe then you *would* have fired me."

"I would never fire you."

They looked at each other for a moment.

"Can I tell you my news now?" she said.

He nodded.

"Our stock went up four dollars a share and was still rising at the close. Cliff thinks it may go over thirty dollars a share by the end of the week. There was record volume in that half-hour after your announcement." She searched his face. "Aren't you pleased?"

"I'm pleased. Now Manuel can call his mother for free."

"You really are strange, you know that?" She leaned over and kissed him on the cheek. She wanted to tell him something else. It was still so difficult to get close or be intimate.

"Shall we leave early today?" he said. "Go see if Sammy approves of my new career as a radio celebrity? Then we can go for sushi."

"Yes, let's."

They paused, still a little awkward with each other.

Jay broke the silence: "I don't remember seeing Duncan when I came in—"

"Oh. I forgot to tell you. You better go and talk to him."

"Why, what's up?"

"He did something stupid, and he's very angry. *Very*. I've never seen him like this."

"What did he do?"

"Maybe he should tell you."

"Tell me."

"Well . . . he sold all of his LiveCell stock this morning."

TWELVE

Friday morning of the same week that Jay made his radio announcement, Mary left a note for her house cleaner: *Dear Trisha, I have company coming this evening. Please wash the ocean-side windows and check the wine glasses for spots.* She realized it was a silly request as soon as she was in her car. Trisha always did a fine job on the glasses, and Jay probably wouldn't notice the windows anyway. For a moment she considered going back and tearing up the note.

On her way home from work she picked up two bottles of very expensive champagne, and again she wondered if she wasn't being foolish. But what was more seductive than good champagne? At least the ceviche, which she'd prepared the night before, he would enjoy since he liked sushi. She wanted the evening to be special; there was so much to celebrate.

As Cliff Thompson had predicted, LiveCell's stock price accelerated throughout the first week and passed thirty dollars a share like a Porsche around a hay wagon. LiveCell now sold two versions of their phone— with and without the black box, the plain one fifteen dollars less. Though the naked phone could only communicate with other LiveCell phones, almost everyone ordered this version. Who wanted to pay for phone service when it could be had for free? The night after the interview, Mary

watched the news, and the story of the free telephone crossed the nation like a cheer. Two days later the media attention disappeared without explanation. This worried her, and she wasn't sure what she could do about it.

But the influx of phone inquiries was staggering, and within less than a week LiveCell was swamped, then deeply submerged with orders. To ease the demand, Jimmy Hakken suggested he run his crew around the clock in eight-hour shifts, and Jay had to agree, stipulating that the extra work load only last a few months until they were caught up. He also explained to Hakken that he required ten minutes alone with each batch of newly matured phones, which occasionally was as often as three times a day. Hakken never raised an eyebrow: he never questioned a Chevalier decree. Deirdre ran two shifts yet produced almost double Hakken's output because of her factory's extra capacity. Jay worked constantly, administrating the company, infusing phones at both factories, fending off reporters. Yet even in his exhaustion, Mary had never seen him so content.

Now as she waited for him to arrive, she kept impatiently walking to the window to check for his car. Finally, at the end of her road there was a drift of blue smoke, and the Cutlass thumped up her driveway. She went down the stone steps to greet him.

"You finally made it," she said.

"Sorry I'm a little late."

"I mean, you finally made it *here*, to visit me." She gestured for him to come in, feeling slightly awkward, excited to be alone with him again.

He followed her into the house, and ignoring the expensive fawn-gray interior she was so proud of, he headed immediately for the floor to ceiling windows. He looked out across the water for a moment as she waited; then he reached into his sports coat pocket.

"I brought you something." He held out a small unwrapped pale-gray box on the flat of his palm.

She lifted it from his hand. "Shall I open it now? Or would you like something to drink first?"

"As you wish."

She studied his expression. "I'll open it." She delicately lifted the lid, her heart pounding more than she would have liked. She unwrapped the blue tissue paper. When she saw the face she knew what it was.

"Your watch."

"Swatch mailed me an early prototype."

The three colors of orbiting light radiated just on the surface of the crystal.

"Jay, it's beautiful."

"I think they're doing an okay job. You said you wanted one."

"It's mine?"

"Of course."

She leaned over and kissed him on the cheek. She placed the watch on her wrist, buckled the muted-silver band, held out her arm to admire it, viewing it from various distances. "It's even more incredible than I thought it would be. You really are something." She continued studying it, thrilled when the color mixed to neutrality for an instant as the dots of light met. "Would you like some champagne? I don't even know if you like it, but I bought two special bottles."

"I'm not sure I've ever had good champagne. You are my guide in these things."

She went to open one, pleased to be his guide in something. She returned with tall flutes, handed him one, the bubbles rising madly. "How about a toast?" she said. "To LiveCell."

They drank. "It's very good," he said. "You keep introducing me to new things."

They walked out through French doors onto the large crescent-shaped redwood deck and settled into two teak Adirondack chairs angled toward the sea. The gilded rim of evening was just beginning to show as a mid-September breeze lifted off the water, blunting the warmth of the sun. Jay still removed his jacket and tossed it over a vacant chair.

"Your arm looks much better."

He glanced at the scar on his bicep and rubbed it slowly.

"Do you ever get cold?" she said.

"What do you mean?"

"You always wear just a T-shirt, no matter how cold it is."

"Where I grew up we didn't have coats, just big wool shirts. I guess people donated more shirts than coats, so we would just keep piling on the shirts the colder it got outside. If it was anything above the mid-fifties we wore T-shirts. I got used to dressing that way."

"Do you ever buy anything for yourself? Except those toy trains."

"How about a car? I was going to ask you what to get."

"You're going to buy a new car?"

"The Cutlass is burning oil. It won't pass the emissions test again without major work, and the body's not that great, so I need something else."

"Let's go tomorrow," she said eagerly. "I'll help you find the perfect car."

"Not new though, and nothing fancy."

"Jay, why *not*? Do you realize how much you're worth? You could buy anything you wanted. We could get you something really nice. A Ferrari maybe. I've always wanted to test-drive a Ferrari. Let's." Her eyes pleaded with him.

"I'd rather have an old car. A fancy new car would make me uncomfortable. Besides, I like bench seats. I bet Ferraris don't have bench seats."

"Do you only like old stuff?"

"I like things people have touched, with their marks on them. They absorb joy and pain and a sense of time, or at least a sense of time passing. And if they haven't been discarded over the years, there must be one good thing about them. Maybe they develop a kind of integrity for me because they've survived."

"You still don't have to drive the worst car in California."

He smiled, and she shivered a little. She excused herself and went inside the house, returning in a button-down cardigan, carrying a silver bucket with the champagne bottle sticking out of it.

"Are you hungry?" she said, filling their glasses.

He shook his head, examining the champagne against the light of the sky, the thin lines of bubbles rising. "I'm surprised I like this wine so much. You know, I think I prefer drinks with carbonation."

"Didn't you drink in college?"

"I just studied."

She took a long sip. She knew what that was like, but she didn't want to interrupt when he might talk about himself.

"Remember when I told you about my grandfather?" he said.

She nodded.

"What I didn't tell you is that he made his own liquor. In the two years I was with him I became quite a drunk."

"*You?*" she said.

He nodded.

"No way."

"*Way*," he said and smiled a little. "We drank every day. It was a wonderful couple years."

She never knew when he was going to surprise her. "Is he still alive?"

"He died a few months after I left him. Sometimes I think he was waiting for me to come to him before he died. He taught me so many

things I needed to know." His eyes went out to the horizon. She followed his glance. The gradual shifting tones of sunset had intensified over the darkening water. He took a long sip of wine, examined the horizon again. "I think we might be in for quite a storm."

"I doubt it. It would be very unusual for this time of year." She paused. "Jay—" He turned to face her.

"Will you tell me how the phones really work?"

"You've already sensed that I want you to know." He upended his drink and nodded slowly, set the glass on the arm of the chair. "This wine is wonderful. Nice to drink it outside like this with the air so fresh and clean."

She noticed again how much he enjoyed certain things, how he paid careful attention to everything around him. He would be a good lover, probably a great lover. She filled their glasses, emptying the bottle, thought of getting another but wanted to hear what he was going to tell her. Maybe champagne was the secret to loosening him up. She hoped so. He rubbed his scar again absentmindedly, glanced out at the ocean and began talking.

"The phones can communicate with each other because their final matrix is identical, because they are all cloned from the same cells, all modified by the same viral DNA."—*his*, she couldn't help but remind herself—"Just as two similar human brains can sometimes know what the other is thinking, like identical twins for instance, LiveCells, being exactly the same, have complete synergy."

His eyes came back to her. "This sameness is a rare occurrence in nature, and LiveCells don't have chromosomes that alter genetic makeup over time—they remain identical. This makes them unique, like nothing else in nature. When two LiveCells communicate with the black boxes installed, the boxes send the call and log it for billing, but, as you now know, they aren't required."—*maybe that's why Duncan was so confused*— "I wanted to keep that secret, until LiveCell gained more momentum. When LiveCell calls are being sent over conventional pathways, the black boxes translate the brain waves into digital code to be sent as radio waves. I had hoped to leave the black boxes in longer, but my hand was forced." He took a slow sip. "I knew once the phone was free and the calls untraceable, real trouble would start. Now you understand why I couldn't patent the phone, besides the obvious fact that DuPont would've sued for the intellectual property. If certain people learn how the phone works, LiveCell will be simple to destroy."

He searched her face as he took another sip. She remained quiet, hiding her emotion.

"So two human brains can hear each other talk through the LiveCells, and depending on the natural intuitiveness of the user, sometimes more. As the human brain forms low-frequency wave-code, as it thinks words, the LiveCell absorbs the code over the short distance we hold the phones from our brains, and instantly the other person's LiveCell knows the coding, and that user's brain absorbs the words through their LiveCell. At first I was worried that LiveCells wouldn't be able to differentiate specific users, but through my program infusion they can. The unusual part is really in the programming." He paused, as if deciding how to tell her.

"Mary, I believe there's a continuum of energy. Anyone who really wants to can access this energy in varying degrees. It allows one to perform and create beyond conscious ability, to understand things outside of conscious thought, and it allows one to simply know things; it's like the clarity we sometimes get in pure nature. You and Kelly can both access it, I know that. Others can, even if they're not sure that's what they're doing. There is so little that we really understand about the human brain."

She hugged her chest, felt the cold air on her face, her hair unruly in the increasing wind.

"I program the phones by accessing this energy. My brain becomes a conduit from this vast intelligence into the LiveCells. When I'm infusing, the closest phone responds and then the energy spreads rapidly through the other phones. You've seen it, but it happens so quickly it seems as if they all infuse at once.

"I think much of our creativity or wisdom comes from this same source. Those years with my grandfather changed me. Without realizing it at first, my intuitive abilities, or my abilities to access this energy, kept increasing. It guided me in my eight years at the forgotten laboratory."

She still said nothing. Her mind was a confusion of conflicting thoughts and emotions, not to mention champagne. He watched her now expectantly, as if he needed her to say something, to respond to what he'd told her. He reached—she thought almost nervously—and picked up his glass from the teak arm, was about to take a sip when he noticed it was empty.

"Shall we open the second bottle?" she said.

"That's up to you."

"Let's." She reached for the empty bottle. She wanted to stand up and do something. *Anything.* She really needed another drink. She was realizing more and more that LiveCell wasn't just another phone company, and Jay certainly wasn't just another CEO.

"Can I get it for you?" he said.

She shook her head. "I'll be right back." She watched him from the French door, his head leaning against the slats of the Adirondack chair, above him infinite chaos, the minute points of colored light that make up an evening sky.

She retrieved the wine and handed him the bottle. He screwed it down into the ice of the bucket.

"Jay, I think I'm getting overwhelmed by all this. I mean, you definitely told me all along what LiveCell was up to; I guess I just didn't realize the magnitude. This is all much more involved and complicated. It's giving me a very odd feeling."

He reached down for the fresh bottle. His hands made quick work of the neck-foil, and after a moment's study he unwound the wire stay to the cork. He looked at her. "I've never opened a bottle of champagne."

All she had to do was imagine opening it, and there was a delicate *pfft.* She'd chosen the brand simply because out of all the expensive bottles in the wine shop, the silver of the neck-foil was her lucky color.

He poured. "I have a toast." He lifted his. "To you. We could never have accomplished what we've done, without you." He leaned toward her, stretched out his arm, and they touched glasses.

She wasn't sure if she believed him—he still acted as if he didn't need anyone. But maybe he did need her?

He'd been correct about the storm. The summit of color at the horizon was past, the advancing clouds a dark blind slowly and methodically pulled shut. They listened to the call of a last mockingbird as it found a roost for the night, the only voice besides the wind and the waves, the rumble of breakers brought to them more and more fiercely as the storm approached.

"I have a favor to ask you," he said. "More than just a favor."

She waited, conscious of her own breathing. *She knew there was something else!*

"It's crucial to what I'm trying to do."

"Tell me."

"I want you to learn how to infuse the phones."

"*Me?*"

"Yes."

"Jay, that's crazy. How could *I* learn to infuse the phones? You think I can simply connect to this continuum thing?"

"Mary, I shouldn't tell you this. And I don't want you to worry, but I've had a death threat. It's most likely a prank, but it made me realize that as things now stand, if they kill me, LiveCell will end. I need someone to carry on if I'm not here."

It was then that the storm reached them from out of the blackness—first a wave of sweet ozone, then large raindrops striking the deck with careless fury. She just sat there, feeling even more scared. Neither moved. Eventually Jay drained his glass and stood, gathered his jacket and the bucket.

"Shall we?" he said.

Once they were inside sitting at the dining room table, with only a low table lamp on, the storm lashing the west-facing windows, he filled their glasses again.

"This is so odd, this storm. It never rains this time of year." She tried to see out through the streaming glass. Just saying something simple made her feel better.

"You're wet."

"I don't mind." She took off her sweater, draping it over the back of a chair. She combed her hair behind her ears with her hands. The rain had soaked the front of her blouse and her bra straps were visible under the dark-pink linen. She could feel the wet material against her breasts, against her nipples. She heard the heat in the house come on.

"Do you have any idea who the death threat is from?"

"Does it matter? When they figure out what I'm up to, that their imperium might be in jeopardy because people's consciousness is changing—you know they're going to have to stop me."

She nodded. The anxiety she'd been feeling on and off for months was clear now. A violent gust drove a sheet of rain against the window and she started.

"Maybe I shouldn't have told you all this," he said. "I thought if you understood, it would help you find what you need to infuse the phones."

"You really think I could infuse the phones?"

"You once asked me why I wanted you to work for me. I always had the gut feeling, ever since Kelly told me about you, that you were the one who could do it."

"You're a very unusual person with abilities others don't have. I'm just ordinary."

"You know that's not true."

"Jay, I'm not sure I understand all this. I don't know what to say."

"You don't have to say anything. Let's not worry about it now. Let's drink our wine."

She sensed that he was embarrassed, that he felt he'd revealed too much, been too vulnerable for a moment. He was beginning to withdraw again. She got out of her chair, walked behind him, put her hands on his shoulders, his muscles reacting to her touch. She wanted to slide her fingers over his damp chest. Did he want her to? All these months and she still didn't know. If only he would give her an indication, any kind of a sign about how he felt. She waited. Then her hands took on a will of their own, the champagne guiding her, her emotion guiding her, and she began to massage his arms, the lean dense muscle under her touch. It made her feel calmer immediately. He turned his body toward her, rose out of the chair.

"Mary!" But as he started to say more, she brought her hand to his lips. Her mouth followed her hand, and with her heels lifting off the floor a little, she kissed him, his mouth at first unyielding, then beginning to open, her tongue now tracing the inside of his lips in a slow circular pattern, the wet tip against his teeth. She felt him shudder, a spasm that ran through his entire body; felt him harden against her center as she clutched him tighter, her hands working across his back. She was getting very excited, and feeling more daring, slid her hand lower to his front, rubbing him through his jeans.

And he pulled away.

Even in the dim light his eyes looked frightened. She had never seen him like this, and she couldn't move. He seemed about to speak, but suddenly his body brushed past her. She still didn't move, her heart hammering in her chest. She heard the door open and click shut, the storm louder for that instant. Heard his car start. Heard him turn in the driveway. Listened until there was only rain lashing the windows.

She walked into the kitchen and opened the fridge door. She lifted out the plate with the thinly sliced translucent snapper carefully arranged

in a circle on the ivory ceramic with tomatoes, peppers, and olives in the center. She forced herself not to remember what she'd been thinking about him as she prepared the fish. She carried it into the dining room and set it gently on the table as if she were serving him. About to return for a fork and a clean plate, she saw his jacket still hanging over one of the chair backs. She sat down next to it and almost reached for it. Instead, her left hand moved to her face; her thumb and forefinger gripped the bridge of her nose as her eyelids squeezed tight to the point of pain.

THIRTEEN

Telecommunication stocks had been down before Jay Chevalier's announcement of free phone service, but in the months after, they began to plummet, and many companies were going bankrupt. There was even speculation that e-mail and the post office would be severely affected. It was conceivable that in the near future all verbal personal and business communication would take place over LiveCell phones. Most people simply preferred it. Jay Chevalier refused another buyout offer. Those who had tendered this—as they thought of it—*final* offer, were stunned and angered that he wouldn't sell the company at any price, that he would not listen to reason.

Two weeks after their unfortunate evening, Jay had asked Mary again if she would attempt the phone infusion. She'd turned him down, telling him he was wrong about her, she wasn't capable of something like that. Hoping more time would heal the rift, he'd waited and tried once more to convince her. She'd flatly refused. Jay continued working as if none of it mattered, but he wasn't the same person he'd been two months ago.

"Mary?"

"Hey Deirdre, what's up? Still at the factory?"

"I guess you're working late too. How's it going over there?"

"You mean besides this FDA thing?"

"What *fucks* they are. I couldn't believe it when I heard. *Headaches?*

Nightmares? Come on. That is *so* lame. I mean, we've been using these phones constantly for way over a year now. Do we have headaches? No. Like *hello!* I mean—*buzzer!*"

"It's ridiculous, but we still have to deal with it. I just wish the media hadn't turned so against us. That makes it worse."

"I can't believe these people coming up with the complaints, and the FDA buying it, or pretending to buy it. First it was cell phones, now they're fine and it's us. Like, check the bank accounts of those complaining."

"Duncan has."

"Really?"

"Almost every one of them he was able to check . . ."

"Can't we use that?"

"Legal says it's only circumstantial proof; all were cash deposits."

"How is Duncan anyway?" said Deirdre.

"He's still depressed he sold his stock. He gets more and more upset about it, calculating how much he's lost—not made is more like it—he says *lost*. Almost every day he says he's going to buy in again, but he doesn't. He should have bought back in after he first sold. Now the stock is so high I'd be worried about buying it, especially with this FDA thing hanging over our heads. That's already affected our stock price a little, and the press is probably just revving up. I'm sure it'll only get worse. The media thrives on nailing us. Somebody out there hates LiveCell, and they must have a lot of power." She paused. "Anything from Wendy Smith?"

"Nothing since she disappeared. But you know, I think someone tipped her off. I mean, we were *that* close to a deal, and then she's just gone, no trace. It didn't make any sense. You know, after I revealed her real name at the meeting, you'd think Duncan would've found something out about her like he can, but nothing."

"When phone calls were still traceable, Duncan told me he'd found that Wendy'd made two calls to Alden Stone Associates. Then a few days after Wendy disappeared and I asked him about it, he denied it."

"*Too* weird. You think Wendell Alden is after us?"

"I think it's the father and his connections. I'm not sure how much Wendell has to do with it, but the father has connections everywhere. He's in the Republican inner circle, and the corporate inner circle. They *all* have every reason to hate us."

"Did you tell Jay?" said Deirdre. Mary didn't need to answer. "And you got the usual? Figures. He can really make you so mad sometimes." A pause. "There's something about Duncan that's been bugging me. He's

changed and something about him isn't right. You know what Jimmy Hakken calls him? . . . The donut."

They both giggled for a moment.

"I feel the same way," said Mary.

"You do? Really?"

"Something about him *isn't* right, but Jay insists he's okay, so what can we do? Does he try to get information out of you?" A short pause. "He's obsessed with figuring out how the phones work."

"You know, don't you?"

"Did Jay tell you I knew?"

"I think we're the only ones who know. Don't you love talking on these phones? You can say whatever you want." She hesitated. "I can't be in there when he infuses. I've tried it a bunch of times, but it like really freaks me out. I feel so weird. He tells me it's because I fight against it, but I can't help it I guess. Did he tell you about the first time?"

Mary didn't answer. *So*, he's been trying it with Deirdre. This upset her though she realized she wasn't being fair. It wasn't as if they were having sex.

"His heart stopped," said Deirdre. "I had to like give him CPR."

"*His* heart stopped?"

"It was awful. I thought he'd died. Like forever."

They were silent for a moment. She wondered why *he* hadn't told her any of this.

"Do you know Luke Delamar?" said Deirdre.

"I don't think so."

"He's one of Jimmy's original gang members, like was his lieutenant or something, you know how they have all those Army positions. Jimmy insisted I take him for security. I just can't get a read on him, so I thought you might have an idea about it. He never talks, I mean like, *not at all*, and he stares at me so strange I get shivers."

"What's he look like?"

"Big. Really big, with long black hair and beard. Rides an old Harley."

"Oh, yeah, I've seen him. He *is* scary."

"I just don't know what to do about him."

"Have you asked Jay?"

"You know how Jay is about that kind of stuff, the weirder they are the more he seems to like them, and I can't bother him with things that are my responsibility."

"You can't tell Jay this either, but there's something I need to tell you," said Mary.

"What?"

"I don't know if I should tell you. I don't want you to be frightened."

"*Please*, tell me."

"My place has been gone through, all my stuff. I know someone has been in my house."

"*No way*. Are you sure?"

"As sure as I can be. At first I thought it might be Trisha, my cleaning lady, but when I asked her I could tell it wasn't her."

"That is *so* creepy. Who do you think it was? What do you think they were looking for?"

"So it hasn't happened to you?"

"I'm pretty sure not. I'll be way more alert."

"Now every time I go home at night I wonder if someone's waiting for me."

"How about new locks, or a security system?"

"I did the locks already, and I guess I'll put in a security system. Though by the time the cops . . . I wanted privacy, living out there, but now I wish I had some close neighbors."

"You want to stay with me for a while? I got plenty of room with Wendy gone."

"I'll be okay."

"You sure? It would be fun."

A pause.

"Hey, you eaten?" said Deirdre.

"Not yet."

"Dos Reales in half an hour?"

"Give me forty-five, I have a few things to finish up."

"Cool," and they ended the call.

Deirdre was relieved Jay had insisted her factory go back to one shift. After two months of doubles everyone was exhausted; she didn't know how Jimmy Hakken's crew had managed the triple shifts; those gang guys really were tough. Neither factory was meeting demand anyway, even at a combined output of fifty-thousand phones a day. Jay couldn't keep infusing phones at the rate he was—even he had limitations.

She locked both the inner and outer doors and walked across the empty parking lot to her station wagon. No sky tonight, just a cold

swirling November fog, the two parking-lot lights wreathed in hazy incandescence.

When she arrived at Dos Reales she had to circle a few minutes to find a place to park in the overfull lot. Then she waited outside by the entrance, listening for the Porsche. She'd already called Ricky, so she wasn't concerned about getting a table. Soon there was a flash of silver and Mary pulled in, one smooth line to the only empty spot—just vacated, right in front. *Such style.* It made her feel awkward and gawky. Silver must be Mary's color, again realizing her lack of one. They hugged each other—Deirdre held it a little longer than necessary—and they entered the restaurant.

"It's strange being here without Jay," said Deirdre, once they'd been seated in a corner booth.

"I've never seen it so crowded." Mary looked around. "This place is getting very popular."

"Yeah, almost *too* popular, but Ricky still takes really good care of us. He treats Jay like a big celebrity now, and Jay is so uncomfortable about it, it's like *way* funny."

"Jay uncomfortable?"

"Absolutely. He can't stand being fussed over. He was in and out of the factory quick tonight; he seemed preoccupied. There's like, a lot of pressure on him." She leaned closer and lowered her voice. "The really weird thing to me is that Jay can't sell the company anyway, because without him to infuse the phones . . . There must be all these tech geeks trying like crazy to figure out how the phones work."

"He thinks I can do it."

"What?"

For a moment, Mary glanced away. "He thinks I can learn to infuse the phones."

"No way!" She said it louder than she expected and told herself to calm down. Being alone with Mary excited her more than she liked to admit.

"I know I can't do it. I told him I don't even want to try."

Like, why not? she thought. Like what would be cooler than that?

"He wants to run this experiment," said Mary, "and he wants you to be there."

"What kind of experiment?"

"I'm supposed to be at the factory, and Jay would infuse from his

office through two LiveCell phones—his and mine. He says he wants you there in case something goes wrong. After what you told me about these severe reactions, I finally understand why he's concerned."

"Are you going to do it?"

"I don't think so. Don't tell him this, but I actually used to *love* being there when he infused. But I can't handle it anymore."

Deirdre studied her face. "Mary, can I ask you a personal question?"

The waiter stopped them, placing fresh-made tortilla chips and salsa on the table, apologized for keeping them waiting and asked if they wanted a cocktail. Deirdre ordered a vodka rocks and Mary a beer. They decided to share appetizers.

As the waiter left, Mary said, "You want to ask about me and Jay, but I can't talk about it." She looked away.

Deirdre reached over and touched her hand. "I'm sorry; I shouldn't have asked. I just know something has changed between you two—like way icy."

Mary continued to look out at the restaurant; then the stunning gray eyes found Deirdre's again.

"Seriously, it's like Antarctica," said Deirdre, trying to lighten things. "He told me something a few weeks ago. He said that when we really love someone, it's difficult for us to understand if our love isn't returned with the same intensity that we give. We believe all we have to do is love that person more, like more intensely, and eventually they'll love us the same way too."

"He told you that?"

"I kind of think he told me so I'd tell you."

"I wonder if he's ever been in love. He's such a loner. I keep wondering if he's ever truly loved anyone. Maybe he extracted too much of his damn *pineal* gland."

Now Deirdre knew there was something really wrong. Worse than she'd thought. "You know, I asked him that, about the loving somebody thing. He wouldn't answer."

Mary didn't respond.

"I guess you know me though, Miss Persistent."

Mary still said nothing.

"Okay, okay. He said—'For lack of a better word, God.'"

"*God?*"

"But when I asked him if he was like religious, he said not at all. He went into this whole weird thing about nature being God, and about this

continuum of energy, about accessing this energy and understanding that there are things like more important than your personal desires and everything."

The drinks and appetizers arrived and they ordered the rest of their meal. They worked at their beverages, cactus salad and flautas. Deirdre reached over and took Mary's hand again, turned it so she could see her watch; it was just an excuse to touch her. She was so damn horny with Wendy gone.

"Those colored dots are amazing, so beautiful like colored stars. The things he thinks of. I can't wait to get one."

"He said Swatch snagged on something, but they should be in production pretty soon. You should tell him you want one, maybe he can get you an early sample." Mary pulled her hand away.

"I can wait. Besides, he gave it to you, that means a lot."

They paused, and Deirdre felt awkward. "Did you hear about Jimmy and the whole Native American thing?"

Mary shook her head. "I think the Jimmy Hakken gossip must stay over at the factories. Most everyone in our office is still nervous about him."

"Besides Duncan?"

"Cliff Thompson seems sort of all right about him, but everyone else? Yeah—but tell me the story."

"Jimmy's talking with Jay at the factory and like *all* serious tells him he thinks he might have some Native American blood on his mom's side. And Jay's all, *So?* You know, like he would, and Jimmy gets quiet. So Jay, of course, senses Jimmy's all upset, so he asks him what the Hakken is and Jimmy tells him. Then Jay says according to his mom his father was half-Finnish, so now Jimmy's forgotten all about the Native American thing. Now he's all Nordic, which fits. The guy might as well be a Viking."

"Jimmy Hakken might actually have another side."

"Yeah, you don't see it at first, not right off, but he does. Like me, he's trying to educate himself more."

"Hakken has worked out. I *never* would've believed it. I remember Jay telling me he was going to run the old factory after you went to the new one. I thought he'd really lost it, that maybe his arm had poisoned his brain." A pause. "Deirdre . . . I'm sorry I doubted you about the Wendy Smith thing."

"That's okay, I think everyone did."

"Not Jay."

"No?"

"I think he may have been a little concerned, but I remember him saying that he trusted you and that was the end of it."

"That whole Wendy thing was kinda weird, but the sex was *really* great, her body was just incredible. Probably not as lovely as yours though."

They were both quiet.

"You're blushing," said Deirdre.

"Sorry."

"Have you ever had sex with a woman?"

"No."

"Really?"

"I haven't had much sex," she said, kind of blurting it out.

"*You?* No way. I can't believe it. You're so incredibly attractive. You're actually beautiful, *really* beautiful. Aw-oh, I'm making you blush again."

"Maybe we should talk about something else?"

"I didn't mean to upset you."

"It just never worked out for me. I never met the right person. When you grow up on a farm, particularly a dairy farm, you have to be home a lot to do chores, so in high school I rarely dated, and then in college I was still living at—"

"*Mary*, I think it's sweet, really. You don't need to apologize. I think it's really cool and appealing. It just surprised me because you're *so* beautiful and *so* smart you could have like anyone you wanted."

"Not anyone."

Deirdre broke the silence again. "I wouldn't give up." She placed her hand on Mary's once more. "I'm *really* sorry I upset you. There I am again, Miss Say-the-wrong-thing." She searched Mary's face. "If you ever need someone to talk to or anything, anything at all . . . okay?"

Deirdre wasn't sure what made her return to the factory that night. It wasn't like she didn't sometimes come back to check, but she was almost positive she'd locked both sets of doors and knew everything else was okay. Maybe it was just restlessness after her dinner with Mary and an excuse not to go home to an empty bed. She kept thinking about Mary. In so many ways Mary was more beautiful than Wendy, not in the same flashy way, but in a quiet one that Deirdre found more and more appealing. It was her coloring rather than her features: that glowing skin and gray eyes, all that rich brown hair, and lately, she could sense Mary's emo-

tion and sensuality beneath her polished manner. After talking with her at the restaurant, she was positive Mary wasn't having an affair with Jay. Though Deirdre knew she didn't have a chance with her, she couldn't help dreaming about it. For the past hour she'd been driving around aimlessly, and since she needed something to do besides obsess, she ended up at the factory.

The wind had abated and fog was draped like a damp hush over the world, only electric lights and neon transcending the monochrome gloom. Two mercury-vapor lights were casting ineffectual violet halos in the factory lot. As she parked the wagon she almost changed her mind and headed for a nightcap before the bars closed. But she was already here, she might as well check.

She shuffled across the gravel; finding the front doors was like reading Braille. She tested the knob and it turned. "Huh," she said out loud, still sure she'd locked it. She pulled open the door and—

A hand grabbed her arm, wrenched her inside. She screamed. Her arm was forced up toward the center of her back. She couldn't see who'd attacked her, the alcove illuminated by only a flashlight. She stopped screaming as the pain intensified. Couldn't believe this was happening—again.

"That's a lot better," said a male voice. "Not that anyone can hear you out here."

"What do you want?" She couldn't move. "Who are you?"

He paused, then chuckled to himself—a hollow nervous chuckle. "I can't fucking believe it. It's you."

"What do you want?" she said again.

"You could start by opening this *fucking* door." She didn't answer. "Did you hear me? Open—the fucking—door!"

"I can't."

He drove her arm farther up toward her shoulders, forcing her onto the toes of her sneakers.

"I can't, *really*, I don't know how."

"The fuck you don't, you goofy bitch. I've been listening to your stupid voice for an hour. For some fucking reason my recording won't activate the voice code. Now, *Open it*."

"Please, you're hurting me."

"If you don't open this door . . ."

"You're breaking my arm."

"Open it."

"Let me go. *Now!*"

He hesitated, lightening his grip for an instant; she was able to drop back on the soles of her shoes and get her balance. She sensed uncertainty, so she kicked back as hard as she could. The heel of her sneaker collided squarely with his shin. He cried out, hopping clumsily on one foot as he attempted to maintain his hold. It was this cry that alerted Luke Delamar.

"Fucking goofy bitch," the guy yelled. As they struggled, he lost his grip on her arm. He barely managed to contain her flailing arms with his, trying to subdue her attack by hugging her from behind. But his efforts were futile anyway; a black fury was approaching by the second.

Luke burst through the open door. "Fuck me!" the guy screamed. He released Deirdre, backing madly. Luke charged, bear-hugged and tackled, his entire weight crushing the guy into the floor. There was the tremendous crash of bodies against planks, and then a long silence, neither moving.

"You okay?" Luke asked her quietly over his shoulder.

"I'm all right."

The guy began fighting for breath, an awful strangled gargle emanating from his gaping mouth, eyes bulging like a dead cod. Luke disengaged himself, patted down the intruder for weapons, and stood.

"What're you doing here?" she said to Luke.

He kept his eyes on the intruder. "I check the building twice a night." He leaned down, a look of concern on his face. "Just try to relax, buddy. Relax and the breath will come." He turned to her. "Who is this guy?"

"I have no idea."

"I guess I whomped him kinda hard."

"He wanted me to open the voice lock. He seems to know who I am."

"Did he try to hurt you?"

"He tried . . . no, not really. He just talked big." A pause. "Luke?" His wary expression. "Thanks, thank you," she said.

Just for an instant he grinned, then kneeled back down. "Buddy, you got to relax, okay?"

Finally a gasp, his ashen face wet with sweat, his lips blue. After a fourth or fifth attempt, he managed a few breaths and lifted his head. Saw Luke. "Don't kill me"—a labored breath—"*please*—just don't kill me." He started coughing, nearly vomited.

"Who are you?" said Luke.

"*Fuck*—what a day. I knew—I shouldn'ta—taken—this goddamn job. I even got lost—stumbling around—the goddamn fog—trying to find—

this place." A wheezing pause. "Fuck *me*. Then it takes an eternity—to disarm the security system. I told her—I don't want—this goddamn job. But she—'*We need the money*,'" he imitated a shrill female voice. "We always need—the money—because she spends—*all* the money. *Fuck!*" he yelled out to no one in particular. "Now I'll be back in—and she'll be fucking—everybody in town—again. I *knew*—I just knew—I shouldn'ta taken—this job."

Deirdre noticed a backpack and small tape recorder resting near the flashlight. She turned on the alcove overhead, everything blinking into bright focus, and opened the pack. "Luke."

He walked over and examined the contents of the pack. "C-four, plastic explosive." Luke went back to the intruder, glaring at him.

"*What?*" said the guy, looking up at Luke.

"Why?"

"Why what, for fuck's sake?"

"Why blow up our factory?"

"What are you talking about?"

Luke continued to stare at him. "Why?" He said it very quietly.

The guy raised his eyebrows. "*Money?*"

"Someone hired you?"

The guy nodded.

"Who hired you?"

"You think they tell me? *Hi, my name is Fuck-head and I want you to blow up this building, so just in case you get caught you can tell everyone.*"

"Who?" said Luke again.

"Don't look at me like that. You already broke my back, my ribs—and my head is killing me. I think I got fucking whiplash."

"Who?"

"I don't know *who*, okay?"

"Who?"

"What're you? A fucking owl from hell?"

Luke reached down and slapped him across the face. The force of the blow snapped his head around like a chiropractor adjusting someone's neck.

"You need to learn better manners," said Luke. "And you swear too much. There's a lady present."

It took the guy some minutes to recover from the slap, and he wasn't quiet about it. A red welt was blossoming, and his eye was beginning to swell shut. "Look, I'm sorry," he finally said, trying to sit up but only

managing to drag himself slightly against the wall. "It's just been a bad fuc—a bad day, *okay?*"

"Who paid you?"

"Listen, *honest*, I just get an envelope. At a drop-off point. Inside is the address, half-payment, and any particulars. In this case it was the recorder that was supposed to open the fucking—sorry—the voice lock and some info on the security system. That's the truth."

"Wendy Smith, she must have recorded my voice," said Deirdre. "*Goddamnit!* How could I have been so stupid?"

"We changed the outer locks," said Luke.

"It wasn't enough."

"It was." He grinned. "Should we kill him?" He winked at Deirdre so the guy couldn't see.

"Sure, why not? Let's kill him, but I want to like torture him some first."

"Wait a minute, what the fuck're you two talking about? It was just a job. I own two LiveCell phones for fuck's sake. They're great phones. Really great phones. *Fantastic* fucking phones. That's why I didn't want to take this job. Listen, let's talk this over. You can have all the money. Or all the money I got—half the money for the job. That's ten thousand, five thousand each." He watched them intently.

"I think I'd rather torture him," she said.

"What the fuck's wrong with you? Did I hurt you? *No.* I was just trying to do a job."

"You called me a *goofy* bitch. Twice."

"Listen, you're not goofy at all. Not in the least, and I mean that. It was that door. I mean, a fuc—sorry—an hour I couldn't get it open." He was near tears, his pain probably increasing as the shock wore off.

"You come in here to blow up our livelihood. You won't tell us who paid you, and you don't expect us to kill you?" said Luke.

"Just listen—" He cowered, attempting to inch farther away along the wall. "Listen to me. I told you: I just get a phone call with a pickup point. That's *all*. Fuck, stop looking at me like that. Listen, I can get more money."

"How should we torture him?" said Luke over his shoulder.

"Let's burn him. Like real slowly."

"What the fuck's wrong with you? I don't know *anything*, you gotta believe me. What a day," he muttered. "What a jewel of a day. She's probably already out fucking somebody because I'm late."

Luke was beside Deirdre. "Should we call Mr. Chevalier?" he whispered.

"I hate to bother him. I'm sure he's asleep. Jay would probably let him go."

"Police?"

"They didn't do much last time. Do we want the publicity? You know how the press has been like savaging us lately? They'll probably say he tried to blow up the factory because of headaches he got from his Live-Cell."

"I think he told us all he knows."

"Hey," begged the guy from the corner. "Just listen, *please!* You gotta believe me. I told you the truth. Besides, I'll probably never walk again, isn't that enough?"

"You want me to call an ambulance?" said Luke.

"And bring the fucking cops? I was thinking you might wanna accept my offer."

"Not if you keep swearing."

"Sorry, really, I am. Lady, I'm sorry." He paused, brightening. "So we've a deal?"

"Hey," Luke said, *"fuck you."* Deirdre started giggling. Luke moved in the guy's direction. "If you take their money and don't blow up the building what happens?"

"They're gonna come after me."

"Who will?"

"The contact person. Whoever's the go-between. Somebody."

"And?"

"Fuck if— Never happened to me before. They'll want their money. Who wouldn't? Are you gonna let me go? Listen, you want me to ask around. They'll figure me for a snitch, but fuck it, I could try."

"Where's the money?"

"In my jacket."

"Let me have it."

The guy reached slowly into his pocket, groaning, and pulled out an envelope. Luke reached down and took it, handed it to Deirdre.

"If you find out who set this up, you can have this back."

"You serious? You're gonna let me go?"

"You think we want you here?"

"I know this sounds really stupid, but I don't think I can get up by myself."

"Try," said Luke, "before I change my mind." He turned back to Deirdre and whispered, "This okay with you?"

She nodded.

The guy rolled slowly onto his side and attempted to get his feet under him, yet with each movement he yelped louder and the sweat poured. He gave them an embarrassed smile.

Luke lifted him onto his feet, the guy biting his lip to stifle the scream.

"Listen," he said once he was more or less standing, leaning heavily against Luke. "You two've been real decent to me. I'm really sorry about . . . you know. Nothing personal. *Okay?*"

"Shut up," said Luke. Then to Deirdre, "Can we take him in your car? I always park a couple blocks away not to alert anyone. Besides, a ride on mine might kill him. We better drop him at SF General, though it's more than he deserves."

Luke emptied the guy's pockets, stuffed everything into the backpack, and tossed it into the wagon. The guy screamed at every step down, but Luke finally got him into the backseat. She drove, the fog still so thick she pulled on the wipers. At the hospital, they propped him up against a wall near an emergency room door. With all the noise he was making, they knew it wouldn't be long.

As they rolled again, Luke said, "Can I buy you a drink?"

"Aren't the bars closed?"

"I know a place—and we can certainly afford it."

She grinned at him, and Luke winked.

FOURTEEN

"Come on, man—*one* more. Come on, baby, juss one more time." Sammy guided the bar as it slowly moved downward, his massive cupped hands as if in offering under the knurled metal. The bar rested across Jay's chest for less than an instant, and then Jay drove the weight upward, his arms quivering slightly as the bar hesitated in mid-stroke, Sammy's two index fingers assisting fractionally. "That's it, come on, baby, you got it, you got it," he said again. With a last reserve of strength, Jay forced the bar to the full extension of his arms. Sammy immediately gripped it and settled it with a loud clank onto the steel bench rack, the six big cast-iron plates rattling against each other.

"Man, I think you stronger now than before. *Damn*, that's seven reps. What you weighing these days?"

"I'm back around one-eighty," said Jay as he lay prone and panting on the weight bench.

"Man, I don't want to hear about it. You lifting almost as much as me, and I got close to sixty pounds on you."

"When I boxed I didn't lift that much—Pete wouldn't let me—but it feels good now."

Jay popped up off the bench and stretched his arms out behind him, enjoying the burn in his muscles. His wounded arm was finally normal again. Looking around he was relieved the Cyclone gym hadn't decorated

for Christmas. It was the time of year when he felt he didn't fit anywhere, a time for families, not orphans. It brought back bittersweet memories of the Northeast and his mother, or at least some vague early memory of Christmas there. He wasn't sure how much of it was really his and how much of it he'd invented as a child. His grandfather had said that Christmas wasn't his people's holiday—wouldn't have a thing to do with it. And now, with him gone, there would never be anyone to ask. It also dredged up those leaden holidays at the orphanage, or his Christmases as a young man when he waited the time out alone in diners or cheap rooms. It was not his favorite couple weeks.

"You ready?" he said to Sammy.

"Naw, man, enough is enough."

"You sure?"

"I gettin' soft in my old age. You must have real strong ligaments." Sammy shook his head. "You too strong for your own good."

"Shall we hit the heavy bag for a while?"

"Let's shower and head down to Felix's for some of that crazy hop water they got down there. You know, that stuff that foam up, come in those little glasses? bubbles all running around inside? all you got to do is ask for it? We'll play some soul music on the juke. Man, I got to hear that Bobby Womack—I love that shit. I got a CD in the Benz now, but it sound best at Felix's on a Saturday afternoon. We get Felix to turn it up for us. I wanna show you his place. An icon 'round this neighborhood." He paused. "Where you park?"

"On Edes around Ninety-sixth Street."

"Then you walk right by. Blue neon say *Lounge*?"

"I've noticed it before. A beautiful old sign."

"Wait till you see the inside. Oh man, I *love* this time a year—and I got me the day and the night off, too."

"Where's Jolene?"

"Didn't I tell you? Jolene and the kids on the plane to Acapulco yesterday. I couldn't stay down there no full two weeks; Nick need my ass at the room, and I get all bored lyin' on a beach anyhow, so I go down later and join 'em for Christmas. Can you believe that shit? Acapulco for Christmas. But she want it so bad, I say, honey, you want an *A*-capulco Christmas, you got your sweet self an *A*-capulco Christmas. Man, I got to haul all the gifts down there on an air-o-plane. And I'm talking these two monster motherfucking suitcases. That why I not working out too

much today—got to save my strength for them suitcases. But today, today baby, daddy gonna drink some beer and rye whiskey."

"Nice to see you in such a good mood."

"Christmastime, man. I got that holiday spirit pumpin' my veins. And thanks to you I don't got to struggle my ass no more. Thanks to you, this the best year of my life, and my family's life. Man, I set up college funds for all my kids a month ago. I didn't tell you . . . I done sold all my stock."

He watched Jay for his reaction. "Not 'cause I don't believe in your ass, you know I do. I done it 'cause I don't need no more money, I make enough, and I didn't wanna worry no more about it." He put his arm around Jay. "Man, I knew you was good luck the minute I laid eyes on your ass. I never told you, but I borrow that first twenty large I put in LiveCell, Jolene screaming at me when she find out. '*How we ever gonna pay this back?*' she said. '*Are you out of your damn mind?*' And now—I her fucking hero, and it all 'cause a you."

Jay looked embarrassed.

"Man, you juss shrivel all up anybody say they love you. You quiet again today. Few months ago, you start to defrost, now you all on quiet again. Jay, you can't let those motherfuckers bug you. I been readin' the papers, and I dig they after your ass again, but I telling you man, those fucks will never rest till they own it all. They coded to do juss that. They got to make sure we *all* juss as fucking miserable as they are. They can't rest till they make everybody on earth miserable."

Sammy studied him again. "Maybe you juss sell it to them? They ain't gonna rest otherwise, you and I both know that. And you got to ask yourself why? I mean, you give the world this beautiful thing, and now everybody talk all over for free, but they got to fuck with it." He examined his friend. "Come on, man. We don' worry about it none today. We go talk with my man Felix. We let those beer angels soothe your weary mind. And Felix got a holiday special you got to try. Let's shower up."

They walked out of the free weight room into the boxing part of the gym. As they headed for the locker room everyone greeted Sammy and gave Jay the nod.

"You change a lot of people's lives around here. They too shy to tell you, but they tell me." He paused. "Man, there you go again, looking all funny. We got to find you a good woman, get on with the *de*frost."

"Sammy, I'm fine," he said.

"Yeah, you fine, I know you fine, I juss wanna see a smile on my main

man." They stripped down for their showers. "You gonna take some steam today?"

"You?"

"If you want. Man, I all ready right now for my holiday afternoon."

"Let's just shower and head to the bar then. My treat."

Sammy glared at him. "No way. This my afternoon, my place, my treat. Right?"

Jay nodded, and finally smiled at his friend. Sammy winked, grabbed a clean towel and headed for the showers.

" . . . across a hundred and tenth street . . ." Sammy sang quietly along with Bobby Womack. Then at the *uhh-wu-wu-wu* part he allowed his voice to rise above the volume of the jukebox. Nobody minded in the least.

Entering Felix's Lounge for the first time was like entering a still photograph from a book, *Lost Barrooms from the Late 1930s*. Of course in the thirties the windows wouldn't have had iron grates, and the door, now protected by steel mesh, would have opened with a push—no wait until being recognized and buzzed into the place. The bar itself had remained the same though, with its horseshoe shape at the entrance-end and its thick curved mahogany lip, the top a sanded and alcohol-stained teak. The same huge mirror corralled by polished wood, a graceful arch with vertical amber lights resembling Grecian pillars, sentinels of the liquor-bottle forest. Mahogany booths and tables lined the right wall beyond the horseshoe section. The cornice of a rusty and tarnished tin ceiling was hung with paper streamers and oversized Christmas decorations. In the center of the bar was a massive punch bowl surrounded by mugs as newborns surround a mother, next to this a red plastic ladle, and on the red glass bowl and mugs, white silk-screened script that read *Tom and Jerry*.

Sammy'd started with one, a Christmas tradition, Tyrone adding rum and boiling water to the egg mixture ladled from the punch bowl, topping it with a *pfft* of whipped cream and a shake of nutmeg. Since Tyrone had inherited the lounge twenty-four years ago, most of his patrons called him Felix though no one remembered the original Felix. When Sammy introduced him to Jay, he shook Jay's hand with great seriousness and told him his money was no good in his place; whatever he wanted was on the house. Sammy told Felix he'd have to wait in line.

Sammy emptied his Tom and Jerry, got up and walked to the front door, signaled Felix to buzz it open. Holding the door with his foot to

keep it from springing shut, he leaned forward and looked down Edes
Street in the same direction Jay had parked the Cutlass. Then he came
back and sat down again.

"They gone," he said to no one in particular.

"What's at?" said Felix from down the bar.

"Man, you running craps in the back, you peddling crack, you serving minors?"

"Sammy, *what* you talking about?"

"You know anything 'bout a chocolate sedan with two ugly white
boys inside? Look like an unmarked."

"Never seen it before."

"Man, juss look wrong to me, but they gone now. Look like some
stray vice boys or some shit like that." Felix went back to stacking glasses.

"You want another Jerry?" said Sammy. Jay told him one was enough.
"You right," he said quietly so Felix wouldn't hear. "They lovely, but they
awful sweet, and I like sweet." Then, calling down to the old bartender,
"Felix, my man, set us up a couple of frosties."

"Blue Ribbon?"

"What else."

"Shorts?"

"Now you talking, brother."

"Calvert?"

Sammy just grinned. He turned to Jay. "So what's going on? I know
there something. Company stuff, the bad press? There something else?
You got woman troubles? I hate to see you with the blues at Christmastime."

"I'm fine," he said as Sammy searched him. "Truly, I'm okay." Jay
watched Felix pouring the drafts, then back at Sammy. "This is a wonderful place. Thanks for bringing me here."

Sammy placed a hand on his shoulder. "You need something, all you
got to do is ask, but you know that."

As they talked and drank, customers began to drift in, the door
buzzer heralding each fresh group or single—that vague nudge of cool
air moving down the bar—almost everyone already gussied up for the
holidays though Christmas was still a week and a couple of days away.
The bar began to fill; another bartender arrived to help Felix pour drinks,
and a waitress began working the tables. Only a few patrons seemed surprised to see Jay on a stool beside Sammy. Many came over to say Hey
to Sammy, ask about Jolene, the children, and meet Jay. There was a lot

of laughter, and after a couple hours Sammy leaned over to his friend and said, "Baby, you finally on *de*frost."

"I'm better, thanks to you."

"You really can't tell Sammy what's bugging you?"

The bar was busy now, which offered its own kind of privacy. Jay felt he should tell Sammy something; he knew Sammy would be hurt if he didn't.

"I'm worried about my people."

"LiveCell?"

"Someone tried to blow up one of our factories."

"*Motherfucker*."

"It was a paid job. Untraceable. Two of my people interrupted the man in the middle of the night. It was a fluke they happened to be there."

"Damn, man. Now they trying to burn your ass out." He shook his head in sadness. "You use David Artega?"

"Unofficially, but the thing was confused. My people dropped the arsonist off outside San Francisco General. A man was admitted that night with broken ribs and internal injuries, but he disappeared sometime before morning. The ER doctor assured Artega the guy must've had help leaving. We have the wallet, but the information was a dead end, an alias. He even used a different alias at the hospital. Artega thinks he was out of the country by that afternoon. My people also took ten thousand off him, which he told them was half the job, but Artega thought fifty-thousand was probably the figure."

"Why didn't your people turn him over to Artega?"

"I don't think either of them have much faith in the police, and though Deirdre saw Artega once, it's not as if she knows him. And you'd have to meet Luke to understand. It takes some people a long time to believe in a good cop."

"I hear you. David didn't clue me in."

"I asked him to tell no one." Jay drained his beer. "Let me buy you and Felix a drink. Let's get back in the spirit."

"Man, glad you told me. I understand better. I told you man, you making some waves; you changing things for them big money boys. I love you for it brother, and I respect your ass all the more. But, baby, you can't let this shit get you down—it bound to happen. They bound to try and set you back, but I know you, you keep coming. Man, I wish I coulda seen you in the ring, I bet you never quit coming."

Jay didn't tell him about the death threats. There'd been a second one

since he'd mentioned the first to Mary. The second was identical: DESIST OR DIE across plain white paper. He hadn't told Detective Artega either. Jay didn't take the threats seriously—how could he? It seemed too stupid, too amateurish. The people after him were not amateurs. They had every possible resource available and no one watching them. They could do what they liked as long as they kept the truth out of the media, and therefore from the public. He understood that the rules were inequitable.

Felix was pleased that Jay wanted to buy him a drink. He opened one of the latched doors and reached far into the cooler, pulled out a big brown bottle, brought it over with a glass to their section of the bar.

"This the Xingu beer, the *black* beer, come all the way from the Brazil jungle. Make a man strong where it counts." He poured it out—it looked like oil—and raised the glass. "Thank you, Jay. Merry Christmas."

They all raised their beverages and toasted each other, Felix draining off half his glass and humming his approval loudly.

"Felix, I don't know how you can drink that skanky shit," said Sammy.

"You juss don't know what's good."

Sammy pretended to strangle himself with one hand, his tongue sticking out. He started chuckling. "Man, you juss like that shit 'cause it got snakes and crocodiles on the label. Remind you a your two ex-wives." Sammy slapped his thigh now, winked at Jay.

Felix said, "Even at Christmastime he got to fun an old man."

"You ain't that old."

"Jay, how old you think I am?"

Jay examined him. "Mid-fifties?"

"I be sixty-seven in June," he said with pride.

"You serious?" said Sammy, no longer laughing. "Man, I had no idea you that old. Maybe I should start drinking that shit."

"You juss keep drinkin' what you drinkin'," Felix said, grinned at Jay, and went off to serve a customer.

"That Felix too much. I remember him from when I's a kid, coming in here after school when it empty, juss the regulars nursing hangovers, and he give us pop—but I never figure how old he must be. He never change. Only his wives." He looked around. "Man, I got to go play that juke again." Sammy sauntered over to the throbbing jukebox and began feeding it dollars.

Jay did feel a little better. The joy and faith in Sammy relaxed him, and he decided his premonitions might be wrong. After all, it was Christ-

mastime, a time of goodwill and fellowship, not a time of fear. Everyone in the bar exuded positive feelings. Why couldn't he? These past months he'd fought an underlying uneasiness that wouldn't rest, and he worried he was putting his people at risk. Was he pushing too hard, too quickly? Had he calculated everything carefully enough? Had he underestimated the viciousness of the opposition?

After the bomb attempt he'd called a special department heads meeting and cautioned everyone that working at LiveCell might be a lot riskier than he'd foreseen. He'd asked each of them how they felt and what they wanted to do.

Jimmy Hakken spoke first. He said, "My crew are ready for anything—*period*. We're on constant alert. Got sentries posted around the clock. No one is blowing up my factory—*period*."

Jay knew that in Jimmy Hakken he'd fostered something that was getting out of hand, yet he also sensed how content Hakken was, as if he'd lived his whole life to fill this role, and if anyone knew the importance of that, it was Jay. However, though Jay would never admit it to anyone, Hakken's devout loyalty made him very uncomfortable.

Deirdre, though she'd absorbed the brunt of the physical attacks against the company, said, "Like I'm going to worry now? Like I'd ever let you down after what you've done for me?"

Her words moved Jay so much that he'd gotten out of his chair and looked out the window at the small rectangle of bay, a silver-gray on that morning. He noticed Mary examining his eyes as he sat down. She was always observing—so astute.

Mary addressed the group. She said, "LiveCell is doing something important, something worthwhile, and that's worth the risk for me."

Jay knew he'd hurt Mary deeply, but she seemed to manage to hide her pain in public. How could he make amends? He couldn't tell her the truth, that was for certain. But now she was unwilling to attempt infusing the phones—he wasn't sure why—and he felt daily that he was running out of time. Time was always the problem.

Chet Simmons was next. Since the day Jay hadn't blamed him for the black-box fiasco and had reassured him that he would never be fired for doing his best, he viewed Jay with quiet but intense fondness. It was as if he'd never had an adult male friend and thought of Jay as his best friend.

At the meeting, "I'm in," was all he said. After he spoke, his eyes flickered downward in embarrassment, and then he glanced shyly at Jimmy Hakken. Hakken gave him a closed-fist salute.

Both Cliff Thompson and Randy Dyer said they would do whatever it took. They were outraged and stunned by the surreptitious undermining and violence. They'd been in the corporate world all their working lives and had never imagined anything like this. It brought the fight out in both of them.

Cliff Thompson said, "I'm agonized by the drop in stock price, but I'm certain it'll rebound once the press and the Food and Drug Administration back off. In some of the smaller newspapers, a counter-attack has surfaced, which is great. People's loyalties to the phones have strengthened, if anything; sales are up, and worldwide sales are just beginning. We've lost a few battles, but we're certain to win the war."

Duncan had been drawing further and further into himself over the last months. He must have sensed that Mary and Deirdre were privy to things he wasn't; of course, his suspicions were grounded. Then there was his sexual obsession with Mary, which had only intensified.

As they waited for his decision at the meeting, he said, "LiveCell is garnering some very powerful enemies. It doesn't seem worth the risk to hold on to it. Jay, as you said, it's getting dangerous for everyone. Why don't you just sell it? I'm sure the new owners would allow everyone to remain, the sale would ease tensions, and we could still achieve the same goals. I don't see any reason not to sell."

Jay asked the others how they felt. They were unanimously against him selling. "There's one reason," said Jay. After more discussion, Duncan finally agreed to stay.

Sammy walked back from the juke, dancing to The Spinners doing "I'll Be Around," his big body imitating a steam locomotive pulling out of a station, his arms churning like the engine's drivers. He took his stool beside Jay again, singing the refrain: "*Ba*by, whenever you call me, I'll be there; whenever you want me, I'll be there; whenever you need me, I'll be there—I'll be around." He gripped Jay's shoulder. "Man, this one *sweet* afternoon."

"The best," said Jay. "I feel renewed." But he didn't; there was still a nasty pressure in his chest.

"That those beer angels doin' their strut. They make a new man outa ya. *For they are the beer angels, and they comfort and make new the weary.* Psalm One-Fifty-One." Sammy chuckled. "Man, I love this place."

Jay nodded.

"Juss seein' you smile, pay me back. You *need* take some time off like

this. Man can't work all the time. We should do this every Saturday."

"Next time is my treat."

"Now you talking."

Sammy signaled Felix by swinging his hand as if he had a lasso. After the round arrived, he said, "Where you wanna go eat? Or you want something right here? The cook be in anytime now, and she fry a mean steak. Or we take the Benz, go anywhere you say. My treat, wherever you wanna go."

Jay looked up at the clock over the bar again, though he knew the time. "I have to take off after this beer. I still have a few things to do at both factories."

"Ah, man, no way, we juss gettin' started."

Jay saw the disappointment. "Let me have about an hour and a half and I'll meet you back here. Save my stool. Actually, I would love to eat right here."

"Now you talking, baby. We have some steaks, bake potatoes, biscuits and beans." He slapped Jay on the shoulder again. "I walk you to your car. You still driving that jalopy?"

"It's time for a new one. Just haven't gotten around to it."

When they left Felix's Lounge, the twilight had reached that exact interval between day and night. A time when we believe everything appears more beautiful and magical. The blue neon of *Lounge* against its metal signboard appeared almost transposed from the vibrant hue of the sky. The *Felix's* had been long burnt out. Below the sign, the street was fairly busy on that Saturday night; maybe neighbors were less afraid to be outside because of the holiday season. Some teenagers on skateboards and high-tech scooters clattered and banged along the sidewalks as they practiced stunts, a few leaners and stragglers in big down parkas watched their kids or argued and chatted with each other, drinking from screwed-up paper bags.

Sammy inhaled the cool evening air and let out a sigh. "Man, I must be crazy, but I always think Oakland have a special smell. Smell like home to me. Tonight it smell like happiness." They turned left out of the door, walked slowly down Edes. This time Sammy didn't notice the dark-brown sedan as it jerked out of a parking spot and drove at them. If he had noticed, he probably wouldn't have recognized it—the headlights on bright blinded his view. He didn't pay enough attention either when the sedan skidded to a stop just in front of them, about ten yards away. At that

moment, Jay was looking across the street at two young kids playing tag and giggling, so it was only Sammy who vaguely saw the sedan's door swing open. A white man leapt out, double-gripped an automatic, pointed it at Jay. Then Sammy reacted. With a sudden violent spasm he sprinted at the gun. He was already running hard, his head down, hunched over, when the man fired twice in rapid succession; a silencer muffled the explosions. The first bullet struck him in the chest but did not slow him. The second shot hit him high in the stomach. The gunman, seeing this huge black man charging him, jumped back into the sedan and screamed, "*Go, go!*" The tires squealed and smoked. The sedan lurched forward, careening away, the car door slamming shut from the acceleration. A third and fourth shot were fired out of the passenger window at Jay Chevalier. Only one of those bullets was ever found.

Sammy stopped running. He swayed as Jay caught up to him. Jay grabbed him as he collapsed, attempting to cushion his fall as best as he could. People on the street started yelling, running toward them. Jay begged someone to call an ambulance. For this one thing his LiveCell wouldn't work without the black box.

He looked at his friend lying on the sidewalk, at Sammy's face gray in the twilight, at his usually animated eyes dull and half-closed, at a small bubble of blood forming on his lips. He didn't want to look any lower. He pulled off his sports coat and gently covered part of Sammy's body with it. He wiped blood from Sammy's lips and chin, wiped the sweat off Sammy's forehead with his fingers.

"You're going to be okay," he said. "You're going to be okay. Just hold on."

Sammy seemed to hear him and his eyes focused a little.

"You're going to be okay," he said again.

He heard a siren. He sensed people gathered around him but didn't listen to what they were saying. Most just stood and stared, a few of them spoke:

"Damn, that Sammy—Sammy Holmes."

"Samuel Holmes, yeah, I remember him, he use to be a boxer."

"Why somebody shoot him? What the fuck?"

Jay saw Sammy's lips move. He bent down close, placing his ear next to his friend's lips.

"Jolene," he heard him say.

Jay waiting.

"Jay? You there?"

He told him he was there, *"I'm here. You're going to be okay."* Sammy tried to say something more but his eyes went dull again, and they closed. A minute passed. Jay didn't notice Felix's hand on his shoulder, or all the people murmuring. Another minute. The wavering cry of a siren growing louder. Sammy not moving. Jay not moving, his eyes locked on his friend's face, his hands trembling.

It was then, during that eerie period of empty waiting, when everyone standing there was startled by a horrible sound. Jay Chevalier looked toward the heavens and he bellowed like a wounded animal.

FIFTEEN

Detective Artega was off duty, leaving San Francisco by the Bay Bridge on his way home, when he heard the call on his radio. He was considering dropping by Felix's for a holiday drink anyway, so he responded to the call, joining the scene shortly after the arrival of two other cruisers and an ambulance. Artega pushed through the dark huddle of spectators, approached the victim being loaded onto a stretcher, saw the face in the electric glare. He looked around in disbelief. Then he recognized Jay Chevalier against the darkness, being questioned by an officer. He walked over to them. Though Artega lived nearby, he didn't have jurisdiction in Oakland. However, by pushing the issue, he managed to free Jay from further questioning. He told Jay he'd meet him at Highland Hospital when the police had finished. By then the EMTs had loaded Sammy into the ambulance, and the siren pierced the subdued street. Artega watched Chevalier hurry to his car.

Jay followed the same route as the ambulance in his Cutlass, assailed by blurred images of tubes and IVs being stuck into his friend, wires being attached to his bloody chest. By the time he'd stashed the Cutlass and entered the hospital, Sammy was already in the operating room. Fighting to stay calm, Jay inquired at the front desk, then cornered the triage nurse. He told her he'd pay for everything, to *please* spare no cost, just

save his friend. Twice he consulted the head ER doctor who reassured him that the surgeon was extremely capable and that someone would alert him immediately when the operation was finished. Finally he found a seat. Marooned in the crowded waiting room, he looked like a week-old piece of lost luggage that no one would ever claim.

Jay was suffering from a pain just beneath his ribcage that made it difficult for him to breathe. He knew he needed to livecell Jolene. He wondered if Artega was aware that she was in Mexico. The image of Jolene and the children at the beach—the kids giggling, jumping together, turning their naked backs to the waves, chasing each other along the smooth sand—was randomly spiked by the memory of Pete's heart attack in the boxing gym. He tried to concentrate on the phone call he had to make. But what was he supposed to say? "Your husband has been shot in front of a bar so he won't be going anywhere for Christmas. He saved my life and would be fine now if it wasn't for me."

After managing to remain in the waiting room for about half an hour, he walked outside into the night air. Below him he could see Christmas lights shaken onto the dark hills like a rain of colored stars. The sight sickened him. He took out his phone.

"Mary," he said when she answered.

"Hey, it's you. Deirdre just livecelled and asked why you weren't answering calls. She expected you at the factory a while ago." And then anxiously, "Is something wrong?"

"There's been an accident."

"Are you okay?"

"It's Sammy. He's been shot."

"*Shot?*"

"A man jumped out of a car near the gym and tried to kill me. Sammy—" His voice broke. "Sammy saved my life."

"Oh my God. Is Sammy all right?"

"He's in surgery. I'm at Highland Hospital. He ran at the gun and he was shot, twice."

"Oh *no*."

A pause and he sensed her question.

"They assured me that everything possible is being done."

"Is Jolene there?"

"She's in Acapulco with the children. Sammy was going to meet them there for Christmas." Again, he couldn't speak. "I need to call her. I need to tell her."

"I'll call her."

Another silence. He shivered in his T-shirt, his blood-soaked sports coat gone.

"Jay, you don't sound good."

He didn't answer.

"I'm going to close up here. I'll be there in forty minutes."

"Mary?"

They listened to each other.

"Sammy can't die," he said. "You should have seen him today, he . . ."

"I'll livecell Jolene and I'll be there as soon as I can."

Detective Artega arrived at the hospital alone. He spotted Chevalier standing outside and headed over. They talked about Sammy. Then he suggested they go inside—it was damn cold as far as he was concerned—and they walked back in. The waiting room was over-crowded, so he asked a nurse if there was a vacant area to use, and she reluctantly pointed out a small cubicle down the hall. He perched uncomfortably on the examining bed and Jay took a plastic chair.

"I made some calls. Oakland's allowing me to assist. I figured you'd rather talk to me than a stranger."

Jay didn't respond.

"Did anyone know you and Sammy were going to be at the Lounge?"

Jay shook his head. "I didn't even know until he suggested it."

"And you walked directly there from the Cyclone?"

Jay nodded.

"What time?"

"We left the gym around two."

"So you were at the Lounge about two and a half hours. You ever go to Felix's after workouts?"

"Never."

Artega paused for a few seconds, thinking. "I know you gave the other officer your description of the shooting. If you don't mind, give it to me again."

Artega listened: how Jay's attention was drawn from the kids across the street by Sammy's sudden movement; the dark sedan; the man dressed in black, maybe dark-brown or blue, dark gloves on his hands, white face, black hair, medium build, no one Jay recognized; the two shots. Sammy had blocked much of his view of the gunman, and Jay hadn't seen the driver or noticed the car leaving; his attention was on Sammy. Artega wrote it all down.

"Why?" said Jay.

"Why what?"

"Why did he run at the gun? He could have saved himself."

"You think they wanted you?"

Jay nodded.

"You didn't mention this before."

"I've had two death threats."

"When?"

"First one was four months ago, the other a few weeks ago."

"How were they delivered?"

"What do you mean?"

"Phone call, message machine, e-mail, letter?"

"Letter, regular mail, sent to me at LiveCell, Harcourt Building address."

"Do you have them?"

"I threw them out."

Artega looked away, tempted to shake his head. Why had Chevalier kept them to himself? "What did they say?"

"Desist or die."

Artega saw in the sick pallor and eyes what Chevalier was putting himself through, how badly he was beating himself up. "Jay, listen to me. Sammy's street smart, and he knew the gunman could kill both of you no matter what either of you did. His best chance was what he took—for both of you. Maybe the shooter would abort the hit, or panic and miss. Sammy might have gotten to him before he fired. From what you tell me, he almost did." He looked away from Jay's face. He didn't like what he saw.

Sensing a call, he pulled out his LiveCell phone. "Artega," he said. He listened, keeping his eyes off Chevalier. "The trunk? . . . Couple rounds missing? . . . *Four*? . . . Prints? . . . Potential DNA? . . . Anything else in the vehicle? . . . Let me know." He slid the phone back into his pocket. "They found the car and the gun. They're still searching for evidence, but I don't think there'll be much. Gun had four rounds missing. There were two other shots fired?"

"After Sammy went down. As they drove away."

"Listen to me. You don't *know* they wanted you. No one knew you were in the bar, so it might be much more random than you think."

"He was shot because of me." Chevalier glared, jerked out of the chair, and banged out of the room.

Artega found him outside. He was standing with his arms across his chest, staring out at the city. Artega lit a Camel and stood some yards

away, idly chewing his thumbnail on the hand that held the cigarette, flicking a stray fleck of tobacco from his lip. He didn't know what more to say to the guy. He'd already tried a few explanations, attempting to give the guy an out, though he figured Chevalier would never take the false way out of anything.

One thing was likely—if Sammy hadn't reacted the way he did, the gunman would have killed Chevalier. But how did the killers know they'd be in Felix's Lounge? That bugged him. Who tipped them off? It also bothered him that Oakland had been chosen for the hit, though the intelligence of it was obvious: if Sammy and Jay had both died, the killing would have appeared to be two more inextricable drug-related deaths, and even with Jay Chevalier's celebrity, any media attention would have died down quickly. He was not going to let that—

"Mr. Chevalier?" a nurse called from the brightly lit entrance of the hospital. Chevalier spun and headed toward the building. Artega cringed when he caught his expression. He hated to see a tough man unravel. "Is he okay?" he heard Chevalier say. "The doctor will speak with you now," was all she said. People working in hospitals all used the same clichés, he thought. He guessed they needed them. What the hell, he used them too. He extinguished his smoke in the outdoor canister, exhaled before the doors, and followed.

He joined the surgeon and Chevalier, who'd just been introduced. As Artega shook hands, he couldn't help but notice how doctors' hands were always the same—cool, baby smooth, and dry. Unlike a cop's.

"Mr. Chevalier," the surgeon said, employing that classic solemn manner, "I've just gotten off the telephone with Mrs. Holmes in Mexico, and she tells me you're a friend of the family." Jay nodded. "Detective, she asked if you were here. Mr. Holmes is in serious though reasonably stable condition, for now. We abated the internal bleeding though reoccurrence is always a concern. We are re-inflating his lung. One lung was severely damaged. We removed the bullet that entered the lung, but the second is too close to the spinal column to remove. He's lost a great deal of blood, which is being replaced. Both bullets entered at a fortuitously angled trajectory. If either had been angled differently he would have died instantly. He's a strong man." He paused. "We'll keep him ventilated overnight. I wish I had better news."

"So he's going to be okay?" said Jay.

"It's too early to tell. As I said, he is a very strong man."

"May I see him?"

"Let him rest for some hours. If his signs are good, you can visit him for a few minutes, though it's unlikely he'll be conscious. He's being kept heavily sedated while on the ventilator." He started to turn away, then rotated back. "By the way, your phones are an incredible product. We use them in the hospital; they save time and therefore lives."

When Mary arrived it took her a while to find Jay. He was in a small sitting room on the second floor down the hall from where they'd wheeled Sammy, the trauma ICU, a wing for patients requiring constant monitoring. When she found him, they embraced.

"How is he?" she said.

He told her.

She didn't ask him how *he* was doing. That was obvious, and it scared her. Now she wished she hadn't been so cold to him after he rejected her.

"I spoke with Jolene," she said, trying to sound normal. "I booked them a flight. They'll get in tomorrow. The last flight today from Acapulco to Oakland left at three. They arrive at eight tomorrow night. I offered to rent something and pick them up at the airport, but Jolene's sister's going to do it. I gave Jolene all the information I had. Did she call here?"

Jay nodded.

"I also let Deirdre and Jimmy Hakken know what happened. And I told Nick Brignolia at the poolroom."

Jay just stared at her.

"Do you know that man?" she whispered, noticing Artega watching her, the only other person in the sitting room.

"Detective Artega. A friend of Sammy's."

Artega got up and was introduced.

"I can't believe this happened," she said to him.

"We don't know anything yet. Though some people noticed the car, no one except Jay admitted to seeing the actual shooting or the face of the gunman. I told Jay there's no proof they were after Sammy or him. It might've been a mistake."

"Sammy noticed the car," Jay said, almost to himself.

"What?" Artega said.

"Sammy," Jay said louder, "as we entered the bar, he noticed the car. I remember he went back outside to see if it was still there. He said it looked wrong to him. He thought they were vice cops. He asked Felix if he knew anything about it."

"Was your Cutlass parked beyond the Lounge?"

Artega saw it now. The hit was supposed to take place as Chevalier left the gym alone. The gunman had waited between the gym and Jay's car to intercept him as he walked back. Simple. Going into Felix's and the presence of Sammy had been unexpected. At first the killers had aborted the hit, then changed their minds. They'd circled back and waited until Jay exited the bar. Shit, *everyone* must have seen them. White people were always noted in that neighborhood.

"Who knows you work out on Saturdays at the Cyclone?" he said.

Chevalier turned away and slumped into one of the chairs. Artega watched Jay's hands wash back and forth across the pallid brow, the fingers pressing at the eye sockets. Artega sensed what he was thinking: that it had stared him in the face. Chevalier would realize he could have saved them both, that he should've known what the car meant when Sammy spotted it. The death threats should have alerted him. That was probably their intention, to alert Chevalier. Professionals don't alert victims. *Shit*, the poor bastard. Many times it was that way; once you knew something and all the pieces fit, it seemed so damn obvious—afterwards.

The woman answered his question about the Cyclone: "Many people at the office know. They think it's odd that Jay goes to Oakland to work out. Most of them wouldn't have much to do with that neighborhood."

"I suppose we don't have the best reputation."

They sized each other up.

She said, "Jay thinks someone was trying to kill him. Do you think that's true?"

"Seems likely. Sammy was in the wrong place at the wrong time." There was no longer any point in giving the guy an out.

The woman sat down. Sat next to Chevalier and placed her arm around him. Artega stood awkwardly not knowing what to do. He thought of calling to see if anything new had turned up, but he'd just be killing time. He wanted to find the shooter, though not as much as he wanted whoever ordered the hit. But he recognized the futility of any emotion. The only chance was if someone had made a mistake, and professionals rarely made mistakes.

He glanced back at Chevalier, watched him straighten, scrub his forehead with his fist, turn to the woman.

"We will suspend all operations at LiveCell until further notice," he said. "We'll close it down."

She removed her arm. "*What?* My God, Jay, what are you talking about?"

"This can't go on. I can't put anyone else in jeopardy."

She looked as if she were trying to accept what he'd said, but wasn't doing a very good job.

"I think you need to give this a little more time."

He didn't answer.

"You're upset right now. We all are. I really think it would be a mistake to decide this now."

"I've decided. I want you to let everyone know," he said. "I want it in all the media."

"When?" she said, sounding frustrated. "Can't you at least wait until tomorrow?"

"No. As soon as possible. There's no time left."

"Shouldn't we at least have a department heads meeting first?"

"No. I won't take the risk. If LiveCell shuts down, there will be no reason for them to keep trying to destroy us. They win."

It took the press about four hours after the fact to discover that a seemingly random shooting in Oakland of a retired second-rate boxer and bartender, Samuel W. Holmes, was a huge story. LIVECELL TO CLOSE was the first headline to saturate the streets. Detective Artega kept the press away from the sitting room by stationing an officer in the hallway. Jay refused to leave the hospital and wouldn't eat. He left the room only once to go downstairs and donate blood, shoving silently past a few pushy, diehard reporters and television people. Some of Sammy's close friends and relatives arrived—Artega monitoring who should be allowed in—and they settled around the room, no one saying much, a few of the women in tears.

When the doctor checked his patient again, he decided there could be no visitors in Sammy's room that night. Artega exited to eat supper, and then at about ten-thirty he went home, leaving the stationed officer. Most everyone else had left as well. Mary retired at quarter past eleven. She told Jay she'd be back early in the morning before she officially shut down LiveCell as he requested.

Just after Mary left, Nick Brignolia entered the sitting room. He'd closed the poolroom early. He shook hands with Jay and took a chair across the room. The old man didn't look much better than Jay did. After half an hour, he withdrew as well.

Sometime after midnight the hospital finally drifted into a hush, and the ICU nurse appeared preoccupied. Jay sneaked down the hall and into the dimly lit room of his wounded friend. He stood silently beside the bed, gently cupping Sammy's shoulder. The ventilator tube in his mouth, Sammy didn't respond to his presence, each machine-controlled breath and the inertness of the big body so painful for Jay.

Jay Chevalier had reached a moment in his life when his intentions and actions, no matter how carefully considered, generated currents that he couldn't foresee or control. He'd already known this intellectually, but now he felt slammed by the reality, and it broke his confidence. He still believed in what he'd been doing, yet for the first time, the cost had changed, and the price was too high.

He'd always known that the end never justified the means. His phones were the means, and though he had visualized his prayer for what they might offer, about what the phones might help accomplish for humanity, an increased closeness to the continuum, he accepted that the end would always, and should always, be out of his control. Otherwise he would be like them, like the Wendell Aldens of the world—dictating, controlling, deciding the fate of others. Even at DuPont, he'd immediately sensed that his discovery would generate conflict and violence. He just hadn't realized it could be directed at anyone but himself. If only Sammy hadn't offered to walk him to his car. He saw Sammy running at the gun, saw the recoil from the automatic, the bullets striking the body, felt himself embracing his falling friend, felt the overwhelming weight of him in his arms, the acrid smell of the gunpowder—

And then Jay had an intuition.

He walked quickly over to the closet in the corner of the room, and though the closet was dark, he found what he was looking for. He grabbed the plastic bag with Sammy's belongings, and reaching inside, his hand rummaging, located the bloody pants. From one of the pockets, he pulled out the object he needed. He moved to the bed and placed it next to Sammy's head. Jay retrieved his own LiveCell.

"Sammy," he said, though his mouth didn't move and there was no sound. "Sammy, it's Jay, can you hear me?"

He waited. Nothing. He repeated it. Still nothing.

Then, "You?" he heard in his mind.

"It's me . . . Jay."

He waited.

"Jolene?"

"She's on her way. Be here tomorrow, with the kids. They're flying up tomorrow."

A pause.

"Fucked up, bad."

"Sammy, you're going to be okay, you just have to hang in there. You've been—"

"Jolene . . . love her . . . my babies . . . love 'em so much."

Jay felt the tears on his cheeks. "I'll tell her. Don't worry about anything, everything will be taken care of. Sammy, I'm . . . what you did for me. I'm so sorry, I wish it had been—

"Naw, don't you be—"

"*What* are you doing in here?"

Jay turned. The night nurse. Steel-haired, stout, the bosom of her white uniform like a spinnaker in a gale.

"I see you on the monitor, hiding in the shadows. You can't be in here," she said, looking around the room. She snapped on the lights and walked over to Jay. "What you doing with his stuff on the floor? . . . You crying," she said matter-of-factly. "What's this by his head?" She reached over and picked up Sammy's LiveCell. "This his?" Jay nodded. "Come on now, you got to leave him alone so the man can res' hisself." She guided Jay to the door with her large hand. "You that phone man, ain't you?" He nodded again. "Son, don' you worry yourself so much. He in the Lord's hands. He gonna be all right."

He searched her face. She wasn't going to let him stay no matter what, so he returned to the sitting room.

After ten minutes she brought him a styrofoam cup of coffee. "You drink this. It good and hot with plenty sugar an' cream. I can tell you ain't gonna sleep."

"Can I see him again?" he said.

"You let him res'. That his best chance." She looked down at him. "Son, you got to let the poor man res'," and she went back to her duties.

As the elderly nurse had predicted, he didn't sleep. His mind toiled all night with the relentless momentum of a dam run-off. When Mary arrived a little after six, she carried a white paper bag with some warm bakery rolls, butter, cheddar cheese, and a plastic bottle of fresh carrot juice.

"You have to eat something," she said.

He sipped tentatively at the juice.

"Jay, you really look bad. I'm being serious."

"I'm fine," he said.

"You *have* to eat something or you're going to collapse."

She handed him a buttered roll with cheese in it. "Please!" He ate it. There was no news on Sammy.

At around noon, when Mary returned from closing down LiveCell and the two factories, she found Jay in the same place—emotionally and physically. She'd no sooner greeted the people she knew in the sitting room than everyone's attention was drawn to a commotion in the hallway. After twenty minutes they saw a doctor walking slowly toward them.

Jay stood. The doctor told them what had happened. Jay staggered over to a wall. He punched it so hard that his fist went clear through the Sheetrock.

On the following Tuesday afternoon, Jay huddled at his desk and stared out the window. All three of LiveCell's floors in the Harcourt Building were vacant and dark. It was like an old school after hours, so dead and lifeless it almost provoked the need to shout. He sat in his orange office, drinking Lord Calvert out of a coffee mug with his left hand, his right hand swollen and bruised. His phone had been paging him constantly. He ignored it. All he did was focus on the gloomy rectangle of bay as rain washed down the thermopane. The wake and funeral were tomorrow. Both would be held at the Oakland Baptist Church. Jolene had asked him to say a few words in Sammy's memory. Would he have refused her anything?

There was a knock on his closed door. He ignored it, but after a moment the door opened.

"Hey," a voice said. "Chevalier."

He glanced over; there stood Jimmy Hakken—wet, dressed in black. A grim sight.

"Man, I know you ain't seeing nobody. Believe me, MacKensie made that *really* fucking clear. I'm here anyway."

He lumbered in, set a paper bag on the floor, ripped it open, separated two sixteen ounce cans of beer from their plastic carrying caddie, snapped in the pull tabs, and placed one on the desk in front of Jay. He tilted back the other for a lengthy drink and settled in the chair in his awkward, sprawled way. He didn't say a word for five or six minutes, until he'd downed the beer. Then he reached for the bag and exchanged cans, opened a second one.

"You know I ain't no good at talking." He took a sip. "I'm gonna any-way."

Jay had barely moved since Hakken had walked in, but now he reached for the can of beer.

Hakken reacted by holding out his can in a particularly solemn way, and he drank when Jay did.

Jimmy Hakken was never in a hurry to talk. Today he needed words to serve him and he was probably worried; they'd rarely served him in the past. He tried anyway: "I asked MacKensie about what happened. She don't give information easy—I'll give her that. But then I said, look, we are on the same fucking side here."

Jay sipped at his cold can.

Hakken leaned forward in his chair, set down his beer, and stared in his intense way.

"Listen," he said, "Chevalier—I'm just gonna tell you straight what's in my heart. That's all I can do, okay?

"This thing you started, it's bigger than you now. I dig you made it, like it's yours, but it's *ours*, too. I understan' Holmes is dead. I know how bad that hurts, because I lost my mom when I was young, and I lost a best friend, got his skull on my desk. It still hurts me, *all* the fucking time. But by quitting, you hurt all of us. And not just your crew. Bunch of people count on us; they need our phones. Lives're changing 'cause of us. Listen, the stock got fucking hammered yesterday—*hammered*. Everyone suddenly all paranoid that LiveCell is closed down for good. Fuck that—we can't close down. What matters is that we get more phones out there. You always said that, right?" He paused. "You can't quit on us. *Please*."—the last word a croak.

It was probably the longest speech Jimmy Hakken had ever made, and might have been one of the few times in his life that he'd said please.

Jay stared out at the rain again. Maybe three or four minutes passed, neither of them moving. Jay turned back to Hakken.

"Sammy is dead because of me. He has five children. Any one of you might be next."

"When you stand up for what you believe in, when you change things, there's risk. It shows we got 'em scared, Chevalier. Think about that! Yeah there's lots of fucking risk. They make sure of that. But quitting's worse."

Now Jay stared at the beer can.

"Listen, would you have taken a bullet for Holmes?"

Jay nodded.

"Would you take one for me?"

Jay nodded again.

"So let's fucking get back to work."

Nick Brignolia did not open the poolroom on Sunday. Sunday afternoon, when Mary called him from the hospital with the news, he'd gone back to bed. Monday he'd only left his bedroom to eat a little reheated spaghetti. Tuesday around noon, he showered, shaved, dressed, then huddled in his recliner, trying to listen to Puccini's *La Bohème*, but before one side had played, he turned it off.

He couldn't believe Sammy'd been shot down too. Was everyone he cared about going to be taken from him? Gunned down?

After three hours of sitting in the growing darkness, he got up and looked for the LiveCell phone his brother had sent him from Boston with a note that said: *You ever need to call me use this phone. Nick, call me, I miss you. We are getting old.*

Nick had never used the phone; it seemed too strange to him, but he knew all he had to do was pick it up, say his brother's name, and then "okay." As he held it, the phone began to luminesce in the darkness. He pronounced his brother's name very loudly at the phone and placed it against his ear, not expecting it to work. But soon he heard a "Yeah."

"Anthony, that you?"

"Nicky. Jesus! You called me."

"Yeah."

"How are you?"

Nick couldn't answer.

"Hey, you okay? You sick? You don't sound so good."

"Anthony, I need to ask you for a favor."

"Go ahead, Nicky, *anything*," his brother said.

SIXTEEN

The day after Sammy's funeral, Mary was exhausted. She couldn't dim the image of Jolene and her five solemn children huddled together near the grave as the coffin was lowered slowly into cold darkness. A damp morning fog had changed to a chill drizzle, the group of mourners shivering as the first shovel of dirt struck the mahogany. It wasn't going to be much of a Christmas for any of them. Weeks before, Mary had planned to return to Vermont for the holidays, but now she didn't have the heart for the trip. Her mother had begged her to come home anyway; it had been too long between visits. However, Mary had still reluctantly told her she simply couldn't this year. Christmas at home was emotional enough under normal circumstances.

The second day after the funeral, Mary showed up for work at the usual hour. Jay had livecelled her the evening before and said, "Do you want to go back to work tomorrow?" She was very relieved by his decision; a farm girl believed in working through sadness and depression. She wondered what had made Jay change his mind, but she didn't ask. For most of the morning she fielded phone calls from inside the company and attended to writing a press release about LiveCell resuming production. In the afternoon she brought it to Jay to be reviewed. A silence caved in on them—they could barely look at each other—but at least it was a start. Mercifully, Jay decided they should quit around three.

As she headed home from the Harcourt Building she drove too fast, was frustrated by slower cars, used the shrill cry of her horn twice and got the finger once. She realized she deserved it and slowed down. No sense in someone else dying. Tears edged into her eyes. She turned into her long driveway and pulled up in front of her place but didn't get out right away. Ever since her house had been searched, she was alert on coming home, always slightly nervous. But today she merely stared dully at the rain-stained windshield, too done in to move.

When she unlocked the door and entered the hall, she immediately knew something was wrong. It was the smell. No sooner the thought than a man walked out from her kitchen. She didn't scream, she froze, terrified.

"Miss MacKensie?" he said.

He wore a pale gray suit with the jacket open, a coral tie and matching shirt. He was straightening the jacket as if he'd just put it on. She'd never seen a man of his modest height with a thicker chest. Was he the one who'd shot Sammy?

"Are you going to kill me?" she said, her mind churning, but strangely calm now that it was actually happening. Could she make the door before he caught her, or pulled his gun? She saw the dark edge of what must be a holster. Would it hurt terribly? Could she reach her car before he shot her? She doubted it. He looked extremely capable, and her body felt like lead, her legs immobile. "Are you?"

"What're you talking about?" He smiled. With the smile she couldn't help but notice that he had a surprisingly handsome boyish face, probably wasn't much older than she was. His black hair was freshly combed straight back, not a strand out of place, his accent probably Massachusetts Italian. She didn't know if it would matter to notice these details; her mind recorded them involuntarily.

"Come in here, I want you to taste something," he said.

What was he talking about?

"Come in the kitchen. I want ya to try somethin'. Tell me what you think."

She continued to stare at him.

"Miss MacKensie, please. Just a taste. I been cooking all afternoon."

"Who are you?"

"*Me?* Frankie Demanno. Who do ya think?"

"Do I know you?"

"We never met." He glanced away for an instant. "Nick didn't tell ya?"

"Tell me what?"

Now he looked embarrassed, and this reassured her just a little.

"Miss MacKensie, *hey*, I'm sorry. I'm Frankie Demanno, from Boston. I work for Nick's brother, Anthony Brignolia. I'm here to keep an eye on you. Now, please, come in here. You gotta try this," and he turned and walked into her kitchen.

She stood rigidly, her legs still weak at the knees, but then she did, not even sure why—she followed him into the kitchen. He waited there holding something out. A brand-new wooden spoon—not one of hers—his other huge hand cradled underneath to catch any drips. He guided the spoon slowly to her lips, and she, not knowing what else to do, tasted his sauce.

Her eyes lit up. "My God, that *is* good."

"You like it?"

"It's fantastic."

He reddened a little, reached for an almost empty bottle of wine. He poured a glass, offered it to her. Then he quickly cut some bread from a crusty loaf and held out the board with the slices on it. "Here, dip the bread in the sauce if you want. I'll have dinner ready in a couple minutes. I'm gonna fry some sole to go with the linguini. That be okay?"

She took a piece of bread and dipped, washed it down with the wine, which was dry and delicious.

"Where did you get all this stuff?"

"Nick and I did some shopping before he dropped me off. We know a grocery out here. I'm sorry I surprised you. Nick was supposed to call you and explain things."

"This sauce is unbelievable. Really."

"My own recipe."

"You shave the garlic with a razor?"

He looked at her and smiled. He really had quite a smile. "I just chop it fine, cook it very light in lots of olive oil, a good olive oil, first press. That razor stuff is for the movies. But my secret is Parmesan rind. You cook it right in the sauce, remove it at the end. And I use canned tomatoes, they taste better than fresh to me, and to cut the acidity I cook some carrots in the sauce. Nothing fancy. Simple is better."

"I need to sit down," she said.

"Sure, sure, whatever you want."

Mary moved to one of the dining room chairs and slumped down. The adrenaline that had pumped through her system while she was wait-

ing to be shot had left her weak. Not to mention everything else. Frankie brought in his wine and sat beside her.

"I'm sorry about the death of your friend," he said, his earnest face showing concern. He had lovely eyes too, amber-brown, long lashes.

"Mr. Dematto, let me get this—"

"De*manno*, but please call me Frankie."

"What are you doing here? How did you get into my house?"

"Mary—can I call you Mary?" She nodded. "I'm sorry I scared ya. Like I said, Nick was supposed to call and tell you. I'm here to see nothing bad happens to you. It's that simple. Nick figured you might not go for no protection, so I thought if you met me first, you might see it's not such a bad idea. I hoped maybe you taste my cooking, you might like to keep me around a while. I love to cook."

"You're going to cook for me?"

"If you'll have me, yeah, 'course."

"You came all the way from Boston not knowing if this would work out?"

"Sure. Why not?"

"So Nick asked his brother for this?"

"Yeah."

"I still don't get it."

"Nick can't lose nobody else. He thinks very highly of you. Tells me you're some kinda pool wizard." He grinned then, as if he sensed he was winning her over.

"Maybe I should call Nick?"

"Sure, you want. Maybe you wanna eat first? You look a little peaked. Here, lemme get ya another wine."

He brought back a fresh bottle, filled their glasses with the deep-red liquid. They sat and drank, both looking out the window at the last hesitating light over the ocean. For Mary, the situation was extremely awkward, but though she didn't like to admit it, she felt a great sense of relief. And it didn't hurt that he was so good looking. She was too exhausted to figure it all out; she trusted Nick, and for the time being that was enough. Besides, if Frankie's sauce was any indication . . .

That evening Frankie Demanno moved into one of Mary's guest rooms. He cooked and did the dishes. She didn't know a man could be so neat. Nevertheless, if the house hadn't had two bathrooms, she wouldn't have accepted his staying with her. He rode with her to work the next day, complementing the Porsche, asking questions about Cali-

fornia, San Francisco, the car, borrowing it the second day to shop for groceries and sightsee while she remained at LiveCell. He nicknamed her Virgin Mary, probably wanting to make it clear to others what their relationship was so as not to embarrass her. The nickname upset her, though he couldn't know why. When her cleaning lady came on Friday, Frankie said he'd take care of the house cleaning. Mary insisted Trisha continue, and he looked relieved. It was Frankie who suggested they should invite everyone to a big Christmas dinner. "We all need some cheering up; something good to eat never hurts," he said. "I'll take care of everything." And he did.

First he asked her about her traditions: how did she celebrate Christmas with her family? She explained about how her grandfather cut a balsam fir tree on the farm a few days before the Eve, soon to be decorated with dozens of live candles; about listening to Dylan Thomas reading *A Child's Christmas In Wales* on the old phonograph in the parlor as the candles burned and the scent of balsam was released from the heat of the flames; about her mother baking all kinds of special cookies and fruit breads. Frankie asked her, with a worried look that made her laugh, if live candles weren't dangerous on a Christmas tree. She told him only if the tree wasn't freshly cut. He quizzed her about the bakeries and wanted some of the recipes. When she livecelled home, her mom said she would e-mail the recipes and asked Mary, again, to come home: "Why would you bake those things there when I've already made them here?" Mary reassured her that she would visit in the spring. She couldn't seem to mention her new roommate.

To the Christmas dinner they invited Deirdre and Jimmy Hakken; Duncan, sounding disconcerted by the invitation, decided to stay home with his mother; David Artega, very busy now with the Samuel Holmes case, had family as well; Mary thought of Jolene and the kids, but knew they'd be with her parents and sister; Nick Brignolia simply asked what time and what to bring; and Jay, hesitating at first, accepted. Mary, disliking herself for the thought, knowing it wasn't the time for it, still hoped that Jay might get a little jealous of Frankie Demanno. "But he just doesn't think about me that way," she admitted, and didn't have a clue how to change it. "I don't want to be *virgin* Mary much longer."

Mary and Frankie spent the next two days shopping and preparing for their party. They found gifts for everyone, and her spirits continued to improve. It was during one of these shopping trips that an incident occurred. It altered her perception of Frankie Demanno.

They'd been walking back together across an unlit gravel lot to where they'd parked, Frankie carrying a bag of smoked salmon, fresh clams and mussels. As they approached her Porsche he slowed, set the bag quietly on the ground. He motioned for her to stay put, his face set in an alertness she'd never seen. He unbuttoned his jacket and walked toward her car. Then Mary saw the two men.

"What're you doin'?" said Frankie, his voice cold. It was still calm, yet without any trace of humor or softness. The inflection was new to her.

"What's it to you, chief?" one of the men said.

Frankie moved in close to the guy who'd spoken, standing only a few feet away.

"You got a problem, chief?" the man said.

"Yeah. You."

The man's hand snapped toward his pocket. Before it got there, Frankie reacted. Mary had never seen a person of his bulk move so fast. His right shoe stamped on the guy's foot, the hard edge of the sole scraping down the length of shin. At the same time his open hand chopped the guy in the Adam's apple. In seconds, the guy was on the gravel choking, grabbing his shin. Later, Mary would remember it as rather comical.

Frankie turned to the other one. "You too?"

That guy grabbed his partner and dragged him across the lot.

Frankie returned to Mary, picking up the bag of seafood. "Sorry you had to see that," he said, looking embarrassed.

He definitely had two sides. "What *were* they doing?" she said.

"I think they liked your car, maybe too much."

She could tell he was protecting her from the truth. She knew then that the Aldens, or whoever, were still after LiveCell. Anger flooded her. It wasn't that she hadn't expected it, but something about Christmas had made her less wary. Had they sent these two men so she'd tell Jay? So that she'd be scared? Were they testing Frankie Demanno? She questioned him again about the incident, but all he said was, "You don't need to worry, Mary, that's why I'm here."

Frankie liked to read different newspaper articles to Mary as they breakfasted. She was reminded of an angelic, aging choirboy as he sat there in his reading glasses and perfectly ironed sports shirts. He was actually in his early thirties, his birthday four years and a few days from hers, but sometimes he could look so young. The coverage of LiveCell in the smaller alternative papers fascinated him. "The only papers not owned by the corporate political dynasty," she told him.

A grass roots movement supporting LiveCell had emerged in ever-widening circles since the FDA had attempted to undermine the company with the allegations that the phones caused headaches and disturbed sleep. Many people had responded in defense of LiveCell, yet the mainstream media had ignored their rebuttals, which only intensified their certainty that something was wrong. As people used LiveCell phones, many developed an intuitive awareness and became progressively more difficult to dupe. They felt that with the nation's economy ruined, with the leaders of big business having looted half of America's corporate wealth, with civil rights being removed in the false name of Homeland Security, that LiveCell phones were one of the only good things they had left. The shooting of Samuel Holmes had further fueled the movement and intensified people's anger. Many were demanding that his killer be found, and conspiracy theories were voiced. Many sensed that Jay was the actual target of the Holmes hit, and they wanted to know who'd ordered his death.

Frankie read to her: "One columnist writes in here, 'A senator and his family were murdered to gain control of the house, why not Jay Chevalier?'" The primary media ignored all the real stories, yet the discrepancy in reporting was becoming embarrassingly noticeable. "This Jay Chevalier guy," Frankie said, "is becoming a people's hero, same as that Cuban guy, Che Guevara."

On Christmas morning Mary was as excited as a child. She'd bought something special for Jay. It was quite a find, and she believed Jay would be thrilled, though how could anyone ever tell with him? Mary got up early and took a leisurely bath. She dressed with care, the smell of coffee and bacon from the kitchen mingling with her bath oil and lotions. Having Frankie Demanno around was like having a gentleman's gentleman. And it was all free, courtesy of Mr. Anthony Brignolia. But is anything ever really free? she wondered. Anthony Brignolia must want something. As she combed out the tangles in her wet hair, she glanced at one of the Christmas cards leaning against the bureau's mirror: a Santa Claus on a reindeer roping a steer. It seemed ages ago that she'd ridden in Garland's pickup truck, and she wondered if he was maintaining his indomitable spirit. There was also a recent letter from Kelly Harris; she reread a few sentences.

> *With all these LiveCell phones not many people are writing letters anymore. Strange to think of myself as old-fashioned. I have to admit something about those phones: I find them almost too intimate, too intense. I look forward to seeing you for Christmas—*

She thought about Kelly for a minute and was startled that her perception of him had changed. She still loved him dearly and missed him, yet he was no longer quite the hero, or mentor, that he'd once been. It was because he had never accomplished anything, she realized, he hadn't used his abilities—he had hidden from them. But she was sure he'd done the best he could. And he'd always had plenty of heart; that was why she loved him.

Had she changed that much in a year and a half? Something passed through her, an energy that shot up her spine, and it forced her to sit on the bed. Then, in a moment of pure calm, she could feel the entire planet surrounding her with all its complexity and all its contrast, all its desire and all its need, all its anger and all its love. As if she could almost touch everyone she cared about, and she felt Sammy somehow with her as well. Was this what Jay meant by the continuum?

After a while she breathed deeply, stood, checked herself in the mirror one more time, and went to wish Frankie Demanno a Merry Christmas.

A few minutes after they finished breakfast, a courier knocked on the door with a long cylindrical burlap-wrapped package addressed to Mary MacKensie. Frankie carried it inside for her. "Fresh cut," he said. It was a balsam fir tree. From his bedroom he hauled a bright-green metal tree stand, Christmas tree candles, and shiny tin holders that clipped onto the branches and pivoted to allow the candles to point vertically.

"I can't believe this," she said. They set up the tree in the corner of the living room facing the ocean. He brought out multicolored lights and an overly generous assortment of ornaments.

"I made a few phone calls," he said. "They shipped everything. I hid the boxes under my bed. I thought that tree guy was never gonna get here. 'Course he'd be dead if he didn't." He winked at her, but she wasn't absolutely certain he was kidding.

Around noon, Frankie, wearing an apron with an embroidered elf over his big chest, started preparing crostini in olive oil to be served with fresh ricotta, anchovy slivers, and a cannellini puree with herbs. When the guests arrived, these would be flanked by a slab of Parmesan and shaved Percino, crisply fried whole baby artichokes, clams casino, and grilled marinated plump Mediterranean sardines. A chestnut and mushroom stuffed goose to honor Mary's New England roots was ready for the oven. Yesterday he'd prepared a spicy tomato sauce for the spaghetti; today he'd add chopped lobster claws.

Soon it was early afternoon, the kitchen exhaling a variety of won-

derful vapors. They opened a bottle of champagne, toasting the day, sitting out on the deck in the Adirondack chairs facing the sun. Frankie, though he enjoyed his red wine while cooking, wasn't really much of a drinker. Their first night had been an exception, and with a tiny smile she realized even he might get nervous on occasion. There is something in life to frighten everyone.

Nick Brignolia was the first to arrive, dressed in a black suit, starched white shirt, and cardinal-red tie with a modest diamond tiepin. He carried an enormous bouquet of roses. While Mary went into the kitchen to arrange them in a vase, Frankie offered Nick a glass of wine. The old man shook his head: "Later, later I will have one. I talk to Anthony this morning. My brother wish everyone a Merry Christmas."—calling this to Mary as she walked out of the kitchen. "Frankie, he thinks he make a crazy mistake to send his best guy out here. He miss your cooking."

"He may miss it a long time. I like it out here." He glanced at Mary, or where she'd been a moment ago setting the flowers on the table. She was fiddling with something on the tree. His eyes followed her, as if he were hoping for a reaction.

"He might be coming to visit," Nick said to him.

"When?"—a flicker of concern.

"In a few weeks."

"Why?"

"I don't know, maybe for your cooking."

"Maybe to see you?"

"Maybe."

Deirdre and Jimmy Hakken arrived together in her station wagon. Hakken was his usual black-clad tattooed self with the addition of a pendulous candy-cane-striped stocking hat and a cloth bag full of presents. He made a very ominous Santa. Deirdre wore a new pants suit and a fresh stylish hairdo. After Mary hugged her, she looked her up and down still holding her hands.

"Deirdre," she said, "you look fantastic. What a beautiful suit."

"I just bought it," she said, blushing.

"What a great color on you."

"I hoped you might like it; I mean, the suit. They called the color like antique plum or something. Silly name."

"Fantastic color though."

Mary introduced everyone, and Frankie greeted the new guests with

a wide smile. Deirdre shrieked on seeing the table of food, and he explained his appetizers to her. Jimmy Hakken was mute as usual, first setting his big bag near the tree, then observing Frankie carefully, probably having heard something about him, maybe noting how relaxed and easygoing he seemed. Regardless, Hakken remained withdrawn and serious. Mary offered champagne, which everyone but Hakken accepted. He had a beer. Always the outsider, she thought.

"That tree is so beautiful," said Deirdre. "And all the red candles look really nice. Oh, my, God, they're real."

"We're going to light them," said Mary.

"No way!"

"Frankie had the tree cut in the wild. That way it has the right spaces between the branches for candles. With pruned Christmas trees the branches are too close together, and you never know when they've been cut."

"That is *way* cool. I didn't know anyone still did it. I mean, have real burning candles." A pause. "Is Jay coming?"

"He said he was. He's a bit late, isn't he? I'll livecell him." She set down her glass. "Jay? . . . okay, good. We were just making sure." She turned to Deirdre. "He's on his way. I don't think he's so big on Christmas." She glanced at the three men talking around the dining room table: Frankie telling a funny story, Nick carefully sipping his champagne, Hakken listening with rapt attention, the strange stocking hat such a contrast to his demeanor.

Deirdre leaned closer to Mary, lowered her voice. "We're always going to worry about Jay now, aren't we?"

"At least he decided to go back to work. I was terrified he wouldn't reopen LiveCell. The idea of being beaten by those bastards irked me to no end, but I knew Jay had to work through it in his own way. Remember Detective Artega?"

"Sure. Tall, lanky, dark. From the shooting at the factory. The only cop that seemed to believe Jay."

"In the last few days he's made some headway on Sammy's death. Michael Pegonis has—"

"Who?"

"From that night, the ex-security guy who shot Jay in the arm."

"That big asshole."

"He worked for Alden Stone Associates. He's contacted Artega and says he has information on the shooting. He wants immunity and pro-

tection from Artega, and two million from Jay. Jay doesn't trust the whole thing. Artega wants him to go along, see where it leads."

"Are you and Jay doing better?"

"Because he's telling me these things?"

"Not just that."

Mary examined her. Deirdre wanted to know if she was going to attempt the phone infusion. Had Jay been talking to her about it? Asked her to say something? She couldn't open herself to him like that again, it was too destructive. Or what if she fought against the infusion as Deirdre had? What if Jay's heart stopped?

"I don't think I can," she said.

"It's like, *real* important that you try."

Mary only nodded, then glanced over at the men.

"Frankie's awful cute, isn't he?" said Deirdre.

Mary suddenly felt that maybe Deirdre was getting too damn intuitive.

"Aw-oh, I'm making you blush again," she said.

"It's not that way with Frankie and me."

"Hey," said Frankie from across the room, his ears burning. "What's the huddle about? Come on and join us."

"He's right," said Mary. "It's Christmas." Besides, she wanted off the subject.

Jay finally arrived, Cutlass sounding terminal. It had developed an ominous rapping, a noise that secretly pleased Mary. She'd heard him coming—who couldn't?—and stood now in the open doorway as he parked. Everyone had kept the space free in front of her two-car garage as she'd requested, and Jay followed suit. He jumped out and walked toward her, dressed the same as on the first day she saw him.

"Merry Christmas," he called. "Sorry I'm late. Car isn't running so well."

They embraced. His body just seemed to fit hers. He was warm too, even in only the T-shirt. Why hadn't he dressed up? Was it from being preoccupied, or from being a bit of a Scrooge? But being an orphan, what kind of good feelings could he have about Christmas? Of course, he never dressed up except in Deirdre's jacket anyway, which, come to think of it, she hadn't seen in weeks.

When they entered the house, everyone got up to greet Jay, even Nick. Deirdre threw her arms around him, and Mary again felt jealous; they seemed so close, their relationship uncomplicated. Frankie and Jay

had met briefly at the office, but they shook hands now with no readable expression. Mary wondered how they felt about each other. Frankie treated Jay as if he were a celebrity. Maybe he was? Would she ever stop feeling this way around him? She tried to put him out of her mind and concentrated on her hostess duties, taking beverage orders, pouring champagne, passing out plates and napkins. Jay decided to join Jimmy Hakken and drink beer. He *would*.

After about an hour Mary couldn't contain her excitement, couldn't wait any longer. She also wanted to do it while there was still plenty of light outside. She double winked Frankie—their signal. He excused himself, and she kept Jay occupied. She'd made sure the CD player was loaded and that the volume was up enough. She gave Frankie five or six minutes and glanced outside. She told Jay she needed to show him something in the dooryard. He followed her.

Resting in front of her garage was an arctic blue 1965 Chevrolet station wagon with an enormous red ribbon and bow around it. "Merry Christmas, Jay," she said.

He walked up to the car, caressed a fender for a few moments, turned back to her, put his arms around her, kissed her cheek. "It is beautiful," he said, releasing her.

"I know the paint isn't perfect," she said, ignoring the placement of his kiss. "Especially on the roof. And it has the one dent, but it *is* all original, even the paint. You can see cracks in the lacquer. I thought you would prefer it that way. It runs like a top."

"It's perfect," he said. "The best."

By then the others had come out of the house and gathered around. "Oh my God, it's an Impala," said Deirdre. "And not a lowrider. Like how did that happen?"

They told Jay to get in, to try it on, see how it fit. Behind the wheel he actually looked like a tough celebrity as he smiled out the rolled down window at them. The car really did fit him.

"Let's all go for a ride," said Mary, and they climbed onto the blue Naugahyde bench seats. Jay fired up the rumbling engine and backed up the wagon, Mary beside him, Frankie riding shotgun, the other three behind. His old Cutlass wasn't a small car, but he acted as though he were backing up an ocean liner.

They drove slowly, coasted through the Christmas day, the road all but empty, hazy afternoon sun in the yellow grass as they paralleled the shoreline. Nick told them how his first car in Boston had been just like

this one: "A sixty-nine Buick sedan, maroon color with the black seats."
Frankie looked over his shoulder and said, "Same car exactly, Nick," and
everyone laughed. For the first time since Sammy'd been shot, Mary felt
some life come back into Jay.

As the sun began to color the sky over the Pacific, Frankie said he
hated to end the family outing, but he had to get the goose out of the
oven. Jay carefully turned the big boat, and with the water on their right
now, motored back.

It was still light when they returned but it was whispering. After
mooring the Impala, Jay walked over and popped the trunk of the Cutlass, removed five packages. Jimmy Hakken, still in his incongruous hat,
helped him carry them into the house. Frankie had shot into the kitchen
and was a whirl of activity. He explained he didn't need help, just quiet
to concentrate. Everyone else settled in the dining and living room as
a hot appetizer of fragrant steamed mussels strayed from the stove
accompanied by loaves of crusty Italian bread. Though another bottle
of champagne was opened, Jay and Hakken stayed stubbornly with beer.
Nick sipped his one glass of red wine, commenting twice about how
good it was. Mary had vodka for Deirdre, but after one on ice, she
joined the champagne drinkers. Mary played Perry Como and Frank
Sinatra for Nick, and Nat King Cole sang "Chestnuts Roasting on an
Open Fire." As dusk gently dimmed the room, they turned on the tree
lights.

Mary and Jay set the table, and soon everyone except Frankie was
seated—Jimmy Hakken finally removed his hat, exposing his freshly
shaved head—and a procession of food began to arrive from the kitchen.
First there was a chilled seafood salad with fresh squid, sea scallops, and
shrimp, the pale creatures glistening in herbed olive oil, capers and hot
peppers, each glass bowl containing a tentacled squid head like a small
violet crown. This was followed by his spaghetti with signature red sauce
laden with lobster bits. Accompanying the goose, steamed broccoli rabe,
and mashed potatoes latticed by fried sage leaves. A salad of radicchio,
arugula, and frisee, a turbulent coil of reds and greens finished the main
course.

"Everyone get enough to eat?" he said.

"Frankie, best meal I have since I leave Boston," said Nick, setting
his napkin firmly beside his plate.

Mary raised her glass. "I'd like to propose a toast. To Frankie, who
not only supplied us with one of the finest meals I have ever eaten, *and*

provided the beautiful tree, but also, with his humor and his calm, helped at a very difficult time."

He looked down as they drank to him, then his eyes came up, searching hers.

"That was like, unbelievable. Everything was *so* good. I don't think I've ever eaten so much. I mean, my God, who has?"

"Is everyone ready for coffee and dessert?" said Mary. "Frankie baked some cookies from my mother's recipes."

"Nick, I picked up a pannetone for you. Traditional recipe. And I got a bottle of anisette, of course."

"I think I call Anthony, tell him you staying here now with us."

Jay said, "Mary, and Frankie. It was a lovely idea to have this meal, and to invite all of us to share it. This is the nicest Christmas I've ever had. You've all been very considerate not talking about Sammy's death. If I may, I would ask that we drink to our friend's memory and to his family. I talked with Jolene earlier today, and she asked us to drink to Sammy's memory tonight." He looked above their faces. He held out his glass, and they waited. "Sammy . . ." If he had more to add, he couldn't manage it. They all drank.

Jimmy Hakken, standing on a chair, lit the top half of the tree candles. Frankie, after giving Mary another gift, a CD with *A Child's Christmas in Wales* on it, lit the rest. They sat on chairs and sofas, each person with a full beverage, all other lights turned off. " . . . *and out of all sound except the distant speaking of voices I sometimes hear a moment before sleep, . . . All the Christmases roll down toward the two-tongued sea, like a cold and headlong moon bundling down the sky . . .*" Each of the three-dozen candles with a starred halo, the tinsel icicles wavering restlessly in the rising heat of the flames, the ornaments reflecting, the warmed balsam sap beginning to scent the air. " . . . *I said some words to the close and holy darkness, and then I slept.*"

"I've never seen anything so totally beautiful," said Deirdre, after they'd blown out the candles and put the room lights back on. "I mean, it was just *so* amazing."

It was time to open the rest of the presents. Mary gave Frankie a pair of handmade Italian loafers in oxblood-colored leather, Deirdre a visit to a fancy spa, Nick season tickets to the opera. Mary and Deirdre gave Jimmy Hakken an exact plaster copy of a winged gargoyle cast from Notre Dame cathedral for his office.

"I wondered what that blanket-wrapped thing was in the wagon," he said.

Nick gave everyone a very delicate hand-blown glass ornament imported from Italy. Deirdre gave Mary hand-embroidered silk pajamas with a matching robe, and Jay a new sports jacket.

"What happened to your other one?" said Mary.

"It got lost," he said.

Jimmy Hakken presented each of them with a wrapped box, each box a different size and in a different wrapping paper. But inside, each person found the identical chunky silver pendant, cast from the same obviously hand-carved mold, attached to a leather lanyard. Everyone was a bit dumbfounded. At the silence, Hakken said, "Luke Delamar's buddy, he does metal, he made 'em up for me. I told him to go all out, no skimping, real actual silver." He looked around at their faces. "It's the eye inside the hand . . . I got one too. We all got one." Still no one spoke, they just kept staring at their pendants.

Finally Frankie said, "Keeps off the evil eye?"

"Right," said Hakken, brightening. "*Right*, they're real good luck."

Jay gave each of them a framed drawing by a Maine artist. All five drawings were of falling lit matches, the burning matches and flames realistic against backgrounds more sketchy, dark and brooding as if with an ominous hint of storm, the paper itself scratched. Mary said the drawings reminded her of the painting in Jay's office. Jimmy Hakken kept examining his drawing, nodding his head as if the image made special sense to him.

Nick excused himself around ten, kissing Mary carefully on each cheek before he left. It was the first time he'd shown such affection. When it was near midnight, the others decided it was time. Mary saw them off as Frankie began to clean up. Soon Deirdre's station wagon roared down the road, Hakken at the wheel. "I only had beer," he'd said as if beer didn't count as drinking. Jay abandoned the Cutlass, told Mary he'd have it towed tomorrow, and the Impala's round taillights slowly disappeared down her road. She stood looking into the darkness long after he was gone. Then she turned abruptly and went back into the house.

After Frankie finished cleaning the kitchen—he insisted she didn't help—they sat together and drank a last glass of champagne.

"I think it went really well," she said, feeling a tiredness beginning to tug after the long day. "First time I've seen Jay come out of his shell since the shooting. I was glad he brought up Sammy. Maybe he's beginning to heal. Maybe we all are."

"He's a very tough guy. You see that right away."

"You haven't seen him at his best."

"Don't need to. I can tell. I also see the loyalty he generates."

She looked at the tree, the stubs of the burnt-down candles, the multicolored lights still on. "Your food was beyond belief, and the tree, and everything," she said.

"Mary?"

She heard something in his voice.

"I have here one last little present for you." He took something out of his pocket. "I know we haven't known each other very long, but I wanted to get this for you." He slid it toward her. "Merry Christmas."

A flat box wrapped in blue paper with a white ribbon.

"Please," he said.

She slowly unwrapped it. Found a felt-covered box of the same shade of blue. Inside were two large pearl earrings. She didn't speak right away.

"Frankie, these are very beautiful, but I don't know if I can accept them."

"I don't have no family. I got no one to spend money on. It would mean a lot to me if you'd accept them as a token of my friendship."

She stared at him, and he glanced away.

"Don't decide right now, okay? Just give it a few days. What's it gonna hurt—a few days. *Please?*"

She continued to look at him, and finally, unable to make up her mind, she said she would give it a few days.

SEVENTEEN

Two and a half weeks after the holidays, Jay Chevalier sat at his desk, working. Though he'd been showing up at LiveCell every day since Christmas, it was only in the last few days that his former motivation had returned. He reached for his phone: David Artega.

They greeted each other, and the detective said, "Normally I'd come see you in person to tell you this, but I'm gradually getting used to the fact that these phones are secure."

Jay waited. Something had gone wrong. Lately, Artega had been having trouble with the Samuel Holmes case. Jay knew it was partially his fault because he'd refused to negotiate with Michael Pegonis.

Artega said, "They've removed me from the case without explanation. Even the Chief couldn't believe it. He told me off the record that he had no choice, the pressure came from high up."

"Did they replace you?"

"If you want to call it that."

They were both silent.

Then Artega, "It gets to me, putting up with this kind of political bullshit year after year. I know it's part of the job, but it shouldn't be."

"It can change," said Jay with more emotion than usual.

"What do you mean? No one can change that shit. Those assholes know they can get away with it; they always have. At least the public

around here seems to be on LiveCell's side. Just when you think America is asleep, it wakes up."

Another pause.

"Michael Pegonis," said Artega.

"Yeah?"

"Gone, disappeared. Untraceable."

Jay's expression darkened further. He waited for Artega to speak.

"Listen, you need me for anything, livecell, okay?"

"Done."

"And listen, I haven't given up."

They ended the call. Almost immediately Jay had another, but he ignored it for the moment. He waited until he no longer felt like punching something.

"Hey, Jay, how's it going?" It was Frankie Demanno.

"Good. You?"

"Perfect, perfect. So we still on for three-thirty?"

Jay was silent.

"Perfect. I'm picking him up at the airport and bringing him directly to you." Jay didn't respond to this either; they'd already discussed these details. "Okay, see you then."

"Frankie?"

"Yeah."

"Are you nervous about something?"

"'Course not."

They said good-bye.

Jay got back to work, yet after only ten or twelve minutes, Mary appeared in his doorway. He motioned her in.

"You look upset," she said.

"Artega called. He's been taken off the case."

"It's been too quiet lately. Almost three weeks now and nothing interesting happening—no one shooting at us, no demolition attempts, no false press, no new spies, even the FDA backing down a bit, or at least no fresh attacks."—she hadn't told him about the two men waiting for her and Frankie by the car—"I'm glad I have a bodyguard. I don't know why you refuse one."

"He just called."

"Was he out in his new car?"

"I think so."

"He's like a kid with that car. Frankie always drove Cadillacs. He'd

never been in a Porsche until mine. You never know what will get to someone."

"How's he been lately?" said Jay.

She hesitated. "A little preoccupied, now that you mention it. Why?"

"Has he ever asked about how the phones work?"

"Never. What's going on?"

"You know who is meeting with me today?"

She shook her head and waited.

"Anthony Brignolia."

"Wow."

"I had Duncan check him out this morning. He found almost nothing. Surprised even Duncan. Brignolia doesn't seem to exist in the form of digital information. Duncan's been at it for hours."

"Is he coming to visit Nick?"

"Nick hasn't been mentioned. He's coming here directly from the airport. You'd think after all those years, something like twenty, he might want to see his brother first."

"I wonder why Frankie didn't tell me?"

"He was instructed not to. Frankie asked me to keep it quiet as well, and asked that our meeting remain secret. Brignolia doesn't want anyone to know we're meeting."

"Do you know what kind of business he's in?"

"Frankie wouldn't tell me."

"Sammy revealed a few things one afternoon at the poolroom . . ." and she told him about the shooting of Nick's wife and son and how it was connected with his brother's business. As she told the story, Jay got very still. Every shooting would bring back Sammy's death for him.

"Will you greet him when he arrives?" he said. "I want your impression."

At precisely three-thirty, the front desk rang. Jay livecelled Mary to meet the guests. Within perhaps five or six minutes, the three of them entered his orange office. Jay came around from behind his desk and extended his arm.

"Mr. Brignolia," he said, "Welcome to LiveCell. I see you've met Mary MacKensie." He said hello to Frankie Demanno.

Anthony Brignolia was younger than his brother and of a more delicate stature. His hair was black and expensively cut, and Jay wondered if he dyed it since Nick's was almost white. He also lacked Nick's humped nose—maybe his had been fixed. His midnight-blue hand-tailored

English suit hung perfectly, a pale-ivory Egyptian cotton shirt and deep-maroon silk tie matched the understated taste of his faux-tortoiseshell wire-rimmed glasses. A glance at Jay's blue T-shirt and worn jeans brought a ripple of surprise across his brow. It was instantly suppressed.

"Doctor Chevalier," he said, "this is a great honor for me." Jay's hand surrounded the gentle clasp of Brignolia's fingers.

Frankie waited by the door, his posture more rigid than normal, a box under one arm. Brignolia made a slight movement of his head and Frankie set the box on the desk. "That'll be all, Demanno," he said, and Frankie turned to leave.

"Mr. Brignolia," said Jay, "would you care for a coffee, something else?" Brignolia shook his head curtly. "Thanks Mary, thanks for showing them up. So long, Frankie."

Frankie nodded, Mary winked so only Jay saw it, and they both withdrew.

Brignolia glanced back at the open door.

"I always leave it open," said Jay. "Would you feel more comfortable if it were closed?"

"If it isn't a problem."

Jay was forced to circle around the motionless Brignolia to close the door. "Please, sit down." He gestured toward his collection of mismatched armchairs.

Brignolia ignored his offer and stepped over to the framed Ryder reproduction, studying it for an unhurried moment; then he chose a chair.

Jay settled in behind his desk again. He wasn't going to give Brignolia any advantages; it fascinated him too much to watch the man work.

"Ryder's *Toilers on a Sea*, isn't it?" Brignolia said.

"Yes," said Jay, though the title was *The Toilers of the Sea*. Still, the man must know something about art, and wanted him to realize it.

"I thank you for seeing me. I've brought you a small gift."

Jay glanced at the plain cardboard box, rectilinear and about as long as his arm.

"Please," said Brignolia, gesturing slightly toward it.

Jay stood up and slid the carton to his side of the desk with one hand. Using a penknife, he cut through the packing tape, opened one end, and pulled out a second box. This had a tight fitting lid that needed to be slowly lifted to break the suction of air. Inside, protected by gray foam, was something long and plastic-wrapped. He knew what the gift was and carefully loosened the almost twelve-pound object from its foam cradle,

unwrapped the plastic, and set the model train engine on his desk. It was a masterpiece in brass, handmade in Korea, each part faithfully reproduced and painted just like the original engine. It could run, sound, and smoke just like a real one.

"A Union Pacific Big Boy," said Jay. "Many consider it the most powerful steam locomotive ever produced." He actually preferred smaller engines like Berkshires and Hudsons.

"I asked the man for the finest one they had. Did he do all right?"

Jay nodded. "How do you know I run O gauge trains?"

"I know a great deal about you, Doctor Chevalier."

Jay looked up from studying the model. "Then you should call me Jay. Thank you for the gift, it's very thoughtful."

"If it brings you pleasure, I'm pleased." The minimal smile was something the two brothers had in common, though Anthony's was even less demonstrative than Nick's. Where Nick's grimace had some warmth, with Anthony, there was none.

Neither said anything; both waited for the other to speak. Jay didn't want his silence to become rude. "So why are you here?" he said.

Anthony Brignolia searched Chevalier's face and spoke immediately. "LiveCell is changing the world. This change has only begun." He paused. "The world runs on information. Up until your telephones most information could be accessed, traced. All conventional methods leave footprints and can be bugged—until LiveCell. Your telephones are secure *and* leave no trail—it changes everything."

"I thought the world ran on commodities?"

Brignolia almost smiled. "You're right," he said. "First salt, then oil, now drugs and silicon chips, maybe water or LiveCell phones soon—but with information you control those who control the commodities."

"Is that what you do?" Jay said.

Brignolia stared at Jay as if he were attempting to look into him. "I am going to be honest with you. I understand you're an honest man. A rare thing at your level. And I know why you're honest. You care more about honesty than money or power."

Jay was silent.

"What I do is leverage situations for clients. I do this with information."

Still nothing from Jay. His silence irritated Brignolia.

"You might be surprised at some of the things we've handled. For

instance, a recent Supreme Court decision over an election. I don't tell you this to impress you, only so you know at what level we operate. Most people have things to hide, and usually these things can destroy them if made public. Of course, much of the media can be controlled, either for or against someone. Many times people have something they want very much and can be manipulated that way. But then there is you. Seems you have nothing to hide and no price."

"Do you know who killed Samuel Holmes?"

"Holmes, the black man. He had courage—a waste. I know he was your friend and I'm sorry for your loss. I know the bullet was intended for you. You've been very lucky, and now I watch as the small newspapers take up your cause. It's given you a little more time."

"Did you have anything to do with it?"

Brignolia was startled. "Of course not. Such methods are barbaric and stupid; they're from thirty years ago. There's rarely a need for killing. It should always be avoided. It's messy. Jay, I fear you misunderstand me. I do not like or respect these people."

"Yet you work for them."

"It's my business."

"Don't they have their own organizations?"

"They fight amongst themselves for power, they're not secure, they have no loyalty. Look at the mess the FDA made. Headaches? What fools. They spent a fortune and it hardly affected LiveCell at all."

"What do you want from me?"

Brignolia stopped talking and looked down at his pants. He needlessly readjusted the crease at each knee.

"I fear I've given you the wrong impression, though it's refreshing to talk with someone so direct." Brignolia waited and received only silence again. "If you want the killer of this Samuel Holmes, I will get him for you."

"Mr. Brignolia, what is it that you want?"

"I want to save your life."

"And you think it needs saving?"

"Yes."

"Why do you think my life is in danger?"

"You don't know?" Brignolia sensed he'd gained something, finally, and paused. "You're a dangerous man. To those in control, you are upsetting their world, the very way that it functions, the fundamental laws under which it operates. You don't think they realize that people using

LiveCell phones are changing? And now the public is believing in you more and more."

"That's ridiculous. I only invented a new kind of telephone."

His mouth flashed the cold half-smile. "You're teasing me now. Do you know that DuPont Chemical Company has a team of lawyers that have been desperate to sue you? But you're too smart, and do not patent your telephone, so what can they do? And still no one can figure out how it works. You're an amazing man, Chevalier."

They were silent again. Brignolia wondered if his outburst had been advisable. How can you read a man like this? How can you figure out a man when you don't know what he wants, or what gets to him? At least he knew that everyone wants to stay alive, no one wants to die.

"So?" said Jay.

Chevalier was going to be killed and this was how he responded? Brignolia decided he hadn't made himself clear enough. "I can keep you alive. It will be difficult, but I believe I can do this. Without me you'll be killed. This I have no doubt about; this I know."

"I thought killing was out of style?"

"You joke with me again, but they're desperate, and they'll kill you. It's their only solution now."

"So what do you want from me?" Jay said it once more.

Brignolia paused, wondering if it was the right moment. He'd waited a long time for this, and he wanted it more than anything he'd ever desired. He kept the excitement out of his voice.

"You need me. I offer the network to protect you and all your people. I can leverage the press in your favor, which will bring the masses behind you, which will further protect you. I know you say you don't care about money, yet this I bring also. I'll assist you in managing the business so that every person on earth has a LiveCell telephone. China alone is worth billions. With this income, and the changes it will bring to the power structure, we can take control. Then we do whatever you want. We destroy corruption, dishonesty, we build all the orphan houses you want."

"You know about that?"

"Most altruism, everyone does it for reward, for publicity. They even pretend they don't want publicity and then quietly allow their altruism to be discovered. Not you."

"And what do you want in return?"

"Half of your stock holdings in LiveCell, which I believe is thirty per-

cent of the company, and my people will make up half your board of directors."

"Does Frankie know?" he said.

Brignolia was shocked. He makes his final offer and Chevalier asks him about one of his employees? "Know what?"

"Why he was sent out here," said Jay.

"He was sent out here because my brother called me and asked for a favor to protect the girl. There is no one better at that than Demanno. Besides, it had to be someone the girl would accept."

"And that was the only reason?"

"I sent Demanno for both reasons. That is the truth."

Jay paused. "I think LiveCell is fine as it is."

Brignolia looked down; he did not want Chevalier to read his expression. He faced Jay again. "I don't think you realize the truth of what I am telling you. You do not know these people like I do."

"But you work for them?"

"Without their approval, very little is possible. They destroy what gets in their way, and they'll destroy you. You need me."

Brignolia sensed he was losing him. He didn't understand this man who seemed unafraid to die. Was he bluffing? He knew Chevalier was too intelligent not to see some truth in what he was saying, yet he wasn't interested in his offer. And he was offering the man his life, for God's sake. He knew Chevalier had turned down every financial offer. Where was this man's weakness? Everyone had something. *Everyone*. Chevalier didn't appear to be involved with anyone and seemed impervious to coercion. A very difficult person.

When Chevalier remained silent, Brignolia said again, "I work for them, but I don't like it. They treat me always as if I'm beneath them, with their careful condescension, and talk to me as if we're in a stupid gangster movie, only because I was born Sicilian. They hide behind their manners, yet their arrogance is sickening. And they're not that smart, this I know, but they're ruthless when it comes to protecting their world. They consider it an untouchable right, something they've been granted by being born into it. They know nothing about working people, people like you and me. These are men who would allow their own buildings to be bombed and children to die, just to remain in power. Chevalier, we can bring them down. Together, we can beat them." It was as close to a plea as Anthony Brignolia had ever made.

Jay got up from his desk and walked to the window. The blue-green in the bay was fading to a blue-gray. He could see a few white caps, the red stern of a boat and its wake as it disappeared behind a building. It was probably going to start raining again. For a moment his mind went to northern Maine. He imagined the snow there now, that crystalline blue curve of a snow field on a clear late January afternoon, maybe a sliver of moon just showing in the eastern sky. He thought of the snow covering his mother's grave; he thought of his grandfather and wondered if the cabin was still standing. He turned back to Anthony Brignolia.

"Mr. Brignolia, I appreciate your offer and your belief in LiveCell. I know you came a long way to talk to me. Allow me a few days, perhaps a week, to consider your proposal. It would not be just my decision, many people make up this company. Would that be okay?"

Brignolia stood. He extended his hand. They shook.

"Yes, that would be fine," he said. "Any details you would like from me, please call."

Jay examined him, and just as Brignolia was about to turn away he said, "Is Alden Stone Associates one of your clients?"

There was a minute jolt in Brignolia's eyes; he didn't need an answer. "I'll walk you down," he said.

It was almost dark outside. San Francisco pulsed with electric light as most offices and stores were still open for business. She'd brought them each a mug of coffee from the lounge.

"So what did you think of him?" said Jay.

"He looks a lot like Nick except for the hair and the nose, but that's where the resemblance ends. He has none of the vulnerability or tenderness. Not that Nick doesn't try to hide his, but if Anthony is hiding his, he's doing one incredible job. What did he want?"

"Half of my LiveCell stock and half the board."

"*Jesus!* Why does he think you would sell to him if you turned down all other offers?"

"I'm not sure. He wants it badly. I know that."

"Don't they all."

"If he has other holdings, which he probably has, he would take control of the company."

She looked at him—at his calm eyes, a bit tired since Sammy's death; at the strong jaw, the carved angles of his pale, battered face; at the close-cropped hair with its increase of gray. Her senses almost too aware when

she was with him, still so affected by his presence that it annoyed her. Then she noticed the locomotive on his desk.

"Was that in the box? How did he know you liked trains?"

"He seems to have researched me rather thoroughly."

"He doesn't know about the Siuslaw Road house does he?"

"Can't imagine how. I bought the trains here in San Francisco, so that was easy to trace. He possesses a great deal of information though. He calls you *the girl*."

"The girl—that's kind of funny. My mom and grandmother always call themselves girls, so I'm not so hung up about that as some women are. It's kind of a New England thing, I guess, older women calling themselves girls, but of course he's Italian, isn't he? So, tell me, are you going to consider his offer?"

He glanced over at the train. "Probably not."

She felt instantly relieved. "Jay, let me take you out tonight," she said, even though she knew how it would end.

"Okay," he said. "Where to? Your choice."

"How 'bout Italian?"

He laughed. "Brignolia said to me, '*Now you are joking with me*,' I don't think he was used to that, anyone kidding him."

"Did you really tease him?" she said.

"Sure, why not?"

And then, in this moment of happiness, she said, "Don't you want to have children?" And though she didn't add, "with me," it was obvious.

It stopped him. He went to the window again, gripped the frame above his head, stared out at the lit windows of other buildings. Rain was just visible in puddles on some of the lower roofs and in the reflected surface of the pavement below. In some of the adjacent offices, a few people were standing much as he was, gazing out at other buildings, or at the rain, or at a moment in their own lives. Everyone has these complicated lives, he thought, all of us battling with our desires and our needs, and all of us connected in a way that so few realize.

"I'm sorry," she said. "I wish I hadn't said that."

He turned back to her.

"I'm glad you said it. I'm just not sure how to answer you. It's not a simple answer."

"Let's forget I said it. *Please*."

"I know you've been upset with me for a while."

"Let's talk about something else, okay? Where shall we go eat?"

He relented for the moment. "Your choice, but my car."

She brightened. "How's it running?"

"It purrs, and as you knew, the color is perfect and even the dent gives me pleasure. The fact that the paint is so old, I can imagine the person who sprayed it at Chevrolet in the sixties. It's like an antique that's never been refinished with all its stories intact in the finish." He walked back from the window. "Even with all the fancy cars in California, people wave at me. Seeing the car seems to cheer them up, allows them to remember something, maybe a more carefree time in America when people still believed in the promise."

And then he said, "Mary, I want to answer what you said before. It's important."

Noticing her face, he continued anyway.

"As you can imagine, because I was an orphan, parenthood would be a very serious thing for me. I'd have to be sure that I could be there for a child. As things are, I have to concentrate on LiveCell for now. I can't think about anything else."

He sat beside her and placed his hand gently over hers.

"I know I upset you when I ran from you. It had nothing to do with you, or your attractiveness, or what I feel for you." He paused. "You have given so much of yourself to LiveCell, and I hate to ask for anything more, but Mary, I still need you to learn how to infuse the phones. We are running out of time."

It was Mary who looked out at the rain now.

EIGHTEEN

She stood in the humid gloom, her LiveCell held tightly to her ear. Jay was talking to her from his office, explaining a few last details, telling her not to be nervous. How could she not be nervous? Deirdre appeared to be just as uneasy. Mary gazed out into the shadowy stillness at the rows and rows of inert vesseled telephones, each waiting to come to life.

The evening after Anthony Brignolia's visit, Jay had taken her out for dinner. He didn't bring up the infusion experiment again, but she sensed it was on his mind the entire time. She could tell how worried he was, and when she got home she decided she was being selfish and called him. Jay was right: personal needs were not a priority, LiveCell was what mattered.

The next day after work she drove over to the factory. The crew was gone, the parking lot empty except for Deirdre's wagon, and something about that solitary car surrounded by all that vacant gravel made her realize that Deirdre must be lonely too. In her own way, all she had was Live-Cell and Jay. He'd taken them both over. As she parked and got out, her stomach fluttered. Deirdre met her at the door and led her into the clean room.

"I sure hope your heart isn't going to do anything weird," Deirdre said. "Of course, I wouldn't mind so much giving you CPR, you know?" Mary looked at her. "Sorry, I'm only fooling. I guess I'm a bit jumpy."

Mary stood where Jay usually stood. "Why does he always have the lights off?"

"I'm not sure," said Deirdre, "he just always asks for it that way, so I figured you'd want it the same. Maybe it's so he can tell, like when the phones are infused, you know, when they start glowing and all."

Mary livecelled Jay.

"Open yourself," she heard him say. "Don't *try* to do anything, except remain empty of fear, and if you feel strange don't react against it, allow yourself simply to embrace it."

My God. Does he do it on purpose?

"I don't believe this could hurt you or I wouldn't experiment with it. If you have random thoughts, don't suppress them. It's a kind of concentration, yet you don't concentrate on anything specific. Allow the continuum to do all the work. Remember you and I are only a medium."

"Can I stand? I notice you kneel."

"Yes, kneel, definitely kneel. Sorry I should have remembered that. For one thing your mind won't waste effort balancing your body, and in case you get dizzy, you won't have so far to fall."

Great. "Why do you always keep all the lights off?" she said.

"It reduces your visual-stimulus input. I recommend you close your eyes as well. Are you ready?" he said.

"I think so."

"You sure?"

She told him she was. Kneeled on the cool vinyl tile. Glanced at Deirdre and winked. She didn't want her to know how nervous she was. Deirdre gave a tentative half-smile. Mary gripped her LiveCell and closed her eyes.

Immediately thoughts and remembered sensations tumbled through her brain: The first time he stared at her in the boardroom. The time he told her she was fired and then their embrace. The way he looked on Christmas sitting in the Impala. Her hand rubbing his jeans the evening he ran from her.

At first she had only these random images and feelings, along with an unusually vivid sense of him. But then why wouldn't she? She could imagine him behind his desk with the phone to his ear. Or maybe he was kneeling? Gradually an energy began to flutter inside her, fill her, a kind of tingling pulse, starting at her brain and reaching out toward her extremities through her arms and legs. *Oh no*, this was what she had been afraid of: what if *that* happens? And in front of Deirdre. She remembered

Jay telling her not to resist, and she tried to calm herself. It wasn't easy, but she knew how important this was. It wasn't the moment for personal reticence; it was all just in the line of duty when you worked for LiveCell. At least it was dark in there.

She allowed it, and the tingling grew in intensity, and then the sensation was so overwhelming that she was beyond concern or fear, or even, in a strange way, sexual feelings. It was a connectedness with Jay, or maybe something way beyond him, something she hadn't known existed. And then came the realization that she was vibrating; not that her body was moving, but that her mind was vibrating at a perfect frequency. It was almost a second orgasm but at the same time it was like the one perfect moment after, prolonged and with a purity of emotionlessness that transcended everything. After an indefinite interval—she had no concept of time—she opened her eyes. She realized she was crying. She got clumsily to her feet and saw the field of phones glowing and pulsing gently in front of her. It was like a field of soft light caressed by a tender breeze.

Deirdre let out a cry. "Oh, my, God! You did it! Mary, you did it. I can't believe it. This is *so* totally amazing."

"Mary?" she heard Jay whisper inside her brain. He seemed far away and very close in the same instant. She couldn't respond. She wondered if this was like giving birth with the pain inverted to pleasure. "Mary? Are you okay? I feel like we did it," he said. His voice still came from a tremendous distance. She realized she'd been holding the LiveCell next to her hip. She brought it closer, but still couldn't say anything.

"Are the phones infused?" he said.

Why did she have to answer? He must know. My God, why is he doing this to me? Doesn't he realize how this makes me feel? It was exactly what she had been frightened of.

She turned to Deirdre, her tears probably visible in the gentle yellow radiance of the LiveCells.

"Mary, are you okay?"

They looked at each other, and Mary's arms opened, and with only an instant of hesitation Deirdre embraced her. Mary felt the strong arms tighten around her and buried her head into Deirdre's neck and shoulder. They held each other for some minutes. Finally they separated.

"I have to go home," said Mary. "This is all too much for me."

Deirdre nodded.

It was then that Mary realized Jay was still on the phone. "Every-

thing's okay," she said to him. "The phones are infused." She ended the call before he could speak.

"Are you, like, sure you're all right?" said Deirdre.

"I need some time alone. I can't even begin to tell you what that was like."

"You want me to drive you?"

Mary shook her head.

"This might sound, like really corny, but I'm *so* glad I know you. And no matter what happens, I wouldn't trade any of this for the world."

Mary thought a moment. "I guess you're right. I wouldn't either."

She left Deirdre in the clean room, went down the hall, stood at the doorway of the factory, trying to get some equilibrium back. The early darkness submerged her in blueness as she crunched unsteadily across the gravel to her car. She slumped onto the familiar leather seat, but didn't reach for her keys. For a second she considered just going to the office to see him, but she couldn't face his presence right then. Where she really wanted to go was home, back to Vermont. To see the farm again, and her parents. To run her hands through Pilgrim's fur and throw the old dog some sticks. She wondered if Pilgrim could even run anymore, with that strange three-legged gait. She wanted to waste away a lazy afternoon of nine-ball with Kelly on that cranky old pool table. She wished Jay would just forget everything and fly to Vermont with her—just for a week. Of course Vermont would be snowed in, but no one would care. The fireplace at the farm would be roaring with maple and oak and birch, her mom would bake a ham or roast a turkey; they'd all sit around the big dining room table and sip hot mulled cider and talk. At night the full moon would illuminate silver-white ferns of frost on the upstairs bedroom windows, those patterns that were like overdrawn constellations with meteor tails, the lacy mappings of a frozen winter sky. They could go cross-country skiing or snowshoeing or even sledding. She imagined Jay on a sled in his blue T-shirt screaming down an icy hillside, grinning madly. The whole idea excited her unduly. "My God, what's wrong with me?" she said out loud. She knew nothing would have changed for him. And then somewhere deep in herself she realized that what Jay wanted would never be what she wanted.

And she sensed he was trying to livecell her. She didn't answer. Let him suffer too!

She wished she could at least head for Jake's poolroom and practice some nine-ball. Her hands itched to hold her cue again. Anything to take

her mind off this feeling. Since Sammy died, she hadn't been back to Jake's. She still didn't have the heart to walk in and not find him behind the bar in one of his crazy bowling shirts, setting a draft in front of her, saying, 'Hey, girl, how's things?' and sliding her the salt shaker, then turning, his big shoulders moving under the shirt, to fix her a crab roll. Would Nick keep the poolroom open? But what would he do if he closed it?

Her mind was untethered, ricocheting from thought to desire. Had the infusion affected it somehow? Maybe the continuum was too much for her? No, she felt connected to everything in a way she never had, as if she could almost see all the infinite particles that formed existence.

Finally she fired up the car, headed toward the highway as it started to rain. Snarled in traffic approaching the Golden Gate Bridge, she waited as all that was visible through the windshield was reduced to streaming red and gray. She didn't even play a CD while the Porsche crawled forward in line. Instead she thought about her life, and realized it would always be a complicated layering of things to deal with and sort through. It was her nature to become involved, not to retreat from emotion or what scared or confused her. She also newly understood that something incredible held all of them in its embrace, whether people were aware of it or not. Knowing this was miraculous, even if it didn't change anything else. No wonder Jay missed those days with his grandfather. We must all have a core memory that we love.

Then Frankie livecelled. "Are you on your way?" he said.

She touched the wiper control, and the world beyond the windshield popped into focus. "Just clearing the bridge."

"Dinner'll be ready by the time you get home."

"I'm afraid I'm not that hungry."

"Don't worry, I'll hold it back—no problem. We'll have a couple wines—build the appetite. Or you want champagne? I got something real important to discuss with you. Okay?"

Oh, great. Is everyone always in love with the wrong person?

Frankie hadn't been with her on the drives back and forth to Live-Cell for almost a week; she'd insisted on going alone. Since Christmas, he'd become progressively preoccupied and distant, almost sulky, yet this change in him was subtle because he hid his emotions. Regardless, she could tell something was up. Was it the pearl earrings? She'd tried to give them back a few days after the holidays, but on witnessing his brave smile and the pain in his eyes—a new expression and one she never wanted to see again—she'd told him she'd keep them. But maybe the damage was

already done? Some situations just don't have good solutions. The earrings had remained untouched on top of her bureau, deserted in their blue box.

When she arrived home, she was greeted by the familiar smells of Italian cooking. Frankie came out of the kitchen in another apron, this one with a big bunch of sprouting carrots on it, and handed her a glass of wine.

"How was your day?" he said.

"Fine, the usual," she said. She'd only infused twenty-four-thousand living phones by being a human medium as a continuum of energy passed through her body and mind, giving her the strangest orgasm she'd ever experienced, and now she was even more in love with this guy whose pineal gland was missing and who insisted on saving the world instead of fucking her.

"You work too much," he said.

"You think so?"

He snapped around and went back into the kitchen. Had her tone been nasty? She hadn't meant it to be. She followed him.

"And your day?" she said, trying to sound friendly.

He looked at her. He sure had romantic eyes. Maybe she'd been missing something that was right in front of her?

"I've been called back to Boston." He was watching for her response.

"Why?" she said. "I don't need protecting any longer?"

"Mr. Brignolia doesn't give explanations."

"And?"

"I like it out here."

"So, stay."

"You don't understand."

"What's there not to understand? If you don't want to go back to Boston, stay here. Are you worried you couldn't find another job? I'm sure Jay would hire you. I know he likes you. I don't know how much Brignolia pays you, but I'm sure Jay would match it."

"Mary, that's not the problem."

"What is?"

He glanced around the kitchen as if seeing if anyone was listening. "You don't say no to Anthony Brignolia."

"Jay did." She regretted it instantly.

"I know," he said.

"Anthony told you?"

"Mr. Brignolia never says anything he don't have to. I got a friend in the organization. There're always leaks, always ways of finding stuff out." He paused. "Let's sit down, okay?"

Frankie adjusted a few things on the stove, and they brought their wines into the dining room.

"If it got out that I told you this, it'd be real bad for me," he said.

She said nothing.

"Mary, I'm gonna be dead honest with you, because it's important and there isn't much time. You know I have feelings for you. I know you don't have the same feelings for me. I accept this." He held up his hand. "Please, let me finish. I really can't do this twice. I know who you have feelings for, and I see he's an incredible man, more than I could ever hope to be." Again he quieted her with his hand. "What I'm about to tell you, you must pass on to him. I do this because of how much I care for you. I do it only for you."

She waited.

"Jay's in danger. Mr. Brignolia was dead serious about that." He saw her expression. "Didn't Jay tell you any of this?" She shook her head. "I guess he wouldn't. He wouldn't wan' you to worry. Besides, the guy's a loner, a true loner." He glanced out the window. "They know Jay needs to attend the phones every day. Without this, the phones won't work. This true?"

Mary wasn't sure how to answer. She was frightened he knew that, and even more frightened that others outside the company knew it as well. Had they found out about the infusion process or were they guessing? But how could they find out? Deirdre would never tell, and of course Jay wouldn't. Who else had found out? Jimmy Hakken? No way—he'd sooner die. And then she felt even more afraid. Was Frankie Demanno really on their side, or was he setting up something for Brignolia? Had he been sent out here by Brignolia to spy on her? No, Nick called Brignolia. But what if—

"You don't have to tell me," he said.

Her intuition said to trust him, but she was still worried. "He doesn't need to be with the phones every day," she said. At least not after today. Jay always seemed to do things in the nick of time.

"Good. That's critical. Then you got to prove this by having Jay disappear. No one should know where he is. No one. This will give them pause, and give LiveCell more time. Right now, they think all they have to do is off Jay, and LiveCell's finished."

How the hell had they found that out? She attempted to keep her emotion out of her voice. "Brignolia's going to kill him?"

"Mr. Brignolia does what serves Mr. Brignolia. For now, saving Live-Cell fits his interests. I think he's waiting for Jay to change his mind and accept the offer. The people after Jay are the same fucking inner circle that call all the shots in this country. Brignolia works for them, not the other way around."

"But you work for him."

It stopped him. "I'm questioning that."

"Were you told to spy on me?"

"Yeah, but also to protect you. Once I met you, I never spied." He searched her face. "Mary, you gotta believe me. I'm on your side."

"Why not quit Brignolia and work for Jay then?"

"You mean that? I mean, you personally? You want me to stay?"

His intensity scared her. "Will Brignolia have you killed if you quit?"

"Mary, I grew up real hard. I been with Mr. Brignolia since I was a teenager. He kinda took me in, took care of me. But everything has a price. You're right, I don't think I can work for him no more. Being out here with you has forced me to look at a lotta stuff. I never considered other ways to live. His way was what I knew, and I didn't question it. Not until I came out here and—"

She knew where he was headed again. "I'll talk to Jay."

"Yeah, warn him. He needs to disappear—soon."

"How soon?"

"He probably has a couple weeks. Hard to tell."

"I'll call him tonight. I'll also talk to him about hiring you."

"Wait a bit. Give it a few weeks. I've gotta go back to Boston. There's no way around that, but I'm gonna try and talk to Mr. Brignolia, not that—"

There was a piercing wail. They saw smoke coiling in from the kitchen.

"Oh, shit," he said, jumping out of his chair and plowing into the fumes.

She sat, stunned by the entire day. She could hear Frankie banging around, a window being opened, a dishtowel slapped at the alarm, which finally chirped silent, Frankie muttering under his breath. She went to the door and peered in.

He stood near a couple smoldering pans. "Dinner, I gotta say, is nowhere near my usual standard. I turned the damn oven heat in the wrong direction."

"Can I take you out for dinner?" she said.

"You want to?"

She looked at him, this stocky Italian in his silly carrot apron, holding a dishtowel. "I'd love to."

"Really?"

"Yes, really."

"Your Porsche or mine?"—a big smile now.

"Yours." She headed for the door.

As he was putting on his sports jacket, he noticed the apron. He untied it and tossed it into the kitchen.

NINETEEN

Frankie Demanno orchestrated the disappearance. Jay grumbled about the procedures being excessive, and Frankie said, "Hey, please, this is what I do, allow me to take care of it." He wasn't worried about outside surveillance but saw no reason not to be thorough: "Hey, what's the point otherwise?" He insisted that only Jay know his destination and that his departure be kept secret except among the three of them; Mary could fill everyone in after Jay was hidden. His disappearance had to be sudden and unexpected.

The day of Jay's departure, Frankie again checked the Impala for tracking devices. If there had been any kind of transponder signal he would have picked it up; it was clean. Renting or buying another vehicle would be more obtrusive than using the Chevy. The car could be ditched later, but changing cars before the departure left tracks unless the second car was stolen. He couldn't imagine Jay agreeing to steal cars.

That night, he had Jay drop off the Impala in a quiet parking lot where he was waiting. He watched Mary pull in and collect Jay. Frankie planned to rendezvous with them later at a rest stop on the 101. From there Chevalier would be on his own.

Frankie waited about fifteen minutes before walking across the dark lot in his new charcoal-brown trench coat, pleased it was raining. He didn't look around, but went directly to the Impala, unlocked the door with

a spare set of keys, hopped in, fired the engine, and eased the wagon into the street. Just the right amount of traffic, he thought, checking the rearview mirror. With his hand on the spindly wheel, he felt as if he were maneuvering a barge. He understood the car had been a gift, but still didn't get why Chevalier didn't drive something else; the man could afford anything he desired. These people really do need looking after, he muttered. It would be so easy for him to slip a tracking device into the car now. Chevalier was a strange guy, trusting, but at the same time he seemed to know exactly what he was doing, and maybe even what other people planned to do. As if he were able to see into a person and—

A strangled cry from right behind him. Frankie jolted. What the fuck was that? Without turning, he noiselessly released his nine-millimeter Beretta from its holster, his ears searching madly. Approaching a red light on Market, he hit the brake and rotated, the barrel instantly locating the culprit. A very ugly cat with a missing ear, yellow paws gripping the back of the rear bench, was staring at him. The animal opened its mouth and squallered again. Two more cats slunk from hiding. Jesus, these must be Chevalier's goddamn cats. He's bringing them! But then, why the fuck not? He holstered the gun and looked around for more surprises. He noticed the floor of the backseat was jammed with paper grocery bags, and he reached over and opened one. It was full of frozen chicken pot pies, starting to thaw, soaking the bottom of the bags. Another held cat food. Christ, what a character this Chevalier was.

Someone blipped a horn. Frankie straightened and the light was green. As he drove again, the ugly yellow cat leapt forward and started to purr on the seat beside him. Frankie scratched along the animal's backbone. The tom arched, bounded into Frankie's lap, nuzzling an elbow with his teeth. Damn thing was gonna get yellow hair all over his new coat, maybe even fleas. Nonetheless, he allowed the cat to remain in his lap. So, Chevalier was going to hole up somewhere. And the poor guy would be forced to eat those horrible pies—*sacrilege*. For a moment he considered accompanying Jay to make sure he had something to eat, but it was an idle thought. Mr. Brignolia had let him know again that he was expected immediately. He had to face whatever it was, try to reason with the man. But why did it have to be right then? What a mess they were all in.

On the outskirts of San Francisco he checked to see if he was followed. This was second nature; he merely backtracked a few times, pulling over occasionally and watching. Assured, he entered the designated rest stop, berthed the barge in the darkest corner, doused the lights,

the rain collecting on the windshield, muddling the view of the on-ramp lights and the highway. The other two cats wandered forward, probably relieved the car was stationary. Out of curiosity, he opened the last shopping bag—those same damp awful pies and a six pack of canned beer. It was too cruel to contemplate.

Within ten minutes a silver Porsche pulled up behind him, switched off its lights. He met Jay halfway between the two cars.

"You leave first," Frankie said. "We'll check your back for a few miles, then you're on your own." Jay nodded. The guy really does look right into you, even in the dark. They stood in the rain for some moments. Since Jay said nothing, he said, "I figure to be in Boston maybe a week, hopefully no longer. I'll try ta get back as soon as I can." A pause. "Jay, I really appreciate your offer. Oh, and hey, remember, cash only, no cards." Jay nodded again. "Keys are in it." He motioned to the Impala. "I didn't lose any cats. That yellow guy with the ear is real friendly."

"Had him since Delaware." Jay gave Frankie's wet shoulder a firm grip. "Thanks for everything. Take care of Mary. She needs you."

Frankie walked to the idling Porsche and slid in beside her. She was staring straight ahead. The Impala's four brake lights flared red for an instant, then slowly diminished like a closing aperture.

"He's gonna be fine," he said. "There is no way anyone can track him now. Okay, let's follow."

Mary engaged first gear and accelerated up through two gears hard enough to wiggle the rear-end on the wet tarmac.

"Easy," said Frankie. "Are you okay?"

"I don't have a good feeling about this. I'm not sure why."

"Hey, nothing can go wrong. He disappears for a while, no one can get to him because no one knows where he is. LiveCell runs fine without him, it takes some pressure off, we figure our next move. It's our best option, until we got a better one. Besides, you'll be talking to him every day on a phone that can't be traced. Where's the problem? Anything looks suspicious, he calls."

Soon they identified the unique iconography of the Impala's taillights in the distance. Frankie said to hang back and maintain distance. He'd checked all the cars they passed, but at this point he wasn't concerned; being thorough was habit. "Okay," he said at the next exit sign. Mary live-celled Jay and told him they were headed back, she'd call him tomorrow. Frankie studied her again, knew she was upset, but didn't know what he could do about it.

The next day she put Frankie on a flight to Logan. He'd stored his car in her garage, staying up until eleven the night before to wax it. She hadn't waxed hers once. "It's leased for heaven's sake," she said, watching him polish, laughing at him.

"Who cares if it's leased. It's a fine machine and deserves to be pampered. I want it to be puffed when I get back." He draped it meticulously with a new high-tech car cover.

"And I thought I had it bad."

Mary ran LiveCell while Jay was absent. Heading the company was overwhelming, not to mention needing to infuse new phones every day. No wonder Jay had so little time for anything else. Of course, *he* didn't have a near orgasm every other time he infused.

Four days after Frankie left for Boston, she heard from Detective Artega.

"Something is wrong," he said over his LiveCell.

"How? What?"

"You're under surveillance, and it's not our people."

"Are you sure?"

"Believe me, cops know how to recognize other cops. But these guys—I have no idea. Maybe Feds, but not your usual Feds. Both factories are being monitored, and your offices at the Harcourt. These guys are extremely professional."

"What do you think it means?"

"Must have to do with Jay disappearing. Maybe they want to validate he's actually gone."

"They must be looking for him then," she said.

"Likely."

"One lucky thing is that the public doesn't know what he looks like. With virtually no photos in the media except the high school and Harvard shots, he'd be difficult to spot."

"These guys probably have surveillance shots, but at least his face isn't part of the public consciousness like most celebrities' . . . Mary, do you know where he is?"

"Why?"

"He won't answer his phone."

"I spoke with him today. He's fine."

"Thanks for telling me. Know you're being watched every minute."

"We really appreciate all your efforts."

"Sorry if I scared you."

"It's creepy, isn't it?"

"A lot of stuff has been surprising even me lately. I thought I'd seen it all."

After finishing with Artega she immediately livecelled Jimmy Hakken. He muttered that he'd thought the same thing but didn't want to alarm her until he was absolutely sure. His crew had spotted them. It had started three days ago.

"What bugs me is how quick they knew Chevalier'd gone to ground. MacKensie—we might have a leak. You want my boys to take care of this? Feds don't scare us none."

"It would only make things worse."

"We're on full alert. Just give the word."

Jesus, did he think he could fight anyone? But he probably didn't care. He was probably ready, maybe even eager, to die for his cause. He really was like a medieval knight. Jimmy Hakken also wanted to know if Jay was okay. Jay must not be taking calls from anyone except her, but why?

She called Frankie about the surveillance. She could tell he was trying not to worry her; she wasn't fooled. He said he'd check around and see if he could get a read.

The next morning Mary felt so restless she figured she must be getting sick, but she didn't have any other symptoms. Too busy to listen to her uneasiness, she decided it was probably stress. But by the middle of the afternoon she knew it was something worse. Kelly Harris called her from the farm.

"Mary," he said.

That one word turned her uneasiness to dread.

"Where's Jay?" he said.

"He's in hiding."

"Have you spoken with him?"

"Not today. Yesterday, last night late."

"Can you call him?"

She only nodded but she knew he heard her.

"Call him. I can't get him."

"What's wrong, Kelly?" She knew Jay hadn't been answering other people's calls. This was different.

"Something's not right."

"I'll call you as soon as I can," she said, her heart pounding.

She livecelled Jay.

He didn't answer. She tried to stay calm. It doesn't mean anything yet, he could just be away from his phone. But Kelly's fear tortured her. He could be wrong this time. He has to be wrong! She forced herself to wait five minutes by her watch and tried again. Fuck! She waited and tried one more time. She didn't call Kelly back; she couldn't handle it.

At about fifteen minutes before four, Frankie livecelled from the North End.

"Mary?"

"What's wrong?" she said, her heart already lurching in her chest.

"I found this out minutes ago. You got a rat. I don't know who it is, but someone way on the inside sold you out."

"Fuck," she said.

"Mary, hold tight, it might not be too bad. I'm gettin' the next flight out in the morning—I already missed the last one today. D'you have any idea who it might be?"

"Yes."

"I'll be in at ten-twenty-two, United one-sixty-three. Can you meet me?"

"Yeah."

"You should call Jay right now. We're gonna need him to figure this out. Something is real fucked 'cause I never seen Mr. Brignolia this pissed. Something or someone has screwed him big time. Is there a way the rat could guess where Jay is?"

"You can never tell with him, if it's who I think it is."

"When I get there, I'll get it out of the bastard, *believe me*. After you speak with Jay, you call me. And Mary, please don't worry, we'll straighten this out when I get in."

They ended the call.

She tried Jay again. She wondered if Duncan had left for the day. She livecelled him. He answered.

"Duncan, can I see you in my office for a minute?"

"I'm almost out the door."

"It's important." As she spoke she started walking toward his office—quickly.

"I really can't because I have an appointment."

"Duncan. *Now*, please." *Stay calm*, she told herself again. She needed to get information out of him.

"Oh, all right," he said. "I resent that tone though. Frankly, I'm sick

of that tone. I'll be there in five or ten minutes. I have something I forgot to do first."

She caught him as he was leaving his office. He had his coat on and his briefcase in hand.

"What do you want that is so goddamn important?" he said, backing away, retreating into his office again.

Just by the look in his eyes, she knew. She kicked the door closed. "Duncan, what have you done?"

"What are you talking about? . . . Why are you looking at me like that?"

"Duncan, what have you done?"

"I'm going home. I have better things to do. This is ridiculous." He started to walk around her. She didn't move.

"Duncan," she said as his hand touched the doorknob. "Would you rather talk with Jimmy Hakken?"

He stopped. A sick smile came over his face. "You think I'm worried about that scarecrow any more? He's being watched as we speak. All I have to do is say the word."

"You sold us out." She didn't even raise her voice; she was stating a fact. It was all so clear. She realized she'd sensed it all along.

"LiveCell was going down anyway," he said. "You didn't have a chance. It didn't matter what I did."

"How could you?"

"Do any of you have any idea how the real world works? Do you even have a clue? You're such a bunch of idealist misfits you're blind to reality. Don't you realize what a mess it would be if the Third World had free, secure communication? Or the Chinese? Or the Muslims? But do any of you geniuses ever think of that? And look at all the trouble you've already caused in this country. His phones are stirring people up, changing people, don't you see that? We could have a revolution in this country and then where would we be? You think this can just go on?" He shook his head. "Well, it's not going to happen."

"You hate him, don't you?"

"What are you talking about?"

"A truly decent and kind man and you hate him." She tried to keep the anger out of her voice, but Duncan reacted anyway, his voice louder.

"Hate him? Who do you think tried to warn him? Who sent him two warnings? Who pleaded with him to sell the company? Who tried to make all of you see reality? And all I got in return was his holier-than-

thou attitude. Who does he think he is always running around in that T-shirt showing off his muscular arms, always pretending to be so calm, *so* together like nothing could ever get to him. He treated me like a servant: '*Duncan* find this out, *Duncan* find that out,' but where it mattered he wouldn't listen to me. And you. I loved you. You have no idea how much I loved you." His voice broke with emotion. "I would have done anything for you if you had given me a chance, but instead you wanted *him*. What was it about me that you couldn't give me one single chance? And to think I would have made you rich and treated you like a queen."

"Did they pay you yet?"

That stopped him. "Not all of it, but they will."

"Who? Alden Stone Associates?"

"When the dyke told us about Wendy Smith and the possible information deal, I paid attention."—*so that's who had tipped Wendy off*, thought Mary—"You all figured I was so devastated about selling my stock, but I saw a way to make even more money. I could see with Chevalier's stubbornness and inability to compromise that eventually LiveCell had to go down. It was only a matter of time. So I contacted Wendell's father."—*he must have contacted him through Wendy*—"Mr. Alden and his connections are the people who are actually running this country. They control things you could never even imagine. They listen to me and treat me with respect, not like you and Chevalier and that dyke and totem pole."

"You've been working for Alden." She knew it was true but could barely believe that anyone could be such a traitor.

"If Chevalier had been allowed to continue, look who he would've sold out to. You think I was going to let that happen? You think I'd work for Brignolia? Wouldn't that have been great—to give *those* people the most important technology on earth."

"How do you know about that?"

"I bugged his office."

"You bugged Jay's office?"

"You and Chevalier are so naive."

"And I suppose you know how the phones work? Is that what you sold to Alden?"

He smirked and stood straighter. "I know he has some kind of device that implants intelligence into the brain-like cell aggregate. I know he used it every day and now you probably are. If that scarecrow didn't have the factories crawling with thugs, I'd know more. With my help, their lab techs can almost produce the supposedly magic cell mutation by now.

Once we get whatever device imparts the intelligence, we'll have it. We'll get it soon, believe me. And we'll patent it!"

As Duncan talked, Mary quietly tried to reach Jay again. She knew she had to keep Duncan talking. Anything he revealed might be helpful.

"If the phones are supposed to be a menace," she said, "why does Alden want them so badly?"

"For themselves. Not for everyone else. Chevalier could have been selling those phones for a fortune—to the right people. But did he listen to me? Think of the military and corporate applications. Think if our generals and leaders had increased intuitiveness over everyone else? We would control the world. Instead he lets the masses have them, cheap, ridiculously cheap, and the sales are spreading outside the country. We'll see if his beloved masses can save him now. Or that scarecrow and his goons. You're all being watched. You can't go anywhere without being tracked. So try to go to the media, or the cops, or the supposed Mafia. See how far any of you get. You can't move an inch without being followed and stopped."

"They'll never find Jay."

A laugh escaped him. "Shows how much you know. I suppose you think your fancy hit man is infallible? Well he isn't. There are three tracking devices already implanted that will lead our people right to Chevalier."

"We checked. There are none." She was feeling ill.

"You didn't check the cats, did you?" He laughed again. "A simple little dime-sized transponder was cyanoacrylated in a small slit in the epidermis under the fur of each cat. Virtually undetectable. It couldn't have been easier getting someone into that dumpy room of his at the Y. I knew Mr. Love-every-fucked-up-misfit would take those mutant cats with him no matter where he went. They've probably found him by now, no matter where he is. And he thought he was smarter than me." He was chuckling with satisfaction.

Mary put her phone to her lips, the bitterness in her heart almost choking her. Her call was answered within seconds.

"Duncan has sold us out," she said. "Because of him, they may have gotten to Jay already. I think Duncan has caused enough trouble, but be careful, he seems to think his new friends can protect him."—she watched Duncan's arrogant face change to concern, veins appearing on his forehead—"He's right here, in his office at the Harcourt Building."

Jimmy Hakken merely grunted, and she could imagine him already running to his car. She was glad he wasn't after her. She couldn't think of anything worse.

"Who was that?"—his voice shrill. It was now Duncan who looked sick.

"Hakken," she said.

"You, fucking, bitch!" he screamed and ran at her with his arms out as if to strangle. She waited, not moving. At the last instant she drop-kicked him in the groin. He fell to the floor, writhing in pain, grabbing himself, moaning. Though it disgusted her to get close to him, she reached down and slipped his LiveCell phone out of his suit coat pocket and left the office. She tried to get him out of her mind; she had too many other things to do.

TWENTY

Mary headed toward her car out of habit. As she walked she livecelled Deirdre, putting her in charge of the company, explaining most of what had happened as quickly as possible. She also talked with Chet Simmons and Cliff Thompson, telling them Deirdre would now be the acting CEO, but not mentioning anything about Jay. On reaching the parking-garage door she hesitated, her mind racing.

Maybe Duncan had lied about the cats? Maybe they wanted her to run to Jay so they could follow? She tried him again and told her Live-Cell to ring him every ten minutes. Now she had to assume the worst. Kelly wouldn't have called otherwise. She forced herself to remain logical and suppressed her worst fears.

She had to get to Jay, yet travel undetected. With everyone in the company being watched, she could rely on no one. Any member of Live-Cell could be picked up and held on some pretext. But if they'd found Jay, she'd need help. Frankie would arrive in the morning, but hours could make the difference. She couldn't wait. She needed a gun and someone to help her, someone they weren't watching, someone outside the company, someone willing and tough. Artega flashed into her mind, but who knew what his orders were? Nick was too old. If only Sammy weren't—

Garland McKeen!
She livecelled.

"Yeah-boy."

"Garland?"

"Naw—nobody here by that name."

"There isn't?" LiveCells never misdialed.

"No, ma'am."

She could hear a faint metallic noise of maybe a horse shaking a bridle, rain drumming against what might be a tarp, and just then the bellow of a steer. Sounds that made her instantly homesick.

"I'm trying to find Garland McKeen . . . Hank. Do you know—"

"Hell, why didn't you say so? Thought you were a bill collector. Who's this?"

"Mary, Mary MacKensie."

"Oh, boy."

"I met Hank about—"

"Believe me, I know. Know *all* about it."

"Who am I speaking with please?"

"Hank's pa, who d'ya think?"

"Mr. McKeen, I really need to reach Hank."

"Hell, he's out by Taylor Creek. Suppose I could get him. He know your number?"

"Does he still have a LiveCell phone?"

"Yup."

"Then if he just thinks of me, it should work."

"All he does is think of you," he muttered. "These new-fangled phones do that?"

"That's why I don't understand getting you instead of Hank."

"Hank juss give me his phone for today 'cause I done left mine at the house. It musta confused the little critter. You know these dang phones amaze me. Sure makes things a heck of a lot easier around here. Hank kept trying to convince me, and I gotta admit—"

"Mr. McKeen, it's urgent I speak with Hank right away."

"Gotcha. Light's draining fast anyway. Hank'll be headed back any time now, but I'll try to get him for ya."

"Thanks."

"You bet."

Mary didn't enter the parking garage. It might be under surveillance, or her car bugged. But she had to get out of the building undetected, before Jimmy Hakken arrived. He might be tailed, and who knew what would happen when he found Duncan. She didn't want to know. Quickly,

she walked back to the elevator and rode down to the main floor.

"Manuel," she said, approaching the front desk.

He looked up from a magazine. "Oh, hey there."

"Is there a way of sneaking out of this building?"—her tone light-hearted.

"Someone you don't want to see out front?" He grinned, and she winked back. "Of course, dear, I know a way. All you do is take the elevator down to the basement . . ." and he explained it to her. Didn't ask any questions, just told her what she needed to know. Some people just understood. She thanked him, and he returned to his magazine.

She followed Manuel's directions, and in six or seven minutes, after lots of duct work, conduits, throbbing machinery, hard-to-find light switches, one wrong turn, she shoved open a rusty door and stepped into an alley. A light rain. She cursed—her coat was still in her office. At least she had her purse; she'd just buy another coat. Why hadn't Garland called? Hadn't her urgency been clear to his father? Should she livecell Frankie? It had been almost half an hour; he was probably getting anxious. But she needed to talk with Garland first. She still couldn't bear to talk with Kelly again. She shivered—the drizzle was worsening—and headed down the alley away from the front of the Harcourt Building. Without a glance, her head down, she entered the sidewalk at Ellis and blended into the crowd of pedestrians. Frankie had told her, "Someone looking around nervously is easy to spot. Why wave a flag?" Every morning he'd shared tidbits like this at breakfast. The memory made her long to be back at her dining room table, listening to Frankie over a cup of his coffee. It's true: we rarely appreciate what we have until it's gone.

In a clothing store, she found a grayish green raincoat, wondering if she was thinking camouflage. Her shoes were okay, they had decent soles. She was relieved that she hadn't chosen heels or a skirt that morning. As the sales girl handed back her card, she asked to use the washroom.

Mary locked the door, took out her phone, thought "Garland," picturing him vividly.

"Yeah-boy."

"Garland?"

"Mary! That really you?"

"It's me."

He let out a hoot; he hadn't changed.

"So how you been? *Dang*, is it ever good to hear from you."

"Didn't your father let you know I called?"

"He told me you might ring, not that these ring. Give me my phone back in case."

"He didn't tell you to call immediately?"

"Pa's not real good at messages. You sound a little bit upset. You okay?"

"I'm afraid I need some help."

"Anything. You know that."

"I hate to ask you this, but I need to get to the Oregon coast—tonight. Some people are watching me. I can't use my car, and I don't dare rent one."

His voice changed. "Who's after you?"

"This could be very dangerous."

"Bet this has to do with your phones. Been reading every newspaper with any coverage. I can guess what's going on. Listen, gonna tell Pa, chores is most done anyway. I'll get the truck and bet I can be in the city in something like four five hours. That be okay?"

"Yes."

"Goddang, I'm on my way then."

"Garland, I think we might need a gun."

"Rifle, shotgun, or handgun?"

"I'm not sure."

".357 long barrel. Matched pair, used to be Grandpa's. They'll be loaded and ready—Remington Golden Sabers. I'll throw a rifle on the rack too."

She wasn't sure exactly what he was talking about, but at least they'd have guns. "I hate to put you in this mess," she said.

"There's some things I just know about, shooting's one of 'em."

"Garland?"

"Yeah?"

"This could be dangerous. *Very* dangerous. I have no idea what we're headed into. It might be nothing, but I doubt it. We might get shot at."

"So?"

"I just want you to be really sure you want to do this."

"Yep, sure do."

"You're really something, you know that?"

He hooted again and they ended the call.

Though she tried to hold them back, tears filled her eyes. She saw him galloping a horse through the rain, grabbing and loading the guns,

jumping in the truck, roaring along a dirt road to the highway, sliding onto the pavement and accelerating toward her.

She pulled herself together. Called Frankie and filled him in. When she got to the Garland part he went cold.

"Who is this guy?" he said.

"Hank McKeen. He's a cowboy." She didn't use *Garland*. Maybe that's why he preferred *Hank*.

"A cowboy?"

"From up north."

"What kinda *cow*boy?"

"His family runs cattle."

"But how do you know this guy?"

"Frankie, we don't have time for this."

A pause. "But you can trust this guy?"

"I believe I can."

"Okay, sorry. Damn, if only I was on that last flight out. This is driving me nuts. And I still think you gotta wait for me. *Please*. I'm trained for this. You and the cowboy aren't."

"It might be too late. Who knows what they might be doing to Jay. You know I have to try."

He fell silent.

"Maybe I could get a flight into Portland?" he said. "Closer to Chevalier. Only trouble might be getting a gun. I'm not sure who we got up in Oregon, not one of our big areas. This new airport security sucks. Anyway, either airport, I get in, I rent a car—use my alias—head to Siuslaw, or however you say it. You still trying to reach Jay?"

"Every ten minutes."

"He told ya where he was gonna hole up?"

"I just knew."

"Shoulda been a perfect location." A lull. "The *cats*! Those people are sick. Mary . . . I'm so fuckin' sorry."

"You're not to blame."

"I'm supposed to be a professional. I shoulda debugged the car one more time."

"Frankie, don't beat yourself up. No one would've suspected the cats."

They stopped talking.

He broke the silence: "Please wait for me. I don't know nothing about this *cow*boy."

They'd already been over it, and he knew she had to go.

"Okay, okay. On the map, there are only two direct ways to get there—one-o-one, or interstate five. You and the cowboy are gonna get stopped."

"But they don't know his truck."

"Don't matter. They only gotta watch two roads, and real soon they gonna know you're missing if they don't already. They'd be fools not to stake out the two roads, especially at night with light traffic. Even if the cowboy's truck crossed a few checkpoints, that right there, it's over. They only need six men. Let me think on it and call you back. And Mary, I'll check in every hour, okay?"

"Thanks."

"You're doing fine, lose the purse and keep moving. They gonna have a hard time finding you in the city, but they'll be looking, *hard*. Be a disaster for them if the two major players in LiveCell vanish at once. Even they couldn't keep that out of the media. The public would demand an explanation. Try not to worry too much about Jay, we don't know nothing yet. He could be all right and just not answering. At the worst, they just want information outta him. He's too popular right now for—"

A knock on the bathroom door. "Miss, are you okay in there?"

"Yes," she called. "Be right out."

"What was that?" said Frankie.

"Store clerk. Got to go."

"Okay, later."

Exiting the washroom she assured the clerk that she was all right, just an upset stomach. "You do look a little pale," said the girl.

Back on the street, she tossed her purse into a trash bin, stuffing only those things where a transponder couldn't be concealed into her raincoat pockets. Duncan's phone she threw into the bin as if it burned her hand, but it upset her to lose the purse—she remembered the day she bought it, so pleased to find that rare shade of silvered leather—but what else could she do? Maybe someone would find it and be delighted. Frankie had told her he wasn't worried about her shoes or clothes. "You got way too many to bug 'em all," he'd muttered. "Take a thousand transponders." She was relieved to hear him joking, knowing he was going through hell. But weren't they all.

Mary tried to keep out of the rain, stay in peopled areas, and avoid doing anything unusual that might draw attention, which wasn't easy since she constantly imagined a hand grabbing her: "Miss MacKensie, come with us, we have some questions to ask you," or whatever that kind

of agent said. She'd never dealt with the FBI, the CIA, or whoever had been directed to watch LiveCell. She'd never even had a speeding ticket, which was a miracle considering how she drove. What lies had the surveillance teams been fed about Jay and LiveCell? She knew cops did what they were told and kept their questions to themselves. And to think that America had been founded on the right to question authority.

Even with her LiveCell trying Jay every ten minutes, she called every five, knowing it was pointless. She had to accept it. He was in trouble. She finally livecelled Kelly; they could barely speak. She couldn't afford to break down again and ended the call. It was the same with Deirdre. Frankie called but hadn't solved the problem of getting Garland's truck to Oregon undetected.

And then Garland checked in: "Mary. Got her running at over eighty. Hit ninety on the hills. Be there even sooner." She could hear the thing hammering down the highway.

"Don't get a ticket."

"Don't plan on it. Not many cops on these roads anyhow. Never knew this rig could run this fast. Just passed Red Bluff. Dang, can't wait to see ya."

God, was everything a delight to him?

They decided to meet in the parking lot of a Safeway off Market—full of cars pulling in and out, a busy Friday evening. Mary wheeled around an empty cart, not really sure why, it probably looked silly, maybe even suspicious, but she needed to do something other than stand. Garland would be there any minute. As she glanced at some of the other shoppers, she yearned to be worrying about what flavor of ice cream to buy, the price of lemons, or even calming an upset child. Again, she forced herself to remain fixed on what she had to do.

She heard it though she didn't realize it was his truck. She just wondered who was driving around without a muffler. It was a sound you heard in Vermont, where road salt ate exhaust systems, not San Francisco. As the deafening rumble pulled into the lot she saw who it was. Nothing like a clandestine operation.

He parked in a space close to her, shut off the truck, and hopped down. He was still wearing his yellow rain slicker and pants from ranching, the same battered Resistol set back on his head. Well, at least he didn't have the guns out, firing them into the air.

"Sorry 'bout the racket," he said, a sheepish grin on his face. "Frigging manifold pipe come loose at the muffler. Musta been jarred a bit on our road, and then the backpressure at ninety blew her apart. She was

holding up pretty good till she sheared plum off."

"Let's talk in the truck." She shoved the shopping cart near the front bumper and got in. He jumped up behind the wheel, and she scanned the parking lot, nervously. No one seemed the least bit interested in them.

"You made great time," she said, and he grinned. He really did look a bit like James Dean—James Dean with a smashed up nose. "Don't worry about the muffler. Frankie doesn't think it's safe to take your truck anyway."

"Who's *Frankie*?"

"A friend of mine."

"He goin' with us?"

"He's in Boston."

"Then how would he know?"

"Believe me, he would."

Something touched his features. But only for an instant.

"Garland, I think Jay's in trouble."

"Chevalier?"

She explained the situation to him. "We have to get to Jay. Obviously your truck's out—too late to get it fixed. Maybe *you* could rent a car at the airport? No one would be monitoring your credit cards. *Shit*."

"What?"

"I bought this coat with one of my cards. They probably already know about the transaction."

He squirmed in his seat, reached inside his rain pants for his back pocket. "Mary . . ." He hesitated.

"What is it? Tell me."

"Don't have my wallet." He hammered the dash. "Dang. See I never take it when I'm working, and I was racing to—"

"We'll just have to think of something else."

"Forgot the rifle, too." He rubbed one of his huge hands across his forehead, stomped his boot into the floor pan of the truck. "God dammit!"

"Garland, come on. It's just great you're here."

She reached for her phone and thought Frankie. He answered instantly. She explained the current complications. He said, "Any rental at the airport be checked no matter whose card you used. No muffler? And you're sure about this cowboy?"

Did men ever stop being roosters? And then she thought of Jay and had to stem her emotion once again.

"God*dang*, I know what we can do." It was Garland.

"Hold on one second, Frankie."

"Freights! We can hop a freight out. They run right up near the coast in Oregon."

"You mean get on a train?"

"Sure."

"We can just get on one?"

"Sure. Hop on and ride. Be easy."

"Where do we get on?"

"Just find a freight yard. Follow the tracks."

"You've done this?" Something in his voice concerned her.

He hesitated. "Not exactly, but kinda."

"Garland, do you know how or not?"

"Well, a guy working at the ranch talked about it. He hopped freights when picking apples and got to liking it. I know we can do it. We just check and see if one is heading north. They move good too, once they get rolling."

She relayed this to Frankie. He was reluctant at first but came around to the idea. "They'd never look for you there. You're safe and it gets you north of any checkpoints. We stay in constant touch. I book into Portland and pick you up in my rental." Frankie checked MapQuest and found a big yard in Oakland. She vaguely remembered seeing it and thought she could get close based on his directions.

"Let's get moving," she said to Garland. He ignited the truck—it sounded like an ailing Nascar—and they rumbled out of the Safeway lot and pointed the Chevy for the freight yards.

Frankie continued, "The cowboy have a gun?"

She told him.

"What's he got?"

She asked Garland and relayed it.

"Dinosaurs—but a good weapon and a great bullet. Okay, you get close if you can, but not too close. Wherever the train stops, livecell me from there. I pick ya up around noon, we head to the house, the cowboy and me got guns. If those fuckers have Jay, I want them."

Maybe the overt noise of the muffler worked as a cover? Who on surveillance would take notice of anyone drawing so much attention to themselves? Besides, would one of the principles of the multi-million-dollar LiveCell be driving around with a grinning cowboy in a battered ranch truck with all the windows rolled down to prevent carbon-monoxide poisoning? Mary still hid behind the hood of her raincoat and hun-

kered down on the bench seat. She wasn't taking any chances. It also protected her from the cold drizzle blowing through the window.

They found the freight yard in Oakland without too much trouble—
and without a ticket for noise violation. Locating one of the roads that
led down to the yard took a few extra minutes. It was almost nine-thirty
by the time they parked. Garland put the guns in a dirty canvas tote from
which he'd removed some fencing tools. He'd left the top chamber on
each gun empty. "Pa calls that the dead man's chamber. Ten shots should
be enough anyhow." He suggested she stash anything loose in the bag as
well. "If we have to run for a train you don't want things jumping out.
Your pockets don't even have flaps." She handed him her wallet and
phone. He wrapped everything carefully in a small wool horse blanket,
secured the brittle leather straps, checked the buckles. He tossed it over
his shoulder, and they walked out over the thistle and weed-studded
ground toward the rows and rows of dark freight cars.

"Guy told me you just ask any brakeman and they'll tell you what's
headed where. Though we got to stay clear of the bull; that's a railroad
cop. They drive around in unmarked cars. If you see somebody let me
know."

"Garland, are you sure we can do this?"

Shrouded in cold fog, the vast freight yard brooded, the distant
noises of the city vague from across the expanse. Though she could hear
a diesel switcher revving and the bang of an occasional coupler, it was
oddly quiet, even the traffic on the freeway above her more muted. As
they walked, a gentle rain became visible in the puddles. Large mercury-
vapor lights on long masts strained to illuminate central sections of the
yard, managing only a dead silver against darkness and the dull orange
sky. A heavy smell of diesel oil, creosote, and tar mixed with the earthi-
ness of ground and the freshness of rain. As they approached the freight
cars, she felt vulnerable surrounded by so much ominous steel.

"Guy said never walk between cars. You never know when they're
gonna move. Always climb up the rungs and over the couplers." As if on
cue, a string of five coal hoppers whispered out of the fog, rolling omi-
nously toward them. They jumped aside, their backs against the graffiti
and rust-covered flank of a car on the adjacent track.

"There isn't much room," she said. There wasn't. She couldn't
stretch out her arms without touching freight cars. "I'm really not sure
about this."

"You'll be okay once we get on board."

"Why were those cars moving around like that without an engine?"

"Hump yard. They run 'em over a big hump back there and a computer sets the switches so they end up on the right track. That's how they form trains. That's why you never step between switch points, 'cause you can't know when they're gonna close. Take your foot right off."

Great. "How do you know all this stuff?"

"Same guy. We worked together over a year. All he talked about, every day. Obsessed with it. I been wanting to do this ever since."

They came to the end of a long string of auto carriers and crossed over more tracks. She'd never realized there could be so many tracks, must be well over two dozen. She glanced down for snapping switch points that could bite a foot clean off, checked for more stealth freight cars creeping out of the mist. Then at Garland—headed into the unknown, rain dripping off his hat and slicker, the bag of guns over his shoulder, that incurable grin on his face. She was stunned that her life had arrived at this place, that this was her only moment of reality, that such a moment existed at all, accompanying this cowboy through a freight yard on a rainy February night hoping to save—

"Hey, look." He pointed.

Leaning between two freight cars, a guy was checking something with a flashlight. He straightened, spoke into what looked like a LiveCell phone, and waved the light beam above his head toward the front of the train.

They walked up to him.

"Hey there, bub," said Garland.

He didn't turn, continued talking into the phone.

"A brakeman," Garland whispered to her. There was the long blast of a diesel horn, a wheel creaked and they heard a distant metallic groan. The sound increased, reached them with a tremendous *k-chang*, and the train jerked forward a few inches. The brakeman faced them.

"Say what?"

"We're looking for a train north," said Garland.

"North?" His gristled face peered at them, his cap pulled down against the rain. The train was beginning to rattle and moan as it slowly gained momentum. "Where you people want to go to?"

"Oregon," said Garland.

"Well," he said slowly, pointing his flashlight. "That's the OAPO headed for Davis. She'll be dropping some there, and then heading on up past Redding to Klamath Falls."

"So it's going to Oregon?"

He thought a minute. "Sure thing. Where else would it go?"

Garland turned to her. "Quick, unbutton your coat so you can run. That's our train."

"Hey," the brakeman called after them, "I wouldn't be trying to get on that; she's already goin' way too fast."

Garland jogged beside her in the loose gravel ballast as a variety of freight cars slowly passed. "There's an open boxcar," he said. "Can you make it? We got to be quick."

For all Garland's railroad explanations, he hadn't mentioned how to jump a moving train. It was too late to ask now. She ran beside the box-car and placed her hands on the wet wood of the floor. A lot higher than she would have liked, almost at her shoulders. She hesitated, felt a flush of sweat, but knew she had to try; the train was moving faster and faster by the second. *Now!* She threw up a leg, her heel catching in the iron door guide, her ass hanging in the air. Her hands started slipping, a splin-ter bit her palm, her body began to fall backwards. She screamed.

Suddenly strong hands found her and pitched her into the car. She quickly got to her knees. Garland was still running. He'd lost a little ground against the increasing speed of the train. "Come on," she cried. He gained on the car again, reached out for the floor, but just when his palms were on the boards, the canvas tote swung from his shoulder. He caught it as it fell in front of him. The save threw his body out of balance and he careened toward the car, his shoulder whacking the side, spinning him askew. "No!" she yelled. Somehow he righted himself and managed to keep running.

"Come on, Garland. You can make it. Come on!" Again he was abreast of the car, his feet flying, the bag held tightly in his hands. "Here," he said, and tossed it at her. She reached out frantically. A leather strap scraped her fingers as she grabbed for it. But the bag fell between them onto the gravel and disappeared in an instant. "Dang," he muttered. With a last crazy lunge, he caught the edge of the metal door with his left hand and hung there for a moment, his legs dangling over the blurred ground, his other arm flailing like a rodeo rider on a bull. She leapt toward him to pull him into the car. Somehow he maintained his grip on the door edge, brought his other arm into steadiness, and grabbed the rusty door runner. From there it was a matter of seconds and he was lying on the boxcar floor, his small chest heaving, his left hand bleeding.

"My God," she said. "Are you okay?"

"I lost—the guns."

"My fault. I should've been ready. God, I can't believe you made it." She looked down at him—being small and very strong had its advantages. No one else could have possibly managed that. "Maybe when we come back we can find your guns. Or let's call someone to pick them up." *Oh shit!* "Do you have your phone?"

"With the guns."

"We don't have either phone." It was a statement of dread. It had been so long since she'd been without a LiveCell; she felt utter panic, cut off from everything. But she didn't want Garland to realize how upset she was. No guns, no phones, no money. It was a complete disaster.

He got slowly to his feet and looked at his hand.

"Is it okay?"

"Just a gash. Had worse."

Blood cleaned most of the rust from the wound. She tore some strips from the lining of her coat and bound his hand, his missing finger looking so sad.

The freight continued to pick up speed, the boxcar vibrated and rattled, the wheels pounding on the rails. They gripped the edge of the door opening to keep their balance, their feet spread wide. It would've been difficult to talk above the racket. The sound of clanging crossing gates approached and receded, the flashing disks visible for a few seconds, an explosion of red across their faces. Streetlights and waiting auto headlights swirled around the interior of the boxcar like search beacons, then left them in darkness again. After perhaps fifteen minutes, the rough track improved and they tried to talk.

"What we gonna do without guns?" he said.

She gestured at her ear.

He said it again louder, almost shouting.

She shrugged. "Maybe Frankie can get a gun."

"You think there's a bunch of 'em got Chevalier?"

"I don't know anything. There's no way of knowing."

"Suppose not. You cold? You're shivering."

"I'm okay."

He took off his yellow slicker and pulled his sweater over his head and handed it to her. "Sorry it's not too clean."

She accepted the sweater.

"You all right?" he said.

"I guess. This has been a long day."

She took off her wet raincoat and got the sweater on, smelling cattle in the wool as she pulled it over her head. They were the same size, she couldn't help noticing. She put her raincoat back on, thanked him, and he grinned. Within ten minutes she stopped shivering so badly and felt somewhat better. They'd left the lights of the city behind, loping now through long fields of soaked fruit or nut trees. Every so often the diesel horn cried out at the far front of their train.

"Are you going to be warm enough?" she said. He looked miserable in the rain slicker with his arms wrapped across his chest.

The roadbed had smoothed still more, and they didn't need to shout any longer.

"I'm sorry about your grandfather's guns."

"First the muffler, then no wallet, forgot the rifle, dropped the guns. Sorry I made such a frigging mess of this."

"You didn't. God, I thought you were going to fall. I'll never understand how you did that." She glanced out at the blurred darkness. "I'm just not sure what to do now."

"We go up there. Maybe there ain't too many of 'em. They got guns, just got ta take one."

Garland really was an eternal optimist. His courage was as natural to him as his joy in being alive. She was still terrified. Now she couldn't contact Frankie, and the only place to meet was at Siuslaw. If only she had a LiveCell, maybe Jay would finally answer and this would all end.

They rode through the wet night, the rain occasionally intensifying, blowing in through the open door. Garland used a scrap piece of two by four and closed it some. He then jammed the lumber in the door guide. "Guy told me these doors can slam shut. Sometimes riders get locked in. Ain't good."

At Davis the freight stopped and either picked up or set out some cars, just as the brakeman had predicted. Garland hung in the doorway and tried to see through the drizzle, the shimmer of electricity that was Sacramento behind him. "She's a long one. Bet they got half-dozen engines up there." He hopped down onto the gravel ballast, looked up at her. "Not that you'll need it, but you ever wanna jump a freight again, this is how you do it." He positioned his hands palms down on the floor, and in one quick motion rotated his body onto his ass and rolled into the car. "Shoulda shown you that before. Practiced it at the ranch." He came and sat beside her. She looked at her watch, the familiar glide of the colored light. The blue dot was past ten, the red after six. Garland noticed

the watch and she told him about it. She silently prayed once more that Jay was all right. The train creaked, humped, and began rolling again.

They thundered through the darkness. As the miles clicked past, Garland got quieter, almost sullen. She'd never seem him like this. Nearly an hour had gone by and he'd said almost nothing. Something was wrong. Maybe he was having second thoughts?

"You okay?"

"Yep."

"Is it the guns?"

"Naw."

"You sure?"

"Yep."

She continued to examine him.

"Just hungry. Shoulda et something. Nothing since lunch."

"You know, I didn't eat either. That was a mistake. I'm hungry too. Very hungry."

After a few more minutes, he said, "I ain't so good if I don't eat."

"What do you mean?"

"Don't run too good."

"Blood sugar?"

"Yep."

"Oh no. Are you diabetic?"

"Naw. Ain't that bad. Just hypoglycemer. Be okay."

"We should have brought something to eat."

"I'd justa dropped it."

"We're quite the pair aren't we?"

This brought a bit of a grin, and they both started giggling.

They crossed a long girder bridge at Lake Shasta, and for an instant it was as if the boxcar had rolled into black nothingness; then they wound along Sacramento River Canyon. Though the rain had stopped, the air felt like snow. It had been a couple years since she'd seen snow. Above them, in the higher elevations, vast reaches of vague whiteness were spiked with pine. The freight slowed somewhere north of the lake and eventually lurched to a stop. The silence was more pronounced after the racket of the moving train. They sat on the wet doorsill, their raincoats protecting them, waiting for the train to begin moving again. Garland was shivering badly, and she kept rubbing her arms with her hands, her feet frozen.

"See that yellow sign?"

He glanced toward where she was pointing.

"Maybe it's a bar or a gas station. Too late for a store to be open. We need to get something to eat and we need to warm up." And maybe someone there had a LiveCell phone. That would be a godsend.

"Can't," he said.

"What do you mean?"

"Might be left here. She won't stop long."

"It's more important we get food."

She let herself down, held out her hand to him. "Come on."

He shook his head vigorously, the brim of his Resistol shuddering. "Be okay, really. Got to get to Chevalier. Maybe there's only two or three of 'em."

"Garland, come on." She had to say it a few more times. Reached up and took his hand. Pleaded with him in a way that got him moving.

They walked along the gravel beside the dark freight, passing articulated auto carriers and chemical tank cars, a few fruit reefers. He said they'd been real fortunate to find an empty boxcar. Soon a cracked plastic illuminated sign, Trackside Bar, and a *Rainier* neon clarified out of the icy darkness. Like two coal miners who had been trapped in a tunnel, they trudged toward this one spot of brightness.

TWENTY-ONE

On entering the Trackside Bar, they were swamped by a warm fetid haze with a stench that almost drove Mary back outside; she had to remind herself why they were there. Garland had guessed the train would pause for around fifteen or twenty minutes before heading north again. That might be enough time unless it left sooner, but the diesel horn would likely signal twice—then they had to run, immediately. At least the tracks were directly across the street.

She peered through the rank smoke. A pool table. All four patrons and barman turned as they approached; only the jukebox ignored them, strumming out a bleary country ballad. Not one of them looked even remotely like a LiveCell user. She planned on asking anyway. The bartender, his eyes mere slits, exhaled and stuffed out his cigarette in an overloaded ashtray.

"Hep you?"

"Kitchen still open?"

"Nope."

"Is there anything to eat, anything you could make us? We're pretty hungry."

The bartender shook his head curtly. "We're 'bout closed."

Someone sitting at the end of the bar mumbled, "Honey, I got some-

thing . . . eat," and two or three of the others started snickering. She ignored the comment, hoping Garland hadn't heard it.

"Just some chips, pretzels maybe?" She glanced at a snack rack behind him.

There was no reaction.

"Please. We're really hungry."

The bartender swiveled and grabbed two small bags of chips and tossed them on the bar. "Dollar."—sounded like a grunt.

"Any coffee?" She got the *Nope* again. They needed something to drink, something to bring up their blood sugar. "Two drafts then, Rainier not Bud, and two bags of those pretzels, and some Slim Jims." As he started pulling the beers, Mary walked down the bar, his pig-like eyes following her. Garland was watching her as well, it probably dawning on him that they didn't have a dime. She singled out the one who must have made the nasty comment—mullet haircut, bulky steroided muscles, low forehead, and an open short-sleeved shirt cheerfully printed in pineapples. "So, any of you play pool?" she said to him.

"And I suppose you do?" said Mullet.

She nodded.

"How much you wanna play for? Or maybe a sweet innocent thing like you wants to play for something asides money?" He gave her a confident leer. *Jesus*, this guy was too much. A skinny woman next to him whacked his arm. She sniffed a few times and her rabbit eyes darted nervously.

"How about if we play for fun?" said Mary. She looked right at him, though it disgusted her.

"I won enough fun. Don't your little cowboy there play pool?"

She shook her head.

"You think you can handle me?"

"I haven't been playing much lately, but I still think I can beat you." *God*, this was awful.

"Why not put your money where your mouth is then?" He stood, made a show of expanding his hairy chest, and took some quarters from his change pile. "Allow me."

She glanced at Garland eating chips ravenously. The bartender set down the drafts, and Garland drained his. He asked for another, the bartender said something, and Garland pointed at Mary. His blood sugar must be climbing, his body warming; the grin returned. He was like Popeye with his can of spinach.

Mullet fed the pool table quarters, slammed home the chrome lever, and fifteen balls dropped onto the shelf with a *ker-blunk*. Mary examined some cues. She didn't eyeball the shaft for straightness or roll the cue on the pool table to see if it was warped. All that mattered in a cue was the condition of the tip, and she selected the best one. Garland brought her a draft and the bags of snacks. She couldn't believe how good they tasted, stale pretzels and cheap beer.

Mullet racked the balls, ordering the solids and stripes obsessively. She winced, the clock ticking in her mind. It took him forever to rack the balls, sliding the triangle back and forth along the felt. He was probably showing off those puffy muscles. They didn't have time for this. Her ears kept listening for the call of the diesel horn; if they missed the train, what would they do? Steal a car? Did Garland know how? She just wanted to get out of this place.

Mullet looked up from his completed rack. "So what you wanna play for?"

"Two dollars?" she said.

"How about a fin?"

She nodded. At least some of it was easy.

"You can break," he said.

She intentionally held the cue wrong, forming a clumsy bridge with her thumb sticking up and gripping the stick at the very end of the butt. On her break, she purposely miscued. "Oh, damn." She wanted him to break the balls.

"Go again," he said with a wave of his arm.

"No, not when playing for money. It's your shot."

He turned and retrieved his drink, took a long sip, grabbed his smokes and lit a cigarette, inhaling deeply. Only then did he approach the pool table. This was all driving her crazy, but she knew she had to remain calm. He broke with a big flourish, sank two balls, both stripes. He looked to his audience for approval. Sitting beside the skinny woman were two men, both in camouflage pants. To Mary they all appeared to have been hatched from the same egg. They matched the place—fake wood paneling, filthy plywood floor, rotating plastic beer light featuring the Budweiser Clydesdales, the pool table lit by a miniature Nascar.

Mullet hammered in two more balls and missed a cut shot by three inches. He still seemed very pleased with his performance. "Okay, honey, your turn. Let's see what you can do."

She missed. "Nice try," he said. But by missing she locked a solid in

one of the pocket jaws, leaving it just at the edge of the hole. "Didn't leave me much, did ya?" he said.

Garland brought her more food and beer, and a glass of orange juice. It had been a long time since she'd eaten a Slim Jim. Did they even have any nutritional value? The juice was a good idea, she should have thought of that, but the situation unhinged her.

Mullet tried a bank shot and missed. Why did they always shoot so hard? She holed two solids, exclaiming as each ball fell. Don't overdo it, she told herself, trying to settle her nerves. She locked another solid in a pocket. He sank a couple more, squinting through the smoke of his cigarette. He was left with one stripe and the eight now. Since Mary had two of the pockets bottled up, his only choice was another bank shot. He missed. She allowed herself to sink only two more, but left him nothing, snookering the cue ball. He stared at the table. Did he suspect something? He missed his ball entirely.

"Isn't that a scratch?" she said, knowing it was.

"No fucking way. Only on the eight. You scratch the eight, you lose."

Time-wise, she had to end this, and did. She drove the cue ball off three rails getting position for an easy shot down the rail on the eight so it looked like luck.

He scowled and threw a five at the table. "Let's play for twenty, see how good you really are." He was irritated now, hopefully not too irritated. There was something behind his sexual bluster that was disturbing.

She approached the bartender, placed the five on the bar. "How much?"

"Fourteen-fifty," he said. More than she figured. For an instant she thought she heard the train call out.

"You gonna play or not?" said Mullet, loud, right in her ear, his breath like rotten meat.

She jerked away from him. "Rack 'em."

"For twenty?"

"Twenty. Let's go." She glanced back at the bartender. He was still staring at her through those slits, but she couldn't read his expression.

She waited again while Mullet went through his inane racking procedure. He kept looking up at her, and it went right into her stomach. She wanted to get out of there immediately—something was beyond wrong. She glanced at Garland; he winked at her. Nothing ever seemed to bother him.

This time she broke using her normal stance. One solid fell and she

quickly ran through the rest of her balls; Mullet, seeing she wasn't missing, tried every obnoxious trick—screeching the chalk, saying, "Don't miss," just as she stroked, moving around in her line of sight. As she got ready for her easy eight-ball shot, the bartender called out, "Hey, you."

She straightened and turned.

"You gonna pay me or not?" His arms across his chest, those eyes.

"Just a second." She leaned back over to play her last shot.

A striped ball blocked it.

"What are you doing?" she said to Mullet.

"What're you talking about?"

"You moved one of your balls."

"Fuck you, what're you talking about?"

"You moved that fourteen ball. My shot was clear before, now it isn't."

"You sayin' I cheated?"

One of the louts got up off his bar stool and headed toward the exit. The skinny woman licked her broken-out upper lip and sniffed. Garland moved quietly beside Mary.

"You moved the ball," he said to Mullet. "Bub, that's no frigging way to play pool. Put it back."

"Dickhead—stay out of it before you get hurt."

Mary addressed the bystanders. "Did any of you see him move the ball?"

"Nope," said one. The others shook their heads.

"It's your shot, *dearie*," said the skinny woman, her eyes gleaming. "Either make it or pay up."

The bartender: "You don't hit that eight, you lose. Them's house rules."

They all watched her. She saw what she'd only sensed before—real trouble. This was no longer about an uneasy feeling, bad smells, or a pool game. They all knew something she didn't. Her heart raced. She stared at the table, not sure what to do, her mind numb.

Then Garland whispered, "The curvy thing."

Inverting the cue stick to a forty-five degree angle, she masséd the cue ball around the fourteen and into the eight, sinking it perfectly. A silence. A very ominous silence. It was broken by the mournful blast of a diesel horn.

"Just pay the bartender the twenty," she said to Mullet. "We have to go."

His face made her flinch.

"Maybe you need a *real* fucking lesson on the pool table—with your legs spread. Dickhead the toy cowboy can watch."

The skinny woman, spit spraying from her mouth, said, "Now you'll get yours, you uppity bitch."

The one at the door snapped the deadbolt.

It was then that Garland reacted. He picked up the heavy bar-table cue ball, and with a throw that had made him a local legend when he played shortstop as a teenager, he threw hard to first. He got the man out at the door; the cue ball ricocheted off his jaw, whacked into the wall, and down he went with a screaming thud.

"Run!" Garland yelled as he grabbed her pool stick. "Don't think, just run. I'll be okay."

She did. Found the door, stepping over the body lying near the threshold, the man holding his mouth, bellowing. The bartender yelled something she didn't understand, peripherally someone was darting toward her. She could almost feel him grabbing her when she heard a sharp crack. She fumbled with the bolt, her hands shaking. Got it turned, threw open the door, and plunged into the darkness.

She ran, cold fresh air surrounding her like a blessing. For an instant she slowed and glanced back. Through one of the windows was Garland, a pool stick gripped in both hands. He swung, struck Mullet squarely on the side of the head, the mouth opening in a contorted scream. Garland must have been one hell of a batter, too. Then she saw a body darken the doorway and she ran again.

Life sometimes works out for just a moment. Sometimes that moment is when we need it most. As she ran across the street to the moving freight train, there in the dull light of the bar sign was a vacant boxcar gliding toward her. She ran beside it, and remembering what Garland had shown her, managed to get in without too much trouble; thank God for his quick lesson. Her heart pounded as she kneeled on the wet boards, looking for him to appear. "Garland," she yelled. She repeated his name over and over, searched the retreating door of the bar, saw only what looked like the bartender standing in the road. He saved me, Garland saved me, he saved me, the train wheels chanted. Some part of her was still back there with him—

The freight cried out again as it surged toward the north, toward Jay Chevalier.

The temperature began to drop as the train struggled up a long grade. Snowflakes flew in out of the darkness until a barely discernible band of dim white formed on the boxcar floor. She jumped up and down, her feet frozen, teeth chattering, body shuddering, her coat pulled tightly around her like waning hope. Without this wool sweater . . .

Garland's courage overwhelmed her again; she could see his face and body, the pure force of it in that small frame. That incredible power and agility had always been just beneath the grin. And then she remembered about borrowing a phone. But she was almost certain no one would've had a LiveCell in that repulsive place.

The train had passed Klamath Falls about an hour ago, her watch the only light—a prayer for Jay. The freight crested a summit and began a long downhill run picking up speed with every mile, brakes and flanges squealing, the acrid-smelling smoke of overheating metal biting her sinuses. The train charged into the icy blackness like a runaway nightmare, and all her thoughts were eclipsed by the cold. She'd never known the fear of freezing to death. She did now, and forced herself to keep moving, tired as she was, the short meal and beers having long deserted her. "When this train stops and I can see any kind of civilization, I have to get off or I'm going to die."

Outside Eugene, Oregon, the freight finally came to rest. She'd noticed highway signs for the city when the tracks paralleled a road. The radiant colored dots read a few minutes before six. She let herself down out of the boxcar and immediately fell onto the gravel, her joints that cold. She picked herself up and walked stiffly up the yard, one hand bruised, her shoulder aching. Garland had been right, it was a very long freight. Though the temperature was milder, she still shivered and knew it would take her a long time to get warm. At least she was shivering; at her coldest during the night, she'd stopped. That had scared her the most.

Out of the chrome pre-dawn there appeared a concrete structure with a half-dozen work trucks and pickups angled next to it. Not seeing anything besides more tracks and freight cars, she approached the building, the metal door with YARD OFFICE above it. She stood, uncertain. After last night, she was leery entering any place where strange men would be. But she had to take the chance, and opened the door.

Two men were sitting over some papers at one of the cafeteria-style tables. They looked up, their faces unfriendly. Regardless, she forced her-

self to walk a few feet into the room, the heavy door drawing shut behind her with a *clunk*. The older one got to his feet.

"What do you want?"

She couldn't seem to say anything. He approached her tentatively, warily.

"You're not allowed in here."

He looked her up and down; she instantly got a queasy feeling.

"Did you just come in on the OAPO out of Klamath?"

She nodded. He came closer.

"You look awful cold."

"I am." Her teeth started chattering again from the heat of the room. She felt her legs go weak and knew she was about to fall again. There was a bench near the door and she just made it.

"Bill," he said over his shoulder. "Get the little lady a cup of coffee, lots of cream and sugar." He addressed her again: "You must be froze. It was goddamn cold even in the cab up there tonight."

"You drove the train?"

"Yeah, what else? We just switched out crews. I logged my twelve, or a few minutes less, and another crew will take her into Portland. You trying to get to Portland?"

She shook her head. He moved towards her, sat down beside her. For a long second she was terrified he was going to reach over and touch her. She sensed that he wanted to. Not again! And without Garland to protect her.

"All my years with the railroad, I've never seen a lady riding alone. Rarely see wimin ridin', alone or not. If I'd known you was back there, I would've let you ride with me in the unit. We could've kept each other warm." He showed his yellow teeth, his eyes moving down to her chest and staying there. The other man approached with the coffee. She took the styrofoam cup, and he returned to his paperwork without a word. She sipped the coffee hungrily, feeling the hot liquid running into her stomach. She needed to get her strength back.

"Are you staying here in town?" the engineer said.

"I'm trying to get to the coast." She could tell he couldn't figure her out. That was in her favor.

"Where about?"

Should she tell him? She was too exhausted to care. "Near the Old Siuslaw Road."

"At the edge of the National Forest. You got family there?"

She nodded. Then added, "My husband."

"He lets you ride freights?"

"It's a long story," she said, unable to think of anything else.

"What's his name?"

For a frantic moment she couldn't remember the name on the mail-box, then realized it probably didn't matter. "Madsen," she said as it came to her. "John Madsen."

"Don't think I know him."

He seemed to reach some kind of decision about her. "I live over in that direction. Tell you what, let me finish up a few things here, and I'll take you part way."

Should she do this? Would it be safe? But what other options did she have without any money? Was the five dollars in her pocket? She was too exhausted to think clearly, so she agreed, finished the last of her coffee. "Is there a washroom?"

"Right through that door down the hall on your left."

She stood. "Thanks, that coffee really helped. I can't tell you how much." Be polite with him, but not friendly.

"You want another?"

"Yes, please, in just a minute."

He smiled and she got that queasy feeling in her stomach again. She set her empty cup on the bench and headed to the washroom.

What Mary saw in the mirror was a shock. She barely recognized herself. Only ten hours and she looked like a vagabond. Her skin was grimy and smudged, her eyes laced with red, her hair a tangled mess halfway to dreads, and with the filthy wet coat and Garland's sweater . . . She made only a few minor repairs, realizing she shouldn't make herself more attractive.

He still looked her over strangely when she returned from the wash-room. She accepted a second cup of coffee, followed him outside to his pickup. As they got rolling he slid on the heat, turned up the fan. She no longer shivered and chattered, but the cold from the train was still in her bones and the heat was welcome; she held her wet shoes near the hot-air vent. Rain came down again, the wipers beat back and forth. The engineer tried to make conversation at first, but she told him she was too tired to talk, if he didn't mind. The less familiar, the better.

She looked out at the illuminated triangle of highway through the rain, a gauntlet of dark pine on each side. As she got closer to Jay, the reality hit her. If only she had a gun. That jolted her mind to Garland.

She might have gotten him killed by asking him to help her. But Garland had to be okay. Somehow she couldn't imagine that he wasn't. He'd have gotten out of that bar; she'd never seen anyone who could move so fast. She thought of Frankie flying across the country, probably somewhere over the Midwest by now. He would drive directly to her when he got off the plane, but he probably wouldn't arrive until noon. He'd be frantic. If only she had her phone—

"You know," said the engineer, "I keep thinkin' I've seen you some place before. You look kinda familiar to me. Could I of seen your picture somewheres?" He was studying her again with quick glances as he drove. Men and their fucking glances.

She kept her eyes on the road ahead. "No, I couldn't imagine where." He'd probably seen her in one of her TV news interviews, or maybe in one of the magazine articles. Should she ask him to help her? Maybe he had a LiveCell phone, or even a gun. But could she trust him? Would his sympathies be with LiveCell? Was it worth the risk? After what had happened in the bar, her faith in strangers was gone. He might do just the opposite of what she asked. She wasn't sure what to do, so she did nothing.

He stopped at the junction of the 101 and Old Siuslaw Road. As she reached for the door handle, he grabbed her arm.

"Why not come to my place for breakfast? It's ridiculous lettin' such a pretty young thing as you out in the rain like this. You could dry off yer clothes. I got an electric drier. You could take a shower an' clean up. I bet you clean up nice."

"My husband's waiting."

"Funny kinda husband, lettin' you run around like this."

She pulled away from his grip, jumped down, shut the door, and prepared to run—but he simply drove off. The queasy feeling in her stomach receded as his truck headed into the gray light of morning. She waited a few minutes in case he came back, ready to run into the woods. Blessed silence. Fixing her hood against the rain, she began walking along the pavement, and before too long, she reached the graveled section of the road. She forced herself not to run; she needed what little energy she had left.

Eventually the mailbox with Raymond Madsen came into focus out of the fog. She angled past it, left the Siuslaw Road and headed along the drive rutted with scrub-pine roots. The rain had abated somewhat; it was fully morning and she smelled the sea. The wet pine and brackish fog

revived the memory of when she'd been there before, stopping her new Porsche to check her face and hair in the vanity mirror. Though only a bit over a year ago, it was an eternity away.

Mary examined the ground for tracks, not sure what she was looking for. In the thick pine-needle bed she couldn't tell much. At least one car had driven along it, maybe two. "I don't know what to expect. I don't know how to do this." If only she had Frankie telling her how to approach the house, or Garland beside her—Garland *and* two guns. That had been the plan, not this. She couldn't slow the beating of her heart.

The distant thundering of breakers, muted as it attempted to breach the fog, made her think of the painting in his office. The image plagued her; she couldn't shake it in her exhaustion, and she started to envision Jay as the boat careening above the turmoiled waves, the chaos of the world. And she was merely a passenger in the boat, the violent sea supporting them both, allowing them to thrust toward the sky, toward their dreams, yet also just as willing to destroy. And then she remembered the moon, saw Jay as the moon, and started to run.

There was his blue wagon with a black sedan parked tight behind it, blocking it in. The sight of the strange car stopped her. A sudden pain between her eyes almost knocked her down. She knelt for a moment on the wet pine needles, fought back the nausea, attempted to calm her breathing. She listened. Nothing, only her heart pumping madly. The house was dark. The smell of burnt wood. She noticed a faint drift of smoke at the chimney. What appeared to be a body was lying on the porch near the door.

Slowly, with careful steps, she approached from along the edge of the drive, her hurt shoulder brushing wet pine, her mind screaming, *Don't let it be him.* If someone glanced outside, they could shoot her, and she didn't care. The front door was open. She saw that though her eyes were fixed on the prone body. A *suit*! It was wearing a suit! A gun lay beside it. She picked it up, the pistol heavy and alien in her hand—evil. The body lay face down against the rotten porch boards, a dark stain under it. She couldn't bring herself to examine the corpse from any closer, and she didn't check if the gun was loaded—what would it matter?

She tried to think logically. If one of them was dead, maybe the others were dead too. If not, would they have left the body? Wouldn't they have dragged it inside? Taken the gun? Or was it a trap? She wanted to call out for Jay. She studied the darkness beyond the doorway. Just some derailed toy train cars on their sides, some disheveled track. She crept

along the porch as quietly as she could, praying she wouldn't break through one of the bad planks and make a noise. She peered over a windowsill. There, barely visible in the firelight, propped up against an armchair, was Jay. He held a gun loosely in his hand. Another body was on the floor. She ran.

"Jay," she called. "It's me—Mary." She listened at the doorway. Silence—the ocean—silence. Entering the front hall she called out again, the gun ready in her hand, stepping over ruined trains and track. She heard a faint something. When she got to Jay his cheeks were wet. She crouched down next to him, the gun falling from her hand.

"You're okay," he said. She could barely hear him, his voice a whisper, his lips almost blue, his face like wax. "They told me they had you, that you'd be tortured—"

"—You've been shot. You need an ambulance."

He shook his head very gently, his eyelids wavering with the pain it caused him.

"Where's your LiveCell?" she said.

"Destroyed."

She looked around the room quickly; were there only two men?

"Mary . . . you're okay. Everyone all right?" His eyes searched her face.

She told him yes, though she had no idea. "Were there only two?" He nodded with his eyes. She noticed his hands. "My God, what did they do to you?" His hands and especially his wrists were burned, blistered. She reached down and carefully removed the gun from his right hand. The fingers seemed to be numb, the knuckles chafed and covered in dried blood.

"Taped," he said. "Hands. Dragged myself to the fire." She cringed at the horror of it.

"Jay, we need to get you to a hospital. Did they have phones?"

"Won't work." And she realized the frustrating truth of it. Though Jay had created the phones, they would still only work with permission from each owner.

"I'll drive you. Can you move?"

He shook his head again, winced. "May I . . . a glass water?"

She stood up and ran to the kitchen, found a clean glass, turned the tap, heard a pump and generator somewhere below rumble on, let the water run cold a second, filled it, ran back. Though the burns to his hands were not on his fingers, she held the glass to his lips; she didn't think he had any feeling in his hands.

"Thanks," he said after he drank, his voice a little louder. She fought back the tears again.

"What can I do? You need help. I can't carry you by myself."

"Don't be upset."

She tried to quiet herself. "Is there anything I can do?"

"Thought they . . . more time." His eyes half-closed, the lids flickering.

"How bad is the pain?"

He opened his eyes, gazed at her for a long time with such overwhelming love that she began to tremble. "For once, I'm not so fine," he said, and attempted a smile.

Her tears fell then, running down her face, completely beyond her control.

"Mary, please . . . it's okay. What matters . . . you're safe, you're here. I knew you would come." His eyes flared for an instant and then shut tight. A spasm ran through his body as if it were her own.

"Jay? . . . Jay? . . . No—" she cried. "You can't die, please, don't die. God, please don't die. I can't live without you." She placed her arms around him and pulled him to her, his head resting against her chest, against her soaked raincoat. "I love you," she whispered. "I love you so much."

She was never sure how long she held him. She remembered eventually setting his head gently on the floor, carefully straightening his body. She remembered stroking his face, bringing her lips to his, their second kiss, her tears landing on his forehead, running along his broken nose, down his pocked temples. She remembered finding Jimmy Hakken's gift of the ugly silver pendant around his neck, and starting to laugh hysterically, uncontrollably. She remembered taking off her raincoat and covering him with it. She remembered walking into the kitchen and staring out the window, her tears like the rain on the glass, moving down her face in the same hapless way. She remembered thinking about what they'd done to him. The anger, the straggling rage poisoning her until she screamed; she must have kicked something repeatedly, her foot was still sore. She remembered drinking a beer with his blood on her hand. She remembered managing a few bites of cold leftover chicken pot pie, telling herself she had to eat or she'd faint. The cats finally came out of hiding and rubbed against her legs. She fed them and realized that she had to get out of the house, that soon others would know something was wrong and come looking.

Her mind began working logically again, and she reconstructed what might have happened. The two men must have surprised and bound Jay the previous morning—if only she'd tried to call him then, if only she'd listened to her premonitions, if only Kelly had known a few hours sooner. The two men worked on him all day, threatening him with her torture and who knew what else, not realizing the rage they were generating; he would have remained calm, waiting, unyielding. They must have attempted some kind of injection because there was a hypodermic on a table. Maybe Jay was immune from drinking so much of his Grandfather's distillate? Her mind drifted to the evening when they sat on her porch as the storm swept in from the Pacific, Jay sipping champagne, telling her about his grandfather, about the phones, about how they could stop him; and then Jay walking away, leaving her, and she started sobbing again—

She controlled her thoughts. Anthony Brignolia must have known about Duncan and the plan to interrogate and possibly kill Jay. That's why he was so angry; he must've attempted to dissuade Alden and his connections and failed. He probably hoped Jay would still come around to his offer in time. Frankie learned part of this through his contact, and he called just before four, warning her about Duncan. It was obvious Jay gave up nothing important over the last twenty-four hours or the men would have been gone when she arrived.

As she'd ridden the freight through the mountains, the two men must have left Jay alone for a moment, or dozed off. Jay freed himself by inching to the fireplace and burning through his bound hands, ripping through his leg bonds—she found burnt and torn tape. He attacked one of the men, killing him and taking his gun. The second man had fired, the bullet striking Jay in the stomach, and Jay had shot him, the man struggling to flee until he collapsed on the porch.

Then she thought: Jay didn't ask her who sold him out, or how his attackers found him, or even why she'd arrived alone and soaking wet. All he'd said was, "I knew you'd come." And for a frightening instant, she wondered how much Jay had known all along. Had he known he was going to be killed? Had he believed that only by dying he could save Live-Cell?—and save her?

He must have foreseen a lot of it. He'd probably known all along that Duncan would betray him, that she would find him here, and that Live-Cell would be saved because of his death. Maybe that's why he couldn't allow himself to love her? Why he ran from her? He knew how soon he was going to die. She wished they'd shared those moments together any-

way. How could someone who knew so much, have known so little about some things?

But Jay Chevalier had his dream, his vision. Whatever had happened to him in the northern Maine wilderness as his eyes locked on the heavens had changed him and guided him. He'd been willing to do anything to realize that dream, this vision he had for humanity, his belief in the continuum, even up to extracting cells from his own brain and accepting that he would have to be killed in order for his prophecy to continue. For her, that held something far beyond any unfulfilled yearning or unrequited feelings.

Mary walked outside, limping slightly from her sore foot, her whole body aching. The Impala. She considered using it to escape. But it was boxed in, and there was no way she was going near those two corpses for the sedan's keys, and besides, she'd be more exposed in a car. Frankie would be there soon enough anyway. He'd have landed in Portland by mid-morning and should arrive within an hour. He'd be able to find the Old Siuslaw Road and the mailbox.

And once she got his phone, she'd livecell Deirdre and Artega, engage enough media and police so that no one, not even the Aldens, would be able to cover up Jay's murder. What they'd managed with Sammy's killing would not happen again. And once the world knew what the Aldens and their associates had done, they would be forced to leave LiveCell alone. Frankie could handle things until the press and police arrived. She needed desperately to find out how Garland was, but wasn't so sure she wanted to know what had happened between Jimmy Hakken and Duncan. She tried to lock her mind on the future.

As she headed down the drive toward the mailbox—ready to jump into the pines if she heard a vehicle—she saw the rain had stopped and that it was going to clear, the sun already working through the fog. She heard a tremendous *whoosh* and glanced up.

Above her, in the open lane between the low trees, the sky was filled with birds, hundreds of them, maybe thousands, all flying silently until they turned together in great synchronous arcs of dark pearlescent color. A part of her was drawn up toward the myriad beating wings, and somewhere inside her mind she felt a voice. She didn't hear it, it didn't speak in words, it spoke in feelings. And then she knew why Jay had needed her to be next to him when he died, and he was there, inside her, and she almost laughed at the pure wonder of it. She listened and she knew exactly what she had to do.

EPILOGUE

Frankie Demanno and Mary MacKensie gazed out her dining room window at the Pacific Ocean. Each held a flute, the chill of the white wine dulling the sides of the glasses. Two cases had been delivered by a special courier, sent from Anthony Brignolia's native village in Sicily. The attached note read: *The world has suffered a great loss, but for you Mary it has been the greatest. Wise people in my village say that this wine can bring the soul back to life. Please drink it in the memory of a great man.* Brignolia also made Frankie a rare gift; he released him from whatever unwritten contract had bound him.

Over the past three weeks, Frankie had been very gentle with her, saying little, respecting her grief, but finally she had to ask him to stop cooking so many special dishes for her. Every time she stepped in the door, he was bringing her something else. If only she'd been the least bit hungry.

From the moment she'd spotted his rental car on the Siuslaw Road, he'd assisted her in every way. He'd summoned the local police and the press to the murder scene and protected her from too much questioning. He'd driven her home, prepared hot chicken broth and fresh vegetable juice with ginger, brought it to her in bed. He'd stayed up most of that first night, sitting at the dining room table, sipping coffee with anisette, glancing in at her every so often during her fitful attempt at sleep.

It was Chet Simmons, LiveCell's meek purchasing head, who asked Mary if he might be allowed to organize Jay Chevalier's funeral. The event was national news, all the major media in friendly attendance—they had switched sides just as Jay had foreseen. Thousands of people came, some from as far as Iceland and Australia. Kelly Harris and Mary's parents flew in from Vermont, staying the week with her. Kelly looked so bad she worried he was back on heroin. "I'd look a lot better if I was," he said. "Believe me." Frankie moved to a motel during her parents' stay, but still came by to cook, her mother eyeing him strangely at first—after all, he was from Massachusetts—but relenting slightly after she tasted a few of his specialties.

At the funeral, the Brignolia brothers were standing side by side. Detective Artega—he'd been put in charge of the Samuel Holmes case again—and what appeared to be at least half the San Francisco police department were there. Almost everyone from the Cyclone gym and most of the staff from the Mexican restaurant Dos Reales. Everyone from Live-Cell and all their families. Manuel, who cried the entire time. But no one had anticipated the intensity and breadth of emotion surrounding Jay Chevalier's death. It seemed as if the entire nation was in mourning. Frankie suggested Mary give a eulogy. He said she was head of LiveCell now; Jay had left her his sixty percent of the company, and she needed to show the world that she was unafraid and ready to continue his legacy. He felt it was important. And when Mary finished speaking, she was about the only one without damp eyes. What she felt for Jay was beyond tears.

The procession of thousands was led by Luke and Jimmy Hakken along with the entire crew, many on choppers, all dressed in black, armbands across their tattooed biceps. The gang had voted to make Chevalier a Druid posthumously, the first and probably last time such an honor was given. Mary had offered Hakken the blue Impala, and he'd accepted, along with adopting the three cats—no one else wanted the mangy creatures. "It wasn't their fucking fault," he said. And then he stared at her for a long Hakken moment. "MacKensie, you know I ain't gonna let this end here." She wasn't sure what he meant, but it chilled her nonetheless.

"So they dropped the charges?" Frankie took a sip of wine, looking out over the ocean.

"Garland's so famous since the story got picked up, they'd be idiots to sue for assault."

"He put three of 'em in the hospital? They were kinda vague in the paper."

"The one he hit with the cue ball has a broken jaw and missing teeth. The one who tried to grab me has a smashed knee. The woman tried to attack him and scratched him, doing more damage than the men. He told me he couldn't hit a woman, but he managed to throw her off, and she disappeared when she heard the siren; the bartender had called the cops. He was the only lucky one. When the cops got there, Garland was having a beer, the bartender in awe. He told the cops what really happened. I guess he'd been scared of that one guy for years and was relieved to be rid of him."

"That the guy who wanted to rape you?"

She nodded.

"What happened to him?"

"Garland said to me, '*I don't usually lose my temper, but the way that guy was talking to you made me frigging mad.*' I guess that guy is still in the hospital. They're not sure when he'll be out. And Garland did all that with a bandaged hand."

"You were right—he's some cowboy."

"I offered him a job at LiveCell, at any pay. You know what he said? '*Naw, I just know ranching. Wouldn't be no good at nothing else.*'"

"You got his accent down."

"That was a good suggestion about buying him the exact same guns. Thanks again for that. I just wish I could do something more for him."

They paused, sipped their wine.

"Frankie . . . I want you to work with me at LiveCell."

"As a bodyguard? I used to think I was the best, now I'm not so sure."

"I want you to be in charge of public relations, but I also want you to be my right hand."

"Public *relations*?"

"You'd be very good."

"Really?"

She nodded. He hid behind another sip of wine.

"So how did Jimmy Hakken do it?" She changed the subject. "You know about that stuff."

"Duncan?"

"Yeah. They couldn't find a mark on his body. Nothing. It took the cops weeks even to figure out he'd been in the room."

He shook his head. "I really don't know. Something I never learned. That Hakken is one strange bird."

"Duncan still hasn't spoken or moved. They have to feed him."

"Do they think he'll ever come out of it?"

"I talked to the neurologist at the hospital a few days ago, and he said a massive trauma like this could take years."

"Hakken's a scary guy. Probably good he disappeared."

"Even for you? I didn't think you were scared of anything."

"Everybody is scared of something. The only person I met not scared of nothing was Jay Chevalier."

They both went silent. She excused herself and left the room. He worried he'd said the wrong thing. When she returned a few minutes later, her hair was pulled back.

"The earrings," he said.

"They look okay?"

"You kiddin' me?" He couldn't take his eyes off her. "Mary, you know—"

"Not yet. *Please.* Give me a little more time."

He nodded. After some awkward moments she checked her watch. "I need to go over to the factories. Deirdre will call any minute if I don't get going. She's become a wicked worrywart. Not that I blame her."

"You go over there every day now."

"You want to come with me?"

He shrugged.

"So, you accept my job offer?"

"You kiddin' me? You know how I feel."

"Then I want to show you something."

"At the factory?"

"Yeah."

"What?"

"If I told you, you wouldn't believe me."

THE END

Eric Green *lives on the Maine Coast with his wife. He was born in northern New Hampshire, rode freights across the country as a teenager, made his living as a visual artist for thirty years, and writes the syndicated award-winning column "The Penobscot Falcon."*

FIC
GRE

02/18/2012   **5CLY0016912**

Green, Eric
Livecell

DATE DUE			

CPSIA information can be obtained at www.ICGtesting.com
Printed in the USA
LVOW041622140212
268675LV00002B/131/P

9 781937 644031

CPSIA information can be obtained
at www.ICGtesting.com
Printed in the USA
FSHW020508261019
63402FS